TO LOVE
AND CORRUPT

TO LOVE AND CORRUPT

To Love and Corrupt is a dramatic novel about a self-made construction tycoon who built cities and destroyed people. Joe Naples is a multi-millionaire building contractor. Born and raised in a poor immigrant family in the slums of New York, ill-educated and coarse, he manages by immense energy, ruthlessness and intelligence to reach a position of astonishing wealth and power. Joe prides himself on his ability to handle men, and his ambition is to be in the fullest sense patron (padrone) of all those he can gather into his organization. But he receives a terrific setback when he becomes the object of a very thorough-going investigation by a U.S. Senate Committee.

For the first time Joe really faces the years and the activities that have brought him where he is. He had done what he thought he had to do to accomplish his ambition: to build houses better and cheaper than other people could build them. And, at last, to build a city that bears his name.

Joe Naples is an extraordinary character – lusty, powerful, rich with sentiment and a sense of his own destiny. He is a man full of responsibility for those he loves – provided they will lean on him!

The extraordinary thing about this novel is that the reader is on Joe's side despite the things he does, and few readers will be able to put the book down once they have started it, for it is a fascinating character study from first to last page.

Also by Joseph Viertel

THE LAST TEMPTATION

TO LOVE
AND CORRUPT

by

JOSEPH VIERTEL

LONDON
HAMMOND, HAMMOND
AND COMPANY

Printed in Great Britain by
Cox & Wyman Ltd., Fakenham
for Hammond, Hammond & Co. Ltd.,
87 Gower St., London WC1
862

Like everything, this is for Janet

One

JOE was startled out of his bleak reflections when Cathy buzzed and said over the intercom, 'Mr. Poltek is here to see you.'

'Ask him to wait.' Joe Naples leaned back from his desk, opened the humidor, pinched out an Upmann Special, pulled it from its aluminium cylinder, glanced at his own signature reproduced on the band and, with a reflex he had never been able to overcome, nipped the tip of the pre-cut cigar with his front teeth. As he lit it, he saw his hand trembled.

What should his attitude be with this Washington lawyer? What was his name again? Polecat? Something like Polecat. Didn't like his voice on the phone yesterday – too oily. He pushed his rolled shirt sleeves up above his elbows, examined the greying hair on his arms, leaned back in his swivel chair and laced his fingers behind his head, making his knuckles crack. This was a hell of a time in life to be facing this kind of a louse-up. Fifty-two, going on fifty-three. 'Counsel for the Senate Investigating Sub-committee on —' the thin but aggressive Bostonian voice had said. What sub-committee again? Milt had told him only fifty thousand times. On government-assisted private enterprises – something like that, something ridiculous. These U.S. Senators didn't have enough to keep them busy, all they thought about was getting elected instead of worrying about the Bolsheviks and doing something for the poor Indians on those crummy reservations; always poking their noses into legitimate guys' businesses. Well, it was a new experience for Joe Naples; he welcomed new experiences, even bad ones. Anyhow, what did he have to worry about? Guys had done a lot worse. He got up and walked to the window.

Looking down from the top of this modern country office building set in the midst of the shopping and commercial centre, Joe could see the roofs and neon lights of his major tenants, J. C. Penney, Woolworth, W. T. Grant – all the rest. To him it was like no other shopping centre in the world. It was part of The City, *his* city,

Naples, New Jersey, which lay beyond those thousands of cars parked below. From the city's heart, beginning on the other side of Miller's Road, he could see the roofs of the thousands of houses.

He walked back to his desk, his teeth tightening on the cigar, and he tasted the tobacco juice. That guy waiting out there, let the son-of-a-bitch wait. He pressed the button on the intercom. It had taken him two hundred years to figure out how to work that thing, but now he had it. Mechanical goddam genius he must be.

'Yes, sir?'

'Come on in a minute, Cath.'

As always, Cathy was neat as a pin, white shirt, grey skirt, and pretty – not like Marilyn Monroe, more like a young Irene Dunne. She knew where every clip, rubber band and piece of paper in the place was. Joe paid her two hundred dollars a week, and she was worth twice that.

She had also been Joe Naples's Wednesday-night mistress, briefly, ten years ago. She used to rent a room every Wednesday at the Peter Minuet Hotel in Newark, that was exactly how circumspect she was, *she* rented the place, so he wouldn't have to do anything but get in the lift and climb into bed for a tune-up.

She was a good kid, but five hundred per cent off her wack about sex, and after a while he'd given her up, but not as a secretary. She was a good kid about it too, didn't seem to mind. Still, he felt sorry for her. She ought to get married. He'd have to dig up a boy for her sometime.

Now she was standing cool and neat in the doorway. 'Yes?'

'Come on in, Cath.'

'Shall I bring my book?'

'No, no.'

She sat opposite him, her knees primly together, smoothed her skirt and folded her hands, waiting.

'What's whozis out there look like?'

'Mr. Poltek?' She gave a tiny shrug. 'Short, very polite. Rather dark, with one of those crew cuts. Quite serious, I'd say. I wouldn't trust him. But then, I've only just met him.'

'Your instincts are damn good.'

'I never set eyes on him before. I could ask around Washington about him. I have a girl-friend at the Justice Department, where he used to work before he went with this Senate committee. Should I?'

'I'll let you know. Is Milt Jason in?'

'I believe so.'

'Okay', he said. 'Tell that sneaky bastid Polecat to come on in.'

He took a deep breath, rolled his sleeves down, buttoned his onyx cuff links. A moment later Cathy was holding the door for Mr. Poltek. She closed it from the outside, carefully.

About thirty-three or thirty-four, Joe judged, as he shook hands with the young, sallow man, shorter than Joe, yellowish teeth, oily skin, crew cut, somewhat abrupt, with one of those phony-baloney smiles that make you feel for your wallet. He wore a dark grey pin-striped suit which fitted too loose. His features were gross: over-lipped, broad-nosed; and he carried a despatch case, which he placed ominously on his lap. 'I hope I'm not interrupting anything', he said unctuously. His voice was like steam under pressure.

'Nah', Joe said. 'Have a seat.'

'I'm only doing my job and it isn't always a very pleasant one', Poltek said.

'Then why not give it all up?' Joe said, and laughed. 'What the hell. There's other jobs.'

Sam Poltek's lips smiled. 'P'raps if we can get your attorney in with us,' Poltek said in his flat New Englandese, 'if he's available, that is.'

'Sure', Joe said, and pushed the intercom. 'Ask Milt Jason to come in.'

'Lovely place you have here', Poltek said as they waited. 'What's the panelling, walnut?'

'Teak', Joe said. He noticed that his visitor had a pronounced body odour.

'Ah, very nice. And those are beautiful paintings. Should I know them?'

'That there's a portrait of my wife.'

'Mmm', Poltek said. 'Lovely.'

'Some guy named Shatzen did her. Hell of a guy, though. You'd swear he's a poet until he slips you the price. Shatzen, that means jokes in German, but his fee is no joke. And that one, the little old house, curio shop – whatever the hell it is – we got that in Paris, costs more than the whole goddam actual whatzis shop it's a painting of, including the merchandise *in* it. Mister Utrillo. I don't know – twelve, fourteen thousand bucks. My wife and I collect those whatzises. Mostly kids painting today. Some of 'em damn talented. My wife knows 'em all.'

Poltek's gaze travelled around the walls. 'Who's the boy in

uniform?' He pointed to the portrait of Carey, sitting on the rail of an iron spindle fence, shoulders drooping slightly, hands at ease, a cigarette between his lips, almost smiling, looking damn near alive.

'My boy, Carey.' Joe felt the customary stab of pain and the churning in his gut.

'Is he in business with you?' Inquisitive little guy.

'He was killed in Korea.'

'Oh. I'm sorry.'

Joe turned away. 'You got children?'

'I'm not married' Poltek said.

Some girl was goddam lucky. 'That's my other son over there – Andy. He's in his last year at Harvard Law School.'

'I went to Harvard College', Poltek said. 'And the Law School as well.'

Maybe there'd be a little *noblesse oblige*. 'Never went to any college myself', Joe said. 'De Witt Clinton's my Alma Mater. Quit in my junior year. The old building down on Fifty-ninth Street.' No use telling the little bastid how nearly he'd gone to Princeton. There were days he wished to hell he'd gone to Princeton. More often than he cared to admit.

The door opened and it was Milt. He looked expectantly towards Sam Poltek, and Joe introduced them.

Milt could smile as phony-baloney as Poltek. Must be something they taught them all at law school.

'Mr. Poltek's from that Senate committee.'

'Oh, yes.' Milt pulled up a chair and sat down. He took the yellow pencil he was carrying and balanced it behind his ear, like a grocer. His long, narrow face was serious, almost mournful and showed a good bit of scalp at the temples.

'The Senate Sub-committee on Government-Assisted Private Enterprise', Poltek said easily. 'We call it GAPE.'

'Yah', Joe said. 'Ain't Harold Brice on that committee?'

'Senator Brice heads the full committee, the Senate Committee on Government Underwriting. But he's not on the sub-committee. Senator Owens of California is chairman of the sub-committee.'

'I know Harold Brice pretty well', Joe said. 'I knew him when he was only the Mayor in Allenburg and after that merely a lousy Lieutenant-Governor in Trenton.'

'Wonderful man', Poltek said with no enthusiasm. 'I've only met him twice.'

'He was ambassador to somewhere for a while. Where was it, Milt?'

'Burma', Milt said. 'Liberal America's gift to the Far East. Probably even did some good out there.' Milt carefully removed and cleaned his gold-rimmed glasses.

'I supported him when he ran for Governor here', Joe said lamely, and caught Milt's wretched look. Timid Milt no doubt figured he ought to have kept his big mouth shut.

A moment of silence and leg-shifting made a gap that was noticeable enough to be uncomfortable.

Milt took a long breath, put his glasses back on. 'Mr. Poltek, would you care to tell us a little something about the purpose of your visit?' He took the pencil from his ear and reached for the yellow legal pad on Joe's desk, placed the pencil eraser under his lower lip and leaned back in the chair, sliding his feet forward.

'Be glad to', Poltek said. He opened his despatch case and took out a file folder, from which he drew forth a single closely printed page. 'This is the Senate resolution authorizing the Investigating Sub-committee on Government-Assisted Private Enterprise', he said. 'Would you care to look it over?' He handed it to Milt.

As the conversation continued, Milt pushed his glasses down on his nose and glanced at the printed sheet. Give Milt anything to read and you damn near lost him. He couldn't take his eyes off it, including a daily paper, stock-market report, or the phone book.

'We plan to investigate individuals and firms who've benefited from government guarantees or government insurance in the housing programmes, shipbuilding programmes and farm-subsidy programmes. We cut clear across the Maritime and Fisheries and Agriculture Committees. Our purpose is to establish whether new legislation should specify more precisely what kinds of persons or firms should be eligible for government assistance. For example, whether they should be required to be of good moral character. Right now, even a convicted felon is eligible for almost any kind of government assistance.'

'Any such limitation sounds as if it would be unconstitutional', Milt said morosely.

'P'raps.'

'How can any government agency be expected to know at the time a man applies to it for assistance if he's of good moral character? It's impossible to police. Each agency would need its own FBI.'

'P'raps. But proposals are being made to require applicants to file affidavits with their applications as a condition of receiving government assistance, certifying that the applicant has not in the past paid any sums, provided any services, or given any gifts to federal, state or municipal government employees or to officials of any labour union with which they have had dealings. Then, if a man is caught five years later, the government has him on a perjury count, and it gives the Justice Department one more string to its bow. People who *have* given bribes or done any other hanky-panky might think a long time before they sign an affidavit like that, don'tcha think?'

Milt shook his head. 'Nope. Guys like that wouldn't give it a second thought.'

'Well,' Poltek drawled, 'p'raps their attorneys might.'

'I absolutely don't understand this kinda talk', Joe said grumpily. 'Are you saying we gave bribes?'

'Oh, my, I haven't said anything like that', Poltek said. 'Our job is simply to investigate. When we're through we may try to write legislation to regularize the relationship between government employees in these agencies and the people who look to them for government assistance. Some kind of code of ethics with teeth.'

'Great idea', Joe said wryly.

Poltek took out a round-stemmed pipe and carefully stuffed tobacco into it. 'Mr. Naples, you're one of the largest government-assisted home builders in the country. The NMIA has insured over two hundred million dollars' worth of mortgages for you. A third of your buyers have used VA guarantees. We want to know a little about your history, and we want to know how you've operated. We expect you've done everything completely above board, and if so, it'll be a shining example to all the others who receive the same type of underwriting. And, frankly, if you haven't we'll want to know about that, too.'

'Sure.'

'We know that some people did not – behave themselves.'

'I want to read this more carefully', Milt said, rattling the printed page. 'Do you mind if I keep it?'

'By all means', Poltek said sharply.

'You mean if I bought lunch for some joker at the NMIA, that's important?'

'We're not children', Poltek said. Reminded him of Carey there saying, 'I'm *not* a little boy, I'm a *big* boy.'

'Do you want to ask my client any questions now?' Milt sat up straight, pulled his knees in. His smile had disappeared now and he was all earnestness.

'Not at this time', Poltek said. 'P'raps later. But we expect that for a while now we'll have him under active investigation. What I would appreciate now is an opportunity for my accountants and staff to look over your books and records.'

Joe half rose. "Ey! What —'

'Certainly', Milt interrupted. 'Would you prefer to examine them here or in Washington?'

'Here would be fine. It's a more luxurious atmosphere, you know those creepy old government offices. My own office is in a cellar.'

Joe was beginning to be irritated. 'What's this crap about good moral character? What does *that* mean exactly?'

Poltek smiled. 'Frankly, I don't know myself. That's one of our problems.'

'Well, I got nothing to worry about', Joe said. 'I'm a member of the Diners' Club in good standing. But now I think of it, I once snitched ten cents off a news-stand when I was five years old', Joe said. 'How bad is that?'

'You want to know something?' Poltek said, smiling steadily. 'So did I. In fact I stole a quarter.'

Joe felt the knot around his duodenum. 'You're a lot younger', he grumbled. 'It's this goddam inflation.'

They all chuckled, Poltek's stomach going up and down while he held it.

'I was probably just a little poorer than you, Mr. Naples', Poltek said pleasantly. 'I probably needed the money more.'

'I was pisspoor', Joe said. 'I lived in a goddam slum till I was in my twenties. Milt'll tell you. He knew me then – thirty-five, forty years ago.'

'Well . . .' Poltek zipped his despatch case. 'You've done right well since.' He scuffed the thick carpet. 'Thanks for your co-opera-tion. It's a nuisance to have to subpoena books and records. Makes it unpleasant all round. My feeling is if you're clean, you're clean, and you may as well establish it right away. There are plenty of crooks and chisellers for us to go after.'

'Sure', Joe said. 'By the way, have you ever been around my little town?'

'No, not really', Poltek said without interest.

'You got time?' Joe could hear the eagerness in his own voice, although he tried to control it. What did he have to prove to this kid? 'I'd be glad to show you around.' He wanted to show everyone around.

'Well', Poltek hesitated. 'I have to catch the five o'clock at Trenton. That would get me to Washington in time for a late dinner.'

'Sure,' Joe said, 'plenty of time. You want to investigate, you should see it all. Come on, you get the two-dollar tour from the padrone himself.'

Milt was silent. He had already had the two-dollar tour. Ten thousand times. But he'd go along for protection. And probably he'd end up having to drive this guy to Trenton.

TWO

JOE pulled his Abercrombie & Fitch Eisenhower jacket from the back of his chair, jammed his short arms into it and led the way to the lift. Next to an empty parking space with the sign *J. Naples*, a car was parked before a gold-lettered sign *Mr. D. Naples*. Its licence plate, which Tony Ferrara had got for Dino, contained only the letter N. 'Is that N for Naples or Napoleon?' Poltek said, and Joe did not bother to respond. If Dino wanted to live it up, that was his own business. Joe jumped into the driver's seat.

'First Cadillac station wagon I've seen', Poltek said as he got in. 'I didn't know they made them.'

'My brother's', Joe said. 'You think it's a little showy? You should see his Ferrari, mister, you oughta get a load of that leopard-skin upholstery. My brother knows how to live. You want to investigate someone, you oughta look into my brother Dino. My own self, I use a jeep, but it's in the shop today so he lent me his car.'

As they drove slowly by the stores, Poltek said, 'I understand you own an aeroplane.'

'Yah. Fly it myself, if I have to. Twin-engine Beech. Hot little plane, and damn useful. I can get you down to Washington in an hour. Fly you there myself, if you like.' Poltek smiled like a sphinx, not a word.

'That's probably not such a hot idea, huh? Free rides. Bad ethics between a Senate sub-committee and private enterprises.' He laughed as they drove into Miller's Road, but Poltek and Milt were silent.

They were just leaving the centre of town, passing the school, the synagogue and the churches. 'That's St. Theresa', Joe said. 'Girl I know asked me to name it for her name saint, so I did it. What the hell.'

Now they were into the first residential section. 'This first batch of houses over there on the right, that's where the city of Naples got started, Mr. Poltek. There's the first slab we ever poured – 1947. It was my first model. Dino designed it. Six thousand families in this section, all rented at sixty bucks a month when they were first built. They're all sold now, of course. You ever seen the inside of one of these houses?'

'No', Poltek said.

'For the average guy,' Joe said, 'nothing like it.' He stopped the car in front of a grey house. 'Come on.'

He knocked at the door, and a young woman, her hair in curlers under a bandana, answered the door. Young she was, but she looked used up and discarded. Bad complexion. Dirty nails.

'Yes?' Dark suspicion in that ugly young face.

'I'm Joe Naples', Joe said. 'I got some men here from Washington wanna see the house.'

'You're Mr. Naples? Honest to God?'

'Yes, ma'am.'

'OhmyGod. The furnace makes such a terrible noise, Mr. Naples! I don't know what you got in it! Scares the wits outa the poor baby. You should see him jump when that furnace goes on. Jesus! He'll be a psychosomatic wreck.'

'I'll have it looked at', Joe said, taking out a small black book. 'What's the address?'

'Twenty-two-A Heather Lane. OhmyGod, am I glad you came! Who'd believe it! Wait'll I tell my husband. The name is Swaboda.'

Joe said, 'All right if we look around?'

'Sure, sure. Help yourself. I'm sorry the place is such a mess.'

'They're all a mess', Joe said.

'It's the babies', she said.

Joe showed Poltek the trick two-way fireplace that could be used for cooking and winter warmth but was at the moment strewn with dirty laundry; the large living-room (18 × 12), with the picture window in the rear facing the yard, not the street, like some of these idiots were building now; the masonry chimney (no tin or asbestos crap for Naples); the sliding aluminium windows; paved terrace outside; and the unfinished attic.

'My husband's gonna finish the attic next spring. We're kinda short right now.'

The Swabodas had bought the place a year ago from the Naples Foundation for $8,890. It was nine years old, but Mrs. Swaboda still thought Mr. Naples should look after the furnace.

'It's supposed to last more than nine years, right, Mr. Naples?'
He laughed.

Poltek fingered his unlit pipe throughout the inspection, backing
fastidiously away from Mrs. Swaboda and mucus-covered baby
Swaboda, who crawled, babbling, after them.

Milt said nothing, but Joe could read his mind. Nine years, what
a ridiculously long guarantee.

They drove through streets past thousands of identical little
houses – all ranches in this section. Joe had always tried to feel for
the underprivileged, but he had a sense of having been driven away
by them. They considered him an enemy, like that Mrs. Swaboda.
He was damn unhappy about it, too. Did *they* have to worry about
the complexities of the '54 Revenue Code, the ever more strangling
regulations of NMIA, the agencies regulating charitable trusts, and
now a full-blown Senate Investigation? Did they worry about a
million pygmies working for the government, lurking in a million
offices waiting for Joe Naples to make one single mistake? They
were goddam lucky, the underprivileged. They never had it so
good. He'd like to swap places with them, almost.

Joe drove to swimming pool number one. The water was still in
the Olympic-sized blue tile pool, but it was too cold for anyone to
be swimming, and no one was on the sand around the pool except a
lifeguard dressed in white slacks and shirt, reading a paper.

'I got sixteen swimming holes like this', Joe said. 'Olympic size.
One for every thousand families. Problem is to keep the kids from
peeing on the sand. They drop their old tomatoes and orange peels.
Most of 'em never saw anything like it. People, Mr. Poltek, are the
sloppiest creatures in the jungle, but they have a helluva time. Just
lookit that pool. Where'll you find anything like that? When I was
a kid on Ninety-eighth Street, we were glad when the fire department sent a guy around to open up the hydrants.' He jerked his
thumb towards the crystalline pool. 'Lookit. Put a dime on the
bottom, that water's so clear you can see if it's heads or tails.'

'In Dorchester we couldn't even get them to open the hydrants',
Poltek said grimly. 'But this place ought to keep the peasantry
happy. Make them forget their real troubles anyway, a lovely pool
like that. Tremendously effective opiate, I'd say.'

'I think it's great', Milt said loyally. 'It shows what can be done.'

'The new America', Joe said as they drove through Morning
Glory Lane. Son-of-a-bitch, talking about opiates. Sounded like
some kinda Red. 'The fresh start. All the old barnacles scraped

away. Lookit all that grass and trees. These kids, they're damn near all young couples. Happiness on the instalment plan. And they damn well get it or Joe Naples wants to know the reason.'

'Anybody's not happy here, they've got to answer to Joe Naples,' Milt said cheerfully, 'and they better have a mighty good excuse or off with their heads.'

'Kid it all you want', Joe said. 'I've seen entire cities smashed, every house knocked over, people living in caves and crates, sleeping in the streets, kids trying to sleep in the rain, not even trying to get in outa the rain, and I don't forget it. Not for one goddam minute.'

'I personally smashed up a few cities myself,' Milt said, 'and I never regretted it.'

'Milt was a bombardier with the Eighth Air Force', Joe said.

'Oh. In the Second World War?' Young Poltek made it sound like it came just before the Battle of Saratoga.

'Yah', Joe said. 'That's it. I've been tryin' to think of the name of it.'

'I watched those cities blossoming up like volcanoes and never felt the slightest qualm', Milt said. 'Of course, it was at night and they were only German cities. I feel bad about it now. But it's a different atmosphere.'

'He's a Jew', Joe said. 'Catholic now, since he married my kid sister, but what the hell.' He was sorry he'd said it when Milt flushed. 'Can't expect the Jews to have any romance for the Nazis. But those cities I saw were all Italian. My own kind. Terrible. And I'm not kiddin'.'

'What did you do during the war?' Poltek asked.

'Oh, I was in Engineers. We built the airfield at Fondi. Then I went into Military Government. I was Town Major in a little burg right on the Gulf of Gaeta called Bellanza. You ever wanna see a town beat up, mister.'

'How many people living here in Naples?' Poltek was not comfortable with the Second World War.

'Ninety thousand, ninety-one thousand some odd, last census,' Joe said, 'and growing fast. I'll show you the new stuff in a few minutes.'

He twisted his cigar expertly with his tongue, pushing it to the corner of his mouth, gripped the holder with his back teeth, glanced briefly at the miniature ivory Virgin hanging over Dino's dashboard and turned the Cadillac wagon off Miller's Road, past the corner with the four petrol stations, and up the long hill. As he came over the crest, they saw more houses ahead as far as the eye could see. Joe felt almost a wave of sentiment. He had rarely, if ever, tried to grasp the full implication of the whole city. Yet now when he tried, it was a thing almost totally apart from himself. As if it owed him nothing. The street signs, like the houses, were pure Dino – Songbird Lane, Larkspur Road, Peacock Place, Weeping Willow Drive. Kids were playing in the dusk, screaming and running, kicking each other and digging up the lawns. Men and women were tending piles of leaves burning neatly, their thick white smoke fusing with the bluish evening sky.

'Back that way, I got nearly three hundred acres reserved for a university and hospital. The Naples Foundation already put up the hospital, but we need a little expansion now. Three hundred beds aren't enough. Last year we had almost a thousand babies in maternity. How d'you like that?'

They were passing a cemetery, small but neat and very green. 'We got separate sections in there for Catholics, Protestants and Jews.'

'A real cross-section', Poltek said laconically. 'Any Negroes?' Joe took his foot off the accelerator and gently touched the power brake. It could have been for the approaching intersection. After the intersection, he resumed speed.

'Nope.' He twisted the cigar to the other side of his face, jauntily, the way FDR used to cock his cigarette. 'We got almost a thousand graves in there, and the way Milt figures it, thirty or forty years, we'll make more dough out of this cemetery than the entire shopping centre. Reason is this is a dead sure thing.'

'I can believe that.'

'My old man is buried in there. Grave number one. I had 'im moved. He was in some Godawful place up the Bronx. I gave this little old cemetery to my Foundation', Joe added. 'I'm not interested in making this kind of money for myself personally. Better if charity gets it.'

'You got 'em from maternity to the grave', Poltek said.

Joe swung off at the Candystick School, also Dino's creation – Candystick because its chimney was painted like a striped candy cane – drove by community swimming pool number four and rolled into an area of fifty acres of scarred earth. Everything was red clay and everywhere were buildings under construction. Three ten-story towers of brick and glass dominated the site. To the north beyond the ten-story structures, a score of long two-story brick buildings were going up, patterned around large courts.

Yellow carry-alls, with *J. Naples* painted on their sides, raced by at forty miles an hour, pregnant-bellied with ten-ton loads of clay. Backhoes were digging trenches in future streets, and bulldozers pushed earth, back-filling. Joe drove the Cadillac over a hump to a treacherous temporary road, and on beyond the ten-story structures. Hundreds of bricklayers were working like ants on the long low buildings. Several of them, noticing the Cadillac, stopped long enough to wave. "Ey, Joe! Joe!" Farther along, carpenter ants were framing, setting girders and joists, nailing the black Gyplap underskins to the buildings. 'Joe! Whattaya say!' Joe waved back. "Ey, Frankie, Dominick, Arturo. Whaddaya know!'

'All new apartments', he continued. 'We think Naples oughta have some apartments. My brother designs alla this. Up there' – he pointed to the tall buildings – 'he's got so much glass it'll be like living in a helicopter. These two-story buildings here are garden apartments. Dino loves 'em. He's a great guy for open space, he's in love with the open. All the open ground we saw when we were kids was over to the other side of Ninety-eighth Street.'

Milt managed a sad smile.

'Naples has no slums whatever. I am interested in this slum-clearance programme, Mr. Poltek, all over other cities. The way I see it, it's goddam important to tear 'em down. Those filthy rat traps and germ factories, every time I see that wrecking ball smack into an old-law tenement, I feel I'm getting a big splinter outa my foot, with all that pus building up around it. When you get that old splinter out, brother, it feels good. Title One. That's the pro-gramme.' Why was he bothering to say it all to this kid?

Poltek was listening expressionlessly. 'It must be very profitable, too', he said.

'There's a *fortune* in it', Joe said sarcastically. 'An absolute mint, or a guy like me wouldn't touch it, right? And if you know the right people, oh, brother.' This kid bit his tail, some new kind of federal wise guy. 'That's all I'm interested in, is profits. That's 'cause I'm starving. I need the money.'

'Are all these apartments being built with NMIA mortgages?'

'Yep,' Joe said grimly, 'Section 207. Hope to make lots of money on *them*, too. Not this building over there though, this is gonna be a grade school. But I must be completely off my head, trying to get schools up, right? Can't make a dime on a school. Naples is one

town has plenty of schools. But that's because I'm as wacked up as
a fruit cake. I don't know what the hell they teach in 'em, but *my*
part of the deal is to get 'em the buildings.'

He made a wide turn and headed back to the main road. As they
passed the bricklayers again, he said to Poltek, 'That's how I got
started – laying brick. Why waste time on education? I was too
goddam busy. Great exercise, laying brick. You lawyers ought to
try it some time.'

Now they were back in the familiar wooded area of Heathcote
Drive beyond which the houses were all abruptly twenty thousand
and up. 'This is my buffer zone', Joe said as they drove through a
small parklike area. 'No-man's-land – for keeping the classes
separated. You guys read the *Status Seekers*? I keep up with all that
stuff. Guy wants to change his status, he's gotta move.'

Joe kept up the running commentary. 'Naples is in two coun-
ties,' he said, 'four townships and God knows how many school
districts, water districts, sewer districts. We got more jurisdictions
than the Supreme Court. We got some houses – their kids go to a
school in one district, they dump their sewers in another and if
there's a fire, the trucks come from still another. Milt's trying to
get all *that* straightened out.'

Poltek stroked the bowl of his pipe. 'You must have had to
persuade quite a few public officials in all these jurisdictions to do a
number of unorthodox things.'

Joe looked angrily at the dark young man. The little bastid,
accusing him of bribing these local yokels. How else did he think
anything got done?

'Patience did it', Milt said. 'Persuasiveness and being right.'

'I suppose', Poltek said.

Soon they were in the forty-thousand-dollar-home area, with
plots up to an acre and a half, heavily shrubbed, carefully mown,
each with its own two-car garage where Chryslers, Oldsmobiles
and small Caddies nestled. A teen-age boy washed a car in a driveway. Two girls biked by. Beyond that, brown elms, yellowing and
reddening maples and the rust-leafed dogwoods retired splendidly
for the cold weather alongside the undaunted evergreens. The
road curved more dangerously and grew narrower. The pavements
had ended, the street signs disappeared, and as the houses drifted by
farther apart, the road became barely wide enough for the big car.
Rural, NMIA called it.

At the top of the next steep rise there was a small break in the woods, a surprise of meadowland on the right, and the unique street sign – a bark-covered pole with a pillow-shaped sign, bearing the legend in old English letters: *Easy Street*. He had completely forgotten that sign, which he now saw through Poltek's eyes. Goddam.

He turned the station wagon into the driveway and saw his own house, four hundred feet back on the hill, surrounded by twenty acres of flawless lawn, a twenty-nine-room stone-and-brick Tudor fortress atop the highest hill in Midbergen County. It looked something like old DeWitt Clinton High School, except instead of being on West Fifty-ninth Street next to the Roosevelt Hospital morgue, it was set in the midst of one hundred carefully cultivated acres, a helluva piece of property. The pool below the house was eighty feet long.

'Whose place is this?' Poltek said.

'Mine', Joe said. 'A lot less trouble than building our own place. This was the old Woodman estate. We got it for nothing. Thrown in with the land.'

'Very nice. Who named the street?'

'I did', Joe said. He was going to add it was a gag, but didn't. The hell with you, Poltek.

At the entrance to the drive was the simple sign, *J. Naples*. Everything was simple like that, including the massed salvia on either side of the drive, just like Jock Dennison's place in Deal. Beyond, as he made the turn, they could see a sign in the driveway a quarter of a mile up Easy Street, one with green reflector letters: *Milton Jason*.

'The little place down there is mine', Milt said with diffidence. 'That Tobacco Road place.'

'Like to come in for a drink?' Joe said, 'Maybe meet my wife?'

'No – thank you kindly. I'd love to, but I'd better get over to Trenton.' Poltek looked at his watch after he had said it.

'Sure', Joe said.

'Why don't you go ahead in, Giusepp',' Milt said, 'I'll take Mr. Poltek to Trenton. It'll give me my big chance to drive Dino's Caddy. I may even use the phone in it. Always wanted to try it.'

'Sure', Joe said. He knew Milt was trying to tell him he had said too much, opened his big yap again. God knows what big fat cat he'd let out of the bag. Milt was the super-secretive type. He hid things from his own self. He had separate compartments in his mind and kept each one under lock and key. Milt had been the greatest poker player in the entire American Air Force. He had won twelve thousand bucks in two years in England, then put it all in common

stocks, never told Joe which or what, or how he was doing. Probably had made a fortune. He was as top secret as a piece of Russian
military intelligence.

'So long, Mr. Poltek.'

'Good-bye. Thanks for the two-dollar tour.'

'Sure. Here, have a whatzis.' He offered the kid an Upmann
from his breast pocket.

'No, thanks. I'll stick to my pipe.'

Joe noticed that he had never lit it. 'I've been thinking, Mr.
Poltek, this good moral character fascinates me. When I was a kid
I used to visit this joint, you know, a hoor house up on Hundred
and Third Street. Stephanie, I think the chief hoor's name was.
Wasn't it Hundred and Third, Milt? Milt never went. He's a guy
with abso*lutely* good moral character. I was around fourteen, fifteen. Used to be ninety cents. Those broads, they were real pigs,
especially Stephanie. But the ninety cents we always came by
honestly, we used to grab it off some kid over on Park or Madison.
Those kids didn't need it like we did, they had money to burn.
You think the Senators on the committee might want to put that
in their little black book? When I think back on some of the things
we did, it's a wonder I got any character at all.' He laughed easily,
shook Poltek's hand and watched Milt drive around the circular
drive and back out to Easy Street. He was glad to get away from
Poltek's smell. It wasn't the same healthy odour that men got working on a scaffold. It was more of a skunk stink.

In the dark vaulted foyer, with the kidney-shaped tropical fish
bowl under the gargantuan chandelier, he gave his Eisenhower
jacket to Josh Cibulkas, who maintained his customary mournful
mien.

'Mrs. Naples in?'

'Yes, sir, upstairs.'

'Feed the fish, Josh?'

'Sure did, Major.' In every word and gesture Josh Cibulkas'
devotion spoke.

Joe yanked off his French maroon knitted tie. As he passed the
large, panelled library he could see the teakwood desk Hetty had
had specially made in Japan – he was surrounded by teak these days
– and the façade of leather book backs that filled the shelves. Why
couldn't Hetty go to one of those book stores down town – one of
those 'Any book in this store 49 cents' – and buy a thousand or so
and put a few books on the shelves?

Jesus, he was exhausted. He hunched by the entrance to the music-room with its two Cézannes and a smaller crystal chandelier and started up the sweeping marble stairway towards the bedroom. Even the stair walls were littered with oils of all sizes. Hetty knew the whole crowd – Max Weber, Darrel Austin, Fletcher Martin, Feininger, some dame named Georgia O'Keeffe, around eight million others. He felt like an interloper in the place.

'Joie, is that you?'

'Yah.'

'I'm in the tub. I'll be right out.'

The highball glass on Hetty's table in her dressing-room had her lipstick mark on the rim. In spite of himself he sniffed at the glass. Bourbon. She was at it again. He wondered how many and what for.

He went into the bedroom, examined himself carefully in the full-length mirror. As he pulled off his shirt, he blinked in puzzlement at himself. The growth of hair on his chest, he noticed, was whiter than that on his head. His full face was more drawn than he ever remembered seeing it; his usual ruddy-pink complexion yellower; his blue eyes were cloudy and a trifle bloodshot. The softness that his full, almost pretty, wavy hair had begun to give him was lost in the lines of fatigue and tension. He studied his own pugnacious face in a photo on Hetty's bureau taken eight years ago aboard the Hetty II – there he was, chin out, fist clenched, stripped to the waist, like Jack Dempsey, the photo oozed potency. No question, he was softening up lately. His sister Luce was always saying how handsome he'd become, he looked almost exactly like Ezio Pinza. Even the scar on his right jaw was hairline, almost invisible, and the one on his neck scarcely more than a white-healed scratch. He placed the cigar on Hetty's night table, with the ash end over the edge, jutted his tongue out and leaned towards the mirror to examine it. Madre Maria, what a colour! He had to cut down on cigars.

Without untying his grey suède and leather shoes, he let himself fall backward on one of the monstrous Louis Quatorze twin beds, not bothering to remove the peach satin spread. He reached under the satin spread for the pillow, punched it into a fluff, rammed it under his head and settled back to stare at the fantastic glass chandelier. It was hideous.

He heard Hetty's bare footsteps on the thick carpeting, opened his eyes and saw her standing, head cocked, the tailored navy and white dressing-gown tightly drawn, watching him like a tall, curious bird, her lips pursed, eyes squinted. In spite of the boyishly-cropped blondish-grey hair, the thin, pale lips and the lines at the edge of her green eyes, she was still a goddam striking woman. At fifty-three she was lean, almost athletic, her high cheekbones and slightly gaunt face giving her small features added delicacy. Her drinking, in some miraculous way, left her body untouched. Maybe it was the massages she got. One thing you could say for Hetty, she was still feminine. She had a musical voice and a rolling, high way of laughing, almost a giggle. The only trouble was that he missed the crawling, delicious sensation over all the surfaces of his own skin, and in his loins. It was not the old loin-type passion, too much hell had been kicked out of it. Not that he still didn't think Hetty was the classiest woman he knew. He felt sorry for her, and when you got down to it, there wasn't much else that held them together. He did have to make up to her for Carey in whatever ways he could, he thought illogically.

Hetty walked to her dressing-table, carefully lifted the grey-rimmed wide-lensed glasses and adjusted them on the bridge of her slight, narrow, upturned nose She peered at him, untrusting, suspicious, as she always did after three or four bourbons.

'Did you see that lawyer from the Senate committee?' Her voice was in its high range today, and unlike her piercing eyes, her words slurred. He could smell the booze as she sat on the edge of the bed to untie his shoes.

'Yah.'

'Whatever did he want?'

'He didn't say. They're looking for monkey business. Anyone who ever got a buck from the U.S. Government.'

'Like your NMIA mortgages?'

'Yah.'

'What kind of funny business?'

'You know – pay-offs, free lunches, Christmas presents. How the hell should I know?'

'Darling, don't be so tense. I only asked.' She put his shoes on the floor and got off the bed.

'Me tense? Are you off your head?'

'You never bribed anyone, did you? Not seriously?'

'Do I look like the bribing type?'

'At least you're smart enough not to tell anyone, even me.'

He sat up. 'Now what the hell kind of crack is that? Ah, look,

I've been two hours with that suspicious whozis, Polecat, or whatever his name is – the kid from the committee. A child. On a
Senate sub-committee, can you imagine? Why do they get such
young boys to do these jobs? The government must be in a hell of
a fix.'

'They probably don't pay much,' Hetty said, 'and it can't be any
fun.'

'Yah. I ought to find out exactly what they pay them.' He lay
back. 'What's new here?'

Suddenly she saw the cigar burning the rosewood top of her
night table. 'Oh, Joie, look what you've done!' Her voice for the
first time came down to its normal, lower range. She lifted the
cigar with a terrible distaste. 'It's a simply enormous hole, Joie,
couldn't you be a little more careful? You know how I love that
table. I try so *hard* to keep things *nice*.' She sounded almost as if she
was going to bawl.

'I hate that table, Mullaly', Joe said. 'Here, gimme the cigar.'

'Couldn't you smoke down in the study?' She spoke with the
pathos of long suffering. Then suddenly she brightened, popped her
lips together and made a tiny shrug. 'Small loss', she said.

It occurred to him that they had been married more than thirty
years and she was still complaining about exactly one hundred per
cent the same things she complained of their first week in the house
on Elm Street. 'There's gotta be one room in the house, Mullaly,
where I can do anything I want – sleep, smoke, tune-up – anything.
Nothing *proibito*, okay?'

'Now I've made you angry.'

'You're out of your mind.'

'It's not my drinking, is it? This is my first." Oh, Hetty, come,
come.

'Lookit, I'm tired, Mullaly. I need this Senate investigation
exactly like I need the septic tank to back up into my bed. They're
sending examiners up to look over the books and lawyers to look
over documents. I'm under what they call active investigation.'

'But why?'

'Who the hell knows? I suppose beause I got two hundred million
bucks of NMIA mortgages.'

'What can they find?'

'How the hell do I know? Not a damn thing.'

'Would you like something to drink, Joie?'

'Yah. Maybe whozis could bring me up a little Chianti.'

She pushed the intercom on the wall over the bed and Cibulkas' voice said, 'Yes, Major?'

'Bring Mr. Naples a bottle of Chianti', Hetty said.

'Okay, ma'am.'

'Now lie down,' Joe said, 'you make me nervous pacing around and about.'

She lay still on her back on the other bed. 'Darling,' she said, 'you've been working too hard.' He took her hand gently across the open space.

'What's new?'

She'd been to New York all day, they were beginning to walk through the new play, *His Majesty Regrets*. 'The director, Mickey Mann, is simply wonderful. Very young, but so vital, and so sensitive and understanding. You ought to see how he handles Miss Evans. She eats right out of his hand. So do I, for that matter. I think we may have a hit, Joie.'

'Yah?' Those sensitive guys absolutely knocked him off. He recalled, darkly, that other great director, Trick Potamos. It made him sick thinking of *that* moment of discovery. Well, he was goddam sure nothing like that was going on with Hetty now. At least, not probably.

And, oh yes, she said, her brother Michael was getting out of St. Francis Hospital next week. While she was in town she called in to see him.

'They think he'll be okay now?'

'Until the next time he takes a drink. You know how it is, darling.' She was devoted to her family.

'Yah.' At least taking care of her family kept her out of trouble. That and the Broadway stuff they had money in and her interest in paintings and painters, the entire culture jazz kept her plenty busy. She was now on the committee to select the Naples Foundation's literary award for books which sold under five thousand copies, and she did a hell of a lot of reading for *that*. Joe Naples giving literary prizes. Would you believe it? It gave Hetty a little standing and him a little laugh. 'How's Mammina?'

'Fine. She's having her regular Scopa party over there this afternoon with all her cronies. She expects to raise a fortune. Maybe ten or fifteen dollars.' His mother never rested. The misdirected energy of that woman should be bottled. Always surrounded by a dozen old broads, Mammina was great, the Queen of the Mob.

'She got a letter from Rosina today. Mammina's as pleased as Punch.'

It was lucky, he was thinking, he had Hetty keeping track of both their families. Made his job of looking after them easier. She got a kick out of seeing her family living in comfortable houses, doing respectable jobs, even Michael when he was not out on a tear. She used to tell him ten million times a week how happy she was for all he'd done for her family. What the hell, why not? It made Hetty happy. That is, in the days when there were still a few things that could make her happy.

Be a helluva shock to all these good people if this Senate investigation turned up serious things against him. What'd they call it in Washington – derogatory information?

'And there was a letter from Andy this morning.'

'Yah? You mean he actually took pencil in hand and wrote his mother and father? *Miràcolo.*'

'Typewriter, Joie. He's been talking to Professor Summers. Andy thinks he'd like to teach Government at Harvard.'

'*Dio mio!*'

'That's what he says he wants. Here.' She pulled the letter out of the night table. '"Mother, you have no idea what a terrific man Summers is. We were talking the other day and he told me that in the election next month, he is going to have the privilege of voting for former students of his for President, Senator and Congressman, and he expects to have the pleasure of seeing them all elected. Good men who might never have gone into politics if it hadn't been for him. How I'd love to be able to say anything like that some day!"'

'He just a few months ago told me he wanted to come into the building business with me, for God's sake.'

Hetty sat up abruptly and spoke with unintended sharpness. 'You wanted him to come into the business, darling, I think.'

He laughed. 'I guess he didn't hear me so good. And what's so terrible about the building business?'

'Nothing. It's just apparently not what he wants to do.' She stood up, walked into her dressing-room. He could hear the ice rattle in her glass of bourbon and he heard her pour another. When she returned she was holding the glass defiantly.

Cibulkas knocked. He left the Chianti and she poured Joe a tumblerful.

'How does he know what he wants?' Joe said. 'He's twenty-three goddam years old. That kid don't know to come in outa the rain. I'll talk to him.'

She said slowly in a barely audible voice, 'So will I.' He often wondered just how much she guessed about Carey.

'You didn't hear me so good.' Joe raised his voice.

'Go ahead, Joie, talk to him, talk. I don't know why I should mind. You love that business of yours so, I suppose you have to fight for its preservation.'

'He don't have to come into *my* business', Joe said. 'He can do whatever he damn well pleases. *You* know that. The name is Naples, not Ming.'

Wearily she said, 'I guess Andy's big enough to fight his own battles, even with you. And you'll never say anything unpleasant or disagreeable to him anyway. You never do. You'll probably expect me to do it for you.'

'Now look', Joe said. 'I'm not trying to tell him what to do. But let's be honest – what kind of a whatzis would he make?'

Hetty smiled wryly. 'You're about to endow an entire university – how much did you say – twenty million to get it started, or was it thirty?'

Joe shook his head. 'Teaching's for Mr. Chips. Andy has more on the ball than Mr. Chips. Locking himself up in some college all his life. He's been in school so long, he's afraid to try himself outside. What it is, it's plain cowardice.'

'You sound like Jock Dennison', she said wearily, and took a long swallow.

'I wish you'd lay off that stuff', Joe said, trying to make his voice gentle.

'I wish you wouldn't wish quite so many things, Joie. Have a little wine yourself. You'll feel better.'

He drank wine like a soft drink. 'Probably the mistake was sending Andy to Harvard in the first place. He oughta try new things. Hell, I was laying brick when I was thirteen. Carey was out on the job with me summers when he was fifteen.'

'Oh, talking of new experiences, I think Andy's in love, too.' The way she changed subjects. You mention Carey and you'd think Carey had never lived at all.

'Yah. Well, at least *that's* normal.'

'He doesn't quite come right out and admit it, of course, but it's there between his dispassionate lines. This girl – Cynthia Schiller her name is – is *the* most sensitive, warm-hearted, generous, and Lord-knows-what girl. I don't think she has any discernible law.'

'She must be built like Sophia Loren. Andy goes for girls who are solid. Now don't get jealous, Mullaly. The kid's gotta get married sometime.'

'Oh, I'm all for it, darling. Andy's always been wild about girls as a gender. I'm amazed he's held out this long.'

'Yah. Be a helluva husband on a teacher's salary, won't he? How does he expect to support this broad? How does he think little Cynthia's gonna like it?'

'I suppose he expects we'll help out.'

He reached for the wine and drank the rest of it directly from the Chianti flask. 'Let's see the letter.'

Hetty handed it to him and sat behind him as he read, looking over his shoulder. Harvard Law School, the letterhead said in crimson engraving over a seal that said *Veritas*.

The letter started 'Dear Mom and Padrone', and the rest was about the way Hetty had said, neatly typed, words like Torts and Contracts, referring to courses he was taking. Hetty kept track of all that stuff. This business about Professor Summers '– and I'm giving serious thought to teaching when I leave school. There are lots of reasons, not all of them tangible, why I want to do it. I can hear Dad saying, "Those who can, do; those who can't, teach". Maybe. But I think I want to teach because I have a tremendous desire to communicate. I'm excited enough about our government, its beauty, its intricacies, its peculiarly involved relationship to the people to want to make others as excited about it as I am – to get into other people the *why* and the *how*. Maybe to inspire some good people to make a better government and a better world. I don't think I'll ever get tired of it or restless with it, because it's such a big order and such a tremendous challenge, and I think well worth one lifetime – mine at least. If Carey could go out and give his life in one day in a gesture for it, I think it's worth my doing in a slower, different, and conceivably more useful way, not that I underrate Carey's sacrifice. He just had one tough break. Summers says he's sure I could get an instructor's job here.' Then a paragraph about the girl he took to the Dartmouth game, Cynthia Schiller, sophomore from Radcliffe, came from Chillicothe. Where the hell was Chillicothe? Not one single thing in the entire letter was familiar to him. You have these kids, they grow up, and you haven't the foggiest idea what goes on. They've also got no idea what goes on with you or what you're all about. What would Andy think if he read in the paper some fine day that his old man was mixed up in some pretty seedy stuff, and maybe not just bribery and corruption? The papers could make things look pretty loused up. Andy would no more understand him or why he did the things he did than some poor bastid from Mars. And what if he ended up on television the way Tony Ferrara did, before the Hendrickson Committee that time? When was it – 1951? Tony thought he'd done great, but no one did great in that kind of a deal. No sir, TV he would not like. It would absolutely have to be prevented at all costs, no matter what. The thought fatigued him.

'Hetty,' he said, 'let's not you and me fight. If he wants to teach, let 'im teach.'

He got up and changed into a Hawaiian sports shirt. He washed his face, snorting like a buffalo into his wet hands. He was suddenly impatient because he could barely wait for Milt to get back from Trenton. They had a lot of ground to go over. They had to be ready for any curves Polecat might throw. Milt would know what to do, how to go about it. Milt had certainly not seemed particularly worried . . . had he? Hard to tell about Milt.

Joe trailed downstairs, into the dark, high-ceilinged living-room, to turn on the last game of the World Series while Hetty dressed for dinner, as she always did. You'd think she was born over on Park Avenue. Well, Second Avenue was only three blocks from Park.

Then the phone started to ring. There must have been four, five calls one right after another. Cibulkas got the first one. Joe got a kick out of the way he answered it in that southern drawl, 'The Naples' residence.' It was Cathy O'Neill from the office, and Joe took it. Simon Cutler, her old boss, and his old friend, had called Joe twice from Washington, said it was important. He'd seemed agitated, Cathy thought. He would be called back in a few minutes.

Si Cutler? Jesus. He suddenly focussed with new vividness on that entire deal in Las Vegas. He'd damn near forgotten all about it. Must be ten, twelve years ago. When you are good friends for so long, you forget the specifics, you bury them. There must be a statute of limitations. Sure, why shouldn't Si have called him at home, he was an old friend. A hell of a dear old friend.

Then it was Seth Ferguson, the managing editor of the Allenburg *Courier*. Nice boy, Seth, always gave him the space he needed. There had just been a visitor at the *Courier* office, Seth said, from Washington, looking through the files of back numbers, way back.

Wanted every story the paper had run on the murder of a guy named Gamboretta, a labour leader back in the twenties. Twenty-seven. Seth Ferguson himself was born in '27 and in Topeka at that, so he hadn't been able to be too helpful, but they had found a lot of stuff, July '27 it was. Did Joe remember anything about it?

Gamboretta? Yah, yah, sure. There was this guy, union official, either with the common labourers or the bricklayers local back there. Had one eye or one ear, one something. Had a reputation for being a son-of-a-bitch and a crooked bastid. Someone shot him or stabbed him. You know how those things are. Joe was only a kid then himself. Twenty-seven. Hell, he was just twenty-one.

Another thing, Seth Ferguson said, this guy from the government wanted stuff on the first houses Joe had built in Allenburg, way back before the depression. Those houses he'd done with Jock Dennison – on Montgomery Street, weren't they – and everything the paper had on him since, even social items. Every mention of the famous house on Elm Street.

What Seth Ferguson wanted to know, did Joe have any idea what all this was about? The guy from the government, he was definitely not from the FBI, he said he was from some Senate sub-committee staff. He didn't offer a thing, just asked questions.

Joe couldn't help him.

Next it was Tony Ferrara from his little fortress in East Orange. Joe hadn't seen Tony for years, but they kept in touch by phone every few months.

At first it was chit-chat. 'Whaddaya think, Joey? I just got married.'

'No! Anyone I know?'

'Great girl. Cookie Muller. You remember her?'

'Nope. I hope you're happy as hell.'

'Well, at least I'm gettin' a little again. Listen, Joey, why I called you, you wanna hear a hot one? A guy just come up with a sub-poena for all my books and records. Some bastid from this new Senate sub-committee. Boy, have I got my bellyful of sub-commit-tees! They never forgive me for tellin' ol' Senator Tobey off. You know what one of these bastid investigators over the Treasury Department tells my accountant? He says I give Senator Tobey the apoplexy the old guy died of. That little Senator didn't die of apoplexy. He died from religious prostration.'

Joe could scarcely make head or tail of Tony's comments,

although he always enjoyed Tony on the subject of Senator Tobey.
It was Tony's open boast that he had killed Senator Tobey by
aggravating him to death. He told this even to people who had
long since forgotten the holy-rolling, peppery Senator from Vermont. 'And I'm gonna outlive that Hendrickson', he usually concluded.

'Well, did you give him your books, Tony?'

'How could I give him my books? The Treasury Department
already got 'em. They took 'em last year. And when they get
finished with 'em the Justice Department got ickies on 'em. They
ain't my records any more, they're theirs. But what the hell, I got
nothing to worry about, they're all doctored up', Tony roared.
'There ain't one right figure in the whole goddam shootin' match.
What right they got to know my business? My business is private,
ain't it? It's very private, that's my position. Ask Milt, the legal
beagle. The hell with 'em. We're living under a Constitution,
ain't we? Not under Ivan the Terrible. This guy Ike, he's no bargain, in fact, he's terrible, but he ain't *Ivan* the Terrible.'

'Tony, do these books show the extent of your interest in Naples?'

'Look, Joe, boy, these books are so loused up, I don't know what
they show. I wouldn't be surprised they show I'm bankrupt. You
know my old book-keeper, poor fella, you remember Herman
Maibaum. When he knocked himself off, that did it. Now nobody
can figure the books out. Believe me, the government ain't had a
problem like this since they broke the Japanese code.'

Joe found himself smiling. Tony had always lived at the edge of
prisons and once or twice inside them, and even, on one occasion,
in the shadow of the electric chair. He was under two indictments
now. To hear him talk, nothing was the least bit serious. But Tony
did not sound like he was at any Mardi Gras either. He kinda
breathed heavy.

'Harold Brice is connected to this deal somehow', Joe said.

'Harold? Bigger jackass never lived. He is the most unwholesome man I ever met. He won't take a dime for anything any more,
and *he's* a Senator, you'd think he'd know better.'

'He took thirty grand from me once.'

'Yah. That was way back, Joe. Forget it. He's a different man
today. He wants to be Vice-President of the whole United States.
I never met a man outside of him in the entire state of New Jersey
wanted to be Vice-President.'

'Tony, did you give him that money personally?'

B

'What do you think I did, spend it? It was a campaign contribution. He was running for Governor. How could I forget it?'

'Well,' Joe said, '*his* sub-committee is investigating me. At least he's chairman of the full committee.'

'Yah. That's what I hear. That's what I'm just tellin' you.'

'Doesn't that thirty grand mean anything to him?'

'Nah! Like I told you, the guy's unwholesome. He's nothing but a thief. You buy him and he gets unbought. I don't trust a single goddam soul in the government these days. All your buddies, but when you need 'em, *nothin'*. I know from experience. What'd you do for him lately?'

'I'll do plenty if he doesn't get his dogs off me', Joe said.

'Hell,' Tony said, 'if you want me to talk to Harold, lemme know. I might be able to do something with him.'

'Thanks, Tony, and thanks for calling.'

'Hope your phone ain't tapped yet, Joey. So long.'

While he was still talking, the other phone had rung. Out of the corner of his ear he heard Cibulkas drawl, 'The Naples' residence.' It was Piggy Banks, chief underwriter of the Trenton NMIA office.

'I'm calling from a booth, Joe.'

'Yah?'

'Everyone at the office got questionnaires today.'

'What about?'

'You know. The usual. It's on something called Form SS-2461. To be filled up by all personnel, regardless of classification. Listen: "Have you accepted the hospitality of any sponsor or builder at luncheon or dinner on more than one occasion? If so, please name sponsor or builder and state approximate number of occasions. Have you ever received Christmas gifts from sponsors or builders? Do you know any sponsors or builders socially? If so, list them. Have you accepted other favours from sponsors or builders, such as (a) Hotel bills or car-fare paid for by sponsor; (b) Vacations paid for by sponsor; (c) Trips or outings paid for by sponsor; (d) Medical bills paid for by sponsor; (e) Indirect gratuities from sponsor via members of your immediate family? Were you previously employed by a sponsor or builder for whom you subsequently processed NMIA mortgage insurance as a member of the Administration? Are any of your brothers, sisters, parents, children or their spouses now employed by a sponsor or builder who is actively processing cases in your field office?" Can you imagine it, Joe, it's the full treatment! And in affidavit form. Criminal penalties for falsification. It's this Owens sub-committee, I suppose.'

Joe grimaced. Piggy could be pretty dense. 'I wouldn't be surprised, Piggy.'

'Can't Harold Brice help us?' Piggy said pathetically.

'Who knows?' Joe said.

'I'm not listing all those boat trips, Joe. It was only a few little old fishing trips, boy. And the form doesn't say fishing trips. You know how charged up the atmosphere can get.'

'Yah.'

'I'd like to go over this questionnaire with you, Joe, before I fill it up. At your convenience, of course.'

'Sure, Piggy, come on over the house Sunday. Things'll be a little quieter around here then.'

'Thanks, Joe. You know I've always worked pretty close with you, boy. I'm glad you're going to work with me.'

'Sure, Piggy.' He hadda get the hell outa the house before the phone drove him out. He'd drop over and say hello to Mammina. He walked across the length of the courtyard in the dusk, two hundred feet, past the fountain and the statuary he had brought from the Villa Berta in Bellanza, and stepped into Mammina's separate vestibule. Great idea, creating this separate entrance out of what had been the delivery portico, almost a city block from the front door. Kept Mama close by; yet she and Hetty were out of each other's hair. At this distance, Hetty could go on pretending as she had for years that she found Mama a simple, sweet, adorable little old lady, and Mammina could go on saying that Hetty was justa the right girl for her Pepe.

Three

THE two entrances were separated by more than space. There was half a century between them. Mammina kept the damnedest junk in the house, some from the house on Elm Street, some of it even from the Ninety-eighth Street days – the old upright nobody played, and Pop's stuffed rocking-chair which he had got second-hand in 1910, and here in the midst of a hundred carefully cultivated and landscaped acres, Mammina still nurtured three beat-up rubber plants in her bedroom.

In the small sitting-room, lit gently with the latest indirect cove lighting, he saw his handsome, stout, seventy-four-year-old mother, her still-jet-black hair strewn cyclonically about her head, and seven other women – all the regulars – standing, facing a folding bridge table on which had been placed the smallest American flag ever made, flying from what seemed to be a toothpick. The ladies were looking towards the tiny flag, holding fervent hands over their hearts.

'I pledge alligence to the flag a the United Stetts of America. . . .' All hands shot from full hearts towards the flag in a passionate gesture of love. Mama's mob: her sister, Zia Mathilda, a refugee from Ninety-eighth Street, and a widow of that old bastid Uncle Giovanni; Mrs. Rino Sacchi, Mama's oldest friend from Ninety-eighth Street; Mrs. Fortunato; Mrs. Benello, Sal's mother; Mrs. Serafino, and the two youngest, Mrs. Pasquale Baccio and Emily di Roberts. Joe could already see tomorrow's social item in the *Naples Sentinel, Mrs. C. Napoli Entertains*. If the newspaper readers could only see these old broads.

After the pledge to the flag, the meeting adjourned and the ladies carefully, but hurriedly, straightened their relic hats, flower-or fruit-laden, and prepared to go, while Mama flung the miniature flag into a cabinet alongside the niche containing her beige plaster Virgin, right under the sepia picture of Pop. Joe never failed to see that picture. It was like Carey's portrait in the office, it drew him with a kind of morbid fascination. It was Pop to a T – handsome, brooding, strong. Joe could remember the uneven furrows even now, forty good years later, and the strong tobacco and wine smell from the great yellow teeth under the drooping moustache. He also could not help seeing the twisted, lopsided head with its eyes rolled back.

Each of the women greeted Joe with the special smile that older women reserve for the children of friends, and took their rightful kiss – each bowing slightly with her kiss as if she were not entirely worthy. Only Emily di Roberts spoke out. 'Joey, you're a sight for sore eyes! I hardly ever see yuh. It's not like the old days, when you first come up to see Curly, remember? Who's better than you, hey? Look at this fantastic place yah livin' in! Well, I'm glad for yah, Joey! Honest I am.'

Joe asked after children, husbands, and assorted dependents, all of whom he tried to keep precisely in mind.

'Whatta you think?' Mama glowed. 'The leddies' auxiliary of-a the Italian Centre has-a raise seventy-one dollar and-a fifty cent in today's mitting. How you like that, Pepe?' She gestured grandly towards the ladies of the auxiliary. Mammina had plenty of *padrona* in her. 'Mammina' was a misnomer, for Mama was diminutive neither in body, voice, nor spirit. As a girl she had been a big-boned, broad-backed, full-breasted *contadina*, daughter of the coachman for Signor Vicenzo Florio, the leading citizen of Palermo. She had always had black, lustrous hair, rarely combed, white large teeth, and a face that was constantly on the verge of violence, laughter, and lust, needing only the subtlest stimuli to release some explosive tempest within. She could be a human *uragano*, or more precisely, a cyclone, for wild as the storm might rage, it would whirl always on itself.

'Seventy-one bucks!' Joe said cheerfully. 'How'd you do it – sell each other cookies?'

'Stop makin-a fun. We're-a play briscola.'

'What are you doing with the money?'

'We give to Mr. Serafino. Belivva-me is-a plenty poor pipple nidda the money.' The women of the auxiliary nodded as one.

'I think you ladies oughta be congratulated, one and all', Joe said. And the ladies' smiles lifted them into the air. At last they left, kissing Mama's overblown cheeks, and each other, telling Mama and each other how nice it had been, glowing with their good deeds, and with the pleasure of having had an opportunity to visit the Palazzo Napoli.

During all the good-byes Mama peered at him and smiled with her wide-spaced gold teeth shining; she was fantastically proud of him.

What the hell for? Because he'd made a lot of money? Built a city? What did all that mean to a woman like Mama? She was supposed to be interested in the Blessed Mother, in sweet Jesus and the Holy Spirit. Mammina could just as soon drop down on her knees and start praying as blink an eye. She talked to the Virgin as if she were her own mother. She was a one hundred per cent supporter of humility, loving your neighbour, alla that stuff. What did she give a hoot in hell for his making ten, twenty, fifty million dollars. Yet lookit the pride! Would she have been just as proud if he'd ended up a jerkwater professor at six thousand a year? Probably. And now with this investigation, what would she think if she saw her son marked derogatory?

When the women had gone, Mama took his arm. 'Come on, we sitta here a few minoot, we talk. How'sa Hetty? She'sa behave herself?'

'Now, Ma!'

'Why, she'sa drinka so much, Pepe? Is notta do her no good.'

It was not any of his mother's business, but she'd say anything that came into her head. 'She just has to have a drink now and then, Ma.'

'When you lose-a poor Carey' – she made a quick sign of the cross – 'he's-a *you* boy, too. *You* no have-a to drink.'

'Yah, Ma, but I got a lot to keep me busy. There's times when I can get Carey out of my head. Hetty can't.'

'She's-a Catolica, *no à vero*? She's-a gotta find Madre Maria. Why she no go talk to Father Ritucci? He's-a help. Whisky no gonna help.' Mammina shook her head sadly and added brightly, 'I'm glad I remind-a myself.' She lurched for the cupboard alongside the plaster Virgin, pulled out a bottle of Lacrima Christi and poured two glasses. 'She's-a okay', Mammina said happily, forgiving everything in a flourish. 'She's-a good-a girl, right-a girl for you, Pepe. You very lucky boy. An' she's-a lucky she gotta you.' She took a deep slug. 'Of course my kids gone away from me a long time and I no midda whisky alla time. Oh, I forget to tella you – I getta letter from Rosina, Sister Angelora.'

'Yah, Hetty told me. It's a dog's age since I saw her. Christ, she must be forty years old, little Rosie. Jesus, Mary and Joseph, Ma, think of poor old Rosie holed up in that God-forsaken place way up there in Massachusetts all these years.'

'Shame, Pepe, you no talk-a like that, you know what's-a gonna happen to you!'

'I know, Ma. I'm goin' to hell in a gondola.'

'What's the matter with you,' his mother said, almost angrily, 'you no fill-a good?'

'Sure, sure, Ma. Fine.'

'You no look-a so good to *me*', Mammina said. 'You look-a lousy. You worry about something?'

'Not a thing.'

'You work-a too hard, Pepe. Take it easy. What you nidda for?'

'You got something to do tonight?'

'Shu, shu, tonight's *I Love Lucy*. After that I'm a watch *T-Man* on Channel Nine. Is-a verr good. I see twice already.'

'Good. See you soon, Ma.'

They walked slowly towards the foyer. 'I hear on-a TV you gotta some kinda difficult in Washington.' She spoke with as little concern as if she had just noticed he had a bloodshot eye, and Joe was startled, defensive.

'Alla this investigaysh, was announce on-a TV.'

'You kidding?'

'You no hear it? Shu, shu. I'm-a tell the girls. *Everybody know*. Everybody filla bad for you. But not *me*. I say to the leddies, I say, you no have-a to worry about my Pepe. He's-a never do *nothing* wrong, alla his life. He's-a good boy – *perfetto*. And belivva me that'sa the true!'

He regained his composure. 'It's nothing, Ma. Big fuss about nonsense.'

'See, I tell-a them', his mother cried triumphantly. 'Stupid politish. Same like in Sicilia! I tell-a them.'

He had to laugh. 'What makes you so sure, Ma?'

His mother laughed, too, her vigorous, unrestrained laugh, as if his question were ludicrous and the answer obvious.

'Because you my *son*, Pepe. You never do wrong. Because I'm you *Mama*, that's why. Stupido! I brekka you neck.' She pushed him playfully, then embraced him. 'Okay. Is-a time for my programme. Hetty's-a wait for you. You no kippa her.'

Four

H E started back slowly across the courtyard. He took great satisfaction from the way he'd set his mother up – kitchen, TV, her old buddies nearby. No matter what happened to him, she was all set.

The sky had darkened and the first stars were out in the cool October night. Joe heard the crunch of Dino's Caddie on the bluestone driveway and saw the headlights inching towards the house. Milt drove Dino's Cadillac wagon with all the respect due to a noble steed and fourteen thousand bucks. Joe could not see Milt's expression clearly when he dismounted, but he could tell that Milt was preoccupied.

'Find out anything?' Joe said.

'Not much.' Milt spoke vaguely, and started towards the door. 'Master Poltek wanted to talk mainly about fishing. I can now tell you the characteristics of every variety of fish in Cape May waters, not to mention the best bait and rig for each.'

They walked into the palazzo-like foyer. Milt carefully placed his Panama on the guest-closet shelf and followed Joe around the fish pond into the forty-foot living-room. A tremendous Campigli dominated the room – two women playing cards. No matter what they did they could never get the mustiness out of this old barn.

'Now what the hell is that Poltek kid all about?' Joe said, as if it were somehow Milt's doing. 'You tell me, because I have absolutely one hundred per cent no idea.'

Milt's face was drawn. With great effort he brightened and smiled wanly. 'Frankly, I'm not wild about the entire situation. It's sure not going to do our Title One programme any good. You know how these things are, Joe; in any business if they're looking for something, they'll find something.'

'I don't even like the way that Polecat smells', Joe said, and Milt grimaced ruefully. 'I'll see Harold Brice myself', Joe continued. 'He's this kid's boss and he owes me one big one.'

'Sure, but what have you done for him lately?'

'Tony said that. You think maybe Tony can get to him? He might hear Tony good.'

'If you get Tony into this act, I want out, and I'm perfectly serious.' Milt spoke ominously, ponderously.

Joe pretended to be surprised. 'Fine way for you to talk about one of your oldest clients.'

'Joe, please. I've represented Tony before the Hendrickson Committee. I'm defending him in the tax courts. I've defended him in God knows how many criminal courts. And we're not winning. But this is not Tony. It's you. I don't want his name to appear in your show unless we simply can't avoid it.'

'Okay, okay.' Joe was impatient. 'But if you can prevent it, you're a cockeyed wonder.'

'At least we can try. I'm a great one for trying.'

Milt was a genius the way he kept his mind in separate compartments, Tony in one, him in another. And the compartments kept secrets from each. Milt pulled the plug out on the normal lines of communication within himself. It was a trick lawyers seemed to have.

This entire deal was being blown up completely out of proportion. There must be someone he could find to get them to drop it. There always was. Who was the focus of the louse-up? The Polecat boy no doubt. He definitely had to straighten that kid out. No doubt Poltek was misguided, a little green. The facts of life had probably not been explained to him clearly. He recalled Tony's performance before the Hendrickson Committee. Tony thought he'd done absolutely great at the time, a second Milton Berle. But you could win on points, get all the laughs on TV and knock yourself one hundred per cent dead. Old Senator Joe McCarthy had found that out. He was another great man for winning on points. Point of order, Mr. Chairman, who could forget that one? And though Tony did all right the two days he was on television, he was still ducking every time the Treasury Department sneezed or the U.S. Attorney-General's office called, and here it was seven years later and now they had these committees on Rackets and Improper Labour Practice, and Tony would hear from them both, no doubt. Some guys were fighting contempt or perjury charges, or worse, deportation proceedings. He didn't need any of it.

Try to make absolutely a bum out of him, these politician wise

guys would, they couldn't tell the difference between an unadul-
terated gangster, a red-eyed Communist and a strictly legitimate
businessman – anything for a TV rating or a headline. But that
upstanding Honourable Senator Harold Brice would absolutely
have the good sense to try to keep the mud from splattering all over
his own trousers. Joe Naples knew a few points about friend Harold,
faithful old servant of the Commonwealth of New Jersey. It
wouldn't look nice in front of all those voters.

Hetty came flowing into the living-room – still in the navy
dressing-gown – magnificent, smiling, offering Milt a drink.

'Darling, the way you treat Milton is a sin. Can't you see he's
dying of thirst?' High as the Eiffel Tower she was.

'Milt and I got some ground to go over, Mullaly. He's trying to
keep me out of the clutches of the law.'

She said sharply, 'I don't think that's funny. Here, Milton, as you
like it. Nothing but gin and lemon peel.' She stirred Milt's Martini.
'And if you two are going to keep working,' she said, 'why don't I
call Lucy to come join us for dinner?'

Milt gave her his lawyer's smile, operated purely by muscle.
'Sure. You know Luce. Do her good to get out. She's probably
been pulling up spring bulbs all day. With the girls away at school,
she goes nuts around the place.'

Hetty went to the telephone-room and they could hear her
dialling.

Milt slouched abruptly, the image of sudden, total dejection,
sprawling on the nine-foot couch which Hetty had had made in
Stockholm, crossed his legs, his head and eyes cast down, the tilt
making his long narrow nose longer. Only his eyes rolled upward;
at last he adjusted his glasses and leaned back into the cushions as if
he needed sustaining. His best friend, Joe thought, had an exhausted
black look tonight, as though he clearly saw disaster.

'Believe thou me, I can use this drink', Milt said, sipping slowly.
He spoke quietly, as he often did, almost in a secretive whisper.
Joe knew if he just waited, sooner or later Milt would work himself
up to saying what he meant to say.

'You know, Joe, Washington hasn't changed a bit, has it? They
still have a few of these eager young boys working in all these
government departments, or for congressional committees, every
one of 'em anxious to get attention, stirring the trouble pots, a little
scandal, a little perjury, a little larceny. Mix well and bingo, you've
got the headlines. They are *tenacious*, believe thou me. Now this

boy Poltek. Harvard College, Harvard Law School and all told maybe thirty-two years old.'

'I'd say thirty-four', Joe said.

'Maybe thirty-four. The way he sees it, this is his season for slaying a dragon and he probably *will*, Joe. This is a formidable young man. Don't underestimate him. These boys all have to slay at least one dragon or they get terribly frustrated and hypertense, and when you've got a kid loose like that in a Senate committee you simply have to duck and dodge and keep out of the way to make sure you're not the dragon he's slaying. Remember Rudy Halley in the Hendrickson Committee? He had his Frank Costello. A nice, respectable dragon if ever I saw one. They were so busy with Costello, old Tony was almost able to stay entirely out of Hendrickson's way. He wasn't entirely, of course, but he never was hit with the full treatment. Last couple of years they found a few new dragons – Dave Beck and Sherman Adams and Bernie Goldfine. By special courtesy of Dragonslayers Bob Kennedy and that boy Schwartz. And this year – well, we have to hope that Sam Poltek can somehow find a bigger, juicier dragon than you.'

'What the hell are you *talking* about?' Joe exploded. 'You comparing me to Costello? Or Whozis?'

'Oh, Joe,' Milt said, glumly, 'be reasonable. You made fifty million dollars in four years. You've always had a good sense of what the average guy thinks.'

'I don't any more', Joe said. 'I swear to Christ I don't.'

Hetty came back. 'Lucy's coming', she said. 'So just relax. I'll go see about dinner. If you want another drink, ring for Cibulkas.'

Milt tilted his Martini and drank the rest of it appreciatively, warming to his subject. 'Anybody makes forty, fifty million fast, starting with nothing, it arouses strong emotions in many breasts. And in the frustrated breast of a man who considers himself your superior in every way, envy could lead to fury. Envy is strong medicine. Maybe you don't understand envy, Joe, I don't know. Probably you don't, because you've never suffered from it. I doubt if you have an envious bone in your body. Friend Poltek thinks to himself, did Joe Naples go to Harvard or Harvard Law School? Did he make *Law Review*? Does he have the *brains* to have made *Law Review* if he *had* gone to Harvard? He doesn't think so. *I* do, but he doesn't, and he's thinking with *his* mind. Then how did he make all this money? he says to himself. Could it possibly have been legitimate? Never. Then what kind of a creature must this Joe

Naples be? All right, I'm glad you asked. Now, remember, I'm Samuel Poltek, boy genius, dragonslayer, protector of the underdog, darling of the common man. Mad at the world, and especially successful people. I'm writing headlines for the *Daily News*. You see, Joe, we have to understand where our opposition is heading. As a lawyer, it's the only way I can work, and I'm too old to start learning new tricks. I'm the devil's advocate, okay?'

Milton's mobile face grew cruel, suddenly his eyes were slits in a deep, exaggerated squint. He was young Tom Dewey, fighting District Attorney. 'You're a man, Joseph Naples, who has fed at the public trough, taking advantage of – no, more than that, abusing – yes, *abusing* the government and the people of the United States. You took money that was supposed to help builders put up homes and apartments in a hurry and you used it for your own *profit*. Ugh! Profit's a horrible thing nowadays, even a little bit of profit. But you took so *much* profit. It's downright *disgusting*. Can't you see the horror of it all, the big black headlines?' Milton's face became an exaggerated leer, a menacing, hating accuser. 'You're a greedy, acquisitive monster, and what's perfectly clear, you couldn't possibly have done it honestly. Otherwise, why wouldn't *everyone* have done it? Everyone knows he's as smart as you. Only *they're* all *honest*. Isn't the conclusion obvious?'

Milt stood up, and now he was declaiming, a silver-tongued William Jennings Bryan. 'There's only three or four, perhaps five men like you in the entire country. For heaven's sake, didn't you build a complete city which bears your name now? Isn't it obvious that you must be the crookedest son-of-a-bitch alive? Isn't it clear that Naples, New Jersey, *your* city, is rotten to the core? Set aside that it's jerry-built. That goes without saying. People always knew the houses couldn't last a year. The mere fact that they *have* lasted eight or nine and are selling for fifty per cent more than you sold them for proves *nothing*. That's merely an Act of God. An accident. Inflation. The only truth is what these people have hypnotized themselves into believing – that Naples is built on a foundation of corruption, nailed together with bribery and, yes, outright theft, and its streets are paved with God only knows what, the pay-offs, the bodies of the prostitutes you fed to other corrupt and evil men to do your bidding. Maybe even – violence!' He threw up his hands in horror and turned away in mock revulsion. 'How else could you have got all that mortgage money – how much was it – two hundred million? How else could you have got all that shoddy construction approved? How else could you have beat the unions? You're Svengali, boy, with a thousand helpless Trilbys doing any damn thing you tell them. Thin out that concrete, boy, leave that nail out – man, any dope can build houses using nails! And the poor veterans, helpless, maybe even paraplegic, are *suff*ering and they'll continue to suffer for – how long are these mortgages? Thirty years. Unborn generations of veterans will suffer, all because of your terrible, consuming, insatiable greed.'

'What'd I ever do that wasn't a hundred per cent?' Joe snapped, knowing this was no question.

'This Poltek is a smart boy, Joe, and thorough. Somewhere, at Harvard or at his mother's knee, they taught him thoroughness believe thou me. Details. This boy is a digger. He'll have two or three of his younger eager beavers digging and gnawing at our records, and God knows who else's, and how far they'll dig nobody knows. Certainly your old friend Milton does not. But this I do know. They'll dig far enough to answer your question – what did Joe Naples do that wasn't a hundred per cent; and the answer is: Plenty.'

Joe was silent. The room was warm.

'If you must know, Sam Poltek didn't just talk about fishing all the way to Trenton. He had me sparring questions about all kinds of miscellaneous matters – wanted to know if I ever knew Giacomo Gamboretta, and how far back does *that* go? Jock Dennison, and even, for God's sake, poor old Marge the Barge. *She* must be dead ten years, or at least not very useful. He knew you were a friend of Anna Landos. She's big headlines these days, Joe. Big star, what the hell. And he wanted to know how close you were to Simon Cutler and some of the boys at the Trenton NMIA. Piggy Banks, for instance. He was also mighty curious about Everett Henderson at Merchantman's Trust in Newark. Believe thou me, they're digging in all directions.'

'Giacomo Gamboretta,' Joe shouted, 'why that no-good bastid died thirty years ago.'

Milt's face squinched. 'He was killed, Joe. And for a Senate committee, there's no such thing as a statute of limitations. They have a right to *know*. Or at least to ask.'

'What the hell are they trying to prove? What's this entire investigation exactly going to prove? That Joe Naples is a no-good bum? Don't forget I got a few absolutely decent citizens are gonna talk up for *me*. Guys like Jock Dennison, not a breath of scandal in

seventy years. Is lousing me up something to consume the efforts of
the mighty Senate of the United States?'

'This is only a little bitty sub-committee of the Underwriting
Committee – just a few of the boys whooping it up. Theoretically
they're trying to find out if there isn't something terribly terribly
sick sick about the entire housing industry from top to bottom so
they can write corrective legislation and revamp the whole housing
establishment. That's the theory. It's a totally screwy idea. More
than that, it's totally dishonest. The NMIA is here to stay. But
what it is, in words of one syllable, is they're looking for a mess, the
usual mess in Washington. One gentleman on the committee, our
old, dear friend, Senator Harold Q. Brice, would enjoy very much
to be nominated for the Vice-Presidency, and young Poltek would
like to be a Congressman from Massachusetts some day. Harold
Brice may not even know Poltek's started on *you*. But if he did,
what could he do about it? He's in a spot. He's got Mr. Owens
heading the sub-committee. And the way Poltek and Brice and
Owens see it, there's no group of just folks who are as all-out
popular with the American public as, ugh, those ugly builders and
landlords. So they're going to serve up a whole slimy mess of them
done to a nice brown turn. Yich! When they get through, you'll
be disgusted with you your ownself.'

'But, Jesus, One-eyed Gamboretta – that was thirty years –'

'And since you're the fellow once had your picture on the cover
of *Time*, that could make you king dragon number one.'

'Are you kiddin'?'

'On the other hand, my own favourite candidate for number-one
dragon is poor old Si Cutler, National Project Director of the
National Mortgage Insurance Agency. Si's even got the name for a
first-class dragon: Simon Cutler. You can see the long, black
moustache, the sneaky eyes.'

'Simon? As harmless as a flea. And a hell of a sweet guy. I
wouldn't want to see anything happen to Si.'

'Oh yes? How about the four months he held *us* up? When was
it, back in forty-seven? You remember that particular wringer he
put us through? Some old friend! I've checked around here and
there. He did the same thing to Martinson in Chicago and Levine
in L.A. My theory is they all took care of him. Tell me, Joe, did
you ever give him any money?'

Joe went to the doorway. 'Josh! Dammit, this old house is so
long you have to use a telephone to get ahold of anyone. It's a barn.

You know how far away my mother lives? One entire city block. Two hundred feet. And in absolutely the same house. On Ninety-eighth Street, Milt, Jesus, there were a million people within a block. Cibulkas! There must be a bell around here somewhere.'

'There's the intercom over there', Milton whispered.

'Where? Oh, yah. Pantry.' He pushed the button, fumbled with the switch. Mechanical genius. 'Josh, you hear me?'

'Sure do, Major.'

'Bring me another bottle of Chianti and a Martini for Mr. Jason. No vermouth.'

Joe turned back to Milton. Almost unconsciously he mimicked Milt's intonation and rhythms. 'What a day! This morning I had a talk about the Polo Grounds with Bob Moses. He's talking about doing a redevelopment job, and I'm thinking to myself, here I am, up on Coogan's Bluff, and they're grinding up my entire goddam life. So help me – *our* Polo Grounds, Milt. This is *us*, these Polo Grounds, and they're getting ready to tear 'em down. Selling the steel for scrap, and I might even be the bastid to do it. Just to build a few apartments, maybe for niggers yet, and I think to myself it's like chopping up a beautiful woman and selling her for meat.' He sighed. 'I don't want you to get discouraged now, Milt. You're gonna knock this guy Poltek on his can. Sooner or later you're gonna see this thing clear. Remember I'm no Tony Ferrara. I'm a legitimate guy.'

Milt removed his glasses. 'It's good to know you have that much confidence in me, Joe.'

'Why wouldn't I have confidence? If I'da always followed your advice, I probably wouldn't be in this spot, would I? Of course, there wouldn't be any Naples, New Jersey, either. You've gotta admit that.' He laughed hoarsely, while Milt shifted his weight and smiled forlornly.

'I suppose there did have to be a Naples, New Jersey', Milt said reflectively. 'It couldn't have been otherwise.'

'That's neither exactly here nor there', Joe said. '*Certainly* I got confidence in you. I got a hundred *per cent* confidence in you.'

'I do have a few surprises for Samuel Poltek up my sleeve, at that', Milt said, making an effort to concentrate and managing a new and slowly rising enthusiasm of his own. 'Believe thou me.'

'Before you're through,' Joe said, 'I bet you surprise the piss out of him. He'll be sorry he tangled with *this* dragon, I tell you, because he doesn't know this dragon happens to have the smartest lawyer in the entire country. I've got absolutely one hundred per cent faith in you, Milt. I leave the defence up to you. You handle it.'

Milt looked nine parts worried and one part exultant, but he drawled soberly, 'I just have the feeling that before we're through, you'll be running your own defence, Joe. And probably doing a great job at it. You know how *I* feel, I've always said you'd make a great lawyer.'

Josh interrupted from the kitchen. 'Mr. Cutler's on the phone for you, Major, calling from Washington on three five eight five.'

Milton squinted his eyes and blinked fiercely. '*Now* he's calling you. Fine, *calling* you on the *phone*. No wonder this man has trouble.'

Joe walked into the sound-proof phone closet, Milton crowding in behind him. He could hear the voice of the tall, brawny man in Washington. Si Cutler was an old friend, and he was troubled that Si should be in distress. Even over the wire Joe could hear that his friend was talking more out of the corner of his mouth than usual. But the voice had a brand-new tremor to it.

'I've, ah, been trying to get you all afternoon, Joe, sweetheart. This, ah, fellow Poltek called me over to his office yesterday asking me all kinds of questions, y'know, sweetheart. The little runt, ah, wants to know every breath I ever took, every word I ever said to you or you said to me. I haven't even had a chance to consult my own attorney. Keeps asking me all about Anna Landos out there in Las Vegas, ah, how do you suppose he ever got hold of anything like *that*, sweetheart, and is it any of *his* business, is that the business of the U.S. Senate boy? Just because you introduced me to a lovely girl. I mean she's a fine lady, big film actress, and all that. Are they trying to drag her name through some kind of mud? It's a cheap publicity stunt, that's all. It's persecution, Joe, nothing but political persecution, because I'm too damn liberal a Democrat.' His voice now had an hysterical quality to it. No doubt it had been a tough day for Simon Cutler.

'Las Vegas?' Joe said. 'Now who got them started on that kick?'

'Shh!' Milt hissed. 'You're on the phone, for God's sake. Not ... on ... the ... phone. Tell him not to worry. Tell him to keep calm. Hang up.'

'Anna's okay, isn't she, Joe? She's an old friend of yours. She's not likely to say anything rash, is she?'

'Just keep yourself under control, Simon', Joe said, like a great white father. 'Everything's gonna be okay.'

'They said they thought I might prefer to resign!' Simon Cutler emitted a controlled but agonized wail. 'After twenty years in the service, my friend. Consider that! What do they expect me to do, go back to selling brick?'

'Now you aint' done a goddam thing, Simon. They can't prove a thing. Keep your shirt on! So long, Simon.'

'I'll be up to see you, Joe. As soon as I can get away.'

'Sure.' Joe hung up.

Milt sipped at his Martini as they walked thoughtfully back into the living-room. 'Simon Cutler', he murmured. 'Just take Simon Cutler as a for instance. Do you think that I, as your lawyer, know everything there is to know about you and Simon Cutler? Is there anything you think you ought to tell me?'

'Simon Cutler is one sweet guy,' Joe said, 'but he's a horse's ass.'

'Well,' Milt said quietly, 'there's five of them for every horse.'

'You know that time he held up our whole programme?'

Milt was up and pacing, his head thrust slightly down and forward, his hands in his pockets. 'Of course. And then out of the blue the Trenton office got that gobbledy-gook letter from him approving six thousand units. Came right after that trip you made to Las Vegas.' Milt's face was a sudden light.

'Yah!' Joe laughed. 'Yah!' He laughed harder, until he began to cough. 'The poor bastid. I'll never forget the look on his face when he met Anna. You'd a got a kick outa that!'

Milt squinted. 'I'd have got a bigger kick out of meeting Anna Landos myself', he said, putting on his most lecherous leer. 'That's for sure. Oo, my achin' back!' There were moments when Milton changed from lawyer to leprechaun without warning.

'You just keep your mind on old Luce, friend.'

'There are moments,' Milt said wryly, 'when I think you take better care of your sister than I do.'

'Why not? Don't I have a responsibility? It's in black and white. Be your sister's keeper.'

Joe thought Milt winced – an odd ball, Milt, when you knew him inside out like Joe did.

'Joe, how about letting me be *your* keeper for a while? I've been around Washington, man and boy, ten years now. I've been through one Senate investigation, soup to nuts. I know what Tony's been through since, and I think I am beginning to perceive the bare outlines of what we're up against. It's not all peaches and cream, believe thou me.'

'So I gather.'

'Be prepared to have your life picked apart by experts. Clawed and scratched over the way only a relentless bureaucracy can scratch. For dirt and nothing else. Nothing good you ever did will see the light of day. This is not a *Time* cover story. This is very dirty pool. "Good moral character." There's a broad underhanded phrase for you. On constitutional grounds, even if they ever could write a law to prohibit government assistance to people of not good moral character, I don't think it would ever hold up in the courts. Gosh, I don't see how authorization for this sub-committee ever got through the Senate. Not a leg to stand on. Who'd decide what was good moral character? Some pygmy-minded bureaucrat? Or worse – a committee of them? It's ludicrous. It's phooey law in spades, but every day we learn something new.'

Joe chewed the now unlighted cigar, a soggy, juicy end, getting some small comfort from the familiar taste of tobacco juice.

'On the other hand,' Milt went on pontifically, 'as to the questions they can legitimately ask you, the court decisions set up one yardstick: it is germane to the subject of the inquiry authorized. And the courts are getting narrower in their interpretations all the time.'

'Is that good?'

'That's good. Still, if this investigation has been authorized on a basis that's as wide open as a barn door – good heavens, good moral character – then damn near any question is germane to that issue.'

'You can cut me outa *that* deal', Joe said shortly, and cracked his knuckles. 'Anyhow, I absolutely don't understand what you're talking about.'

'I've known you nearly all my life, Joe', he heard Milt saying. 'We've been close, probably as close as any two people can get, but there were moments – crucial moments – when you wanted to go it alone. I'm sure you'll recall. You didn't ask my advice, or anyone else's – not that I blame you. You've got your own methods, and no one can say they haven't worked. Joe, you *know* me. I've never tried to pry. Here we are pushing our way through our fifties, kiddo, and I certainly wouldn't want to start prying now. But if I'm going to be of any help, if we're going to build a defence, I'm afraid I have to know everything about you that, as of right this moment, I simply don't.'

'My entire autobiography?'

Milt gazed at him with disconcerting steadiness. 'The works. But with special emphasis on your sins and transgressions. And *why* you committed them, that's crucial. Motives, buddy. And remember, Joe, I love you. If I loved you any more, I'd have to see a psychiatrist.'

'Are you kidding? This is a helluva way for a lawyer to prepare a case.'

'It's not a case, Joe. It's a defence against a nebulous set of un-defined charges that haven't even been made yet. You've got to have experienced this sort of atmosphere in Washington. There'll be a million rumours about you. The one thing we can't afford under any circumstances is for me to be surprised during any part of the hearing. Stuff I hear for the first time you know I'm hopeless on. I have to have a chance to masticate the stuff. I have to be prepared. Digest. That's the way I am, slow and steady. You want me to handle this for you, you have to submit to my disciplines.'

'I see.'

'And if you're in doubt as to whether some particular act is a sin or transgression, then for God's sake, tell me about it. We can't afford to be polite with each other – Alphonse and Gaston.'

'I gotta laugh. In England they'd've made me a Knight or a Sir or maybe given me some kind of order of the garter for building a city like Naples. Here they *investigate* me. What a laugh!'

Milt Jason was his friend and his lawyer, but there were a few things around and about through the years he was damn sure he did not want to tell Milt Jason or anyone else. Milt thought Joe Naples was the world's greatest, keep it that way. The trouble was Milt was always making judgements. Should've been a judge. Milt believed in right and wrong, justice and injustice. Alla that. Terrific guy to have in your corner, fought like a tiger, but why did he or anyone else have to know every last thing about Gamboretta or Simon Cutler or Anna Landos? Hell of a lot of it he didn't remem-ber so good himself. There were a million things a guy wouldn't tell his wife and quite a few he'd just as soon keep from his closest friend.

Milt must have read his mind. 'If you'd prefer to do this with some other attorney, Joe – if you feel you'd find it easier —'

'Hell no', Joe exploded. 'That's not it.' He couldn't stand the way Milt read his thoughts.

'I was going to say there's a hotshot lawyer in Washington we could use, specializes in these cases. Fairly young fellow, knows his way around Washington, especially on the Hill, Theodore Keller. He'll probably hit you for fifty or seventy-five thousand.'

'It's deductible,' Joe said, glowering, 'isn't it?' He hated to be taken by these thieves.

'Sure. And it might well be worth it. If you think Keller's your man, I'll call him and make a date in Washington. We could fly down tomorrow in the Beechcraft. I may insist that you do it anyway when I know all the facts.'

'Let me give it a thought', Joe said. 'This is pretty complex, and I'm only a lousy bricklayer, for Christ sake.'

'Joe, kiddo, believe thou me, I don't want to be a nudge, but if I were handling it, one thing I'd want to know, for example, is what took place between you and Simon Cutler in Vegas in '47. All I'd want are the facts, man. It would be the only way I could help.'

Joe closed his eyes and kept them closed. 'Tomorrow, Milt. I'm too damn tired tonight. And for God's sake, don't get Luce or my mother or Hetty all stirred up about this. I don't want the family worrying.'

They heard the front door open, and Lucy called in her cheery Tallulah voice that sounded like a new-world version of Mammina's, 'Joe . . . Milt . . . Hetty. Let's eat!' Then they heard Hetty in the foyer, offering sisterly greetings.

Five

I N the dark Joe tossed in bed. Hetty often said that when they turned out the lights, she could hear his deep sleep-breathing before the room was dark, but the fact was that he resented sleep. Took too bigga bite outa your life. He lay there as he always did, passing his future triumphs through his mind like soldiers on review. There was so much demanding his attention – the new apartments in Naples, those redevelopment jobs in St. Louis and Philadelphia that were being held up by bureaucrats (have to light a few fires under those bastids), the University still on Dino's drawing board, the hospital extension, the beginning of another new city outside Pittsburgh – Naples, P.A. Be a hell of a big thing if the ball team ended up in the first division.

He heard Hetty, who usually took a pill or two to get to sleep, breathing peacefully. He was in no mood for this Poltek louse-up, and he had absolutely not one spare minute to recall a lot of ancient history for Milt. It was a goddam nuisance. He needed this entire deal exactly like a sprinter needs a middle leg.... Something peculiar about that Poltek boy. Something eating him. Not the normal type at all. He'd have to give that runt a little thought. A Harvard boy. Maybe Andy could find out something about him in Cambridge. No wonder he couldn't sleep and itched all over, restless, turning from side to side, getting snarled in the bedclothes. Lookit him. A nervous wreck. It was horrible to be kept awake this way. He closed his eyes. If he could concentrate, all these fragments would straighten themselves out, form themselves into a pattern the way iron filings do when you put a magnet to them. He wasn't used to tossing like this . . . And that was the last thought he had before he was in a deep sleep. He had tossed around for nearly eight full minutes, and now he slept eight hours without changing position.

Joe was up at dawn, out at the apartment job by seven. The fifty-acre site was as silent as the early-morning fog, the D-8 and D-9

Caterpillars a study in motionless potential power. The night-watchman, waving forlornly from the shanty, was the only living creature in sight. Joe loved the damp feel and smell of the job in the early morning; at this hour the job was a hundred per cent his. By eight o'clock it would belong to the thousands of men and machines who would crawl over it and grind it or hammer it one day nearer completion. All the unfamiliar fears that Poltek and Milt had set swirling in him were pushed down deep when he smelled the reality of wet earth, the fresh cut lumber stacked, damp sawdust, millwork neatly piled in the dry sheds. This incredible potential, the astonishing power to build, gave him peace. He scanned the brickwork with practised eye from the moving Cadillac, then parked at one of the ten-story buildings, took the lift up and walked briskly from the top story down, jotting notes: Base warped, doors binding, windows open n.g., qu.-rd. missing in kitchens – detail on detail. Then he walked the garden-apartment site, erect, fast, as if he were still in the army. Backfill not tamped, stakes not laid out far enough ahead for water mains, 2 × 9 planks being used for masons' platform instead of plywood. When he left, workmen were beginning to arrive, parking their jalopies, opening the various shanties. Never failed to remind him of the old days when he and Pop used to show up on the job with nothing but their bare hands and their lunches.

By eight-thirty he was back in his office, and Julius the barber was there to shave him while he worked. Joe put a call in to Curly di Roberts. "Ey, Curly, remember you were telling me that idea you had to use plywood instead of plank for the masons? Try it. It's your own goddam idea. Do me a personal favour. For me, Curly. 'Ey, I saw Emily last night over at my mother's. She still looks great, boy, what's your secret? Yah? At your age? Lay offa *that*, kid. Yah, now lemme talk to Gravel . . . Gravel? There's something wrong with the heating unit at – lemme see, I wrote the address right in here – Twenty-two Meadowlark Lane. People named Swaboda. Yah, I *know* it's nine years old. Don't you think those heating units oughta stand up more than nine years? Yah, I know all about it. Swaboda, yah, you know 'em? Okay, so they're trouble-makers. Have a look anyhow.'

Julius removed the barber's cape from round his neck, shook it out, and took the money Joe gave him, smiling like an idiot, bowing and retiring backwards, as if Joe was some kind of king.

He buzzed for Cathy. 'See if you can get Andy up in Cambridge.' Milt poked his head in, and seeing Joe on the phone, withdrew.

'Andy?'

'Gee, Dad, you woke me up.' He could picture his son lying in bed, that sharp and delicately featured, mussed-up head so like Hetty's peering out over the sheets – a thoroughbred head on a workhorse body. Looked a lot like Carey did, but he was a different boy.

'It's nine o'clock.'

'Okay, okay, Dad. What's the word? How's Mother?' Joe would never become accustomed to Andy's smooth, almost glossy manner. His voice, like his eyes, was sharp, fast, sometimes staccato.

'Fine. Is your room-mate around?'

'No, Bob has a nine o'clock class. Why?'

'Good. Get a pencil. I want you to do me a favour.'

Andy must've groped around for three bleary minutes looking for a pencil. How these kids learned anything was a wonder. You want to see illegible handwriting, you take a look at Andy's. Like some bird had walked across the page. Best schools.

'Okay, Dad. Shoot.' Andy's diction was like Harold Brice's, as if he was some kinda duke. You send 'em to Lawrenceville and Harvard and you can't tell 'em apart – like penguins.

Joe had trouble deciding how to begin. 'They're off on another one of these investigations, the Senate, and they're investigating your old man.'

'The United States Senate?'

'Yah.'

'Is investigating you?'

'Yah.'

'Hey.' Andy was impressed. 'You made it, Dad.'

'I'm serious. Now lookit. The man who's chief counsel of the sub-committee is a guy named Poltek. Samuel Poltek. Take it down.' Joe spelled it.

'Okay, Dad, got it.'

'Whozis graduated from Harvard and Harvard Law School. Strikes me as being a weirdie. Something wacked up about him.'

'In what way?'

'Like one of these Red wackeroos.'

'A Communist, Dad? Oh, you're kidding. He's working for the United States *Senate*.'

'I'm serious. You ever meet a Communist, Andy?'

'I don't think I have, Dad, but —'

'Well, I have, my friend.'

Andy thought the whole thing over a minute. He must've been awake by now, because no one asleep could've been that silent. Finally he said, 'What do you want me to do, Dad?'

'Find out about this guy. He must've graduated outa Law School there, maybe nineteen forty-six or -seven. Talk to his profs. Anyone around remembers him. Ask around and about. Let's see what kind of detective you make.'

'Hey.' Andy was pleased with his role. 'I'm with *you*, Dad. Is anything bad likely to come out of this investigation?'

'I have no idea what kinda dirt they're gonna dig up on your old man, but it'll be lousy publicity, so brace yourself for it. Might hurt business a little. And if I get fresh to these Senators, I might end up in the pokey. You know your old man. He won't stand still for any nonsense.'

'I know.' Andy was thoughtful again. 'Take it easy, Dad, will you? Listen to Uncle Milt's advice.'

'I hope I don't louse you up with your girl friend, boy.' He couldn't remember her name.

'Gosh, how can you think of a thing like that? Don't worry about Cynthia. And don't worry about me.' Joe could picture that intense, serious face, full of concern. Jesus, how he'd love to have that boy at Naples and Company. Naples and Son, yessir, that was the ticket. Something always squeezed inside him when he spoke to that kid. Not like Carey, but there was something there.

'Okay, Andy, you can go back to bed.'

'I'm wide awake now, Dad. Ellery Queen, on the job. I'm off to buy a deerstalker and a pipe.'

'This is serious, Andy.'

'I understand', Andy said solemnly, as if he were talking to a four-year-old child.

'So long.'

'So long, Dad.' Andy's voice softened. 'I'm glad you thought of me to help.'

Milt poked his head in again, cautiously. 'Counsellor, you ready to take confession?' Joe shouted. He felt good early in the day, especially when he'd been out on the job.

'Well, yes. But there's one thing first, kind of pressing. You know the Howard-family case? We've got to make a decision on that today one way or another.'

'That coloured family? God, do we have to?'

'Afraid so. The Civil Rights Commission's ruled against us. Just got the decision this morning. We have to decide whether we want to sell 'em a house, or take the case into the courts.'

'God, Milt, I hate the idea of coloured families living in Naples. It's my city, isn't it? I built it. The bastids are always on your back.'

Milt sighed. 'It's less within our control than that. The Howards, I hear, have offered to buy another house from someone who's moving to St. Louis. People named Lewin.'

'Oh, yah. Phil Forney told me somethin' about that. Well, what do we do about it?'

'As far as I'm concerned, nothing. I think it's pretty hopeless.'

'Milt. You're losing the old zip. Cathy! Come in here. Cathy, you call a man named Lewin. What's his address, Milt?'

'Seventy-one Heather Road.'

'Yah. You call him and ask him if he wouldn't be good enough to drop into the office sometime at his convenience. I'd like to talk to him.'

Cathy left.

'You're not, Joe.'

'I am,' Joe said, 'and let's file our appeal on the Commission's ruling right away. You know this goddam anti-discrimination law's unconstitutional.'

Milt looked sad. 'You know what you're doing, Joe?'

'Lookit, Milt, I don't have anything against coloured people personally. Of course, I never had any good experience with 'em. Every one I ever had on a job was yellow, surly bastids, and always had it in for me. And you remember that Hundred-and-Fourteenth-Street gang. What was that kid's name? The Blade. Yah.'

'That was forty years ago, Joe. We were kids. Things change.'

'Even so. You know I'm not against 'em personally. Hell, didn't I offer the President to build apartments for 'em from here to Baltimore? Their own places. But they're not for Naples, Milt. Not for my town. They'll ruin the place. It's a big country. Let 'em go somewhere else.'

Milt continued to blush unhappily. 'Don't you see how this ties into the investigation, Joe? It'll make you look bad. Real bad, buddy.'

'I don't give a damn how I look.'

'Ah, now, Joey! This man Howard is a chemist. He has a job at Sanders and Sanders. He makes twelve thousand a year, and his wife is a registered nurse.'

'Yah, I know. They got kids?'

'Two boys and a girl.'

'There's your answer', Joe said in triumph. 'How's all the whozises gonna like it when these three nigger kids move in next door?'

'Joe,' Milt pleaded, 'this is the last half of the twentieth century.'

'You didn't hear me so good. The goddam law's unconstitutional, and we all know it. The Attorney-General knows it.'

Milt shrugged. 'Okay, Joe, if that's how you feel.'

'That's how I feel. Now about getting back to the confessions of Joe Naples?'

'Sure.' Milt acted uneasy. 'Why don't we call Cathy and let her take it all, as we talk? I'd like to get it down in black and white so I can study it.'

Dictate the stuff to Cathy O'Neill? Not while he was in his right mind.

'Let's just talk, Milt. We don't need Cath. You got a good memory, keep it in your head.'

Milt bowed his head, acquiescent.

'I was thinking last night,' Joe said idly, 'we could probably kill this whole thing by finding the right guy to take care of it.'

'Please.' Milt suddenly looked near tears. 'Please don't think about anything like that. Someone tried it a couple of years ago, and he's had nothing but grief since.'

Joe had no idea just how much Milt did not know, but he had decided one thing: he would rather spill himself out to Milt than to some hotshot lawyer in Washington who wouldn't understand one absolute word he was talking about. His friend would not only understand, but, Joe realized, Milt had no choice but to forgive. Joe had thought for so many years of Milt as a separate person from himself with a separate destiny, but when he looked back, he realized Milt was the rung of the ladder and he the support. There was no independence. They were parts of the same structure.

'Cathy, hold all calls for Milt and me. We don't wanna be disturbed.'

'Yes, Mr. Naples.'

If Joe Naples was a man of no moral character, an associate of a man like Tony Ferrara, it was all no doubt traceable to Uncle Giovanni. The psychiatrists were always starting you off back in your childhood. 'That old bastid,' he heard himself saying to Milt, 'he hated himself, he hated his wife, he hated his own kids. Any time he could do a first class louse-up in this world he was a happy man. This guy was an upside-down Boy Scout. At least one foul deed a day. When I try to think about my own self, I don't need a psychoanalyst. I know one thing – I've been fighting Uncle Giovanni a hell of a lot of the time.'

'How did you ever happen to get into his clutches in the first place?' Milt asked. 'I was never very impressed by him. I can't imagine your submitting to an old fossil like him.'

'Who else was there? When Pop was killed, I was twelve. The only one around from that day on was Uncle Giovanni. First shrewd deal, he advanced us money for the funeral. We never heard the end of *that*. You remember the afternoon Pop got it?'

'It was before I met you.'

'I ever tell you about it?'

'No.'

'Jesus, I'll never forget it. Tony remembers it. Ask Tony sometime. Just this morning out on the apartment job reminded me of the whole thing. Watchin' all the brickies getting ready to go out on the scaffold. And all of a sudden it was like this thing just happened to Pop ten minutes ago instead of forty years. Of course, that morning was a lot colder. . . . In fact, it was as cold as a witch's tit. . . .'

Six

An icy Monday before Christmas, and maybe Pop should have stayed at home altogether. In the first place he wasn't feeling so hot. All that Spanish flu around, like Mammina said, lotta people sick, look-a the funerals, all those funerals on Fift' Avenue, why you wanna take-a chance, Carmine, such a day? Why you no stay in-a bed? She'd call the doctor. Mammina was adamant. She loved the opportunity to baby Pop.

But Pop thought that by eight it would not be too cold to lay brick. It was twenty-eight or -nine, and with the sun coming up, it would soon be warmer. And he wasn't sick. Just-a little headache. 'Carissima' – he never failed to use endearments to Mama when he felt most condescending – 'how can the family of a bricklayer afford to lose a day's work?'

The argument went this way and that until Joe hadda open his big mouth. 'Aw, c'mon, Ma, Pop's okay. You're okay, right, Pop?' Joe was anxious to get out on the job himself, to be with Pop, that was the only reason he said it, but it tipped the scales. Pop said, 'You see? Pepe's a know.' And miraculously Mammina retreated. His big mouth.

He and Pop walked west on Ninety-eighth Street to Park Avenue – it was always a marvel to Joe to see how abruptly the neighbourhood changed as you went west, slum to luxury – down Park to the job on Eighty-sixth Street: Carmine Napoli and son. He felt ten feet tall just walkin' with Pop. Pop was a strapping strong man. Joe slapped his hands together and blew hard on them; Pop's moustache drooped with tiny particles of ice. 'Mama, I think she's-a not like-a see her little Pepe go on-a job', Pop kidded, chuckling. 'Too *delicato*.' From the moment Joe started going to school, Pop had always spoken English to him, his own brand, anyhow. 'She do anything kippa me home. You ask-a her, it's a like Nort'a Pole. For man from Napoli where I'm-a come, is-a fine,' he shrugged, 'but for Mammina, whatta she know, a Siciliana! For

Siciliana is-a *goddam* cold.' He reflected a moment. 'An' I no think-a Mama want-a you go on job inna first place. She no like-a you lay brick. She wanna you wear stiffa collar. *Cosi.*'

He made a priest's collar with his palms, covering his leathery neck. Pop had no use for priests, but Mama used to put her hands over her ears and refuse to listen to his blasphemy. Pop wanted Pepe to be more than a bricklayer, too, but Pop's ambition was for him to become a schoolteacher.

'Is-a plenty time, Pepe. Plenty time to be Padre or maestro. You smart-a boy. You watch. First-a gotta grow up, see how's-a life. How's-a da men gotta dig – dig outta one penny, two penny witta fingernail.'' He held up his own blackened nails – almost a defiant gesture. 'Poor people. Is-a no use be teach if you no understan' how's-a da worl'. *Capito?*'

Joe nodded. He was not quite sure what Pop meant then, but he thought he knew now.

'Is-a good you come on-a job with you Pop. You see wit'-a you own eye how they tritta the man. You big boy now, you ready to see. Job is-a like farm, and the man, he's-a the ox, the horse. Boss who run-a the gang, he's-a the push. He's-a yell, holler, make-a big noise, no work. The man, he's-a pull, push-a the barrow, lay the brick, carry the hod. One getta sick, maybe die, is-a no diff. Getta new man. You watch, you see. Kippa eyes open. Maybe when-a you grow up, you no wanna be profess', you gonna fight for the man. You fight so the man stan' on-a two feet, up in the air, instead-a four feet, like-a some kinda sheep.'

'Don't the union do anything for the men, Pop?'

'Hah! Is-a no union. Is-a buncha crook. You know the shop-stew? Gilardi? He's-a no lay one brick. Rich-a man. Bigga crook. You know how's-a everything run? On graft. Boss pay. Union man take-a money, no care for men. Is-a joke. First thing you gotta do, you get rid all-a the crook.'

They walked through the door in the protection fence. Steel on the new apartment job was topped out and brickwork was sill-high on the twelfth story, just before the set-back. 'Some day we gonna live in house-a like-a *this*. See some green-a grass. Inna spring see yellow dandelion out-a da window, notta for eat, just-a for look. Is-a pretty nice, ah? Okay, I think-a we take.' They went into the mason's shanty and Joe put the coffee on. Men were opening tool boxes, putting up lunch boxes, getting out trowels and jointers, changing trousers, warming their hands and backsides at the kerosene

salamander, waiting for the steward's whistle. Joe enjoyed the
smell of their bodies, the strong-smelling breaths of men who
worked as hard or harder than Pop, the insults they flung at their
tenders. Rino Sacchi, Pop's great friend, who had waddled in after
them, took a large onion out of his lunch box and bit into it like an
apple to keep him warm for the morning.

'Ey, Carmenuche. How's-a the profess?' Rino slapped Joe's
back with his pudgy hand while Joe watched the coffee boil on the
kerosene stove. Other men took nips of gin or swallows of red wine
and no one gave the liquor much thought because this was 1919;
talk of Prohibition was only an unbelieved rumour to the men on
the job; they did not take national legislation seriously.

Lou Gilardi, the shop steward, looked at his great gold-fobbed
watch as carefully as a timer at a track meet, took a deep breath
and blew his low-pitched whistle. But there was this difference
from a track meet: no one ran. The bricklayers and labourers
ambled to the hoist, silent, with the measured pace of men who
must conserve themselves for a long day, men who had done this for
a thousand or ten thousand mornings. And no one said or thought
this morning was different from any other.

Joe was water boy for Christmas week – Pop had pulled strings
with the foreman to arrange it. Mr. O'Connor, the foreman, had
never heard of a water boy, but for twenty-five cents a day he was
willing to try it. Pop assured him a water boy would raise production fifty bricks a man each day. Work had scarcely started when
the men began to shout for hot coffee, and Joe, his kettle hung in-
geniously round his neck, made his way along the scaffold on the
twelfth floor, for brickies were not the kinda guys to be kept waiting. "Ey, Pepe!' 'Joey!' 'Professore!' 'Get the lead out, boy.'
'Hey, Teach, shaka-a you ass.' The coffee had also been Pop's idea,
and the men had chipped in a nickel each for it.

'Zucchero?' For those he liked, he added sugar: half a lump for
Little English, one for man Sacchi and Mr. Benello and Lupo the
Fortunate, and, of course, all there was for Pop. These were the real
old pros who knew how to lay brick, not the dogmeat you see
around forty years later. Some would slip him a nickel for the
sugar once or twice during the week, and all the time, hour after
hour, the Irish foreman, his tenor shout at top-lung, his vocal cords
straining in his throat, would roar, 'Lay *brick*, lay brick! We don't
wanta all grow old and die on this job. Get that mortar tub outa the
way, Pete. Let Charlie get them blocks by. Come on, men, for the

luvva Gawd, wake up. Open yer eyes and lay brick.' Like a crazed cheer leader. There was rhythm to his shout, and the men paid exactly no attention. None. It's doubtful if they even heard.

Joe went easy on the scaffold, picking his way; after all, he was only twelve. It was not so much the twelve stories to the pavement or the lack of protection as it was the ice. The five-foot wide scaffold was always open, without rail or rope, and all you had to do to reach eternity was step off. Most days Joe took fast giant steps to show himself and the men how brave he was, but today the week-end snows which had melted and frozen alternately made dangerous glassy patches. Everyone moved with caution.

By the lunch break, the weather had not warmed up enough to get the thermometer beyond thirty-four; the sun had been covered by a grey blanket of snow-laden clouds.

In the shanty, Pop was eating Mammina's huge bologna sandwich without his usual zest, and Joe noticed that he was sweating pro-fusely in the sudden heat of the shanty salamander. With con-siderable effort Pop ambled over to the tall foreman who was gob-bling into an enormous slice of blueberry pie, eating from the point outward, holding the golden crust with both hands.

'Mist' O'Connor.'

The foreman nodded and continued to gobble into the purple goo. Pop shifted his weight from one foot to another, embarrassed.

'It's-a no good up onna the scaffold, Mist' O'Connor. It's-a fulla ice.'

O'Connor swallowed what pie he had in his mouth and licked his lips with his blued tongue. 'Sure, Carmenuche, pee on it, why don'tcha? That'll tend to melt it now, won't it?' He grinned at the other men. 'When that Dago red turns to pee, it'll be pure liquid fire, now, an' you not puttin' it to any use at all. Shame on ye. Here, have a bit o' pie.' He handed Pop a small crust.

'Should-a be a little protection onna the scaffold, so much-a ice', Pop persisted doggedly. He wiped small beads of sweat from his forehead. 'Wotta the safety inspector say? Little rope maybe, or littla fence. Don' cost-a so much.'

O'Connor swallowed the pie crust and carefully licked his fingers one by one.

'Now don't be givin' me no safety inspectors, Carmenuche!' Then softening, 'Complaints, complaints, Napoli, you always jeopardizin' yer job complainin' and never a thought in your head for your poor wife an' kids who are needin' the day's pay. And yer own boy standin' there, listenin' to every word, Carmenuche, m'boy. Have ye no shame now?' He smacked Pop on the back a smashing blow of friendship, and uttering the short snort of a good-will laugh, turned and left the shanty.

Pop looked about in puzzlement, muttered, 'Is-a fulla ice. Is-a no joke', shrugged and went back to his sandwich. 'Shu. Some-body pay off safety inspector. Pay, pay.' For an instant Pop's face was drawn. He looked like an old man.

'Whatta *he* care!' Rino Sacchi said. 'Slippa, break-a you neck. Compensaysh. Doc, he fix-a you up – mebbe.'

Joe was worried by the way Pop sagged. Maybe Mammina was right. Maybe he had flu or something. But suddenly Pop grinned and he looked fine again. 'Maybe Mist' O'Connor gonna fall on *his* own ass-a.' He and Rino were cheered immeasurably by this thought.

By three o'clock Joe was a tired boy. The men were cold and taking huge quantities of coffee. Here and there a man's knuckles bled and were sucked on or urinated on to stop the blood. 'Come on, boy, get the lead out', the Irish foreman screamed at Joe. 'Let's have the coffee, boy!' There was no shortage of bullies on the scaffold in those days.

'You take your time, kiddo', Little English said from the corner of his mouth. 'Cahn't the bloomeen heathen see the bloomeen ice?'

'You're bloomeen well ry-t, Gov'nor.' Joe could imitate Little English even when he was a kid. He could imitate O'Connor, too, but he didn't dare. 'Sugar, friend?'

He was putting a lump in Little English's coffee when he heard the terror-filled shriek, and he knew it was Pop. How, why, he could not explain, but he knew it. It was an offended cry from Pop's throat as if someone had tripped him or played him a dirty trick. Then he heard the terrified words in Italian: 'God! Help me! Help me! Help me!' It was Pop's voice plainly now.

Heavy footsteps thundered on the scaffold. Reverberations of the bouncing plank echoed in his ears; men came trotting across steel I-beams. Not able to get rid of the coffee pot, Joe ran as fast as he could. He heard a jumble of voices. 'Slipped on the friggin' ice.' 'Just slid an' hit the ice. There! There e' is!' And Pop still scream-ing as if no one had heard. 'Help me, help me, help . . .' Everything happened in seconds. Not thirty feet away Joe saw his father's head just below the level of the scaffold. Pop was clinging to the plank, holding on, it seemed, by his fingernails, his body convulsed, his legs, twisting and kicking as if he were trying to climb the air back up. Heavy men stampeding, and Pop grunted painfully, his eyes blank with terror. 'I . . . can . . . still be . . . saved!' Then before the first man had reached him, he let go. Three seconds made the difference. Ten steps. His father's unearthly scream, Pop's last animal protest against every injustice in the world and in his life and especially his sudden, involuntary leaving of it, was a sound which Joe kept permanently in his ears – sharp, falsetto, piercing, the scream of terror fading to the street below, falsetto, receding. And the sick thud. The sound of life decapitated. For seconds the world was silent, the men frozen. Joe rushed to the hoist which was already crowded, but someone – old man Sacchi probably – shouted, 'Room for the boy! Make-a room!' And as if he were some kind of prince, two men stepped back for him. He remembered the damnedest details about this moment: the breaths of ten or twelve brickies in the hoist producing smoke like a steam engine, a green truck rumbling below covered with a sign that said 'Read the Journal'. When he arrived below, the men at the mortar mixer had already covered his father with a tarpaulin, head and all. Not thirty seconds dead and already covered by some neat bastid who stood, hat in hand, and looked at the small pile under the tarp as if it were a mound of holy sand. The slightest thing and they couldn't wait to cover you up. You gotta hold your ground, tooth and nail. The bastids couldn't wait.

Joe pulled the coffee urn off himself roughly, spilling coffee on his hand, not noticing the scald. He rushed to the small pile, yanked back the tarp and no one tried to stop him. His father was crumpled in relaxation, unharmed in any way, except that he was dead. Then Joe saw the blood on his moustache, the ripped trousers, the mixture of blood and excrement in a tiny pool. He now saw that his father's head appeared to be out of shape, strangely lopsided. The eyes stared as if Pop were beholding the most terrifying sight ever seen. Joe threw himself on his father, suddenly broken in unmanly tears, calling, ''Ey, Pop, Pop! C'mon, Pop, will ya?' and shaking the limp body. All he could hear was, 'I can still be saved!' Three seconds. 'He's warm', Joe shouted. 'He's still livin'! Get a doctor somebody!' But Little English only shook his head. The other men would not look back at him. Pop and he had worked together, rubbed each other's charley horses, Pop had told him everything, always the truth, and now there he lay in this heap on the ground

C

like a sack of cement that had been split open. Joe screamed out his protest like an animal, guttural nameless sounds of grief. 'I can still be saved!' Ringing in his head were words like words he'd heard in church. Pop must be in heaven now. Heaven was the only place good enough for him, and he thought how surprised Pop must be to find that heaven was there and that he was in it. He ought to go fetch Father Ritucci at once. Just make sure.

"Ey, you better call your Mum, kiddo', Little English was saying. "Ere's a nickel.' He rose and saw the men, coming back to time and place, not only brickies and labourers were there, but steam-fitters, plumbers, electricians, the super himself, blowing cold smoke into the frost-laden air, and the superintendent shouted, 'You get Bellevue, Jerry? All right, men, it's not a circus. Whyn't you be good guys and get back to work? Come on, men. Nothin' we can do standin' around.' He took off his hat as if to make his own gesture to the mystery of death. Joe saw O'Connor and lost all idea of what he was doing. 'Bastid, bastid, bastid!' he screamed, and he felt O'Connor's cheek under his fist. He saw the surprised look in the foreman's face. 'He told you about the ice, I heard 'im, I heard 'im myself! Rino! Rino, you heard 'im, didn't he tell 'im, Rino?' He was now totally out of control, crying fiercely, not see-ing. He felt the steel fingers of strangers pulling him, hauling him away from O'Connor. He saw Rino Sacchi standing beside Pop, Rino weeping, choking, his body racked. 'Carmenuche, Car-menuche . . . *Amico mio*. . . .'

'Your fault, you bastid, *your* fault!' Joe screamed, kicking, but the men were pulling him away from O'Connor.

Mr. Whitman, the superintendent, motioned to the men peremp-torily and they began to drift off, as if a half hour at two dollars an hour per man was already too much to have wasted on a corpse.

'O'Connor, why don't you watch that ice on the scaffold?' Whitman said. 'Get a little rock salt.'

The men let go, Joe backed away and started heavily through the door in the protection fence, dragging himself, as if someone were tugging him into the earth. He'd heard Pop say after another acci-dent on the Forty-third Street job, 'Who's a-gonna break-a the news to the Missus?' His own terrifying duty loomed clear. He was head of a family. As he stumbled homeward, he heard the ambulance siren racing up town from Bellevue.

In later years Joe had seen a whole netful of men dead – that nineteen-year-old kid from Fort Wayne knocked off in Fondi by a

bulldozer, two women-victims of jeeps speeding through Bellanza
– and he himself had used the phrase, 'Come on, men, it's not a
circus', so you couldn't blame people for not pausing. Death was
there, that was a simple statistic; you couldn't hold up the works for
it, unless it was your own, and sometimes not even then.

Maybe it was to put off facing Mammina that he walked so
slowly. At Ninety-sixth and Park, Joe saw Tony Ferrara race
around the corner towards him.

'Hey, Joey, c'mon, there's been a helluvan accident! Some bastid
falls off'n a scaffold! C'mon! Let's get a look before they take 'im
away!'

Joe shook his head. He could not see Tony, he could not see
anything.

'Whatsamatta?'

Joe closed his eyes and just shook his head, as if he were trying to
get rid of buzzing in his ear, and felt the hot tears on his cold face.

'*Yaw* job? Some friend a *yaws?*' Tony said. 'Someone offa the
block?'

Joe could still not say a word. Goddam if he'd start bawling in
front of Tony, he'd never hear the end of it. Remembah that time
your old man falls off'n a scaffold, an' croaks, an' you come runnin'
home bawlin' like a friggin' infant? Nosir, not Joe Napoli.

'Who, then?' Tony said relentlessly.

He managed to mumble, swallowing the huge lump. 'Pop.'
And he started quickly across town towards St. Cecilia's as much
to get away from Tony as anything. But in a few seconds he felt
Tony's arm on his shoulder. Tony trotted along, not saying anything except, 'Jeez, Joey, 'at's tough, kid. Jeez', right up to the time
they reached the church. Pop had never set foot in the place, not if
he could help it, but Mama spent so much time there she oughta be
paying rent. Joe had served Father Ritucci briefly as altar boy, not
long after his First Communion, but he soon found that being an
altar boy cut into the block's one-a-cat session, and he *had* to give
up Mass. Some things, they were *impossible*.

Now with Pop lying out there with the sand and cement, Joe
wished he'd stuck to the altar-boy deal a little longer. He walked
unsteadily up the steep front steps, pulling himself up by the black
iron railing, peered about the dim, empty church. He and Tony
shifted uncomfortably. Joe genuflected, touched his forehead with
holy water and walked towards the altar. Tony did the same.
Father Ritucci must have heard them because in a few seconds he

was there, too, with that tough smile. The scar on the priest's chin
was an ugly red in those days, especially in the hot church. He put
his hand lightly on Joe's shoulder. 'Pepe, you boys looking for
me?'

'Joe's Pop just been killed, Fahder! He fell off'n a scaffold!'
Tony spoke gloomily. Joe had not been able to get his mouth open.

Joe turned towards the priest, and saw in his hard, lined, dark face
a flash of naked fear, covered instantly by the solemn ritual expression of sorrow and grief. Oh, you gave yourself away then, Father!
From that terrified look, the transformation from life to everlasting
life was not the sure easy thing you've been talking about. Joe had
never doubted heaven and hell until that instant – Pop's scepticism
always seemed like some kind of comic act – that was Pop, always
kiddin' around, anything for a laugh. But Father Ritucci's tough
face crumpling – boy, it musta been a jolt!

He was clutching the priest's cassock, and repeating crazily, 'I
seen 'im! I seen 'im!' The priest walked to the altar and knelt. Joe
knelt beside him, and Tony stood there. Father Ritucci spoke to
God in Latin in a kind of mumble. Joe didn't like it in Latin.
Usually he didn't care, but this was his own father; he thought he
had a right to know what was going on between Father Ritucci and
God, the Father and the Son.

The priest led the two boys through a side door to the rectory,
into his tiny study, lined with books. On the wall over his desk
hung an ivory crucifix. A photo of Pius the Tenth was on the
opposite wall.

'Sit there, boys.' Joe watched him, mesmerized. 'Have you told
your mother yet?'

Joe squirmed. 'Notchet.'

'She's gonna take it lousy', Tony said gloomily. 'Remember that
Morelli dame? *She* tried a kill herself.'

'Where's your father now?'

Joe hesitated. 'In heaven – I guess', he said, as if he were repeating
a lesson from catechism. The priest almost smiled.

'I mean his – uh – body.'

Jesus, how he hated that. 'They come for 'im in the ambulance.
I dunno. Bellevue, I guess.'

'Arrangements have to be made', Father Ritucci said gently. 'Is
there someone in the family —'

'Me', Joe said at once. You could cut Uncle Giovanni outa *this*
deal. Giovanni never thought much of Pop.

The priest studied him. 'I don't see why not', he said slowly. 'You're pretty well grown up. How old are you now?'

'Twelve', Joe said.

'Would you like me to help?' Father Ritucci said.

'Sure, if ya wanna.'

'Well, let's see. . . . Today's Monday. We can have the requiem Mass Thursday. Does your family have a cemetery plot?'

It must have been the first thing Pop had done when he got off the boat. 'Up the Bronx', Joe said. 'St. Benedict's. Pop was always talkin' about it. I never was there.'

'Good', Father Ritucci said. 'I know St. Benedict's.' *Jesu*, even the priest couldn't wait to get poor old Pop into the ground – covered and forgotten.

'Your family can be over at DiStefano's funeral parlour tomorrow and Wednesday', the priest was saying. 'They're over on a Hundredth and Lexington. They do a dignified job. It'll cost some money over there. Maybe seventy-five dollars, Joe. You realize, all the arrangements, the rooms, the coffin.'

'Okay, I s'pose we can use the compensation money.' There was always the mysterious compensation money when a thing like this happened. Where it came from Joe didn't know, but it always came.

'I suppose. But meanwhile someone will have to advance the funds.'

Uncle Giovanni. It would have to be Uncle Giovanni. Dammit. Dammit to hell.

Joe's eyes narrowed, his bargaining look. 'How about the Mass, Father? How much is 'at?'

'Whatever the family wants to give, Joe. The church is a beggar. Five or ten dollars, it's up to you. It goes for the Lord's work. Of course, if you want more than one priest to serve the Mass, it's usually ten dollars for each priest.'

'How many's the most priests ever do a Mass like that?'

'Well, we've had as many as three here.'

Joe whistled, then spoke slowly. 'We'll have three for Pop', he said. His voice had regained its hoarse stridency. 'I wouldn't wanna take any chances.' It meant Uncle Giovanni again, but Uncle Giovanni made real shekels out of that grocery store of his. Thousands.

The priest smiled wanly.

'You don't dare take no chances on a thing like 'at', Tony said. 'Especially your own fahder.'

'I wouldn't worry about *your* father, Joe', the priest said. 'His soul is immortal – like yours and mine – and even Tony's here, with or without a Mass.' He rose abruptly. 'Hadn't we better get on home to talk to your mother? Wait here, boys, I'll get my coat.'

He left the study and Tony snorted, 'Oh, Fahder, are you full-uvit!' Pop had died and no one would ever know he'd lived. Oh, Jesus, help Pop to Grace.

'This guy is a real louse-up', Tony said. 'You wanna be immortal, Joey? Be George Washington or Babe Ruth, or somebody. Get a statue a you built in Central Park or better yet, have a street or a whole city named after ya, like them old-time bastids did. *They* got immortality, kid. An' if ya notice, they didn't have it so bad while they was aroun', too.'

Father Ritucci was ready, and the three of them left St. Cecilia's to bring the bad news to Mammina.

Just outside the house, Tony pulled Joe aside and whispered cheerfully, "Ey, Joey, when ya get through tellin' ya ol' – ya mother, c'mon out, we'll take the gang up a Hun' Tenth Street and knock the livin' crap outa them Black Owls.'

Mammina was as bad as Tony had predicted. She screamed and sobbed convulsively. It was impossible to get through to her. And when the children returned, her shrill and unrestrained grief set the girls off in terrified wailing. Even Dino was racked with sobs. Next day at the funeral parlour, Mammina calmed down enough to be able to nod to friends, but she could say nothing, because the effort would bring on uncontrolled shrieking and hysteria. For two days she clutched her rosary in a vicelike grip and prayed incessantly. Joe himself could not bear to look at Pop, lying in his good blue suit on a platform in the front of the room at DiStefano's, his moustache and face neatly powdered.

He never passed a skyscraper under construction after that, but ya, ya, ya, he heard their hoists screech, knocked yer old man off! He wanted the fist of a giant to ram the steel work into a twisted mess. Ya, ya, yourself. So's your old man, the buildings whine. Ya, ya, ya. No more goddam accidents for Joseph Napoli. He had as much intention of letting any accident louse him up as going to visit Queen Marie over in Ruritania for a quick tune-up. As they lowered Pop into his grave, Joe Napoli swore an oath that he would see things happen his own sweet way, and not by any goddam accident.

Seven

AFTER that it was only a matter of time before Uncle Giovanni Castanello drove him out on the street, right into Tony Ferrara's arms, no question about it. The old bastid was as tight as a hoor's girdle and as irrational as the Katzenjammer Kids. As long as Pop was alive, the flat on Ninety-eighth Street had not been a bad place. Not quiet or orderly – that was impossible with Mammina and all the kids, but there was plenty of disorderly love around the premises. After Pop's death, though, when there wasn't a dime to pay the rent, Uncle Giovanni and Aunt Mathilda insisted that the entire Napoli family move into their flat, which was directly across the street on the top floor. The old-law tenement in which Uncle Giovanni lived was a comparatively new building, only thirty-five or forty years old. Some of the fire escapes still had paint on them. The flat itself had three rooms and a kitchen. Giovanni and Mathilda slept in one room enjoying a privacy that was the last word in luxury; the ugly little twin girls, Maria and Teresa, had a double bed in another, and Mammina, Rosie and Lucy – three in a bed – moved into the tiny room with them. Joe and Dino took up residence in the small parlour with Uncle Giovanni's fourteen-year-old son, Enrico. Joe slept curled on the floor between the sofa and Morris chair, and for four years never was able to straighten his legs at night. Ten people in three rooms, which was no worse than the neighbourhood average. The gas-lit toilet was out in the hall.

When Mammina insisted on moving all their furniture across, including the old black upright and Pop's three rubber plants, the place did get a little crowded. You had to pick your way around it carefully, but this, too, was no different from all the neighbours. What was absolutely different was Uncle Giovanni. A thick, pompous, overgrowing man, he looked as if he had gone to grass : black hair grew in profusion everywhere, out of his nose and ears, on his neck and on the backs of his hands. His moustache and clothes overflowed as though no human hand had ever trimmed or arranged them. All shapeless herbage and no stem, Giovanni had as little character as a weed. He was driven by a consuming miserliness which was only occasionally overcome by a desire to please his wife, who, Joe decided, must be a fantastic tune-up, because she was the only person Uncle Giovanni would do the slightest thing for. Giovanni, bent over with arthritis, was usually tanked up with wine; and Joe never remembered seeing his slit eyes when they were not shockingly bloodshot. Fear made him mean, and his wild temper made him frightful.

Within two weeks of the funeral, he began what became an endless tirade about the expenses and his generosity. 'Seventy-one dollars for a plain box not worth twenty-five and three priests for a Mass! People with nothing to eat trying to be buried like princes. And how much did we get from the compensation? Not a cent over twenty-five. Banker Giovanni Castanello, step right up with forty-six dollars, sir, and *I* am supposed to be a shrewd businessman! Stop shrieking, Annunziata, I hate women yowling. Tears will not buy your brats groceries.'

Giovanni organized the Napoli family while Mammina, too stunned and terrified to protest, stood by impotently. He commanded like a general, his straggling moustache quivering imperiously. The family Napoli, he shouted one night, was a disastrous economic drain on the family Castanello and he had hoped that after a week of receiving charity, they would have the sense to realize it was necessary to bring a little money into the house. However, they were not very sensitive. No feeling whatsoever. Somehow they thought they were living on Easy Street instead of Ninety-eighth Street. Therefore, 'I have given each one careful thought, Annunziata.' He turned his spread-toothed smile at Mammina, licking his lips like a hungry dog. 'You can go over to the park in the mornings and collect vegetables; dandelion plants are growing everywhere and Mathilda fixes them so they're delicious. In the afternoons you can do laundry for the millionaires who live on Madison and Park.' Turning to Lucy and Dino, 'The law in this country says children must go to school; the law is the law, and I am not going to break it. All right then. But there's also a law which says he who does not work does not eat. A law of the universe. Dino can deliver papers before he goes to school in the morning and when he gets back in the afternoon to the big apartment houses.'

Giovanni's friend, Kaufmann, who had the stationery store next to his grocery, had generously consented to give Dino this lucrative job – worth fifty cents a week. As for Joe, he would work in the grocery after school, waiting on customers or delivering, like Enrico; Saturdays he could be a mason's tender on a construction job; and as soon as he became old enough, he could lay brick.

Pointing at nine-year-old, olive-skinned Lucy, Giovanni said, 'After school your Aunt Mathilda will teach you to do embroidery on that frame, the way she did when she was a child. Little lace things can always be sold to the millionaires on Park Avenue. Those nitwits will buy anything.'

All the money was to be turned over to Giovanni and no nonsense.

Within a few months Lucy had indeed become a proficient lace worker. Once she protested feebly that all her afternoons at the lace frame were hurting her eyes and Giovanni shouted maniacally, 'Out of the house, Mathilda! Mathilda! Get your lazy relatives out of the house! This is the thanks I get.' Mammina had struck Lucy's mouth, so hard it cracked her lips. Then when Lucy wept, so did Mammina. But Mama knew no other way. Joe could feel his stomach churn.

Working in Giovanni's grocery was detestable and boring, Joe was accustomed to Pop's neat, clean brickwork. Giovanni had his stock arranged as if it had been struck by a cyclone, and Giovanni himself walked about, hunched over, in the filthy little shop, pencil behind his ear, glowering in arthritic pain at Joe and at Enrico when there were no customers, shouting at the customers when they did come, cheating everyone he could on quality, weight, and price, and complaining bitterly about his competitor, Martinelli, on Ninety-fourth Street, who was stealing customers with cheaper prices and inferior merchandise.

Friday evenings the family gathered, and the week's earnings were solemnly delivered up to a red-eyed Uncle Giovanni. Aunt Mathilda sat quietly, trying to smile and biting her nails. Mammina was always first, usually with five or six dollars. Then came Joe with three, Dino with his fifty cents, a dollar or two from Lucy, and the six-year-old Rosie with a few pennies she had stolen off the news-stands. 'So what are they going to do if they catch her – put a six-year-old child in prison?' Giovanni glowered, counted, rammed the money into his pocket, grumbling incomprehensibly. 'That all?' he invariably muttered. It was never enough. Joe stood sullen without reply. Dino and the girls nodded mutely in meek misery as they saw their money snatched by the big, hairy hand and rammed into that bottomless pocket.

Joe found relief from the Giovanni louse-up and from the monotony of poverty out in the street and, after he was thirteen, down at DeWitt Clinton, where they not only taught him geometry, history, English, and Latin, but where he was a track hero. In the street gang, he and Tony Ferrara were the unchallenged co-kings. After supper each night they shared the one-block realm on Ninety-eighth Street bordered by First and Second Avenues. Together with Milt Jason, who lived up at a Hundred and Second and First Avenue, they formed a distinguished triumvirate, both at DeWitt and on the block. Tony and Joe had discovered Milt at DeWitt, the smartest bastid in school, and though he lived almost five blocks away, they made him a member of the Ninety-eighth Street gang, a privilege he earned doing Tony's homework.

'Wit' his brain,' Tony said, 'an' my hands, we'll cockalize 'em. Anyone lays a finger on my friend Milt gets his head kicked off.' Milt, for his part, admired Tony, who was everything he himself was not – possessor of reckless courage and the strength of a jungle king. Everyone was terrified of Tony, but Milt had harnessed him, and Milt was drawn to Joe when he discovered they were both dependent on relatives they hated – in Milt's case, a cousin he called Aunt Rosel.

During a gang fight, Milt would rush to the fifth-floor roof of 321 and begin to peer up and down Second Avenue through his spectacles, like a look-out on a crow's nest, scanning the Ninety-eighth Street seas for blue uniforms on foot or horse. Milt had once entered active combat, but had lost his glasses, been knocked cold, and later required so much first aid – a bloody nose, a cut lip – he was deemed worse than useless on the street. Honoured by his wounds, he accepted with secret relief his mission on the roof. When he saw cops, he emitted a piercing whistle that could turn a milk nag into Man O'War. They heard him in Brooklyn. He whistled a kind of melody – so-me, so-fa – in perfect pitch. Thirty seconds after Milt's whistle, Ninety-eighth Street was as empty as Wall Street on Sunday.

You don't find hitters like Tony Ferrara any more. Those were the days before knives were put in the hands of ten-, twelve-year-old kids, they still used fists. To Tony the sight of anyone standing around was a tremendous challenge, and frequently an unbearable insult. He liked people to lie flat. The only living things he was kindly disposed towards were Joe, Milt Jason, his old man's monkey, Stupido (his old man was the world's most alcoholic organ grinder), and an emaciated white mongrel dog named Scummy. About the only thing Tony loved as much as Scummy and Stupido was a good cold glass of beer. At nine, Tony could hold fantastic amounts of beer. No one knew where he got the money for it, though everyone assumed it was from pockets he picked along Madison and Lex, but he could drink five, six bottles standing up. In fact, Tony was a completely wacked-up kid, which he came by honestly because his old man was the number-one champion drunk of the block, and against tough competition at that.

Joe rounded out the trio. What Milt was to the gang's intelligence service and Tony to its military arm, Joe was to its body politic. There was practically no guy around for whom he hadn't done at least one small favour. 'Throw 'em a fish', he'd say to Tony. Whatever little things guys wanted or needed done, it came natural to him. He hocked quite a number of bags of immies for Sal Benello out of old Fart Feinberg's candy store because Sal was absolutely nuts for immies and always losing them; he could lose 'em faster than Joe could hock them. Or if someone wanted a quick tune-up under the stairs, Joe would get Rudy Meraglio to send for his sister. Or if one of the boys needed someone banged around, he would get Tony to do it. Well, it was like that, one good turn after the other.

Of course, across town at DeWitt Clinton, at Fifty-ninth and Tenth, the same three guys were the pillars of society, all Doty boys – school police under Mr. Doty – students selected because of a keen sense of responsibility, with the job of maintaining law and order. Hell, when you got right down to it, there wasn't a hell of a lot of difference between maintaining law and order and defying it.

To start with, you had to have everyone's respect, which to Tony meant regularly beating the crap outa some bastid or other with everyone watching.

Milt was the business manager for almost every team DeWitt had. Doc Guernsey took a shine to him and he practically ran the Guernsey squad. He controlled more athletic equipment, tickets and paraphernalia than Tex Rickard. Everyone would always trust Milt with the *money*. Even Tony never tried to lay his hands on *that* dough. Milt's soul lacked a basic ingredient – a deep, compulsive sense of larceny.

But Joe's was the name you heard on every tongue. He could

run faster than anyone in DeWitt's history – the backbone of the track team. His time for the hundred was college time, ten flat, and his picture in the New York papers sent his fame skyrocketing far beyond DeWitt's old classrooms.

They were the three musketeers.

Once the new anti-liquor law was in force, Tony took up with a funny little guy – a dark, pock-marked runt of a man in dark clothes and a black felt hat, who met Tony almost every day across the street from the Roosevelt Hospital morgue to deliver a slip of white paper and a few confidential words. Carting whisky those days became such a good thing, in fact, that Tony quit school before he finished his junior year and got himself a licence to drive a truck which, the way Tony drove, would have been dangerous even *without* whisky in the truck. If Joe didn't know Tony so damn well, he'd say Tony had got sort of cracked in the head on the subject of liquor from his old man's drinking. But Tony was like that – fighting the problem. And maybe that was what gave Joe such a soft spot for him.

Take the time they went up to Harlem. The summer before Tony went into bootlegging in a big way, when Joe was fifteen and Tony sixteen, Tony had this thing about the Black Owls. Every so often, usually when he'd just had the can kicked off him by his drunk old man, he'd start talking about they hadda go up to Harlem and knock the guts out of the Owls. The Owls had already terrorized every other Negro outfit north of Central Park to a Hundred and Sixteenth Street, and inflamed by success, had begun to make forays into pure white territory, using hit and run tactics on stragglers. Until the night they waylaid Rudy Meraglio coming out of Stephanie's place on a Hundred and Third. Rudy got off easy, taking treatment for bruises and contusions at Lenox Hospital, because he got hit with nothing but shoes and fists. These Owls were reported to be wizard razormen in close-in fighting, and while other gangs used bottles and rocks at long distance, the Owls' special artillery was the broken bottle, the neck of which they used for a throw-handle. They had at least two deaths to their credit. Their leader, whose fame had spread as far south as Fifty-ninth Street, was The Blade – quick and elusive, described by one of his victims as so long and skinny you could shove him up a snake's ass. It was The Blade that Tony was out to get. Nobody was gonna mess up Rudy Meraglio or any one a his boys.

For weeks after the attack on Rudy, The Blade and his Owls were elusive, but every couple of weeks Tony'd lead the gang, swinging up town, a dozen or more, with Scummy yapping along behind, they'd lay two or three slobs out flat on the way, just for exercise, and fix up a couple of tyres good. They must have gone up there eighteen million times, and by the time they reached a Hundred and Eleventh Street, they were always pretty keyed up, but they never did see any Owls. Seems like these black boys were pretty goddam wise old Owls. Tony, flanked by Milt and Joe, and surrounded by their cohorts, would strut up and down the centre of the block and bellow up at the cold-water flats, from the bottom of Slum Canyon, 'C'mon out, ya filthy owls! Ya yella nigga bastids, c'mon out an' fight!'

There was never the slightest response – not even the giggles or the ya, ya, yas the cops usually got. Silence reigned in Slum Canyon. Then they'd go on up to a Hundred and Twelfth and Tony would repeat the challenge, and so all the way to a Hundred and Sixteenth.

After a few such abortive trips, Tony revised his challenge, screamed up from Slum Canyon: 'C'mon out, ya yella bastids. Ya sons a hoors. I'll take on any one-a yaz. I'll fightcha myself. Fair fight, One ta one. Winna take all!' But this Goliath-like appeal went unheeded, and in desperation Tony got carried away and one day on a Hundred and Fourteenth Street he shouted, 'I'll take on *two* a yaz. Two ta one. Winna take all, you yella bastids!'

For the first time, after a long reflective silence, there was an echoing voice from the walls of the canyon. 'How 'bout all dem boys you got witchu? How 'bout *dem?*'

And Tony roared back, 'They ain' gonna do nothin'! I don't need nothin' but these!' He shook both his fists up at the windows.

A high-pitched voice screeched, 'Ya'll Tony Ferrara?'

'That's me!'

Suddenly there was a chattering, like the noises of the jungle.

'Fungoo! Fungoooo! Fungoo la sis!' There must have been twenty of them.

'Send down The Blade', Tony yelled. 'I'll take on The Blade an' anyone else. Two ta one. Winna take all!'

Joe said, 'Can it, Tony. These bastids'll take y'up on it. Can it, boy!'

'Lemme be', Tony screamed, shaking loose from Joe's restraining hold. 'I'll kill any two a these bastids, one han' behind my back.'

From a fourth floor window came a long whistle. 'One han' behin' yo' back, white boy? You *mean* dat?'

Milt's face, which had been clouded with concern, was furrowed in pessimism. 'Tony, for God's sake! These guys are going to expect you to deliver. Be *careful* what you say.'

'Let's sherry outa here', Joe said. But Tony had gone berserk. No one could shut him up.

'One hand behind my back, yah!' Tony screamed. 'Yah! *Yah*! *Yah*!' He was completely out of control, smelling blood. 'Two a yaz!'

' We comin' out!' These were the fateful words in Harlem that day.

Two Negro youths, one tall and thin and the other just as thin but shorter, emerged to the stoop of one of the buildings. They walked gracefully, almost gliding. With a flamboyant gesture the taller one pulled a folded razor from his pocket, snapped it open so that the blade caught the sun, and tossed it with elaborate non-chalance down the stoop, publicly disarming himself. No doubt about it, this slump-shouldered, skinny guy was The Blade. His eyes were narrow yellow slits, and his teeth were bared like a barra-cuda's. His companion took out a razor and made the same gesture of disarmament.

The Blade carried a small coil of clothes line. The Ninety-eighth Street boys lined up watching. Joe could hear his own inhalations.

'Dohne staht nuthin'', The Blade said. 'We got guys on the roof up theah. They got bottles. Busted ones.' Joe looked up to the roof top. He saw a body move. They were there.

'We ain't afraid a no goddam bottles, ya black bastid', Tony said. 'When I give my word my boys don't get in it, they don't, under-stan'?'

'Ah'm jes sayin'', The Blade said softly, oh so softly.

'You gonna fight us two, one han' behin' yo' back, lak you say?'

'You heard me!'

Milt turned away; he could not bear this tightening noose.

'Ah'm comin' ta tie yo' han', guinee-boy.' The Blade advanced cautiously while his companion remained behind, just in front of the stoop. The Blade stopped at Tony's side. 'Which han'?' Tony seemed to hesitate as if only at this last moment he realized what he was doing. Then he jerked his left hand behind his back. The Blade set to work at once, winding the rope around his wrist and then running it around Tony's waist. 'Y'all tell me if dat too tight 'cause I dowanna choke yo' stummick', he said seriously.

'Gowan. Tie the damn thing', Tony snarled.

The Blade tied and tied again. 'How dat?' he asked politely.

Joe saw it coming. Before The Blade's question was out of his mouth, Tony had hit him with a blow that started from the ground and ended in The Blade's solar plexus. The Blade rocked back too surprised to recover, and Tony was at him with another right to the side of his head and another to the eye. The three blows were struck so fast and so hard that it was almost impossible to see them as distinct blows. It was like an animal attack, fierce, unexpected, irresistible. The Blade went down, and Tony was kneeling on his chest, beating his face with his free hand. It was sheer beauty and slaughter.

'Georgeee!' The agonized cry came from the lips of The Blade. George had been paralysed by the speed of the first attack, but now he made his move towards Tony on the run, fast. Fast, Joe thought, that boy could break ten seconds easy. Tony had jumped off The Blade's crumpled form, but not quite soon enough. He was able to ward off most of George's blows, but could land none of his own, and occasionally George would land one, not serious, but one to the neck that hurt a little, and one to the nose, which started a trickle of Tony's blood towards his mouth, into which he sucked it. Scummy began to bark and snap at George, and Tony called, 'Milt, hold Scummy! Don't let no one hurt Scummy!' Milt managed to catch the dog and held him in his arms.

The Blade had now recovered sufficiently to get up on one knee, and he remained in that posture for thirty seconds or more, staring at Tony Ferrara, who had injured both his body and his pride. He kneeled there, letting George do the work for a moment, bathing in the pleasure which was to come. This guinee boy would get his.

At last The Blade stood alongside George. 'Now listen heah, George. We jes' gone get in each other's way. You get holda his loose ahm. Jes' get hold, an' hold on, then ah gone give it to'm. Maybe ah take his both eyes out, or mebbe leave him one. Ah ain' decided yet.'

George made several attempts to seize Tony's free arm with both hands but each time Tony landed a blow and George fell back. 'That ahm is slippery, man!' George complained to his leader. The Blade stepped behind Tony, and Tony, sensing that The Blade was preparing to attack from the rear, whirled rapidly, first in one direction, then the other, trying to keep both his adversaries in sight, but the struggle was uneven. George landed a stiff one to Tony's ear, and Joe shouted, 'Pull your other arm loose, Tony! Pull it loose!'

Tony shook his head. 'I said one hand!'

George landed another heavy blow, this time in the gut, and Tony rocked. From behind Tony, The Blade's hand flashed, and he had Tony's free arm, flailing, but prisoner. Exerting all his strength The Blade twisted. It was slow motion, Indian wrestling, but The Blade used both hands on Tony's one, twisting, twisting, until the white boy's free arm was turned behind his back. From fifteen feet away Joe could hear the breathing of all three.

'Yuh got eeem!' from one of the windows. 'Keel eeem!'

'Now George . . .' The Blade was panting, but he had lost none of the sardonic touch which delighted his followers. 'Now George, now that . . . ah done the man's job . . . how boutchu . . . jes' hole ontuh this heah ahm? George . . . Ah hope ah . . . ah ain' axin' too much?'

'Ah got it!' George cried triumphant. 'Ah got it!'

'Now —'

The Blade knew how to punish, and if ever he hated anyone, it was Tony Ferrara. He hit him alternately in the gut and the eyes, his blows snakelike and swift. There were no sounds but Tony's grunt and the sound of a hard fist striking flesh. Tony's face was all blood. 'Winna take all, guinee bastid.' The way The Blade spoke, it was almost a caress. 'Winna take all.' Tony's right eye was closing, but he said nothing, all there was to be heard were the grunts.

Joe could no more have restrained himself than to hold his breath for five hours. He hit The Blade with all his strength as The Blade came at Tony again.

Tony, summoning strength from some unsuspected reservoir, shrieked, 'Stay outa this, Joey! I said two ta one . . . I said one han' behind my back. . . . You heard me . . . Joey . . . I said . . . I said . . .' His voice trailed off in a wail.

The Blade, recovering, taut, said, 'Y'all heah dat, man?'

Joe headed in, The Blade's hands went up, and everything happened. From three of the old buildings streamed Negro boys, God knows how many. The sound of bottles breaking in the asphalt gutters was heard under the howling of the Owls and the equally deafening shouting of the Ninety-eighth Street gang. Scummy got loose, barked and yipped and ran up and down the street like a mad dog.

Joe met a sea of fists. Over all the yelling, he could hear Tony screaming, 'Joey, you son-of-a-bitch, Joey. I said keep ya nose outuvit.' It was as near as Joe had ever come to hearing Tony sobbing. Of course, he was so punchy he didn't have the first foggy idea what he was saying.

Then he heard Milt's fantastic whistle, that damn perfect pitch, if it was half a tone higher only dogs would've been able to hear it, it was so piercing. Sure enough it was Milt, right with the cops, leadin' 'em to the scene of battle. That was Milt, all brain.

'Cossacks! Cheezit, cossacks!' So-me-so-fa!

Everyone scattered – the Owls into the tenements, the white boys towards Second Avenue. Joe headed east with the others, and that was the last he knew. The sky cracked open, and whatever there is behind it, all of it fell and hit him and down he went into blackness. . . . Later he discovered that the jagged edge of a milk bottle, thrown from a roof by an Owl marksman, had caught him in the neck.

In the ward at the hospital, they had ten million beds, every one filled with some sick bum. A few looked dead and maybe were. In the bed next to Joe's lay Tony Ferrara, and he had high colour – purple mostly, with small patches of red, yellow and orange.

Milt Jason was sitting on one of those hard wooden chairs they use to discourage visitors in the free wards of hospitals. He had managed to get rid of the cop, but he had had to do quite a bit of talking.

Tony lay there, silent. Finally he rolled towards Joe, as carefully as if his bed were full of eggshells, and his voice sounded far away, but what he said was plain. 'You son-of-a-bitch, Napoli. I says I'm gonna fight them two boogie bastids and you make a greaseball outa me. Just when I am gonna finish them jigs off. I don't like that one goddam bit.'

Joe said, 'Two more minutes a you not bein' a greaseball an' you'd be deader than McKinley, ya crazy no-good Siciliano bastid.'

Milt said, 'Please, men. You're in a respectable hospital.'

'Shaddup, ya nut, running fa the cops. Whattsamatta wit' *you?*' Oh, Tony was boiling over.

Milt's eyes were soft and brown and you expected them to fill up with tears. 'Tony,' he said very quiet, 'there's a time when it's an excellent idea to call the cops. I always keep that in mind and you should, too.'

Joe turned on Tony angrily, 'You unthankful bastid! Milt and me . . .'

Sick as he was, Tony sat up in bed. It must've tortured every inch of him, but he started shouting so the veins stood out in his neck. 'So yaz saved my life! What's so big about *that*? Ya two louse-ups! Fa Christ sake, I *made* the rules and if I can't do it on my *own* rules, I shoulda got cut up in a million pieces and served on a roll with cat-soup. You two bastids a got the hundred per cent wrong *idear*. Milt's always tryin' to go by rules everyone *else* makes. Milt keeps offa the grass, fa Christ sake. But, Joey, you never hearda rules of any kind whatsoever. You'd do any goddam thing comes into ya head. Even ya friends don't know what t'expect. What's everyone gonna say about me now? You ain't *trustworthy*, Joey, that's whatsamatta wit' *you*, ya bastid. Nice guy, save my life, an' crap like that, but I don't trust ya. Where the hell are you gonna end up? In the gutter!'

Joe said nothing. He brooded over Tony's tirade, the unthankful bastid. No gratitude whatsoever. What the hell was he talking about? Trying to put a label on him, some kind of unprincipled bastid. He absolutely had principles. Good ones. Maybe he couldn't list them neatly, but take care of your friends, wasn't that one hell of a good one? And the bastids in this world, if you couldn't make friends outa them, you had to knock hell out of 'em. You had to be out of your head to worry about the rules on *how*. That wasn't principle, it was suicide. He'd stack his principles against Tony's any time.

Eight

Now some wise-aleck Senator or Sam Poltek, boy prosecutor, was going to ask him why he was having this and that deal with Tony Ferrara, the gangster, gaolbird, twice convicted on assault, once with intent to kill, almost indicted for murder, and presently under federal indictment for evasion of income tax and God knows what else – every louse-up in the book. How come Tony Ferrara was a one-third partner in Naples, New Jersey? And he was supposed to tell this fine Senator exactly in three or four well-chosen words the entire facts. We're old friends, Senator. Great! That would make about as much impression as a drop of Chanel No. 5 in the East River.

Maybe somewhere along the line he could have got away from Tony, torn himself loose from his evil influence. But the trouble was he liked Tony, he always got a kick out of him, and by the time he realized the danger, it was too late. There was one occasion just after he was fifteen, a junior at DeWitt, that the opportunity to break with Tony and Ninety-eighth Street – and in fact everything that had gone before – came knocking at the door with both fists. Milt would certainly remember all that without Joe's reminding him.

The first hint of it came at that four-way track meet. This smooth and pink-cheeked character, all dressed up in a great big raccoon coat, was there. No one could figure out who the hell he was. He stood out in the crowd of kids and teachers. It was in the fall of '22 at the meet between Eramus, DeWitt, Evander Childs and Stuyvesant – the day Joe first broke ten seconds. God, that was a day! He ran like a bolt of lightning. And after the race, when he was breathing so hard he thought he'd pass out, who walks right into the gang of kids whamming him on the back but this man in raccoon.

'Sonny', the fancy old guy in fur said; it was the first anyone ever called him Sonny. 'What do you plan to do when you finish high school?'

'Lay brick', Joe said. He thought he saw the man swallow a smile. 'Anything wrong with that, mister?'

'No,' the tall man said, 'nothing at all. Joe, I think I might be able to change the future for you. Drop in to see me at my office – any time it's convenient for you.' He handed Joe a business card and disappeared.

Joe scarcely gave it a thought after that, all the guys were hollering, Joey, Joey, Joey, whacking him and shaking his hand. But he glanced at the card and held on to it. The Woolworth Building, it said, 233 Broadway.

Having lived in New York all fifteen years of his life, Joe Napoli had naturally heard about the Woolworth Building, but until this bleak day in January, 1923, he'd never seen it, much less set foot inside it, though Ninety-eighth Street was only six miles up town from it and Pop's friend, Rino Sacchi, had personally laid brick on it. There before him, through grey snow, loomed the even greyer tower, its green pyramid top pointing skyward – the most beautiful and moving work of art he had ever seen. With gothic windows, dripping architectural curlicues, it was like a series of baroque spires on seventy-story stilts; and he was going into it. He slowed his stride, licked a snowflake from his lower lip and without a word pointed to the tower, while his companion trudged unaffected and silent through the snow and hiked his mackinaw higher. This pillar of grey stone made his muscles ache, he could feel the sweat of the thousands of men who had built it, the men who had worked with him on other walls, his father and his father's friends. 'Lookit that son-of-a-bitch', he said reverently. 'That is *built*.'

The lobby, vaulted with gold mosaic, was the inside of a cathedral, and the office on the forty-third floor was the most elegant place he had seen outside the films. The sight of this elegance aroused new emotions in Joe – awe mixed with an old resentment. Quite a few shekels went into this joint. The letters on the door – Webb, Tyson, Warfield and Ballantine – were gold leaf and so were the dozen smaller names below, and when Joe and Milton stepped into the panelled reception room Joe uttered a piercing, uninhibited whistle, removed his cap and twirled it around his forefinger to control his swirling emotions. '*Jesu*', he said, his voice hoarse and high.

'Mmmm', Milton responded judiciously, doing his best to keep his eyes from bulging beneath his gold-rimmed glasses. Milton was a frail young man those days, not much different from the way he was now, stooping slightly, and the glasses made him appear older than his sixteen years. His narrow, straight, down-pointed nose was set in a thoughtful, gaunt face, giving him an air of added wisdom. He, too, removed his cap and took his glasses in hand for a careful, quiet cleaning. The blonde receptionist looked up and yawned. Joe saw she was pretty in an upturned way – the corners of her mouth, nose, lashes, even her eyes had a small, oriental upturn. When she saw the two tieless boys still red from the cold, Milt practically shrinking up the way he always did, and Joe, his finger-nails cracked, black, and hands raw, in clothes indescribably shabby, shoes that tracked wet dirt on the immaculate green carpet, she probably made up her mind to throw them out. But Joe walked up to her and stood there, seeming a foot taller than his friend though actually the same height, his black, curly, cascading hair shining, his full lips smiling with his own awe, pleasure and contempt. In spite of herself, she smiled back.

'Beautiful', Joe said without restraint, not acknowledging her smile.

The girl said, 'Whom do you want to see?'

Joe fished out the calling card from his mackinaw pocket. 'This here – Mr. Webb. H. Stotesbury Webb.' He laughed, snorted, rather. 'Is that an honest-to-God name?'

The girl shrugged. 'Do you have an appointment?'

Joe twirled his cap impatiently. 'He said I should come in to see him any time it's convenient for me. He says he's gonna change my entire future. *He* says. So I thought *now* is a pretty convenient time for me to have my entire future changed.' He scuffed the rug. Snow had made its way into the big hole in his sole, and he had just begun to feel it. He needed new shoes. That old bastid Uncle Giovanni was getting tighter every day.

'Your name – sir?' There was no trace of irony in the 'sir'.

'Joe Napoli. Guess he'll remember me all right.' He did not add he damn well better.

'N-a-p-o-l-i?'

'Yah.'

'Will you wait?' The girl rose gracefully.

'Sure, sure.' He took her arm as she turned to go and squeezed her elbow. ''Ey, it's not gonna be long, is it?' She looked at his hand as though it had struck her, then she smiled secretly and covered his hand in a lightning gesture. 'Just a second', she said, and was gone.

'Sit down, Milt. You make me nervous, pacing around and about.' Milt sat stiffly and set his cap down; with his head inclined downward he looked like a poised bird. 'Lookit these leather chairs. That's genuine leather, Milt. Feel that. And feel the rug. Jesu, it's three, four inches thick!' Joe twirled on his heel in half a dozen revolutions, taking in the Spy prints, the mahogany panelling, the intricate plug board. He bent his knuckles back slowly, one at a time, making each crack. 'And the tune-up is built.' He jerked his chin after the receptionist. In a moment the upturned girl was back, her upturned smile intact. Joe widened his eyes expectantly. 'Mr. Webb will be with you in a few minutes', she said.

'Exactly how many minutes is a few?' Joe continued to flick his cap in a circle and thrust his head forward in a gesture of belligerent curiosity.

'He's on the phone.'

He jutted his lower lip and thought for an instant. 'The hell with that', he grunted. 'I'm not hanging around for Old Stotes. Come on, Milt. Let's get out of this firetrap.'

Milt stared up at him as if he were out of his head. 'Joe,' he pleaded patiently, 'we walked a hundred blocks in the doggone snow. I almost froze my – uh, knuckles off. And now —' He shrugged hopelessly.

The girl looked up and said in a friendly way, 'Did you boys really walk a hundred blocks in all this snow?'

'Not exactly *walked*, Miss', Joe said. 'Actually, we ran most of the time.'

'Why didn't you take the subway?' the girl asked.

'She thinks we're made outa money', Joe said. 'That's a hot one, subway.'

Milt turned to the girl and in his slow, controlled voice spoke with open admiration for his friend. 'He's the fastest sprinter in New York. Does the hundred in under ten flat.'

'Ah,' Joe protested, 'twice only.'

'Mr. Webb was a four-forty man at Princeton, you know', the girl said.

The plug board's buzz forced the girl to turn her back. 'Yes, Mr. Webb. And – Mr. Webb – the young man here says he's terribly sorry, but he can't wait much longer. He has another engagement which is rather important. Oh, yes, he's *very* upset that he has to leave. And I – yes, sir.' She flipped the plug out and smiled. 'Mr. Webb will be right out.' Her voice was as soft as wine. Joe examined her. She had taught him a lesson he would remember: that receptionists and secretaries, glistening and complicated at their switchboards or desks, presumably out there protecting the big shots, were the keys which opened vaults of treasure and favour. Use 'em, treat 'em right, and the vaults were open. Then all you gotta do is help yourself. He twirled his cap and for the kindness and lesson he smiled slowly – a half-whistle, half-kiss twisting into a youthful, secret smile. His smile was a caress and she returned it vaguely.

Mr. Webb stalked blithely into the reception room – tall, lean, athletic, his forty-five years showing only in the greying and thinning of his sandy hair. He looked a little more human than he had in the raccoon coat at DeWitt. His voice was brisk and friendly. 'Napoli, glad you could make it. Come along, will you?' He turned towards Milt, and, as if he were repelled by the sight of him, turned away and put his arm lightly at Joe's elbow. 'This way.'

'Don't go 'way, Milt', Joe called back, as if he were cautioning a retarded child. As he passed the receptionist, he touched her shoulder and winked at her. He saw her blush. Mr. Webb led him into a room that contained a gigantic mahogany board-table with sixteen chairs. A clothes tree in the corner was covered with Mr. Webb's raccoon coat. Mr. Webb settled at the far end in a swivel chair with Joe on his right. His gaze was friendly, but he was unable to hide the fact that there was something slightly repulsive in what he saw. He spoke with speed and vigour as if to get it over. 'Napoli, you've got good stuff. I think if you train right, get into the right hands, you can break nine and four-fifths next year. By George, I love to see a boy who can run like you. Pleasure to watch.' Joe was studying the man, rather than listening. Spoke like hot potatoes were in his mouth. By George and hi-de-ho. Mr. Webb's hands drummed impatiently on the highly polished table. The fingers were soft and pink, the nails polished and evenly white at the edges.

'Yah, yah, up at DeWitt they make a big deal outa my running', Joe said, much too loud for the room. Mr. Webb almost winced at the raucous, reverberating voice. "Ey, my ol' Uncle Giovanni gets a big horse laugh outa *that*. He thinks Americans are all nuts. He says what's the big deal if you're born so you can run fast? I tell you, I don't get it my *own* self. Like Pop used to say, if you don't have it *here*' – he tapped his temple – 'God puts it in your legs or your ass. So I guess I don't have it here.'

Mr. Webb smiled somewhat fishily. 'Napoli,' he said, 'when do you finish high school?'

'I'm in my third year', Joe said. 'I got one more year. Only I'm not graduating! I'm gonna get my working papers as soon as I'm sixteen.'

'Have you ever thought about going to college?'

College? Was this man serious? 'Nah. Oh, the old days when I was a kid, Pop useta say I was gonna be a professor. Wanted me to study hard, all that. Maths I'm not too bad at, in fact. Pop, he was up to his ass in ambition. He wanted me to go to college, but now Uncle Giovanni, he's a whole different proposition. For him to give away a buck is like for me to give away both my ears.'

'I take it your father has passed away?' Mr. Webb said softly.

'Fell off a scaffold on an apartment job. Slipped on ice. Jesus, like that, in one second. No protection. Yah, on account of Pop they changed the law. Maybe you heard about that, you're a lawyer. I was on the job, too, that time. Three years ago.'

'What did your father do?' Mr. Webb spoke as though the entire subject had become distasteful but necessary.

'Laid brick. Fact, he got friends worked right on this building.'

'That's rather a coincidence, isn't it?' Mr. Webb's interest was at the vanishing point. 'Tell me, Napoli, how would you feel if I told you I could arrange for you to go to Princeton? That you wouldn't need this – uh – this Uncle – uh —'

'Giovanni?'

'Yes.'

Joe knew this must be a joke so he winked with his greatest *savoir faire* and made a smacking sound at the corner of his mouth. 'Princeton, hah? Great.' Then, as he realized Mr. Webb might be serious: 'Where *is* Princeton, for God's sake? Somewheres out West?'

Mr. Webb closed his eyes. 'In New Jersey', he said quietly. 'Some of the alumni, like myself, are on the look-out for good college material. We like to help boys like yourself, who can do something for the school. And at the same time the boys we help – well, sometimes it changes *their* lives a bit.'

Joe stared at Mr. Webb in amazement. He had never really talked to anyone who had gone to Princeton or Harvard or N.Y.U. or any of those pay colleges. Change his life, why Jesus, he might

end up in a fancy office just like this, next door to God. His head
swam, but he forced his mind back to reality. Mr. Webb was clearing his throat to try again. 'If Bill Denny got his hands on you, in
my opinion, you'd be cut out for the Olympic team next year. Or
if not next year, surely in '28. I know potential when I see it. I'm a
four-forty man myself.'

Four forty? This decrepit old bastid looked like he could barely
crawl his stiff lanky self across the street.

'I'm certain you could shave a fifth of a second off your start.
Then you have to train, boy, train and I'll wager you'll break nine
and four-fifths. Do you smoke?'

'Nah', Joe said. 'Look, Mr. Webb, couple things you maybe
don't understand. Why I couldn't pay the *car-fare* to Princeton.
My family, Mr. Webb, I mean, we're piss-poor.'

Stotes Webb swung on his swivel chair coughing spasmodically.
In the days when Stotes Webb went to college, it was possible to
tell a Princeton man merely by his clothes and gait. If they had
made too great a fetish of uniformity, at least there was comfort in
knowing that you were with other boys from homes much like
your own, from good stock. But in his four years he could not
recall one boy at college remotely resembling the creature before
him – 1923 was certainly not 1908. Perhaps he ought to let Old
Nassau struggle along without his track discovery. But if this boy
should win the Olympics, they'd say, You have to hand it to Stotes;
he can pick 'em.

But there was something more: here was something tossed up by
the sea, the scum of some Dago village, the 'wretched refuse' of
Miss Liberty's sonnet, but good raw material, bright, the DeWitt
principal had assured him, even if he didn't always work at top
level, and he, Stotes Webb, had it within his grasp to make something of this ghastly mess. Raucous voice, unkempt hair, callused
hands, and yet in four years this boy's mother might scarcely recognize him. Pygmalion Stotesbury Webb, surveying the clay of Joe
Napoli from his high seat in the Woolworth Tower, swallowed his
distaste and issued a friendly chuckle. 'Joe,' he paused to let the
familiarity make itself felt, 'Joe, I don't think you understand. My
friends and I take care of *all* your expenses. That's the entire
point.'

'Yah?' Joe's eyes narrowed. 'You take care of car-fare and
clothes? Guess I'd have to have new clothes, place like Princeton.'
He held out his shabby arms with their ravelled cuffs.

'Everything.' Stotes Webb waved his hand with finality.

'And all I have to do is run the hundred?'

'That's it.'

'Supposing I don't feel like running sometime? I get canned?'

'Now, Joe, why would you *not* want to run? To people like you and me, running is being alive.'

'Oh, Jesus, Mr. Webb, maybe I get cramps, maybe something I ate. What's so important – what bothers me – if I *can* run a hundred yards a fifth of a second faster than some other guy? Who gives a good —'

'Now listen, Joe. You're an ill-mannered dirty boy with incredibly offensive characteristics. But you do one thing in this world better than anyone else – in the rest of the whole bloody *world*. Don't sell it short. That's a gift of *God*, that's something rather unique, isn't it?' Joe shrugged. 'As sure as God made little green apples, Joe, it's unique.'

'Ah,' Joe protested, 'what the hell *is* it?'

'There must be *something* to it, Joe, or why do you bother to run for DeWitt Clinton? I don't know what it is that drives some fellows to want to do better than all the rest. But they do, and all their lives. And p'raps next year, surely in '28, mark what I say, you could well win the hundred-metre dash at the Olympics. I don't say you *will*, but you *could*. And Joe, there's nothing like the Olympics. Winning some scholastic meet in New York is nothing. You'll march out there in front of a *hundred thousand* people in some foreign city three or four thousand miles away – Paris, next year. People will be there from all over the world to see you. You're out on that field with the best athletes on *earth*, you and your team-mates, in white flannels, marching along behind the American flag – I don't care how jaundiced or jaded you are, something gets you, whether you're black or white or Anglo-Saxon or Mediterranean or wherever your parents happened to come from. *You* know you're representing the United States of America, and you'll run your heart out. I did. And Joe, if you're ever lucky enough to be up on that top platform, as I was, and they've called your name out to the world and they're playing "The Star Spangled Banner" and a hundred thousand people are on their feet for *you* and the music – that's something, that's a thrill you'll *never* forget if you live to be a hundred. I know I never have.' Mr. Webb had to clear his throat, he was so choked up at the memory. 'And when you hear that announcer's voice through the megaphone: "A new

Olympic record . . . a new world record . . ." I'm telling *you*, son, it won't seem asinine to you then.'

'Princeton sure must have a crappy track team', Joe said, and laughed.

In spite of himself, Stotes Webb was blind with exasperation. He said coldly, 'What do you say, Napoli?'

'Well, if they need me that bad —' Joe was talking absently. He was thinking, My chance, oh Christ, what a chance.

'Let's keep one thing clear, Joe. The people at Princeton don't know a thing about this.' Stotes Webb spoke sharply. 'Just a few friends and myself.'

Joe shook his head. 'It's a goddam outrage', he said suddenly. 'Did you see that friend of mine sitting outside? Milt Jason? *There's* a smart guy. I mean real smart. He can do maths' – he snapped his fingers – 'like that. In his head, a problem with three unknowns. Brain at English, whiz at history, terrific in anything. *He* should go to Princeton. Well, it's too late to get him, he's already been admitted to C.C.N.Y.'

Stotes Webb said bluntly, 'Marks aren't everything in this world, boy. They don't necessarily reflect your natural abilities, you know. My own marks were never so hot. Oh, I got by, but I mean, all C's and D's.' He chuckled. 'How are your grades, Joe?'

'I'm lousy in English. *The House of the Seven Gables* or *Ivanhoe*, boy, that stuff puts me to sleep. Maths is okay, I do okay in maths. But you take Latin. Will you tell me what the hell am I gonna use Latin for?'

'Well, you could always get tutoring help at Princeton. There's always some smart scholarship kid, some grind like your friend there, willing to earn a few extra dollars to help you cram.'

'Tutor?' This guy must take him for Little Lord Fauntleroy. A tutor! La-di-da! 'See that?' he said to Mr. Webb, leaning forward and pointing to the white scar on his neck. 'You know where I got that? Kid from the Hun' Twelfth Street gang lands a broken milk bottle on me. Big, black boogie bastid. Split right into my neck.'

By now Stotes Webb didn't give much of a damn whether Joe Napoli went to Princeton or the University of Heidelberg. 'See here, Napoli, this is a tremendous opportunity, a boy like you – from a foreign family. All you have to do is say "Thank you" and you're in.'

Joe felt his ears getting red. Santa Claus coming out from behind

the whiskers. Always some smart guy like Webb or Uncle Giovanni trying to do him favours. 'Mr. Webb,' he said, and his voice
for the first time was so restrained it cracked, 'lookit, I tell you what.
If I can do something for Princeton, okay, sure, I'm happy to do
something for Princeton. But in ten million years nobody is gonna
do me any favours. I'm serious.'

Stotes Webb stared at this snot-nosed kid from Naples and the
East Side of Manhattan and for ten seconds couldn't decide what
to do. Ultimately he had to laugh. The kid had the brazen gall of
the most genteel of the Wall Street sharks. All Princeton had to
do was smooth him out, polish him up, teach him to speak, and he'd
be right at home down town.

'We don't have to decide anything just now, Joe', Mr. Webb
said. 'Think it over carefully, Princeton isn't going to run away
and neither am I. Come see me in June.'

They shook hands and Mr. Webb reached into a drawer for
application blanks. 'Take these home, Joe. Talk to this uncle of
yours. When you come in June, I hope you bring these back to
me.' Hah! Talk to Uncle Giovanni! Go talk to Columbus up on
Columbus Circle.

Joe folded the application forms carefully and stuffed them into
his mackinaw, as he and Milt stood waiting for the lift. He felt
completely weightless. Downstairs they pushed their way out
through the revolving door into the sobering snow. Joe pulled his
cap lower. Princeton, for God's sake, who did he think he was?
He'd be sixteen in June, the end of compulsory schooling and then
come hell or high water he was going to get the family out of Uncle
Giovanni's place. Princeton might want him; okay, he could stretch
his mind to believing that, but they weren't giving him free schooling and fifteen hundred bucks a year to support a family besides.
It was impossible. Not just for running the hundred. Maybe if he
was one of those hot football players . . . Ah, no use living in a pipe
dream.

'What'd he want?' Milt said as they were approaching Canal
Street.

'Nothin'', Joe said. 'He asked me if I wanna go to Princeton
College.'

'Princeton?' Milt was bug-eyed.

'On a scholarship.'

'Wow,' Milt said, 'if that isn't the cat's meow!'

'Yah. I thought so my own self.' They were approaching a

drugstore on Canal Street, and Joe stepped inside. He suddenly felt as large as a giant, anything was possible. The world could be remade. 'Gimme a couple cigars', Joe told the clerk.

'Nickel or ten cents?' the little clerk said.

Joe looked in his pocket. He had accumulated forty cents, car-fare saved over two weeks.

'Ten cents', he said.

He nipped the tip off one of the cigars with his front teeth. Carefully he lit it with the match the clerk had given him. 'Milt, have a cigar.'

Milt was smart enough not to refuse. With no relish he, too, bit the tip and allowed Joe to light it for him. Joe looked at Milt with enormous satisfaction. Then he took three quick puffs. 'C'mon, let's go.' Princeton College, by God. It would have to be *made* possible – somehow, somewhere there must be an answer. The two boys walked out into the snow, puffing hard on the cigars.

When they had reached Ninety-eighth Street, Joe turned east from Park Avenue, after waving to Milt, who continued up town through the snow. Joe saw Ninety-eighth Street through entirely different eyes now. The smell of stale urine hit him as he passed Second Avenue. It mingled with other effluvia as he went past over-turned garbage cans, stacked ash cans and eight- and nine-year-old kids in a screaming, battle-scarred crap game for bottle tops. As he walked up the five flights in 371, he saw clearly for the first time the broken newels, missing stair treads, a scurrying rat, peeling paint, and the gas jets, which on some floors emitted a feeble light and on others only escaping gas. They lent the place a flavour which had taken years of neglect and mismanagement to achieve. Yet the residents had become so accustomed to it all that an amazingly high proportion survived – a testimonial to human resilience. But Joe was thinking of the path out.

Standing in the gas-lit hall outside the flat, Joe could hear Uncle Giovanni's outlandish howling: nothing extraordinary, only that the gas bill had been a dollar ten more than last month. The high living of the royal family they had taken in was pauperizing him. The gas was always turned on when there was plenty of light from the windows. This terrible extravagance must stop, and everyone had better understand it. He was a man of infinite patience, but even he, in the face of base ingratitude . . .

Joe made up his mind to wait, not to mention Princeton yet to anyone. No rush, Mr. Webb had said. Some miracle, somehow, somewhere. He would keep his eyes and ears open. He would find the moment, the occasion, the opportunity, the sign. He was to wait almost three months for its appearance.

One morning Mammina complained of a toothache. For three days it grew worse, until Joe could hear her lying awake, moaning at night after the girls were asleep. On the third night, he heard her sobbing frantically, and he got up to sit with her and hold a piece of ice to her jaw until she said it felt better and sent him to bed. In the morning, Mathilda interceded with Uncle Giovanni.

Giovanni was almost sympathetic. 'Ah yes, toothache,' he said, judiciously, 'terrible thing. Terrible.' He seemed uncharacteristically pleased at being able to help. Shaking his head sadly he slowly sipped his breakfast coffee; then he took Mammina gently by the hand to the window, stood over her as she sat in terror on the edge of the Morris chair. 'Open your mouth', he commanded. Mammina did so. 'Wider. Way up. Now where's the pain? Exactly which tooth?' Mammina said 'Anh' with her mouth open, and gestured towards the upper right molars. 'Anh!' Uncle Giovanni pushed his face to within an inch of Mammina's mouth, peering like some microbe expert, the light from the window completely obscured by his own head. He peered into the total darkness of Mammina's mouth for several moments. 'I do not see it', Scientist Giovanni announced at last. 'It is nothing.'

'I cannot bear it', Mammina wailed, holding her jaw. 'It's unbearable.'

''Nunziata, you are teasing me. It is your imagination.'

The tears welled in Mammina's eyes. She held her jaw with both hands and rocked her head from side to side. 'I have not slept for three nights. If I could only sleep! The pain is terrible, I swear it. Shooting pains all through here! I wish you could feel it, wild, wild, wild! It's a nerve. God! I cannot sleep, Giovanni. I'm tired, Giovanni. I don't know what to do. I'm exhausted. Please. What must I do? Anything, Giovanni, anything. In the name of God, believe me. I need a dentist, I must go right away. I must have the money.'

'I do not see it', Giovanni said sanguinely. He pulled out the spectacles he used for reading the paper, placed them carefully on his nose, and peered into Mammina's mouth again. 'I cannot see any sign of pain whatsoever. If your face was swollen or there was pus around the tooth, I could see it, true?'

Mammina slipped to her knees, her arms embraced Giovanni's

legs. 'Please, please, Giovanni, I am in pain. In the name of my children, in the name of my beloved Carmine, in the name of the Holy Mother, I am in great pain, terrible pain. I will do anything. Whatever you wish! I must go to a dentist, I need money for the dentist. Be merciful!' The tears flowed.

'I cannot see the slightest pain', Giovanni said blandly.

Joe found his fingers around his uncle's hairy neck. 'Bastid. Give her the money. You hear what I'm telling you? My mother gets the money or so help me, I'll . . .' He realized that Giovanni was gasping, struggling, breathing with great difficulty, and his mother and Mathilda were shrieking. He felt the older man sag, and released his grip.

'Pepe, Pepe. Let go your Uncle Giovanni!' For a moment her fear was stronger than her pain. Aunt Mathilda was wailing and whispering prayers.

'Hit him', Dino cried. 'Sock the old bastid!'

'Two dollars', Joe guessed aloud. 'Gimme two bucks, Uncle, for the dentist!' He tightened his fingers. 'Two dollars for my mother, Uncle.' He squeezed tighter with almost all the strength in his fingers.

Uncle Giovanni, kicking and struggling, tried to twist away, and with great effort he fished into his pocket and found a roll of bills. He threw a two-dollar bill to the floor and Dino grabbed it and gave it to Mammina.

'Go ahead, Ma,' Joe called, 'go find the dentist.'

Mammina hesitated for an instant, then turned and ran down the stairs, holding one hand over the shooting pains of her jaw, exultant in her agony, while Giovanni, eyes blazing, kept his distance.

Joe understood dimly at that moment that he was born to a special kind of slavery. He was the champion of those he loved. Giovanni, the inglorious son-of-a-bitch, had made Joe's nature clear to himself. Some people made a big deal out of favours they did their families, held a halo over their own heads, but Joe knew absolutely it was nothing but a sickness and a special form of slavery. Every guy in this world goes around with some kind of sandwich sign: Doctor, Phony, Humble Man, Crook, and a helluva lot just said Nobody. The single Italian word which was Joe's sign had not changed since that day: Padrone.

Joe sat at the kitchen table and wrote on his best white, blue-lined paper in the approved business-letter form out of a DeWitt text book.

Mr. Stotesbury Webb
233 Broadway
Woolworth Building
New York, N.Y.

Dear Sir,

With reference to your offer to provide the undersigned a scholarship to Princeton College after I graduate from DeWitt Clinton High School, I regret that because of a previous commitment, I am unable to accept. I am sorry I am not able to be of service to you. I absolutely hope you find a good hundred yard man for your college.

Truly yours,
Joseph Napoli

He never heard from Mr. Webb.

Nine

'I VE always wondered,' Milt said pensively, 'why you didn't jump at the chance to go to Princeton. That's probably the difference between us. I'd've let my whole family go down the drain if I had had an opportunity like that.'

Joe laughed. 'Sure. You had no family. Anyhow, you never had to live with Uncle Giovanni.'

'I had Aunt Rosel', Milt said. 'Luce has told me a bit about Giovanni. Real charmer.' He was running his hands up the sides of his face as he always did when he thought hard.

'Yah', Joe said dryly. 'Well, I hadda get the family out of *that* place. Before I quit at DeWitt I went down to see Lou Gilardi at the masons' local, and I know Louis was usually a son-of-a-bitch, but he was okay to me when I needed him this time. He got me my apprentice card, and the sentimental old bastid kept saying he was doing it just for Pop. "How I loved dat man", Louis used to say. "I mean a foist-class prince!"

'So I started laying brick on a school job, P.S. Eighty-two, up on Washington Heights, for diSala. Pop used to work for diSala in the old days, and Louis put in a good word for me with them, and I was set. I could beat all those bastids hollow on the wall. Well, you remember how I laid brick. I was goddam good and fast.'

Milt nodded. 'Do I remember? Are you kidding?'

'We got the hell out of Giovanni's place and took that flat up the block on Ninety-eighth Street, you remember, where you used to come looking for Luce. Beautiful place, wasn't it?'

'It was home,' Milt said, 'and I thought it was pretty nice because Lucy was in it.'

'Yah', Joe said. 'I used to love the stink especially. If you stayed awhile you got used to it, but if you went out and came back, whammo! Right in both nostrils. And the goddam bugs, you know we tried everything they had those days but never got rid of the bugs; and Dino, he comes back from down town one day and he says we are very lucky. He's been to the flea circus on Forty-second Street – you remember that joint – and they are making a mint down there showing off trained fleas at twenty-five cents a look, and they haven't got one-millionth the number of fleas we got. So all we have to do, Dino says, is train our fleas to jump through hoops and our fortune is made. It was a lovely hole, but I liked it anyhow because Uncle Giovanni was damn near a whole entire block away.'

The intercom buzzed insistently even though Joe had told Cath no calls; Cathy sounded flustered. 'There are two men here – uh, Mr. Rose and Mr. McGill from the staff of the Senate sub-committee, Mr. Naples.'

'Yah? Tell 'em we'll be right with 'em.'

Milt's face squinched in pain. He opened his mouth and started to speak, then changed his mind.

Joe snapped the intercom. 'Ask Woody Faber to come in. And, Cath, get Chuck Rossmore on the phone. And while I'm talkin' to Chuck, get everyone in the entire office together in the conference room, and Cath, see if you can get Curly di Roberts and Sal Benello in from the field. I just want to have a little talk with everyone.'

'The girls, too?' Cathy said with some surprise. Cathy considered the girls in the office, including herself, as a kind of human under-stratum.

'Yah. Girls and men. Everyone.'

Woodrow Faber, the head of the book-keeping department of the Naples Company, was a stoop-shouldered, grey-haired man in his early forties. He was ten years younger than Joe and looked ten years older, and there was no mystery as to why. He'd done at least twenty years more worrying. His hands were clasped ner-vously before him, and as he spoke he wrung them; this habit had taken the place of biting his fingernails which he had been forced to give up when he was sixteen.

'Woody,' Joe said, 'there are two examiners here from a Senate investigating sub-committee looking into our business, and we've agreed to let them examine our books and records. Milt'll handle the legal stuff with them. You make your books and records avail-able and give 'em a place where they can work.'

'Examiners?' Woody was terror-stricken. 'Uh – *all* the books?'

'Yah.'

'Uh – the general ledgers, too?'

'Of course.'

'You-uh-well, Joe – uh – Do we *have* to?'

Joe looked at Milt, and Milt nodded.

'It's only a matter of time, Woody. Sooner or later they'd subpoena everything.'

Joe thought Woody Faber was going to cry. He turned without a word and left the room with his head bowed low, as though he were going to his own execution.

The phone rang. 'Chuck? Joe Naples. Listen, boy, I don't know, some crazy bastid decided the United States Senate oughta investigate the builders again, so here we are, we're right on top of the list. Now what we need real fast is some first-class public relations, because Milt tells me these Senators have absolutely no intention of proving what a useful citizen Joe Naples is. In fact, they are going to try and show what a complete no-good s.o.b. I am, and, if possible, maybe try sending me to the pokey. This is not a technical proceeding. It's a kind of circus, with headlines and all that stuff like Goldfine had a few years ago, or old Dave Beck. Gee, these fellows fade so fast I can hardly remember who they were. So I'm gonna need some pretty damn nice things written about me in all the papers and magazines you can break into, and I don't mean *House and Home* or *Architectural Forum*. You got it?' He could hear Chuck Rossmore nodding. 'Come on over this afternoon, Chuck. Four o'clock.'

'Okay.' Chuck got paid for his words and used them sparingly.

Joe switched the intercom. 'Cath, ask those two guys from the Senate committee to come in.'

Mr. Rose was a medium-sized, sallow, dark-haired young man who wore bifocal horn-rimmed glasses over his small brown eyes. This body odour must be an occupational disorder. Rose was as bad as Poltek. Mr. McGill was round and short with water-blue eyes, rosy-red skin, greying hair, and a thin smile. Mr. Rose had a letter of authorization from Samuel Poltek and he gave it to Joe to read, while Mr. McGill made sucking-smacking sounds with his throat, as if he were telling a horse to giddap.

Joe glanced at the letter, stood up and introduced Milt. 'You boys see Woody Faber. He's our comptroller.' He had never before referred to Woody as anything but the book-keeper and wondered as he said it whom he was trying to impress. Like these hot shots who keep saying ne-go-see-ay-shun. 'He'll show you anything you want and he'll give you a place to work. Okay?'

McGill nodded cheerfully as they started out of the office. Rose's face, as he turned for a final look at Joe before he closed the door, was a study in scorn. No doubt he could see Joe Naples with an apple in his mouth, slowly turning on a spit.

'Rose and McGill', Milt groaned, rubbing his face with both palms. 'Rosencrantz and Guildenstern we got now.'

'Guildenstern looked like a good egg. At least he smells good.'

'I don't trust him', Milt said. 'It's not exactly *him* I don't trust. What it is, is I don't trust anyone.'

Joe pushed himself up and started for the conference room. His spirits were rising, as they always did when he faced a new obstacle. While he would rather have been working on Naples University and his Title I jobs, this was a more exacting challenge. He'd built Naples his own way; now he'd have to justify it. He'd, by Christ, come out good.

More than ninety people from the office and a few from the field were now crowded into the fifty-foot conference room, standing along the walls and sitting at or on the conference table. When Joe and Milt walked in, they all became silent. Brother Dino sat at the head of the table in his English yellow-and-brown-checked waistcoat, his wide, handsome smile intact. 'Hi, brother Joe', he said cheerfully as Joe stood behind him and placed one hand fondly on his shoulder.

'Jesus, Dino, those Naples University studies were absolutely the nuts', Joe said in a low voice. 'You got the preliminaries on the administration building finished so we can go over 'em?'

'All set', Dino said.

'Right after this meeting then.'

Dino looked happy. Any special attention or recognition he got from his brother publicly always set him up.

Milt protested, 'Joe, we haven't the time —'

But Joe was now on display. 'If you think I'm gonna devote all-a my time to this goddam sub-committee nonsense, you got another think coming', he said. 'We got things to do in this office. Everything can't stand still.'

Milt shrugged hopelessly.

Joe cleared his throat. He was good in a small group, six or eight, but now, suddenly, he felt formal. Same people you see every day, he thought to himself. Pick out one. Not Woody Faber, still wringing his hands. Curly di Roberts, in work clothes. Sal Benello. Pasquale Baccio. The old crowd, he could talk to them. Maybe having the girls in was a mistake; he couldn't talk in quite the same way, but it was too late to get rid of them now.

'Some of you, no doubt, have read in the papers about this Senate sub-committee investigation,' he said, 'and it's no secret they're getting ready to investigate Joe Naples. Now some of you know me a long time, most of my life. You know I got my own way of doing things, I take care of my own people, try not to let anyone down. My conscience is clear. I don't think I ever did anything wrong. We'll see whether the honourable Senators agree. I'm hopeful that every one of you will stand by me and your job, and keep on in the same old way with the work we're doing in this office.'

Milt saw that Joe intended to go no further, and so he spoke finally. 'May I say this, Joe? As part of this investigation, there are two men here going over all the books of all the companies. They're going to want all vouchers, all legal documents, and I want every-one in book-keeping and legal to give them any paper or book they want. On the other hand, there's no reason to volunteer any information, and if they ask you a direct question, please refer them to Mr. Faber if it's book-keeping, or to me if it's legal. We're not trying to hide anything, but we have to go about this in an orderly way.'

The meeting started to break up; both Curly, now in his early sixties, and bent a little, and Sal, turned to touch Joe's shoulder by way of a vote of confidence; when brother Dino spoke, his voice was charged with emotion. 'I don't think we ought to let my brother go without knowing how we feel about him. Joe, I've talked to a lot of the boys. We all think it's a damn shame and an outrage against decency. Maybe it's the price you have to pay for being the outstanding man in your field. Speaking for myself, everything I've accomplished I owe to you. You're the guy who put me through architectural school, encouraged me, I don't know, in a million ways. I've sure I speak for every last one of us, even though I'm your brother, when I say, give 'em hell, Joe. We're with *you*.'

Joe could feel the tears welling in his eyes. He swallowed hard and someone started to sing 'For He's a Jolly Good Fellow'.

Joe looked around the room of singing faces. He was astounded at the number of people he had touched. Here in this room there were only ninety-odd, but outside there were literally thousands – workers, the people who had bought his houses, shoppers at the Centre God knows who or how many. Millions of people he never saw or even thought about. Here in this room were some people he had known since he was a kid. Fat old Rino Sacchi over there by the window, Pop's oldest friend, damn near eighty, existing practically on a pension; Curly di Roberts, who had given him his first instruction in estimating; Little English, who estimated the brickwork nowadays; his brother Dino, whom he put through Rutgers School of Architecture, and a damn good architect he had turned out to be, even if he was a completely mixed-up man; Sal Benello, whose mind was still on girls; Pasquale Baccio, whose kid he had tried to save in vain; Cathy O'Neill, his Wednesday night tune-up; Woody Faber, the gaolbird he had given a new lease on life, now a twentieth-century slave; Gravel Larson inherited from Jock Dennison; Oscar Swanson; cynical Dulian, best damn flyer in Jersey; and Milt. 'For he's a jolly good fellow.' Goddam, Joe thought, I guess I *am* a jolly good fellow. Guy like me. I don't have just one family with a wife and kids, I got a thousand wives, a million kids. He pressed the tears back when he saw how loud and how sincerely everyone was singing. Suddenly he had a vision of all Mammina's old cronies as he had seen them standing last night, one hand over their hearts and another flung out to the flag. It struck him that Joe Naples was the flag of everyone in this room. I pledge allegiance . . . He oughta have a twenty-five-year club like Macy's, give out pins and buttons and watches. But what he had you couldn't buy for pins and watches. Macy's never got anything like *this*.

Though he knew it to be a sacrilegious thought, he understood for the first time how Jesus must've felt on the road to Calvary. Hetty maybe needed the applause an actress must hear in the theatre, but all Joe Naples needed was the 'Ey, Joe, which was his applause wherever he went day in and out. Now to expose his soul, to admit he had lied, cheated, bribed, procured, almost murdered for them, to hold their complex machinery together – to be persecuted for their sakes could be a martyrdom which might be greater than the entire row of triumphs behind him. Hadn't the crooked union leaders who'd been pilloried, the Communists who were persecuted for making deceit a tenet of their faith, the early Christian martyrs who dissembled and stole for their faith – hadn't they all felt something like this – an inside-out exhilaration, a burst of emotion that carried them along like a tide?

Milt said quietly, 'I only hope that before the cock crows thrice, someone in this room doesn't betray the master for thirty pieces of silver.'

Those nearby stared at Milt in shocked silence, and Joe said, 'Now, that was a goddam sacrilegious thing to say, Milt.'

'I'm only a Christian lately', Milt said wryly. He'd never made any bones of why he'd become a Catholic. 'Maybe I'm too suspicious.'

'That administration building of Dino's is gonna have everything', Joe said, as he and Milt walked back. 'Dino is a genius, and he's the right guy to do it, because if anyone likes his comfort, it's brother Dino. He's got refrigerators hidden for snacks for the girls, he's got the desks and light arranged so scientifically, people are gonna be beating the doors down to work there. This is gonna be the best goddam university in the entire state.'

'I believe it', Milt said. 'Now —'

Dino stood nearby with the roll of plans in his hand. 'Ready, Joe?'

The buzzer rang. Mr. Lewin was outside to see Mr. Naples. Mr. Lewin?

'You know', Milt said. 'He's the one who wants to sell his house to that Negro family.'

'Oh, yah.' Joe shook his head sadly. 'I'm sorry, Dino. To-morrow morning first thing, eh?' Dino made a long face and trailed back to his office like a boy whose candy had been taken away.

Mr. Lewin, a tall man with glasses and a crewcut, entered as if he were trespassing; he held his felt hat before him as though to ward off a blow and his eyes seemed distracted and troubled behind the lenses. Although Joe asked him to have a seat, he did not.

'I'm kind of in a hurry, Mr. Naples. My wife's packing and the kids are underfoot. We're moving to California.'

'I heard', Joe said. 'Heard you've got a customer for your house pretty quick, too.'

Mr. Lewin seemed to back away and said, 'That's right. A fellow I work with over at Sanders and Sanders – boy named Mal Howard. Awful nice chap. We're signing contracts tomorrow.'

'Is someone kidding me?' Joe said. 'I hear he's coloured.'

'That's right, Mr. Naples. But you know, if you work with a man a while, you kind of forget it.'

'We don't have coloured people living in Naples. You oughta know that, Mr. Lewin. They got their own places to live.'

'Gee, I *didn't* know it', Mr. Lewin said. 'Naples is a pretty big town, and I just hadn't noticed one way or another.'

'Didn't you know he brought a case before the Civil Rights

Commission to force us to sell him a house? How's he think his kids are gonna get along? People'll get sore as hell, maybe heave rocks through his window. God knows what. People get pretty wrought up.'

'Gee, I didn't discuss that part of it with him. He's a pretty bright boy. Ph.D. in chemistry, seems to have a pretty good head on his shoulders. I guess he's thought about it and decided to try it.'

Joe got up and felt his face flush. 'Goddamit', he said, his voice rising. 'I'm not gonna have any broken windows or burning crosses in *this* town. Nosir. What made you think you could do a damn-fool thing like this?'

Mr. Lewin clutched his hat slightly out of shape and lowered his shoulders further. 'Gee, I just thought – it *is* a free country, isn't it?'

'Don't gimme *that* crap', Joe said. 'You know what you're doin' and so does this nigger. Starting trouble. And right now I just happen to need that kinda trouble in the worst way.'

Mr. Lewin was plainly flustered and distressed. He looked pleadingly at Milt, backed away another half step, and cringed further. 'I don't know, I just told the boys at the lab I was being transferred, and Mal congratulated me and asked me if I'd sold my house. He has to commute all the way from New York, and I guess it's pretty rough. So he came out and liked the place, and I figured I wouldn't have to pay a broker – and I thought, why not? I wish you could meet him. Really, Mal's an awfully nice –'

'Yah, I know. So you saved the brokerage. How much is he paying you for the place?'

'Eleven-five. That includes the combination storm sash and screens I put in, and the finished attic, and –'

'Look, I got no time to argue', Joe said abruptly. 'I'll give you twelve-five.'

Mr. Lewin looked deeply agitated. He took his glasses off and blinked his eyes. He was slightly cross-eyed. 'Gee, a thousand dollars.' He turned this huge fact over in his mind, studied Milt, looked around the room, saw Carey's picture, the Utrillo, then laughed nervously.

'Wow, Mr. Naples, I sure appreciate that offer, but I don't think I could back out now. I told Mal the house was his.'

'Thirteen thousand.'

Mr. Lewin put his glasses back on. He seemed to stiffen a little and he stood ground as if the force of a hurricane were being blown against his spindly frame. 'Gee, I think not, Mr. Naples. And I sure wish you wouldn't do this.'

'Why not?' Joe said. 'It's a free country. Thirteen two fifty, and that's it.' But as he said it he sensed that the numbers had stopped having any meaning for Mr. Lewin.

The phone rang. It was Jock Dennison's office. Joe held the phone away from him. 'Excuse me a minute, Mr. Lewin.'

Mr. Lewin clutched his hat. 'I don't think there's any more we have to say', he said. 'We've about covered the ground.' He shook hands with Milt – 'Sorry, I really have to hurry back' – and escaped.

Joe watched him leave, glanced at the phone in his hand a moment. He had the wretched, unfamiliar feeling that people were not reacting properly, that the rope was unravelling in his hand.

'Did you hear me, Mr. Naples?' the operator was saying. 'Mr. Dennison's office.'

Good old Jock Dennison, there was one guy he could count on. Breeding. No doubt Jock had heard he was in trouble, and here he was, coming to the rescue. This was a gent. 'Yah. Put him on.' But it was only Billy Snow, Jock's male secretary. He had just been talking to Jock in Paris.

'Are you doing anything special next Friday afternoon, Mr. Naples? Mr. Dennison is flying back Thursday and he'd like to drive out to see you.'

'Sure, Billy. Look forward to it. Hope Jock's not exhausting himself on all those two-legged French deers.' Billy chuckled. 'Over seventy and getting more lecherous every day, eh?' Joe said. 'And me, I haven't even got *time* for women, with this goddam investigation. They got me thrashing around just to stay even.'

'Mr. Dennison'll be out about noon', Billy said, and hung up.

'Now there's a real padrone', Joe said. 'Jock Dennison. Like the Commendatore in Bellanza. Coming all the way from Paris to give me a hand. How d'you like that? I'd go to hell and back for that man. But it takes a few generations to breed one like him.'

'What d'ya think he really wants?' Milt said. 'Coming all the way from Paris.' But Joe ignored the scepticism.

'You know, Milt, Jock's a hell of a lot more to me than just a partner in Naples, New Jersey. When I first got to know Jock, why, Jesus, he practically wanted to be my father. I got a hunch he's heard about this investigation and maybe he's got some idea, some angle to give me a hand. Sweet guy. What the hell, didn't he give me my first break?'

'And he introduced you to Hetty, too, didn't he?'

'Yah. Jock and me have always been close. Not just business-close. I remember one day we even had a long talk about Gamboretta. In fact, we've been through a hell of a lot together when I think of it. You could say him and me have certain responsibilities in common.'

Milt knew most of it, but with notable exceptions. 'Joe, let me ask you a few things about you and Jock.'

'Sure.' Joe poked the intercom. 'Cathy, see if you can reach a man at Sanders and Sanders named Malcolm Howard. Ask him if he can drop over and see me any time at all. And hold all calls for Milt and me, right now. We're in conference. I'll have lunch in. Get me a bologna sandwich on a roll and a beer. Milt?'

Milt shook his head. 'Can't we go out for lunch?' he asked sadly. 'All this rush – it's bad for you.'

'We got no time', Joe said. 'Cath, order a chicken sandwich for Mr. Jason – and tea.'

'No mayonnaise for me', Milt called. Joe snapped off the intercom.

'Now where was I? Oh yah, Jock Dennison.'

Ten

O N a Saturday in May when Milt was still a senior at City College, and the alteration job Joe was working on as a bricklayer was shut down, Joe called to pick up Milt on the way to the Polo Grounds to see Artie Nehf pitch. This was 1927 and since the Napolis were now living on what Joe earned, he could do a few things that had been impossible in the days of Uncle Giovanni's tyranny.

Walking up Convent Avenue towards the trolley, Milt's books tied in the end of a strap and slung over his shoulder, the two boys approached the six-story apartment job Curly di Roberts was running for diSala. 'How's the family?' Milt was saying. 'How's Lucy?'

'Fine.' Joe gave him a funny look. Why was Milt always worrying about Luce?

Squeal and whine of hoist, scrape of trowel on wall and slosh of mortar were all as familiar to Joe as the back of his hand. Carpenters hammering and sawing, the mingling of shouts – sounds and sights of the old tyrant, The Job.

'Let's stop in, see Curly's job. We got time.'

'Well, you're predictable', Milt said. 'We haven't passed it yet without going in.'

Joe opened the temporary door in the protection fence. As soon as he set foot inside, he felt at home. They passed two labourers wheeling mortar towards the hoist.

''Ey', Joe said. 'Sally! Whaddaya know! How's little Sal? Where's Curly?'

'Oppa stair', the short, red-faced one said grinning. 'Fort'a floor. Littla Sal, too. Looka, Pete,' he said to the sallow one behind him, '*il professore*! 'Ey, Joe, Howsa *you* job?'

'Okay', Joe said.

The two men set down their wheelbarrows and tipped their hats to Milt as though they were greeting a priest. It was all those books. Joe and Milt scrambled up ladders to the fourth floor.

On scaffoldings around the perimeter, men were laying brick. Labourers who were wheeling brick or mortar over planks moved in slow, measured rhythm, pacing themselves for an eight-hour day. A large man wearing a beaten fedora, smoking the tattered remnants of a cigar, carrying a rolled sheet of blueprints like a baseball bat, shouted instructions in Italian to one man and then another. He turned towards the hoist impatiently, saw Joe, and his face brightened. This was Curly di Roberts.

'Joey! *Paesano*! Ain't seen you in a month. Whattsa matter, you lose interest?' He removed his hat to scratch the top of his bald scalp. The little dark, curly fringes made him look better than he would have looked with no hair at all, but not much. His square, arrogant face gave him the prime pre-requisite for a foreman on the job – he looked ferocious.

''Ey, how's the boy?' Joe said.

'Great, Joey, great.' Curly pounded Joe's shoulder with one great blow. He nodded at Milt and, like the men below, tipped his hat in deference to the college student and his books.

'How's Emily?' Joe said.

'Whaddaya think she gives me yestiddy? She's gonna drop another bambino. In December! Makes five, and I'm not thirty-two. It's takin' it out a me, I'm tellin' you.'

'Out of *you*?'

'Now don't go worryin' about Emily, Joe. She's crazy for kids. Makin' 'em, havin' 'em, baptizin' 'em, beatin' 'em. She's nuts for kids.'

'This is absolutely fascinating', Milt said mildly, looking about at the shouting activity. 'I never come here without being fascinated.'

'Just another lousy six-story crap job', Curly snarled. 'I hate 'em. This summer I'm gonna run me a man's job – Brentwood, Long Island – big nut house, State Hospital, for the loonies. Real nice work. Flemish bond they got. That'll be a job, eh, Joey? Hundred men, may be hundred and fifty. Eight million brick.'

'Understand those State inspectors stand over ya.'

'Them guys? They don't know their ass from their armpit.'

Suddenly Curly turned to the scaffold behind him. 'Get it up, Pete. Get it up. Lay brick! Lay brick! Sal, let's go. Let's get that line up.'

The bricklayers continued to work at the same steady pace.

Curly's screaming caused not the slightest change. Joe judged they were getting a thousand a day. They could move a lot faster if they wanted to. Curly knew it, too. What he didn't know was how to make them do it. Curly could threaten his men, but couldn't get work out of them.

'How I hate this lousy job!' Curly growled. 'You shoulda been here an hour ago, Joey. See all that water? They put the test on the damn water lines and, Jesus, it was like Niagara Falls! I never seen a test like it. Those guys musta been puttin' pipes together wit' chewing gum and spit. You think they caulk? You think they wipe them lead joints? I'm tellin' yuh, Joey, all the trades are goin' to hell – plumbers, steam fitters, not just the brickies. No young blood. Guys like your old man, where we gonna get 'em? They're a dyin' breed, I tell yuh. They stop immigration, so where's the young blood comin' from? No pride in the work! Guys like you'n me, we want to be supers, bosses – work in a department store wit' a goddam flower in our buttonhole, dentists, teachers, for God's sake. Who the hell's gonna make the buildings go up?'

'Seem to be going up', Milt said, looking around.

'Yeh, but lookit how! What a shortage!' Curly said. 'I been offered *three* jobs this summer. They come to *me*. Yah! Brentwood, Mount Vernon and Allenburg, New Jersey. They can't get men, Joey.'

'New Jersey?' Joe said. He could hear the interest in his own voice. Tony Ferrara was out that way somewhere, married a cousin of Vince Barciano, too, Rosalie her name was, and the word was that Tony was becoming a big man there. Not just liquor, but Tony was rumoured to have big friends in politics and the labour unions. He glanced at Milt and somehow he knew Milt was thinking the same thing.

'Yep. Sounds like a honey of a job, only I already got Brentwood for diSala. I stick to diSala, diSala sticks to me.'

'What's the job in New Jersey?' Joe asked.

'They puttin' up one of them A & P warehouses in Allenburg. Dennison's the owner. You know 'em, big real estate outfit. Five million brick. Dennison's his own GC and I hear they're thinkin' o' doin' their own brickwork, but there's a tough brick ring out there.'

'I once worked on the wall for Dennison', Joe said. 'So did Pop.' Joe turned his back on Milt for an instant and took Curly into a two-man huddle. "Ey, Curly, tell me somethin'. How much a pusher make these days?'

Curly spoke defensively. 'Ninety a week an' expenses – like travel when I gotta travel – like out to Brentwood.'

Joe made a smacking sound with the corner of his mouth. It was a mixture of envy and admiration.

Curly turned to the scaffold. 'Hey, Charley, come on, shake your tail, can't you see they runnin' short o' mortar over there?' He started towards the scaffold on the far wall, shouting between cupped palms. 'Gino! Felice!'

'Okay if I say hello to the men?' Joe called. He had just got an idea that was to change everything.

'So long as you leave 'em lay brick', Curly shouted back.

Joe walked out on the scaffold, Milt pacing slowly after him like a faithful dog.

"Ey, Lupo il Fortunato! *Amico* – whaddya know?' Lupo looked up and grinned. *'Com' è la bambola?'*

Lupo the Fortunate spoke a pure Sicilian dialect, always at the top of his lungs. 'The news is excellent, friend. The little pigeon has thrown away her crutches. She walks like a robin. My old woman prays and, by God, God listens. He's afraid not to. She was getting ready to throw a picket line around the church.' He crossed himself and laughed.

Joe responded in Neapolitan, in the same half-shout. 'Excellent! Excellent!'

'Your friend, Giusepp'?'

'You know Milt Jason. Studyin' to be a lawyer. He's been around before.'

Lupo, like the men below, tipped his cap and Joe said to Milt, 'Lucky Lupo's little girl had infantile, but she's okay now. Little doll.'

'She's-a fine', Lupo said apologetically to Milt.

'You'll be topped out soon', Joe said, peering towards the roof.

'Next week. Then a little inside work – the partitions in gypsum, I believe.' He returned to his work, pacing himself slow.

'How many brick a day are you giving Curly?' Joe asked in a low voice.

'Ah, some countryman! A man without a heart!' Lupo said with deep feeling. 'All he does is make babies.' He made an obscene sign with his fingers. 'Four already, another one coming.'

'I heard.'

'But does he once ask me about poor little Carlotta, so pale? No! For the men – no heart. Never even a bottle of near-beer, not to mention wine. *He* has wine, but always for himself. Never a hand except to take. You know he owes me twenty dollars?' Lupo hawked and spat noisily.

'How many brick you give him?'

Lupo lowered his voice. 'Nine hundred a day, may sweet Jesus forgive us. When we can't help ourselves, like now in the spring, perhaps nine fifty.' Lupo shrugged as though he were ashamed of himself. 'For one thing, the shop steward – he watches everyone like an eagle. He's a terror. He will permit nobody to work too hard. A true terror.'

'Who is the shop steward?' Joe said.

'I', Lupo said. Joe roared, and Lupo enjoyed his own joke.

"Ey, Lupo, supposin' I was to run a job in New Jersey this summer. You wanna work for the old professor?'

'You?' Lucky Lupo said. '*You*, a foreman?' He squinted at Joe thinking how fast children grow these days.

Joe nodded. 'One hour overtime a day for all', Joe said. 'Time and a half for the extra hour. Two dollars a day for travel and we can set up one car for five men, eh? And free wine at lunch hour made by my own mother with her own hands.'

'Where is the dagger hidden?' Lupo said.

'No dagger', Joe said. 'But the absolute necessity would be two thousand brick a man every day without fail.'

'Yi-yi-yi!' Lucky Lupo said. 'The men will keep their waistlines, eh? But some are too old for two thousand.'

'If my own father was not too old for two thousand,' Joe said, 'from everyone I will expect at *least* two thousand.'

Lupo stood for a long time. 'May God bless his spirit', he said awkwardly, memorializing Joe's father. Then he laid half a dozen brick. Joe maintained the silence between them, but said a silent prayer: 'My first promise – may I keep it.'

The silence was unbroken while Lupo laid four more brick. At last he straightened. 'I believe you could expect me', Lupo said.

Joe took Lupo's shoulder in his fingers and squeezed. My first, he exulted to himself. Then with Milt following, he picked his way along the scaffold, watching warily as bricklayers and labourers moved in their aching rhythm. He greeted the men in passing and stopped finally beside a short, thin man with pop eyes. Milt had heard Joe Napoli imitate all the accents on Ninety-eighth Street before, but never one like the cockney he now heard.

"Ow, English. 'Ow the 'ell's the old bugger doeen?'

Little English jumped up excitedly and put out his cement-stained fingers. 'Joey, m'boy!' he screamed.

"Ow's the owld trouble an' strife?' Joe shouted.

'She's fine, the owld thing. Wot's new, Joe, boy? 'Ow's tricks?'

'Okay. Now look 'ere, English', Joe said. 'I'm thinkin' o' runneen a bloody job in Jersey this summer. 'Dja like to come out with me?'

'Wot's the word?' English said as he turned back to work slowly and steadily. He placed a brick carefully in a rowlock course.

'Three, four months' work, and an hour overtime's in it', Joe said. 'That's the word, at time an' a 'alf. Ayt bits for travelleen and I furnish the crossword puzzles for lunch hour, one per dye.'

'I s'pose it's a nice, cushy job, m'boy', English said. 'M' back's been killeen me.'

Joe said, 'Two thousand brick a dye, fice and back-up. Solid miceonry walls. Two thousand – dye in an' dye out.'

For a moment English hesitated. Then he broke into a grin. 'You're on, Joey', English said, winking at Milt. 'I gotcha, m'boy. I'd not do it for anyone else, 'ear? Certainly not for this 'ere pig Curly.'

"Ere', Joe said. 'Let me 'ave your trowel a minute. I want to show my friend 'ere genu-oine talent. I know the bloke since we're kids, an' 'e's never seen me lye brick proper.' He took English's trowel and laid four brick deftly, filling the joints quickly, striking them expertly. 'Like 'at.'

"E's good', English said. 'Good as his old man any dye.'

'Wot's good about me I owe enteyrely to my English blood, which I got through my mother, Gawd bless 'er. Surrounded by Irish an' Americans we are, but are we daunted, English, m'boy?'

'I am!' cried English. 'I'm daunted, I'm damn well terrified.'

'Never', Joe crowed. 'Gawd bless the English.'

With no wasted motion, almost effortlessly, as he talked, Joe sloshed the mortar bed evenly, the brick, mortar, tap, tap; mortar, brick, tap, tap . . . In sixty seconds six more brick had been put in place for a hundred years or more. He struck the joints.

'Twelve in less than two minutes', Joe laughed. 'Know 'ow many that is a dye? Over three thousand. I've lide more. Lide in bed the 'ole bloomeen week after.'

'Okay, English!' Curly bellowed darkly across the open floor. 'Get movin' or I'll have Joey stay an' you go home an' listen to the radio.'

English picked up his trowel and winked at Joe. ''E owes me thirty smackers, 'e does. If 'e fires me, I'll foreclose on the bloomeen son-of-a-bitch.' Disdainfully he started to lay brick again.

'I'll let you know when', Joe called. 'Cheery-bye, English. Got to shoot the moon.'

'Bye-bye. I'll wite to 'ear from ya.'

Joe stepped along the scaffold and Milt, not daring to look down the forty-foot drop to the pavement, minced gingerly behind him, perspiring freely. Before he was through, Joe had tapped Art McGregor, the great, red-faced Scotsman, Little Sal Benello, son of Sally the labourer, and Moe Schwartz; he tapped them as if he were the representative of a secret honour society. Many more were passed by than spoken to and none of those invited refused. Joe promised McGregor a lunch-hour checker game, Moe Schwartz that he could use his old Franklin for transportation and collect a dollar a man in addition to his own travel allowance; and to Little Sal he held out the prospect of a speakeasy in Allenburg where they would meet the 'finest two-legged deers in the East. Sal, there's one – Francesca – she's put together outa pieces of cloud, the spongy kind that floats in the sky on hot days, only this one you can reach out and grab. When she bounces, *they* bounce, only one second *after*. Sorta nice like. Very ticklish she is, too. She likes ya to take little bites outa her. She's a friend to man. You gotta meet 'er.' Sal's young eyes opened appreciatively.

As they left the job Milt said, 'What the devil's in your mind, Joey?'

'Why not? I'll be a hell of a sight better foreman than Curly.'

'You've got nerve, Joe, I'll say that.'

'The only thing is,' Joe said, '*you* know I'm a foreman and *I* know it, but does Mr. Dennison know it?'

Milt was silent and hiked his books higher up on his back.

'I met Dennison twice on a job', Joe mused aloud. 'Pop was layin' brick for him so it ain't as if I don't know the man.'

They ran for the approaching trolley and just made it. It was one of the open kind, crammed with people hanging off the edges, going to the ball game. Joe could feel Milt's breath on his ear.

'Curly's like a million other foremen', Joe said. 'He's a mongrel. Nice guy, but he's got all the faults in the trade – bullyin', buddyin' and borrowin'. He's into every brickie on the job for at least a fin. More as the job goes on. Maybe's even put the bite on the labourers. He buddies around with 'em, hoorin', drinkin' – one o' the boys. Positively, how can he fire 'em? So they dog it, maybe he gets nine hundred, nine fifty brick a day. Costs shoot up and then *he* starts worryin' about his own job, starts bullyin' and screamin' at 'em and it ends up they don't even like the son-of-a-bitch. How he keeps gettin' jobs I don't know. Not that he's not a hell of a nice guy. I like the bastid. Maybe he lends money to *his* boss.'

'You mean there's guys'll lay two thousand brick for you and only nine hundred for Curly?'

'Nine hundred's *good*. Over on my alteration job, we're givin' our slob eight fifty. Hell, these guys could lay twenty-five hundred for me. The real brickies can do it, every last one a the bastids. They're good if they wanna be.' Milt was silent, and for a long time all Joe heard were the trolley wheels.

'Joe,' Milt said tentatively, 'why be a foreman? Sure, ninety a week sounds like a lot of money, but figure it out, Joe. The difference between two thousand brick a day and nine hundred. How many brick are there on the job in Allenburg? Five million, Curly said?'

They were at the ball park and it was early. They bought bleacher tickets – now that they were older and Joe was in the money, it was more satisfactory than Coogan's Bluff – got a hot dog apiece, and half ran up the ramp to grab the best seats they could find. The Cards were warming up on the field and someone was hitting flies to the outfield. Joe watched each player with the eye of a connoisseur, but Milt had his books on his lap and was jotting numbers on the flyleaf of his philosophy notebook. 'Sit down, Joey, and listen to me. Look at these figures.'

'Lookit that! Hornsby can handle anything', Joe said as the shortstop made a one-handed stop. 'Atta boy, Rajah!'

'Joe, for crying out loud sit down and listen to me. This is *important.* I'm going to show you how you can be a zillionaire, so stop worrying about Hornsby.' Joe looked at the columns of figures impatiently. 'See this', Milt said slowly. 'If you could get a contract to do the brickwork based on the men laying nine hundred a day and then they actually lay two thousand, you know how much money you'd make on that job?'

'How much?' Joe said.

'Sixty thousand bucks', Milt said.

'Ah, Milt,' Joe said impatiently, 'dry up. You're outa your mind. Have a look at Freddy Lindstrom. I think he's still got a limp from yestiddy.'

'Sixty *thousand* bucks', Milt said. 'Jesus.'

'You gonna sit there and dream about money all afternoon,' Joe said irritably, 'or are you gonna watch the ball game? Lookit Nehf lay it in there.' But he had already done the arithmetic in his own head.

'A guy like you shouldn't walk around loose', Milt said sadly. 'You need a business manager.'

'Okay,' Joe said, 'you're elected. Now shaddup, for Christ sake.'

'What's a "ring", Joe, what does Curly mean by a "brick ring" in Allenburg?'

'Coupla wise guys, brick bosses, get together an' keep everyone else out. They rig prices, like that. They work close with the local union.'

'Is it something Tony could take care of?'

Joe looked sharply at Milt. 'That's what I been figuring.'

'You'll go to see Dennison Monday? For sure?'

'Okay, okay.'

'Remember, you don't want to be a foreman. You want a *contract*. Understand? It's very simple. You get the highest price you can, do the job as cheap as you can, and pocket the difference. It's fundamental.'

'Okay, okay. We'll talk about it tonight. I haven't got a thing to do tonight. Right now there's a ball game goin' on. Jesus, we paid fifty cents for the damn seats. Whatta you trying to do, waste money?'

Milt subsided for the moment. At the end of the second inning, the announcer took the field and his voice boomed slowly through the megaphone: 'La-dies . . . and . . . gentlemen . . . we have just received word that Lucky Lindy, our own American eagle, has been sighted over Ireland!'

There was a tremendous roar, as great as any the old Bambino had ever stirred with a clout to right. People were on their feet, shouting and congratulating each other. When the crowd had subsided, the voice boomed slowly again, in a kind of tidal rhythm:

'In tribute to the courage of this great American youth . . . la-dies and gentlemen, will everyone please rise for one moment . . . of silent prayer. May God help the lone eagle to reach his destination.'

A mass of fifty thousand was on its feet. The silence was sudden and complete, and a fluttering of a handkerchief could be seen here and there throughout the stands and bleachers. The silence seemed much longer than the regulation sixty seconds; the ball-players removed their hats on the field and in the dugout and stood motionless until the plate umpire's high voice shouted, 'Play ball!'

As they settled back in their seats, Joe said, 'That's the way to do it. Fly across the ocean, an' everyone knows your name. This guy is bigger than Jack Dempsey and Gene Tunney *combined*.'

Milt cocked his head and studied Joe. 'You believe that? Listen Joey, in two years nobody will remember this man's name. Gosh, I've almost forgotten it already. What was it again? Lindenberg, Chester Lindenberg? It's a fluke, pure and simple. You can't really succeed by some kind of trick. You'll never be great just because you could run the hundred in ten flat, or even nine and three-fifths. Who cares? But listen, if you can get men to lay twice as many brick for you as they will for anyone else, then you can get other people to do a lot of things for you they won't do for anyone else. *That's* what'll make you famous, believe me. A thousand times more famous than Bill Lindbergh, or Sam Goldberg, or whatever his name is.'

'What crap', Joe said, and heard every word.

'Remember,' Milt said quietly, 'Dennison's office Monday morning.'

'Okay, okay.'

Eleven

DAWN on Monday brought the clatter and chaos of every new day. The girls, Dino, and Joe squalled and brawled, slamming in and out of the three-room flat to compete for the toilet with the Sacchis, the Shapiros, and the Meraglios. Scarcely a calm, unshouted word was spoken. Mammina stood firm in her black morning dress, which made her look like the steadfast peasant she was, ladling thick coffee, cutting thick slices of bread, and cleverly setting the children one against the other to achieve a maximum din. She liked teasing her girls and she liked din. 'Look, Rosie, Lucy's a-lika you cake so much, why you not letta her have-a the rest?'

'Lucy! Gimme my cake! Ma! She took my cake!'

'Lucia! Give Rosina back her cake!'

At six-thirty the exodus started, not only from the Napoli flat but from all the apartments in the house. To the street-cleaning department and to the tailor's shop downstairs – up town, down town, across town the men fled. When Joe left, Rosina and Lucy were still squealing in the toilet in the hall, and Mr. Meraglio was screaming to get in; Dino was already on his way down to DeWitt and his friends (Dino was going to finish high school and go to college if it was the last thing Joe did); in fact, the street teemed with people – kids playing ball, two fights going full blast, two men on a street-cleaning-department truck flinging presumably empty cans to the pavement spilling surplus garbage everywhere; the uproar of every day.

Joe, standing in the packed subway, read the *Daily News*. Lindbergh the darling of Paris; President Coolidge sending destroyer; New York preparing hero's welcome. The stock market had taken another big jump and the Giants had blasted the Cards again yesterday. Those Giants. And some guy named Lowell in Boston had made another wisecrack about Sacco and Vanzetti. Joe knew by heart the burning words Bartolomeo Vanzetti had said in court, two, three years ago to the judge. He would never forget them:

'I never commit a crime in my life. I have never steal and I have never kill and I have never spilt blood, and I have fought and I have sacrificed myself even to eliminate the crimes that the law and the church legitimate and sanctify . . . I am suffering because I was a radical and indeed I am a radical; I have suffered because I was an Italian and indeed I am an Italian; but I am so convinced to be right that if you could execute me two times and if I could be reborn two other times I would live again to do what I have done already. I have finished – thank you.'

Very nice. Couple of years ago the words had moved him to angry tears as he read them. But this guy Lowell was now going to arrange the public ceremony for Vanzetti to be killed, so where was the percentage? Was it so damn different from Pop's falling off the scaffold? Accident accompanied by some fancier speeches. 'We are the oppressed class', Nicola Sacca had said to the judge. 'You are the oppressor. You persecute . . . tyrannize . . . kill . . .' *Mama mia*, how these guys could *suffer*.

Joe studied the features of Bartolomeo Vanzetti. He looked a lot like Pop. That droopy moustache, the deep-set eyes. Well, you could cut him outa *that* deal. He'd be goddamned if he'd be oppressed. If he had to be something, he'd rather be the oppressor, like Mr. Lowell or the judge. No, you could cut him out of the entire idea of belonging to any kind of class. He was Joe Napoli. He didn't even feel especially Italian. What did being Italian have to do with anything whatsoever? Sacca and Vanzetti may even be nice fellows, but they had the altogether wrong idea. Get right down to it, Pop was better off. At least he didn't *suffer* so loud. He just went fast.

As the subway shuttle neared Times Square, behind every line of print, every picture, Joe began to see images of Mr. Dennison. Sixty thousand bucks Milt had said – *Mama mia*! No man with sixty thousand bucks can be oppressed. To face the truth, however, he remembered Dennison only vaguely. It was five years ago when they had met briefly on the scaffold. Tall, blond, bronzed, regular-featured, he recalled, slightly cadaverous. He would have to be careful of what he said because everything in his future would depend on it. He would, of course, remind Mr. Dennison of the conversation Pop had had with him on the scaffold ten years ago.

Down town the city was seedier and richer. Broadway was like the inside of the subway at rush hour. There was the Palace Theatre right under the Dennison office. Lou Holtz, Lyda Roberti and

Irene Bordoni. Trucks and cars, trolleys, and only a few blocks down he could see the garment carts loaded with dresses; traffic clanged, snorted, ploughed, stalled, started and honked itself to a cacophonous stand-still in mid-town Manhattan. Buildings reached into the air, gasping for light. It was the louse-up of mankind – like the photos of the old Sicilian hillside outside Palermo near where Mammina was born, house glued on house, worse than the East Side tenements. Give him a place of his own, a little land around, there was plenty around, he'd seen it himself in the Bronx, in Long Island, in Jersey, out by the beaches.

The panelled waiting-room of Mr. Dennison's office on the fifteenth floor was clean and neat; it wasn't up to Mr. Webb's office in the Woolworth Building, but it was not bad. The well-stacked receptionist was cool and remote in her white blouse and black skirt, about as high-toned as you'd want. She even had a pencil behind her ear and rimless eyeglasses hanging from a ribbon. Her face wasn't much to look at, so he avoided looking at it. She was sorry, but Mr. Dennison was all tied up. Would he care to see Mr. Dennison's secretary? You come right down to it, she was goddam ugly. Mr. Dennison's secretary turned out to be a man who said, 'I'm Billy Snow, may I help you?' Joe had the uncomfortable feeling the young bespectacled man was flirting with him. He tried to explain what he was there for, and the boy said, 'Would you see Mr. Larson?' What the hell, might as well start somewhere. Sure, he'd see Larson, whoever *he* was. This boy really got him. He ought to get him a box of candy some day, maybe he wouldn't have to wait out here so long next time.

Gravel Larson at least *looked* human even if he didn't sound it. He was of medium height, with a broad face, balding head, and an eagle-like beak on which was precariously mounted a pair of bifocals. His body was stooped and humble, but his impatient voice was pure gravel. Although he was thoroughly unfriendly and suspicious, Joe felt his was a human animosity, probably springing from dyspepsia. He told Joe he was Dennison's chief estimator. Gravel Larson had good reason to feel insecure, having accepted substantial under-the-table gifts from a number of sub-contractors to whom he had given jobs. On the Allenburg job, he was expecting something substantial for the masonry work from McMahon. He and McMahon always worked pretty close. He hobbled through the hall, leading Joe into a long, narrow room with three large plan tables on which blueprints were spread.

'D'you have a card, Napoli?'

'Card?'

'Business card.'

'Hell, no. I wanna talk about the brickwork in Allenburg. You guys gonna sub-contract that job?'

'We plan to sub-contract everything, Napoli.'

'Then how about getting a set of whatzis – plans?'

'We've never done business with your outfit before, have we?'

'My old man once did a little business for Mr. Dennison', Joe said.

'How about letting me have a couple of references, then, Napoli?' Gravel rasped, holding pencil to paper. 'And your bank?'

'*Bank?* Wait'll ya see my price.'

'No use giving us a price if you have no references, Napoli.'

He rose with a gesture of dismissal, and started towards the door.

'You mean to tell me,' Joe shouted, and pulled at Larson's sleeve, 'you gonna let me walk outa here? You gonna throw maybe thirty, forty thousand bucks out of the window? Is that what whozis – Dennison – pays you for?' Joe's loud shouting gave Gravel pause.

Jock Dennison might hear this idiot. Gravel sat down at his desk and sought to restore tranquillity. 'What the hell are you talking about?' Gravel rasped impatiently.

'Look, Larson. You got five million brick in the job, right?'

'Yes . . .' he answered suspiciously.

'I suppose you're figuring nine hundred brick a man a day?'

'Well —' Larson himself had used eight fifty in his estimate.

'I can get over fifteen hundred a man. Average.'

'Now, Napoli, cut it out. One or two men, maybe, but average? You invented some kind of a bricklaying machine?'

Joe snapped, 'I invented my men.'

'How many men like that you got?'

'As many as I need.'

'You'll need over a hundred brickies and fifty labourers.'

'Only fifty brickies. See, my men get maybe twice the production, so I only need half as many. One to one is my system. They all keep movin'.'

Gravel Larson leaned back in his chair. Slowly he rose, walked to the plan table and smoothed a half unrolled set of blueprints. 'You want to take the job off, Napoli? Give us an estimate? I suppose it can't do any harm.'

'Yah', Joe said promptly. Not that he'd ever done it before.

'Do you think you could have your figure in by Thursday?' Larson said. Get this kid out of the office.

'Sure', Joe said.

'Tell me, Napoli,' Mr. Larson said dryly as they passed into the waiting-room, 'how come you can get fifteen hundred a man these days? I thought the days of the lash were over. What's your secret?'

'I'm sorry, Larson', Joe said loudly. 'I could only tell that to Mr. Whozis himself in person.'

'Okay,' Larson forced a smile. 'Maybe Thursday.'

'It better be Thursday', Joe said loudly.

'You know there's a brickie ring out there in Allenburg', Larson said.

'The ring don't scare me. I know a few guys out there my own self.'

He carried the plans in a great roll under his right arm and the large, soft-covered book of specifications in his left hand, feeling for the first time in his life like a person of importance.

Joe knew nothing about taking off quantities or pricing a job. But as he had explained to Milt, Curly di Roberts would. And why wouldn't Curly help him? He loved Curly, and after all, it was Curly himself mentioned the Allenburg job only Saturday.

Emily di Roberts answered the phone. 'Joe? How are you, Joey?' Emily had lived on Ninety-eighth Street till seven or eight years ago. She had married Curly when she was sixteen. She was an old friend.

'I hear good news. How's the new baby?' Didn't Whozis, Curly, say something about havin' a new baby? Boy or girl? he thought furiously. I have to learn to remember these things. 'Take after Curly?'

'Oh, Joey, news travels so fast. I haven't even had the baby yet, not till December, and here you're congratulatin' me already.'

He laughed sheepishly. 'How *you* holdin' up, Emily? I ain't seen you in a dog's age. I always think you're just a kid and here you got four of your own already – five coming up. Holy smoke! How are they all?'

'Fine, Joey. But they always got somethin'. Mary Frances had the mumps last week.'

'What you need is a vacation', Joe said. 'Trip to Florida.'

'That's a hot one', Emily said. 'You're a regular comedian, Joey.'

"Ey, is Curly in?'

'Not yet. You know how it is. He's probably layin' out to-morrow's work.'

'Could I come over after and talk to Curly?'

'Sure, Joey. If you can stand all the kids hollerin'. Bring your Ma. Maybe you boys could play some cards or dominoes or somethin', an' us ladies can discuss somethin'.'

'I just wanna talk about some business to Curly. See you around eight.'

'Okay, Joey. I'll tell him.'

Curly was seated at the radio listening intently to a series of squawks and squeals when one of the kids opened the door for Joe, with his roll of plans, and Milt, who trailed behind.

'Pittsburgh', Curly called in a hushed voice. 'KDKA. Listen.' A faint sound of two tin voices: 'Yes, sir, that's my baby, no, sir, don't mean maybe . . .' faintly from the speaker. 'That's the Happiness Boys, Billy Jones and Ernie Hare. Listen. Last night we had Washington, D.C., didn't we, Emily?'

'That's what the man said', Emily called from the kitchen. She came out, wiping her hands on her apron. 'Hello, Joey. And Milty Jason, where you been? Long time no see.' Emily was a short plump girl with sallow skin, dark eyes, and black straight hair. She weighed twenty pounds too much. They shook hands all round. 'D'ja see Billy? Ain't he grown?'

'I hardly recognized him, Emily, that's a fact', Joe said. 'How's the boy, Billy?'

Billy, who was six, ran into the kitchen and began to bang a pot on the kitchen floor.

'Cute', Joe said. 'He's a real cute kid.'

'Shaddup. Stop makin' a racket, Billy, or I'll take a strap to ya!' Curly shouted. 'To what do I owe the honour?' he said, changing his tone abruptly, his ear still half-cocked to the loudspeaker.

'I wonder could you give me a hand with this?' Joe said.

Curly rose, took the set of plans and opened them on the floor. He unlaced and yanked off his heavy shoes and placed them on either end of the plans to keep them from rolling up.

'What the hell is it?'

'That warehouse job in New Jersey you were telling me about Saturday.' A four-year-old and a five-year-old, whom Emily addressed as Josephine and Mary Frances, took to turning the four dials of the radio. The children and the radio emitted tremendous, spine-chilling squeals.

'Yah.' Curly examined the first sheet of the blueprints and flipped the huge, rustling page. 'Yah.' He turned to the specifications and spoke to Joe narrowly. 'Where'd you get these?'

'Dennison's office. I figured, seeing you're going out to Brentwood this summer, I might as well run this Allenburg job.'

'*You? Run* the job?' He put a fatherly arm around Joe and said in a confidential tone, 'Joe, this ain't an alteration or some little crappy piece-a work, this job's got five *million* brick, friend. More brick than a twenty-story apartment house. This job, fa Christ sake, will run over a quarter of a million bucks with the back-up and spandrel waterproofing. This building's gonna be four *blocks* long. You must be crazy with the heat, boy. You, fa Christ sake, you're only twenty-one goddam years old. What do you know about drivin' men? You gotta drive 'em, Joey, you gotta put the fear-a God in 'em.'

'I have a few ideas about running men', Joe said. 'But I don't know the first damn thing about taking off quantities. I thought maybe you'd give me and Milt a hand with the estimating, you being in the business so long and all.'

Curly beamed in spite of himself. Emily strained to see over his shoulders. 'Well, I ain't been to college like your friend Milt here', Curly growled.

'You know,' Emily said, 'I never seen a roll of plans before. What the dickens is it gonna be?'

The racket from the children was deafening. Curly turned a menacing glare at Emily, but Joe shouted, 'An A & P warehouse, like Curly says, four blocks long.'

'It's interesting', Emily said, ignoring the kids. 'You'd think bein' in this business Curly would take the trouble to explain a few of the more interesting things to his wife. He thinks I got no head.'

'Listen', Curly snapped. 'Mike is banging *his* head against the crib again.'

'Let him', Emily said. 'He got a good, strong skull. Takes after his father.'

'So what you want me to do?' Curly growled.

'Give us a hand taking the job off. Just show us how', Joe said.

'That's a hot one. Look,' Curly said, 'you guys must be, fa Christ sake, out of your head.'

'You listen to me, Curly,' Emily said suddenly. 'Joey's got a good chance at somethin', at least it sounds like it, and you're gonna help him, you big gazebo. Be a good egg for once in your life. *Do* somethin' for somebody.'

Curly looked from Emily to Joe and back. He heard the banging of the pot which Billy was smashing beyond recognition against the kitchen floor. Mike in the bedroom was rattling the crib timbers, and the two girls kept madly turning the dial of the radio set. 'I got China. I got China', Josephine chattered. 'She got China', Mary Frances screamed.

'Okay!' Curly shouted to Emily. 'You keep the kids quiet, chloroform 'em anything, you got a deal. Anything for a quiet night. Come on, Joe, if you're gonna be in this business, you better learn somethin'.'

Curly pulled a six-foot rule out of his back pocket, a pencil from his breast pocket, and Joe provided the paper – Rosina's copy book. The three men squatted before the great roll of blue-prints. "Ey, looka me, Emily!' Curly called, 'I'm teachin' the professor himself!'

Emily took the kids into the bedroom and somehow managed to get them to sleep.

Curly grunted and bellowed while squatting or kneeling on the parlour floor; the architect was a horse's ass, where the hell was the details, sloppiest drawings he ever seen in his whole life. What are you gonna do without details? By ten o'clock Joe realized that Curly had only limited knowledge of estimating and plan reading. but that he did recognize the masonry work and knew enough about taking off quantities to make substantial progress and to give Joe and Milt the yardsticks with which they might finish the job. Scores of numbers were jotted on the lined white paper in Rosina's copy book. Milt was quiet and listened intently.

'*Artch*itects!' Curly raved. 'This guy calls himself an *artch*itect. He don't even provide sleeves through mason-ary walls.'

By eleven Curly had exposed the sum total of all his technical knowledge. 'It's getting late, Curly. 'Ey, Milt, we better get going, 'eh?' Joe rolled up the plans, carefully folded the work sheets and put them in his pocket.

As they started for the apartment door, Curly said, 'Whatcha gonna do for men?'

'Oh, they got plenty of men in Allenburg', Joe said vaguely. 'It's a big city.'

'Them bums will slaughter you', Curly said. 'Ain't you heard about Allenburg? Toughest bunch east of the Mississippi, incloodin' Chicago. Guy out there, Glass-eyed Gamboretta, or One-eyed, somethin' like that, runs the local. He got the town wrapped up. Him an' the ring. Tell 'im you're a friend o' mine. I met the bum a coupla times. An' hey, tell 'im you're a friend o' Tony Ferrara. That's even better. Tell 'im about you an' Tony.'

'I'll do that.'

'I heard Tony's gettin' to be a very big man in Jersey.' Suddenly an idea struck Curly and he turned pale. "Ey, Joey, what was you talkin' to *my* men about on the scaffold Sattidy?'

Joe shrugged noncommittally. 'This and that.'

Everything came clear to Curly in a burst of insight. He grabbed Joe's lapel. 'Why, you son-of-a-bitch, you was stealing my men! I seen you talkin' to English and them guys!'

'I *asked* you, could I talk to them!'

Milt said quietly, reasonably, 'Nobody steals men, Curly. It's a free country. Slavery went out with Robert E. Lee, remember?'

'I wasn't here them days, friend,' Curly shouted, 'and neither was you. Stealin's stealin'.' He turned on Joe. 'You goddam crook. Wadja offer 'em, ten bucks an hour?'

Joe lowered his voice, 'Lookit, Curly, you don't own those guys, they own you. How much you into them for – two, three hundred? What do you do with all that extra dough they lend you? You give it to Emily, *paesano*?'

Curly started to shout, 'Why you son —' But he quietened himself as suddenly as he had started. 'Get your goddam ass outa here', Curly said with as much ice in his voice as he could command.

'Don't get yourself in an uproar. Those guys don't *want* to work for you. You're into 'em too deep already. They don't care for having the bite put on 'em so regular. I said to 'em, what the hell, what's the tragedy? So it's twenty bucks or ten bucks – but, boy, you should hear them holler, ten bucks is like a million to those guys.'

Curly's face was a puzzle, dark, full of fear and hate, yet poised in a sickly half-smile, ready to swing either way.

'I guess that's a couple of hundred bucks Emily don't ever see, 'eh, Curly?' Joe slapped his thigh and laughed hoarsely. 'What you do with it, I figure, that's not Emily's business, right?'

Curly said warily, 'Whatcha mean, Joey?'

'I figure what's the whole thing amount to? Maybe two, three hundred bucks. So I told the men *I'll* give it back to 'em and that'll save you the trouble, right? Besides, from you they figure they'll wait ten years to get it. You're such an unreliable bastid.'

'How *you* gonna . . .'

'Don't worry, you just leave it to Pepe.' Joe smiled his slow kiss-smile. 'The men are better off with me, *you* can see that, 'cause they won't be worried about you putting the bite on 'em again, and you won't be worried about them ragging you to get their dough back. You can break in a new bunch who maybe won't start out so aggravated or so wised-up. There's a million brickies around'll give you eight, nine hundred brick. Right?'

Curly's face broke into a grin of relief. 'Boys,' he said, and hushed his voice, 'what a woman don't know won't hurt her, right?'

'Right.'

'I guess God helps them who help themselves, friend', Curly said.

'Let me ask you,' Milt said smiling almost too pleasantly, 'when you started running a brick gang, where did *you* get *your* men?'

'Here and there', Curly said defensively. Then he roared with appreciative laughter. 'Stole 'em from Ricci! An' Flato. Sure. Yah, an' what I promised them guys to get 'em! *Mama mia!*'

'And you'll steal others before the week's out, Curly', Joe said sharply. 'You always have. *Ecco la vita.*'

Joe left the parlour and headed towards the bedroom. He tiptoed in and tapped Emily, who was asleep in a rocker with Mike, her one-year-old, in her arms. 'Night, Emily', Joe whispered. He squeezed her shoulder.

'Oh, you boys through?' She rubbed her eyes and carefully put Mike in his crib. The other three children were sleeping askew in the big bed. Emily led the two men back out to the parlour.

'Night, Joey. It's always a real pleasure to see ya. The kids get a great bang outta ya. Come over and see Curly any time.'

'Sure', Joe said, shook Emily's hand and took the roll of plans.

'Everything work out okay?' Emily said. 'Ya get the help ya wanted?'

'Sure', Joe said. 'That Curly, he knows everything.' He could see Emily smile with pride. 'Thanks a lot, Emily.'

'So long', Curly growled.

'Good night', Emily called, when Joe and Milt were halfway down the stairs.

Milt shook his head admiringly and said, 'I sure envy you, Joe. I just can't like everyone the way you do. Never could.'

'Who, Emily? I'm crazy about Emily. Good kid. And that little bitty Mary Frances, how can you help lovin' *her*?'

'What about Curly?'

'Underneath, Curly's a good hearted son-of-a-bitch. Give you the shirt off his back – or the brains out of his head.'

Twelve

NEXT day Mammina rattled from kitchen to bedroom, shaking blankets and sheets out of the window, sweeping dust under the living-room carpet. Joe and Milt sat at the kitchen table, plans outstretched, with work sheets, adding and multiplying man-hours for scaffolding, unloading, mixing, lay-out. Mammina fed them coffee while they worked, and when Dino and the girls came home from school, she pretended to try to shoo them all down into the street so Joe could work without interference. The girls, who normally never spent an unnecessary minute in the dark flat, immediately besieged Joe and Milt, especially Lucy, who was now sixteen, damn striking with that olive face of hers, and really beginning to bust out all over. She peered at everything with one hand glued to Milt's shoulder, her cheek always within inches of Milt's, and brought him cookies and a glass of wine, until Joe had to throw her the hell out personally, especially since Milt didn't seem to mind having her around. In fact, Milt seemed to enjoy the whole idea. Dino, however, stood his ground, quietly fascinated by the blueprints, which he examined over Joe's shoulder. Dino was seventeen and finishing his junior year at DeWitt Clinton. Once Joe looked up and saw his brother curled in a kitchen chair with the specifications, reading avidly.

"Ey, Joe, what's spandrel waterproofing?'

'What's lintels, Joey?'

"Ey, Joe, what's a continuous fin?'

'*Silenzio*!' Mammina cried to Dino repeatedly, shattering the peace.

Joe and Milt drank their fifth cup of coffee, and worked steadily. Brick and back-up – column on column of figures. Joe could feel his fingers trembling, his stomach churning. Milt stayed to a gulped supper, and they were back at the kitchen table with Mammina feeding them more coffee until ten; and after the rest of the family was asleep they worked until two, until figures jumbled and reformed before their eyes and turned meaningless. Checking, they found errors in arithmetic. They snapped at each other and blamed each other. And at last Milt went home. To-morrow Joe would go to Allenburg alone, because Milt had to study for a final exam. And Thursday, Joe would recap the figures before going down to Dennison's. For a while, as he lay listening to Mammina's and Dino's snoring, he could not get the numbers out of his head. They danced before his eyes, multi-digited, mean-ingless scrawls on a page. Who was he to be talking of hundreds of thousands of simoleons? He lay appalled at his own effrontery. Hell, Joe, it's as true as your lousy ten bucks a day. Talk big when you meet these guys, ten thousand, ten million, it's all the same. Numbers on paper. This guy Larson, that's all he talks about, big numbers. Big man. Probably makes fifty bucks a week his own self. Before he fell asleep, he got out of bed, knelt and prayed. Gentle Father . . . Deliver us from poverty, give us a chance to show that bastid Uncle Giovanni, lead us to abundance . . . I don't want to be one of the oppressed like Vanzetti. And I'm not going to be. In the name of thy Son . . . And then he lay there while his golden future, a new car, a house in the country, passed in review . . .

In the morning, Joe withdrew thirty dollars from his eighty-three-dollar savings account at Corn Exchange and took a train from Penn Station to Allenburg, carrying his visa of authority – the plans. By nine-thirty he had visited the job site, examined topography and soil condition, and concluded a most instructive conversation with a fat, sly and informative Mr. Flugelman at the dusty offices of the F & S Brick Company in New Brunswick. Mr. Flugelman was tickled with his own new brick, and Joe was intrigued by everything Mr. Flugelman told him and particularly by the unusual brick he showed him.

Taxis were expensive, but he took a cab to Perth Amboy. Thirty bucks was a big investment, but what the hell, time was short. As he rode through the flat Jersey countryside, he noticed the small, white bungalows in neat rows of four and five, tiny picket-fenced homes rammed together on huddled forty- or fifty-foot lots. Here and there two or three small frame homes, tents of matchwood, were under construction and usually there was a huge sign almost as large as the houses: TWO BEDROOMS $5,990. MORTGAGES AVAIL-ABLE. Must be money in those wooden sticks.

Even out here in the Jersey flats, they built like it was Broadway.

E

Why not spread the houses out a little? The world was full of louse-ups. Oh, what he'd give to get out in the open! Just let this crazy idea of Milt's come true, hell it was his idea as much as Milt's, doing this job for Dennison, let it come true, and he'd move Mama and the kids out here where they could get some fresh air.

The taxi pulled up – buck and a quarter. Joe wondered if he should think about a tip. Hell, he'd never see this pug-nosed bastid again. Go peddle your papers.

'Thanks, brother', he said. Then at the last moment, 'Here, buster, this is for you', and he gave the driver a nickel. He felt better. Who knows how many kids the driver was trying to support.

In his office at the Finlayson Brick Company, Perth Amboy, Simon Cutler, the tall, hefty and muscular, dark-haired salesman, greeted him with a twisted smile, talking always from the corner of his mouth. Simon Cutler was a man in his late twenties with a face like Francis X. Bushman's, a frame like one of those physical-culture ads, and a manner that was all illicit intimacy. Through the window behind Cutler, Joe could see brick in huge stacks, and alongside them the long kilns hunched low to the ground, their chimneys spewing smoke. On the walls were photographs of Clara Bow, Pola Negri, and Theda Bara, each half clothed.

'All the brick you want, sweetheart', Simon Cutler said, opening his hands in a gesture of welcome. 'As long as Dennison's credit is behind it. Isn't Dennison one swell guy?'

Joe said, 'But twenty-two bucks a thousand. Holy Christ!'

'That's cheap, Joe.' Those hands were so sincere. 'In fact, it's a very, very special price for Dennison's job. After all, we don't sell five million common brick every day.'

Joe scowled glumly. 'Maybe you won't sell five million today, either.'

'I think we will, Joe, m'boy. After all, we're the brick specified. Right in the book – Finlayson or equal. And nobody's equal. Our product is swell.' He winked.

'You and the architect must be old buddies', Joe said.

'Bert Winters and Mr. Finlayson happen to be married to sisters', Simon Cutler said offhandedly, winking. 'That's the way the world whirls. Bert does all A & P's stuff,' he continued smugly, 'does a swell job, too, sweetheart, and Finlayson brick is about all the brick Bert likes. Quality. Even the building inspector hates that Flugelman brick, it's full of lime. He hates it. You'd have a million rejects. Incidentally, the inspector's a friend of mine. Swell guy. I got him his job.'

'Maybe we can get A & P to use something else besides brick', Joe said darkly.

'Block?' smiled Simon Cutler. 'Cinderblock? Been tried. A & P will never go for it. Look, sweetheart, man is a political animal. Play a little ball. Boys will be boys. I'm a committeeman, and you learn things in the Democratic party here they don't teach at Rutgers.'

'There's a new brick', Joe said. 'Something they call over-sized brick, around eighteen per cent bigger than common. F & S makes it. Lays just as fast, get the same production, cuts down labour eighteen per cent.'

Si Cutler said blandly, 'F & S makes it because that old Kraut Flugelman is trying to stir up a revolution, but you know the building business. Hardest arteries in the world. No one wants anything new, we're still building pyramids like Egyptians. Bert Winters won't take F & S product anyway – too damn much lime, like I said.' He smiled broadly. 'And we don't make the big brick.'

'Why *don't* you?'

'We sell more brick this way, Joe boy, eighteen per cent more. Sell more brick, we make more money, you can see that.' He extended his hand palm up, engagingly.

'Listen to me, Si, my old political friend', Joe said hoarsely, in a sudden staccato. 'Pay attention now, 'cause man is not only political, he's also mathematical. Five million common bricks on the job, twenty-two bucks a thousand. Say you make three bucks a thousand profit, okay?'

'Okay . . .' The customary suspicion.

'How much more d'you think it costs per thousand to make the oversized – labour's same, material's peanuts, right? Fifty cents a thousand, maybe?' A sheer guess.

'Well . . .' He could see from Simon Cutler's face that it was probably not even that much.

'I figure you oughta get twenty-four bucks a thousand for over-sized. You make four and a half a thousand instead of three bucks.'

'Who said we'd ever get twenty-four dollars?'

'I said so. I just made it up, Si. That's what we'll pay. Me and

Dennison —' Joe put two fingers together and held them aloft to show Simon Cutler how close he and Mr. Dennison were. 'I know F & S gets only twenty-three fifty for their oversized but, Si, they got too much lime, like you say, right? That's a hell of an advantage for you guys. Quality. Figure it out,' Joe said, 'four and a quarter million oversized at four fifty profit against five million standards at three bucks.'

Simon Cutler was now writing on a long estimating pad. He mumbled to himself, checked his arithmetic, then he looked up. 'We'd have to make new moulds', he said uncertainly. He was figuring his commission in his head.

'So it's a few hundred, maybe a thousand bucks, chicken feed. Then you're all set up to compete with F & S. In five years everybody'll be using the big ones.'

The friendly smile had left Simon Cutler's face. There was pure avarice, and he licked his handsome lips. It was an expression Joe would come to see more and more. In Simon's case, it was accompanied by a half smile, and a licking of the lips; on other faces it came as a frown of concentration, the lips usually tight; still others emitted short, nervous laughs; but always there was the same inner spring – the inner flow of happiness, mingling with the flow of funds.

'How much you want out of this?' Si Cutler said in a low voice, so casually Joe wasn't sure he'd said it.

'Me? You don't understand, Si. Mr. Dennison and me are like that.'

Simon Cutler studied Joe for an indecisive moment. 'Wait here', he said abruptly.

After twenty minutes, Si returned with an older, red-headed man whose face was heavily freckled.

'P. N., this is my old friend, Joe Napoli. This is Mr. Finlayson, Joe. Joe's got an interesting idea, P. N.'

They shook hands. It was apparent the older man had been briefed.

'I've just spoken to Bert', the older man said. 'All the courses would have to be changed, all his sill heights, lots of little stuff if we change the brick size. It'll cost Dennison maybe a couple of thousand in plan changes.'

'Okay,' Joe said, 'I'll see Mr. Dennison tomorrow.' He was thinking of the savings on material and labour. The figures stunned him. Such small ideas multiplied so many times. Milt Jason wasn't kidding, Joe Napoli was a walking gold mine indeed, if he had to say so himself.

'You've got a deal', he heard Mr. Finlayson saying from a distance. 'We'll start making the moulds as soon's we get the order.'

From Finlayson's, Joe went to the Saunders Block Company in Allenburg, and before the day was out, he had met an even dozen men, cigar-chewing, cigarette-smoking, doodling men with black fingernails, or manicured, snapping, compulsive or indifferent men in the business of selling brick, cement and sand. He lined up planks, putlocks, wheelbarrows and mortar tubs on rental. He made notes and jotted columns of figures on the back of the plans. By the time he was home at seven o'clock that night, the thirty dollars was reduced to two sixty-five, but he had ten million dollars' worth of answers.

Mammina had kept some gnocchi warm and there was liverwurst in the icebox. She took down an unopened bottle of white wine and insisted that Joe eat properly, take off his coat and tie, roll up his sleeves, relax. 'The wine is good for you, rest, rest. You worka too hard, Pepe. Look-a how you look-a so worry.' Dino and the girls dashed from room to room. Joe stood in the kitchen gulping his food, drank two tumblers of wine too fast and, although his head rocked, he shouted at the girls and Dino to be quiet, get the hell outa the kitchen, he had to finish his work, couldn't they see he was busy? Milt came over and he and Joe, now more facile with figures, sat down at the kitchen table to resume their estimating.

Four times during the long night, when the cobwebs in his mind were thickest and his eyelids heaviest, Joe had to get up to put his head under the kitchen spigot.

By seven o'clock in the morning the figures were recapped. They were all there; common brick converted to oversized, material prices as he had eked them out in Jersey. Plant calculated and overhead estimated. General conditions: hoist engineering, washing down, patching, everything. If he got eighteen hundred brick a day, he could do the job for two hundred and twenty thousand, including a profit of forty-five thousand. This would stun Gravel Larson, that fat old eagle, Joe thought as he shaved. And if the men really gave him two thousand brick a day, he could make over sixty thousand dollars. Probably he'd have to cut Milt in somehow. How would it feel, he wondered idly, to be rich and have a good night's sleep without Dino snoring in his ear.

This time, he thought, as he waited in the outer office, he would by God get in to see Mr. Dennison or know why. But first Gravel Larson gave him a good going over. Even Larson's dead pan flickered and the rasp in his voice was eloquently silent when Joe told him the figure at the bottom of his sheet. Larson had two hundred and sixty thousand on his sheets and he had to swallow hard. His gift from McMahon was drifting out of reach. At the same time, here was a grand coup.

Gravel wanted details. Joe described the oversized brick, of which Larson had never heard. By the time he was through, Gravel Larson looked jumpy. This crazy kid was there all right, he knew exactly what he was talking about. What the hell would he tell McMahon, whom he had promised a first refusal at two fifty-five? But this was too dangerous to bypass. He left the room, and in a few moments, returned, all joviality.

'Napoli,' he said, 'Mr. Dennison would like to meet you.'

'I hope the air ain't too thin up aroun' Mr. Dennison for me to breathe.'

Larson glowered alongside at him, then decided to laugh. 'Don't get the wrong idea. Jock Dennison's a regular guy.'

Inwardly Joe Napoli was not the assured young man he seemed to be when they walked into Dennison's mahogany-panelled office. To tell the truth, he was shaking in his shoes, but he did what he could to keep from showing it. Every word and gesture counted from now on. This was the day for Joe Napoli to get out of Vanzetti's class. It was no time for a single louse-up. He bent his head and crossed himself mentally as they went through the heavy flush door marked JACQUES DENNISON.

Jock Dennison was the sole owner of a real-estate empire. At the moment when Joe Napoli walked in to see him, he was reviewing a consolidated balance sheet of his forty-odd properties – office buildings, lofts, apartment houses, taxpayers, in New York and Jersey – as of December 31, 1926, which showed total assets of fifteen million, and a net worth of six million, seven hundred thousand. Going over the details of the statement was necessary, but boring. Since his father's estate had been settled last year and the estate taxes paid, and since everything but a single trust for his mother had been left to Jock, there was now little to occupy him but the accumulating of more money or the building of more buildings; and although he had just turned forty, he had done enough of both. Nevertheless, he moved easily along the path his father had prepared, building for Woolworth or A & P, according to plans by Bert Winters, collecting his rents, paying his taxes, commuting to the big house in Deal, taking a great interest in his various philanthropies, playing backgammon at the Yale Club and bridge at Canoe Hill.

In the last few years Jock had also put more than fifty thousand dollars into plays. Some had clicked, others had folded, but it gave him an opportunity to read *Variety*, meet producers and directors, and to take out actresses.

What Joe Napoli saw behind the old mahogany desk was a tall, thin man with straight, blond hair and concave cheeks, and a large mouth with prominent teeth. His smile was controlled, but friendly. His watery grey eyes were restless. He rose when Joe came in.

'So you're Napoli? Sure, that's right, I met you out on a job with your father. You were just a kid. I mean a real little kid. Where was it? The Flatiron Building? Sure. How've you been?' He reached across the polished desk and shook hands. Dennison's warmth was genuine, although his hail-fellow manner was obviously achieved with effort, and was neither natural nor effective. Under everything, there was the kind of steel that one associated with army generals.

'How's your father?'

'Pop was killed, slipped off a scaffold, nine, ten years ago.'

'Oh, gosh, I'm dreadfully sorry to hear that.'

'Yah.'

Joe saw the accountant's folders, another open folder with several pages of single-spaced typescript, two paper weights and two photographs – one of a smiling older woman who resembled the man behind the desk and who, Joe decided, must be his mother, and the other of a young, skinny, waif-like girl, looking scared in the picture, under bobbed, blondish hair. This one bore an inscription, 'To Jock – the show's Angel – and mine. Hetty.'

Mr. Dennison was talking. 'Your father said you were planning to be a lawyer or an accountant or something, didn't he? What was it again?'

So he remembered that, did he? 'Teacher', Joe said. 'Pop always said "professor". Pop used to take that stuff pretty big.'

'I remember being impressed, he was so damn proud of you. The way he looked at you. And you weren't that much at the time.' He smiled to indicate he intended no offence. 'Mr. Larson's been giving me the gist of your talk. It's rather fascinating, your approach.'

Could be, Joe thought.

'But it doesn't surprise me. I've always felt brickwork was way overpriced,' Mr. Dennison said, 'especially where they have one of these rings. You've been out to the job site?'

'Yah', Joe said.

'You talked to the suppliers?'

Joe nodded. Mr. Dennison never took his eyes off him.

'And have you seen the union delegates?'

'Not yet.' He saw the disappointed expression. 'But I know the right man out there. Guy named One-eyed Gamboretta.'

Mr. Dennison swung away and turned towards the window. 'I understand you have to make your peace with him. Rough bunch.'

'Peace? Those guys ain't gonna give me trouble. I can handle 'em.'

'I don't know', Mr. Dennison said vaguely, 'Allenburg —'

'Just don't worry about it, Mr. Dennison', Joe said. 'I can get along with that crowd.' Showed you how easily he might've slipped up on something important. He might've hesitated, said ah-ah-ah. Thanks were due to Curly, being ready for this one. And of course, Tony was his ace in the hole.

'Your figures are attractive. I'll be completely frank, too attractive. Almost forty thousand under our lowest bid. But figures are funny. They're one thing on paper and another when the job's done.'

'Sure', Joe said. 'Only these'll stand up.'

'This oversized brick is a great trick if A & P will go for it.'

'Why shouldn't they?' Joe said. 'Nobody in the entire world could ever tell the difference. I've seen 'em. As long as Finlayson's gotta get the brick business, it's a break for him. Before he's through, he'll sell eight trillion of 'em.'

'What do you mean, Finlayson *has* to get the brick business?'

Joe told Mr. Dennison about Finlayson and Bert Winters. Mr. Dennison smiled sagely. There was a subtle change in his attitude, a hint of admiration as if for a clever child, amusement, but tolerant amusement.

'What about this figure here – twelve thousand for miscellaneous?'

'That's the most important twelve thousand bucks on the sheet, Mr. Dennison. That's travel expense for the men from the East Side – five guys in a car. Each guy has to get a buck a day for travel, plus ferry fare, labourers and brickies, maybe sixty, eighty guys. And there's beers, wine – hell, I'll have to buy six, seven hundred bucks worth of grapes for my mother to make wine, and, oh God, crossword puzzles, cigars, what not. And another thing, these guys have been working for a foreman who borrowed money from 'em, three, four hundred bucks maybe. That's big dough to them, and this foreman, he's *never* gonna pay 'em back.'

'Who is he?' Larson growled.

'I'd rather not say', Joe said belligerently. 'And I know it sounds crazy, but we've gotta get that money back to 'em.'

Larson was incredulous. 'You're going to pay off some other guy's debts?'

'Sure,' Joe said shortly, 'but it just has to be done, otherwise, the men are mad and worried all the time and they can't work when they're worried. We give 'em this few hundred bucks and they'll lay, I don't know, maybe fifteen hundred, even two *thousand* a day. You can't tell.'

Mr. Dennison's face clouded, but Larson spoke. 'That's another thing, two thousand brick a day, Napoli, Jesus!'

Mr. Dennison lit a cigarette and asked, 'How do you hope to get that kind of production across the board? I mean, an occasional man, yes, but to average two thousand.'

Joe took a deep breath. Here goes. 'Mr. Dennison, maybe you don't understand how us Italians work. With us,' he continued, 'you know how it is, everything's for the family. Y'ever hear of a Padrone? Okay, my old man, he was the Padrone a the family, his old man before him, so when he cashed in, it's me. Padrone. You understan'? There ain't exactly any word in English for it. I got, geez, I don't know how many relatives – friends, ya know, uncles, aunts, cousins. Ten *million* of 'em. Those people kinda depend on *me*. I get 'em jobs, someone's sick, I take care of 'em – all that crap. Kinda small, family-size Tammany Hall I run. So they work their tails off fa *me*. Those guys, they'll gimme fifteen hundred, two thousand brick, or bust. It ain't like I'm some outside boss.'

Jock Dennison was nodding his head in satisfaction. 'You see,

Larson, didn't I tell you all this? I know how these Italian folks operate.'

Gentle Jesus, forgive me, Joe prayed. Pop dead, Uncle Giovanni in his grocery store, all Pop's brothers back in Italy, they hadn't had a letter from Pop's father for twenty years, and he'd parlayed that up to an entire living crew of relations for the Allenburg job. 'They're scared pissless o' me', Joe added. 'It's as good as having a whip. An' I got no mercy on 'em.'

'How many of these relatives do you have?' Jock Dennison said.

'Well, Mr. Dennison . . .'

'Look, Joe, call me Jock, will you? All the boys around the office do. Ridiculous in this business on a Mister basis.'

Joe breathed deeply. He knew he was in command. Nothing he said now could go wrong. Jock Dennison was nodding happily. Still, he'd watch his step. He tried to remember the names of his Neapolitan uncles. 'Well, Jock, lemme see, Uncle Luigi, his boys . . . Uncle Giovanni, nine . . . mmm, *mama mia*, around, I would say, thirty, thirty-five guys. Few men I gotta get in Allenburg.'

Thus far he had six men who had agreed to go, including Pop's old friend, Rino Sacchi. Not one was a relative.

'Where do you live, Joe?'

'Ninety-eighth Street, 371 East.'

Jock Dennison's face clouded as if he had a terrible headache. 'We used to own that building. My father got rid of it twenty years ago. I don't like those old-law cold-water walk-ups. They make me sick at the stomach.'

'It's home', Joe said. He was Bartolomeo Vanzetti. We are the oppressed . . . you the oppressor.

'Lousy', Jock Dennison said. 'In fact, I never stay in the city unless I have to. Wednesday night for backgammon mostly, and then I stay at the club. I like it out in Deal. Mother and I have a nice place there. D'you have any children?'

'I'm not married', Joe said.

'Neither am I', Dennison said. 'But I don't recommend bachelor-hood for too long, Joe. A fellow needs children, especially boys. I've waited too long. Don't make *that* mistake.'

'I got two kid sisters and a brother. Nice kids. Smart guy Dino is, my brother. I think he's gonna be an engineer or architect or somethin'. Smart as a son-of-a-bitch. Crazy about building.'

'That's no place to bring up children', Jock said gloomily. 'You ought to get them out of there.' This guy was trying to be some kind of father to him.

Joe laughed. He held out his cupped hand palm up, rubbed his thumb across two fingertips. 'Gotta make a few shekels first.'

Jock Dennison made up his mind then he was going to help this loud, confident, but talented kid one way or another. Nice Italian boy. He knew the type, all right. Usually it was all brashness, but this kid had the brains – you could see it from the estimate. And he could make Jock Dennison some money, too. No substitute for someone who's still running hard. He'd make one more try at breaking the bubble. 'Look,' he said offhandedly, 'even if your figures are optimistic and let's say you don't do quite as well as you hope. Even if you overrun your estimate, let's say we don't save forty thousand, let's say we only save thirty or twenty thousand, it'll still be pretty darn good, won't it? I guess we ought to be satisfied.'

Joe said nothing, but looked hard at the sheets.

'After all, every last figure doesn't have to be perfect, Napoli, does it?'

Mr. Dennison was so agreeable Joe's instinct was to agree, but he did not. He rolled up his estimating sheets for emphasis. 'No sir,' he said, 'my figures are right. I'm bettin' my life on 'em. My whole goddam, slummy life. This I will absogoddamlutely do. No sir, Jock, I think if I can't make sixty thousand on this job for myself, and get you a job at two twenty, I lose all the marbles.'

Jock Dennison leaned back and stretched. The expression Joe saw on Jock Dennison's face was one of relief. It was over; he was in. Now was the time to move fast.

'One thing, Jock. I ain't got a dime for payroll. I gotta rent equipment. And I need guarantees from you for all my suppliers.'

Jock Dennison leafed through the accountant's statement and, preoccupied, turned to Larson. 'What do you say, Howard? We take a chance on Joe?'

'Whatever you say, Jock. It's a hell of a long shot. If he overruns, it'll be your dough, not his 'cause he's got none.' He resisted saying, 'And it won't be mine.' He was thinking of what he'd have to tell McMahon. McMahon would be burnt as an ash.

'I'd better start drawin' a hundred and twenty a week starting right away, same as any foreman, and my business manager, he gets seventy-five.'

Jock Dennison stifled a smile. He thought he'd heard everything, but never before had he heard of a business manager for a masonry contractor. It sounded more like something for an opera singer. Joe saw the smile and added hurriedly, 'He keeps track. I run the job. I can't stand all that paper work.' Actually he rather liked the paper work, the numbers racket, as Milt called it. It was amazing what you could do with figures, but he had to keep in character. He was a hard-hitting, straight-from-the-shoulder field man. Mr. Dennison would expect him to be impatient with office work.

'Joe, I think we may go along with you', Jock said. 'Howard, get up a scope of work so we'll be sure we have everything. You'll hear from me in a few days, Joe. Now don't count on anything.'

Outside Gravel led him back to his own office.

'You could have knocked me over with a feather, Napoli. Jock Dennison's not the man to even think of taking a big gamble.' His gravelly larynx had a touch of bitterness. 'His old man was a gambler, but Jock plays it safe. This was a job I had all figured for diSala.' As long as McMahon wasn't going to get it, might as well spread the word of his good intentions to diSala, too.

'Jock's a hell of a good guy', Joe said. 'But I hope he's not trying to be my father. I already *had* one father.' Gravel said nothing and Joe rambled on. 'He seems to think he's doing me some kinda favour, Larson. Who's doing favours is, I'm doing *him* a favour. Let's keep *that* straight. I don't need anyone lousing me up with favours.'

The next week was the longest in Joe's life. Almost nothing happened. But on the second day a man wearing a business suit came to the job where Joe was still laying brick, and asked a number of earnest questions about Joe of the super. 'Wanted to know if you wuz conscientious an' all that. If I knew of any bad habits. What's going on, you in some kinda trouble? Is he from the parole board?'

Joe shrugged. 'Anyhow, you got nothin' to worry about. I told him you were okay. I can't afford to lose no bricklayers offa *this* job.'

Another guy called Milt and visited him at City College. 'Must be for Dennison', Milt said.

Even Lou Gilardi called on Joe to tell him about this guy who was down to the local making inquiries about Joe, and years later at a DeWitt renunion, old man Doty told Joe there had been inquiries there. Jock Dennison left no stone unturned.

On the eighth day, a telegram was delivered that said, 'Please call. Jacques Dennison.'

Jock was, he thought, a little too friendly this time, hardly looked at Larson and treated Joe like the Prince of Wales. They talked about this and that, the way executives do.

'We might as well call a spade a spade', Jock said reluctantly, after he had asked about Joe's entire family. 'I've made a few inquiries about you, Joe. In general, everyone thinks pretty highly of you. But you just don't have the capital for a job of this size.'

'Hell, I told you that last week.'

'I know. But where does that leave me? The risk's all mine. If you overrun your contract, you disappear; and I'm left talking to a contract, a piece of paper. You ever see a contract lay brick? So I have to do it. And if there's anything I don't look forward to, it's getting into the masonry business on a half-finished job. On the other hand, if you do well, you make all the profit. So it's my risk, your profit. It looks to me like a one-way street. Now I have a proposition for you that I think is a little fairer than that. Now, Joe, hear me out.'

Joe subsided, decided to keep silent. Jock Dennison seemed not entirely to have his heart in what he said. Maybe it was all for Larson's benefit.

'I'll put you on as my masonry superintendent. We pay pretty well, Gravel can tell you that. We'd pay you ten thousand a year. And that means year in and year out. When this job's over, there'll be another. We have an active shop. Good steady work, year in, year out.'

Joe looked from Dennison to Larson and back, as if somehow he had been betrayed.

'If you do real well on a particular job, we might even work out a bonus arrangement.'

Joe found himself shaking his head, more in wonder than in opposition.

'If you take this contract instead, Joe, when it's over, then what?'

Joe realized then just how high he had allowed his hopes to soar. Hell, nobody ever offered him anything like what Jock was now, but there was no elation. The preconceived picture would not go away. Once he had a picture of things, he could never seem to make it go away. He scarcely knew what he was doing.

It was either being his own boss or to hell with it. 'Jock,' he said, and leaned forward to shake hands, 'thanks anyhow. It's just a goddam shame we can't do any business together.' He was going to be no man's man. He'd rather lay brick.

He turned to go and had his hand on the door. 'Joe!' Jock's voice was sharp. He turned and saw Jock standing behind his desk, smiling, those large, almost buck teeth a friendly reassurance. 'You got yourself a brick contract. Two hundred and twenty thousand. They'll be ready first thing in the morning. About nine, Gravel?'

Gravel nodded glumly.

Joe took Milt, who wouldn't believe it, up to Dennison's office, where Larson had the printed and typed four-page contract already signed by Jock Dennison. It was rather formidable, with a corporate seal affixed and a place for Joe's signature over a typewritten line – Joseph Napoli d/b/a the Napoli Contracting Company. He signed it and handed the executed document to Milt, who started to read it carefully.

'You shouldn't sign a contract till you've read it', Milt said.

'Don'tcha think I trust Jock Dennison?' Joe said for Larson's benefit.

'Joey, please. You're inevitably going to get yourself into a jam that way sooner or later. I'm sure Mr. Dennison wants you to read it. He won't be insulted.'

'Your friend's right', Gravel said.

'I can't stand reading', Joe said. 'I got enough trouble with the *Daily News*. That's why I got a business manager.'

'Here', Gravel said with disgust. 'Here's the dough you said you needed. Personally I think Jock Dennison's gone soft in the head.'

As soon as they were out of the door, Joe slapped Milt over the back vigorously and jigged around his friend. 'Lookit *that*, Milt. A genuine contract.' He held the document up high. He slit open the envelope and looked at the thousand dollars in twenties. He showed Milt. They both stared at the money. This was the day he was leaving the oppressed class. Good-bye, slobs. Until today he had never wanted to admit, even to himself, that the trouble with being poor was that it was goddam boring and plain monotonous. Poor was brown. 'Starting today, Milt, you're getting seventy-five bucks a week. Jesus, that's more than

Pop ever made, isn't it? And if the job comes out good, I'll give you a bonus.'

Milt started. He cleared his voice. 'I – ah – I – ah – thought —'

'Yah? What?'

'I just assumed —'

Milt flushed. His expression was difficult to read. 'Nothing.' It could've been appreciation or sharing the kick, or it might've been he was sore at something, so Joe added, 'You want to be a lawyer, Milt, don't you? Now you can start going to law school at night and be making good money during the day! That's not a bad set-up, is it? You just stick with me, Milt! I'll take care of both of us!' What the hell was Milt looking so puzzled about, what'd he expect?

Thirteen

THE three best places for the recruitment of bricklayers were on the steps of Santa Cecilia's, up at the local union hall, and in the homes of the men, and Joe recruited in all three. He attended all four Masses two Sundays running and there enlisted twelve hand-picked men for his job. The men he approached had all been okayed beforehand by Rino and Little English. The inducements Joe offered included overtime, travel allowance and a higher rate than union scale. Two of the men, who had long since become revolted at the sight of their wives, responded to Joe's lure of getting a job out of town, with its inviting freedoms and an interlude of all-male society; but for the most part, it was necessary to charm the wives of the candidates and joke with their children.

A handful of the old-timers who resented the intrusion into the foreman ranks of such a young man were outraged at the recruitment on the church steps, but by the second Sunday the gossip had got around that Joe had chosen only the gifted, the artists, and it became a triumphant moment of journeymanship to be invited to New Jersey. Those who were not sulked and swore you'd never get them out on any lousy outa town job. Especially Jersey where that crook Gamboretta had everyone scared pissless.

Joe's activity was called to the attention of Father Ritucci by his assistant, Father Ryan, after the third Mass on the first Sunday. 'And have you noticed young Joe Napoli down front at all three Masses, Father?'

'I have indeed.'

'The spirit must have seized him by the throat', Father Ryan said.

'He was one of my altar boys,' Father Ritucci replied, 'a good kid.'

'The spirit that's come to him is somewhat commercial. Between Masses he's recruiting brick masons for a building job he's to do in Jersey.'

Father Ritucci grinned and shrugged. 'In here we implore "Give us this day our daily bread", and out there, just as they leave church, right on the very steps, who stands there but Providence disguised as Joseph Napoli to answer their prayers on the spot with an honest job.'

At the union hall in a loft on East Eightieth Street, Joe met Lou Gilardi in the small, bare room which served as an office off the meeting room. Gilardi was talking with one of his stooges when Joe walked in.

'Beat it, Chris', Lou said as if he were addressing a cocker spaniel. 'I gotta talk to the famous Mista Barnum an' Bailey here of the famous Barnum an' Bailey Construction Company, the miracle boy hisself.'

'Right', the stooge said faithfully, and lowered his head to nose his way out. "Ey, Joe', he mumbled as he passed.

'Why all the wisecracks?' Joe said, though he had no trouble holding his temper in check. 'You think I'm some kinda big joke? I just came down here to do you a little favour.'

Lou Gilardi rose and bowed ceremonially. 'I am honoured to loin that *you* could help *me*, perfesser.'

Joe said, 'I need men. Good men.'

'So that is why you are standin' on the steps o' the choich, leadin' my good men out-a the Manhattan wilderness into the green pastures of New Joisey? I was wonderin'.'

'Look,' Joe said, 'we're in the USA, aren't we? It's a free country, I heard.'

Lou Gilardi rose and his smiling face turned into a fearsome scowl. His hands went to the table as if for support, and his knuckles turned white. He spoke softly, almost caressingly. 'It aint' free for hi-jackin', Joey.' He came around the table. Lou was well under six feet, but his desk was on a raised platform, and he towered over Joe.

'See, Joey, the men o' local three-o-one belongs to local three-o-one. They like us. We like them. We loined 'em everything they know. We got 'em right offa the boat. We got 'em their foist jobs. Manhattan got all the woik we can handle an' it ain't nice if some little feller who ain't even dry in the diapers, just 'cause he had one o' the nicest old papas ever lived, tries to take advantage o' dat fact an' attempts ta take them men outa this here bailiwick. See what I mean, Joey? What the hell business they got in New Joisey?'

Joe looked up at this towering, gently-speaking man with modest respect. He was studying him as if he were a specimen to be mastered. Lou Gilardi had got where he was with a cajoling voice, a blackjack, and some loyal lieutenants. Lou liked the position he had achieved among the men and their families, and he liked the way the union treasury was always handy in case there was any little thing he might need. Anything that threatened the constant monthly flow of funds into that treasury threatened his life. Men were not as likely to be prompt in their payments when they worked in New Jersey, and they might even tend to forget where their first loyalty lay. Out of sight, out of mind.

'Looey, you're a hundred per cent right', Joe said. 'I'm not using the brains God gave me. I should've come to you first, Looey. But better late than never, 'eh Lou?'

Gilardi's eyes narrowed.

'What it comes to, Looey, is I need co-operation. And if you co-operate, I'll remember it and that might mean something someday.'

'Who can wait for someday?' Lou Gilardi said mildly. He did not underestimate this kid, in fact he rather liked him, always had. And his old man was a regular. 'What happens *now*?'

'Well, this is what I have in mind, Looey, and you'll tell me if I'm way off base.'

'Yeah?'

'About the dues. I'll guarantee every man pays his dues as long as he's on my Allenburg job.'

'You'll guarantee. With what?'

'I'll deposit with the local, Looey, six months' dues for each man. Twelve bucks a head, including myself. If they don't pay it, you'll take it out of my deposit.'

'Yeah? What else?'

'That's all as far as the local goes', Joe said. 'The rest is between you and me.'

' What's that?' Lou Gilardi said.

'I'd like you to do a little recruiting, Lou. You know everyone – who's good, who's a dog. I need fifteen more men. They got to be good. I have to get two thousand brick a day – average.'

'*What?*' Lou said. He was genuinely shocked. 'This is a *union*, Joey. Not a sweatshop. We gotta make things *easier* for the men. How would I talk about two thousand a day?'

Joe put his hand on Lou Gilardi's shoulder and spoke confidentially, almost like a father, '*You* have to make things easier in *Manhattan*, Looey. Not in Allenburg. You can do it, Lou. I have an allowance of fifty bucks a head for every man you get me. For you personally, since this has nothing whatsoever to do with your duties for the local, right? Just a special commission from me to you.'

'You mean *I'm* workin' for *you?*' Lou Gilardi said darkly. His face clouded ominously.

'Hell, no, Looey. You're *co-operating* with me and I'm co-operating with you. I'm one of your boys. You brought me up from a pup.'

Gilardi's eyes burned bright. His lips hardened with the familiar line of satisfaction. 'Where you gettin' all this dough, Joey?'

'I'm getting it,' Joe said dryly, 'from my godfather.'

'An' how about them jokers you been talkin' to on the choich steps? I get my cut on them?'

Joe hesitated. He had twenty men in all, church steps, friends of the family. Quickly he said, 'For them, half. Twenty-five bucks a man. I didn't need as much help from you with them, Lou. You just give 'em your blessing. Okay?' Joe slowly took out his wad and counted out five hundred and handed it to Lou Gilardi. 'There's for the twenty brickies I already got.'

Lou Gilardi's eyes glowed. He took the money. 'Fifteen men. Whadda they get?'

Joe described the terms of employment, and Lou Gilardi promised to go to work. He'd start on the telephone, he'd visit pool rooms and bowling alleys. Seven hundred and fifty more bucks were worth working for. He liked the feel of the five hundred in his pocket so much, he hardly remembered to say good-bye to Joe.

At the bottom of the hierarchy of men working on a construction job is the labourer. He is not the deepest thinker, but he is the hardest working and the lowest paid. And while there is a knack to being a good mason's helper that makes him something more than common labour, the mentalities fall roughly into the same class. To get labourers required radically different techniques.

Joe went to see Frank Lanczycki in his flat. Frank, who was a good man with a wheelbarrow, had taken out first papers two years ago, and his English was now obscurely comprehensible. Frank was thirty-three and was married to a slovenly stray-haired woman who looked more like his mother. A number of filthy children rambled through the place.

Frank was drinking cheap bootleg gin and playing solitaire in his dark, damp flat on Mulberry Street, while all around the family was in confusion. On the table with the cards was a cap pistol, and as he talked to Joey, Frank periodically lifted the gun, aimed it at one or another of the kids, and shouted, 'Bang! Bang! Bang! You dead, Nickie! Bang! Bang!'

Nickie fell to the floor dutifully, and Frank continued with his solitaire and listened to Joe with no apparent interest.

'Where'd you get the gun?' Joe asked.

'I foun' it on Gran' Street in a ash can', one of the kids screamed.

'Bang, bang!' Frank Lanczycki said. 'You dead, John.'

John, who was six or seven, shrugged.

'You dead!' his father shouted angrily. 'Roll over, dead!'

The kid stuck his tongue out.

'Fresh!' The father got up. 'When I say you dead, you roll over. An' don't stick tongue out to Papa!' He gave the kid a tremendous clout across the head. The child started to howl.

Joe picked up the gun himself, held it to his own temple, 'Bang, bang!' he cried. 'Bang, bang, I'm dead!'

He fell to the floor in the accepted film style, clutching his breast even though the bullet had entered his head. The gun clattered to the ground, and Joe lay stretched out.

'Good', the kid said, stopping his bawling. He jumped on Joe and started to hit him, but Joe lay motionless.

'Look, looka Joey', Frank said happily. 'Dead. He don't move.' He sat down and started to push his solitaire cards.

Joe got up and said, 'I gotta go, Frank. How about it?'

Frank screamed to the kitchen at his wife, 'Marcia! Joey wants me I should go to New Jersey on job. Is okay?'

'Is good pay?' Marcia called glumly.

'Yeah. Overtime.'

'So why not? How you get there?'

'Car. Some men drive.'

'So why not?'

Frank turned to Joe. 'Okay.'

'Good', Joe said. He leaned forward, picked up the cap pistol, and aimed it at Frank. 'Bang, bang. You're dead, Frank.' Frank clutched his heart, rolled off his chair, strewing cards everywhere, and stretched out on the floor.

'You see, John? Like that.' He snarled out of the corner of his mouth, 'Dumb goddam kid.'

Joe left Frank stretched on the floor, and Frank was thinking to himself that Joe Napoli sure was a regular fellow. A prince of a fellow.

Once the brickwork started on the A & P job, Joe was out of the house each morning by four-thirty. Milt, now a full-fledged college graduate, met him each day at the Lexington Avenue kiosk and took the subway to Thirty-fourth, the cross-town to Penn Station, the Pennsy to Allenburg, N.J., and the Morris Avenue bus to the job – four separate vehicles, consuming fifty-five cents and almost two hours each way. A few weeks earlier, fifty-five cents had been a potful of money, but with their fabulous salaries, it was now exactly car-fare. Joe read the *Daily News* and the *Graphic* to and from work. Milt peered avidly through his gold-rimmed glasses, down his long, straight nose, at his Blackstone, like an owl, whistling through his teeth as he read. Joe liked those early-morning rides, looking forward to the job. If the truth be told, he couldn't wait to get started, and some mornings he was up by three. The days were not long enough.

Once they got to the job, Milt would call Si Cutler at Finlayson's, and the other suppliers to confirm material deliveries for the day. Joe had the scaffold men out at six-thirty, setting plank and put-locks, and got the mortar mixing started at seven. By eight, when the brickies trudged out on the scaffold, Joe had done half a day's work.

The steward blew the starting whistle and it was one thing after another for Joe: conferring with Rino Sacchi, now his pusher, who griped about the incredible laziness of the local men; working with Little English and Lupo the Fortunate, now lay-out men, who complained about the oversized brick; defending himself against the superintendent, a red-faced Dutch giant of seventy, and a small wiry, greenish man who was the steam-fitter boss. For the first time in his life, Joe felt he was fully awake and going at all his nerve ends. It was ten cups of coffee.

At first amazed by the chaos at the top level of supervision, Joe soon became accustomed to the fact that nobody kept a promise or intended to. A promise in the construction business, he learned, was simply a way of terminating a conversation. Every trade was in business for itself; everyone was in everyone else's way. Co-ordination was a matter of getting your men there first, finishing your job, and letting the other bastids worry about how to work

around you or through you or after you. The howls from the
carpenter boss, the steam fitter, the plumber and the electricians
went in one ear and out the other. The lather boss belted the
carpenter foreman so hard he had to be taken to the hospital with
a bad cut under his eye. Joe wasted no time arguing or fighting.
Ready or not, here comes Napoli. He graded for the foundation
man, scaffolded for the carpenter, to help them get out of his way.
He got his own lines and grades, using the transit himself. Spend
a few extra minutes or extra bucks. To the shiner-eyed carpenter's
threat, 'You backcharge me, you crazy guinea, I smack four by
four on you head', he shrugged, 'No spik Swedish, Oscar.' Nothing
could stop his men, and to hell with technicalities and arguments.
Let Milt fight for the backcharges or the extras. That was all peanuts. Just give me two thousand oversized brick a man a day,
face and back-up, and I'm in. The rest is conversation. The concrete boss saw his backfill work being done free, and gave Joe
a cigar. 'You're a good egg, Joe.' Joe was not deterred by Milt's
complaint that he was a sucker. 'When our brickies have to stop
for five minutes,' he shouted to Milt, 'I'm standing there pissing
money on the ground.' He lit the concrete man's cigar and smoked
it, even though it smelled like a chemical factory. He looked more
like a boss with a cigar in his mouth.

Milt spent his days raising quiet hell with suppliers. Milt never
raised his voice, never threatened, but he was persistent. He smiled
in a chummy fashion, even over the phone you could hear his
smile. He wheedled, and got what was needed. He checked material
in, checked time and production, and walked the scaffolds once or
twice to be sure the men were all there. You had to watch these
guys; they could take off for a beer or a walk around the block.
On the first Friday, he paid the men, including himself and Joe,
in money-bulging, yellow envelopes brought out to the job by
Dennison's book-keeper, Gert Saunders, a skinny woman with the
face of a cigar-store Indian. Milt liked the feel of the crisp new
money, it was silk to him, he caressed the bills. Joe never even
looked at his money or thought about it, except to know he'd got
it. Pfft. He was too busy enjoying the job and planning for next
week.

Milt also prepared a voluminous weekly report on costs and
progress for Dennison's secret service, Gravel Larson. Joe loved
Milt's neat columns of cost and production figures, giving meaning
to the brick walls everyone could see rising so fast. And the profit

figure for each week was more than just a number. It was the very artery of life, the pump of Joe's contentment.

At lunch each day, Joe had Little English's crossword puzzle book out, a checker game set up for himself and McGregor; and the wine flasks he had got from Mammina were pulled out of the padlocked locker. Young Sal Benello, who watched the checker game, which Joe almost always lost to McGregor, sipped his wine thoughtfully. "Ey, Pepe, how 'bout this floatin' cloud – what da hell wuz her name again? Francesca? At dat ol' speak? When we gonna see this fabulous babe?'

'Ya, ya, ya, Sal. Just stick around. Soon as we're roofed out, we'll all go up to Francesca's. What a broad!' There was a great deal of speculation about her, and Joe knew that sooner or later he would have to produce Francesca's lily-white body.

Within a few days Joe's masonry shanty with its crudely lettered NAPOLI CONTRACTING CO. over the door became the centre of the job, not only for brickies and labourers but for steam fitters, carpenters and the electrician foreman, all of whom hung out there for laughs and to hear Joe cry to the lather, 'Gawd bless the Irish, Dana! Go ahead and lath the bastids in! Sure, Dana, I'm for *you*, 'cause wasn't me old lady born in Galway?' Or to the steel man, 'Greenstein, after what you done to me, you should sit shiva for a week! I'm ashamed to tell my old orthodox mother what a good Jewish boy did to *me*.'

By the end of the first week, ten New York brickies had checked in with Gamboretta's Allenburg local, paid their permit fees, got their books, and started to work; in order to keep the local out of his hair he put on five of their men, including one Pasquale Baccio as shop steward. Their rules required at least fifty per cent local men, but that would have been murder. Baccio was a small man of indeterminate age, who never showed up on the job without a day's growth of bristly beard. He must've used a scissors instead of a razor. The five local men gave Joe *exactly* five to six hundred a day average, and it was clear from the outset that the greatest hurdle of all would be Union Boss One-eyed Gamboretta, whom Joe had never met, but about whom among many disquieting things he had heard, was the fact that Gamboretta carried a pearl-handled revolver. On the fifth day, he fired two of the local bums, who, glowering, went to Milt for their pay-off money. Sooner or later the problem had to be faced.

The morning after that firing, two men drove up to the job in a long, black Buick to see Joe. Both were heavy-set, tall, and in their middle twenties. One was dark and always smiling, the other was light, and squinted as if the sun were constantly in his eyes.

'Who the hell allowed you to come here to Allenburg to build?' the Squint said, without preliminary greetings. He flashed an agent's card.

'Mr. Dennison gave me a contract,' Joe said, 'being it's a free country.' He jerked his chin towards the scaffold. 'As long as Mr. Dennison keeps paying me, my men are going to lay brick.'

The Smile said softly, 'Why don't you just take your men and equipment and get the hell back to New York where you belong? We got plenty good brickie outfits in Allenburg to do this job.'

'Look, Mister,' Joe said, 'I'm not looking for trouble. But I'll tell you guys one thing – I'm a nervous type, and don't start trouble for me, 'cause someone is going to get hurt.'

'That's fa sure', Squint said. 'That's fa goddam sure, someone is gonna get hurt.'

'You tell friend Gamboretta,' Joe said, 'that I'll be glad to come down and see him and talk. All he has to do is invite me. But under no circumstances am I going back to New York.'

'Sometimes some of our guys get outa hand,' the Smile said, 'and the first thing ya know, there's an explosion, like from dynamite. Does a lotta damage. The kids come for miles ta watch. Kids is quite easy to amuse.'

'Now that you mention kids, you tell Gamboretta I'm a very close friend of Tony Ferrara', Joe said. 'Him and I were kids together. Very close.'

The two men looked at each other as if this were something they had not been briefed on.

'We'll tell 'im', Squint said. They turned to get back in the Buick.

Nothing happened after that for a week.

By four in the afternoon, Joe and Milt had put in twelve hours. They had to run like Man o' War to catch the four-fifteen bus, and it was almost six-thirty by the time they reached home. In different ways they were slaves to the job. To Joe, it was a ruthless master – a tyrant beyond Ernie Schaf, the super, or Swaltzer, or the menacing, unseen Gamboretta. It was a smoke-breathing, whining, clattering God-giant – Job: growing, having to grow before the eyes of the men who made it grow, created by them, and master of them all. It required rigid sacrifice, demanded full attention, although each man knew finishing it meant unemployment and a new beginning. Nothing else could be served – though family, or self-interest or pity or love might clamour. Not until Job had been served first.

After supper Joe kissed Mammina, kidded Lucy to eat less because her backside was getting fat, Indian-wrestled with Dino a couple of rounds and was out of the house to visit men with sick kids or to play cards with lonely ones until nine, ten o'clock. These were the men who were giving him two thousand brick a day. In return he gave them Joe Napoli. He could have used a ten-day week and thirty-hour day. And on his rounds everywhere he went he asked about Giacomo Gamboretta, trying to piece together bits and pieces of what he heard. Sooner or later he would meet someone who really knew the man.

About all he discovered – and from Lou Gilardi – was that Gamboretta was Sicilian, came from Palermo, which was Mammina's home town, and he kept meaning to ask her, but Palermo was a big town, and though he had spoken to nearly everyone he knew who had come from there, Giacomo Gamboretta was not a well-known man on the New York side of the Hudson. Then one night he did mention the man to Mammina.

She screwed up her face in doubt, shaking her head slowly. 'Gamboretta?' Then suddenly her face lighted. 'Si! Mio ricordo! The Gamboretta boys! Shu, shu. Old Man Gamboretta was Palermitano, was contadino for the place where I'm-a live, takes-a-care-alla legumi, fiori . . . The signore who owns-a the villa, man named . . . Pop, he's-a rememb' . . . Oh, Vincenzo Florio, si. Ver' nice-a signore. Always wear a fine-a white linen suit, I rememb' always has bigga pearl inna tie, gold-a chain, bigga watch. Ride on bigga black horse. An' such a nice-a place . . . bellisima! Look-a way down over the sea —'

'How about this Gamboretta, Ma?'

'Oh, Gamboretta was bigga family. I dunno, five, six boy, five girl. Shu, I useta know. Two the boys useta go dance with me, before I meet-a Carmine.'

'You remember their names?'

'Oh . . . it's-a so long. Giorgio maybe. One's-a Giorgio, the bigga one. Lemme see . . . Gianni? No . . . Giacomo. Si Lo. credo, Giacomo —'

'Ma! You kiddin'?'

'Why I'm-a kiddin'? You no belivva me? You ask-a you Aunt Mathilda.'

'This Giacomo, he useta dance with you?'

'Sure. Lots-a boys dance with me. When I'm-a kid I'm-a verr', how you say, cutie.' She stood and whirled girlishly. 'I'm-a dance good, too. You should-a see. Annunziata's-a bigga, how you say? Sport. I like-a the boys, boys like-a me. Giacomo he's-a live on same-a villa ground as me.'

'You *serious?*'

'Whattasmatta? Why not?'

'Oh, nothin'. He lives out in New Jersey.'

'Out where you doon-a work? No kidda you Mama!'

'Yah. Maybe I'll run into him one of these days.'

'Whattayou know!' his mother said. 'Small-a worl', ah?'

He leaned over and kissed his mother. 'You sure must've been a real sport, Ma.' His mother was grinning, remembering the days when she had been a silken black-haired, gusty girl, the darling of the *contadini* of the big villas and farms around Signor Florio's Villa Igiea.

Milt, though he was running as hard as Joe, did not feel anything about the job the way Joe did, for he was running in a different direction. He proffered his twelve hours a day for the money. After supper he took a subway down town to night classes at Fordham Law School, where his last class in torts let out at ten. And it was during those hours in Law School when he came alive. Milt got five hours sleep every night, and if he was losing weight and his face was taking on a drawn, dehydrated cast, he probably comforted himself with the picture of himself in the dignified, black robes of Mr. Justice Brandeis, handing down the Word. Because while Joe wanted action, Milt's love was first, last and always, the Word.

On the job, Milt tried to be conscientious, but already in the first two weeks he had made several costly mistakes. Like he forgot to call the block man one day, and when the previous day's deliveries had been used, there the men stood, tubs full of mortar, brick laid out, and no goddam four-inch block. Two hours for fifteen brickies and fifteen labourers, while they waited. Joe could see all Milt's strings weren't tight, and, in fact, he had a kind of faraway, moony expression on his face, the kind you see on high school kids when they think of their first piece of tail.

On the subway, going home one night, Joe studied his friend's increasingly pale face which was deep into *The Principles of Contracts* or Henshaw's *Bankruptcies and Reorganization*. This guy was being held together with spit and chewing gum. Seriously.

"Ey, Milt, come on up for air! Listen, you're looking *lousy*. You're working too *hard*. You're walking around the job like you lost something. Stop reading a minute, will you? You'll be a lawyer five minutes later, what the hell! Breathe in, breathe out!'

Milt smiled wanly behind the gold-rimmed glasses. '*I'm* working hard, Joey? You're a fine one to talk.'

'Yah, only I don't forget a thing like ordering block. And I don't lose weight. Lookit me. I'm *exactly* a hundred and fifty, fifty-five pounds. Lookit you. You look like a walking stiff. You must be down to a hun'twenty. What's your trouble?'

Milt lowered his book and closed his eyes gently. Then, peering up at Joe, judiciously, deciding whether to say anything, he murmured. 'It isn't the work, I can tell you that.' He hesitated, then with wretched slowness: 'What's been bothering me is your sister Lucy.'

'Lucy? *Lucy?*'

He knew that since Luce was a child she'd been soft on Milt, he'd seen them peering furtively at each other, but it was one of those kid things. Now, however, his mind fastened on the subject. Lucy was not yet seventeen. but Lucy was a changed girl in the last year or two. She'd given up stoopball and jacks, and was beginning to look like a young and untamed Mammina. Her arms were always fleshly and bare in spite of Mammina's never-ending threats of purgatory or damnation; her teeth were good and white and straight. Her nose wasn't bad either, kind of Roman and narrow, with the faintest Napoli hump; and her hair which had been naturally a wavy brown she had somehow turned black and set in ringlets. Rosina looked upon her older sister with complete admiration and awe, Dino called her Juicy Lucy; Mammina's continuous barrage against the hair-do, the lipstick and the bare arms was a condition of life. 'Pepe, make her *do* somethin'. She's-a gonna go to *hell*. Maybe she listen to you, the *man* of the family.' But Joe had shrugged. Was he a priest? Lucy responded to Mammina's barrage and Dino's taunts by screaming, periodically, 'I gotta get outa this place. I'll go crazy! It's as bad here as with Uncle Giovanni! I'll get married! I'll run away with a dope fiend! I can't stand it! I'm warning you, Ma!' What she did finally was to get a good job as a dentist's assistant. Now Joe recalled that whenever Milt had come to dinner, Luce had been a model of decorum. He had to regard his friend with new interest. Joe, after all, *was* responsible.

'You didn't get Luce in some kinda trouble!'

A flicker of pain crossed Milt's face. Joe thought he detected a touch of amusement.

'Joey. Brace yourself.' Milt peered at him from under his glasses sadly. 'It's worse than trouble. You know I have too much respect for Lucy for *that*. Lucy and I want to get married.'

'Whaaa? You *serious*? Luce – she still – for Godsake – she still eats tootsie rolls! She needs a husband like she needs a bald head! And you need a wife like *two* bald-heads!'

'Lucy's a lot more grown up than you give her credit for. The reason she never got in trouble is not because we never thought of it.' Milt spoke with earnest and compelling sincerity, ten times as sincere as anyone else. 'Anyhow, we'd like to get married. Only —'

'Only what?'

'Well Joe, your mother – you know, she's pretty religious . . . and I'm . . .'

Joe was astounded. He too was thinking of Mammina. 'We're a good Catholic family, Milt . . .' And suddenly he was laughing. 'Oh, yoy, yoy, wait'll Mammina hears about *this*!' He gasped. 'Four hundred Hail Marys, she'll go out and buy up all the candles at Macy's and Gimbel's *together*. Going out, okay. But getting married, oh, poor Mama!'

He peered at Milt. What the hell did Luce see in him? He wasn't pretty with the obtuse triangle nose, the glasses, the black ringlet hair. Well, he was the smartest guy Luce ever knew, for one thing, the only college graduate she'd ever met. And he was probably the gentlest. Milt seemed to be able to feel for everyone. And he was sure feeling sorry for himself right now. Lookit him.

Milt closed his book, took his glasses off, wiped them slowly, then put them in his breast pocket. Joe could see him swallow unhappily several times. 'I'd hate to cause your mother any grief', he said slowly. 'But it's so hard to please *every*one. Lucy and I are very pleased with each other. On balance, isn't that the important thing? I mean we're planning to *live* together all our *lives*.'

Joe could not help being touched by his friend's solemnity. To Milt there was nothing amusing; Milt blossomed on tribulation.

'You really like old Luce?'

'How would *you* know, you're only her brother.'

'Okay', Joe said shortly. 'Stop worrying. Don't love always find a way? I'll fix it up with Mammina.'

Milt stared at Joe through myopic eyes. He reached for his glasses, put them back on deliberately.

'I wouldn't be surprised if you could, Joe', he said with a degree of awe.

'G'wan, read your book about how to go bankrupt without losing money. You and I are gonna need everything in every book you got.' The job just started, Milt absolutely the most necessary guy in the whole works and he comes up with this. Well, Milt was a good guy. He made you want to take care of him.

Milt spoke deferentially, more so than he ever had before. 'You're okay, Joe.' And Joe knew the problem was in his lap, and right now he needed one more problem like he needed ringing in the ears. But he noticed after that talk Milt was more alert on the job. All his mistakes came to an abrupt halt. Mammina was easy. He simply told her that Milt was going to marry Lucy, listened to her scream for five minutes and then added that Milt would, of course, become a Catholic.

Fourteen

THE showdown with Gamboretta started with an accident one hot July morning two weeks after the brickwork had begun. Joe was in the shanty when he heard an eerie cry. Even now he could feel the way his gut had hollowed and sunk; it was that same wailing scream from throat to chest to stomach that had come from Pop's falling, twisting body. But there was no high scaffold on this job, the men were only ten feet off the ground.

He and Milt rushed out to the small cluster of men, and there in the centre was young Sal Benello on the ground, dazed, with a cut head, bleeding badly. Sal, barely able to cross himself, murmured weakly to one of the boys to get a Father, he was going fast. Milt ran to the shanty to call an ambulance.

Lupo the Fortunate turned with fury on Pasquale Baccio, the shop steward, who stood scuffing the ground, 'Sonabitch accident in pigga's assa! You do onna purpose!'

Pasquale Baccio, it seemed, had kicked several bricks off the scaffold at the precise moment that Sal had passed below him, and Sal had fallen under the avalanche. Baccio glowered at the New York men, squinted at Joe, scuffed the ground, pushed out his lower lip in defiance, and snarled at the injured man, 'Why you no watcha where you go?'

Joe hurried to Sal's side, elbowing his way through the circle of men, who fell back to make room. Sal was badly cut up. One look at Pasquale Baccio's face was all Joe needed to know the accident was no accident. His fist shot out, all the strength of his shoulder and back behind it, and he felt his knuckles plough into that whiskery jaw. It was a tremendous, furious blow, and Pasquale Baccio went down in fear and surprise.

'You try anything on *my* men,' Joe shrieked, his veins out in his neck, 'I'll kill the whole goddam lotta you! You tell that to Mr. Gamboretta!' He turned his eyes moist, and cradled Sal's head like a baby in his arm. 'Okay, Sal. Okay, okay. Everything's gonna be okay.' He wiped his own eyes and gently rubbed the blood from Sal's cut with his kerchief. 'Don't stand there, get some water, you lazy bastids.'

Pasquale Baccio pulled himself up off the ground. 'You see', he muttered. 'You gonna see.'

Joe ignored the man. He held Sal's head in his hands, cleaning the cut with the dampened kerchief until the ambulance came, try- ing to stop the flow of blood. 'Stop squawking, Sal. You're healthy as a horse. Lookit all the good blood you got!'

Sal smiled weakly. 'I'm gonna die', he whispered. 'Tell my mother and father —'

'Your father's right here. See? Stop trying to scare him.' Old Sally Benello took his son's hand. He was too choked up to speak.

Sal's head wound was not deep; he was suffering mainly from terror.

'You haven't even got a good headache, Sal. You get yourself stitched up and come right back, 'cause by now I got this Francesca broad all hot and bothered waiting for you. I promised her we're coming up as soon as we're roofed out. She thinks you're Rudolf Valentino. Kid, do you have a tune-up waiting! *Mama mia!*'

Sal dabbed Joe's handkerchief to his head and looked aghast at his own blood, the flow of which had slowed to an ooze. He smiled weakly, as if he had just been pulled back through death's door.

But just before they shoved Sal into the waiting ambulance, he cried, 'Giusepp', you gonna let me die? Joe, you forgettin' me?' You had to hand it to Sal, if he was exactly one thousand per cent braver, he might make coward, first class.

Milt climbed into the ambulance, and Pasquale Baccio demanded the right to go along, too, insisting he was hurt, also. Since a shop steward on a job is as useful as a rainy day, Joe let him go. The whiskery old bastid could spend the rest of his entire life in the hospital for Joe Napoli's dough.

By noon, Milt was back from the hospital to report that Sal was okay, and that they'd sent him home with three stitches, a little weak, but okay. 'And why d'you think Pasquale Baccio came to the hospital? He wasn't hurt. He has a sick kid there, Joey – nine years old. He made me come upstairs and meet him.'

'What's the matter with the kid?'

'Gee, I wouldn't know. I have the feeling he's a real sick boy, the way the nurses treat him. I wouldn't be surprised if he was on his way out. He's had six blood transfusions. Pasquale hasn't the vaguest idea what the kid's got, but the doctors have him worried stiff. He's kind of a sad old horse when you get him off the job.'

'Son-of-a-bitch kicked those brick at Sal on purpose.'

'Possibly, Joey. If you ask me, he's a little sore at the world.'

'What the hell, it probably wasn't *his* idea anyway', Joe said. 'It was that son-of-a-bitch Gamboretta.'

At three o'clock Pasquale reappeared and found Joe on the scaffold.

'Giacomo Gamboretta, he wanna see you, down-a the Hall afta work, Mist' Napoli. Okay?'

'Sure', Joe said. He looked at Pasquale with new sympathy. Poor bastid. Well, at least he was ready for Gamboretta. In the shanty he asked Milt, 'You got that envelope Gravel Larson brought out last Friday?'

'Locked up', Milt said, rolling his lips back in a nervous gesture to bare his teeth.

'I need it', Joe said. 'I'm going to see Mister Gamboretta this afternoon.'

Milt glumly opened the petty-cash box and fished out the envelope. Joe could hear the crisp crackle of currency inside. 'You're sure you want to do this, Joey?'

'Sure, I'm sure. You think I *want* to give away money? *My* money? I *have* to. How else would you get the job done?'

Milt smiled a soft but embarrassed smile and stared at Joe for a spell. 'Well, I just want you to be certain in your own mind.'

'We talked it out a thousand times!' Joe shouted impatiently. 'What do you keep asking me for?'

Milt said nothing, but blinked unhappily.

'Who'll know?' Joe shouted. 'How d'you think I got this?' He struck the envelope against the desk. 'You think I just said, please, Mister Larson, hand me over a couple-a G notes?'

His lips pursed, then broke into his whistle kiss and grin as he recalled how he'd done it.

'First I hadda show Gravel Larson the two thousand brick a man. Y'ever seen such a dopey look on a guy's puss the day we did our count? He was amazed, he was stunned, trying to keep a straight face. So then I tell him, unless we make a deal with Gamboretta, we'll get murdered by the local brickies. Maybe he'll even murder *us*, period. He don't think anything of dropping bricks on people. Gamboretta's demanding one to one, locals and New York men, and the locals are giving us five, six hundred a day. And the goons are coming around to put the fear-a God in me. So when I explain it all, simple and clear like that to Gravel, he goes back and gets this envelope from old Jock Dennison. Plus the fact it's *my* money, coming out of my contract price. And *you're* asking me do I know what I'm doing! *Jesus*, Milt!'

'As a legal matter, you're entitled to know the risks, Joey.'

'Hell, *everybody* does it', Joe snapped. 'There's not a guy in Allenburg doesn't have to pay Gamboretta off. Don't be a complete louse-up.'

'The pokeys are full of everybodies', Milt said wistfully.

'You think I like it? It's pure poison. I'd like to lock every one of these crooked bastids up for life. But how? You expect me to call out the Marines, put the cops on him?' Joe cried. 'Can't you just see me running up and down the street yelling, Arrest that man? I love my family, Milt. I don't want anything to happen to Luce or my mother or Rosie or Dino. This guy's a *killer*. He's got that union where he wants it. I'd have to go to the International in Washington, and even then I'd get my brains beat out. If I start straightening out *that* whole deal, you can forget *this* job. I mean, I have to decide exactly what I'm *doin'*. Am I some kind of cop or D.A. reformer? That's another career *altogether*. You were the one said take the contract. Okay. I did. Now I'm performing under the contract. Pop was always telling me, do something for the men. Well, there's all kinds of ways to help the men. *My* men, not these local stumblebums. Jesus. Action, boy, I've gotta have action. These guys're *murdering* me. These local bums move like they're in divers' suits under water. You've seen 'em. Once they get to *our* men, we're done. I have to straighten 'em out fast. And this'll straighten 'em out!' He smacked the envelope against his leg.

'Joey, shhh! For God's sake!' Milt lowered his voice. 'One thing *absolutely*. If you're going to do anything illegal, like bribery, at least do it' – his voice was a whisper and he scrunched his face and held his hand over an imaginary lid – '*qui-et-ly*. I mean, I'm not a half-wit, Joey. I suppose bribery is resorted to as a last desperate measure. But you're sure there's no conceivable other way?'

'So-mi-so-fa!' Joe sang. 'Still yelling cheez it, the cops. What am I supposed to do, use my charm on this gorilla? It's *impossible*.' Joe folded the envelope and put it in his pocket.

F

'Taking bribes is a crime, Joe. You could report this man to the proper authorities.'

'*Authorities?*' Joe shouted. '*What* authorities? The cops in town? He's their brother-in-law. The politicians? He elects 'em. The International? They're bigger crooks than this One-eyed monster. Stick to your paper work.'

Milt looked as though he had been told to stand in the corner. Then his face took on that familiar, earnest expression. 'I'm thinking only about you, Joe, whether you want me to or not. If I'm going to be a lawyer, I've got to think first about my clients. I'm not a Boy Scout. The way I think of it is this: Would *I* do it? Can it be defended? You see what I mean?'

'Nope. The way I lookit the son-of-a-bitch is what's best for the job. What's the deal? I have to get the brickwork done. It's not my work to clean up corruption in the International.' He walked out of the shanty, leaving Milt still shaking his head sadly.

In Giacomo Gamboretta's 'office', which was the back room of the dingy Hotel Esplanade Grill in New Brunswick, four men sat at a table decorated only with a ketchup-stained tablecloth. Baccio was still in his work clothes; Squint and Smiley were there in their black, shiny suits; the fourth man was Giacomo Gamboretta, chief of the Allenburg local, a man in his late forties with a kindly, Santa Claus face overlaid with shrewdness. His one glass eye gave his entire face an eerie cast. From time to time he consciously narrowed his eyes to indicate his wisdom and to show the wheels were going round. He was a jolly shape – all he needed were the white whiskers and a red suit. Instead, he was clean-shaven and wore a neat, white linen suit, crisp and pressed, a bright red tie and shiny black alligator shoes, which matched his gleaming patent-leather-black hair, pressed thinly to his scalp. His sallow, baby-clean face was still tinted with the white talcum of the barber shop. In his tie was a pearl pin, and alongside the table lay an ebony cane with an old-fashioned hook handle of hammered gold. A huge gold fob hung from a heavy gold chain across his white linen waistcoat. His shirt-sleeves stuck out far enough so you couldn't miss the gold cuff links. Although he was president of the Masons' local in Allenburg, he had perfectly manicured fingers – fingers it was difficult to believe had ever handled brick and trowel.

He was jovial, but there was a thick irony in his voice. When he spoke, you could not be sure he was an immigrant. 'Siddown,

Napoli. Siddown. Beer for Mister Napoli, Tomaso.' Squint went off for the beer.

Joe felt in his pocket for the envelope.

'You know Baccio here, Mister Napoli. Steward on your job. He's been tellin' me the pertection onna scaffold is so bad on your job he drops a brick and it hits one-a your men. We don't stan' for that crap, Napoli. Things like that don't happen aroun' here. We're here to watch out for the men's good, see what I mean?'

Squint came back with beer for all. It was viler than most. Only Baccio abstained, because no beer was delivered for him.

'Men goin' to the hospital is *bad*, Napoli, so you know what I think we gotta demand? You gonna hafta build a pertection fence all around them scaffolds so nothin' else falls off. That poor boy in the hospital is a stinkin' shame.'

Baccio lit a cigarette.

'It happens to be *exactly* one-a my *own* boys', Joe said. 'Think how I feel.'

'Bosses got no feelings', Gamboretta whispered. 'You know that. You was once a brickie yourself. What's brickies to a boss – each one brings in so many shekels, am I right?'

Joe could feel the hate boiling up, but he kept the lid on. 'My old man fell off a scaffold, so don't start givin' me lectures about *protection*, for Christ's sake. And not only was I and my Pop both brickies, so was *his* father back in the old country. I take *care*-a my men. I like my men. I grew up with my men. You can't talk louse-up stuff like that to *me*.'

'You're the worst kind', Gamboretta shrugged. 'Usin' your own friends to line your pockets with gold. An' that's another complaint the boys've got. Too many-a your New York men. We don't allow more than fifty-fifty. It's in the by-laws. You got the book. You on'y got five-a my boys an' twenty-two New York men. That don't look good. Our men needs the work.'

Joe laughed. Gamboretta laughed. Smiley kept smiling and Squint kept squinting. Pasquale Baccio smoked his cigarette in thoughtful silence, looking from one black suit to the other.

'You call it work, what your men do? Five hundred brick a day? They're bricklayers like I'm the Prince of Wales. Those guys are all under water in iron divers' suits, and someone turned off the air on 'em – that's how they lay brick.'

'We don't like to see our men sweatin'', Gamboretta said smoothly. 'We don't like to see *nobody* sweatin'. A job with a lotta New York men, workin' too hard for their own good, scaffold without pertection, bricks fallin' on guys, Jesus, Napoli, we on'y got about four, five rules *in* this union, an' you just about broke 'em all.'

Joe reached into his pocket for the crisp envelope, placed it carefully on the table, and caressed it twice, causing it to crackle.

'Okay, Baccio', Gamboretta said abruptly. 'Okay, boys. Me an' Napoli are gonna handle this here now. I'll get in touch wit' ya if I need ya.'

Smiley and Squint left without a word; it was like one of those gangster films. Baccio got up to leave, hesitated, and Joe called after him, "Ey, Baccio! Wait around outside, I want to talk to you about your boy in the hospital.'

Baccio flinched, turned and spoke trying to conceal his surprise. 'Okay. Sure.' And he closed the door after him.

Without a word, Gamboretta now slit the envelope open, pulled the bills out, counted the first few, then riffled through the rest, and tossed the money in Joe's face with calculated casualness. The bills hit Joe's cheek, scattered on the table and a few fell to the floor. 'This is not money', Gamboretta snapped. 'We're just gonna hafta close down your job, Napoli.'

'Not money?' Joe shouted hoarsely. 'Not money? There's two grand here!' He picked up the stray twenty-dollar bills, stuffed the money back in the envelope and left the envelope on the table.

'Make it twenty thousand, maybe we can talk business', Gamboretta said.

'Twenty?' Joe shouted. 'Are you *serious?* Look, Gamboretta, I'm new in business, I need a fight with you exactly like I need a permanent wave under both my arms. But twenty grand! I'll just have to sherry out of here and we'll have to battle it out.'

Gamboretta tilted his beer into his gullet in a single gesture and patted his handkerchief delicately against his fat, pursed lips. 'Five million brick is a lotta brick. The way we work in Allenburg, we do things a little different, see? We got three, four brick contractors, they figure on gettin' just about all the work in Allenburg. We don't get an A & P warehouse every day. So they ain't too happy seein' five million brick go to a New York outfit. An' we like them fellas, we do a lotta business together. You, ya finish the job an' you go back to New York.'

Joe watched him narrowly. Gamboretta did not seem like such a tough character. In fact, he seemed rather soft and gentle.

'You yourself, of course, were born and bred right here in Allenburg, New Jersey?' Joe asked.

Gamboretta smiled craftily, took a gold nail clipper from his waistcoat pocket and meticulously clipped one cuticle. Then he snapped the clipper shut, put it back and drew out a small emery board. Slowly he began to file his left thumbnail. Joe peered at him over the edge of his glass of vile beer.

'Every once in a while,' Gamboretta said, 'some wise guy comes aroun' thinkin' he's gonna buy this town. Well, I got news for guys like that. I bought this town long ago. An' right at the moment it ain't for sale.' He held up the file and shook it slowly. 'You know what it means to have a town – like that?' He placed a half dollar in his palm, closed his fingers slowly and put the half dollar in his pocket. 'Halfa my brickies jump ship before they come out here to see me. I know what that is, 'cause that's how I got here myself. Heart always right up in the throat. Got a job on a freighter in Palermo and jumped ship in Hoboken. Scared pissless. And when I come they didn't have these immigration laws. Now I'm an American citizen, see, but I know just how these poor bastids feel. I get 'em a place to live, give 'em a work permit, find 'em jobs. But if they look cockeyed once, back they go to sunny Italy. Ya see, I got the whole immigration service workin' fa *me*. I don't like it, but sometimes you *gotta* do these things. The boys understan'. These boys'd do damn near anything I ask 'em. You know, they're loyal boys. That kinda loyalty don't come cheap. I think for me they'd trip up their own mother. When you got things like that, you know you own somethin'. Naturally, I gotta get a little help, here'n there. Coupla guys in Jersey City, coupla guys in Trenton, guys in the International, guys in the Immigration Service. You know it kinda branches out, an' whatever I get, I gotta spread it around. 'Cause when you don't spread it, some-a these boys, especially the young ones comin' up, they'd just as soon knock you off.'

'Listen, *paesano*, I can understand all that. What part-a Italy you come from?'

'I come over from Palermo, an' I was fulla vinegar like yourself. Used to lay tufo there when I was a kid. You know, kind of a soft stone. But there's no future in layin' tufo. So I got to thinkin', with all the Indians here, it's only a matter of time till Gamboretta takes over America. Then I find out you gotta work with all kinds-a guys. Like your friend, young Ferrara. I understan' you know Tony

Ferrara. An' workin' with guys like him means you never have
nothin' a hundred per cent. Settle for fifty. Settle maybe for
twenty.'

'So you're from Sicily! Whaddaya know. My own mother's
born in Sicily.'

'Everyone is born in Sicily', Gamboretta said. 'The whole island
is a baby factory.'

'Palermo', Joe said. 'That's the town she's born in.'

'Yeah', Gamboretta said, not rising to bait.

'Maybe you knew her – Annunziata Perini?'

Gamboretta filed his forefinger, scowled. Something was going
on in his round, thick head. Slowly he began to nod and he
repeated the name half to himself. 'Annunziata Perri — Shu, shu.
Big, wild girl with black hair, big, shiny teeth . . . black eyes?
Shu, shu. Jesus, she was a wild girl! Lived on the same place I did.
Signor Florio's. When she'd laugh, you could hear her allaway in
Messina. She could scream like a cyclone. She useta wear these
two gold rings in her ears – big ones.'

'Still does', Joe said.

'Jesus, what a figger', Gamboretta said. He was suddenly back
thirty years. 'She gotta tremendous pair-a tits – built like — That's
your *mother?*' Gamboretta stopped filing his nails.

Joe said, 'Her hair is absolutely black, not one lousy grey in it,
but she put on a little weight.'

'I useta take your mother *dancin'*! Shu, do I remember! Then
this bastid – Carmine Napoli – comes down from Naples to do
this job for my boss – changin' the old Villa to a hotel. I understan'
these days it's the fanciest place in Palermo. Villa Igiea. We poor
slobs did the tufo work, but this Napoli – Christ, *he* must be your
old man – he was a specialist in settin' marble.' He put the emery
board back in his pocket. 'Good-lookin' young fella, this Napoli,
looked a lot like you, except he had a big, black moustache, always
workin' with them short, tight trousers an' no shirt, and got them
nice, round muscles. Girls loved them muscles . . . And Annunziata – her old man was Florio's coach-driver – she is always out
there teasin' the men on the job, screamin' at them, laughin' at
them, hollerin' back an' forth, showin' herself off to them, then
the next thing I hear, she run off to Naples with this guy. So that's
your mother, hah? Got fat, hah? How's your father?'

'Like I said,' Joe said, 'he got killed fallin' offa scaffold.'

'Killed!' For a minute Joe had the impression Gamboretta was going to laugh. 'That's bad', he said. 'Bein' a brickie is a tough business. You see how important pertection is?'

'Why don't you come out to the house, let my mother dish you up some of her lasagna, that's her speciality.'

Gamboretta took the envelope with the two thousand dollars and fingered it thoughtfully. 'I tell you what, Napoli. I'll take this for the time being. Then you bring me fifteen thousan' more. Meantime we'll let the job go ahead for a while.'

Joe took the envelope back gently, and Gamboretta made no move to stop him. 'No deal.' Joe held the envelope loosely. 'Seventeen grand is too much. Sure, I'd like to make a deal. But lemme think it over. I'll talk to you again next week. Meanwhile, how much harm am I doing keeping my job going?'

Gamboretta leaned back, squinted sharply. 'Yeah, you ain't doin' too much harm at that. I can wait a week. I just wanna tell you one thing, Napoli. Talkin' about old times. This man Florio was one of these old-time padrones like they don't have no more, not even in Sicily. People were scared out of their skins by him; all he hadda do was drop those eyelids down when he got mad, people pissed in their trousers.

'Well, here in Allenburg I seen plenty of builders thought they was some kind-a small-time padrone like that; but lemme tell you, don't you try bein' one, because there is only one real one in this town and that is Giacomo Gamboretta. I take care of my friends and I take care of anyone ain't my friend, too.'

'A padrone has gotta treat his people decent just to stay where he is', Joe said.

'I love mine', Gamboretta said. 'Like the Statue of Liberty says, They are the crap of the world. They come to me an' they are all mine.'

Fifteen

PASQUALE BACCIO did not have the highest I.Q. in New Jersey, but he had the good sense to know you had to walk a careful line if you were just an everyday brickie, particularly if you were in this country illegally. Waiting outside the Hotel Esplanade's restaurant for Mr. Napoli, he had good reason to think of his father's most succinct advice that foggy morning he had bid farewell to Pasquale on the dock at Messina. 'Hitch your wagon to a winning horse,' his father had said, 'but be sure you do not end up with an eyeful of manure.' These days he had a cautious hand guarding his eyes constantly. If there were some way of getting unhitched from Gamboretta now without being invited to depart for the old country, bag and baggage, oh, he'd like that. This Napoli boy seemed to know how to handle Gamboretta. Pasquale Baccio had a low opinion of most bosses, but this Napoli – oh, yes, he'd agree to shakedown money all right – but he didn't shiver when the great Gamboretta snapped the whip. He was brave and strong, as the lump on Pasquale's jaw testified. And although he surely had things of weight on his mind, young Mr. Napoli seemed to have taken an interest in his boy, Robby, about whom Pasquale was tremendously worried. All those blood transfusions, and now there were no more donors. Pasquale himself had given blood three times. It was not what Doctor Berkman had said, but the way he looked, hiding behind his glasses, always turning away, evading a good, straight look in the eye. And while Pasquale told his wife there was nothing to worry about, he was frantic himself.

Mr. Napoli emerged from the Esplanade's restaurant, stuffing that white envelope into his breast pocket. 'C'mon, Pasquale,' he said, 'let's go see the boy.'

Robby lay on a cot in the kids' ward at the Allenburg General Hospital, white and small. He was not the child his father knew. 'Is always a bigga, strong boy', Pasquale said apologetically.

The crowded children's ward was attended by two sisters. There must have been a hundred kids there, and Robby looked the worst of the lot. His eyes were sunk into huge pits and his narrow, jaundiced face, his newly-erupted second teeth, looked enormous behind the drawn, pale lips. Joe could not avoid seeing the skeleton beneath the flesh.

'Robby, I want you mitta my boss, Mista Napoli. He's-a the big boss on the job.'

Robby tried to acknowledge the greeting, but he whimpered, 'I wanna go home, Papa, Where's Mama?'

'Mama no can come. You rest. You gonna come home soon, you see.'

But Robby shook his head and swallowed dry. 'I'm never gonna go home', he said in deep discouragement. 'When am I gonna get better? I'm never gonna get better.'

Later, out in the hall, Joe said, 'He's a good kid. Most kids would be bawling all the time. Good kid.'

'Oh, yes.' It was like watching a stone wall crumble. This man who had cruelly conked old Sal in the head with half a dozen bricks now had his nakedness totally exposed. He was a woman under the man's exterior.

'Yessir, he's-a nice-a boy, very good-a boy. He's the only one God give us. We gonna keep.' He tried to smile, but his lips froze.

Joe asked the tall sister if he could see the doctor on the case. 'I'm a friend of the family', he explained.

'You wait here, Pasquale', Joe said.

'Yes, yes, boss', Pasquale said. He sounded relieved. He hated to talk to the doctor.

In the small, sterile cubby, Dr. Geoffrey Berkman turned out to be an even-featured young man with horn-rimmed spectacles and a five-o'clock shadow. He had a soft, slightly full face, almost kind, but still too young for mature sentiment. He questioned Joe about his relationship to the Baccios. 'We wish we could do more for the boy', Dr. Berkman said vaguely. 'Our facilities are extremely limited here.'

'Lookit, Doc,' Joe said, 'this man is a very important part of my organization. I have a deep interest here. He don't have the first idea what disease his kid's got and it worries him. When he worries, it's not good for anyone.'

Dr. Berkman turned away; he nibbled at the eraser of an Eversharp pencil he took from his breast pocket.

'The man is entitled to know what's going on', Joe said.

'The boy, I am sorry to say, has acute leukaemia. I have just never been able to bring myself to tell that to Mr. Baccio.'

'That's bad, hmm?'

'Yes, it's as bad as it can be. We've been able to keep Robby alive from day to day with a dozen blood transfusions, but we're no longer able to get donors. His father's given him three pints in the last ten days. We can't let him give any more, and in any case, transfusions won't help the boy much longer. It's a matter of weeks, maybe days.'

'Leukaemia. What's that exactly?'

'It's a form of cancer, Mr. Napoli.'

'Cancer? A little kid like that?'

'It's not uncommon in children.'

'Jesus!' Joe crossed himself. 'Maybe I could give the kid some of my own blood.'

'If you have the right type, I suppose you could. It might keep him going that much longer.'

'You want to see if I've got the right type?'

'Sit right here.'

While the young resident busied himself extracting a sample from the large vein in the crook of his arm, Joe thought of Pasquale Baccio and his boy. It was exactly the worst thing he had ever come across in his entire life. Joe Napoli, still childless, could imagine only one thing worse than losing a father, and that was losing a son. Jesus, you take Pop and me; that's all he lived for. Take that away —

'You absolutely sure about this, Doc?'

The doctor said, 'I'll send this down to the lab. You want to wait?'

'Yah, I'll be out in the hall.'

Pasquale was waiting in the corridor like a kid who had got lost. His head was cocked and he looked hopefully at Joe with great brown, wet eyes. Joe put his arm about Pasquale's shoulder. 'You and the Missus have gotta pray for that boy, Pasquale. Your boy is gonna go to heaven. You've gotta get the Missus ready for that.'

'He nidda more blood', Pasquale said. 'I gonna give him more blood.'

'No, no, Pasquale, listen to me. You can't. They won't let you. If my blood is the right kind, I'll give him some of mine. What you have to do, you've got to pray.'

Pasquale closed his eyes. 'Pray? I'm-a pray all day. All night.

Whatta you *think?*' He shook his head and began to mumble. 'You no tell Pasquale the truth. You no tell-a the truth. You like all the boss. You lie.'

There were tears on his cheeks and he shook his head as the tears rolled down. 'Robby gonna be okay. What's-a the matter with him? I'm-a surprise at you, Mr. Napoli, you wanna give-a you own blood but you no wanna tell-a the truth.'

Joe touched his shoulder and Pasquale was too tired even to pull away successfully.

'I'm-a sorry you no help-a me, Mista Napoli. I better go home. I talk-a to my wife. We get a *specialist*. We gonna fix up.' Without warning he was sobbing uncontrollable deep-throated sobs, hugging Joe for support. Joe felt the tears in his own eyes. Injustice was loose in the world. There was so much that could not be understood. Talk to the priests about it. They know as much about it as Robby in there. Exactly zero. Joe pulled away, took out his handkerchief, blew his nose, wiped his eyes, and then did the same for Pasquale, as if his shop steward were a two-year-old infant. 'Come on, Pasquale, come on.'

Dr. Berkman came by briskly. 'Mr. Napoli, we're in luck. You've got Type A positive, same as the boy.'

Joe felt a trace of exultation in the doc's voice. 'There's so damn little we can do', the young man said. 'It's a relief to do almost anything.'

'I'll be right back', Joe called to Pasquale. 'I'm just going in to give Robby some of my blood.'

They lay three feet apart, facing each other, emaciated Robby Baccio and Joe, not saying anything while the doctor and nurse studied the pressure gauges. There was no sensation. For Robby, it was old stuff. He lay still, a veteran of a dozen blood transfusions, waiting for it to be over. 'Thanks', he said weakly, when Joe got off the bed, as if Joe had brought him some kind of toy.

On the steps of the hospital, Joe waved to Pasquale and headed for the trolley. 'Thanks for you blood, Mista Napoli', he heard Pasquale's tired voice through the dark. '*Grazie.*'

'*Pregor*,' Joe said. He felt faintly light-headed as he walked in the dusk.

Sixteen

'TONY? Joe Napoli. How you, y'old bastid?'

'Joey, 'ey! Whaddaya know? Long time no see. How long is it, four, five years? Where you callin' from?'

'Home, on the old block, you lousy Jersey mosquito. Listen, Tony, an emergency's come up. *Seriously*. I need a little help.'

'Yeah?' A wariness crept into Tony's voice. Five years was a long time. 'Watcha doin' with yourself, Joey?'

Joe said, 'I'm doing the brickwork on the new A & P warehouse out in Allenburg.' As if that were news to Tony.

'Oh – yeah, I heard somethin' around about that.' Tony heard everything in New Jersey. 'What's-a problem?' Joe thought he detected a curt note.

'You remember old Milt?'

'The Brain? Sure. What become-a him?' Tony's voice was relieved.

'He's studying to be a lawyer', Joe said.

'Hah!' yelled Tony. 'What'd I tell yah? That guy was born a legal beagle! 'Ey, I could use a good lawyer around here', Tony roared. 'I wish the old Brain was out here in Newark. My dumb bastid lawyers don't even know the law o' gravity. I bet Milt knows more than most-a them *already*.'

'Hey, Milt wants to marry my kid sister Luce. You remember Luce?'

'Marry? No bushwa? Luce, lemme see. Little snot-nose kid with all that curly brown hair and big brown eyes? Kinda cute little mutt? Sure, I remember her. Married, Jesus.'

'You think you're the only guy in town can get married? How's Rosalie?'

'Fine, fine.'

'Well, Luce and Milt wanna get married, only you know how it is.'

'How is it?'

'Why, you dumb bastid, Milt is Jewish.'

'Oh, yah. Jesus, I betcher old lady is sore as a big yellow boil, eh?'

'You should have been here!'

'An' how about *his* old lady an' man', Tony said. 'I bet they're goddam mad. Hey, you think maybe I should have a couple-a the boys push his ol' man and ol' lady around a little? A couple-a boots in the ass and tell 'em to leave old Milt marry whoever he wants?'

'No, no', Joe said. 'Milt has no parents, you dumb bastid. They've been dead ten, fifteen years. He lives with this cousin. Broad named Rosel. How about you comin' over before supper an' talkin' to my mother? I need help gettin' her to be sensible. Then afterwards, you and I can go out for supper.'

There was silence at the other end of the phone. Finally Tony said, 'That's a switch. You want I should bring flowers and a violin?'

'You do it, Tony?'

'For you, Joey, for the Brain, anything, boy. Didn't you guys once save my life? Where'll I meetcha?'

'Up my place', Joe said. 'Friday night. And when you get here, be damn sure to say something extra nice about Milt. It'll make my mother feel a hell of a lot better.'

Tony rolled into Ninety-eighth Street two evenings later in a long, black Pierce Arrow limousine, which, except for the triple thick windows, might have belonged to a funeral parlour. He was driven by a small man wearing a chauffeur's cap, eyeglasses and some bulky equipment around his chest. The man spoke in a laryngitic whisper; his name was George Pedula. George was never more than three feet from Tony.

'Mrs. Napoli, long time no see, 'ey? How you been? Joey givin' you any trouble? I hear little Luce is gettin' hitched to Milt Jason. Ain't that the cat's whiskers? You're a lucky woman, Mrs. Napoli. That Milt's a fine boy, salt-a the earth. In fact, he's a genius. I mean, bein' Catholic is nice, but it ain't everything, Mrs. Napoli. Take me, I'm a good Catholic, nice Italian boy, alla that, but you wouldn't want me for a son-in-law would you? I mean, I'm always takin' foolish chances. Right, Joey?'

After half an hour Joe suggested they walk out in the soft evening's summer air, but Tony said he didn't care too much about walking these days, as he was getting very lazy; in fact, he was so lazy he didn't even like to use up his strength driving, which was one of the reasons he had George, so he could relax. Because in this day and age, in order to decide who were your friends and who were no good for you at all, you had to have time to carefully relax and think things over. In fact, it seemed that was the main thing a man had to do was deciding who were the friends he could do business with and who were the people that he dast not have anything to do with whatsoever.

They rode down to a brownstone restaurant in the Fifties – the first speak Joe had seen, complete with peep-hole. Inside the fat greeter grinned when he recognized Tony Ferrara. The fancy waiters in red boleros and the head waiter in a tuck couldn't do enough for Tony or his friend, Joe Napoli, or even George, who sat at a different table by himself, three feet away, keeping a friendly eye on one and all, with the one hand always in his coat pocket. Tony took half a dozen beers and ate a dozen clams, small, slimy globs which positively disgusted Joe; and after that they both had fine steak dinners with spaghetti, and talked about old times on Ninety-eighth Street and DeWitt, and Joe filled Tony in on Milt and Luce. But there was no mention of the city of Allenburg, New Jersey, or Gamboretta or the job or what Tony was doing with himself these days.

The owner of the place, a short Russian named Jack, rammed Tony on the back and pointed out Jimmy Walker a few tables away, and said he hoped Tony would be in again soon. The Mayor grinned and waved and called, Hello, Tony.

Joe admired the way Tony was treated, not having to pay for the meal, knowing the Mayor, and particularly the way he had been able to stuff away those slimy clams. Some day, he thought, he would be able to do that and make it look as though he was having a good time, but his stomach was not up to trying it yet.

When coffee came, Joe took the plunge. 'The way I hear it, Tony, you got all of New Jersey wrapped in one hand', he said casually.

'Oh,' Tony said, 'I'm lucky, that's all. I took up with bad companions, that's the secret a my success. An' I ain't afraid a fight. You wanna come out to Jersey wit' me, Joey? The ol' combination – Ferrara an' Napoli?'

It was a totally unexpected invitation. 'I'm so goddam busy', Joe said. 'Right now I couldn't.'

'Yah, it ain't for you', Tony said, and his face clouded.

'You must be doin' great', Joe said. 'When I went out to Allen-burg to see this Gamboretta, absolutely just mentioning your name, it was like hitting the lucky gumball. The bastid lit up. Only trouble is he still wants twenty grand.'

'*What?*' Tony was shocked and shaken. 'Are you *kiddin'*? Twenty grand? For *what*? He told me — Why, that son-of-a-bitch.'

'He cut it to seventeen as a special favour because he knew my mother when they were kids in Palermo. This man is as sharp as a cracker and twice as crummy, Tony.'

'That son-of-a-bitch', Tony repeated, as if he were dazed. 'Seventeen grand. Whaddaya know.'

'I'm a soft-hearted guy', Joe said. 'If it's something he needed that would be one thing. Be glad to help the old bastid out. But if he thinks he's got that kinda dough coming, that's a hundred per cent different idea.'

A girl blues singer began, 'St. Louis woman —' but they paid no attention to her.

'This Gamboretta is a most humorous character', Tony said thoughtfully over the music. 'He gives me one big laugh after the other. Like he goes around telling one and all he owns the City of Allenburg, New Jersey, for instance, like he bought it. Anyone in their right mind knows it's ridiculous, owning a city. Cities gotta be held on to. Well, whaddaya expect? This man is uneducated. He never been to DeWitt Clinton; he never read history like the Battle a Saratoga, the Battle a Verdun, the Battle a Waterloo, all that crap. That's a big advantage I got over him. I'm up on the fall a Rome. Boy, did *those* bastids think they had it bought! All over Jersey nowadays I'm always runnin' into some wise guy thinks he has bought himself a city, and along comes someone else with a couple a trusty friends and zippo! Unbought. Another thing, you ever look in his eyes? Well, you look in his glass eye he looks like Honest John; but if you look in the one which works, you see it's shifty. And I do not like it once I find out that his honest eye is made a glass. 'Ey, *George*.'

George hurried over from his table a few feet away.

'George, I want to see Hutch over our place in the morning. Call him.'

'Hutch?' George smirked unhappily.

'George don't like to leave me alone', Tony said. 'He's afraid he takes his eyes offa me, somethin' will happen. I'm kinda his baby.

Anything happens to me, he's out of a job, eh, George?' He leaned across to George, winked, then sat back. 'Joey, have a beer. Jesus, don't this beer remind you a the days we useta get Scummy drunk? Them were the days, Joey, ya know that? We didn't appreciate them days. Ya know I ain't had a friend like you or the Brain since then? Dog eat dog. It's a lousy life. Here's to Ninety-eighth Street.'

Joe couldn't help smiling. Tony was beginning to remember Ninety-eighth Street as some kind of paradise.

Tony put the beer on the table and straightened up suddenly, as if he had made a decision. 'I tell ya, Joey, we don't have to stand for this glass-eyed nut out there. We can get ridda him, no trouble at all. You just say the word. What the hell, I owe you one, don't I?'

Joe looked from Tony to George and back again. They both looked thoroughly comfortable but alert. He could not believe what he thought Tony meant.

'How d'you mean?' he asked quietly. 'Rid of him?'

'He stops givin' you trouble. He stops givin' everyone trouble. As a matter of fact, he ain't much smarter than my old Scummy. This guy should grow like a carrot, underground. There's a masons' union out there. Once he's out of it, we'll clean it up, run it right, put the proper man in there. A decent, upstanding guy who knows the right people from the wrong people.'

Joe decided against asking any more questions. Tony's business was his own. If he was planning any premeditated violence on One-eyed Gamboretta, Joe did not want any part of it. Perhaps all Tony had in mind was a peaceful rigged election.

'I think life would be easier,' he said at last, 'without Mister Whozis, if you know some way of getting him out of that local. But I'll let you know definitely in a coupla days.'

'That's a funny thing about you, Joey. No rules. Accordin' to the notes on the sheet music, this one-eyed monster already commits suicide. But you do not play by the notes, you play a hundred per cent by ear.' Then Tony said, 'Have a beer, Joey.' It was difficult to tell whether Tony had insulted or complimented him. Was he calling him an unprincipled bastid again?

Joe noticed that George sat back and slumped comfortably in his chair and a cloud descended over his slumbrous eyes.

Even though Joe knew that with Rino Sacchi running the entire job without him, there would be a million louse-ups out there, he

was sure this development was important enough to see Jock
Dennison. Jock was friendly as ever; in fact, he treated Joe like
some kind of child prodigy, as if he were Jock Dennison's personal
boy genius.

'Sit down, Joe. Have a cigar. What's on your mind?'

'Jock, the first day I came in here, you asked me about the locals
out there.'

'Yes, of course, I remember. I mentioned the ring, and the union
problems, and you said you had the situation under control.'

'Yah. Well, control was maybe not the word. This Gamboretta
out there is a one-eyed Siciliano bastid. He's famous all up and
down Jersey. He asked me for twenty grand, Jock. Twenty grand
is a lot of jack. So I says to him, you're an old friend of my mother's,
used to take her dancing in the old country, all that crap. So he
becomes a slobbering, sentimental idiot, and offers to cut it to
seventeen gees. I figure to give him two, so you can see we have
quite a gap. Then I meet my old friend Tony Ferrara, who I think
has some kind of hold on this guy; in fact, I wouldn't be surprised
if Tony has control of all the labour unions out there, and he is a
real old friend of mine. In fact, once I saved Tony's life. So Tony
says, "Why don't I get rid of this so and so One-eyed Gamboretta?"
And frankly, Jock, I am not exactly a hundred per cent sure what
he means. He says it is entirely up to me and once we get rid of
him, we'll have absolutely no more trouble with the Allenburg
local. I should just give him the word.'

Jock Dennison sat entranced. 'That's fascinating', he said. 'That's
what I like about you, Joe. Nothing like this ever happens to me.
What does your friend mean? You know it sounds like they've
got a corrupt situation out there.'

'What they got is absolutely one goddam cesspool of a situation',
Joe said. 'It's absolutely one hundred per cent murder in the first
degree.'

'What do you want me to tell you?' Jock Dennison said gently,
his watery eyes steady on Joe's deep blue ones.

'Should I tell Tony to get rid of this bum?' Joe said. 'It'll make
it a helluva lot easier to do the job.'

Jock Dennison stood behind his desk, his thin frame towering
over Joe. 'How does he plan to get rid of him?'

'I don't know', Joe said. 'Make him walk the plank, for all I
know,' He said it as a joke. 'Maybe have an election and vote him
out. I don't have the foggiest idea.'

'There *is* a difference, you know', Jock Dennison said, then grimaced like a man under pressure. 'I tell you, Joe, I don't think I ought to get mixed into this. I mean, you're the brick contractor. Do whatever you think is best.'

Well, Jock, you're as much help in the decision department as an overcoat. 'It's okay with you?'

'I'm indifferent, put it that way. They're all animals, these people. And in my position I have to steer clear of this sort of thing. I have complete confidence that one way or another you'll get your job done, and do it damned well.'

Joe called Tony that afternoon. 'Tony, what the hell can we do to get this Allenburg local straightened out?'

'I'll think a somethin', Joe. Leave it to me.'

At 10.22 on the following Friday morning, Giacomo Gamboretta was shot twice in the abdomen and five times in the chest by a man with a Tommy gun in a fast-moving Pierce Arrow limousine, just as Gamboretta was coming out of the Hotel Esplanade Grill, and he was dead on arrival at the Allenburg General Hospital. The killer was not apprehended then or later.

When Joe heard the news on the shanty radio, he felt as if someone had slammed into him, as if he were the one who'd been shot. He sat staring at the Fada radio, and then for the first time in his life he was sick to his stomach. Weak and wretched, he sat in the shanty looking at Milt, neither of them saying a word. Each was thinking his separate thoughts, although they both thought of Tony, their old buddy Tony. It was one thing to go up to Harlem looking for Black Owls and trouble, but Jesus, Mary and Joseph! Joe could picture Gamboretta in his spotless linen suit, lying in a pool of his own blood at the entrance to the Esplanade. There are things you know with your mind and things you know in your gut. Joe had never really anticipated this in his gut.

A little after two in the afternoon, two city detectives showed up at the shanty. They were not bad guys, polite and all. The old, tired-looking one was almost fatherly.

'You heard about brother Gamboretta?' he said.

'Yah', Joe said. 'Jesus.'

'You had some trouble with him?'

'Nah. No trouble. He was trying to get me to use more local men. But I brought my own men from New York, I consider better bricklayers, that's my opinion, but any special trouble? No. An everyday argument, part of the business. No strike, nothing of that kind. Happens every day.'

'You been away from the job this morning?'

'You kidding? I'm here six o'clock every day, if I turn my back these guys'll start tearing the building down. I leave four-thirty in the afternoon.'

The two detectives exchanged glances. 'You a friend of Ferrara's?' the young one said.

'Tony? Yah. So's he.' Joe jerked his thumb towards Milt. 'From way back. We were kids on the same block.'

'Mind if we talk to your men?'

'Go ahead. But don't keep 'em from laying brick. These guys get fourteen bucks a day.'

The two detectives wandered out of the shanty, and Joe saw one of them talk to Sal. Sal nodded. That Joe was in the shanty all morning, exactly nine million people would swear to, because he was.

Joe took the envelope with the two grand from his pocket and handed it to Milt. 'Give this back to Gravel Larson next time he shows', he said.

Son-of-a-bitch asking for seventeen gees. No wonder he gets shot. It could've been anyone. He noticed Milt looking at him funny. Milt Jason couldn't get off the Doty squad. He should've been absolutely at least an Eagle Scout. After all, every word he'd told Tony Ferrara about Gamboretta had been the unvarnished truth. If Tony had taken a notion . . . Tony must've had other reasons . . . his own reasons . . . Maybe he wasn't getting his cut. The rules in that business were not written anywhere, but they were strict. And Tony was a man of principle and rules, especially those he wrote himself. Not in his wildest dreams had he thought . . . Anyhow, maybe it wasn't Tony at all . . .

Maybe the job ought to be closed down out of respect to the passing of a distinguished labour leader. He decided to consult his shop steward, Pasquale Baccio. Baccio, Milt said, was not on the job. His kid, Robby, had taken a turn for the worse and Pasquale had been at the hospital all day. So Joe made the decision alone: no work Monday. The men were to attend Gamboretta's Requiem Mass at St. Francis' in Allenburg. He told Little English and Rino, and the word passed.

That afternoon, just before four, he called the hospital and was told that little Robby Baccio had passed away during the morning. It was a great day for the Old Reaper all round.

Almost a thousand men and women, including the tall, aristocratic mayor, Harold Brice, followed the coffin bearing the remains of Giacomo Gamboretta out of St. Francis' Church. Giacomo lay dead in there, clean-shaven, powdered, dressed in a white linen suit, wearing a gold watch on a gold chain, dressed in every detail to match his secret and hated hero, Signor Vicenzo Florio of the Villa Igiea, Palermo. After the Mass, Joe Napoli, alone, of all those who had attended the funeral, waited in the church while at the entrance one sleek Pierce Arrow after another, each holding seven black-suited men, followed the flower-covered hearse in sombre procession. For the twenty minutes Joe waited, he observed first each of the images of the saints and finally that of the Son on the Cross, as he considered the fate of Giacomo Gamboretta and speculated on the portions of his catechism which he knew by heart and which now rambled through his mind:

'The Seventh Commandment of God is that Thou Shalt Not Steal.

'What are we commanded by the Seventh Commandment?

'By the Seventh Commandment we are commanded to respect what belongs to others, to live up to our business agreements and to pay our just debts.

'What does the Seventh Commandment forbid?

'Besides stealing, the Seventh Commandment forbids cheating, unjust keeping of what belongs to others, unjust damage to the property of others and the accepting of bribes by public officials.'

Giacomo Gamboretta had asked Joe for a bribe and no doubt in his time had accepted plenty. He had knocked hell out of the Seventh Commandment of God. He got his, and he would get it worse where he was going, regardless of how hard the priests who had just served his Requiem Mass tried to put in a good word for him.

He stared at the spot where the corpse of Gamboretta had been lying a few minutes earlier, powdered, solitary and still. Joe Napoli had not pulled the trigger, he had perhaps not understood the precise intentions of friend Tony. Joe was shocked, yes; nevertheless, he knew he was the author of this death. Suddenly he felt wildly, feverishly elated, he saw himself in a euphoric hallucination – invincible. A man had to act . . . or he would inevitably become the victim of a series of accidents. Life would be forged for him instead of by him. The world was a jungle, and the best survived. This elation, this sweet self-knowledge was for himself only. It was too dark a truth ever to be shared with anyone. And yet he did not feel an undetected impostor. The destruction of One-eyed Gamboretta was an exhilarating opportunity. It set him beyond the rules, and now he would have to make the most of it, not only for himself, but for all his men, for whom now he truly felt a saviour's zeal and affection. He felt damn near holy.

The door to the anteroom at the right of the altar opened, interrupting his thoughts, and two men wheeled in a small white coffin. The lid was open and one of the men placed a wreath of flowers by it. Joe walked down to look; the small, pale, waxen emaciated face of Roberto Baccio stared back at him. The immaculate blue serge suit made the boy look even younger than he was, as if he were going to First Communion. Joe stepped into the second row and knelt. He closed his eyes, and felt the tears of his own sadness. In the name of the Father, the Son, and the Holy Ghost, protect the soul of Robby Baccio. Bring him peace and Grace. He opened his eyes in a mute appeal to the image of the Son.

Down the main aisle, Pasquale Baccio and his wife, dressed in their gloomy best, walked uncertainly to the front row. From the back of the church Joe saw Dr. Berkman slip inconspicuously into a rear seat. Including the priest, Joe, an altar boy, and one attendant, seven persons were present in the church with Robby. A thousand empty seats yawned behind them. Pasquale Baccio saw Joe, turned and nodded gravely.

The priest made the sign of the cross at the foot of the altar. '*In nomine Patris, et Filii, et Spiritus Sancti . . .*'

Why wouldn't Pasquale Baccio be the ideal man to succeed Giacomo Gamboretta as the president of the local masonry union? It was an inspiration. He must talk to Tony about it. Where Gamboretta had been bad, Pasquale was good, the salt of the earth. And Joe loved him, because, as he had once helped Tony, he had also given his blood for Pasquale Baccio out of the depth of a full heart. It would be a tremendous thing to see Pasquale get a break.

Seventeen

THE Building Trades Council in Allenburg had one hall where on different nights each of the locals held their meetings; it was on the rickety second floor over Hugh's Billiard Parlour on Mott Street. It was bare as a rabbit hutch and bathed in semi-darkness, its most useful attribute, since speakers frequently found it safer to do their bellowing from the shadows. From the moment this meeting of the masons' local opened, a tack piano next door could be heard endlessly banging out 'Me and My Shadow'.

The chairman of this meeting of Local 312 was brother Tony Ferrara, who was ponderously introduced by the overblown Carpenter President, Chairman of the Building Trades Council, brother Newman. He presented Tony to the two-hundred-odd brother masons shifting suspiciously on their folding chairs, benches, window sills, or standing ominously in the rear, wondering who the hell was Tony Ferrara.

Brother Tony, wearing an open-necked, checked sports shirt, rose with lithe grace to speak, and Joe, sitting in the rear of the hall beside Milt, noted the impatient stirring in the crowd. He and Milt exchanged sidelong glances. Suddenly, before Tony could get out his first word, a high-pitched, quavering voice called nervously from the shadows.

'You a member of this local, Mr. Ferrara?'

Tony smiled slowly and spoke in his low, bull voice. 'Who ast that?'

No response.

'C'mon fellas. Leave us see who you are. This is an open meeting. A wide open meeting.'

The fat carpenter delegate rose and said, 'Mr. Ferrara come over here from International to help youse guys get reorganized. I think youse all oughta give him your thousand per cent co-operation. He is the chairman of this here meetin'.'

The high-pitched voice, more querulous than before: 'Are you Anthony Ferrara, the bootlegger?'

There was a moment of reflection. The querulous voice was emboldened to add, 'This guy is one a them strong-arm artists! Are we gonna have that crowd take over the local?' The owner of the voice rose from the shadows for emphasis. He was a tall, lean young man.

A scuffling began. The man next to the heckler slammed his folding chair and flung it into space. In the clatter and bellowing that followed, two lithe men strode with incredible swiftness from their seats, shoving everyone out of their way; before anyone could do or say anything, one of them had hit the querulous heckler a stunning clout below the eye, and the man went down, with a surprised grunt. His two assailants promptly dragged him, kicking and twisting, from the room. 'Get your hands offa me!' The clattering sound of his body falling down the long, narrow flight of stairs over his shout of outrage filled the hall. The clodding footsteps of his two assailants followed him downstairs. Someone else threw a pop bottle which fell to the floor with an ominous clatter.

'Don't anyone else leave yet, fellas', Tony said gently to half a dozen men who had started for the door. 'Not till we get this settled, anyways. Come to order, men. If you please.'

A huge slob had planted himself at the door to add conviction to the advice from the Chairman.

'We don't want trouble', Tony said. 'This is an open meeting. All we ast is you guys act polite and decent and give us your kind attention.'

He had it now. Tony proceeded to tell the men how sad a day it was to him personally and to each of them personally, and in fact to the entire American Federation of Labour personally, that One-eyed Gamboretta had met his untimely end at the hands of some crazed maniac – probably a reactionary contractor, or maybe a relative of one of the hundreds of men he had had deported to Italy, which was one of the bad habits One-eyed had.

'Trouble was,' Tony said, 'maybe Gamboretta was too ambitious.' But they had to understand that if he was ambitious it was not for himself but always for organized labour, and especially for Local 312.

'With this local,' Tony said, raising his voice to the singsong of an operatic aria, 'like with a kingdom, there is no such a thing as

a vacuum. The king is dead, but we're gonna elect a new king right
here, even though it maybe sounds like we got no heart, to hold an
election so fast after – well. We dast not do otherwise, because life
gotta go on. Now the International claims there was stuff goin' on
over here that was kinda lousy. In fact putrid. I don't wanna say
anything about the dead, but they got evidence Mr. Gamboretta
took graft to sell you guys out. Now the International wants no
more a *that*. So they authorized us to appoint a trustee for this local
till we get the situation straightened out. I don't hafta tell you men
what a trustee is. He'll represent the International here. Now I
don't like appointing a trustee any more than you want one. So I
tell you what I wanta do. I'd like you men to elect a trustee of your
own choosin'. Fair enough ?'

Before anyone could respond, he continued. 'The chair will
appreciate any nominations for trustee of Local 312 from the floor
in the regular democratic fashion.'

A hum of confusion and uncertainty filled the hall. No one had
come prepared to nominate anyone for anything. A hand in the
third row shot up.

'What's this trustee stuff ?'

'Don't get yourself in an uproar', Tony said. 'The trustee acts
just till a new slate of officers is elected. Meanwhile he keeps an
eye on everything. That's all. Mr. Drago', Tony said to a raised
hand. 'Mr. Drago got the floor. Quiet, you guys.'

Smiley Drago, former aide-de camp to Giacomo Gamboretta,
stood on his feet and smiled his endless smile.

'As one and all knows,' he said, 'I am an old associate of our dear
departed friend, One-eyed Gamboretta – I have been an apprentice
in this here local since I am old enough to lay brick. It gives me
great honour to nominate the man I know Mr. Gamboretta woulda
voted for if he was here to vote today, and that is none other than
my old friend Pasquale Baccio.'

Almost before he was through, Squint jumped up and roared,
'I second that nomination.'

What had been a hum of uncertainty grew to a staccato of muttering. 'Who the hell is Baccio ?' Pasquale Baccio was not simply a
dark horse, he was an invisible one.

'Mr. Chairman,' called a third purposeful voice, 'I move dat
nominations be closed.'

'I second that', a fourth voice cried quickly.

Slowly Tony said, 'All those in favour a nominations bein'

closed?' Half a dozen shouted yahs rang through the hall; then for a moment the men looked at each other.

Tony lowered his voice almost to a whisper. Slowly he said, 'All those opposed.' Only the shuffle of feet could be heard. 'Nominations closed', Tony called cheerfully.

'Mr. Ferrara!' A red-faced Irishman in the last row was on his feet. Joe had never seen the man before, but his voice had the soft ring of authority. 'Yessir', Tony said.

'Now don't misunderstand me, Mr. Chairman. It's not that I'm an arguin' man, but be damned if I'm not a wee bit up in the air, so to speak. You seem like a fine boy yourself. But might I ask who is the gentleman, this Pasqualey Baccio? I been a member of this local three years, goin' on four, and I've never had the pleasure of meetin' the gentleman. Would he be averse to standin' up and displayin' himself to one and all?'

Tony smiled. 'Stand up, Pasquale, so all the boys can get a good look at ya.' Pasquale stood in the second row, uncertainly shifting his weight from foot to foot.

Several men were beginning to whisper and mutter among themselves. One shouted, 'I don't like this one goddam bit! I'm gettin' outa here.'

A short, fat man lumbered to his feet. 'S-s-s-say', he said, speaking painfully. 'Are we g-g-g-gonna have the s-s-s-same crooks running this local as b-b-b-before?'

'Crooks? Did you say crooks?' Smiley was on his feet and heading for the stutterer.

Two men jumped up on the seats, flanking the fat man in a move to protect him. 'Keep off, Smiley', one of them warned.

Tony said in a ponderous voice, 'Meeting will kindly come to order. Smiley Drago, sit down, you dumb bastid.'

The two men protecting the stutterer were still standing on their seats, scowling, towering over the assemblage. Another Coke bottle went to the wall and crashed. Four or five men began to shout. At that moment anything could have happened to the meeting.

'Mr. Chairman', Joe shouted.

'Shaddap you guys. Man in the back there wants to say somethin'.' There was a moment of expectant silence.

Joe surveyed the two hundred brickies whose faces now turned back towards him. 'A few-a you guys,' he started, 'maybe recognize me. I'm doing the A & P-warehouse job over on Jefferson Street.'

'For Christ sake', someone called. 'Now I seen everything. This guy's a stinking boss. What's *he* doing here?'

'Boss? *Boss?*' Joe screamed. 'I'm a *brickie*!' He slammed his fist into his open palm in white fury, 'Nobody calls me boss. Son of a brickie! Grandson of a brickie! I've been layin' brick since I was thirteen.' He pulled his union work book out of his breast pocket. 'There's my book, wise guy. Laying brick since I'm thirteen.' He flipped the pages and paused to let the sight sink in, then placed it carefully back in his pocket. He took in the puzzled faces, the hostile faces.

'Maybe you guys don't know Pasquale Baccio like I do. He's the steward on my job. One of my New York men got a little outa line tryin' to show how many brick a day he could lay, tryin' to make some of you local men look bad. So we had a little whatzis over there. Yah, you all heard about it. An accident, nothin' too serious, but enough so everyone, includin' me, knew the union was on the job. And who engineered it? I don't wanna mention it in open meeting, but I tell you there's nobody gonna do a better job for the union than Pasquale Baccio. Sure I'd like to make money on my job. But first I'm a brickie even if that means it's gotta cost me something! I want to urge each and every one of you guys to vote for Pasquale Baccio for trustee – for your own damn good.'

Joe started to sit down. Some of the men were far from satisfied. 'What the hell's a boss brickie doing here?'

'Boss?' Joe bellowed. 'You see Pasquale Baccio there? Ask him who's boss and who's brickie! G'wan ask him. You tell him, Pasquale. When your little kid was sick, who came to the hospital to see that boy? I'm not askin' for credit, but I don't like this boss crap. Which one of you bastids came up the hospital? Let's see your hands, brothers.' There was no movement. 'And when God took the poor kid, were all you fine brickies down at the funeral with Pasquale Baccio showing your respect? One brickie was there, and some wise guy is trying to call that brickie *boss*. Lookit Pasquale Baccio sittin' there. He's had it rough, men. Think of your own kids. How'd you like to watch your own kid growing weaker every day? Wasting away until he just breathes his life out. That's somethin' not many men have to take, but Pasquale Baccio hadda take it. I think it's time he had a break, and you men can give it to him. I think it's time we stopped arguing whether this man or that man ever met him before and get together and do the decent thing, the right thing. Do we want to make it any tougher for him than it's already been? *Vote* for him. Why do we have to argue around like a bunch of hard-hearted bastids? Thank you, Mr. Chairman.'

Before anyone else could reply, Tony Ferrara said, 'All those in favour of Pasquale Baccio for trustee of Local 312.' A dozen clear yahs and a scattering of grudging grunts of assent, why the hell not? 'Opposed?' There was no sound except a hacking cough.

'I declare Pasquale Baccio trustee of Local 312 for an indefinite period. The meeting is adjourned.'

From the rear of the hall the Irish brickie's voice cried across the room to a friend like a great amen: 'May the Lord protect me from having Pasquale Baccio fightin' for me rights as a workin' man. And will you have a beer with me, O'Toole?'

'Be damned if I won't', O'Toole cried.

Joe breathed easier as he glanced at Milt. Milt announced he was going home, and left abruptly to catch the Jefferson Street bus.

After the hall had emptied, Tony and Joe went down to the beer joint next to the pool parlour; behind them at a respectful distance trailed Pasquale Baccio and George.

Over beers in the smoky joint Tony and Joe huddled, while Pasquale and George sat at an adjoining table.

"Ey you! What's 'is name again, Joey? *Pasquale?* Hey, Pasquale, come on over here.' Pasquale moved to the table desolately. George stared into space. In a half-mumble Tony was teaching Pasquale his new catechism. 'Okay. Now you understan'? Now whattaya do with collections?'

'Fifty-fifty', Pasquale said like a good mule. 'Half-a to you, half-a to me.'

'Right, and what do you do with your half?'

'Tenna per cent to Squint, tenna per cent to Smiley. Right? Thirty per cent to me.'

'Say, this guy's very bright', Tony said to Joe. 'He gets everything fast.' Pasquale's dull face glowed perceptibly. 'Now, how much you collect?'

'One dollar every thousand brick. Fifty cent a hundred block. Fifty cent every yard-a concritch. Two cent a yard plaster. Okay?'

'This guy's smart enough to teach high school', said Tony. 'I had lots of teachers dumber than you, Pasquale, I swear to Christ. Remember that dumb bitch, Prune-faced Turner, Joe? All she knew was Shakespeare. Now what happens, Pasquale, if you have trouble with one-a these sons-a-bitch bosses?'

'I calla you up.'

'Right. And remember,' Tony said grimly, 'you collect from everybody. General contractors, sub-contractors, no exceptions. Anybody wants-a do masonry in Allenburg, they gotta come across.' He stared grimly at the wall.

'Except me', Joe said in an unusually low voice.

Tony took a long drag of beer.

'Hell', he said, throwing an arm about Joe. 'Hell, everyone except Joe here, that goes without saying. We can't ask Joey for anything. Did you know, Pasquale, Joey once saved my life? Ah, what the hell do you care?' He pulled Joe's head forward so that even Pasquale could not hear, and said into Joe's ear, 'Okay, so *you* own Allenburg. Now don't say I never gave you nothin'.'

Joe said, 'All I want is to be able to do my work and no one should bother me.'

'You got it', Tony said.

'Yes, sir', Pasquale added.

'How about another beer?'

It was Tony who proposed the last toast. 'To the trustee of Local 312, elected with the solid support of the entire rank and file.'

Even Pasquale, who hated beer, drank to that.

Next morning there was a brief meeting of the fifty brickies on the job and Joe stood on a nail keg in the shanty and spoke to them like a Dutch uncle, the cigar always in the corner of his mouth. 'Men, this is a damn fine job. We're getting overtime and all kinds of extras. We ought to get out there and give the job twenty-five, twenty-six hundred brick a day from now on in. If we roof out by September fifteenth, we're going to have one helluva blow-out, men, and I don't mean at the corner candy store.' He winked hugely. 'What's more, there's a bonus if we finish on the fifteenth – a hundred smackers for each one of you guys.' One hundred bucks a man was five thousand bucks – too much dough, but they deserved it if they could do it. He bent to get off the nail keg as the men began to murmur their pleased surprise. Then he changed direction and got back up on the keg. 'Oh, yah. And any man don't put out at least two thousand brick, he's fired.'

The amazing thing was, even the local stumblebums gave him over two thousand a day, and Pasquale Baccio, who put in one last day on the job before assuming his official duties as trustee, which was to look after collections, got over twenty-two hundred, and that was after a helluva lot of beers the night before, and for a man who was in deep mourning. So there was no question that if a brickie wanted to, he could.

When it came to locating the particular hoorhouse in which he would find Francesca and hold the blow-out he had promised the men, Joe could probably have asked the advice of Tony Ferrara, who doubtless had his finger in that pie too. But he couldn't see himself beholden to Tony for that one, so he consulted, instead, Simon Cutler, boy wonder and political man-about-town. Simon offered the information leerfully, along with a brief lecture in comparative hoor appreciation, and Joe settled on an establishment run by a woman Si called Marge the Barge. There were two girls there Si said looked exactly like Clara Bow and Barbara LaMarr. For a grown man Simon was completely dippy on the subject of these Hollywood dames.

Milt accompanied Joe along the tree-lined, sun-mottled block of grey, three-story, porched houses, each scaled by two steep flights of outside steps. The morning was hot, and both young men wore their new straw hats at a jaunty angle. Milt was openly curious at the prospect of seeing a brothel for the first time in his life, but he nodded dutifully when Joe said, 'Remember Milt, you're just going in to look, no touch; I have to protect Luce's interests.' Milt tried a fast impish grin, and ran his tongue over his upper lip.

Marge the Barge opened the screen door herself. She was the shortest two hundred pounds Joe had ever seen. Her powdered jowls billowed over each other in riotous competition. Black, pig eyes crinkled happily at the mention of Simon Cutler and she ushered the two boys into the dark and rancid parlour whose main piece of furniture was a gramophone with a brown metal megaphone horn which had gone out of style fifteen years earlier. The sofa and armchairs were overstuffed and covered in heavily patterned silks and velvets, with purples and browns predominating. Marge spoke with a thick Polish accent in friendly tones clearly inspired by business interest, but also with a tinge of suspicion. Upstairs a shower was running.

'Usually we not open so early, Mista Napoli. We don't expect nobody till 'bout seven, eight clock, but if you an' you friend want, I call down couple nice girl.'

'At eleven o'clock in the morning?' Joe laughed, slapping his thigh.

Marge said, 'I'm not surprise at nutting no more. Last wick was two boy – verr' nice lookin' boy, rich boy – what you think they want? One girl betwinn them – all three in one bed. Such young boy! Where they get such idea?' She shook her head at the increasing decadence of mankind. She added heartily, 'Grown man is different, but such young boy!' She shook herself out of her mental valley of deploration. 'If you no want girl, what I can do for you?' Marge fanned herself and muttered, 'Such hitt, so yumid.' She sat heavily on the sofa and picked up what had looked like a cushion but which, as his eyes accustomed themselves to the darkness, Joe now saw was a large grey cat. Marge's fingers clawed lovingly into the fur and she never left off petting the animal, which kept its eyes closed and purred noisily.

'Is only boy in house', the madam said, looking at the cat. 'That's why all my girl spoil him. Fidd him liver, fidd him fish, everything he like. Look on him. He fetter than me.' Her fingers worked the skin beneath the fur lovingly. 'Okay, boys, what you want? Spick op.'

'How many girls you got, Marge?' Joe said.

'What you minn? Four girl here steady, live with me opstair. We also got couple girl come here when we nidd. You friend, Mr. Cutler, he know them.'

'Six girls. How does that sound, Milt? Enough? We don't want to run out of girls.'

Milt frowned judiciously. 'Sounds about right. I don't know too much about this kind of operation.'

'I got around fifty men workin' for me', Joe said. 'We get done workin' around four o'clock. I thought maybe I'd bring them over here for a party after work. Maybe September seventeenth. Friday. Next Friday.'

'Fifty man!' Marge the Barge was deeply troubled, but her jaws began to work with expectation.

'Oh, they're a nice quiet bunch. All they want is a few jokes, couple of drinks, and a chance for a little tune-up with a girl.'

'Mista Napoli, we gotta nice quiet place here. We don't want no trouble with the neighbours, you know. Big party with fifty man – my goodness, Mista Napoli, is gonna be terrible mess.'

'Oh, I don't think so. You think it'll be a whatzis, Milt?'

'I shouldn't think so,' Milt said carefully, 'not if the girls behave themselves.'

Joe slapped his thigh and roared. 'Yah! Marge, you worry about your girls and let me worry about my men.'

'You look like pretty young fella. You got fifty man work for you?' Marge said doubtfully.

Joe took out his cigar and lit it. 'Please, Marge, I got over a *hundred* men working for me. Show her the time book, Milt.'

Milt dutifully pulled the time book out of his back pocket and flipped the pages of names and hours at Marge.

'I'm only taking care of my own boys. Some men don't mean a thing to me or I to them. But to some of those guys I'm like their old man. I got a duty to see they have the best of everything.'

'Gonna come in afternoon?'

'That's what I figured', Joe said. 'Afternoons you're not doing much anyhow. Now this party has to be good, Marge. The day before I'm gonna deliver maybe fifty, sixty bottles of wine. You feed it to these guys for free. Everything's free to them. You got that? You and I will fix up a price for everything, but for them, everything's free. You follow me?'

'Why not?' Marge said. 'So long as price is good for Marge and girls.'

'Okay. That takes care of the free wine. Now the music. Most of these guys are crazy for music. You got any Italian songs?'

Marge's brow wrinkled. 'I got "Varsity Dreg" and "Charleston". Gotta nice polka.'

'They're okay. I'll bring a few songs, maybe a couple of tarantellas. Those girls a yours know how to dance?'

Marge shrugged. 'I guess maybe, why not?'

'Another thing – I like one of the girls to walk around naked.'

'What you talkin'? You crazy?'

'I mean she don't have to do anything special – she can act completely natural. Have a few drinks and all with the boys, only just so long as she's a hundred per cent naked.'

'But why? My girl don' do that. My girl nice girl.'

'I think it would be a good idea. What do you think, Milt?'

Milt thought it over. 'Oh, I think it would be very nice', he said.

'See, Marge, I want this to be something these guys are never gonna forget. If a girl walks around naked all the time, maybe dances with a couple of guys, gives them a chance to hold on to her real good, they aren't gonna forget it. Tune-ups a dime a dozen. If these guys live to be two hundred and ninety, they gotta be able to say, "Remember the time Joey Napoli took us over to Marge the Barge? Was that a night!" And it's gotta *be* that kind of night. Naked. Maybe a pair of shoes, so's she won't get splinters.'

'I dunno —'

'It's a sight I'd never forget myself, and I'm the absolute normal. How about you, Milt?'

'I doubt I'd forget it', Milt said slowly. 'Only I'm sorry I came with you. I'd rather have been surprised.'

'That reminds me', Joe said abruptly. 'Whozis here's engaged to my sister. If you let one of your broads get near him, I'll get my friend Tony Ferrara to close the entire joint up. This guy is pure virgin, understand? Don't let the girls get a hand on him.'

'Such a shame', Marge said to Milt sympathetically. 'Virgin. Terrible shame, poor boy.'

'Now this naked *bambolina* – she won't want to show up right away. First, the boys ought to have a few bottles of wine, little music, like that. Everyone gets happy. Maybe half an hour after we get here – then she shows up. She comes down the stairs real slow. She doesn't have to say a word. It's — Jeez, I feel like a film producer. You understand one word I'm talking about?'

'Oh, I think', Marge said, somewhat doubtfully.

'Okay,' Joe said, 'now let's have a look at the girls.'

'Ruthie!' Marge called, and set the cat down. 'Estelle, Blanchie, Willow.' She had waddled to the foot of the stairs and was shouting upward. 'Come on, leddies, shake a leg.'

The shower upstairs stopped and in a few moments a tall and a short girl clattered down in high-heeled shoes and kimonos. The tall one wore a towel turban wrapped around her head. After them a blonde came running barefoot, two steps at a time like a kid, wearing a middy blouse and one of those straight pleated skirts that made her seem eighty per cent waist. She had a pouty, tiny bow mouth, almost insolent, but more like a child's than a woman's. Joe did not notice what the fourth girl was wearing because all he saw was that she was Negro. If any of these girls looked like Clara Bow or Barbara LaMarr, Joe Napoli was Fatty Arbuckle. But the middy blouse kid tickled the hell out of him.

He tugged Marge aside into the shadows of the dining-room and leaned close to her heavy face. 'The Black Owl. I don't want her when my men come.'

'Why not? She good girl.'

Joe glared at her.

'She do things others no do.'

'I wouldn't care if she stood on her head in Macy's window. I don't want my men getting mixed up with her.'

'Okay. If that how you like.'

'That's how I like. Tell them to take their clothes off so we can pick out the one we want.'

'I don't think they gonna like.'

'Sure they will, Marge, if you ask them. Why not?'

She led the way back to the foot of the stairs, where the girls were smiling at Milt. 'Mista Napoli gonna bring fifty men here for party next Friday afternoon', Marge announced. 'Want one girl should walk around bare. So now he want to see which one got right figure.'

'Golly damn, *quelle folle idée*', the barefoot girl pouted. 'The living end.'

The girls looked hesitantly at one another.

'Is all right, girls', Marge coaxed.

'They both doctors anyhow, I suppose', the black one said, and without hesitation unhooked her jersey dress and pulled it over her head. She had a firm, compact figure. Milt's eyes bulged behind his glasses as the Negress grinned, swinging her hips and running the back of her right hand over her left breast. The other girls giggled. The two with kimonos opened them up, holding their arms aloft like birds but not removing their kimonos. The tall one was too skinny. The short one had a pleasant upper half, but her legs were heavy and short. The barefoot girl in a single motion stepped out of her skirt and pulled the middy blouse over her head. Joe knew at once she was it. Although still not too much girl, she was rounder and fuller than she had seemed. He noticed for the first time that she had a voluptuous oval face, a broad nose, and wide, slanting eyes. Her heavy lips in a pout made her suddenly sullen.

'Okay, boys?' the Negress said sarcastically. 'Seen everything?'

'What's the hurry?' Joe said, 'I hate to rush things. You – walk up the end of the room. Whozis there.' He jerked his thumb at the barefoot girl. The others covered up unhurriedly. 'Congratulations, Miss America', the tall kimono girl said. 'Congratulations, dearie', the coloured girl said. The barefoot remained expressionless. 'The man speaks haughty, *n'est-ce-pas?*' she said. 'I have to walk around b.a. in front of fifty gents?' she said. 'Yay, team, and razzmatazz. What kind of work do they do, *mon petit cher?*'

'Bricklayers', Joe said.

'Oh, no,' she said, 'if that's not the living end. I don't know

G

whether my complexes could stand it. How much tip would I get?'

'Don't worry,' Marge said, 'leave business to Marge.'

'Not a nickel less than fifty', the girl said. 'Suppose one of my regular friends comes in? Some of my friends are jealous wild cats, *bêtes folles*, and you know it, Marge.'

'Maybe Marge should walk around b.a.!' short kimono said. 'They'd see a lot more for the money.' The girls giggled and Marge smiled good-naturedly. 'They good kids', she said happily to Joe. 'Like my own dutter.' She jutted her chin towards the dining-room and led the way there, Joe and Milt following docilely. 'Toodley-oo, darling', Middy-blouse called.

'How much you gonna pay?' Marge said abruptly, and before Joe could answer, 'Fifty men, usually is five dolla for each. For naked girl is at list twenty-five. And music also extra. Let's see – here —' She sat and jotted figures on a pad on the dining-room table. 'Two hundred eighty dolla.' Marge the Barge was as wacked up as a fruit cake, hallucinations of grandeur.

'Too much,' Joe said, 'I'm bringing my own wine, my own records. You said yourself you don't usually do business till seven, eight o'clock. This party'll be over by seven. It's all found money. Tell you what. A hundred and sixty bucks.'

It was the right figure, close enough to be acceptable, not so low that Marge the Barge would refuse to do business.

'Leave out naked girl, is okay.'

'No deal.'

'One hundred seventy-five dolla is better. You want girls should be happy? Should be good party? So nobody ever gonna forget? Everybody laugh, drink, be happy?'

'Okay, Marge, you got a deal – a hundred seventy-five. You're a pretty smart girl, Marge. Half you get now, half after the party. Okay?'

'Is okay wit' me.'

'Couple more things. The dresses these girls are wearing – Jesus – they are awful. You know any place you can rent real duzie dresses? Maybe gold or red?'

'Sure. Nice place in Trenton.'

'How much it cost to rent a fancy dress?'

Marge hunched her shoulders. 'Maybe six, eight dolla each one.'

'Okay. Forty dollars more for the dresses, but they gotta be beautiful. Slinky. And get the kids to a beauty shop. Get their hair

combed. Stick some flowers around the place. Jeez, if I was runnin'
this joint, there'd be a few improvements. And how about perfume? Not some cheap crap, get the best. One small bottle, but let
the girls sprinkle themselves good. I want the whole room to *smell*
like a hoorhouse. Including Miss America.'

'Good perfume cost lotta money.'

'One bottle ten bucks. Real French whatzis. Remember.'

'How much that make?' Marge asked.

Joe calculated in his head. 'Two twenty-five. Give the young
lady one hundred and twelve bucks and fifty cents, Milt.'

Milt took his payroll envelope from his pocket and counted the
money out deliberately.

The girls who had turned on the gramophone were at the arch
now between dining-room and parlour, ogling the boys. 'Anyone
in a mood to dance?' Middy-blouse said. She smiled and looked at
Joe.

'Why you no go opstair with Willow?' Marge said. 'She like
you.'

'Willow? Who gave you that name, honey?'

'Not my mother, *mon petit;* she gave me my face and figure, my
fortune; but my good name, dear my lord, is my own, my own.
Remember the little birdie who sits and cries so sadly, Titwillow, titwillow? I just kept the willow. I can't *stand* vulgarity.'

'The day when we come,' Joe said, 'your name's gonna be
Francesca.'

'Francesca? Francesca what?'

'Who the hell cares – Francesca Smith.'

'What for?'

'Never mind. Just be Francesca, hear? I'll write it down for you.
Memorize it. There's one fella in particular, he's got his eyes out
for this girl named Francesca and he's been kinda building her up in
his mind, so you keep your eyes out for him. Sal his name is. Treat
him right.'

'Sal? Sounds like a she-girl.'

'Salvatore.'

She put up two fingers in a Girl Scout's oath. 'On my honour, I
will do my best. God and country, and all that. Oh, *quelle idée
drôle, drôle*. I could die. Is he nice?'

'Sal? He's the best. I'm serious. Personally, I think this will be
his first experience. So that's a break for you.'

'Oh, how sweet. I'll look forward.'

'Okay, Francesca?'

'Why not?'

'Why you no take Willow opstair?' Marge urged, counting the money for the fourth time. 'She like you.' She licked her fore-finger to tally the bills more easily. 'Is with compliments of the house.'

'Her name is Francesca, Marge; keep it in mind. I never even heard of Willow.'

'Yeah. Francesca, okay. You a crazy boy. Have it your own way. You want go up?'

'Why not?' He took her elbow. 'Now listen, kid, remember I'm a touchy guy, very sensitive.' He turned to Milt. 'You watch yourself now. Act your age. Don't start anything the minute my back is turned. I'm serious.'

To the girls he said, 'He's engaged to my sister. Keep an eye on him.'

As they started towards the stairs, Willow chattered, holding his hand like a child. 'Do you parla Italiano? I'm studying it, but honestly, these kids, I tell you, signore, non possono parlare one word, not one. It's the most hopeless.'

'Willow – uh, Francesca – verr' smart girl', Marge the Barge called after them. 'Study all the time.'

'I try to improve myself every day', the girl said softly to Joe. 'In every way.'

He put his arm around Francesca's thin waist, tramped noisily up the stairs beside her, thinking that in spite of the natural reaction of his flesh in these surroundings, and in the face of the stimulation which had already been provided at his own request, he was first and foremost doing a thorough reconnaissance job for fifty loyal men. They were entitled to the finest money could buy.

Eighteen

'NAPOLI! Hey, Napoli!' The rasping voice of Gravel Larson reverberated through the hollow job like a hog call. Joe made his way down the ramp and through the concrete form braces towards the long black car.

Progress on the job had become so fantastic that Gravel Larson, in a moment of panic that it might be finished before he received his share of the credit for the miracle, had nagged until Jock Dennison himself agreed to drive out to see it. His tall black Pierce sedan now stood beside the shanty like a royal coach, driven by a distinguished Englishman – Arthur, the chauffeur – who saluted. In the rear seat, both passengers leaned forward, Larson's mouth not two inches from Jock Dennison's ear.

'I always said there was something unusual about the kid', Larson said, as if Joe were not already standing beside the car, pumping Jock's hand.

'No question about it, Gravel. You're the Belasco of the bricklaying business.'

Jock Dennison stepped out of the car and placed his hand lightly on Joe's shoulder. Gravel, scrambling out behind Jock, said, 'A green, wisecracking kid, not even dry behind the ears. He'll be the biggest mason in the East.'

'He's one of the smart foxes on the run', Dennison said. 'Scurrying around that slum on Ninety-eighth Street, breaking his tail to keep ahead of the pack. Right, Joe? You see, that's our problem, Gravel – we just don't have the whole pack after us yelping for our tails. Still, enough's enough. Why don't you move out of that dreadful place, Joe?'

'I will, Mr. Dennison – Jock.'

'Good. When?'

'Pretty soon now.'

'Next week? Next month?'

'Soon as I finish the job, Jock.'

'Good. When do you expect that?'

'I'll have the brickwork topped out September seventeenth if it doesn't rain. Five more days.'

'You'll have to go some.'

'That's what I figure Jock.'

They started on a tour of the job, Jock Dennison searching, seeing everything, commenting laconically. 'Needs pointing. Those holes for the plumber have to be patched. You should've used sleeves there.' And over his shoulder he called to Joe, 'Your paesans are certainly giving you your money's worth. Why don't I have relatives like that?' Not a word of their conversation about Gamboretta. There never would be.

'You're doing okay, Jock. Don't reach for the crying towel. There's no mud on your shoes.'

Jock Dennison turned sharply, stared at Joe's mortar-splattered work clothes, peered down at his own Bond Street suit, and started to laugh. The longer he laughed, the more out of control he became, until he was emitting his piercing, falsetto laugh so hard that he began to gasp.

'Joe,' Jock Dennison said, tugging him out of Gravel Larson's hearing, 'I'm having a few friends out to my place in Deal on September seventeenth. Would you care to join us? You and I ought to celebrate winding up the job.'

'You kidding?' Joe said.

'A little party will do you good, Joe. Everyone needs a little breather. And I think you'll add something to the group. Come about seven.'

'Sure. You suppose any of your friends ever laid eyes on a live bricklayer?' Joe said without rancour.

'Probably not socially', Jock said.

'Don't expect me to walk on my hands', Joe said.

'That never occurred to me', Jock said. 'I honestly think you'll like these folks, they're all really quite simple, and they'll like you. There's one girl in particular I'd like very much for you to meet.'

Joe said, 'I wouldn't do it for anyone else. September seventeenth. Now how the hell do I get to Deal?'

'Easy', Jock said, and smiled his wide, inward smile. 'You go out U.S. twenty-five —'

On the afternoon of the seventeenth of September, those pedestrians on Jefferson Street who happened to pass the A & P-warehouse job were astonished to see the behaviour of the fifty bricklayers and their labourers who were finishing the parapet wall. Labourers pushed wheelbarrows up the ramp on the run. Bricklayers shouted at each other to hurry. Trowels flew. Plumbers and steam fitters, by contrast, worked at their accustomed pace, playing tortoises to the bricklayer hares. Only the Keystone Comedy Cops could cover the screen with such jerking, lightning action as these brickies.

In the Napoli shanty, a single word had been passed before the starting whistle: *Francesca*!

As soon as work was completed on the parapet wall and the brick job was, in fact, wound up, they were all scheduled to pile into the bus which would be waiting. They would be off to hunt two-legged deer. Joe Napoli had done his own computation for the last day and found what was needed to finish the job was an average of three thousand brick per man face and back-up. Without knowing the size of the individual task, but only the communal one which they could see with the naked eye, they proceeded to do it and by three-thirty the top-out flag had been raised to a cheer which only the employees of Napoli and Company fully understood. The usual deal was beer all round. But in the shanty the men gathered like the winning team in a college football game.

'Men,' Joe Napoli said, 'I'm proud of you. Now you remember I told you guys a hundred bucks a man if you finished on the fifteenth. Well, today's the seventeenth. I'm sorry you didn't make it, but we're gonna have our party anyway, and seeing you came so close to the fifteenth, I'm going to give each of you fifty bucks.' Cheers all round. Joe Napoli was one great guy.

They piled into the long red and blue bus parked on Jefferson Street, dragging lunch boxes, loosening their red bandanas about their necks, pushing caps back from lively, smiling faces – men entitled to reward beyond money, beyond overtime, beyond a mere beer. Sal sat in the front behind the driver, his eyes ablaze with anticipation, his face wide with a foolish smile.

Marge the Barge, infected and touched by Joe's desire to give his men something out of the ordinary, had outdone herself. Imported from Trenton were two chic black-haired bambolinas, Eileen and Betty, with the latest bobs and spit curls, the two highest-class girls she knew, complete with mascara, blue eyelids and fringed dresses. Marge had put starched antimacassars on the arms of all the stuffed living-room furniture, and had set out the Chianti flasks Joe had sent over, along with fifty water tumblers; she had asked Jim Zeckenstadt, a tall, jovial, heavy-set, balding gentleman, to act as bartender and sergeant-at-arms. Jim, she knew, could handle the job because he not only could hold his own liquor, but also was a regular member of the Allenburg police force, and she frequently gave him odd jobs like this during his time off, if traffic in the house threatened to be heavy.

Milton went along against Joe's better judgment – but Milt had pointed out soberly and somewhat portentously that since he was not to be involved directly in the proceedings, he could keep order and decorum and see that none of the men was robbed, rolled or cheated of his wine or his trip upstairs. In short, he would be Joe's deputy to see that the men got Joe's money's worth. He would also keep an eye on the bus driver to be sure he remained clear-headed enough to get the men safely to the Weehawken Ferry. This was the more essential, Milt carefully pointed out, since Joe had to leave early for Deal, where he was expected for that fancy Dennison dinner.

The men entered Marge's as quietly and as orderly as children breaking into a penny-candy store at night. They spoke barely above a whisper and, in fact, opened their mouths hardly at all.

The green shades were drawn and the room dimly lit by three lamps covered with hemispheric, red fringed shades.

Sal's eyes darted here and there, settling on the huge conglomeration of fat, powder and gold teeth that was Marge the Barge's happy face. She? Sometimes Joe Napoli was a big joker. He went into the back hall, peered upstairs, walked into the dining-room, peeped into the kitchen. Joe winked at Milt.

Four girls appeared at the head of the stairs – the Negress was not among them – and slowly descended. The tall redhead wore a long gold lamé dress that came several inches below her knees, which, stockinged in net, protruded through a slit in the dress. Her décolleté bodice permitted a good portion of her breasts, which were pushed high by a distorting support, to present themselves in the flesh. Here it was, served on a platter. Behind her the others followed, just as bold – the two girls from Trenton smoking cigarettes which hung from their full, red, glistening lips.

'Come on, boys, let's have a drink', the gold lamé redhead said.

'Drinks free', Marge added loudly, getting Joe's eye.

Timidly at first, then with increasing boldness, the men drifted towards the wine, Jim Zeckenstadt poured with a heavy hand – full tumblers of red, coarse wine.

'Jesus,' one of the high-class girls said, 'this Dago red is awful. Don't you have any good gin, Marge?'

'Drink same wine like men drink', Marge said cheerfully. 'Gin bad for girl stomach.'

'Look, look, look', one of the girls cried, pointing. Old man Sacchi had taken a full flask of wine, tipped it up on his elbow and was proceeding to drink the entire flask without coming up for air. No hands. When he had finished, the girls applauded and the men refilled with renewed vigour. Milt put a tarantella on the gramophone and old man Sacchi seized the girl in the lamé dress. 'In all my life you gonna be the first girl I ever dance made of-a gold', he said, turning her wildly.

Within half an hour there was not a focused eye in the place. The laughter and the shouting was an unshackling. Joe watched the revellers with satisfaction and anticipation. He lifted his chin towards the stairs and looked at Marge, who came close and put her lips to his ear. 'Now?' Joe nodded. She headed up the stairs about half-way. 'Francesca,' she called, 'Francesca, we waitin' for you. Hurry op.' Those who heard her stopped dancing. The word went round the room. Francesca! Francesca! Sal Benello's mouth hung open; he licked his dry lips.

She came to the head of the stairs, wearing only high-heeled shoes and black stockings, held up by pink garters. You never would've believed this was a girl with books littered all over her room. Maybe it was the French books that taught her so much. Every part of her which could tremble did so in a special harmony as she descended the stairs, one slow step at a time. She carried her right hand up, mocking the demure affectation. Her left hand rode the bannister. 'Hi ya, suckers', she laughed, mimicking the queen of the day. Joe watched her a moment, then turned to observe his audience. The stunned silence, the licking of dry lips by nervous tongues – this was a moment they would never forget.

'Darling', Francesca called, her lips puckering to a kiss. '*Pour toi seulement.*'

'Francesca,' Joe said, 'I want you to meet the boys. Hey, Sal – Sal.' Sal came forward, trembling, his eyes expanded to cue balls, his mouth still hanging open, his breath so short, he could've just run the hundred.

'Here I am!' he croaked superfluously.

'Francesca, honey, I want you to meet my good old friend, Sal. I promised him when he first came out here, I was gonna introduce you. But until now I've been afraid to do it. Okay, Sal? Promised, delivered. Be nice to this boy, Francesca. I gotta be going.'

'Going? *Mais pourquoi*, darling? You and your big *bouche*. Oh, there's a rat, rat, rat hidden in every man. Where to?'

'Over to Deal to a friend's house for sup – dinner. Jock Dennison's.'

There was a murmur of appreciation.

'Mist' Dennits, he's a the big *bigga* boss', Rino Sacchi said aside to Marge the Barge. 'He's the riches' man inna New York, except maybe Mist' Rockfella.'

'But not yet, my honey.' Francesca ran the remaining steps, her heels clattering on the bare wood. '*S'il vous plaît*, golly, one dance with me and a little drinkie.'

'Gosh, I'm sorry, Francesca.'

Her fingers were now around his neck, her eyes closed, and she began to sway like a girl in a trance. 'Listen to the music, Joey, hang around.'

The closeness of her flesh, which pressed on him, was not without its effect, but he knew there were also fifty pairs of eyes on him.

'Francesca, kid, I'm not for free. You'd have to pay.'

The men roared. Francesca let her open hand fly and caught Joe in the cheek, flush and loud.

'Keep the home fires burnin', Marge', he called loudly, grinning at Francesca. 'You settle for everything, Milt. See everyone gets what he needs and see they're all out of here by seven; that's our deal. I want everyone home by eight-thirty. I don't want any wives sore at me.' He laughed, and the men laughed with him.

Francesca's lips were at his ear. 'You lousy bum', she hissed. 'Bricklayers, for good God's sake, it's the living end. Modelling was better than this. What am I doing sashaying around here with these *paysans hystériques*? Smell like walking gymnasiums. With my talent. Goddam, I tell you.'

He tried to disengage her vice like fingers from his collar, but she would not let go.

Marge pushed to the rescue and slapped Francesca's rear with a light sharpness and quickness unexpected from all that avoirdupois. 'You be good girl now. Mista Napoli want to go, he go.'

What an impression for his men! A girl mother-naked, as voluptuous as Vilma Banky, tugging at him, begging him to lay his own body on hers, kissing him, importuning him, and he was able to turn away as easily as if he were some kind of God beyond the temptations of flesh. *He* was no boy of twenty-one. Oh, babe, I'll be back. Just hold it open for me. But today – superman. He didn't whore with them. It was an amazing demonstration to the flock.

With a casual word – friendly to all – he was about to leave in his car, Model A Ford though it was, symbol of the new America, to visit his millionaire friend over in Deal; and the amazing part of it was that he was still one of them. He could have been the son of any man there. He had sprung from Carmine Napoli and Annunziata Perini. It was a miracle of the new world and he was its symbol.

Disengaging Francesca's frantic fingers, Joe turned her, put her arms about Sal, patted her rump gently, smiled, waved and went out of the door. 'Can you dance, kiddie?' he heard her pout to Sal. The screen door clattered after him.

It slammed also on his boundless confidence. He was leaving a room he understood, with only a vague comprehension of where he was going. What could he possibly have to say to the Jock Dennisons of this world? He might just as well be going to Mars for tea. Well, he had his instincts to fall back on.

Nineteen

THE Dennison house off Ocean Road was directly on the ocean, fifty or sixty feet from the beach on a plateau high above it. The circular driveway in front of the porte-cochère, which enclosed a blood-red quarter-acre bank of massed salvia, had a number of cars parked in it. In Jock's Pierce, Arthur the chauffeur, deep lines on his drawn British face, concentrated on the *Evening World*.

'That the way in?' Joe jerked his thumb towards the porte-cochère.

'Yes, sir, Mr. Napoli', Arthur said, and folded his paper as if he had been caught in a vile act. 'Lovely night, isn't it, sir? Just have a look at the sky over the water.' Arthur pronounced it waugh-tuh.

'Rahthuh', Joe said, and pushed the bell.

A man in a black alpaca jacket opened the door. Jesus, a real butler.

'Good evening, sir.'

To the left and several steps down was a panelled room, and from the far end of it came Jock Dennison, highball in hand, a strand of blond, thin hair falling toward his eye. His thin lips were pursed in friendliness. 'Hello-o-o.' He dropped the second syllable several notes and held it in a verbal caress. 'Glad you could make it. Come meet a few nice people.' He took Joe's elbow in an authoritative, but strangely ineffectual, grip and led him into the living-room.

As dark as Marge the Barge's had been, that's how this palazzo was lit up like a firecracker. A huge, curved, colonial window gave, through the stone arches of the porch, a view of limitless, restless water. Fantastic joint. And the place was mobbed. In every corner were people of one kind and another, all speaking, like Arthur, as though they had just burned hell out of their tongues, absolutely a different English. Jock introduced him to exactly eight and a half million people; you could never tell them without a programme.

At a bar, standing beside an athletically built man with a square spare face, teeth that were too even, and pepper-grey hair, was a striking girl, trying to decide on a drink. She was as tall as Joe, with the face of an undernourished naughty child. She couldn't have weighed ninety pounds, but she was beautiful in a pale, emaciated way, with high cheekbones, a narrow, slightly uptipped nose, a small mouth, accentuated by an almost-orange lipstick. Her eyes were cat green and seemed at times to stare at him. The girl in the photograph on Jock's desk, he thought. Her blonde, curly hair was boyishly bobbed, and as he came closer, he noticed the faint redolence about her. There was something about her expression – he had the crazy notion that if someone said one stinging word to her, she'd bust out bawling.

'I think that one', she was saying to the square man. 'Chablis Cassis.' She looked up and saw Joe, but did not smile. She spoke breathlessly, timidly, but there was also a sharp, arresting quality to her voice, as if, once raw, it had been refined. Joe had an immediate urge to protect her and a sense that she would welcome protection.

Jock Dennison said, 'May I present Joe Napoli? This is Hetty Marshall. This girl's going to be one of our great actresses one of these days. You just watch.'

Hetty winced. 'Thank you, sir', she said.

Jock Dennison laughed, bent and kissed Hetty lightly on the cheek. 'Mmm, you beautiful creature. Isn't she beautiful?' Joe nodded dumbly. Jock had an arm about Hetty's waist pulling her along wherever they went, and she came without question.

'And this is Ev Henderson. Ev's from East Allenburg, God pity him!' Jock put his other hand gently on Everett Henderson's neck. There was possessiveness in every gesture. 'Runs a bank, poor chap.' The square man with steely eyes. He poured Joe a Chablis Cassis to match Hetty's.

'And Trick Potamos', Jock Dennison continued. 'Trick's assistant director for Hetty's new play. He's a genius. Even he admits it.'

Potamos was a young, short, emaciated man who looked as untamed as his hair, which was lush, black, curly, long and bushy – a Fuller brush gone wild. His smile was absent-minded, and he winced when Joe shook his hand.

'Watch that grip, pardner', he said.

Joe would not have minded so much that he did not know a soul among the many guests, but they all knew each other so damn well! They talked about this and that, the most wacked-up stuff he'd ever heard. Joe tried to listen to some of it, but it drove him off his track. There was a lot of high-class dirty talk, and nonsense about books and the wives of two new members of some golf club – he had about as much interest in that as yesterday's weather in Persia. So he sherried out of there to the sun porch, where who turned out to be lurking but good old Simon Cutler.

'Hi-ya, sweetheart', Simon Cutler cried. 'Meet the wife.' Ellie Cutler was a mousy young woman, sweet, but plain.

Joe was so glad to see a familiar face, he clutched Si Cutler's hand as if it were a life preserver. 'Whaddaya know, Si? Mrs. Cutler, I gotta tell you, it's certainly a real pleasure.'

The mouse's little hand trembled as he shook it, but not from nervousness. She had some kind of palsy. Simon Cutler was so big on Pola Negri and Theda Bara and that Hollywood crowd, and an expert on the hoor situation in Allenburg – a man who really thought about women – that Joe immediately felt sorry for this shaky little mouse who was married to him. 'I had the pleasure of buying a lot of brick from your husband.' Mrs. Cutler smiled, a sweet, grateful smile. How the hell did she ever come to get mixed up with and marry an oaf like Si Cutler? He turned to Si. 'Who the hell figured you were a friend of Jock's?'

'I'm a friend of everyone's, sweetheart', Si Cutler said. 'I'm in Allenburg politics up to my neck. You hear about Jock's new deal?' Si Cutler was speaking out of the corner of his mouth. 'The Mayor wants to sell a few hundred lots the city took for taxes back in twenty-one. Montgomery Street. Mayor's an old friend of mine. can get 'em at a steal. Jock thought maybe we'd put up some houses there on spec.'

Joe was barely listening. Hetty Marshall, sipping her Chablis, had just come out to join them, and the whiff of her perfume was doing something to him that the sight of Francesca, one hundred per cent naked, hadn't.

'How'd you like to be Jock's builder?' Simon Cutler was saying.

'Hm?' Joe said, realizing vaguely that he was being asked some kind of question.

'These houses Jock wants to do on spec – how'd you like to build 'em? I don't think he'll do it without you, Joe. He thinks you're a magician. What do you say, sweetheart?'

'Why not? Anything for old Jock.'

'Isn't Jock one swell guy? We figure about three hundred houses', Simon Cutler said.

'Three *hundred*? Are you kiddin'? Where's all the money comin' from?'

'You met Ev Henderson inside? He's president of the sturdiest bank in Jersey.'

'Looks like a square shooter', Joe said. 'He even has a square face.'

'Banks are where they keep the money, sweetheart.'

'Jock hasn't said a word to me about it', Joe said.

'He won't unless I tell him you're interested. Jock Dennison doesn't lay himself open. Why d'you think he asked us all here tonight? It's not for our wit, sweetheart.' Joe felt a flush of irritation flowing into his face.

'How come you know so much about it, Si?'

'I'm Chairman of the City Democratic Committee. It's my job to know about everything. And I'm the boy who can deliver the lots, which I will, as long as I can sell seventy-five thousand bucks' worth of brick in the deal.' He winked.

'I see.' Joe was taken aback by the realization that he still didn't have the first idea about how things were done in Allenburg. Lots to learn. But he couldn't take his eyes off this girl – what's her name – Hetty. Probably just out of some finishing school. Poor old Milt, stuck at Marge the Barge's with a bunch of brickies and mere hoors.

'I'll think about it, Si.'

'Swell,' Si said, '*do* that.'

Joe waved at little Mrs. Cutler, who replied with her sweet, mousy smile. 'Pleased to meet you, ma'am.'

Four glasses of Chablis had him feeling fine. Hetty drank the stuff as fast as he did, and looked sadly at his empty glass. 'Mr. Napoli, d'you think we might go back and get some more Chablis? Your glass is empty and I – I could use quite a lot of it tonight.'

'Sure.'

She had a smile that broke your heart; it came and went slow the way lights go up and down in a theatre, and you could feel it long after it had disappeared from her lips. But he had no idea whatsoever of what to say to her. She mixed two more drinks. 'Are you really a bricklayer?'

'Yah. Bet you never met a bricklayer before, ha?'

She leaned to his ear. That perfume, sweet Jesus. 'I'll tell you a secret, Mr. Napoli. If Jock hadn't told me, I'd never have taken you for a bricklayer.'

He suddenly realized she had made it her business to follow him. That guy over there – Henderson – was a bank president, this kid maybe was the Rin-Tin-Tin of actresses. She might be a goddam Broadway star for all he knew. He knew exactly as much about Broadway stars as he knew about the champion Lithuanian soccer team.

'You ever been in a Broadway whatzis?'

'She's in one right now.' Jock Dennison appeared behind them from nowhere. 'In rehearsal. *The Silken Rope*, watch for it. This girl will be a star some day, mark my words.'

Joe thought he saw her Tangee-covered lips quiver, and she blinked and tried unsuccessfully to smile.

Dinner was being cooked outside on the barbecue and served in the brick-enclosed patio. Jock Dennison, never without a drink in one hand, insisted on doing the cooking, turning huge steaks on the flaming grille with an enormous fork. Joe watched closely. Learn, you uncouth bastid. The guests merely milled about like hungry sheep.

Everyone was much friendlier than he had expected. They didn't say a damn thing, but they did keep the conversation hopping.

Ev Henderson asked him if he played golf or if he fished with flies, which was the first Joe had heard of *that* idea. Ev assured him that both were rewarding sports, especially fly fishing. Joe must take them up. If it weren't for golf and fishing, Mr. Henderson confessed, he would find life intolerably dull. 'Banking has its rewards', he said. 'I wouldn't want to be doing anything else in the world, but not the least of the job's amenities is the chance to take off for the Club or run up to Maine for trout and landlocked salmon.'

When Joe was a kid, Pop had taken him over to City Island and he'd caught a flounder and two eels off the dock there on these bloody, wriggling worm whatzises; they even had feet, for God's sake. Joe got a hook caught in his hand and it hurt like a son-of-a-bitch and after that he figured this is a sport that's too dangerous. Jesus, those slimy eels. But fishing with flies, how about that?

Jock Dennison was putting a sizzling, blackened steak on a wooden platter, and handing it to the butler to carve and serve.

At the table with Hetty, Joe jutted the handle of his fork towards her temple. 'You got a coupla grey hairs there,' he observed, 'but you look like such a kid.'

'Well, I'm not such a kid', she said. She'd had quite a bit of that Cassis. 'I'm twenty-two,' she said, 'but an elderly twenty-two. A precocious twenty-two, I worry so.'

'Big deal,' Joe said, 'I'm as old as you my own self (he was exactly twenty-one). You don't see any grey hairs in *my* head. I absolutely never heard of such a thing.'

'Both my parents were grey in their twenties', she said. 'I think people who look too young have no character a-tall.'

'You goin' back to New York tonight?'

'Yesss.' It was almost a hiss, she was a little tipsy.

'How you going home?'

'Oh, Jock's arranged it. He always arranges everything. He has Arthur waiting for me, the poor desolate li'l man; I'm sure he'd prefer to be home with his family. But Jock thinks I'm too *fra*-gile for the train. People like Jock make you into whatever they need, d'you notice that? He likes actresses and he needs them *fra*-gile. If I had tuberculosis, he'd absolutely adore me. He's Daddy Warbucks and I'm Little Orphan Annie. Still he's sweet, Jock is, only one mustn't take him too seriously. I try not to.'

'I could drive you in. I live in New York my own self. We could let old whozis, Arthur, get back to the wife.'

'Is that an invitation, sir?'

Joe was silent.

'P'r'aps we should tell Arthur to go, shall we?' She took his hand quite naturally and led him, weaving only faintly, through the arch to the driveway.

Arthur was slumped, dozing, over the wheel. Joe tugged him and the chauffeur roused himself, tipped his hat.

'No need to wait, Arthur', Hetty said gently. 'I've got a lift to town.'

'Thank you, Miss.' He tipped his hat again. 'You're sure Mr. Dennison doesn't want me for anything else?'

'Not a thing, Arthur.'

'Will Mr. Dennison be going into town tomorrow, Miss?'

Hetty called over the wall. 'Jock! Oh, Jock? Will you be going to New York tomorrow?'

Jock Dennison's high, positive voice, 'Sure.'

When they got back inside the enclosure, Jock said, 'Who wants to know?'

'I sent Arthur home, the poor man', Hetty said. 'He was simply exhausted. Mr. Napoli's driving back to town anyway.'

Jock Dennison peered for a brief moment at the two of them in the dark, his eyes shifting from one to the other. 'Arthur is well paid,' he said, 'to exhaust himself.' He turned towards the house. 'Here, have another piece of steak.'

Joe must have eaten four pounds, and was still chewing the remnants of a crisp and tender charcoal-smelling sirloin when Jock Dennison, nibbling on a black bone, turned towards the house and called over his shoulder, 'C'mon, gents, let's get going. Joe, bring your drink. Ev and I have a little proposition we want to go over with you.'

As if on a signal, Henderson and Simon Cutler fell into formation. Joe hesitated. He was having a helluva lovely time talking to Hetty and had no wish to leave her.

'Be sure and wait', he said to her.

'What choice do I have?' she said, pouting for an instant, but then she smiled sadly.

In the study everyone sat around Jock, members of a human solar system waiting for their sun to shine. Joe knew from the looks on their faces that when Jock made a joke, as he would, they would laugh. He did not entirely mind the sensation. Jock was the kind of man took care of his flock all right. He was an A-1 shepherd.

'You fellows realize,' Jock said, 'the tremendous real estate opportunities in Jersey now that they've opened this new Holland Tunnel? There's fantastic potential out in that Jersey clay. More and more New Yorkers are going to be moving out to join the mosquitoes – you wait and see. And once this new George Washington Bridge is built, flying skunks won't be able to stop 'em. There'll be a mass migration of millions of human beasts, the like of which has not been seen since Moses left Egypt – the entire herd who've been caged in New York apartments all their lives. It will be like emptying the zoos. All we have to do is throw ourselves in the path of the stampede, and domesticate a few hundred of them, by which I mean, sell them homes.'

They all chuckled. Jock paused and looked from face to face, but Joe had the feeling Jock's remarks were directed at him. 'The City of Allenburg owns a three-hundred-lot tract on Montgomery Street, land they took for taxes years ago – and they're ready to sell it at auction. And the City will put sewers in for us. Is that right, Si?'

'Right, Jock. A sixteen-inch trunk. The City Engineer is making studies right now.'

'Harold Brice is the mayor out there. Awfully nice chap. Have you met him, Joe?'

'I've only seen the guy once, at a funeral.'

'Prince of a fellow', Everett Henderson said. 'Good old-line New Jersey Yankee stock.'

'But a regular. Right down the line with the organization', Si Cutler muttered.

Ev Henderson smiled superciliously. 'Si was in the Seventy-seventh Infantry with His Honour during the war. Biggest thing in Si's life.'

'It's a lot more than that', Si said with some heat, twisting an angry corner of his mouth and bobbing his head for emphasis. 'I'm the *only* man in Allenburg he trusts, sweetheart. No offence, Ev.' Joe marked Si down for an overgrown booby.

Jock Dennison stood up and the bickering stopped at once. 'Si can deliver these lots for a hundred dollars apiece. That's an important function, don't let's underestimate it. The roads and sewers we'll be getting from the city are worth five or six times that, makes the lots worth a thousand apiece, we owe all that to Si, and heaven only knows how high land in Jersey may go.'

Si Cutler cleared his throat nervously. 'You fellows understand these sewers are being installed to serve a much larger area. These lots will be served only *incidentally*. Harold Brice is going to be very touchy on that particular point.'

'Naturally.' Jock Dennison dismissed the comment. 'Now, Everett here likes our deal so much that Merchantmen's wants all the mortgage loans. With the land worth a thousand, even though we pay only a hundred, we figure house and land might *cost* us thirty-three hundred, and we ought to be able to see 'em for forty-nine ninety, which we all may as well admit is a right nice mark-up. I guess Ev would give us mortgages equal to our entire cost – thirty-three hundred. Is that a fair assumption, Ev?'

'Don't see why not', Ev Henderson said breezily. 'It's a fine neighbourhood. Perfectly lovely homes there. These houses should sell like jelly beans. Of course, it'll have to go to the Committee, you know that, Jock. We work on two-thirds of valuation.'

'The neighbours might raise a stir', Jock Dennison said, brushing the last comment aside.

'They always do, sweetheart,' Si Cutler said, 'but that's *my* problem. I'll work that end of it with Harold.'

'I have only one very serious problem, men', Everett Henderson said. 'I've promised a couple of friends faithfully to meet them down at Matecombe Key for bonefish next month. So we'd have to get the thing wrapped up by then. Absolutely essential.'

'Now,' Jock Dennison said coolly, 'the labour problem. We're novices at that side of it, Joe. That's why I thought of you. How'd you like to join forces with us?'

'I might', Joe said.

'Swell', Si Cutler said.

Jock Dennison turned to the others. 'Joe operates under the padrone system – you never saw the like. He sees all his men are taken care of and they put their hearts into their work. Does that about describe it, Joe?' Jock slid a paternal hand over Joe's shoulders. There was nothing to do but leave it there. 'Takes a unique talent, which I am sorry to say I don't possess.'

Oh, Jock, come, come. Jock Dennison's embrace pulled Joe a bit closer. 'There was a troublemaker out there – Gambo or Gimbo something or other – what was it, Joe?'

'Gamboretta', Joe said. He took out the cigar he'd got from the butler and bit the end of it. 'Guy got all shot up. You guys must've see it in the papers. Don't look at me, though.'

They smiled.

'Not that he was a likeable man', Joe said. 'He was a no-good bastid.'

Jock laughed his uncontrolled cacophony. 'Don't you just love this guy?' he said. 'No respect for the dead – or the living either, for that matter.'

Joe felt himself flush.

'The Dennison Corporation is prepared to furnish all the necessary front money. Joe. All you do is the work.'

'*I'm* not gonna be paid to exhaust myself though, am I, Jock? Like old Arthur?'

Jock looked up sharply, as if Joe had hit him. 'You and I shall split profits fifty-fifty', he said unexpectedly. His voice was cool. 'You take care of Si out of your half. And my principal job's to see that Ev gets off on his fishing trip happy and content.'

Everett Henderson closed his eyes and bowed his head. 'Just so long as I get my bonefish.'

'You'll get your fish', Si Cutler said under his breath, so only Joe could hear. Si took two fast, nervous swallows of Scotch. 'What do you think of it, Joe?' he whispered. 'How's it sound to you, sweetheart?'

Joe took his own drink and the two men started towards the door. 'I'd sure as hell like to help Jock and all you guys out', Joe said. 'Let me think it over.' He started for the door.

'Before you go back out,' Simon said, 'I have a little something I'd like you to have, sweetheart.' He slipped his hand into his pocket and brought out a purple flat box. 'Just a little thing from old man Finlayson; he and I thought you ought to have it for the swell job you did out on the warehouse.'

He handed it to Joe, who took it suspiciously and opened the box. It was a flat gold Illinois watch with jewelled figures. Must've cost a fortune, maybe a hundred bucks.

'Look here', Si said. He snapped open the back revealing the jewelled works, and inside the back cover was engraved 'To Joe Napoli With Gratitude, Simon', and which Simon read aloud in a hushed voice. 'How about that? And we mean every damn word', Si added. 'He made money for you and me both, Jock.'

'I never had a watch', Joe said. He listened to it tick.

'Seventeen jewels', Simon said.

'Nobody ever gives me a watch', Jock Dennison said querulously. 'Why is that, Ev?' He examined the present and handed it back to Joe.

'You know the time better without one', Ev Henderson said dryly.

Joe took the watch, dropped it into his pocket. 'Thanks Si. I absolutely never expected anything like this.' As he left the other three men, he was thinking what a clumsy, heavy-handed oaf Simon Cutler was.

Back outside it was midnight black except for the dying glow of the barbecue fire. Only the occasional crackling of the wood broke the silence. Here and there guests strolled like shadows through the grounds. Joe heard a sudden muffled sound, the squeak of the glider, a man's laugh and a girl whispering, 'Please! Trick! Don't! You're very trying!' Joe could see the outlines of the glider flashing in moonlight, and twisting spasmodically. He heard the squeal of the springs, and he recognized Hetty's voice. 'Trick, please! *Behave* yourself!'

The thick voice of a man, far gone in drink, sputtered, 'Now whooz up on 'r high horse? Thish the twentieth centuree, babee? Nah, nah, nah, nah. C'mon, Desdemona! Li'l ol' honeypot. Ol' Uncle Trick knows who *you* are. Star, yessir. I know it! Brilliant star. You wanna go right through the top? You stick with me, babee. Cantsh see I'm absoluley nuss about you? Who you waiting for, Prinsh Wales?'

A dishevelled Hetty was twisting and struggling with the insistent hands of the facile but liquored Trick Potamos.

"Ey!' Joe heard the shout of his own hoarse voice, as if in absolutely some dream. 'Stan' up, you!' He reached down and lifted the assistant director by the collar until the man was fully on his feet, swaying.

'Pulease', Trick said thickly. 'Mr. Garibaldi. We're busy. Go away. Verry busy. No eeda spaghet' tonight.'

Joe's fist flew from the ground up, there was one hard, solid contact, and Trick Potamos sank slowly to the ground, unconscious.

Hetty jammed her fist in her mouth as footsteps came running on the lawn. Jock Dennison was in the vanguard.

Hetty was gesturing to Jock, shrugging, trying to explain, putting her hair right, giggling and crying.

Jock surveyed the prone form and began to laugh. '*Why*, Joe?'

'He was trying to get wise with Hetty. Miss Marshall.'

'OhmyGod.' Jock Dennison doubled over, his laughter almost hysterical again in a falsetto shriek. 'Isn't that priceless, really priceless! Joe, you're wonderful!' He laughed till tears came. 'Not since King Arthur!' Jock screamed his amusement, and for Jock to be amused was the largest part of affection.

Trick stirred.

'I better take the skunk home', Joe said. 'You know where he lives?'

'I do', Hetty said, her voice still shaking.

Joe lifted Potamos's head and dragged him by the armpits to the Ford, Hetty and the others trailing behind him.

'Here, let's get him in the back seat.'

Together he and Jock lifted the limp body and sat it in the rumble seat like a rag doll. Trick was mumbling and his head was weaving.

'So long everyone', Joe said, and went around to hold the door open for Hetty. She was quite unsteady as she stepped into the car. She must've had a few more Chablis while he was in conference.

Before they reached the Weehawken Ferry, Trick twice asked piteously to have the car stopped for him to be sick, and when they finally deposited him at his flat off Riverside Drive, he must have thanked Joe three thousand times for taking him home from that *dreary, dreary* party.

'Okay', Joe said, when Trick had stumbled into his apartment house. 'Now – where do *you* live?'

'Where do *you* live?' Hetty said.

'In a cosy old-law tenement on Ninety-eighth Street with my mother and brother and two sisters and eight million cockroaches.' He had started across Central Park.

'Well.' She hesitated and almost winced. 'Think of that. I live on East Eighty-fifth Street, not quite old-law tenement, but the next thing to it. And you know something? My name's not Marshall – that's my stage name. May I be frank? I'm Hetty Mullaly. An' my father was a teacher at P.S. 92. Fifth graders. The poor, sweet, frail dear man. He wasn't made for this world. Used to like a spot of old Irish whisky, off and on, mostly on. He loved knowledge, but all those children were more than he could stand. Oh, but he was a darling man, father was.'

'Well, whaddaya know', Joe said. He could not explain why he was suddenly elated, as if he had scaled a mountain peak. 'You kiddin'?'

'You're sweet, too, Joie,' she said, 'to take me home. And to take poor Trick home. Very sweet. Shouldn't have hit him though. Not so *hard*. Trick is quite delicate. No one ever did *anything* like that over me. All my men friends are so civilized, subtle – psychological people, the ones I know, y'know? Too much Freud and T. S. Eliot.'

Whoever the hell they were. Well, they didn't play for the Giants, that he was sure of.

They had parked on her block.

'Are you actually no kiddin' in a Broadway play?'

'I'm not *in* one. Just rehearsing.' Her voice was strangely small and shivering.

'What's it called?'

'*The Silken Rope*. The author's a wonderful love of a man – George Sidney. You've probably heard of him.'

'You kidding? The only playwright I ever heard of was Willie Shakespeare with that *Julius Caesar* number. Friends, Romans, Countrymen. That's the best damn play *I* ever read. In fact, it's the *only* play I ever read. You believe something? I've never been inside a real theatre. Not one. My old man used to go to the opera, sat way up in the peanut gallery. My mother raised hell, spending food money for opera tickets. But that's the way Pop was. He used to make us listen to those scratchy records. I don't know how much money he spent on 'em – Galli-Curci, Caruso – the whole mob. Pop was nuts about Caruso. You really expect to be a big star like Jock said?'

'Now, Joie, don't tease me.'

He bit and lit a cigar. 'I'm serious. I never met any actresses
before. When does this play open – what do you call it – The Silk
Whatzis?'

She turned away. 'I don't really know. In the theatre you're
never sure.' Suddenly she was spitting fierce, angry words. 'And I
don't give one little damn.'

Her shoulders began to tremble, and suddenly her body was
shaking. She had turned her face back towards him, hidden her
nose in the crook of his shoulder, and although he heard her sniffling,
it took a moment for him to realize she was crying. In half a minute
she was going full blast, as if her heart were shattered. He blew a
sparse stream of smoke over her fine hair.

'My one wonderful chance', she wept. 'Oh, I hate them, I hate
them all!'

'What the hell are you *talkin'* about?'

'Oh, Joie,' she said, catching her breath in a sob, 'it's been a
terrible day. I was fired! This very afternoon. You can't imagine
what it's been like. Having to go through motions all evening.
Pretending. Be a good little girl and don't bother us any more,
child. And all the while I'm dyin' a bit at a time. The director was
patient, oh yes, and how kind, but I'm simply terribly wrong for
the part. Not my fault, of course. I'm simply not forceful enough
in the big scenes. They must think it's St. Joan . . . And my nice
Mr. Sidney says not a word. The play must come first, my dear
child. How can they call themselves *human?*' She was all over him
suddenly, shivering as if she had the chill. He had never seen
anything like it.

'Poor kid', he said. He had no idea what it was all about or what
to say. 'Back at Jock's there, I had a hunch you weren't feeling too
hot.'

'Did you now? Do you think anyone else noticed?' she said
bitterly. 'Oh, if I could only show you what it means! Since I was
five years old, Joie, my mother has taken me to acting schools,
dancing schools, speech lessons, fifteen years of it. She used to fight
something terrible about me with father, agents, producers. Every
cent poor, dear father made. I just never knew anything else. Oh,
I've been on radio for a few months, I was little Susan Malone in
"The Merry Malones"; did you ever listen to that?' He shook his
head. Catch him listening to one of those radio serials. 'After father
died, my mother worked like a dog, took in laundry, went to

people's houses to do their cooking, and when I was sixteen I went to work myself at McCreery's, selling dresses to fat women so I could keep up at drama school, nights. Night after night for four years. Not that I don't love the work of acting. It's all I've ever loved. But you've got to be supported by hope and there's this Molly Staver, you know? Who runs the school. She's the one who believes in me. Molly's so sure of me, she's given me confidence and now look. And my poor dear mother, she'll die. Everyone used to say, Isn't she the shy one though? But on the stage, I'm not. Really. You should see me. Anything but. Molly could tell. I'm so free there, I can be anything. I'm not even aware of the audience, I swear. Do you have a handkerchief?'

He put the cigar in his mouth and pulled out his huge, red bandana, patted her tears and held the cloth to her nose so she could sniffle again, as if she were a mewling infant.

'I was so sure I'd be good', she said. 'Damn, damn, damn.' She was whimpering, muttering against him again.

'You'll get into another play – what the hell.'

'But, Joie, I keep being afraid, maybe I *don't have* it. I heard Margalo Sedgwick read for my part this afternoon. I couldn't leave the theatre, I was that fascinated. Oh, how she's got it, *inside* of her. In, in deep where it counts. She's *so* good. I couldn't stand seeing her do my part.'

'Who's Margaret Sedgwick?'

'Margalo. When you have it, everyone in that theatre can tell it right away. I wanted to hate her, but I couldn't.'

'She's taking your part?'

She had stopped sobbing, but the tears kept running down her face as if some wound could not be staunched. 'I haven't been able to tell a soul, Joie – not even Jock, and sure not my mother. You know how scared I feel?' Her face was twisted craven. 'Even Trick doesn't know about it. But they'll all know soon.'

'Why tell me?'

'Because you don't care. At least I hope not, do you? I'd loathe being pitied. Oh, I despise cry babies. Especially when it's me. Look at me. I had to go and get drunk on Chablis, of all things. I'm disgusting, aren't I?'

He tapped the long ash of his cigar out of the window. 'I sure as hell do care.' He didn't know it until he'd said it.

'Oh, you mustn't. You may stop being sorry for me immediately.' She was rearranging herself for greater dignity. Then she

tried to smile, but it was hopeless. And he could feel a great surge
of fatherliness.

He took her by the shoulders and held her away from him to
examine. 'Sure, Miss Mullaly, I feel sorry for you, but not the way
you think.'

She laughed, high, shrill and tremulous. 'You know how silly I
am? I bought two new dresses. I thought after the opening in New
York there'd be Press conferences, the story of my life, Cinderella,
from rags to riches.' She blinked hard and leaned back, more composed, free of his proprietary grip. 'You know why I wouldn't tell
anyone? Didn't dare. I was afraid to be scared. Don't you see?
Too exposed. I've got to be impervious and brave and hard and
untouchable. Always.'

'Boy, do I feel *sorry* for you! Lookit you, nice, high-class girl,
speak like a million bucks, like you're from England or some place,
dress like one of those real society dames – what do they call 'em –
debutantes – act like Mary Pickford. You must be able to act pretty
damn good. I sure believed you came from Ohio or somewheres.
And scared to be scared? All because you don't get one lousy part
in one lousy play?'

'I *had* the part.'

'Okay. But you're so miserable, I figured maybe somebody died.
A kid sister, maybe even a dog. I mean there are people with *troubles*.
Ha! Some jerk director don't know a good actress when he sees
one. So what? With all that stuff you got bottled up, holy St.
Mike, you could be *ten million* stars. Scared to be scared! That's
the absolutely one hundred per cent limit. Lookit all that nice feeling you got inside you it's murder in the first degree. You could
make a helluva girl, a real girl. You oughta try it.'

He had no idea what being an actress was like, much less a heart-
broken one, but he spoke with absolute authority.

'All my life —'

'All your life you've been makin' believe this and that.' He had
worked himself up into a triple-distilled expert. 'Pouring your
whole self into some kind of an *act*. Just feel you shaking. Come on,
now, Mullaly, settle down.' He put one arm around her and she
was soft and the smell went to his brain. 'Making believe this or
that, like some kind of Clara Bow. You know what she is? One
great big tremendous mirage. She's twenty feet long! She's not
real. On Ninety-eighth Street or Eighty-fifth Street or any other
street – I'll give you ten million bucks, you find me one single girl is

anything whatsoever the slightest bit like her. People have to wash diapers, they make real love, they put out the garbage, they don't have time to put their lipstick on perfect, they got a smell to their bodies. The men gotta get to work, women have to get the place cleaned up, kill the rats, step on the bugs, cook dinner, go to the can. They're busy.'

She turned her face up towards him still tearful, but calmer now. 'Joie, you know I feel better. I like to hear you talk.'

He tossed his cigar out of the window and, not roughly as he intended, but with a gentleness he never expected to find in himself, he took her shoulders. The pressure was scarcely necessary. She came of her own accord. Her kiss was grown-up, open, uncontrolled. He smelled the Tangee and then tasted it, it was young and fresh like the mouth it was on, and he had a flash recollection of a rabbit he had once seen hit by a car, wounded, squealing, and seeking shelter.

He was gasping a little for breath. 'Sure there's plenty of guys crazy for actresses. Si Cutler, he must spend half his life in a cinema. Glamour. I absolutely don't get it.'

'Very well, I shan't take myself so seriously', she said. 'Never again.'

'You don't take yourself seriously enough', he said.

As he bent to kiss her again, she made a sound hardly human, like an animal that has achieved its needs, and she clutched him with sudden strength.

''Ey,' Joe said, and heard his own hoarse voice shaking. He let her go. He touched her face, the most delicate thing he had ever held in his callus-covered bricklayer hands, yet he could not hold it because he had absolutely one hundred per cent no idea what was inside. Instead, he took out another cigar and lit it, while she observed him in silence.

'Mind if I smoke, Mullaly?'

'Smoking cigars goes with you', Hetty said, still studying him. 'Not that I'm wild about them, but they do give you an air. You've made a lot of money on this job of Jock's, haven't you?'

'Seventy thousand bucks. I got thirty in the bank already. I got enough money right now even to get married, in fact.'

'I believe you have.'

'And put my kid brother through architectural school besides, and get my family out of that filthy dump. I can do a lot of things. Not only that, but Jock wants me to build three hundred houses

for him, and I can make probably another hundred, hundred an'
fifty thousand.'

He was talking to her about money as he had never talked to
anyone, as if she were, for God's sake, a member of his family.

'That's a lot.'

'For a brickie!' he laughed. 'That's more money than there is
in the world.'

He knew nothing about her, she didn't know a damn thing about
him, and yet so much of his life was being decided with a few kisses
and that fluttering of distress. It was some kind of a miracle, not
logical. But something had hit him, of that he was sure.

'You belong to anybody?' he said at last.

'No.'

'Not Jock?'

'Jock's a love, but you know, he's strange. The only time he ever
touches me or kisses me is when other people are watching. You
saw him tonight. When we're alone, he never comes near me. I
think he uses a girl for decoration. He wears her. That's what I
think.'

'Yah?'

'I think he enjoys his backgammon and bridge at Canoe Hill more
than any evening he's ever spent with me.'

'Nice guy', Joe said sincerely. 'But a hundred per cent fruit
cake.'

'He's very fond of you', she said. 'He's told me so.'

'What are you doin' tomorrow?' Joe said.

'I have my rehears —' Then she smiled ruefully as she remembered; her stomach sank and her spirit rose almost at the same
moment. 'Nothing. Nothing at all.'

'I'll pick you up, ten o'clock.'

'Isn't that a bit late for an evening to get started?'

'Evening?' He laughed. 'You want to waste all day? Ten
o'clock in the morning.'

Twenty

THEY fed pigeons and watched seals. 'Lookit', Joe said, observing the seals at feeding time. 'Throw 'em a fish, they'll do anything. I hear they got one in the circus, you throw 'em a fish, he'll play "My Country 'Tis of Thee" on a saxophone. Like a lotta people I know.' And Hetty laughed.

They'd take a rowing boat or lie on a blanket on the banks of the pond, and they'd kiss fifty thousand times as traffic hissed by and the sun settled for the night. They were with each other fourteen, fifteen hours a day. She was trying hard to be real, to feel what it meant, to listen when he spoke. He told her about himself, which is to say he spoke of the people around him – his mother, Lucy, Rosina, Ed, Uncle Giovanni, the grass-face, and *his* whole miserable clan, Milt Jason and Tony Ferrara, Pasquale Baccio, the men who worked for him from Rino to Sal, and, of course, he told her all about Pop. Always Pop, 'the greatest guy in my life'. What was Joe Napoli, after all? Merely the centre of a constellation of people, each moving in his separate orbit, revolving on his own axis, yet all part of the Napoli gravitational system.

Although their young bodies were not immune from the general laws of polarization, Joe Napoli had made a firm resolve that this was to be no quick tune-up; Hetty Mullaly, his fragile, magic girl, was not to be sullied, even if she were weak enough to soil herself. So far, Buster, and not one step further. Once in your life don't be a bastid.

In spite of his restraint, soon it was as if he had been in her, had inserted the key to the lock and opened some kind of floodgate. Whenever she was with him, her fears evaporated and her love poured over him like an invigorating waterfall. He perceived dimly that he could never provide the same outpouring for her, but she seemed to need only whatever it was he could give. She made no effort to hide her delight in him. In Central Park, in the Model A, or sprawled on the grass in the pussy-willow autumn nights, or in a rough-house, she was always delighted, always fascinated, always wanting to know everything he knew. She listened avidly to him. It was as if she were searching for the key to him, to get inside his skin with him.

Joe took her up the house to show her off to Mammina; and Hetty took him to meet her mother and four brothers, all freckled Irish boys, living in a flat on Eighty-fifth Street scarcely bigger than the Napoli place, but less chaotic and with hot water and an inside toilet. And books, the place was crowded with books. Hetty's mother was a small, sinewy woman, with stringy hair in tangled, grey strands, who walked about in a shapeless brown sweater. She was sprightly, like a Bantam hen, and wore a look of determination on a face that was delicate, as finely boned as Hetty's and with eyes as green. Her tiny nose and thin mouth were lost in a sea of dimmed-with-age freckles. Almost anything Hetty said made her light up; the four boys were a chore. When she first saw Joe, and whenever she saw him afterwards, she would look at him sharply, then go about her cooking or laundering or sewing, as if she were too busy or tired for further social intercourse with one of Hetty's boys.

After a couple of weeks, Hetty took him and her mother to the second night of *The Silken Rope*, the first legitimate show Joe had ever seen. Several times he caught himself falling asleep, but was sensible enough to wake up in time to applaud. The theatre air was stale and the whole entire idea was a big load about this wacked-up old broad trying to keep her great oaf of a kid brother, a goddam booby who apparently didn't do anything useful, tied to her apron strings. And the booby's young wife trying to cut him loose from the old battle-axe. The young and defiant wife was the part Hetty was supposed to do. The entire cast reminded him of the crowd at Dennison's party. The whole play was absolutely no bargain – not that it was as boring as Shakespeare – it had at least a few plain English words in it, but these characters absolutely didn't have enough to keep them busy and naturally got themselves worried over nonsense like this bossy sister crap. Give this old broad a job at some sweatshop sewing machine and you'd have the entire problem licked. Christ! They oughta get a load of Uncle Giovanni and they'd stop worrying about this nice old broad who, after all, *liked* her brother. Too much love. There was something to worry about! The play was a complete Mother Goose from start to finish.

To give Hetty some idea of what was really going on in this world, he took her out to Allenburg. Although the brickwork was completed, he explained the entire building business to her, from the bond in the brickwork to how he had to be a wet nurse to the men and a father confessor to the material suppliers; he explained the difference between making and losing dough – and how it was all in the minds of your men – just how much they were willing to put out; how you'd work those minds and hear all their problems and actually love the poor bastids. They were a seedy lot, and except for that, they didn't ask much. Love, he told her solemnly, is God's word and it's also goddam necessary in your work and in general.

As they walked over the job, plumbers, electricians, lathers called, "Ey, Joe', and tipped their hats to Hetty, as if she were some kind of duchess. Hetty listened as he talked, her eyes shining – those green eyes always looked like they had tears or dew in them – and she smiled back at the men. She was fascinated, a lot more than he'd been at *The Silken Rope*. He thought she was beginning to see the difference.

Back in the Model A, she rested her head on his shoulder in a gesture of absolute satisfaction. 'Joie,' she murmured, 'those men all *do* love you. And so do I. I can't seem to help myself.' He knew that.

They drove over to Montgomery Avenue, to the site of the new housing job and, like Jack and Jill, hand in hand, walked over the site. Beautiful piece of land, good drainage, nice trees and the most varicoloured sunset you ever saw.

This deal could've gone on for months. They wallowed in each other. Until one morning Jock Dennison reached him on the new phone Joe had just had installed in his flat and wanted to know if Joe had thought over 'our little proposition. What do you say, Joe? How about it?'

What a pain in the tail – just when he was living a little. Still it was a terrific opportunity. 'Okay, Jock, okay. What the hell. I might as well come in with you.'

'Good, Joe.'

So that night he took Hetty out in the Model A and from one of those long, trembling, deep kisses, he emerged to say, 'Jesus, I guess this is the entire deal, Mullaly. We better make it permanent.' No use getting poetical, trying to be something he wasn't. 'Okay with you?'

She looked at him a long time. Finally she nodded, and her eyes had real tears in them this time.

At City Hall there was waiting and confusion, and they had to go over to the Health Department to get birth certificates – about as romantic as a bag full of dirty linen. When the clerk handed him his receipt, Joe said to Hetty suddenly, 'C'mon up the house; I been thinking over a helluvan idea.'

On the way up town in the subway, he wouldn't tell her what, but when they came into the building they met Milt and Luce on the stairs just on their way down for a walk, and Joe showed them the licence. Luce screamed with delight.

'Now,' Joe said, 'I got a terrific idea. Listen. What's the reason you two are waitin' around for? It's the season to get married. When Joe Napoli gets married, *everyone* gets married. I'll get it all fixed with Father Ritucci. All you need is a couple of weeks of instruction, and the way you both been carryin' on, it's a goddam disgrace to the entire family. I gotta think of my kid sister's reputation.'

'Holy smoke,' Milt said, 'October fifteenth. I've got two more years of law school and *I* can't become Catholic; I'll never be able to believe all that stuff. Father Ritucci will never marry me.'

'The hell he won't. Leave it to me. You just learn your lessons like a good boy and leave everything to me.'

'You're a terrible busybody', Lucy said. 'Honestly.' But she was laughing.

There were plenty of arguments and tough details Joe had to work out before it was all settled. Father Ritucci explained everything to Joe, who had to get Milt to promise not to use contraceptive devices and bring all his kids up Catholic, and getting him to agree to *that* was no easy job; in fact, it was absolutely a tremendous crisis, with Luce in tears and Milt not showing up for a couple of days. But Milt was so damn anxious to get Lucy, he would have agreed to bring his kids up Eskimo. Especially since he had no idea whatsoever what either having kids or being Catholic was like.

In a way it was lucky Milt's parents were dead. At least they didn't have that complication. Even Milt's cousin, Aunt Rosel, who had no use for him whatever, had a triple-distilled haemorrhage when she heard.

When it was all over and Milt had accepted the inevitable, Joe caught himself thinking that no dame would ever get him to give *his* religion up.

Even after they were over the hurdle of religion, every practical problem that remained unresolved Milt saw as a tremendous barrier. He wanted to finish law school. Luce would not stay at Ninety-eighth Street. No job, no money, two years of school – what business did he have getting married? He didn't want Luce to keep working at the dentist's office. The dentist was beginning to look at her funny.

'Don't worry,' Joe told him, 'she won't stay there.' And it was settled because he said so.

The two weeks before October fifteenth were busy ones. In addition to preparing for the wedding, there was the new job to get ready for. Joe and Milt must have seen exactly eight and a half million people who had anything whatsoever to do with the new housing job. Plumbers, steamfitters, the architect, Tony, union delegates, sub-contractors and politicians. If getting ready for just a brick job was complicated, this was one for Einstein. Joe was impatient with all the preparation. 'Let's go see Si Cutler', he'd say, or 'Let's talk to Oscar Swanson'. 'Let's see the architect.' 'Let's visit His Honour, the Mayor; I hear he's quite a man.' It was a period of self-education.

Oscar Swanson, the carpenter foreman on the A & P job, was the man who really put them on the right track. Joe had brought Oscar over to a thirty-house job someone else was building in Orange. 'I want you to explain everything to me here, Oscar, every operation.'

Oscar beamed. 'Ay do my best', he said pompously. Oscar had new admiration for the boy he had threatened to lay out with a four by four. This boy was yeenius.

The job in Orange was bedlam. Carpenters, plumbers, plasterers were working in chaos, going in and out of houses like ants in ant hills; and the carpenter foreman stamped around the property, with his head down, like a punch-drunk fighter, 'Mike, they're waitin' for six penny nails in fifteen! My God, where's the man with the lath? What happened to that guy with the casings for twenty-one?'

Oscar started at the beginning, as if he were talking to a child: footings, foundations, mechanicals, roughing, framing, all the way to the hardware on the kitchen cabinets.

H

'How many doors a man hang in a day, Oscar?' Joe jerked his thumb towards a man who had been hanging one door in the next room for the past twenty minutes.

'Some better, some vorse. I tank maybe five, six. Got also to do trim, hardware. Is slow operation.'

Joe stepped into the room where the carpenter was working. They stood there, Oscar shifting his weight while the man worked slowly for another three-quarters of an hour.

'Took you over an hour on that one', Joe said. 'You can do better.'

'I'm not tryin' to kill myself with heart failure', the carpenter said. 'I got a wife and kids, mister.' Slowly he planed the edge of a door and stood it on end. He reached for the router.

'I'll lay you twenty bucks to a buck you can't hang four doors an hour. The hell with trim and hardware. Twenty bucks.'

'You're covered', the man said, grinning evilly. 'Put up your dough.'

In ten minutes another door was in. In less than an hour, the man had hung five doors, and Joe gave him the twenty-dollar bill, then took the man's name.

'Union don't allow no piecework', Oscar said, his face clouding.

'Let me worry about the union', Joe said.

They strode down the street in silence.

Joe was thinking hard. 'Every guy gets used to one simple job, just like that guy. Over and over. We set up a rate for each operation. Put every two guys in business for themselves. A lump price for each operation.'

Oscar made a sour face. 'They gonna cheat, leave out nail, botch job. No, no, no. Ay no like lumping out.'

'Yes, yes, yes', Milt said with such excitement as Joe had never observed in his friend. 'Joe, you're on to something. Oscar, your job is going to be to inspect. Before any team gets paid, inspect. All day long, inspect. Not only fast workmanship – good workmanship. Superior workmanship. Quality. The men will put out not only more, but better work. It's the two-thousand-brick-a day theory with a slightly different twist.'

'And who thought of it?' Joe said triumphantly.

'Ain't never been done', Oscar said dolefully.

'Why not?'

'Ay don't know. Union don't like. Men don't like. Nobody doing it.'

'I think the men *gonna* like', Joe said. 'You round up the framing crew, Oscar. We'll lump out everything.'

The architect Si Cutler took them to see was a man named Middlin – a short flabby man in his late fifties, bent low by life's artistic and business compromises and corruptions, his watery eyes uncertain, pudgy face pale, his expression as ineffectual as his features. He had scores of house plans stacked away in great flat drawers. 'Any kind you want, boys – two bedroom, three bedroom, two family, one or two baths . . .' An absolute five-and-dime store of plans, this guy was operating. The man hadn't thought about designing an original home for twenty years.

Joe took Si Cutler aside in the two-man drafting room. 'We gotta use this bum?'

'He's Harold Brice's father-in-law', Si Cutler said out of the corner of his mouth.

'Jesus!' Joe said. 'Lucky you told me.'

Mr. Middlin sidled over from the other side of the room, carrying a coloured rendering that looked like ten million other houses, and spoke with a good-time Charlie chuckle. 'A young feller like you, Napoli, may not realize it, but houses are not a thing to experiment around with. You want to experiment, take a research job with Dupont. Haha! The tried and the true, young feller, it's the only thing. Design something unique and you'll see what happens to you – trouble with the banks, trouble with the neighbours, and no customers. Yessir. Public acceptance. Here's a nice number, all brick. I understand you're a brick man. Two-story job, centre hall, three bedrooms. There must be fifty thousand houses just like it in Jersey.'

He could barely swallow it. Next year absolutely he had to get Dino off to architectural school. Dino was smart – on the honour roll at DeWitt this year, straight A's in maths, tremendous in mechanical drawing. And only seventeen. It would be worth something having a decent architect with some imagination in the family.

When everything else had been ironed out, Si Cutler took Joe to meet His Honour the Mayor, Harold Erasmus Brice, III. Harold Brice did not look unusually tall only because of the high ceiling in his ancient office, but he was six foot six. His eagle face was patrician, noble, lean. If anyone ever looked like a mayor, it was Harold Brice. In fact, put a wreath on his head and he looked like an emperor.

'Every co-operation, Napoli', Joe heard him saying in his resonant baritone. 'My father-in-law was mighty impressed with you, don't mind telling you. Our people badly need decent, moderate-priced, modern housing. Why, half our population is still living in these outmoded Gothic relics or miserable flats unfit for human habitation.' He pulled the phone receiver off its hook. 'Get me the Public Works Commissioner, Polly, my dear . . . Dan? . . . Hal Brice. Listen carefully. Next Council meeting, we'd like appropriations acted on for the sewer and water extensions out to that Montgomery Avenue site. We're all cleared on the bond issue. When you talk to reporters, tell 'em it's for the new city hospital and three hundred new up-to-date houses. Emphasis on the hospital. I'll have the feller who's going to build the houses put in an appearance at the next meeting. Name's Napoli. I'll send him over to meet you now. Oh, you've already seen his man? Good. Well, he'll be over himself. I want you to meet *him*. Oh, and Dan, if anyone asks you who told you to say all this, tell 'em you thought of it yourself.'

Harold Brice hung up without listening to the reply. 'The members of the Common Council are prepared to vote the appropriation unanimously.'

'There's some neighbourhood opposition, Mayor', Si Cutler said cautiously between his teeth.

'I'd expect about five hundred people to come out', the Mayor said. 'Some people will fight to the death against any kind of progress. They'll scream their bloody heads off, as usual, but the Council will be unanimous. You've got my word on it. We're simply obliged to do something about getting decent housing for the folks hereabouts. And it's not only for people in the – how d'you say – the lower echelons. They're important, yes, but don't think for a minute I'm a red-eyed socialist. We've got people, the finest people in town, like my own mother, till the day she died, lived in one of these rambling old barns. Lovely place, mind you, old family homestead, stained-glass windows, huge cupola, beautifully landscaped grounds, but fifty years out of date. I was born in the old place, but I have it on my hands now and haven't the vaguest idea what to do with it. It has no place in our modern society of small families.'

Joe did what he could to conceal his sudden interest. 'How big is this joint of yours?'

The Mayor said, 'Oh, I don't know – eight or nine bedrooms.

Lovely old house, full of musty charm, but thoroughly unpractical. Someone ought to buy it and remodel it into small apartments.'

'Mind if I have a look at it?'

The Mayor raised his brows. 'Simon knows where the place is. I have the key right here. Show him the old barn, Si.'

'How much you want for it, Mayor?'

'We're asking ten thousand', Harold Brice said. 'But I'd take nine.'

The family knew only that they were in for some kind of surprise when they piled into the car two days before the wedding. No Model A was made for this kind of load, but they all managed to squeeze in. When the car rattled on to the ferry, Rosie went mad with excitement. 'Now I know the surprise', she shouted. 'We're going to Europe!'

Hetty said, with a little scold in her voice, 'I can't imagine what you have in mind, Joie. I'm all pins and needles.'

Mammina set up incessant chatter. 'Rosie, kippa still. Dino, sid-down. You sit. You craze? You wanna get kill? I breakka you neck! Here, eat, eat.'

When they drove up to the big old house on Elm Street with its cupola towering over an acre of carefully cultivated lawn, neatly trimmed shrubs, in a gracious neighbourhood, surrounded by other old houses on equally well-tended plots, the passengers looked at each other in puzzlement.

'Okay, gang, everyone out', Joe shouted.

The inside was spacious and in first-class condition. None of them had ever been in anything like it. Two of the windows in the hall were stained glass, maroon and green, most of the furniture sombre mahogany – old, but in good condition. There were five bedrooms on the second floor and three on the third.

Suddenly as they stormed back down into the parlour, they were all talking at once. 'What is it? Whose is it? What's the surprise?'

Joe sat on the sofa, his hands poised on each armrest, a king in court. 'It's ours', he said. 'Used to belong to the Mayor of the whole entire City of Allenburg. We move in right after the wedding. Upstairs on the third floor for you and Luce, Milt. Second floor, Hetty and me. Mammina, you get the red room, Rosie gets her own room. Dino get his own room. The Mullalys get the three rooms over the kitchen, and we got a few guest rooms left over for new kids. How's that? All the furniture goes with the house.' He was pleased indeed. One big, happy family.

Rose and Dino let out cheers and ran all over the house a second time, discovering new treasures, a whole world of wonder.

'Look at the back yard', Dino yelled. 'It's bigger than the Polo Grounds. Hey, Mike, what a place for one-a-cat, hey?'

'Look,' Rosie screamed, peering out the window into the street, 'a penny merry-go-round – just like home.' And with shrieks of delight, she and Dino and Mike Mullaly were out of the house for a ride.

Mammina and Mrs. Mullaly seemed preoccupied with the kitchen, touching the big icebox and oversized range with awe.

But Hetty's brow was creased and Milt and Lucy sat on the arms of Morris chairs, not looking at each other or at Joe. 'Gosh, Joe', Milt said.

'I don't want to hear any thanks', Joe said. 'Forget it'. Then, as only uncomfortable silence followed, "Ey, whatsamatta with alla ya?'

'It's a beautiful place', Lucy said doubtfully.

'You see, I've got to get to night school,' Milt said, 'and we thought if we got married, a little place – maybe two rooms in New York . . .'

'Two rooms!' Joe cried. 'Two rooms! We got exactly ten million rooms here.'

Hetty put her hand tentatively on Joe's shoulder. 'Joie, darling, perhaps Milt and Lucy would like a chance to be more on their *own.*'

'What the hell are you all *talkin'* about?' Joe bellowed. 'Two *rooms?* Night school? I absolutely don't understand that kinda talk. It's exactly half an hour to New York on the train. The family's been together all these years, the whole entire family. Now we got a real beautiful place in the country, trees, for God's sake, grass. You don't know what kind of people used to live in this house. The Brices, Si Cutler says the absolute tops in Allenburg. High-class Society. One hundred per cent best neighbourhood in town – Elm Street. This is the Park Avenue of Allenburg. Milt, you're going to save all that rent, kid. Jesus, two rooms in New York costs *something.* You're going to work out here days on our housing job. And, Mullaly, you and I might as well get used to each other's families sooner or later.'

'Joie,' she said, 'you're so sweet. Are you sure you're going to like living with my whole family?'

'Why not?' Joe said. 'I think your mother is a helluva fine woman, even if I say so right to her face. Give her a chance to get the hell out of that slimy flat, give up doing everyone's laundry. Anyhow, this joint is so big, we may never see each other for months.'

Hetty was laughing.

'What's so funny?'

'Nothing. Nothing.'

Milt smiled ruefully himself. He wasn't happy, but he couldn't help handing it to Joe.

'All settled?' Joe said. 'No more arguments? Now what the hell you bawling about, Luce? This was supposed to be a surprise, and it turns out I'm some kind of a monster. I'm the one who's surprised at all of *you*. I don't understand it one stinkin' bit.'

Suddenly Hetty cried, 'Oh, Joie, look what you've done to that beautiful table.' His cigar had been lying on it and Hetty was rubbing a black burn with her wet finger tips. 'For heaven's sake, let's try not to burn all our furniture before we move in, Joie. That awful cigar.'

'How do you like that, eh?' Joe said. '*Our* furniture. See that? Right? Everybody's problem solved. You and me, Milt and Luce, we have a place to live. A hell of a fine place. Mammina and the kids all set. Everybody ought to be goddam happy. Milt? Luce? Mullaly? Mrs. Mullaly?' Silence was satisfactory enough for him. This, then, was his zenith, the good achieved, and the odds against it a million to one.

'Another thing – the minute we move out here, the family name is changed. It'll be Naples instead of Napoli. Hundred per cent Americans. That's us.' He looked from unbelieving face to face, then in a gesture with both arms, took in the house and grounds. 'If I say so myself, you've got to hand it to me. Wasn't this one hell of an idea?' He was completely happy in his success and all it meant to those around him, and it was beyond his imagination that he may have left in his wake any seeds for bitter fruit.

Twenty-one

'THE old house on Elm Street', Milt said nostalgically, putting his feet on Joe's desk. 'I remember it almost fondly. What an old barn it was. And how I dreaded moving into it.'

'But *why?*' Joe shouted, no less insulted than if it had all happened yesterday instead of thirty-odd years ago.

'Why not?' Milt said wryly. 'I was cursed with an old-fashioned mind. I had this completely ludicrous thought when we were young that Luce and I ought to start off in our own place. One room anywhere, but all our own.' He shrugged. 'Don't get mad, Joe. It just wasn't to be, old buddy. Kismet – Arabic for Joe Naples. The Elm Street place was colourful in its own way. I think six months after we took title to it, they closed down the Elks Club in Allenburg, didn't they? What did they need it for? Every deal that was made was made right in that house.'

'Now, Jesus, Milt, don't start that, from the time we moved in there,' Joe said, 'I mean from the point of view of all this good moral character and all that crap – we've been as clean as a whistle, damn near.'

'Yes?' Milt squinched his face in pain and sorrow.

'What's worrying you, that whoozis campaign? I can absolutely explain that a hundred per cent.'

'Well . . .'

'Harold's not going to say anything, for Christ sake. He's chairman of the entire committee, his own self. What's he going to do – commit political suicide?'

Milt shook his head sadly. 'Harold Brice may no longer be in control of the situation.'

'And that business with Si Cutler out in Vegas, nobody'll ever prove a thing. In fact, nobody even knows about it.'

'Knows about what?' Milt said.

'Anything. And absolutely nothing illegal took place.'

'Whatever it was, Joe, we have to assume Sam Poltek will dig it out, so I sure wish you'd please tell *me*', Milt said morosely. 'I'm your old buddy, old buddy.'

'Don't worry, nothing like the Gamboretta business', Joe said defensively. 'You understand one hundred per cent about *that*? I didn't exactly . . .'

'I understand it just the way you told it to me', Milt said. 'You *didn't* – and you didn't exactly not, either. I want to think about that Gamboretta business – how to handle it if it should come up. The greatest element in our favour is that it's all more than thirty years ago.'

Milt pondered a moment. 'The house on Elm Street', he continued, fascinated by the sound of his own voice. 'Doesn't it roll trippingly from the tongue? Like Mr. Costello's tin box or Goldfine's cashiers' cheques or Alger Hiss's typewriter. You know, you can get hung up on a phrase like that. The House on Elm Street.'

The buzzer rang and Cath said Chuck Rossmore was here and his son Andy was on the phone from Cambridge. Joe glanced at his watch. The day had flown. 'The house on Elm Street', ran through his head as he picked up the phone, holding his hand to the mouthpiece. 'Listen in tomorrow, same time. The sins and the whatzis – transgressions – of Joe Naples. Hello, Andy?' He could hear the suppressed excitement in Andy's voice.

'Dad? Hi. Say, I don't think we have anything definite yet, but we may have hit on a little something.'

'Yah?' Joe said, his colour rising.

'I spoke to one of my professors here. Man who teaches international law – Karpeko. He and I hit it off real fine. He remembers your man Poltek very well. He never had him in class, but he worked with him in the Legal Aid Society. Brilliant guy, the professor says. Mr. P. was here during the war. Graduated in forty-six.'

'Yah?' Joe said.

'Dr. Karpeko thinks he may very well have been – you know, left of centre.'

'Left of centre? Look, Andy, if he's a registered Democrat, I'm not interested. Left of left I'm lookin' for.'

'I know, Dad.' Andy was as patient with his father, as always. 'He belonged to quite a few organizations up here, and we're running 'em down to see if any of 'em are on the Attorney-General's list. Dr. Karpeko's helping me. He says he can't understand how Poltek ever got a job with the government in the first place. The

FBI never asked Karpeko about Poltek. Of course, that was back in forty-seven. Dr. Karpeko's quite hopeful. He hates the Communists, being a White Russian himself. He's really a weird duck, Dad. He claims he has prescience in these matters. I get the feeling he suspects *something*. But we have nothing definite.'

'Prescience? I absolutely don't understand that kind of talk', Joe said. 'But it's the nicest thing anyone's told me all day, whatever it means.'

Andy laughed. 'Karpeko's going to keep after it, Dad. So am I. Maybe he'll have something definite in two or three days. A week at the outside.'

'Yah. You're so busy being a detective, you go to any classes today?'

'I only had two. Couple of cuts won't hurt me.'

'Listen, Andy. Don't get behind in your work. Your mother'll get sore.'

That kid. Anything for his old man. Joe felt the tears fill his eyes. All these years he hadn't given Andy one-tenth the attention he was entitled to. First all tied up in Carey and then a man so damn tied up in work.

Chuck Rossmore ploughed in, a bull of a man – always reminded Joe of Erich Von Stroheim. The slight accent whenever he was excited must have been Alsatian, because it was neither wholly German nor French. Where the name Rossmore had come from was anyone's guess – same place as the name Naples, no doubt. Probably Chuck made it up his own self. Chuck had married a girl from Atlanta, and it was his boast that he knew the mind of the average American as only a one thousand per cent native could. Once when Joe had asked him what part of Europe he was born in, Rossmore had sat upright to his full five four and had snarled, 'Are you crazy?' (The r's gargled in the back of his throat.) 'I wass born in Ohio.'

He was born in Ohio the way Joe Naples was born in Rangoon. The truth was that Rossmore understood the mind of the average American as only a foreigner who has made a study of it could. He was marvellous on what Jock Dennison called the 'beast level'.

'Zo-o-o.' He smiled broadly, showing his white snarling teeth, and placed his briefcase carefully on Joe's desk. 'The cops haf caught you at last, eh?' He chuckled cheerfully. 'Lucky for you you're filthy rich, so you can afford men like me.' He sat down stiffly. 'Now, what's the mission? What notes are we listening for?' He tried heavy-handedly to be Madison Avenue.

For ten minutes Milt outlined the situation. Joe had jobs under construction and on the drawing board, couple of hundred million bucks worth, banks involved, government agencies, redevelopment commissions in three cities. Bad publicity could scare these people and that could damage the Naples deals ferociously. And the Naples Foundation was planning a big financial drive to augment its own funds for the building of Naples University. This would hurt that bad. Furthermore, if Joe got a bad enough Press, the upstanding Senators might even go after him for contempt, perjury, who could tell what? 'Depends on how big a dragon they make out of him, whether he's worth slaying.'

'Another cover story for *Time* won't do it', Rossmore said quickly. 'That caption, Joe – I'll never forget it, under your picture – it was classic – "What have I got to be humble about?" Whatever made you say a crack like that?'

'It just came to me', Joe said, grinning as he recalled the gangly *Time* reporter from Texas who had suggested that he must be full of humility at his success.

Rossmore pulled the old *Time* issue out of his briefcase and studied Joe's picture on the cover. 'I don't know whether that caption is good public relations or not. I think not. Have we ever done a story on the men around you?' Rossmore continued idly. He was playing for time while he thought it out.

'Hell of a good idea,' Joe said, 'and we never have. Big human interest. Why, you take Woody Faber, for instance. When he came around here looking for a job fifteen years ago, you know where he'd spent his last four years? Rochester State Prison. Embezzlement. The guy had swiped sixteen thousand bucks from some bastid of a plumbing contractor in Brooklyn. Well, I liked old Woody. Nobody else would give the poor bastid a job, but I did it. I'd trust that man with absolutely ten million bucks in quarters. I want him to stay late, by God, he stays. If I want him to work week-ends, he works. I mean you can't buy that kinda loyalty. Of course, he knows goddam well if he gets caught stealing, it's twenty years, and if he gets fired, it's good-bye, Charlie.

'Or lookit Gravel Larson. Hell, he'd been taking kickbacks from subs over at Dennison's for years. Had a regular scale. Well, Jock knew it, but he finally got fed up and Gravel came to me one day and said Dennison was making nasty sounds to get rid of him.

So we had a talk, and I asked him to figure out how much these whatzis – kickbacks – amounted to that he could remember. He figured about ten grand, which was an out and out lie, because if it was a dime, it was over a hundred thousand. But why should I argue? I'm not a psychiatrist. I said, Gravel, I'm gonna lend you that ten thousand gees and you're gonna pay that dough back to Jock. And then you can sign a note and pay me back outa your salary here, no interest, mind you. Maybe like fifteen hundred a year. And, by God, Jock was pleased to get rid of him. The ten gees was found money, Gravel was delighted, made him feel all clean, like just outa confession, and I was glad, too, because as long as Gravel sticks to estimating and doesn't buy or sell any contracts, he is the best man in New Jersey for my dough.'

The public relations man looked at Joe as if Joe were some poor slob actor who had done one very lousy bit. Rossmore, in fact, looked ill.

'Very warm human interest stories', Rossmore said. 'Iss great for some other time. All heart, yes. Right now I don't think we mention kickbacks, embezzlement, or state prison. Okay with you?'

Joe laughed. This guy Rossmore was okay. 'The point is,' Joe said, 'by giving these guys a sense of security, you make honest men outa them. That's all I try to do around here, is give my people a sense of security.'

'Well, you don't gif me any!' Rossmore said uneasily.

Joe shrugged. 'You're the public relations man, not me.'

'Hellish thing about this Senate business,' Rossmore said, 'is there are no specific charges. Who knows where the lightning might strike? What'll the ploy be – the usual? Corrupting government officers, loans, pay-offs, improper influence? Who'll they be gunning for besides you – anyone big?'

Milt thought a while. 'We've been close to Harold Brice in the Senate. Joe backed him for Governor eleven years ago. Contributed thirty thousand dollars to his campaign.'

'Oh, very charming and generous,' Rossmore said, 'a double and redouble whammy. I was hoping this could be one of those quiet investigations they'd bury on page nine. What else?'

'Well, I went to see the President once. I don't know what they can make out of that. Harold Brice was on the White House staff those days. He took me in, tried to get me to build housing for coloured people. I damn near did, too.'

'Iss too bad you didn't', Rossmore said. 'You should have. What else?'

'Speaking of housing for coloured people', Milt said, agonized. 'Even though it's not precisely on the point, I think you ought to know it, Chuck. We have a little problem here right now. There's a family named Howard trying to buy a house in Naples.'

'What the hell's *that* got to do with anything?' Joe said sharply.

'Let me hear', Rossmore said quietly.

Milt told Rossmore about the Lewin-Howard house sale, pretty quick for Milt, took him like half an hour, and Rossmore listened intently.

'What else?' Rossmore said, when Milt was through.

Slowly Milt said, 'There's a man named Simon Cutler with the NMIA in Washington. He used to be head of the Trenton office. He and Joe have always been close. We've known Simon thirty years. Used to sell us brick thirty years ago. He approved all Joe's NMIA mortgages for the City of Naples, two hundred million worth.'

'That sounds corrupt even to me', Rossmore roared happily. 'How much did you pay *him?*'

'We thought we could play up the fine things Joe's done', Milt said quietly. 'You know, up from the slums. Built a beautiful new city. Now busy in slum clearance and redevelopment. Horatio Alger, with a heavy dash of public spirit.'

'Please,' Rossmore said, holding up his hands, demolishing Milt, 'don't say Alger to a public relations man. When will these hearings take place?'

'Hard to say', Milt said wryly. 'Pretty soon. Few weeks, a month, maybe.'

'Oh, Gott! We have to work fast. Start with your family. You have a lovely wife, two sons, one lost in the war. Very standard and wholesome. Not enough, of course. This is not for the *Springfield Advocate*. This is AP, syndicated, TV, coast to coast.'

'I want the damn family kept absolutely out of it', Joe said.

'Oh, he wants his family kept out of it', Rossmore said acidly. 'Fine. And who will give a damn about what *you* want?'

'You didn't hear me so good', Joe said loudly. His voice shook. 'I want Carey kept *out* of it. You listen good now. Absolutely one hundred per cent *out*. I'm not waving any flags over my kid's grave, for Christ sake.' He half saw Milt behind him shake his head vigorously at Rossmore. Everyone knew Joe Naples was

kind of a nut on the subject of his son Carey. Harold Brice had
a good idea why, and Hetty had her suspicions, but no one else
knew what it was. Except Carey, and Carey was dead.

"Kay. Now how about all this stuff we talked about in the
Time story? The hospital, the new university – what's been happening to all that?'

'The hospital's built,' Joe said, 'and I've been too goddam busy
for the university.'

'Well' – Rossmore was beginning to bite hard – 'how about a
ground-breaking ceremony for Naples University? President Pusey
of Harvard is there, you're there. America's oldest and newest
university. How about that?'

Joe's brow wrinkled. 'I was just talking to Dino about the plans
for the new administration building for the university this morning.'

Rossmore zipped his briefcase closed and open in a single gesture.
'Let's have an architectural rendering at least. Tomorrow. We
can run that.'

Joe pushed a button on the intercom and another. Finally it
worked. 'Goddam louse-up machine', he muttered. 'Dino, can
we get an air-view rendering on Naples University tomorrow?'

'Gee, brother Joe,' the voice of tin said, 'we're working on it.
For a respectable one, maybe Friday. Okay?'

Rossmore nodded.

'And how about the rendering of the hospital addition?'

'That's ready now.'

'Ask Cathy to bring it in, will you?'

Rossmore put his briefcase on his lap. 'You haf this charitable
foundation, also – the Naples Foundation. You have a goodly sum
accumulated there? How much?'

'Thirty million, isn't it, Milt, give or take fifty thousand? Milt's
run ten million way up in the market these last eight, ten years.'

'Yess? Fine.' Rossmore's eyes flicked at the amount. 'Why
don't you select some worthy institution and make a grant? Not
too enormous. Say a half million. For a settlement house, or to
the Church towards a new school or retreat. Something where we
could have a nice picture with a cheque and a bishop grabbing it.'

Joe grimaced. Fat chance his handing out any real dough to
some faceless institution. Every cent of that pile was for Naples
University. But there was the earned income; he had to give that
away each year.

'Think it over, and let me know what you decide', Rossmore snapped. 'I can't get you a good Press unless you *do* something good. Take this coloured man wants to buy a house. Let him have it. Make a virtue of it. Have a nice brotherhood rally. Whoop it up. We'll get you national coverage. Just let us know when.'

Over my dead body, Joe was thinking.

Milt spoke vigorously. 'I'm not criticizing Joe. Not that, believe thou me. No one knows better than I do, it's not simple, this coloured problem. But Joe hollers at these little guys. Tries to buy 'em off. I mean.' His face was that of a sick man. 'Can't we do something about that, Joe?'

'You got to,' Rossmore said. 'Oh, you got to.'

'First thing you know,' Milt said, 'we'll have the NAACP on our necks; they've got this new anti-discrimination law to work with. We'll be in court, and then the fat will be really in the fire, believe thou me. One fight at a time, buddy, please.'

'You said it', Rossmore said. 'Joe, you got to behave yourself.'

Joe stood up slowly and looked from Milt to Rossmore. 'Horse feathers. Just lemme handle this my own self. It's not gonna get in any papers.'

Rossmore shrugged. 'All I can do is *advise* my clients. I have no police power. Another thing, go to church every Sunday, without fail. It won't kill you. You used to go to half the weddings and funerals and bar mitzvahs and baptisms in Naples. It's all right here in *Time*. You're becoming lazy. Every time you're seen in church, it's a good mark for you.'

'I'm so damn busy', Joe said.

'Go!'

Cathy brought the hospital rendering in and placed it against the wall. It was a handsome modern building and they admired it for a moment.

'Very nice', Rossmore said. 'I'll take it with me.' He glanced after Cathy as she left. 'Now, Joe, I don't want to interfere in your private life, but for heaven's sake, no women. You're a married man. You're going to haf all the scandal we can handle. We don't want someone turning up saying you're playing around with some woman besides. And don't think you can get away with it. Doormen, lift men, motel clerks. Once your face gets in the papers, sonny, everyone will know you.'

Joe was impatient. Tune-ups these days was something he could take or leave alone. 'Are you through?' he asked Rossmore. 'Milt, you got any bright ideas?' He spread his legs. 'Then listen carefully.' He offered Rossmore a cigar. 'This young guy, Poltek, the counsel for the committee – he strikes me like a strange wack. You ever meet any Communists?'

Rossmore shook his head.

'Well, I have, my own self. In Italy, when I was running a little town called Bellanza, all these partisans came running out of the woodwork, and then when we had that tenant committee back in the thirties, remember, Milt? And down the union, all over. Oh, I know the type. They're smart. And you can't satisfy 'em; they just keep boring, looking for trouble. They never get tired. Suspicious, cold as ice. They got their ideas and they're not, by God, the same as *my* ideas. They're not looking for reforms. They'll never be satisfied till they tear everything to pieces and get their man in the White House. Tear down is all they know, at least in this country. Well, I've got a hunch Poltek is one of these bastids. If not right this minute, I'll bet my last buck he used to be. Happens he graduated from Harvard Law, so I asked Andy up there to see if he could find out anything about this cookie during his college or law school days. Andy just called. Turns out Poltek used to belong to a hell of a lot of organizations. Could be one or two were on the Attorney-General's list. There's an old professor up there, Moscowitch or Romanoff or something, used to be with the Tsar, and I got a feeling he's got no use for this type either. Andy's working with this Whoziz-witch. How do you like them onions?'

Milt looked as if he would break into tears. 'Please. Please, Joe, anyone working for a Senate sub-committee has had a security check, a full field check. A thorough one. And Sam Poltek came up all through the ranks at the Justice Department, where he must have had Lord knows how many previous security checks. By the FBI, Joe. In the name of everything sensible, let's not grasp at straws. Straws? I mean *cobwebs*. Let's get back to work on our *defence*.'

'But this could be *fact*', Joe said, irritably.

'Sure, sure, sure', Milt said, leaping up, his eyes suddenly going leprechaunish. 'And I'll turn out to be Heinrich Himmler. Oh, what an investigation! We'll have the whole thing made into a Marx Brothers film.' His hands gesticulated wildly. 'I'll be Mr. Moto.' His face turned Oriental. 'Verr' suspicious, my fran'!'

Rossmore's cat eyes were large with excitement. 'Joseph, are you teasing us?' he said incredulously.

'Absolutely not', Joe said. 'I am giving you one hundred per cent fact. I feel it in my bones.'

'My Gott!' Rossmore was on his feet, calling to Milt like a moose. 'If there is *any* possibility, let's track it down, by all means.' He turned on Milt. 'You're not seeing it, counsellor. You're not seeing it at all. Listen to him. You haf to see the American people as I see them.'

'Fact?' Milt said. 'It's pure pie-in-the-sky fantasy. This man may have met a Communist once when he was twelve years old. I don't believe he ever was a party member, not for a minute, and if he were, what would it prove?'

Rossmore waved his arms wildly. '*Is* a Communist. *Was* a Communist. Even had a long-distance *call* from a Communist. My Gott, counsellor, in this country don't you realize what it means? Poltek a Communist! Why, Joseph Naples would become a man on a white horse, the target of Communists. We couldn't top it. We'd have it made. The man who is pulling the teeth of Communism by providing fine attractive low-cost houses. Smear! He becomes more sacred than Chiang Kai-shek.'

'I could end up being a goddam hero', Joe said catching the excitement. 'I guess I owe that much to all the people who depend on me.'

'When will we know any more?' Rossmore said. 'How soon will you have facts?'

'Facts', Milt said glumly. 'And even if you have facts, so called, not a word to anyone until I clear it for libel.'

'A week', Joe said. 'Maybe less. Andy sounded like he knows more than he told me.'

'Joe', Rossmore said, glowing and rubbing his hands together. 'If this is true! Even if it *isn't*, you know you have a *flair*. At least you are looking for the right note. Oh, what a marvellous public relations man you'd have made. Fabulous.'

'Unfortunately he makes a darn good lawyer, too', Milt said morosely. 'That's the trouble.'

'See?' Joe cried. 'What the hell have I got to be humble about?' He laughed and the other two could not help laughing with him. Joe did not wait for the sycophantic laughter to subside. 'Milt, how's about a quick nine holes? It's a gorgeous day out.'

His change of mood was complete, as if with one heave he had got the world off his back. 'See you around, Chuck, you old horsenpfeffer. I'd ask you to play, but you've got too much to do already, sonny boy.'

Today was Wednesday and Joe knew that Harold Brice played golf every Wednesday except in case of war. Even in Burma in the days when he was ambassador to Rangoon, Harold had two pitch-and-putt holes built right behind his house. In fact, next to saving the world, the only thing Harold gave a damn about was golf. And Harold could absolutely put a stop to this investigation nonsense. Instead of all this end running and dodging of Milt's, why not take the problem right to the head man? After all, Harold was an old friend, and he probably had no idea whatsoever how far off the trolley the Poltek kid was getting.

Whenever Joe drove up the long winding Canoe Hill driveway, as he did now, he felt like a trespasser. How they took him as a member in the first place was a story no one would ever believe. His son might feel at home here, but at every moment he expected to be unmasked by any one of the old dowagers as the snot-nosed kid from Ninety-eighth Street. He always got a big hello from Ronnie who took the car, and by the time he reached the locker room, the word was passed and Charlie had his golf clothes laid out for him. In fact, Charlie did everything but lick the floor to show he didn't care *what* the newspapers said, Charlie loved him. Maybe it was the crisp monthly fifty Joe gave him, or the job Joe got his son, Gene, out on the apartment project.

'Evening, Mr. Jason.' Even a friend of Joe Naples was an automatic prince of a fellow to Charlie.

There was always a crowd on Wednesdays at the club. Half a dozen members in various stages of undress shouted greetings across the aisle as false as they were hearty. Phil Forney was there. Joe was always impressed how little he resembled the old Phil he had first met in Italy. This round faced, jowly man was now a forty-year-old executive vice president at Sanders and Sanders, drug manufacturers in Raritan – an organization man stem to stern, like most of the other members at Canoe Hill. Didn't know the time of day or how to keep out of the rain, but always fitted in, just the right amount of joviality, Dale Carnegie hello, how are you, hear the latest joke, and all that talking in business riddles, a hundred per cent fulla crap. Lucky thing Sanders and Sanders didn't get hold of this joker before the war, or he never could've done what he did. Oh, these organization men were all right, it was just that they all seemed to have been castrated somewhere along the line.

As Joe and Milt passed through the glassed-in grill room, they saw the ageing nine-holers playing backgammon and bridge. Joe missed the familiar face of Jock Dennison, who was customarily there Wednesdays, furrow-browed over his cup of dice. Jock would be back from Paris now though, thank God, and if by any chance Joe couldn't settle things with Harold Brice, Jock would know what to do. Damn nice of Jock to be thinking about him all the way in Paris. It made him feel good.

From the door in the grill Joe saw, as he could never avoid seeing, the brass plaque with the names of the club champions. 'Carey Naples,' it said, '1949.' The name and year blazed in his eyes, seared his mind. Carey had had to get Ev Henderson's tournament committee to waive its rules against participation by juniors. 'Runner-up: Everett Henderson.' That irony always gave him a laugh. He could see eighteen-year-old Carey, with Hetty's finely cut face set on that massive body, the young muscles rippling in the white T-shirt, studying that last fifteen-foot putt as if it were the most important goddam thing in the entire universe, stooping, peering, unconscious of the three hundred people on the terrace watching breathlessly. All those days of practice Joe had seen to might now pay off. Only one quick glance up at Joe, and a wink. If this one went down, down would go Ev Henderson, perennial and never before defeated champ. Carey addressed his ball and stood as if he were never going to putt. At last, the putter blade gleamed and the ball started on its winding course. Was it too much? . . . it looked like too much . . . but the ball broke sharply on the hill, went skimming to the back of the cup, popped two inches into the air and fell backward into the cup. Carey shook his head in wonder at the sudden, shocking applause and finally grinned, the family grin, a kiss. Ev Henderson strutted across the green, shoulders square and shook Carey's hand smartly like some phony Prussian soldier trying to be a jolly good loser with an ingratiating and patronizing smile, and Carey came loping quickly up the hill like a colt to his old man and hugged and kissed him like a goddam baby. 'I did it, Pop!' Then he laughed and said, 'I guess *you* really did it, didn't you, Pop?' That boy —

Bits of Carey popped out at him everywhere he went. Never

could insulate himself from even the most innocent memories. Sometimes he thought he was going off his rocker.

Milt tagged along docilely as he had, it seemed, all his life. Milt could play at Canoe Hill as a guest only once a month; as a member, Milt was unthinkable. Joe was aware that his brother-in-law was a hell of a lot more of a gent than he, but facts were facts, and the unwritten rules at Canoe Hill were absolute.

'Senator Brice?' Steve Madero, the caddy master, said. 'Yes, sir, Mr. Naples, he's over at the practice trap. He missed two trap shots Sunday and he's doing penance.'

Joe asked Milt to wait at the first tee, and Milt peered after him in his troubled way. 'Be careful what you say to him', he called under his breath.

The patrician white-haired figure in the practice trap swung with a grace and precision that belied his sixty-four years. Joe watched him put four shots within six feet of the pin. "Ey, Senator!' he called. 'How you fixed for a game?' Harold Brice stood erect, blinked a moment, and his face lit up. 'Joseph. Are you alone?' the Senator said.

'Milt Jason's with me.'

'Good. We'll do a threesome. But I'm only going nine.' Harold Brice spoke with his famed charm, but the old inner warmth was missing. There was that touch of glassy coolness Joe had first felt ten years ago, the day Harold Brice had stood not far from him and Hetty when they folded the flag and lowered Carey's coffin into the grave in the Naples cemetery. Carey Naples and Carmine Napoli, in the earth side by side, his father and his son.

On that day, Harold had pressed Hetty's limp hand and kissed her haggard cheek in sympathy. Turning to Joe and looking down from his six foot six, he had said, 'Sometimes we love our kids too damn hard, Joe. We try for too much and sometimes in the wrong way.' He said it oh so cold.

After that their cordiality was form without content, for Joe had blamed Harold almost as much as himself. Yet outwardly they continued to treat each other as if nothing had happened.

'Nine's enough for me', Joe said. 'We're just out for a little exercise. Goddam waistline's running away with me.'

The Senator motioned for his shag boy to pick up the practice balls, and they started back to the tee.

'How's everything in Washington?' Joe said, as if aimlessly.

'So-so. Look's like we're in for a rough session. I've been busy as the very devil myself. I'm working on two major committees and trying to get my book finished.'

'Another whatzis on our brown brothers?' Joe did not even try to conceal his scorn.

Harold's pace slowed and he half turned towards Joe, frowning. 'You're incorrigible, Joe. You're a bright fella, you ought to know better. This work I'm doing is important. The book's important. We have to bring some understanding to Americans of the very real problems in southern Asia, and elsewhere, too.'

'Oh, Harold, I know all that.'

'I'm discouraged, honestly, Joe, when I see how little headway I make with a fellow like yourself. After all, you're a thinking man.'

'Who said? Lookit, I got problems of my own, Senator.'

'We all do, but —'

'Listen, Harold, let's cut the crap. This committee with this guy Poltek —'

'Senator Owens's sub-committee?'

'Yah. On publicly assisted whatzises.'

'Yes,' Harold said vaguely, 'and it takes up more of Owens's time than I like. I'm thinking seriously of having him step down. Arthur McLean can do the job, and Owens should be spending more of his time with the full committee.'

Joe studied the carefully barbered face of New Jersey's senior Senator. 'I'm surprised at you, Harold', he said. 'Everyone knows you're America's gift to Nehru, U Nu, Sukarno and that whole crowd. But how are you on the home front? Are you against corruption, immorality, an' all that? Maybe that's the pay dirt you need. It'll round you out– just in case your name's called out at the convention for something.'

'I hadn't thought of that, Joe. Perhaps I'm not so much of a politician after all. *You* should take a more active part in politics yourself.'

Joe laughed. 'Well, I'm dinner chairman of the State Democratic hundred-buck-a-plate thing', he said. A faint, but worried smile played around the corners of Harold's thin mouth.

'You know, Harold,' Joe continued, 'you been in and out of the advertising business so long you're beginning to believe your own copy.'

The senator chuckled a professional non-committal chuckle.

'Now all this digging into people's moral character', Joe said. 'How does it feel, being God up there?'

Harold smiled. 'We're accustomed to it. It used to bother me, but in every society someone has to be God besides God. In ours, why not the Senate?'

They had joined Milt and were starting to limber up with a few practice swings when the caddy master called Joe into the pro house to answer the phone.

It was Hetty and she almost never called him at the club. Her voice was tentative. 'You have a visitor, Joie, a charming lady in a Rolls Royce. With a chauffeur in pearl grey.' Her voice rose higher than usual, trying to be so offhand. Something must be bothering hell out of her.

'Yah? One of those old bags wants a few bucks for a wacky charity? Take care of retired old cats? Tell her to come to the office.'

'Joie, no. *This* is a beautiful, lovely, famous lady. It's Anna Landos.'

'Oh. What the hell's she doing there?'

'She's really most attractive, even off the screen. I admire your taste. She wants to see you. She won't tell me what for. Is there anything you'd like me to tell her?'

'Look, I'm just on the first tee. I'm with Harold Brice. I'll be back in a couple of hours, Mullaly. Be a good kid, could you keep her busy?'

'Oh. Harold Brice, I see. Do you expect Simon Cutler here? She says he's coming. She says she's a very old friend, which, of course, I didn't know, though you'll be glad to know I pretended to. She gave Cibulkas a very big hello. And we've talked about olden times in Bellanza and New Jersey. We've been upstaging each other for an hour, and we're running out of things to say, Joie. Must have been a lovely war, darling.'

'Christ, Mullaly, I haven't seen her in – I don't know – ten, fifteen years. Anyhow, it ain't every day we have a big star at the house. She's a good kid – wacked up, but talk to her about that whatzis, that new show you're rehearsing. Maybe she'll have a coupla ideas. You and she got one or two things in common. I'll be home at six-thirty. Sharp.'

What was Anna doing there? Back out on the tee, even though he took several practice swings to settle his mind, he could not get rid of a sense of gloom. His sense of the fitness of things was outraged at the thought that Hetty and Anna were together. He had never exposed Hetty to anything like it. When he finally stepped up to his tee shot, he topped it miserably.

'Who was on the phone?' Milt asked as they walked towards their smothered drives. Harold Brice had left them to stride down the middle, where he had pasted one two seventy-five.

'One of my oldest sins', Joe said. 'Jesus, I don't have to remember 'em, Milt. They keep coming out of the woodwork at me.' Milt's expression pleaded with him. 'I'll tell you about it later.' Poor Milt looked darkly troubled.

The smell of cut grass, the sight of golfers and caddies walking gossipy and easy in the late October afternoon made the entire investigation seem like the invention of some sick mind. Who needed anything like it? Life could be pleasant.

On the short fifth hole, Milt's tee shot found the deep trap beyond the green, while Harold and Joe were on. Milt was about the slowest player in captivity anyway – he must have come up to the green to look at the pin and gone back to study the shot four, five times, and with all the practice swings, it gave Joe a good chance to talk to Harold.

''Ey, Harold, are you actually thinking about running for Vice-President?'

Harold Brice laughed. 'Propaganda, Joe, pure Jersey speculation, and without my sanction.'

'Jesus, Harold, you sound like a corny politician even out here. I'm your old friend Joe, we're exactly ten million miles from anyone.'

Harold grinned the sly grin that had made him famous throughout New Jersey. 'I can only say this, Joe, as an old-time supporter I s'pose you've every right to know, nobody who means anything has asked me. I like the Senate. And I don't want the job. And even if I did, it would be a little like being struck by lightning.'

'You're not by any chance hoping to get there over my dead body, are you?'

'How d'you mean?' Harold said, squatting to study his putt.

'What's this good moral character bit, Harold?'

'Oh, I suppose it's a little like the days when I was in the advertising business. We used words, but we were never quite sure what they meant.'

'Yah. Well your man Poltek has been around to my place. He has me under active investigation. I think you oughta know that.'

'No!' Harold Brice was surprised and, it seemed to Joe, troubled. 'The sneaky little so-and-so. Digging in my back yard.' He had stood up and was pursing his thin lips in thought. 'I'll have to have a look into that, Joe.'

'If this Poltek starts backing me and Si Cutler and Woody Faber, my poor bastid of a book-keeper, into a corner, it's gonna be no good. No good for me and goddam bad for you, Harold.'

'Joe. I'm surprised. Are you somehow threatening me?'

'I'm doin' *nothing*', Joe said. 'I'm just stating facts. You know the facts as well as I do.'

'What do you suggest?'

'I don't suggest a thing. This Poltek is a little prick. I'm serious. He should have his goddam head chopped off.'

'And how do we do that?'

'How the hell do *I* know? You're a Senator. You're *chairman* of the whole goddam underwriting committee. You got rules. Figure something out.'

'Well, I'll look into it, Joe. But I think you're making a mountain out of a molehill.'

'Yah. Well, while you're writing books about our brown brothers and worrying about foreign aid, your nice little counsel is getting ready to carve you up and cut your heart out. And incidentally, mine too.'

'Mmm.' If Harold Brice was disconcerted, he camouflaged it well.

'If you don't chop him down, Harold, I'm gonna have to. And you know me, when I chop, anyone can get hurt. I sure hope I don't needa do it.'

'Mmm.'

Milt's ball was on the green after three explosive tries. Harold bent to his twenty-five footer and swung. The ball rolled ten feet beyond the hole, an incredibly bad putt for Harold, who was usually death on the greens.

Joe looked at his own twenty footer. This was the omen. If it went down, he'd be all right. The odds were against it, for he knew each of his transgressions, in technicolor. But if this one putt could go down . . . He struck the ball and it took the roll as he had expected, it was going . . . right for the back of the cup. The ball struck the cup and hopped up, an inch from the hole, and stayed out.

Jesus, that close. Was that the way it was to be? Now let's not start getting superstitious at *this* stage of life.

As they walked to the sixth tee, Joe did not like the way Harold's turtle lids closed over his opaque eyes and kept him out. Harold was clearly distressed, but saying nothing.

'Funny boy, Poltek', Joe said. 'Something fishy about him, d'you notice? Have you checked him out?'

'What the dickens are you worried about, Joe?' Harold spoke with a sharp edge.

'I'm not any more worried than you, Harold.' The sentence was not without impact. Harold Brice pinched the bridge of his nose with thumb and forefinger, then dropped his hand.

'You're clean, aren't you, Joe?' Then he chuckled and eased the tension. 'And you have the finest legal talent in Jersey to keep you out of trouble, don't you agree, Jason?' The Senator had introduced Milt to the conversation for the first time.

'I try my damnedest, Senator.' Milt was wry. 'But you know these headstrong guys . . . up late night after night trying to figure a new way to hoodwink the public and make a fast buck. But kidding aside, the thing I don't like is that a man nowadays doesn't know until years afterwards what was moral and what wasn't. You have to hold a kind of retrospective lens to everything, and even then it's not always clear. Like those windfall scandals, so-called.'

'*Now* aren't you sorry you asked him something?' Joe laughed and addressed the ball, but he was still feeling depressed about that putt of his.

'Nice drive', Harold Brice said when Joe hit, and after that there was no more talk about anything but golf. Nothing more needed saying.

After they had showered, Joe dressed quickly, shook hands with the Senator, who sat in his terry-cloth robe drinking a Tom Collins. 'See you around Washington, Harold.'

'In some cosy bar, I hope', Harold Brice said.

'As long as it ain't the bar of justice', Joe said, and Harold Brice flicked his turtle lids. There was something gentle and regretful, almost sentimental, about the way Harold had shaken hands, as though either Joe or he were a dying man.

On the way home, Milt said, 'That man puzzles me, he really does. He's walking a tightrope, believe thou me.' Then after a decent interval, 'Tell me, Joe, I've been consumed with curiosity. The phone call. Who was it?'

'Anna Landos.'

'Mmm . . . great! Nothing like a little glamour to brighten up a dreary case, is there? Even the Trojan War had its Helen. Could you tell me about her? How you met? And what you and she cooked up in Vegas . . . you know what I mean.'

'Jesus, how we met. That's going way back. She was just a kid. We met in Bellanza – you know, in that seedy burg where I was Town Major. I think I first saw her the day after the Fourth of July celebration. I remember it was hot as hell . . . Everything was sticky . . .'

Twenty-two

THAT particular day it was not only the black heat but also these five sabotaging old bastids facing him in the gloom. Joe Naples, Major, A.U.S., paused to breathe, and to revolve and quick-puff his Admiration panetella. His trousers were sticky; sweat trickled down his soaking shirt, though he had twisted down his tie and opened his collar. Two fat green flies buzzed around his nose like lazy Messerschmitts, while overhead the useless electric fan revolved erratically. He seized the straw-covered chianti flask on his desk, desperately lifted the bottle and took a few life-restoring slugs. Painted in black on the outside wall were the words TOWN MAJOR.

Joe had been in Bellanza two months, and he might be here another ten million years. Anyone passing through might think Bellanza was a pretty seedy anthill of a town, but it was only when you knew it intimately, all its workings and its six-thousand-odd human inhabitants, that you realized what a complete louse-up it actually was. Joe Naples was now its one hundred per cent absolute dictator, and he wished the Creator and military government had kept the job.

His netful of officials sat on hard chairs, like the kids who used to get sent up to Doty's office at DeWitt. Mayor Bianco always insisted on a hundred per cent decorum. Mayor Snow White and his four dopies, two of them die-hard Communists, or, as they preferred to call themselves, partisans.

Joe cried again in his hoarse, strained voice, 'Now, gentlemen! The sewers on the east side absolutely must be repaired, and I am not making jokes. If not, the least we'll get out of it is typhoid. You men know what I went through to get that pipe.' The four dopies looked at each other nervously. Christ, that pipe was laying there above ground two weeks now – a hundred lengths of sixty-inch terra cotta, not something you could exactly hide. Any day one of those smooth-faced college kid inspectors would be down from the I.G.'s office and start asking their little questions. Oh, he knew those young bastids. He hoped Carey and Andy would not turn out anything whatsoever like that young lieutenant, no matter what fancy schools they went to. That smooth-faced lieutenant from Newton, Massachusetts, who'd ask him in wide-eyed innocence, 'And where in the world did you ever find that pipe, Major? Did you get it authorized?' You could cut him outa that deal. He had to get the pipe under the ground fast.

'We must dig trenches and put the pipe in – not next week. Right away.' Joe slammed his hand on the desk. '*Subito! Capito?*'

He looked from one to the other of his comic-opera town government. 'You just tell your people in the name of the United States government and President Harry S. Truman, any son-of-a-bitch keeps us from getting those sewers in —' He drew his finger across his throat and made a choking sound. 'Understand?' He turned to flick the folds of the American flag, hanging from the short mahogany pole beside his desk. The mention of punishment seemed to animate them to a kind of jocularity.

The *partigiani* Public Works Commissioner said enthusiastically, 'We could open a concentration camp exclusively for people who will not work on the sewer.'

'Okay', Joe Naples said, ignoring him. 'Get to work.'

'We will hold an impressive ground-breaking ceremony', the Health Officer said eagerly.

'*After* the sewer is in we'll have the most tremendous ceremony ever held in Italy. You can all make a speech', Joe said. 'Bigger than yesterday.' The celebration of the Fourth of July yesterday had been made to seem, somehow, an Italian holiday. All the saints along with photographs of Stalin and Roosevelt had been paraded up and down the waterfront and through the Piazza Vittorio Emanuele during the singing of the 'Star Spangled Banner'. 'But first, let's get the goddam sewers in the ground. We have to get things in shape around here.'

The officials rose and, after shaking hands with him, filed out, but not before Mayor Bianco had handed him the regular typewritten list. Four funerals, three weddings, and three baptisms. Before the night was over he would attend at least one of the weddings and a baptism or two and have Cibulkas send off a fistful of those neat letters of condolence or congratulations, beginning, 'On behalf of the Allied Forces in Bellanza, I offer my sincerest . . .' The things he did for the American Republic!

Sergeant Josh Cibulkas shifted his feet uneasily in the ante-room as he waited for the town officials to leave. Josh was a lanky, enormous boy from Atlanta with a Ukrainian name and a Georgian drawl. When he took his hat off, his straw-coloured hair rushed forward and hung over his face like a theatre marquee. He stood in Joe's office, his face cloudy with a characteristic, blank expression.

'What is it, Cibulkas?'

'Sir.' Cibulkas shifted his weight uneasily and smirked. 'I don't know how to exactly put this, sir.' He twirled his hat like a nervous kid and frowned.

'Sergeant', Major Naples said. 'It's been a tough day.'

'Well, sir, what it is, there's been a kinda invasion of Bellanza by enemy aliens, sir.'

'What the hell are you *talkin'* about?'

'Sir?'

'Ain't you heard about V-E day, Sergeant? The war's over. Stop makin' a jerk outa yourself.'

'Sir, the enemy is right here in Bellanza. Hungarians, Major.'

'Hungarians! Are you *serious*? They parachute troops or what?'

'Not exactly, sir.'

'Will you stop kiddin' aroun', Cibulkas. I got enough trouble with old Snow White and his four dopies. Come on, boy, snap it up.'

'Well, what it is, sir, I discovered this *harem*, sir?'

'A *what*?' Joe Naples spoke harshly. He needed one more problem like he needed a third row of teeth. He pulled out a fresh perfecto and bit the tip off angrily.

'A Hungarian harem, like I say, sir. A whole lot of Hungarian women just come to town, livin' in that old hotel down by the water?' Usually Cibulkas stated things as though they were questions. 'They claim they's wives o' Hungarian officers and their men went north kind of in a hurry, sir? No one come around to get them? I think those dames was run out of Naples, sir, and delivered here by an American truck, an' they plenty insulted. They live in this here *seraglio*? It's kinda two rooms on upstairs there.'

Joe lit his cigar carefully. 'Sergeant, you're getting to be a private eye.'

'Well, sir, the guy down the *albergo*, he kinda keeps me posted on what's new. So me and Palter go down there, sir, and we see this here woman right downstairs in the lobby? And I mean, sir, she ain't just an average woman. So we ast her where she's livin'?

And she starts atremblin' an' takes us upstairs to this place. I mean, you know how them dumps are; and I'm tellin' you, sir, this flat had ten beds in the two rooms, with dames sittin' on all of 'em. *Hungarians?* Talk about an explosive situation, sir. But it ain't no hoor house, sir. Not a man in sight.'

'Is it possible that's because it's two o'clock in the afternoon?'

'Major, no sir.'

Joe Naples studied Cibulkas, who was not more than twenty-one and whose enthusiasm was contagious. 'Are you *serious,* Sergeant?'

'Yes sir, I am. There's all them broads up there, goin' to *waste,* sir?' He looked at the Major, whose face was a blank and added apologetically, 'I wouldn't a bothered you, sir, I know the local police coulda handled it if they'd a only been *local* women, but they're *Hungarians* and Hungarians're enemy aliens, ain't they? So that's how *we* get 'em, sir.' His face brightened hopefully.

Joe blew a magnificent smoke ring and watched it drift apart. 'I gather you consider this a serious security problem?'

'Yes, sir.'

'You told anyone else about this?'

'No, sir, only Palter.'

'Well, let's have a look.' He took a last slug of wine and put his revolver back in its holster. He handed Cibulkas the Mayor's list and followed his Sergeant into the sun. It was one of those days when the sun is small, high and white, and the sky cloudless but not clear blue, rather a blue mist, a merciless desert heat from which there is no hiding. They walked through the piazza, and along the cobbled street towards the waterfront, leaving contrails from Joe's perfecto.

People stopped to wave and shout greetings. An old man tipped his hat; women, old and young, looked up nervously. A few children, many of them bare-bottomed, ran into their houses, while others came out to watch; and the older urchins followed the two Americans, calling, 'Gotta ten lire, Joe?' By God, he could be elected Mayor. He waved, flipped a few ten lire coins, of which he always carried a supply, and gave his cigar band to a curly-headed bambolina. 'Damn brats never leave you alone', he muttered to Cibulkas. 'G'wan!' he yelled in English, knowing they couldn't understand. 'Beat it or I'll call the cops!'

The sight of Bellanza – cuddled in the foot of the palisade which rose abruptly from the water – horrified him: burnt-out ruins; crap;

the old human wrecks walking the streets; kids calling to G.I.'s, 'I gotta sister'; women picking through garbage for food; nine-year-old Enrica collecting cigarette butts under the tables of the Café Lascatti and stuffing them carefully into a paper bag; the bombed-out block in which there had been a dozen survivors who had erected a metal cross and painted a sign *Grazie* for sparing their lives. It all made him sick. Thanks for nothing. Idle men huddled on the beach watching the fishermen working their nets. Everything gone or loused up but the fishing boats. Only the monastery on top of the mountain was intact. Everything else had to be made over. That was all he could think these days; no foundation in the whole deal. Might as well get the bulldozers and level everything in sight; dynamite the bleak school building at the waterfront which looked down on the town's raw sewage emptying into the gulf. Sure, Mussolini had promised Bellanza a new school. Every building in town ought to go. And why did the people have to live on top of each other? The place is so crowded, musta been before the war, too; anytime someone put a can of garbage outside, someone else started building a house on it. He glanced towards the clustered hovels, and his eyes turned towards the palisades. There perched at the top was the protective San Martino which had cast its shadow on Bellanza for four hundred years. Yet here below was enough flat land back from the water before the pre-cipitous rise – he could see exactly where he'd put the new project. Houses, neatly spaced. As he walked after Cibulkas, he was irri-tated. If you couldn't get one lousy sewer in, how could you rebuild the whole town?

They were passing St. Elmo's, the seventeenth-century church, and he crossed himself devoutly for everyone in town to see.

The cluster of the fishing fleet's boats, bottoms up on the beach, freshly painted blue and grey, was a hell of a good sight in the after-noon sun. *His* goddam fleet. They'd be going out tomorrow morning, first time in many months. Men worked their nets repairing, tying, sewing, while a DMS and three trawlers crawled across the Bay of Gaeta sweeping mines. A dozen hulls cluttered the bay, but the wrecks were no longer a menace to navigation or fishing. One of the men on the beach spotted him, jumped up and shouted a greeting that started all the others yammering and hop-ping around like monkeys.

They turned away from the water, picking their way now through the most appalling part of town. The shops were all damaged and indescribably dirty. Filth, flies, and stench rushed to greet him. Shops had been blackened by fire and were littered with everyone's trash. A dozen pushcarts cluttered the narrow street, taking the place of destroyed shops. One-man vendors shouted their wares over their baskets. People bargained and haggled in the heat. To one cart just at the entrance to the *albergo* an old man had tethered a scraggly brown-and-white chicken whose skin showed through its feathers. It was on a rope leash, like a horse. Ninety-eighth Street was Tiffany's compared to this.

Joe Naples was disappointed in himself. If only he had a little intellectual equipment! If he'd read more, maybe he could make something out of what he saw, discover some great truth. Instead he saw exactly what he saw: filth, disorganization, pimps and tune-ups, cut-throat teenagers, chaos; and it only made him mad. He desperately wished to hell he was back in Allenburg. He'd struggled all his life to get out of this kind of louse-up. Maybe Milt could've made something of it, a piece of Jason-spun philosophy. And poor old Milt might be dead for all he knew, probably was. Shows you, all those brains dead in one blinding flash. Like Pop – in ten seconds. Joe had a compulsive desire to sweep away this entire unholy mess of filth and disease, under the rug with it, the way Mammina used to sweep the house. But would a new city make these people any better? And why was *he* trying to neaten things up for these *contadini*? What were they to him? Was it just because he'd been born Giuseppe Napoli?

Cibulkas was picking his way up the narrow winding stairs of the unlit hall of the *albergo*. Buzzing mosquitoes were thick as bees in a rose bed and he had to keep brushing and slapping his face, ankles and hands. At the sound of their heavy shoes on the stairs, occupants opened their doors, and seeing American uniforms, stared with unabashed curiosity. 'The Colonel!' an old woman shouted back to her family triumphantly. An old man slammed his door angrily. They reached the third floor attic, to which there was a low entrance, and Cibulkas knocked imperiously.

The door was opened by a short, fragile girl, who shouted in schoolgirl Italian, emphasizing her words, '*Abbiamo fatto niente!*' We've done nothing! Then, recognizing Sergeant Cibulkas, she smiled obsequiously and said in English, 'What is the friend?'

Cibulkas said, 'How 'bout that, Major? This here's Elena?'

The two men stepped inside the bare, low-dormered flat. Nine girls sat or lay on metal beds, but with the perfume and all that round flesh, it seemed that there were nine thousand. Two of them had pimpled faces, several had their hair tied into tight, unattractive buns and one had a noticeable bald spot. Another sucked noisily on a cigarette, blew the smoke contemptuously towards Joe, and passed the cigarette on to the next girl, who repeated the ritual and passed it on again. None wore any make-up except the girl who had answered the door; she had a wet, carmine lip rouge that made her clay-grey face garish. The cheap perfume smell hung thick in the air.

Joe had barely closed the door behind him when he heard the staccato clacking of sharp heels on the stairs and a cheerful, throaty, woman's voice shouting something foreign. Hungarian no doubt.

The girls jumped up from their beds and rushed for the door, shrieking and clawing at each other to get there. 'Anna! Anna!'

Anna came skipping in with a package wrapped in newspaper, gay as if she were arriving at a New Year's party. The others tore it from her, ripped it apart, pulling out onions, carrots and olives, which they gobbled with silent savagery. Anna had deep, naturally red hair which was strewn about her head like freshly cut hay. Her face was delicate with a far-away, preoccupied look. Her nostrils flared back from upturned lips; she had white, clear skin, widely set grey eyes; her mouth was full-lipped and even her teeth were good – something rare in these parts. Although she couldn't have been much older than eighteen, nineteen, she was full-bodied. Laughing, Anna held up an egg and pressed it to her bosom like a lover. The egg was plainly for her. She said something that made the others giggle like seven- or eight-year-old kids. Suddenly one of the girls shrieked and pointed to a wildly fluttering creature on the floor.

It was a white-and-brown hen which Anna had brought, the same scrawny one Joe had seen below, and still on a rope leash; now it had made the fatal mistake of fluttering.

Joe heard the delighted shrieks. The women surged towards the now thoroughly terrorized fowl, who clucked fearsomely and batted its wings against the wall it had backed into. The girls fell upon the bird, screeching so that their wild cries and laughter could not be distinguished from the chicken's. A short but terrible battle ensued with several girls falling back from the frenzied fluttering. Considering they were nine to one, this was a lion-hearted chicken. But two girls finally held it firmly and a third, a tall girl they called Marta, seized its head in one hand like a club and slowly and pitilessly twisted the chicken's head like a wind-up toy to break its neck.

Anna, who had let go of the leash, saw the two men for the first time, shrugged contemptuously and jumped up on a bed, looking over the heads of the others to see more clearly what was being done. Joe could not take his eyes off the girl. Watching her hypnotized face, he had the sensation of being in the presence of perversion, and had a foolish impulse to draw his revolver and order them to stop. Okay, Naples, you get the Silver Star for saving the life of a chicken against the Hungarian enemy.

Slowly, as if she were labouring heavily, Marta turned the head another notch while the others cheered and urged her to twist harder. But Anna stood silent on the bed, her body writhing slowly as if she were both chicken and executioner. Her muscles tightened, her eyes narrowed, her fingers opened and closed spasmodically and her mouth hung open. In the heat, her brown cotton dress stuck to her body in great wet patches. The chicken struggled, but slowly, inevitably, its neck was tortured round, and the room became silent. Everyone – even Cibulkas and Joe – was quiet. There was a faint cracking sound, but the executioner continued to twist, and on the bed Anna continued to labour, her breathing hard and her fingers working very rapidly now. At last, the chicken's head had been turned clear round – three hundred sixty degrees – and the girl let go. The others let loose and scattered back. The dead chicken fluttered and jumped and in sixty seconds lay still, ten feet from where it had been killed.

On the bed, Anna gasped as if she had reached some climax and stepped off the bed in a dream. The two girls who had held the chicken began to pluck its moth-eaten feathers with fantastic vigour.

Anna approached the two Americans and spoke to them in remarkably good English.

'Heil, Truman!' raising her arm in a half-Fascist salute. Her laugh was scornful.

'Where you from?' Joe asked.

'I already told *him*.' She indicated Cibulkas with a twist of the shoulder. 'We are from Budapest. I myself am the wife of Major Ferenc Andramy of the Hungarian Army, and I claim the protection of the Geneva Convention.' Joe tried to keep his face grave, but the haughtiness of this child tickled him. Instinctively, he tested her accent, repeating her words to himself. Yes, Hunkie, the

sound of Laslo Bornholz, his trim foreman, but with a genteel over-
lay which could come only from schooling.

'It so happens my own mother was Hungarian', he said.

'You? Your mother? You are joking.'

'I'm *serious*. Half the Americans you meet, their parents are from
somewhere else. One chance in *ten million* to meet someone from
Hungary and I meet a whole roomful.'

'Imagine!' she said. She turned to the girls and explained about
Joe's mother in Hungarian. They all seemed delighted, even the
two chicken pluckers.

'You see how famished we are', she added gravely. 'We eat like
animals. I have heard of people who became so hungry they de-
voured each other.'

Joe did not respond.

'I have', she said, her voice trailing away. 'I have heard of it.
It's not just a story.'

'Sure', Joe said abruptly. 'Passports, girls.'

'*Passaporti!*' Anna cried to the girls as if she were now second
in a chain of command. There was a scurrying and fetching of passports from handbags and from under mattresses. They appeared to
be genuine Hungarian passports, but they were all for single girls.

'Officers' wives?' Joe said, and Anna nodded gravely. 'You'll all
have to come with me.'

When this intelligence had been translated, there was consterna-
tion; they all shrieked at Anna at once. Maybe it was a mistake telling them his mother was Hungarian. For an American there would
have been instant obedience, but for a fellow Hungarian there were
only arguments. Everybody gave him arguments. They called
him Colonel, but when it came down to cases, they argued. What
the hell good was this uniform if it couldn't save him a little
arguing?

'They want to know if they can bring everything', Anna said.

'Whatever they can carry.'

'Naturally they do not wish to leave the chicken.'

'Bring the chicken.'

Marta, the executioner, carried the half-defeathered fowl.
Clothes gathered into bundles, they made their way past the desk
downstairs, into the merciless smoke-circled sun and along the cobbled waterfront towards headquarters in the piazza. Joe led the way,
Anna alongside. It was a sight for the townspeople to behold: girls
marching in the Piazza Vittorio Emanuele, each toting her black

cloth bag, while the statuesque Marta carried a still-warm, half-naked bird by the head, swinging it like an overnight bag. Sergeant Cibulkas brought up the rear, his eye on Elena. The bald little man who worked the *albergo* panted after them. 'Signor the Colonel, what has happened?'

'*Arrestato*', Joe said solemnly.

'*Veramente?*' The distressed man continued to trot alongside. 'But who will pay for the rooms?'

'You have been harbouring enemies of the United States', Joe said, drawing his hand slowly across his Adam's apple.

'But they did not look like enemies, Signor the Colonel. How was I to know?' Then, as he saw the fierce look on Joe's face. 'No matter, Signore. It is not important.' He screwed up his face like an old imp and whispered, 'War makes strange enemies, is it not true, Signor the Colonel? Also strange bedfellows.' And he turned to run back to his hotel cackling.

By the time they had reached headquarters, five hundred townspeople were out in the square to see the sight.

There were several things Joe Naples could have done about the ten Hungarian ladies: he could have turned them over to Snow White and his four dopies, or he could have notified Colonel McVay in Naples, or written a report with carbons to everyone in civil affairs right up to Divisional Headquarters, asking for instructions; but what he did was to notify no one. He simply had Cibulkas put the girls up at one of the villettas and when Doc Niles visited from Rome two days later, he asked the Doc to give them all Wassermans. Four girls tested positive, and they got a series of penicillin shots. No one was going to louse up Joe's detachment. Two hundred yards up the hill from Villa Berta, where Joe and his two officers were quartered, were the two villettas also owned by the Commendatore, Count di Bellanza – two four-room apartments surrounded by grape arbours, housing Cibulkas and five other enlisted men. To accommodate the girls, Cibulkas and Palter eagerly abandoned one of the villettas. The entire estate, something more modest than a palazzo, was located on the mountain, just below the great monastery. The farmer's cottage and barn were set in a forest of chicken coops, pig sties, and a fenced-in tennis court gone to seed, where a German shepherd dog paced forever in furious captivity.

Joe told his two officers, Captain Burnside and Lieutenant Barker, about the girls. 'One kid named Anna there, I asked her over the house tomorrow for dinner. She could use a few good dinners. You guys wanta have a look? You might wanta have one over. The Villa Berta, where the elite meet t'eat.'

Dinner next night was a curious affair. Anna, her hair redder and more unkempt than ever, dominated the table; Elena, fragile and diminutive, who was Bill Burnside's choice (Cibulkas, a mere sergeant, had been outranked and out pre-empted); and the tall, imperious Brunnhilde, the girl called Marta, who was young Barker's tune-up, decorated the table. The Commendatore, who had understood that there were to be three extra for dinner, had expected men. He now thanked God the Contessa was up north in their Bellagio retreat and could not witness this disgraceful display of bad taste in her beloved Villa Berta.

The three girls ate the pasta with a curious concentration and scarcely a word. When they did speak, it was to each other in Hungarian. Then they'd laugh like hell. Bunch of kids whooping it up.

'You seem to be enjoying it', Joe said to Anna.

'Of course. We're much hungrier than the average', Anna said, directing her remarks to the Commendatore in Italian. 'We have always eaten very well, and when we stop eating suddenly it is much harder for us. The Italian women have not been eating for years; their stomachs have shrivelled up; for them it's no hardship.'

'Why,' Joe said, 'I been hungrier than everyone at this table put together. My stomach never shrank. Vino, my dear ladies? *Rosso o bianco?*' Although wine had flowed at Villa Berta in the past two months, it had never gushed so freely. By nine o'clock the American officers and their three Hungarian girls were on their eleventh flask.

The Commendatore, a small-boned, slight man in his late sixties with a parchment-like skin and a reserve which he never dropped, watched the proceedings without expression. When coffee had been served in the small red-silk-walled sitting-room, he nodded a silent good night to everyone and gravely ascended the great winding stone steps to his bedroom.

In the small living-room, the three couples had nothing much to say, but they laughed it up. The girls were marvellous gigglers. Each told his or her last name and, using Anna as interpreter, even attempted desultory conversation, but without success. There was an old gramophone with twenty-year-old opera records and they tried playing a squeaky Titta Ruffo doing *Pagliacci*. The effort was a noisy, tinny, ludicrous failure.

"Ey, you wanna see the upstairs of the villa?' Joe asked Anna. 'C'mon, I'll show you the sights.'

Upstairs when he had shown her the five baths, the lift, the bare-walled bedrooms, she said, 'The villa where my husband and I live in Budapest is just as nice. And my parents' house is even bigger. We had fifteen servants – or eighteen. I can never remember.' She walked down the long corridor to look at the master bath again, longingly. 'Oh,' she said, 'there is nothing I like more than a bath.'

'Any time', Joe said. 'Just come up and use it.'

Joe smiled and stood at the door and thought he liked to listen to her lies. His lips formed themselves into a half whistle, half kiss – intimate, inviting – then broke into a lesiurely and asymmetric smile of rare warmth. Anna was thinking people might forget everything else about Joe Naples, but they would never forget his smile.

'Comin' in?' They were at his bedroom door. His two and a half quarts of wine had given him quite a head.

Anna Landos smiled a guarded smile, stepped inside, and waited patiently until Joe had followed her; then, like someone who knew precisely what to do next, she closed the door quietly. The room was barren, unpainted, with wires exposed, lit by two of the feeblest lights in civilization. The Commendatore had never thought of em-bellishing the bedrooms. Even the oak wardrobe, which had been imported from Holland – the Commendatore said it was a museum piece – was dark and ugly and covered with hideous carvings of cupids and swans. On the tiny desk in the corner next to the sink, Joe saw the twenty or thirty letters he still had to answer – letters from the men at home, or their wives or even their kids. Jesu, Maria e Giuseppe, every brickie and hod carrier, every wood-butcher, lather, plasterer or bum who had ever worked on a job for him wrote letters. People who bought his houses wrote to com-plain: oh, great white father, what do I do about the leak under the kitchen sink? From four thousand miles away. He'd been away from Allenburg two years and he had to keep writing to his men and their wives, don't worry, I'm coming back. Stop worrying!

Well, those were the guys that had made Joseph Naples, Inc. the best home builder in the Garden State. He took care of them, and they knocked out seventy, eighty houses a year. It was a living, and a hell of a good one.

The letters the men wrote in painful scrawl – 'We wait for when you get home again, Giuseppe. We wait . . .' 'The wife and kids talk about the old days,' 'My wife says Joe Napoli is the only boss who understands the men.' Several of the wives had sent him socks and sweaters – just the thing for tropical Bellanza.

There were letters from Carey at Lawrenceville, Rosina at her convent, and Hetty and Mammina, and a letter dictated to Hetty by five-year-old Andy.

Anna had begun to take her clothes off, not in any hurry, but as if there were nothing else conceivable for her to do.

The situation was as ancient as mankind. But even in his fuzzy wine-soaked condition he was disturbed. It never hurt a girl to wait till she was asked. Spoke good English, too. Maybe she was from some high-falutin' Hungarian family after all. Maybe one a those high and fancy bitches, spoiled bad. Why not? Who could tell what the war had done to these snobby European girls and their families? She might be anything – the daughter of a countess, or God knows what. He watched her drape her dress carefully over his letters on the desk. Lookit this kid with the face of a goddam *infant*.

'What the hell you doin?' he said uncertainly. She stood facing him in a pair of frayed cotton pants and nothing else.

'Don't you want me to?' she said. Her voice was flat.

I tell you, he thought, give 'em a dinner, give 'em wine, treat 'em good and whattaya get from 'em? A kick in the tail. Lookit 'er, standin' there like I just beat the hell out of 'er. Now she wants me to feel like I'm foreclosing on the old mortgage. What am I – Simon Legree?

'Hell, no', he said. He'd been to that fat hoor Simonette twice last week, and was she a lousy tune-up!

'Don't you read the history books?' she said. There was a faint touch of irony in her voice. 'When I was a girl, I read all the histories, it was always the same for the defeated women. And I was always the defeated woman. It made history fun. Even when I was twelve or thirteen, I didn't really mind.' She stepped out of her pants and flipped them to the desk. 'And you know very well there are much worse things. Men at war have terrible needs. That's what my husband told me.'

She stood before him for an instant in the dim light. The faintness of the feeble electric light added to the illusion, but she was the loveliest creature he had ever seen. Such grown-up eyes in that faraway child face, on what was a full woman's body. Only her red hair, still uncontrollably flung out from her temples, spoiled the physical perfection. Her breasts, though full, were young and light, as if they wanted to rise to some unseen surface. But her belly button, which popped out instead of in, gave her a childlike, almost an infantile touch. She stood before him, her head faintly bowed, a sombre smile on her lips, as if there were no help. Then she crawled silently into bed and pulled the sheet to her chin.

In spite of himself, he could not stop trembling; he began to undress, but she wasn't going to look him over like some bull. His thickening waistline made him self-conscious; he'd look like Fatty Arbuckle to this kid, too damn much pasta and vino. He yanked the old-fashioned pull cord, and undressed hurriedly in the dark. Moonlight was gleaming through the huge window on the pillow and on her face. The hell with it. It was too hot to close the shutters.

When he flung his flesh on hers, he was still trembling. When they kissed, wide-mouthed, she stroked the back of his neck. She was very quick. Guiding him, spreading herself, taking him into her almost before he knew it, she the one in command. He was irritated almost at once. He could feel the tremendous surge of his sex, but this had nothing to do with him. It had just been too damn sudden, and dispassionately he observed himself and the girl. Her body churned and she panted – a cold-blooded act. Even the tune-ups at the local hoor house had more sensitivity, and Joe Naples had his own idea of the act of love. He was the one to smile, kiss, arouse. He was the one to make 'em like it. Even Simonetta thought he was tremendous. He'd make her laugh and then she'd owe him something. Okay, then he could use her, because that wasn't exactly like someone owing him for a packet of cigarettes, or ten bucks. It was something, any kind of real pleasure was a damn rare thing. But this girl he hadn't touched in any way at *all*. Fake she was. He looked down and saw her watching him. She snapped her eyes shut, caught in an act of espionage. Then her face fell into repose, an expression of patient stolidity like a mother coping with the tantrums of an angry child or a nurse holding a pan for a nauseous patient, while her body beat mercilessly like some mechanical apparatus, beating until she was notified she could turn the stop switch, a great controlled rhythm trying to triumph against him. Why, she was nothing but a tune-up machine, without the slightest spasm in all her gyrations. He felt no need to go on. It was not something sudden, a decision, but rather a lassitude that had been building against the natural rising of the flesh; and he had no hunger born of abstinence. He felt profound disappointment, finally revulsion. To hell with *her*; nobody had to do him ridiculous favours like this. He looked at her again, the pale face of a child in the white moonlight.

And with an enormous lunge of will, he pulled away, uncoupled himself, lay listening to his own heavy breathing and heart pounding, disgusted.

'Gowan, get over there', he snapped, pushing her to the other side of the bed. 'I need this deal exactly like I need three eyes in my head.'

'What's the matter?' She opened her eyes wide as she slithered to the other side of the bed. 'You not feel well?'

'Why, Anna, I'm surprised you ask me that. I'm healthy as a bull.' He smiled and she blinked, wondering whether to be reassured by the warmth of his smile. 'But I'm not *exactly* a goddamn *bull*.'

She raised herself on one elbow and regarded him with a mixture of fright and puzzlement. 'You do not like me?'

It was Swede Swanson, the wound plainly in his face, crying. 'You ain' sodisfy wid my work, boss?'

He grimaced. 'Why in the first place you're *exactly* old enough to be my daughter. That's number one. And second place, I don't like this cold-blooded stuff. That's for kids like Barker. But I'm no kid, I'm thirty-eight years *old*. You can count me outa *that* deal. I mean, there oughta be *something*.'

'But how will you . . .? For a man, isn't it difficult?'

Joe laughed. Her concern – the more he thought about it, the funnier it struck him. 'Look, kid, if it gets to that point, I'll take a cold shower. Now stop lookin' so nervous and go to sleep, will you?'

'Right here? In this bed?'

'Why not? Just lay over there on your side, okay, kiddy?'

She rolled over with her back towards him and he pounded his pillow.

'*Buona sera*', she sniffled. Let her sniffle.

'*Buona sera*, kiddy.' Come to think of it, a good cold shower wouldn't be such a bad idea.

When he awoke and looked at his watch it was 6.30. She was not in bed but he heard her splashing in the tub.

'*Buon giorno*.' She sighed when he came in. 'I was just wondering about my poor husband. Do you think he's a prisoner, or maybe even worse – Do you think— Here, wash my back. I itch all over.'

'Husband?' Joe said, scrubbing the washcloth over her back. 'You got no husband.' He tossed the washcloth into the water.

She seemed saddened.

Who cared? Perhaps one day he would find out what went round in this girl. Right now it didn't matter.

'*I'm* married', he said. 'Seriously married.'

'Your wife is a lucky woman', she said. 'I think you must be very kind.' She lolled back in the warm water.

'Okay, if you think I'm so kind, then tell me the truth – how come you're in Bellanza?'

'It's quite simple. I was a film star. You probably never see Hungarian films. But Anna Landos is a big name in Budapest. Not exactly a star – I'm still too young. But on my way up. In Hollywood – how do they say – starlet. I sang sometimes in night clubs – the fancy ones, there are only two big ones in Budapest. And in one, in the Golden Abbey, I met Ferenc Andramy. He was beautiful and tender and he came night after night to see me, drinking sparkling red wine, and he fell madly in love with me. So, I quit my work and followed him to the town where his camp was; and after that wherever he had to go, I went. It was the war, we did crazy things, and that's how we got to Naples. I sacrificed myself for him and now he is either a prisoner or dead.' She sniffled as if she were trying to weep.

'Mmmm. Great. And your parents?'

'My mother was also a great star. She was part of an . . . an acrobatic act. She could walk a tightrope on her hands.'

'You must have had a marvellous childhood – theatres, witty people.' He felt guilty leading her on. He was always running into girls who loved the theatre. Even Hetty was still in it up to her ears, working as a volunteer in New York at something called the Stage Door Canteen, with a lotta big shots in the theatre. Anna was a common hoor, and hoors always had tremendous and glamorous stories. But she was such a young and appealing one.

She studied his face. 'You don't believe me', she said softly. 'I tell you what. I'll make a protocol with you. I'll tell you the truth if you'll promise to believe me. I understand Americans are very high for telling the truth. They don't seem to mind it, like Hungarians. You ought to know *that*, if your own mother is Hungarian. She probably lies all the time.'

'Okay, deal. Tell me one single lousy truth.'

She took a deep breath as if she were going to plunge again.

'I grew up over on the Pest side of the river. My father was a watchman in a factory. A – a shoe factory. He drank all the time. They call the place where I lived the Worker's Section, but it's nothing but an awful slum. When I was a child we never had enough to eat. My mother used to go with men. Many nights my father would be in the kitchen drunk and my mother would be with some other man. Sometimes there were terrible fights. We had to move every few months. Ever since I was seven or eight years old, I dreamed of being an actress, a great dancer. But I found there were so much easier ways to get out of the slums. I learned from my own mother.'

This girl could think up a story a minute. What the hell did she know about living in a slum?

'You think I'm clean yet?' she said. 'I've been here two hours. Oh, I'm so lazy.' Reluctantly she got out of the tub and began to dry herself.

For no reason he showed her the scar on his neck. 'See that? A milk bottle hit me right there. Some son of-a-bitching nigger threw it at me from a roof. They stitched me up in the hospital. When I was a kid, we fought the niggers, the sheenies, the Micks, anyone who came around. That's exactly how stupid *we* were, we used to murder each other – instead of doing something useful.

'You know' – he warmed to his subject – 'ninety-two per cent of the whole stinkin' world lives in the goddamdest junk. In filth. That's the scientific fact. Can *you* tell me what the *hell* this war is all about, if ninety-two, maybe ninety-three per cent of the people are living like that? Nah – how would *you* know? We're fighting the wrong goddam war. I'm *serious.*'

'Americans never know what they are fighting for', she said triumphantly.

'Yah? And Hungarians? I been through France. I been in Germany. Ripped up, houses smashed, so now the people who were in the slums are living in – for God's sake – *caves, sewers, subway stations.* Now that's an improvement for you. It'll be *exactly* ten thousand years before they get *back* to their nice old filthy cosy slums again. Ah – what the hell do you know? You're a child.'

'And you, my Major, you feel sorry for *everyone.* Oh. I've heard. You're too soft-hearted, my darling Major.' She half sat up, snuggled up along his chest, kissing as she went. 'I have heard that you do *kind* things for people. Like stealing all those things from your Navy for the fishing fleet. I heard about that. But I don't think you're so different from other officers. You still like to have power over people. Only you get it in a different way.'

'I use it in a different way, too.'

The warmth was returning to his body as she beat her square, stubby, almost childlike fingers in a light tattoo along his flanks. She was more than a child.

Her fingers and lips made their way along his neck and chest, but she was not going to fake him out again. None of this floating in on him. 'Okay,' he said, 'cut it, cut it.'

She started to grow bolder.

'Hey, I'm serious', he said pushing her away. 'You didn't hear me so good. Get dressed.'

Listlessly she stepped into her unwashed cotton pants, put on her torn bra. 'I thought we were *simpatico*', she said pouting. She picked her dress off the desk.

'You ever been to Naples, kiddy?' Joe said suddenly. And she caught his change in mood.

'Never', she said, then bit her lip. 'Except, of course, that time I was married.'

'Oh, yah, *that* time. Would you like to go?'

'I love big cities.'

'We'll go after breakfast', Joe said.

Downstairs Barker and Burnside were having a huge breakfast of prosciutto and eggs with Elena and Marta; and when they saw Joe and Anna the two men stood up and said good mornings all round politely, as if they were at some middle-class pensione. The Commendatore had kept to his room for breakfast, no doubt informed of the worst by the cleaning woman.

During breakfast the mail jeep from Division drove through the Villa Berta gardens, into the cortile; a PFC who covered the sector from Rome to Calabria brought the detachment's mail into the dining-room, saluted, dropped the letters on the table and, without batting an eye at the girls, returned to his jeep. Joe saw Hetty's V-mail letter at once. And Carey's. He read Carey's short note fast. Kid was okay. Working as a junior counsellor in a day camp. When was his Pop coming home? There were six other letters for him, but one in particular, a thick one, caught his attention and he grabbed for it. That carefully slanted neat hand – by God, it was Milt Jason's! His heart jumped. Milt! Praise Jesus! What about that, the old bastid was alive and sending his patron saint the Word! He put Hetty's V-letter in his pocket to read later and ripped open

Milt's. He could all but hear Milt's quiet, untroubled voice, his studious, painfully slow, hesitant delivery, his professorial manner.

'Dear Joe, old buddy', and he led off with a detailed account of how he'd been shot down over Frankfort and bailed out, and was hidden by a German farmer until Patton's troops came through. Then there was stuff about Lucy and his two girls, and Hetty and the boys. Milt had been discharged and even his mind had quickly become a civilian:

> But what I've really been thinking about, Joe, since I got home, is you – that old habit of mine. You know, there's been practically no new homes built all during the war except in a few defence towns. Do you realize that when this thing ends, twelve *million* guys will be getting out of service and each one *has* to find a place to live? Stop and think about that, Joey. I mean, as you would say, that's *serious*. It's fabulous. Now, buddy, with your talent and know-how you can be the richest man that ever came out of Ninety-eighth Street. You'll make Tony Ferrara, boy gangster, and Rudy Meraglio, restaurant tycoon, look like pikers, and you'll do it legitimately. I'd like to help. Practising law is okay, but I'd like to be part of the brave new world. This is Operation Opportunity. I don't mean a hundred or two hundred houses a year, Joe. I'm talking about *thousands* a year. Maybe tens of thousands. And you can live on Easy Street. We all can for that matter. One thing more: I have the tract. A four-thousand-acre farm that Tony tells me is for sale, the old Woodman Estate, near New Brunswick. I'm sure you remember it, with that great ugly manor house along Route 19. Now you know me, Joe. I think only at the top level. Details like getting all the money for this operation I'll let you worry about. You have freinds who believe in you. Maybe Jock Dennison or even Tony, who sounds interested if you are. What am I, a genius? If I were, I'd be you. If you can't do anything more, Joe, *think* and let me hear from you. If there's anything you want *me* to do, I'll do it.
>
>   Your fellow millionaire,
>   *Milt*

Son-of-a-bitch, Milt was okay, he was all brains. He really was out there operating that old head of his all the time. And usually with Joe in mind. Which was no more than right. Who always took care of Milt in the pinches? What was it he wrote there? Joe glanced back at the letter. Biggest home-building boom in all history. Zoom, zoom, like the '20's, only bigger. Just in time for Joe Naples.

He turned to Captain Burnside. 'Bill, I'm going for the day. Climb up Snow White's back to get those sewers in. If necessary, lend him a few men. And keep an eye on the commie Public Works guy. Don't let him louse things up.'

'I hope you don't mind mah sayin' so, Major,' Burnside drawled in his backwoods Monroe-ese, 'but chew suppose installin' a sewage system is a direct function o' the U.S. Army?'

Burnside disliked work. He could show you documentary proof that absolutely nothing was his function.

'Function, my tail', Joe snorted. 'We'll all end functioning with typhoid.'

'Ah mean, now the manual . . .' Burnside said gingerly.

'Bill, you been in the Army long enough t'know *nobody* reads that handbook. *You* know if we followed the handbook, we'd be under five feet of crap.'

'But . . .'

'What the hell you *arguin'* about, Bill?' He shook his head, snapped out a cigar and bit it; it was one of the Commendatore's best. 'Whatta you guys expect? Y'eat the best food in the *world*, sleep in the old Commendatore's best beds, from a goddam *museum*. Wine for breakfast! Lookit you guys! That's vintage stuff, boys. And y'each got a tune-up, and *Hungarian*, so they can't even talk back, and all I do is ask you to follow a few simple little suggestions. Is that so *impossible?* Don't give me the handbook. You ever run high hurdles, Burnside? All these handbooks, manuals, rules, laws, I've been jumping 'em all my life.'

'You're the Major, Signore, Colonel, suh', Burnside said with resignation.

'Thanks. Then get after that old biddy Mayor.'

'Yus, suh! Maybe some day they'll name the sewers *after* you, Major.'

'See you tomorrow', Joe said. He tugged Anna out after him.

As he left, Joe overheard Burnside saying, '. . . and there goes the last of the world's intellectual giants.'

Dumb college bastids, couldn't come in outa the rain.

Joe Naples hadn't been out just plain riding in the countryside in the sun with a girl – since when? When he first knew Hetty back in the twenties. Just nothing to do – brother! He felt damn near young again.

He drove the jeep along the winding highway south to Naples. On the road, there were only bicycles, donkey carts and an occasional military vehicle. Anna sat demurely beside him holding her dress down, her hair flying like a flag. From time to time from a great height they could see down to the water, a stirring, shimmering flame, glistening in the brilliant sun. The weather had turned somewhat cooler; occasionally Anna sang snatches of Hungarian songs.

No judge of voices, he found hers small and throaty, but gently pleading, urgent, begging, heartbreaking. The jogging of the jeep, the song of this child, the sun and the view lulled him. 'Hey, that's good', he said when she finished. 'Sing some more.'

She smiled. 'You like it? Tell me, what do *you* do at home?' she said.

'I'm a builder', he said. 'I build houses in the country. Little white ones, with grass and bushes and backyards and crap like that.'

'A builder. You know, all the men I have known before have been wreckers.'

'It's a living', Joe said.

'You do it only for the money. All Americans are mad for money, I know.'

'And all you like are the things money can buy.'

She shrugged, and rested her head on his shoulder. 'I don't mind. You're American. Why shouldn't you like money? Do the people who live in your houses love you very much? For building them the nice little white houses in the country with trees around?'

That got him laughing. 'Love me? Ho, Christ! The complaints! The abuse! The can leaks, the furnace is out. They call me at midnight, one in the morning! They, for God's sake, write me letters *here*. They want me to get the squeak out of the stairs from four thousand miles away.' He whistled. 'People who buy houses are the scum of the earth. An' you oughta see how *bewdeeful* these houses are. My kid brother Dino designs'em. Bay windows and fireplaces. Very graceful. But do the people who buy 'em appreciate 'em! Nah!'

'And after all you do for them? Imagine that. Courtyards, flowers. It's not fair. They should love you as I do, and you don't even build a house for me. But if I come to America, you'll build me one, won't you?'

'Absogoddamlutely.'

'Good, I'm coming.' She began to kiss him again without warning. The jeep lurched off the road. He turned the wheel furiously and she laughed. This girl was out of her head. Her kiss was wide, wet, and passionless. It was something she had learned to do proficiently, like dancing. He twisted out of her grip.

'What the hell you trying to do, kiddy?'

She murmured singsong wordlessly at her own amusing secret and smiled down at the back of her hands. At last she said, 'I have it in my mind to defeat you somehow.'

'Are you Catholic?' he said abruptly.

'Of course.'

'Here.' He handed her his rosary. 'Think of your sins.' He nudged her to the far side of the seat. She stared at the beads and cross, placed them quietly on the seat between them, and drew away from him as if he had shocked her. At last she said, 'Can you show me a photograph of your wife?'

He took out his wallet and she examined it, while he drove. 'She is nice, so tall and so young, so long-legged. And the boys are both yours?'

'The big one is Carey. Lookit the size of him. Bigger than me. Would you believe that big lunk was born in a car?'

'You are teasing me. American babies are born in hospitals.'

'They're supposed to be, but not old Carey. My wife looks like some kind of duchess, right? Well maybe so, but she has her babies like those dames in the Po Valley. Can't hold back. We were on the way to the hospital. See that big guy? Well, I delivered that monster my own self with my own two hands and I'm no doctor, kiddy. With these old bricklayer hands.'

'How was your wife?'

'Brave as hell, believe me. They don't come any braver.'

She examined the photograph. 'He is very nice, the boy, so handsome. Is *he* married?'

'Nah. He's fourteen. But spoiled. Oh, I worry about him. Why that son-of-a-bitch is ninety-eight per cent of my entire net worth. He's damn near six feet tall and only fourteen. I'm scared some worthless girl is gonna get her clutches on him. That kid is so smart, he's got professors eating out of his hand. He – you know – *thinks*. He don't just accept what *anyone* says, except maybe from me. He thinks I'm Jesus Christ on horseback.'

'But my darling Major, I think also you are Jesus Christ on a horseback.'

'Don't talk sacrilegious, kiddy. I tell you it's like some kinda supernatural feeling I got for that boy. Maybe it's because I gave him life. I helped anyhow with these goddam hands of mine. From the second I slapped his little round tail, I tell you, I've given that boy everything I got. Anything. And he's alive every minute – not like some kids. Out on the job with me seven in the morning before school. You ought to see that boy lay brick. Great tennis player. And you ought to see him play golf.'

Anna was staring at him in wide-eyed disbelief. 'Major, now, now I know who you are in love with. Your son, and he probably is in love with you. No wonder.'

'I'm in love with the future, kiddy, and Carey's the future. He's got it going for him. The war's over. Peace is just layin' there for my boy Carey to pick up.'

She sat curled in the corner of the jeep like a discarded cat, picked up the rosary and thumbed it idly. 'You are excited by new life', she said. 'The new baby being born in your hands must have given you the shivers. For me, I get shivers from death, especially the kill. I'm not ordinary at all. This is the truth, my darling Major, I never told this to anyone, but you are like a father. Now I understand very well why we are no good together in the bed. You guessed my secret. For me it is the only way to kill, and you probable don't like that. But I hate ugly force; I hate brutality. What a man puts into me is ugly and brutal life and I hate it. I hate babies. Am I unnatural? I want to do only one thing, kill. So I use myself to kill men. Perhaps I give pleasure, but it is only a trap to kill. When I have a man inside me and I bring him to the end and he moans at me, the way Ferenc used to do, and says I die, darling, I die for you, I get the shivers from his death – the death of the monster of life. I take life from him into me and leave a wet rag of the monster. Oh, I get the shivers.' Her face was flushed with a morbid glow. 'And what is nice is that you can kill a man many times, watch his death agony over and over. You must think I'm crazy.'

'You're not crazy, you're just a wacked-up little fruit cake, kiddy. Come around in twenty years. I'll discuss it with you.'

She closed her eyes and slowly her face, which was contorted into a hard, tense ugliness masked by lovely features, relaxed.

When she spoke, her voice was quiet, dull, almost lifeless. 'My parents died in a camp', she said. 'My father was a professor of English. They had nothing special against my mother – my mother was just his wife. Nobody bothered to kill them. They just sent us all to camp and neglected us. By the time they died, even I couldn't recognize them any more. I hardly cared about them any more. I was an animal, trying to stay alive myself. We all were.'

She shuddered. 'My father did not see eye to eye with the Nazis, but by the time he died, that seemed unimportant. It was a strange place, that camp. I fell in love with death there. It was with you every day, and every day you wondered which one of your friends had died or been beaten to death. The only way to stay alive, of course, was to be cleverer than all the others, steal their food or their clothing.'

'Holy God!' he said. 'It absolutely did something to you. Hate maybe.'

'Oh, no, I was so busy staying alive, I had no time to hate anyone. Besides, there was no one to hate. The guards didn't hate *us*, they just did their jobs. They didn't care. I have hopes some day I will have the pleasure of killing someone I do not hate with my own hands. I could be God . . . like the guards at camp. The inner feeling . . . must be quite satisfying.

'One day they came and took a dozen of us girls to an apartment in Budapest, where they brought soldiers back from the front. They were a terrible bunch, but they were not cruel. Some were even gentle, some were lonely and frightened like us. They wanted us to comfort them. Until one day Ferenc talked to the matron and I went away with him. I was really quite lucky. See, there are no bruises on my outside and my appetite is quite normal.'

Suddenly she was quick and animated again. 'Of course, I'm just telling you this nonsense to make you feel sorry for me. They're lies. Americans are such sentimentalists. Especially you. But it goes together. Who else but a sentimentalist would be a builder? You should stay in Europe after the war. Everything has to be built again. All the people in the camps need new apartments, and you'd make a great deal of money. I would stay with you.'

'There'll be plenty to keep me busy in New Jersey. You know this joker, the Count di Bellanza? The Commendatore?' She nodded. 'His great-great-great-grandfather – I don't know how many greats – was a builder. He built half of Bellanza. They named the entire place after him. Used to be called Dalprina. You know how this old bastid spends his days? He goes to baptisms. He goes to weddings. He goes to funerals. It's a hell of an honour in Bellanza to have the old Commendatore to your funeral. These ceremonies are important to people. I'm Town Major so I imitate him.

But that man is a padrone in spades, everyone's papa. All because his great-great-great-grandfather built the place. I'm *serious*. I've learned a lot from that old guy. Okay, maybe the town is run down. All the same, the old man was gloomy as hell when it was shot up, I can tell you that. 'Cause it was *his* town. A whole city with his name.'

'You could surely build a city, my dear Major. Is that what you are thinking? I'm sure you could. The City of Major Naples.'

'We already got a helluva lotta cities in the States named Naples', Joe said. 'There's one in Florida; one in Maine. I looked it up one time. Six or eight of 'em, in fact.'

Then as the jeep bounced along, quite unexpectedly Joe had his vision. Some people have had visions of the Virgin, but Joe's vision, which must be described as a vision rather than a fantasy, because it was so real, was of a somewhat different kind. He first noticed it, when along the barren road he saw a rectangular sign in block letters that said, NAPLES, NEW JERSEY – 25 M.P.H. The vision was then more or less strung out along the highway because before long he saw another sign, this one diamond shaped and yellow, saying, SLOW SCHOOL SLOW, and soon they came to a red-brick building three stories high with a white New England colonial front and a white-and-gold belfry tower with a clock. And the words on the great portico were NAPLES HIGH SCHOOL. Looking into the valley down to the sea he saw hundreds, thousands of frame houses, small, brand new, all about the same size. Yellow and white and grey, each with its blue or red or green shutters and its small perfect garden and lawn, some with white fences. A car in every garage. Kids everywhere, playing in yards, sitting in playpens, sleeping in carriages. Right before him the world was remade. It was immaculate, it was shining, as visions are. War, filth and hate were destroyed by it. Men were watering the lawns. Women gossiped over back fences. The world was new. The vision remained, but the jeep bounced on past it; and before long he could see half hidden beyond the cliff a large, much dirtier city sprawling down to the water. Turning a bend, they observed an old and mud-spattered blue sign, which said NAPOLI. He looked back. The vision was gone, and they drove in silence into the ugly outskirts of the war-torn city.

The dimly lit and murky restaurant they discovered on Via San Carlo was a crowded place popular with American troops and the black-marketeers of Naples. The room was long and narrow like a corridor, and the row of unpainted tables, each to accommodate six, jutted at right angles from one wall, leaving a narrow aisle along the other for passage for waitresses and customers. High up on the far wall at the end of the corridor was a blackboard with the menu. At the table behind them a scrawny woman smoked a long thin cigar. At their table were already seated a Captain and a Lieutenant of the Air Transport Command and two overdressed Neapolitan girls heavily made up, all of whom had been drinking wine for some time. The Captain was prematurely balding, roundish and freckle-faced. His pug nose and stocky frame gave him a powerful, impish air. The Lieutenant was frail with a thin, giraffe-like face.

'*Ciao*', the Captain said, smiling at Anna. He spoke to her in painfully slow Italian. '*Sono – Capitano Forney. Lui é Dulian.*'

'Who the hell is Looey?' Lieutenant Dulian said.

'*Le ragazze sono Gloria e Teresa*', Captain Forney said, pouring glasses for Joe and Anna. '*Piu vino, signorina!*' he called to the waitress. 'Major, may I congratulate you on your exquisite taste. You will observe to what low estate Dulian and I have fallen. You would scarcely believe that he is a Yale man and that I am Princeton '39.' He smiled at the two girls who giggled at each other and twitted their fingers at him.

'Almost went to Princeton myself', Joe said. 'I woulda graduated – let's see – 1927.'

'Princeton, twenty-seven?' Forney said cheerfully. 'What a coincidence! Here's to Ol' Nassau.'

'I'm Major Naples', Joe said. He put his hand across the crowded table.

'Be-bee', cooed Teresa.

'Naples?'

'Yah, and it *used* to be Napoli', Joe said.

'Here's to ol' Napoli, Major Napoli.' Dulian drank.

The food was brought with four additional large bottles of Chianti. The girls ate ravenously, but the men stuck principally to the wine, and in a short time they were peering through the smoke as though it were more or less impossible to see each other. With considerable awkwardness Captain Forney put his arm round Joe's shoulders and said, 'Major, you have certainly come up with the most beautiful girl in Europe, but she has not opened her little red mouth to say one little word, though she has packed away quite a meal.'

'She's hungry,' Joe said, "cause – and you'll never believe *this*

— she's *Hungarian*. Too much, eh ? A hungry Hungarian. I'm *serious*.' He struck the table. 'Which is a helluva coincidence because my mother is also Hungarian', he said reassuringly to Anna.

'I knew it,' Lieutenant Dulian said, 'wherever you go, imported is the finest.'

'What is more,' Joe said, 'she sings *exactly* like a goddam canary.'

'No !'

'Sing something', Joe said. "Ey, Anna.'

'All right,' she said quietly to Joe, as if the others were not present, 'but only for you.'

'Introducing,' Joe said, 'the champeen singer of Budapest. Anna Landos.'

'Shsh . . .' hissed Captain Forney at the restaurant in general. In a voice so small that she could scarcely be heard beyond her own table she sang a wonderfully melodic and wistful song. The notes were small but perfect. Her song created enchantment, even in that place. She became a changed creature, a delicate spirit of a girl. It was a miracle that she could keep her song so small here in this crowded room, the most touching song Joe had ever heard – and she sang it only to him. At no point did her eyes wander from his own kissing smile. Conditioned by wine and touched by song, he was only slightly removed from breaking down. He was homesick. When she finished, everyone at the table applauded and she laughed inwardly with the glee of a child who had pleased herself. It was the first of many songs suggested to her. 'Do you know this one ?' 'How about this ?' And before she had finished, the whole restaurant was applauding and calling for more. 'You should be at the Stork Club. People will pay to hear you', Captain Forney said.

'I'm too lazy,' she said, 'I won't practise. I like too much to have a good time.' She took a long tumblerful of wine and drank it all slowly, her eyes shining. 'I'm having a good time now', she added.

'You know this one ?' Captain Forney leered and leaned back in his chair, waving his arms wildly like a symphony conductor. 'Roll me over, in the clover, roll me over, lay me down and do it again !'

Anna shook her head, but the two Italian lasses knew that one, probably the only English they did know. 'Rollmi oh-va an' oh-va', they chanted. 'Rollmi o-va, lei-mi donn an' do eet again !' Anna said, 'Excuse me', and went to the lavabo while they sang another chorus, and half the restaurant joined in.

Captain Forney said, 'That's an enchanting Hungarian you have latched on to, Major Naples.'

'Don't let the kid fool you', Joe said. 'She oughta be in the hands of a head shrinker. Oh, this is a loused-up kid.'

'She should put herself in my hands', Lieutenant Dulian said.

'Wouldn't you know I'd end up with *her*?' Joe said. 'I must have a sign on me. I dunno what it is, but if I take a nap, I wake up, there's a dozen people on my back. Ah, what the hell's a use crabbin'? Where you from, Captain?'

'Me?' Captain Forney weaved a trifle as he spoke. 'New Jersey, pearl of the Atlantic seaboard.'

Joe groaned. 'Well, well, well . . . whereabouts?'

'At the moment? My wife lives with her dragon of a mother. East Orange. You ever meet a mother dragon?' Joe lifted his head off the table with difficulty; it weighed exactly two tons.

'Yah? An' where you plannin' to live when you get back?'

'Not with the dragon. Tha's for sure.'

'You wanna buy a *new* house, right?'

'Right! A nice postwar house.'

'With water in the basement', Dulian grunted.

'Somewhere out near Raritan. I got me a job at Sanders 'n Sanders. Oh, I'd like rambler roses, car in the garage, washing machine for Susie, darkroom for me, playroom for the kids. We got us two girls an' boy. Coke in the Frigidaire, cook-out in the backyard. Every little ol' cliché. An' up in the attic, a little ol' dragon cage and some tasty dragon seed.'

'Don't forget picket fence all aroun'', Lieutenant Dulian said. 'Obviously.'

'You an' exactly twelve million other guys', Joe said. 'An' you know who's gonna build your house? I'm gonna build it, that's exactly who's gonna build it.'

'Washing machine for the little woman? Darkroom?'

'Yah. An' right in Jersey, too,' Joe said, ''cause I live in Jersey, my own self, and tha's where I build.'

'*Landsman!*' cried Captain Forney. 'My poor benighted friend here comes from blackest Flint, Michigan.'

'Michigan!' Joe said. 'Michigan! In Mongolia, ain't it?'

'Lower Mongolia!' corrected Dulian.

'Ah, well, doesn't matter', Joe said. 'Happens my own mother was born in Michigan.'

'Oh yeah?' Dulian said. 'What town?'

'Town?' Joe said. 'What'm I, a goddam atlas? She wasn't born in no *town*. She was born in the sticks somewheres.'

'What town *you* come from?' Captain Forney said.

'Captain,' Joe said, 'I'm from Allenburg.'

'Allenburg? Think of that, Dulian! Twelve million guys in the armed forces, and I meet this guy. Princeton twenty-seven and he lives only a couple of miles away from me.'

'An' play golf at Canoe Hill', Joe said.

'Hey!' Captain Forney said. 'My sister's member Canoe Hill. You know Sandy Henderson? Married a big banker. Oh, a stuff shirt, but verr-ee nice.'

'My own banker', Joe said. 'Ev Henderson.'

'Why, my God!' Captain Forney said.

'Think of that', Dulian said yawning. The two girls were chattering to each other in Italian.

'This is fate,' Joe said, "cept I don't believe in fate. You guys ATC, *seriously*?'

'Hell, yes, Karachi, Abadan, Casablanca, Natal and all points west', Forney said, his freckled round face coming into focus for the first time.

'New York, London, Paris, Rome and all points east', Dulian added. 'The ATC gets aroun'.'

Joe's eyes narrowed. 'You men been to the States lately?'

'Major, there's something called security, you un'erstan'? Hush-hush.' Captain Forney looked under the table carefully as if a lion were about to jump out. 'I was home last week. Dulian, wasn't that last week?'

'Yes, sir', Dulian said.

'I remember it clearly because I not only saw the little woman and kiddies, but I saw the dragon herself and sir, you couldn't forget a dragon like *her*.'

'When you gonna see this dragon again?' Joe said, leaning forward. His eyes were cool and steady and he was smiling fixedly, the wine notwithstanding. Captain Forney was charmed with the smile. 'Soon, maybe. Two weeks maybe. Right, Dulian?'

'Right', Dulian said. 'To the old dragon!' He took half a tumblerful of wine in a single breath.

'You set down here in Naples?'

'Rome, not Naples. Never Naples. Rome.'

'I got a leave comin' up', Joe said. 'Probably for Cannes or

Paris. But you know something? I'd rather see your li'l old dragon in East Orange. She fascinates me.'

"Markable', Captain Forney said. 'You don't care for the Riviera?'

'Can't *stand* it', Joe said. 'All those international slobs 'r *impossible.*'

'Come wiz me to New Jersey, my fran', Casbah of the new world.' Captain Forney's face was screwed up with pleasure.

'Deal!' Joe said.

'Whoa, whoa', Captain Forney said, holding up his hand like a traffic cop. 'Not so fas'. You inspect to build me a house. Right?'

'Right', Joe said.

'How much you sharge me?' Captain Forney said suddenly. 'I know you builders. Ver-ee trick-ee.'

'Cheap', Joe said. 'Free. No sharge whatsoever.'

'Including picket fence?'

'Joe considered that a long time. 'How high?' he said.

'So high', Forney said. 'No, *so* high.'

Joe scrutinized him carefully. 'Okay. 'S a deal.'

'Okay', Captain Forney said. 'Ciampino Airfiel'. On July – lemme see – July nineteenth. Right, Dulian?' Dulian's head was on the table and his girl was murmuring, '*Bambino mio.*'

'Ask aroun' the field for Cap'm Forney. Name of our plane – Dragonsdaughter. Name' after my sweet wife Susie.'

Dulian spoke up suddenly. 'Why the hell you want to go to New *Jersey*, Major, you got such a lovely pear-shaped picola right here in Naples?' He waved in the direction of the lavabo at the far end of the place.

'I'm the *most* unlucky bastid in the universe', Joe said morosely. 'You should only know!'

'What on earth are you talking about?' Captain Forney said.

'Men, jus' lookit that girl down there, you think she's just another cucuracha, don'tcha, a two bit tune-up? But she has got the absolutely saddest story in the universe. And *I'm* the guy ends up with her problems in my lap. Who else? Are you men sober enough for me to tell you this?'

'I have never been sho sober in my ganzes life', Dulian said.

'Likewise, Major', Captain Forney nodded through a thick blear, trying to wipe the fog from before his eyes.

'Better have one more', Joe said and filled all glasses with Chianti. 'This beautiful creature,' he continued lugubriously, 'with the heart of a goddam *child* has live' in a Hungarian concentration came for *five entire years*.'

'No!' Dulian said. 'Egad!'

'Too much to be'lieve', Captain Forney said. 'Piteeful.'

'Men, I'm *serious*. Dragged away as an infant. Christ, I thought I had a lousy childhood. Did you have a lousy whatzis, too, Captain?' Joe felt himself again at the point of tears. 'Trouble with all this peace, you get thinking. Next thing I'll be goin' to a psychiatrist. Where was I? Ah, yah, so her old lady and her old man are *smacked* into this filthy camp, starved to *death*. Because he did not happen to *agree* with the Nazis. How zat? After a while, she couldn't *recognize* 'em. You know what her father was? A goddam professor of English? A *professor*! How about *that*?'

'Gosh!' Dulian's mouth hung open drunkenly.

'Gentlemen, we gotta do something for this kid with the voice of a bird and a build like a brick sh— I mean this is a number-one champeen girl.'

'You are right, suh, Major,' Captain Forney said, 'an' we are at your command.'

'Men, the only patriotic, red-blooded, hundred per cen' American thing for us, we gotta get this songbird to New Jersey, an' fortunately I got it all planned. Now. Here's the deal. From Jersey, I'll ship her to frien' of mine in Hollywood, California. Old Trick Potamos, big Hollywood director. You ever heard of old Trick? Ain't seen whozis for a long time, but he owes me one hell of a favour. Oh, Jesus, what a favour.' Even in his drunkenness a wave of nausea took hold of him and he closed his eyes as he thought of that disgusting, unbearable nightmare moment when he had walked in on them, Trick and Hetty. 'He'll get her a job as a goddam extra. From there. Christ knows how far she'll go. To the top maybe – or the bottom. I dunno.' He peered intently at his wine glass, which was empty again, and filled it.

Captain Forney studied Joe for quite a while. 'You know, Major,' he said in a low, sincere voice charged with alcohol, 'for a few minutes I was won'ering how come man like you gets to be a Major, an' a foxy college man like me is relegated to mere Captain and Dulian here only Secon' Lieutenant. In fac', I have been brooding over the injustice of it all. But Major, I now take it back. You are a *genius*, Major. You think *strategically*. Why didn't we think of that, Dulian? Take the girl to New Jersey. From there to Hollywood, California. Zippo. Because we are too dumb, tha's why.

No imagination. I take my hat off to you, Major. Say, where's my hat?'

'Now,' Dulian said sceptically, 'this good deed we are about to do, will she go quietly, or do we have to bind 'er, an' gag 'er an' chloroform 'er? Because it's more *com*plicated that way and also *more illegal.*'

'Wise guy', Joe said. 'This girl will be eternally grateful to you, evermore, and you gentlemen – officers and gentlemen – you're the guys to do it.'

'*Bébé!*' cried Teresa, and pouted, too long neglected.

'*Silenzio!*' Captain Forney cried impatiently, and the girls subsided glumly.

Anna returned, her nose powdered and her lipstick fresh and wet. She had even flattened her hair down somehow.

'Okay. Back to Bellanza, kiddy. Back to Bellanza, my little cucaracha.'

He pushed his chair back, placed what money he still had neatly on the table and said, 'Captain, it's been a pleasure doin' business with you and don't you think jus' 'cause I had a fair amoun' a wine that I will not be at Ciampino Airfiel' on July nineteenth. With baggage. And you better be there, too, or absolutely no house.'

In Bellanza next morning, Joe acted swiftly. He stirred Barker to conclude his inquiry into the local black market, which he had initiated several weeks ago on complaints by the Mayor himself. Gagliano in Public Works got a hundred fellow partisans to start digging for the sewer so the Communists instead of the Americans would get credit for *that*. To all the routine meetings of town boards Joe brought his deputy, Captain Burnside, so that in the event of the sudden death, absence, or inability to serve of Detachment Commander Joe Naples, Captain Burnside would be briefed and ready. 'I could go anytime, Bill. Hell, they even shot whozis, Lincoln', Joe reminded his deputy prophetically. Joe took a day off to go to Rome, where he knew a supply sergeant from the old days at Fondi, and got the smallest size G.I. uniform made – 'for a goddam costume party we're gettin' up for the natives. Big comedy routine. This one's for a little chick who does a helluva number.' On the eighteenth of July, Joe announced to his two subordinates that he was taking his ten-day leave with assignment to Cannes, beginning tomorrow. Barker and Burnside were to carry on as though he were there, and if any direct inquiries came from Division, they were to assure Division that he *was* there. He did not need to remind them he had done the same for them.

During these few days Anna slept in the same room, on a cot he had moved in, and oftener than not, stalked about the room bare. When she was not in the bathtub, she cut the Commendatore's roses freely and brought vases of them to the bedroom, which soon looked like a florist's shop. Joe gave her money to buy scarves and trinkets, fed her at the expense of the U.S. Army, whose funds seemed inexhaustible. But Anna was distressed at not being permitted to share his half of the bed. Joe had to laugh. 'Just don't try so hard. You don't owe me a thing.'

'I do. You let me use your bathtub, you took me to Naples, we had drinks together. You let me sing to you. You smiled at me. You gave me money. How can you say I don't owe you anything?'

'Oh, all that crap. Tell me, kiddy, what about somethin' *big*? The biggest thing that could happen to you?' He *wanted* no part of this girl. Only to see the expression in her eyes when he told her. That expression he lived on and for.

She looked at him in wonderful wonder.

'How'd you like to go home, kiddy?'

'To Budapest? But what for? I have no one ...'

'No, no. Not Budapest! Budapest, for God's sake! The middle of nowhere! No, I mean *my* home, the States.'

She stared for a moment. 'My dear Major, do not joke with *me*.' She turned and looked out of the window, and he remained silent. 'Oh, yes, *yes*. To America, oh, my *God*. Now look what you've done.' The tears were overflowing. 'You make some kind of awful joke. I don't want to think of it.' Her breakdown was sudden and complete; she was too distraught to think of him.

He was bursting. 'Okay', he said. 'You're goin'.'

She stared. 'You're *only* a Major', she said.

'I'm sending the rest of the girls back to Budapest.' She laughed at him, harsh, young laughter, as if he were crazy.

'Oh, my dear Major.' She was still laughing, hysterically; then she walked to the furthest point in the room, turned on the water in the basin and talked softly. 'Can you really do it?' She splattered water on her face.

'Yah. And remember one thing, kiddy. When you get to the States, don't squander yourself.'

Although the order to deport the girls was bad news for Barker and Burnside, they accepted it manfully. It had, after all, been a

pleasant interlude. Cibulkas, who was given the honour of driving
the female caravan to Budapest, was furnished with safe conduct
passes for all commands, signed by Major Naples – passes which
Joe knew were worth exactly as much as last week's copy of *Yank*,
but he had limitless faith in Cibulkas. 'You think you'll be able to
handle our Bolshy allies?' he said.

'Major,' Cibulkas said, 'ah'm of Yew-karanian descent, ain't I?'

It was a departure unique in the annals of war. Nine pretty
women, rehabilitated, venereal diseases and pimples gone, loaded
with U.S. Army duffel bags full of loot, climbed into a caisson of
the U.S. Army at the Paizza Vittorio Emanuele and, as the motor
roared and the truck started towards the waterfront highway, fourteen American officers and men, mixing democratically with fishermen and townspeople, waved a reluctant farewell. Anna stood
at Joe's side and, as the truck lurched forward, cried her last farewell and waved a small handkerchief at her less fortunate sisters.

Next day at Ciampino, Major Joe Naples and a silken-faced red-
headed private who was the next thing to a midget boarded an ATC
C-47, the Dragonsdaughter, and landed nineteen hours later at
an army airfield in New Jersey.

Twenty-three

'USED to get a lot done those days', Joe mused. 'Christ, I took whozis to Newark, bought her a dress the same day; Milt, she was the cutest lookin' G. I. you ever laid eyes on, got her a plane ticket to Los Angeles, called up Trick Potamos – he was at RKO right after the war – the boy's a big independent today, and, in fact, he was pretty big then. Anyhow I put her on a plane in Newark – all in five hours. And that night I got to Lawrenceville in time to have dinner with Carey. I mean, I got around, y'know? And was I glad to see that kid Carey. I was amazed how he'd grown, you know he was damn near a man by that time. I missed those years when he was growing up. And that same night I think I saw you back at Elm Street, and Hetty – Hetty must have thought I was completely off my wack. Christ, we hardly had time to hop into bed together, I had so damn much to do. We only had a week. We hadda get the contract signed for the entire four thousand acres in three days. That old lady Woodman was a doll, though. Worked nights, right? They had us scared stiff with that cock-and-bull story that Levitt was negotiating for the site. Remember that? That was the first piece of land we bought by lookin' at it from a plane. Scares me when I think back how we ever did it. All those goddam easements, water rights, paper streets to be vacated, hell. And getting Jock and Tony to put their dough on the line, I really felt like a genius. Remember all that crap when we had 'em in the plane, about my big vision? We must've all been nuts. Probably it was peace coming all of a sudden.'

'You haven't changed a bit', Milt said. 'At least now I understand how Phil Forney got his house. I always thought it was some kind of pay-off to Ev Henderson for getting us the building loans.'

'Why, Milt, you know me better than that. Phil Forney got the sixth house we finished in Naples. A promise is a promise.'

'I've wondered what a guy had to do to get a free house.

Smuggling girls into the country for you. Sure, it's obvious.' They drove in silence for a moment. 'So now here we are, and your past looms up and glamorous Anna Landos, America's dream girl, is home waiting for you with your wife. What for? All you've told me so far is not what I'd classify as genuine first-class *sin*, old buddy. These are simple violations of a few petty army regulations and the immigration code. These are mere boyish pranks.'

'Yah.' The thought sobered Joe. 'Maybe I ought to try to do better for you. Well, okay, I saw Anna once after that. And this may be more like it.' Joe was almost enjoying the recollection. 'Oh, Anna'd become pretty damn famous by then. She was married first to Nicky Stewart, you know, the crazy kid from Houston whose old man hits oil every time he takes a divot, you know. Then she divorced him and married that rich tennis player whozis, you know – complete twit. And then she started that whole revolution because she posed for that magazine *Playboy* . . . hell, she'd pose naked for anyone anywhere. She just doesn't give a damn. I bet she's tuned-up half the guys in Holywood, including Rin Tin Tin. Not that she gets anything out of it except in a wacked-up way. Every time she gets laid, she's getting back at everything lousy in her entire life. It kinda purifies her. Beats me. Anyhow, by the time I saw her she'd been in half a dozen pictures. Trick Potamos's big new hot discovery. The little bastid. That was the week she was on the cover of *Look* and *Life* in that peekaboo dress. At the Flamingo in Las Vegas, they were paying her twenty-five thousand bucks a week just to stand there in that dress and do five songs a night. That's what the magazines said.

'It was in April of forty-seven, I think, the same week we got that gobbledygook letter from Si Cutler, saying he didn't think it was in the interest of the Commissioner to issue six thousand commitments in an untested area. You remember all that crap he wrote?'

'How could I forget it? It put life in my poor ulcer. Our pal. Good old Si.'

'So I called him for an appointment – I said I hadda see him, but he said he hadda go out to Las Vegas. Well, Jesus, a bell rang, you know.

'You know poor ole whozis, Si, had it pretty rough those days. You can't be too hard on him. His wife, with that lousy multiple sclerosis, never out of bed, oh, that Ellie was a sad apple. Broke your heart. I'm not kiddin'. Hospitals bills, and nowhere for Si to go for a decent roll in the hay. Si was not a guy who could go too long without a tune-up. Great big handsome son-of-a-bitch, but he dreamed in dirty pictures, like a high-school kid. So I figured hell, why not meet him out there in Vegas?

'I swear to you, Milt, except I took some extra dough with me – I had Woody Faber give me ten grand, I guess – I had absolutely no idea what was in my own mind to do when I got out to Vegas. I thought I'd play it by ear. I figured I'd get another look at Anna, kill birds with stones, after all, I hadda kind of proprietory interest in the broad. And I'd get that commitment nonsense straightened out with Si. I figured what Si needed mostly was a good loud lecture on what the hell was going on in this country of ours . . .'

Joe had been in Vegas a few times before with Tony and once with Jock, so he knew his way around.

He called Anna in her dressing-room the minute he landed, and you'd think she was Eva Peron these days, the deal he had getting through the switchboard, past her agent and her maid, but Anna screamed with delight when she heard who it was. That was part of her new self-assurance and the phoniness that could only have been acquired in Hollywood. 'Darling, my darling Major Giuseppe, how's your old Hungarian mother? Still living? You old so and so. Where've you been all these years? That friend of yours, that Trick Potamos, I spit on him. He is a first-class louse, my darling Major, did you know that? I do not thank you for him, no. I made him *millions*. *What* a louse. That is the truth, too. Oh, my darling Major, I'm so glad you've not in show business, I couldn't even have *talked* to you unless you were definitely *somebody*. It's like a prison up here in these rarefied clouds. The *mores*! Sometimes I wish I were back in Bellanza! But, darling, you are a pretty filthy-rich millionaire, so I suppose it's all right.'

'Not exactly a *rich* millionaire, but filthy, yes. Kiddy, how about I come over to catch your show and we can have a few drinks together afterwards? I got a friend I want you to meet.'

'But, darling, I'm married twice already and divorced. Men I don't need. I want to see only you. It's not Trick Potamos, is it? Not that rat!'

'Hell no, not Trick.'

'And how's your wife, with her oh-so-long legs?'

'Home with the two boys. No, this guy I got with me is a big shot in the government.'

'Oh, my darling Major, please. I don't like people in the government, even your government. What am I saying? *My* government.
Did I tell you I'm a citizen? By my first marriage, and I even read
the Constitution. That is something, darling. I bet you haven't.'

'You're gonna like this guy, kiddy', Joe said. 'He's got a sad
story. I'll tell you all about him. He's important to me, kiddy.
When's the show?'

'I'm on at nine, my darling. I can hardly wait to see you.'

Simon Cutler's mission in Las Vegas was to pass on a site for
a proposed five-hundred-house job. He could have left it to the
Zone Commissioner, but a trip to Las Vegas sounded inviting.

He did not like the builder of the proposed job. 'Little runt',
he told Joe, over drinks at the Flamingo's bar. 'I think he's in the
liquor business, and liquor's not quick enough for this bird. He
figures building is the quickest, only he wants Uncle Sam to take
all the risks and he'll take the millions. Think of it, five hundred
firm commitments out here in the middle of nowhere. He's a nut,
sweetheart. A complete nut.' He looked around the huge gambling
room lobby at the Flamingo to see if anyone had overheard him.
Out of the side of his mouth he said, 'This house prospector thinks
Las Vegas's population is going to triple in five years. A nut, I
never heard of Nevada till I was a full-grown man.'

Joe sipped his Martini. Si had become even better looking with
the years. His massive frame carried additional authority. Men
who hold authority, Joe thought, sure look it even when they
haven't got the brains they were born with. 'Si, listen to your old
friend. Did I ever give you a bum steer? The little runt, whoever
he is, is right, and after I get finished in Jersey, I got a good mind
to come out this way my own self. California'll be even better. Or
maybe Florida. You know the warm places in this country are
gonna grow like wildfire now that people can get around. Planes
everywhere. You wanna be smart? Give him his whatzis, commitments, Si. This town is gonna bust wide open. The whole country's
ripping at the seams. In fact, the entire world is.'

'And I suppose you're going to nag me for *your* six thousand
commitments, too, sweetheart?'

'In the worst way.'

'Sweetheart, I am damn sorry to be working for John Q. Public',
Si said winking slyly. 'I'd be better off working for you. I know
it. I'd probably like it more and do better for myself. Lord, I think

of the old days in Allenburg. How we scrambled for a buck. But I'm carrying a public trust now, sweetheart, it has other satisfactions, and I tell you, our statistics and surveys just don't show that. It's all imagination.'

'Manure', Joe said. 'What do I know about surveys? All you gotta do is look. The place is busting wide open.'

Si peered at him pityingly. 'Sweetheart, you have any idea what it's like working in a big organization? We have ninety-three field offices, each one with a director; eight thousand employees, almost all in civil service. We fellows at the top are their prisoners. And we're only a small outfit, part of a huge set-up. We have to make our annual pilgrimage up on the Hill and get our little appropriation and our nice fat authorization and explain ourselves. I'm an organization man, Joe. We work in committees. I don't make policy alone. I can't even act alone.'

That burned his tail. Si Cutler not only admitting he was an organization man, part of an ant hill, but bragging about it.

Joe put his drink down, sauntered over to the crap table and got chips for a hundred-dollar bill. Play was quiet, there were only eight people at the table. Si followed him.

'Screw the statistics', Joe said. 'I'll show you exactly how much statistics means.'

'Point coming out', the croupier droned. 'Six. Six the point.' Joe put two chips on five and nine. The rake pushed the dice to a heavily rouged fat lady, a septuagenarian who rolled them as if she were getting rid of a pair of live worms.

'It's a game of crap', Joe said. 'You know what's gonna happen? The guys who have the guts to take chances right *in* government are gonna do okay. The safe players, the hedgers, oh, I suppose they'll hold on to their jobs, but too little too late is gonna get no promotions. No sir. You want to be Deputy Commissioner some day, Si? Or maybe Commissioner? You need a policy.'

The old lady threw three fives and a nine and Joe let his bets ride, until he had a stack of thirty-two chips where two had lain. He picked them up and dropped them into his pocket. 'That's statistics, Si. That's what my ESP tells me. Take that back to your committees.'

'I don't feel lucky at all. Let's eat.'

As they made they way into the gaudy dining-room, Joe said, 'How's Ellie, Si?'

Simon's face clouded, as if someone had struck him in the solar

K

plexus. 'Oh, that girl. Can't even move out of bed any more. Uses a bedpan. Pain, oh my. And never complains. Just gets that terrible white colour. We have round-the-clock nursing for her now. I don't know what I'm going to do about her, Joe. That's a terrible thing she's got. She's lost forty pounds. I just don't know where to turn.'

'Yah.' It was frustrating to Joe that there was someone he knew who needed help and he was unable to provide it.

'I hate to think of my hospital and doctor's bills. You have any idea what a private room costs these days?' Si said. 'I just don't know what to do.' His voice was hollow with despair. He was no longer a man with all the answers. 'I still have some life insurance I can borrow on, but where'll it end? That's what worries me.'

The poor bastid. It was amazing to Joe how many unrelated sides there were to a man. Women, it seemed to him, were more monolithic. Their work, worry and private lives were unified. Their security, like their play, revolved around man, home, sex, and babies – connected. Men, on the other hand, were all over the lot. A guy like Si was trying to protect the interest of the public, do small favours for his friends, house the entire American people, worry about his dying wife, make ends meet on a $12,000 salary, and at the same time look for his tune-ups elsewhere.

Joe said, 'I don't see how you can be figuring four or five million bucks every day, putting your John Hancock on a billion at a clip, and have to be worrying about a few thousand lousy bucks at night. How can you keep your mind on your work?'

Simon Cutler's mouth twisted sheepishly. 'Sometimes it's tough. Lots of temptations, sweetheart. There are many moments I wish I were back in Allenburg selling brick. Many.'

Somewhere, and somehow, he had to find the key to open Simon Cutler, the key to his city. The old days in Allenburg would never be good enough. Si had come a long way since then. Si was a big power now. When Si thundered, plenty of big guys in this business trembled; and Si now had a vision of himself as some kind of public saviour. In his eyes the builders were all out to get something for nothing, and his old friend Joe Naples was no exception. He knew for a positive fact that Joe had bribed half the public servants in Allenburg when he was building houses before the war. Si had even helped him.

The captain showed them to a ringside table. 'Ey, Si,' Joe said, 'you ever seen Anna Landos? She's an old friend of mine. You gotta meet her after the show. Nice cucaracha.'

Si brightened perceptibly. Joe nipped the tip of his cigar and lit it carefully. 'Lemme ask you, Si. You say you work for the people. You ever met any of these people?'

Si smiled. Joe was getting to be a great kidder.

'I'm not kiddin' around, Si. You didn't hear me so good. You're a horizontalist. I think you must see people spread out, acres of 'em, like Fifth Avenue on Easter Sunday. That's where you think your duty lies. To those ants. Who the hell are they – these people by the acre? You probably don't give one good damn about one single one of those poor bastids in the crowd. I've met other guys like you – priests, teachers, politicians. Well, *I'm* not interested in the crowds. I'm a verticalist, Si. Every person I meet is a standing-up guy. I gotta know all about him, his wife, his extra curriculum, his kids, his secrets, his bankbook, his friends and enemies. I can't find out enough about the people I meet, and I like to help 'em out if I can. Most of 'em don't know to come in outa the rain and I feel sorry for 'em. And if I'm so goddam interested in everyone else, I naturally take a vital interest in my own self, my family, my own friends, my reputation, my ambitions, all of that. I don't have *secret* ambitions, Si. They're right out in the open. I'll tell you all about 'em. Let's say I'm a guy looking for lots of everything, making a splash, and for the honour and all that crap. Even I wanna be the biggest guy in the room. Every room, including the lounge at Canoe Hill. So what? Well, the funny part of it is, *I'm* doing more for all those acres of all those horizontal bastids, all those ants, while I'm tryin' to feather my own nest, than guys like you, with your public trust. Because I really *do* it, whether it's good or bad, I do *something*. And just by accident, the crowd's gotta do good, whereas you bastids sit around with pencils in your hand threatening to pin them up our backsides, getting in everyone's way, tripping up anyone who's doing the slightest useful thing. Give me a verticalist any time, Si, much as I like you personally.'

'Sure', Si said. 'I've heard all that before. Sounds like all the conversations I've had these last few months with Milt Jason. Sweetheart, they come at me these days from all sides. I mean *all* the boys want Uncle Sam to play papa – Los Angeles, Cleveland, Chicago, New York. They quote me the Bible, Karl Marx, and Adam Smith if only I'll just put the signature of the National

Project Director of the National Mortgage Insurance Agency of the United States government on five hundred or a thousand or Lord knows how many firm commitments and let some nice fella walk off with the booty, if there is any. But if there's a bath, Uncle takes it. I dream about those fellows all with their hands outstretched, holding their palms up in a universal salute which means "Uncle, *gimmee*".' He winked. 'And did I mention this one gent, an old friend of mine from Jersey, wants *six thousand* commitments, all firm?'

'Why not?' Joe said.

'Six thousand commitments, Joe! I'll go a thousand out there. A firm underwriting. Plus a thousand conditionals. And that's making Uncle Sam stretch it for old times' sake.' Joe shook his head impatiently. 'Suppose I were to give you all you want, Joe, and you sell only half the houses. Sometimes houses don't sell, Joe, you know that. I've been in this game since thirty-five, especially out in the sticks where no one lives. The government takes a bath for three or four million and I'm the guy on the spot. My name's on the paper. Even the local office is off the hook. My neck's out. Why should I?'

'Because guys like me don't have the four million to lose,' Joe said, 'and Uncle Sam does, and we've gotta get the houses built for the good of the entire country, that's why. That's a positive policy, Si, a policy based on self-confidence, confidence in the country, confidence in the future.'

'There are some who'd call it pure recklessness', Si said. 'Everyone's in a rush now, but wait ten years. Some Congressman'll raise a stink and heads'll roll. I've seen it. I'd prefer to take a little longer. Wait till the first thousand get sold. Build a little slower.'

Joe was thinking of the brilliant speech he'd made to Jock Dennison and Tony Ferrara about mass production to get them to put their dough on the line. 'That would increase our costs maybe a couple of thousand bucks a house. I'm planning to set up to build an entire goddam city, our own concrete plant. I got my own timber tracts in Arkansas, our own heating plant. It's a wholesale operation. A house you couldn't build for less then ten thousand, we expect to sell under eight.' He reached into his coat pocket and pulled out an old gold pocket watch. 'Remember when you gave me this, Si?' He snapped the back open, and let Si read, 'To Joe Napoli, With gratitude, Simon'. 'I still got it, Si. You remember,

I came up with those jumbo bricks? Good for you, good for me, right?'

Si took the watch and scrutinized it carefully.

'With six thousand firm commitments, Si, I'll do good, and your horizontal guys will do good, too. They'll get ten-thousand-dollar houses for seventy-nine ninety. And you'll be a bloody hero.'

Si handed back the watch. 'Damn, those were the days, 'ey, sweetheart?'

The waiter brought them new Martinis, as patrons continued to file in from the lobby.

'Don't stand in the way, Si', Joe murmured softly. 'It wouldn't be right, for me or for the country . . . or even for you.' What Si needed was a papa of his own to tell him everything was going to turn out okay. But Joe knew that mere debate was never going to get Si Cutler out of his neutral corner; and he knew just as suddenly and clearly when he saw the way Si looked at Anna Landos, who had just walked out on the stage, what would. Si was just nervous and on edge. He needed loving comfort; comfort would lead to self-confidence and confidence in the country's future. He was pessimistic on account of Ellie. The right kind of woman could mean a lot to a man.

Si held his drink, the stem between his hands, rolled it a moment, and staring at the stage said to Joe, 'Sweetheart, is this your girl-friend?' He swallowed the drink in a single gulp. Joe just puffed and blew one nice smoke ring.

Bathed in an amber spot, Anna Landos stood on the stage, smiling her most intimate smile for the five hundred plush patrons. She was up there alone, wearing a dress which was a layer of gauze on top, covered with sequins. You couldn't tell whether you could quite see all of her or not and what she did was stand there and smile personally at everyone, and make love to the mike and the audience exactly the way she had back in old Napoli. Her songs were sweet and tender: 'Lili Marlene', 'My Bill', 'La Vie en Rose', 'My Man', and she simply stood there caressing the mike with her clever hands, not moving an unnecessary muscle. After the last song and the long applause, she stood silent, smiling. Suddenly she stepped back, a radiant young girl, ninety per cent of the sophistication gone from face and posture, and she said in much more of an accent than she actually had, 'When I am overseas during the war, I have a night on the town in a leetle place in Eetaly with three American soldiers – flyers and soldiers – how you say – pilots. And there for the first time I hear a song, such a sweet song, but I do not understand one word of eet. And one of those boys who sang eet to me in that old restaurant in sunny Eetaly is here weeth us tonight and I'm going to sing thees tender song back to heem, even though I steel do not understand these words.'

Then while the lights dimmed into a magenta spot, she stood back from the mike and blasted in a harsh voice he had never heard her use,

'Roll-me over, Yankee soldier,
Roll-me over, lay me down, and do it again.
Roll-me over in the clover . . .'

The crowd laughed.

She waved her arms and cried, 'Everybody sing – sing!' The orchestra blared out a cover for shy voices and people took heart and sang, at first sketchily, then with lusty voice. During the second chorus, Anna reached for the mike, carried it to ringside, leaned over to Joe and said, 'Come, my Major, come up here. Come on.' Then she asked the audience for support and got it in applause. Joe, who smiled at Si Cutler, shrugged and, feeling the flush in his face, went up to the stage from the ringside table, while the audience and orchestra finished rollicking . . .

'Roll-me over in the clover
Roll-me over, lay me down . . .'

When the applause had died, Anna said in her smallest girl's voice, 'I steel don't understand eet, but I *like* eet. Eet's so – how you say – nostalgic? Now I want you all to meet my darling Major, the man who actually save my life.' She kissed him in the centre of the magenta spot. It was a stage kiss, but there was warmth behind it. She directed him to the stairs and as he started off the stage, she cried to the audience, 'I would do anything for thees man. That ees the truth.'

At the table, as Anna subsided into her farewell, 'Smoke Gets in Your Eyes', Joe whispered gruffly to Si Cutler to hide his fluster at having been pulled onstage, 'She gets twenty-five thousand a week, and I'm in the act and I don't get a dime. Is that a fair deal?'

Si Cutler squinted. 'It reminds me of *my* job.' The crowd was standing, shouting, applauding, and Anna bowed and smiled and threw a kiss to Joe.

After she changed, Anna came directly to their table. Si Cutler behaved like a great oaf, goggle-eyed and giggling. They ordered a drink and Joe took her to dance.

'Kiddy, you look like quite a number. You're all grown up. But look, what's that? A grey hair?'

'Oh, Major, behave yourself. Who is the man? He's beautiful', she said. 'You told me he had a sad story.'

'Oh, Jesus. First lemme tell you about his wife. This guy's got trouble. You ever hear of multiple sclerosis?'

Anna listened with her eyes wide and Joe did not hold back.

'This is a guy who is one of the most important men right now in the entire government. I mean outside of the President and that crowd. And he can't even pay the hospital bills for his wife. Not only that, but he hasn't been tuned-up, you know, in I don't know how many *years*. He was just telling me he can't bring himself to hop into bed with just anybody. For him it has to be something special. Absolutely years, literally that's what he says. What d'you think of *that*?'

Anna shook her head sadly. 'Imagine, strong virile man like that.'

'All mixed up with conscience, you know. He's American, and this is peacetime, kiddy. It's not like during the war. Things were simple then.'

'Oh, it is *sad*.'

'*You're* not going after old Si, now', Joe said. 'I want to keep this guy alive. He's an old friend.'

'Don't worry, the people I kill all seem to come back to life', Anna said as the orchestra stopped for a moment. 'And he seems very nice. I like him.'

The music started again, and they danced in silence for a few moments.

'Anna, listen. I got an envelope with ten thousand bucks cash money in my pocket. I'm going to put it in your purse.'

She stopped dancing. 'Major, are you giving *me* money?' For a passing instant, fury had a grip on her and her face distorted.

'Not for you, kiddy. Oh ho, God, no, not for you. Don't get sore. I want you to give it to *him*. I've been carrying it around, but I don't dare give it to whozis myself. And I want him to have it. Lookit, tell him it's gambling money. Play money. In fact, before you give it to him, change it to chips. Tell him if he loses it, he can forget it. If he wins, he can pay it back.'

'Oh.' Her body relaxed and she wore her most ingenuous smile. 'I just thought – I earn here twenty-five thousand dollars a week, my darling Major, and I have two former husbands who are also rich and contribute a little every month. And for my next picture, I'm getting a hundred thousand. Please don't offer me *money*. Ever.'

Joe laughed. 'Who'd ever think of it?'

'You should see my home in Beverly Hills', Anna said. 'Two sunken bathtubs, both enormous.'

The music was 'Star Dust'. Anna moved closer. 'And you – how you say – you are completely in tune for yourself?'

He pressed her closer to him protectively. 'Don't be ridiculous, kiddy. You're my daughter.'

They glided together for a moment. 'You are a funny man. And some father you are, to ask me to do such a thing! I think I should be insulted.'

'Anna, please. You know me from way back, and I know you. Don't do anything you don't want to do. All I can tell you is he needs the money bad.'

'I'm a big star now. I have to think of my public. What would my agent say?'

Joe shrugged. 'Might make an item for *Confidential*.' Then he saw the angry look. 'I won't be mad, cucaracha, whatever you say.'

'What does it mean to you – just money?'

'Just money. Six or eight million buckeroos. That's all.'

'You are joking!'

'I'm serious! If Simon Cutler does what I want him to —'

'You are dreaming? The same dream you had about your city? Naples, America?'

'The very.'

'I like that dream. You are really asking me to help you build your city?'

'In a way.'

'That's nice. I am flattered. Really. Anna Landos would not do this for anyone else in the world, my darling. Name something after me,' she said, 'when your city is built. Perhaps the church – my name saint is Theresa.'

He said, 'It will be Saint Theresa. So help me.'

They glided back to the table, and when they reached it she smiled at Si Cutler, who simpered. She was holding her purse open under the table and Joe took an envelope from his pocket and stuffed it into the purse.

'Simon,' she said, running her forefinger down his forearm, 'are you for a bit of gambling?'

He continued to simper. 'Miss Landos,' he said, trying not to talk from the side of his mouth, 'I'm not a gambler.'

'Oh, you must try eet, Simon. And my friends do not call me Miss Landos. Some call me Anna, and my darling Major, I am his cucaracha. Come, my dear Simon, let's forget our troubles. You know I've been divorced twice and it depresses me. Anyhow, I am supposed to encourage the very rich men to gamble. It's not in my contract, but my darling, they like me to do it.'

'Let's take a crack at it', Joe said. And inside the casino lobby, he added, 'Deploy, men. I'll take the roulette. Kiddy, why don't you and Si try the crap table. Looks like plenty of action tonight.'

Simon Cutler laughed and said, 'I'll just watch. I study faces, it does something weird and fascinating to people, this gambling. But I can't bring myself to play.'

'Come along, my darling,' Anna said and put her arm around Si's massive waist. 'It's so nice to have a real man for company for a change. Most of the men are so interested in money, money, money. They have no time for a girl, even a nice well-known girl like me.' She ignored the stares of the patrons, and Si Cutler was her only world. 'See, even our darling Major is money-mad to-night. It comes over them when they see the green tables.'

Snaking through the crowd, she led Simon to the crap table. Joe concentrated on roulette and started to spread fifty-cent chips on and around seventeen, wasting time, and when he had lost sight of Anna and Si, he slipped out fast, took a cab down town and saw *The Best Years of Our Lives* at the local cinema; and it was a damn wholesome two-hour picture. Showed what a family could really mean to a man, and Joe liked it. He skipped the news and shorts to get back to the Flamingo. The lobby was now densely packed with humanity, tuxedoed and Hawaiian-shirted men, women in evening gowns, cotton dresses, Bermudas, and slacks, all fogged in by the smoke and smell of tobacco. Joe made his way to the crap tables, now surrounded four deep with spectators and players. 'Four the point', he heard a croupier drone. 'Four the point. Field loses. Twenty on the field coming out, yes sir. Ten on low. Place your bets, place your bets.' He could hear the click of chips and the dice as the roll came out. 'Four!' the croupier said, and Joe thought he detected a note of surprise in the croupier's voice. There was an instantaneous cheer and shout, and all at once Joe saw Simon Cutler, smiling glassily, dice in hand, with Anna Landos beside him watching him happily, sharing some triumph. Simon Cutler was sweating profusely. He licked his lips. The same lick Joe had seen twenty years ago at Finlayson's brickyard when he'd told Si about oversized brick. Joe pushed his way through the crowd.

'Si. How you doin'?'

Anna said, 'He just made five points in a row.'

'I'm hot', Simon Cutler said. This was no longer the National Project Director for the National Mortgage Insurance Agency. This was playboy Simon, cut-up Cutler.

'Where's your bet?' Joe said.

Si Cutler pointed to a fifty-dollar chip on the win line.

'How much you win on the five points?'

'Oh,' Anna said, 'I think three hundred dollars. Maybe more.'

'You kiddin'?' Joe turned back to Si Cutler. 'Si, you're not doin' it right. You gotta back yourself when you're going. Like I was telling you, you gotta feel that ESP and I *feel* it, Si. It works when it's goin' for you. Look, I'll bet 'em, you shoot 'em.' He seized both of Si's stacks, perhaps a thousand dollars worth of chips, and pushed them to the win line. 'Roll 'em.'

Si Cutler closed his eyes. His eyebrow twitched in a tick Joe had never before observed.

'Eleven, a winner', the croupier called. The surprised cheer again from the hot knot of people around the table.

Si reached for the chips, but Joe held his hand. 'We'll ride', he said. The croupier cleaned up the other bets, matching some chips, sweeping others towards himself. New bets went down. Simon Cutler was a man mesmerized. He stared at the dice the croupier pushed towards him. He lifted them gingerly, examined them as if they were the most remarkable contrivances made by man.

He shook and threw them across the baize against the opposite bank of the padded table. 'Six, six the point.'

'Where's the money?' Joe said. 'Where's the rest of it?' Simon Cutler reached into his pocket while new bets went down, and handed Joe a stack of chips, all hundreds. Joe broke the large stacks into ten chip stacks and placed stacks on four, five, eight, nine and ten. 'Roll, Si', he said. 'Let's roll it big.'

Simon Cutler had no idea what he was doing. 'I'm hot', he said.

His tongue went round and round his lips like that of a man dying of thirst. He rolled.

'Five.'

Joe took the twenty-five hundred dollars off five.

'Point is six. Bets down please.'

'Snake eyes.'

Joe nudged Si. 'Okay, boy. Anything but seven. We got winners everywhere. Four. Six. Eight. Nine. Ten. Roll 'em, Si.'

Si Cutler rolled the dice in a dream. He was drowning in moisture. Not only his sweat, but Joe had the queer feeling the poor bastid was crying. He rolled eight times and hit every number Joe had money on. Joe pulled the winning piles down one by one, as each number came up.

'Six, six the point. Six right.' That cheer again. One young frenetic woman screamed, 'I don't believe it!'

Suddenly Simon Cutler seemed to come out of his dream. 'Let 'em ride', he cried. 'Come on, baby!' He had come to life. 'Be good, baby!' He rolled the dice. 'Seven!' Now Si Cutler's hysterical voice could be heard above the cheer. 'Natural! See that, Joe boy, natural! I'm going to make a fortune. Watch this. Let 'em ride!' He made another point, ten the hard way.

They must've had thirty-two thousand dollars in winnings, chips piled high. Simon, vibrating, pushed two thousand of it on to the win line. His tongue was going feverishly and his eyes kept blinking. 'Be good, dice! Be good to Papa!' He rolled them. There was a groan. 'Twelve', the croupier said, and raked in the chips on the line. Simon shoved another two grand on the win line. Joe watched close. 'Come on, dice, be nice!' Simon called, seeing no one, knowing nothing. 'No box cars this time, dice. Let's have a little old *natural* . . .' He rolled the dice. 'Two', the croupier said, 'craps, a loser', and raked the chips again.

Si blinked more furiously as he took the dice again.

Joe saw the wild fever. He knew that in this moment Naples, New Jersey, hung in the balance. Si Cutler was an idiot child over his depth. Before him he had twenty-eight thousand dollars in hundred dollar chips. Si Cutler had never had so much money of his own before. More of it would not be of the slightest help to anyone.

'Come on', Joe said. 'Let's get the hell outa this firetrap.' He began to stuff the green chips into his jacket pocket. 'He passes', he said to the croupier. 'Si, give the man back the dice.'

It took Si Cutler half a minute to understand what was happening.

'Hey!' He stood up, enormous. 'What the dickens are you doing? They're *my* dice.'

Joe tugged him by the arm. 'We're cashing in', he said under his breath. 'You're way ahead.'

'*They're my dice!*' Si Cutler shouted. 'I'm *hot*! I just dropped four thousand dollars I have to get back!' He had seized Joe's collar and was pulling him back. '*Give me my chips.* Give me those chips!'

The hard voice of a woman called from the back of the crowd, 'Come on, roll 'em!' And a man at the table said, 'Let's have a little action!'

The pit boss cried to Joe, 'Mister! Mister! The man had the dice!'

Joe and Si were tugging and scuffling, and Si Cutler clenched his fist and pulled it back threateningly.

'Don't hit me, Si', Joe said, very low. 'Use your head.'

In a moment there were two uniformed, armed guards in the crowd, each with a strong hand on the elbows of the disputants.

'Pass the dice', the croupier cried in vain. 'Place your bets', the pit boss said. But no one placed any bets. Not a chip was on the table.

'*They're my dice*', Si Cutler cried, insanely. He was a hundred per cent gone. '*He's got my chips!*'

'Look, officer,' Joe said quietly, 'it's my money. Miss Landos here will tell you. Si, for Christ sake, wake up.'

'Yes', Anna said. 'I'm surprised at you, my darling Simon.'

Simon Cutler blinked furiously, then blushed. He winced slowly, getting redder, looking over the curious crowd, as if he were coming out of a bad dream. He pulled his arm loose from the grasp of the armed guard.

'Oh, my God', he cried in a hollow voice. 'Oh, Christ Almighty. What am I doing?'

The officer let go of Joe's arm, warily.

'Come on', Anna said. 'We need a drink.' She led them quickly to the bar.

They sat silent at the table for almost five minutes while Si regained control of himself.

'What came over me?' he said morosely at last.

Joe ordered Martinis for them and a half bottle of wine for himself. He looked at his watch. It was eleven-forty. The elapsed time since he had walked into the casino lobby was ten minutes.

When their drinks came, Joe pulled the chips out of every pocket he had. He counted ten thousand dollars worth, slipped them into his pocket, and pushed the rest towards Si. 'Here's your winnings, Buster.'

Si Cutler stared at the chips, his eyes still glazed, and Joe got up to cash his own chips in. Si, Joe estimated, had won over eighteen Gs. The teller counted him out a hundred hundreds; Joe put the wad in his pocket, and went back to the table. Chips bulged from Si Cutler's pockets and he was leaning forward grinning foolishly at Anna Landos, who was talking. 'So, the Irishman said, "From there I go to Lourdes and there you'll see the damndest miracle you ever saw".'

Si Cutler roared. He laughed so hard Joe thought the cops would be back, and Anna's high giggle joined him. 'My darling', she said. 'You missed one of my best stories.'

Joe sat and peered at his drink. 'How much you win, Si? I figured around eighteen thousand.'

Out of the corner of his mouth Si Cutler said, 'I can't do it, Joe.' He turned around nervously to see if anyone might be watching.

'Why? You won it', Joe said. 'And I got my dough back.' He reached into his pocket and pulled out the hundred hundreds. 'Ten Gs. Safe and sound.'

'I might've lost it', Si Cutler said feverishly.

'How could you have lost, Si? Not with our ESP. When you got that going, you're infallible. Only remember one thing, Si, you gotta play it my way. The way I just showed you. You gotta bet big. When you're on a winning jag, it's no good betting ten bucks at a chip. You gotta plunge. Faint heart, Si, never won eighteen thousand whatzis.'

Si sipped his drink, looked at Anna Landos speculatively. 'Faint heart never won fair lady either. I'll bet on that.'

Anna batted her eyes. 'You are so clever, my darling', she said, and covered Si Cutler's hand with her own.

'I don't know about you two,' Joe said, 'but I'm only a brick-layer. Bedtime for me.'

Si Cutler got to his feet with effort. 'Night, Buster.' He was grinning from ear to ear. His hand was in his pocket feeling the nice chips.

'And Si,' Joe said, reaching his hand up around the big man's enormous shoulders, 'don't go getting any ideas and go near that crap table, or I'll kill you, so help me. Dead. You're ahead. Stay that way. You'll see to it, Anna. He needs that dough for a good and worthy cause.'

Anna laughed. 'I'll see to it, my darling, no matter what I have to do to save him from himself.' She smiled up at Si provocatively.

Simon Cutler looked like the happiest man in the world, and it made Joe feel good. Si was a fine man at heart and Joe thought how Si was going to like it when Anna's dynamic tune-up machine began to beat him to death. Everything was gonna go great for everyone, all round.

As it turned out, Joe did not have a chance to see Simon the next day because Joe was able to catch a United flight to New York at eight in the morning. The first thing he did when he got home was to tell Woody Faber to put the ten Gs back in the bank. The next was to call Anna in Las Vegas.

'Major, darling, it's so early. What time is it?'

'Three p.m., my cucaracha.'

'But, darling, that's the middle of the *day*. Nobody wakes me in the middle of the day.'

'Cut the cornball stuff, kiddy. How'd everything go with Si?'

'Oh, Simon. He's sweet really. A little boy. But you know he's a rather perverted little boy.'

'Hell, kiddy, I wouldn't know. It takes one to know one.'

'Thank you. He and I have become good friends. Next time he comes to Los Angeles, he's going to call me. He was very sweet, really, he reminded me of Ferenc. You remember Ferenc. I think I could really love Simon if I could love anyone. Oh, it's so sad about his wife, you have no idea. The poor creature. He cried about *her* half the night. He felt so guilty. Isn't that sweet?'

'I hope I didn't put you to too much trouble, did I, kiddy?'

'Darling, it was my pleasure. Please now, go away. I have only a few more hours to sleep before my first show.'

It was almost two weeks after Vegas that Piggy Banks called Joe from the Trenton MIA.

'Joe, we just got a long letter from Cutler in Washington.'

'Yah?'

'I don't want to read it to you, Joe, because it's three pages long and I can barely understand it myself. I tell you the boys down there have invented ways of saying things that we country boys in the field offices just can't understand. But I've had it decoded and the gist of it is we've got a green light on your six thousand firm commitments.'

'Yah?'

'I thought you'd be interested to hear that. That's why I'm calling.' Piggy was the kind of guy who really was glad, too, as long as he hadn't had to stick his own neck out. Piggy was excited at the prospect of his office's part in building an entire city. 'You'll get a letter in a day or two. That is the mortgagee'll get it. Ev Henderson, isn't it? It'll take a couple of weeks to type all the commitments.' At long last, Naples, New Jersey, was assured.

'Thanks for calling, Piggy. Appreciate it.' He was thinking he really ought to do something for Piggy and Henry Stewart, the chief underwriter and the other boys at Trenton soon. Maybe he could take them all off on a fishing trip at Tom's River some Sunday and get drunk with them and maybe even lose a few hundred bucks to them all at poker, although that was certainly not necessary.

Twenty-four

'OH, so all you did was merely get poor Si someone like Anna Landos to shack up with in Las Vegas. It's lonesome in Las Vegas, everyone knows *that*. Or maybe Simon's afraid of the dark. I have to hand it to you, old buddy.' Milt made his wildest grimace. He could combine his most accusatory trial manner with his cutie-pie Disney-type dwarf in the damndest way.

The trouble with Milt, the way he smiled and squinted and made faces, you could never tell if he was secretly complimenting you or attacking you. In fact, it was a little creepy altogther and always made Joe feel defensive.

'Lookit. I introduced 'em. Period. That was *it*. In fact, they saw quite a bit of each other on the side after that – every time Si went out to the coast.'

'Sure. And all you did was tell Anna to be nice to him.'

'So? Lookit the shape Si was in, I hadda do *some*thing for him. I know Si a long time.'

Milt squinted at him sideways from the other seat. 'That's what I like about you – anything for an old buddy. Would you care to give *me* a send-off with Miss Landos, Joe? I'm an even older buddy.'

'You kiddin'?' He needed Milt's needling like a typhoid shot.

'As a matter of fact, I am', Milt said a bit contritely. 'But not altogether.'

''Ey, Milt, what'd you *think* I was doing in Vegas? I remember when those commitments came through, boy. You did a jig all over the office, I remember *that* good. Running around waving Piggy's letter like you were a goddam leprechaun.'

'Joe, don't get me wrong. Please. I'm with *you*. But I'd estimate you probably violated – I won't say many – maybe five federal laws. Not that anyone would've been likely to notice.'

'What the hell's got you? You asked me to tell you transgressions. Okay, I'm telling you.'

They had just reached Easy Street, and as they entered the drive-way, they saw the grey Rolls, big as life, and the chauffeur in matching pearl grey behind the wheel, with a little Pekinese dog beside him.

'Lucky thing Dino's not here,' Joe said, 'or he'd be out buying a Rolls first thing in the morning.'

Cibulkas greeted them with a big grin. 'Guess who all's here, Major?'

'You mean whozis, our Hungarian war prisoner?'

Cibulkas's face fell. 'How'd you know?'

'I absolutely know everything, Cibulkas, you oughta know that.'

'Damn if you don't. Evening Mr. Jason.'

In the den Hetty and Anna were on the sofa, bent over the new script, while a squat, bullish, kinky-headed man, about forty, with horn-rimmed glasses, looked on indifferently from an uncomfort-able modern chair. Anna was sipping a red wine, while the man and Hetty were working more seriously on bourbon. Anna still looked fabulous, but kind of lacquered up now, as if her whole self had been dipped into some kind of preservative.

Hetty lifted her head to kiss him a bit possessively and then kissed Milt a peck. She spoke over-deliberately – it was the bourbon.

'My husband. This is Mr. Harris, Joie, Miss Landos's lawyer.'

The guy stood up and Joe shook his hand. One of these Holly-wood gents who wears a checked sports jacket in the middle of a business day. 'And my husband's attorney, Milton Jason. Milt, you know Miss Landos I'm sure by reputation. Mr. Harris.' Hetty was cheery and plainly feeling no pain.

'Enchanted.' Milt turned his most leprechaunish smile on Anna. 'I've heard so many things about you, Miss Landos.'

'Not everything, I hope', Anna said darkly.

'Only fabulous things, I assure you.'

'My darling Major', Anna said, and Joe noted that her voice had become huskier and more actressy since Vegas. 'You have a beauti-ful place. I have never seen such a large pool *inside* a house – just for fish. And your wife is even more pleasant than you told me. We have been getting on beautifully.' She lit a cigarette. 'And your lovely little city, I simply adore it. Remember the first time we talked about it?' She turned to the others. 'He had a vision – he told me all about it – oh, he was quite tight at the time, but he des-cribed every detail, on our way from Naples to Bellanza. The houses are so cute and I *love* the sweet little church of Saint Theresa.

Of course, I've seen pictures of it all in magazines, not to mention *your* picture on *Time*. Yes, but it's nicer in the flesh. Both you and your city.'

Joe listened to Anna impatiently. 'How's every little thing with you, kiddy, out there in make-believe land?'

She shrugged. 'Very trying, that I promise you. Nowadays, if you don't have a blockbuster, it's a stink bomb and if you don't get a piece of the picture, it's hardly worth working at all.'

'*A Night for Memory* must've made money', Joe said. 'It was a hell of a show.'

'My darling Major, the picture was good, but I got a lousy hundred and fifty for it. And the government got most of *that*. But now my accountant has a tax gimmick. I am a corporation. You know what I get for a picture today? Three-fifty. A third of a million.'

'Is that *after* social security?' Hetty said, swallowing bourbon.

'You must visit me out there', Anna said. 'Both of you. I sold my place in Beverly Hills, you know. I'm in Bel-Air now. The place is *full* of bathtubs.'

"Ey, how's about some supper?' Joe said. 'We got enough to feed these people, Mullaly?'

'Miss Landos, do you like cold chicken?' Hetty said sweetly.

'Call me Anna, please. Thank you, I love the simple things, cold chicken. You're so nice to ask me. And anything at all for Sugar, my little Pekinese. She would love a bone to play with.' She turned to Joe. 'Dear Simon is coming here, too, my darling, any minute now. We do have a few things to talk over.'

'Yah?'

'I promise you, it's not *just* a social visit, but, of course, it's nice to see you. Your wife – Hester is it? No? Oh, yes, Hetty, how stupid of me – Hetty and I have been having a ball. And Cibulkas has told me all about his trip to Budapest that time, from Bellanza, with all the girls. Very amusing, but thank God they all got there. And thank God I wasn't with them. What they must have gone through with those Russians. He is a charming man, your Mr. Cibulkas. Be careful, or I might try to steal him. Help in California is impossible. No, but my visit's quite serious. We have problems with the United States government, Major. It's almost like the old country – an inquisition, really.'

'I guess I'd better hang around', Milt said.

'I think,' Anna said, 'if you are his lawyer.'

'I'll call Luce', Milt said, and started towards the phone closet.

'Ask her to come over', Hetty called. 'See if she can bring one of her nice shortcakes. We could use a little dessert.'

Mr. Harris put his drink down decisively. 'I don't mean to be rude, but could we get down to cases?' he said briskly.

'Shoot', Joe said.

But the front door chime rang, and it was Simon Cutler. Cibulkas came to get Si's coat and, at Anna's instruction, went out to tell Anna's chauffeur about dinner and to take care of the Pekinese. Simon came in rubbing his hands and trying to smile crookedly as if something good were about to befall him. He was clearly under tremendous pressure.

'Darling', Anna cried, and bit her lip.

'Anna. Well.' He winked broadly at her. 'Everyone here? Even Milton. Must be pretty serious. I don't believe I've met *this* gentleman.'

'He's *my* lawyer, darling', Anna said. 'Lloyd, *this* is Simon Cutler.' The two men shook hands. Milt went to the bar and mixed Martinis for Si and himself.

'We were just about to get down to brass tacks', Mr. Harris said to Si.

'Without me?' Si sniggered. 'A hanging without the prisoner?'

Harris remained solemn. 'Two men from the Senate Sub-committee on Government Assisted Private Enterprise were out to visit Miss Landos last week', Mr. Harris said. 'And she naturally called me for advice.'

'Yah?' Joe said.

'One little fellow named Poltek and an assistant named Fellon', Harris said.

'Ooooo, that greasy little Poltek man', Anna said. 'He really makes me resent my income taxes. To support a man like him, ooogh! I despised him the minute I smelled him. Did you notice? He is the *one* man in this world I couldn't bear to have *touch* me. Such a dirty little mind. Wait till I tell you.'

'They were in my office, too', Simon Cutler said. '*Boys* they are. Kids half my age threatening me, suggesting I might prefer to resign! Imagine that! After all those years!'

'They were interested,' Mr. Harris continued dispassionately, 'in the events of a particular night in April, I believe, 1947, in Las Vegas. I don't think I need to go into the details, but Miss Landos thought it only fair for us to tell you exactly what our position is and will continue to be if she is called on to appear at a hearing, either public or private.'

'Oh, I am so unhappy, Simon. My darling Major, I'm simply miserable. But I don't know what else to do.'

'Miss Landos is an important motion-picture property', Harris continued. 'I'm sure you're well aware of how important. Her agent, her Press agent and I have considered this problem from every point of view and we have instructed her to tell nothing but the precise truth. In fact, we insist on it.'

'What precise truth?' Milt was smiling warily now over his Martini.

Lloyd Harris spoke patronizingly. 'I presume you know all about this, Mr. Jason, about the ten thousand dollar loan. And about Mr. Naples' request that Miss Landos be – uh – pleasant, shall we say? to Mr. Cutler.'

Simon Cutler's mouth gaped and he turned ashen. 'Be pleasant to *me*? Anna, did—'

'Simon darling,' Anna said, 'it was the very nicest thing that ever happened to me.'

'Do you mean to tell me, every time I came out to the coast —'

'Oh, by then, darling,' Anna assured him, 'it was all from *me*.' And Simon brightened perceptibly, but the incurable scar was left.

'It's quite simple', Mr. Harris went on calmly. 'We've reasoned this way. Her handling of the money was no crime. She had no clear idea of its purpose. In fact, she still doesn't.'

'And such a small amount anyway', Anna said. 'Ten thousand.'

'I gave every cent of that back!' Simon Cutler shouted. 'Joe knows—'

'Precisely', Mr. Harris said calmly. 'And my client will so testify. So you ought not have any worry on that score, Mr. Cutler. As for the other, Anna had already been divorced from her second husband, and the American people somehow don't seem to mind such minor – how shall I say – peccadillos in their stars.'

'No, not peccadillos, Lloyd', Anna said gently. 'Please. We had some wonderful moments, Simon and I.' Simon Cutler flushed.

'Take people like Harlow,' Mr. Harris continued, 'and going as far back as Mary Astor. We're persuaded that a star's box office if anything, is, uh, somewhat, shall I say, enhanced by a few harmless – uh – charming – uh, how shall I say it? I hope I don't offend you, Mrs. Naples?'

'Not at all', Hetty said. 'Don't mind me. I'm not 'ffended. Just jealous.' She deliberately poured herself a full tumblerful of bourbon, and began to drink it unhurriedly but steadily.

'On the other hand,' continued Mr. Harris, as if he were winding up a boring business deal, 'Hollywood and the American people, especially the newspapers, take quite unkindly to anyone who challenges the Congress. We have the writers and directors who committed perjury and contempt before the Jenner and McCarthy committees and, take it from me, it cost every one of them dearly. Some of them never worked again. And, of course, there is always the very real danger, which we like not to think about, of being committed to a federal penitentiary. We couldn't take *that* chance. So you see, Anna will not commit perjury and she cannot refuse to answer. It's that simple. It's her own self-interest.'

'It's so *sad*', Anna said. 'But I am a prisoner, as you see.'

''S very sad', Hetty said in a small voice.

'How the hell did Poltek find out anything about any of this?' Joe said.

'Yeah?' Simon Cutler echoed hollowly.

'There were two Treasury men at the Flamingo the night of that little ruckus at the crap table', Mr. Harris said. 'T-men are in and out of Las Vegas spot-checking on the big players. Of course, it could mean a little problem with the Bureau too, unless Mr. Cutler declared his winnings.'

Simon tried to bluff a crooked smile, but failed. 'Sure I declared 'em.'

'Mr. Poltek claimed he had talked to the croupier and the pit boss', Anna said. 'In fact, he seemed to know but *everything*. As if he'd actually been there. It was worse than the Gestapo.' Anna looked almost triumphant.

'Not a single thing happened out there that doesn't have a logical explanation', Si Cutler said, as he had been saying for days. 'And in any case, it's none of the proper business of the Senate. Think of it, my old friend Harold Brice permitting a sub-committee of his to start up with a terrible thing like this. They're out to get me, Joe. It's raw politics. And to think I went through three military campaigns and half a dozen political ones with that man. D'you know I saved his life? Yes sir, in France. You know what that counts for? Nothing. Man doesn't know which way to turn, I tell *you*.'

'How much did you actually tell Mr. Poltek when he came to visit you?' Milt said.

'Hoho, I told him plenty', Anna said. 'I bet he never heard language like *that* before from a lady. The main thing I told him was to get out of my house.

'I said, "Look here, I've been in a concentration camp. I've been beaten with rubber hoses, and I don't intend to start *that* all over again." I said, "Don't think you can use Anna Landos just to get yourself some cheap publicity." I said, "I tell you absolutely nothing." I said, "Mr. Poltek, don't you ever bathe?" And I got a can of that Glade out of the kitchen and spritzed it all around him and all over the room. You should have seen his face.' She laughed, but there was something metallic in the bell-like tone.

Lloyd Harris chuckled appreciatively and Hetty smiled. 'Anna likes to keep these discussions on a warm personal level', Harris said.

Same old cucaracha, lying in her teeth even about her lies.

'That silly little man, I thought he would choke, so I said—'

'What difference does it make what you said?' Harris interrupted. 'You could've said anything. You weren't under oath. But when you are, Anna, you'll tell it straight, that's all there is to it.'

'Yes', Anna said softly.

'Gosh,' Milt said with reluctant admiration, 'you're just the girl for Poltek, Miss Landos, aren't you? He must've said ten Hail Marys when he found you were involved. Manna from heaven to him. The space he'll get on the front pages. Iy-yi-yi. Some guys have all the luck.' He was smiling his most lawyerish smile.

'Counsellor,' Harris said, suspicious and tense, 'please don't tamper with my client.'

'Me?' Milt said. 'Wouldn't dream of it.' But his smile was ice.

Simon Cutler rose unsteadily from his chair. 'Excuse me, people. Anna . . . Hetty . . . Jeez, I don't feel very well . . .' Joe saw that Si's face, which a moment before had been deeply flushed, was now drained of colour. Standing, Si supported himself on the back of his chair, suddenly grimaced, and put his free hand to his chest. 'Oh, boy . . .' he muttered. 'Oh, boy . . .' He doubled over, crumpled in pain.

Joe was on his feet. 'Okay, Si . . . Here . . . here, fella, lean on me.' He helped Si to the living-room and lowered him gently on to the couch. Si's face was contorted with pain, and he was having difficulty breathing. 'Lemme get you a drink. Mullaly! How's about a little Scotch? On the double. 'Ey, Milt!' He motioned Milt to put his ear closer and spoke in a low voice, 'Get Dr. Berkman. Tell him to come right over.'

Milt hesitated.

'C'mon, shake a leg!'

Milt pulled him a short distance from where Simon lay. 'In *this* house?' Milt hissed. 'The newspapers—'

Joe pulled himself away from Milt, turned back to Si, holding the Scotch jigger to Si's twisted lips; he grabbed a cushion, put it under Si's head, gently pulled Si's tie loose and opened his collar. 'There, fella.' Then he rose, turned to Milt, pale with rage. 'How in God's world can you think about the papers or *my* problems? Can't you see the man is *sick*?' he said in a hoarse whisper. 'My friend Si is sick.'

'Okay', Milt said. 'Okay. I'm just thinking about you. That's my job, isn't it?' Joe glared at him and Milt left reluctantly to call the doctor.

Anna Landos was watching Si apprehensively. She and her agitated attorney whispered and she shrugged, watching Simon like a cat, holding her breath. Hetty, too, never took her eyes off him, even as she poured and sipped another bourbon. Si was barely conscious.

After four or five minutes, his breathing began to come a little easier. He began to tremble with chills and Hetty ran to the den to fetch an afghan, with which Joe covered his friend gently.

'Oh, God,' Si said weakly, 'I'm sure glad Ellie didn't live to see all this.' He tried to smile and his face twisted into an agonized grimace. 'Makes a man wonder if it's worth trying to do a job. What if I did give you six thousand commitments? They stood in line to buy your houses, didn't they? Why do they fight with success? Not one default in eighteen thousand houses, Joe. Not one! The government's collected over six million in premiums on Naples. Is that success? Nothing but—'

'Shh!' Joe said. 'Take it easy, Si. Relax.'

Si subsided. His face was still a ghastly grey. Anna said, 'I'm afraid we have to go, Simon. I'm sorry you're not feeling well.'

'Don't go, Anna', Simon said, and Joe had never heard such helpless pleading in a man's voice. 'Not yet.'

'The doctor will be here any minute, my darling. And I have to go, really I do.' She bent to kiss him and when she rose, Joe thought her eyes were malevolent, almost as if she were enjoying herself. 'Good-bye, my dear Major. And Hetty – you don't mind if I

call you Hetty? – good luck with the new play. Come along,
Lloyd.'

They were outside almost before anyone had a chance to say
good-bye. The Rolls started quietly and drove away.

Si looked after her, helpless.

'How baleful', Hetty said in a hushed voice.

'Well, *she'll* be no help to our side', Milt said.

When Jeff Berkman arrived, he gave Si a thorough and pains-
taking going over and took an electrocardiogram on his portable.
'Been under heavy pressure, Mr. Cutler?' Simon nodded dumbly.
Efficiently the doctor administered a shot of Demoral.

Milt and Joe retired to the den for a hurried consultation with
Jeff Berkman, whose opinion was that the patient had suffered a
coronary occlusion and should be in a hospital. It was touch and
go. 'Does he have any family?'

'A sister,' Joe said, 'but she lives in Minneapolis.'

Dr. Berkman shook his head. 'Better get in touch with her. I'll
take him into Naples Hospital.'

'No, no, no, no!' Milt said. 'I have to draw the line on you
fellows somewhere. Bad enough you're here in the first place, Doc.
No one ought to know about this.' He tried to tell Dr. Berkman
briefly about the Brice committee, but Milt was incapable of telling
anything briefly. Jeff Berkman nodded his head impatiently. 'Don't
you see, they'll say Joe is holding Si in his own, ah, personal hospital, ah, to keep him from testifying', Milt concluded. 'Couldn't
we get him into Allenburg General instead?'

Dr. Berkman shrugged. 'Sure, I have privileges there. Let me
call an ambulance.'

'How bad is he?' Joe said, his deep concern for Si clearly in his
voice.

'Week or ten days'll tell the story better', Jeff said. 'He'll either
make it or he won't.'

Joe wanted to go along in the ambulance, but Milt absolutely
wouldn't hear of it. 'Please, Joe, let me go. Listen to me, old buddy.
Jeff'll be with us. What good can you do? All you'd do is expose
yourself to unfavourable publicity.'

Reluctantly Joe allowed the ambulance attendants to cart Si
Cutler out on the stretcher. 'The old ticker, isn't it?' Si asked
weakly as he passed. Joe did not respond for a moment, except
to squeeze Si's massive shoulder. 'Don't be absolutely ridiculous',
he said at last.

'Nobody tells me a thing', Si gasped.

'Crap', Joe said. 'Goddam ambulance is just a precaution. You know these whatzis, doctors. You take it easy now, Simon. Don't worry so much, you hear me good? Everything's gonna be okay.'

Luce, who had come in just after the doctor's arrival, and Hetty, with a glass of bourbon still in her hand, stood in the driveway to watch the ambulance pull away, and without a word they all filed back into the living-room.

'I guess I'd better go', Luce said.

'No!' Hetty cried, almost desperately. 'Stay! Stay! Please. Just a little while? I have to talk to you, Luce. You're only one I want to talk to.' Luce shrugged to Joe, put her arm around Hetty's shoulder and sat beside her on the couch.

'A little while', she said placatingly.

'Jus' a little while', Hetty said gratefully. Then she looked at her sister-in-law cravenly. 'I'm frightened', she whispered. 'This house is bad luck. Bad, bad luck.'

'Any place can look bad on ten drinks', Joe said. 'Can't you put that away?'

Hetty glared at him through her drunkenness. 'Can't', she said. 'An' that's the Lord's truth. Y'know, I finally got to hate the house on Elm Street. But I think I hate this place more. So many bad things happen here, Luce. Y'know? So many . . . I'm gettin' afraid of the dark . . .' She took a long swallow. 'That terrible Landos woman', she continued thickly. 'Terrible, terrible woman. Under that false sad face of hers, she was radiant, wasn't she? Only one thing. She was sorry it wasn't you, Joie darling. Did you realize that? I bet not. What did you ever *do* to her?'

Joe was often startled at his wife's insight, but he pretended to know nothing.

'Me? I helped her, that's all I did. When she was really on her can, too.'

'Knew it', Hetty said in her highest pitch. 'I was sure of it. Ah, Joie, poor Joie . . . Such an easy mark. Everyone takes advantage of 'm. Helps everyone, doesn't he, Lucy? You're so wonderful to everyone, Joie. I don't deserve you. Jus' don't. No, I'm being perfectly serious. Lucy, don't let's talk to him. He's *too* perfect. Let's just you an' me talk. Come on, Luce . . . Over here . . .' Almost blindly, she led Lucy, who half supported her, to the sofa at the opposite end of the room, and unsteadily she settled herself in, peering fondly into Lucy's eyes. Slowly she sipped her bourbon.

'You're a *nice* person, Lucy. I jus' love you. I really do, y'know.
Always have. All my wild brothers . . . what good're they? Can't
talk to *them*. Nah. You're the only *friend*, real one, y'know, I have,
y'know? Better than a real sister. I jus' don't know what I'd do
without you . . . an' Milton too. Oh, here I go again . . . You
mus' think I'm terrible . . . jus' simply terrible.'

'No, no,' Lucy said, 'here take it easy now . . . there', as if Hetty
were an infant.

'You know what today is?'

'October twenty-fourth', Lucy said, and winched at the realization.

'Right!' Hetty raised her voice. 'October twenty-fourth!' She
called to Joe. 'Your son's birthday, Joie. He'd've been thirty today, Luce. Jus' a nice age. Young married.' Her eyes filled with
tears. 'I'd be a grandma by now. So' – she popped her lips – 'instead
of being a young grandma, I'll be an old grandma.

'Poor Carey . . . started life in the front seat of a car . . . Oh, what
a mess *that* was . . . It was jus' awful for poor Joie, too. An' what've
we got to show?' Her words came slowly, interrupted by long
pauses while the now sluggish machinery of her mind groped for
expression. Lucy sat close to her, took her hand occasionally and
listened intently. Joe was silent, feeling sick. What the hell had
happened to his wife? All these years he had never really focused
on the problem, but facing it, here it was: She was absolutely an
alcoholic. Or if not that, a common drunk. What the hell had
happened to her?

Hetty held Lucy's wrist pleadingly. 'Be a lamb and get me a
refill?'

Lucy took the empty glass to the bar, glanced at Joe helplessly.
Hetty lit a cigarette and Joe unwrapped a new cigar, biting the end
viciously. He had a sinking sense of doom now, but he could not
see any escape.

'Mullaly', he half wheedled. 'You're not feeling so hot. Hows'
about getting to bed?'

'Never felt better in my life', Hetty said, spacing her words
evenly and enunciating too precisely. 'Li'l more, Luce, don' be
stingy. C'mon.' Lucy poured another half ounce, stirred the ice and
poured a stiff one for herself.

Hetty did not wait for the drink but started unevenly towards
the bar to get it. As she approached the wing chair that Joe sat
in, she wavered, leaned against the back of it. 'Joie, c'n I get you

drink?' Suddenly she stopped and stared at him as if seeing him for the first time. 'Joie, darling, what're you going to *do*?'

'Lookit, there's nothing to worry about', Joe snapped. 'Stop worrying.'

'Oh, but I do, darling, I do worry', Hetty said with great feeling. 'Part o' my job. Always has been. Darling, you're always so *sure*. Everything's always sure to turn out all right, isn't it? Only it doesn't always. Like – *you* know, *you* know.' She took her new drink from Lucy and let her accusation hang suspended. '"Carey'll be all right", he used to say. "Carey'll be fine." Joie, dear, I want to *help, that's* all. Isn't there *anything* I can do?'

'Nah, nah!' he said impatiently.

'What does Milton think, Lucy? Does he tell *you* what it's all about? Joie tells me abs'lutely nothing. I'm a – I don't know – second-class citizen.'

Joe blew a perfect smoke ring. 'Now lookit, there's not a damn thing to do. There's absolutely nothing that has to be done about anything. The investigation is going to blow up in their faces.'

'But I read the papers', Hetty said. 'Poor, poor Joie.' She put an unsteady hand on his cheek, bristling now with a day's growth of grey whisker.

Suddenly her mood changed. 'Luce, you think the glamorous Anna saw something in poor Simon we don't see?'

'I can't imagine what', Lucy said.

'Well, he's big, an' he's good looking, got' admit that. An' he certainly likes the girls, doesn't he? You 'member back in the house on Elm Street, whenever Simon came, you an' I would run for cover?' She giggled inwardly. 'So *handy* he was. Remember?'

Lucy laughed. 'He used to pinch. One night, I was ready to kill him.'

'Y'know, I think he even made a pass at Mammina.'

Both girls giggled like teenagers.

'How come you girls never told me any of this?' Joe said.

'Oh, what for?' Hetty said. 'What could *you* do?'

'You'da just got sore', Lucy said.

'Lucy dear, you're so so *understanding*', Hetty said in a small voice. 'You're so *good* to me. Not like your big brother Joie. Really, *really* good. You know what I'm really like, an' that's the difference.'

'God knows I try', Joe said helplessly.

'He *tries*', Hetty said. 'Yes, he does. Not his fault . . . 'smy

fault. I know, I know, I'm terrible, terrible wife.' Suddenly her
face contorted, and she was straining to speak without breaking
down completely. 'You know, Lucy, 'fore we were married, we
used to go watch the seals in Central Park. Joie used to stan' there
watching 'em and say, "Look at 'em. Throw 'em a fish, they'll do
anything." Oh, I think of that, and you know what I think? It's
kinda sinister idea, don't you? But Joie's big success in every way,
isn't he? Nature's plan, man suppose to go out, hunt lions, bring
home skins, bring home meat. That's your brother Joie. Very big
in the lion-hunting department. Bank account in eight figures.
Started with abs'lutely nothing. Right, Joie? Ask 'im. Good lion
hunter oughta marry lion huntress. But *unfortunately* Hetty Mullaly's terrible huntress. Jus' no good. There 'e is – Joe Naples, look
at 'im, lion hunter, forceful, masculine. I could tell her, Joie,
couldn't I, ol' lion hunter?'

Joe said, 'Come on, Mullaly, be a good kid. Let's get to bed.'

'Bed? Oh, no. No, no abs'lutely no. What's there in bed? Jus'
sleep and I don' wanna sleep, couldn't sleep, nossir. You're tire',
sure, an' have every right. Out killing lions all day. Pulling Harold
Brice's beard, God knows what. Made a million today I bet. But
not for me, you didn't, 'cause I don't *need* a million. You know
how I'd like it? 'F I could jus' live in one of your seven'y-nine
ninety ranches. Or maybe I'm spoiled now, maybe I'd need the
luxurious eleven nine ninety split level with nice li'l radish patch in
the yard an' a li'l place for mums an' glads an' like that.'

Slowly she looked about the room. 'What am *I* complaining
about, really? Aren't I jus' terrible? Have a husband who adores
me, do anything for me. Won'erful son . . . What's wrong with
me?'

'You know what I think?' Joe said. 'I think you oughta take
a Miltown and get into bed and not get all stirred up. Tomorrow
you're gonna feel good and lousy.'

Hetty said, 'Y'know, he's abs'lu'ely right. Always right. Why
'm I picking on 'im, Lucy? Oh, yes, I'm the one. You know *I*
haven't been much of a wife . . . haven't even been a great mother.
Not to Carey, anyway. No, no, let's be honest. I'll tell you something terrible, Luce. You promise never to tell another living soul?
Promise?'

'Promise', Lucy said patiently. Lucy had been through sessions
like this before, but usually Joe was out and was spared the
details.

'I never was exactly right for Carey. I mean for my own son. Not the way a mother should be. Not till he was much, much older. I re-*sent*ed him, and he was such a dear little boy. Little spoiled, but good at heart. Oh, I've grown up since. But y'know why? I'm ashamed to admit it. Interfered with my *stupid* acting. With th' way I saw my stupid self. Oh, stupid, stupid. Oh, yes, very, very much so. I know whereof I speak. Two years psycho'nalysis, that mush I know, you find out the damndest things, an' that was the *least* of my trouble. See, Joie didn't really steal 'm. Oh, he didn't make it any easier. But they did love each other. I know *that*. Did you ever *see* such father an' son?'

Joe was furious even though he knew it was the liquor speaking. 'You make it sound like something unnatural, like something completely wacked up!'

'Oh, no, no, no. It was beautiful relationship. From the minute he pulled that baby out of me, and took 'im into *his* hands – strong hands. Hetty Mullaly, keep out. Outside completely. But now look, let's face it, reckless our Carey never was. Oh, that doesn't matter. Wasn't your fault, Joie. No, I'm telling Lucy. All those ball games, together, out on the jobs together. Pals . . . That was *my* job. *My* default. Oh, my God.' She snuffled, unconscious of herself. 'What happened to Carey, Joie? All that stuff in the citation. Reckless. Disregard for's personal safety. Daring. False, *false*. *That wasn' our boy Carey!* What could've *happened*? Was he trying to prove something? What though?' Her voice was hollow, empty, like a whisper from the grave. 'All those years. And then, oh, that little telegram . . . little square piece of ugly yellow paper . . . Poof! No more lovely smile all over on one side, no more big hello mom, what's for supper? No phone calls from Lawrenceville or Princeton, how's about you and Pop coming down for the game? See Joie . . . not saying a word. Oh, how awful of me to think it, isn't it awful, Luce? But keeps coming to me . . . I know my Joie. He feels 's bad as I do, maybe worse. Oh, it never shows, but you know something? He cries in his sleep, Lucy. You know that? Nobody knows that. Never tol' you or anyone. I've heard my Joie crying in 's sleep, calling his father, like a little boy. But awake? Never. Never weak, oh no. Rock o' Gibraltar. Don' you need me, Joie? Don' you need *anything*?'

'What kinda ridiculous question is *that*?' Joe said sharply. 'I need everyone. What are you trying to prove? What am I without everyone? Nothing whatsoever.'

'You don't need them, darling', Hetty said slowly. 'You jus need *them* to need *you*.'

Joe was beside himself. He didn't have the first foggy idea what was wrong with this girl or what to do about it. Menopause the doctor said and gave her pills. Well, it would drive both of them off their wacks yet.

They heard the phone ring and Cibulkas came to say Andy was calling from Cambridge. Hetty looked crushed and frightened.

'Oh, my Lord, how can I talk to 'm?' she said. 'Look't me. What'll I *say*?'

'I'll talk to him', Joe said, and hurried to the phone.

'Dad? I think we've hit it. I think Karpeko and I are going to come up with all the affidavits you need. We have one real live witness. Your hunch about Poltek was fantastically accurate. You must have a sixth sense, Dad.'

'You kidding?'

'I wouldn't kid about a thing like this, Dad.'

'Lookit, Andy. Stay right where you are. I'll fly up there in the morning. Get ahold of your Russian whozis, prof, and I'll bring Uncle Milt and maybe we'll get somewhere.'

'Okay, Dad. Right. See you in the morning.' Andy was as high as a flag.

Joe dialled Dulian to ask about weather and to tell him to get the twin Beech ready for take-off at eight. Then he called the hospital and got Milt, who said there'd been no change in Simon's condition. They'd taken a private room for him, and Simon was under sedation, no oxygen needed at the moment, he was resting comfortably. Dr. Berkman had called in a heart man, and Milt had ordered round-the-clock nursing. They'd take new cardiograms in the morning.

After a moment of foot-dragging at the prospect of flying to Boston to see Karpeko, Milt unhappily agreed to come along and to pick Joe up at seven for the drive to Teterboro.

'How's Hetty?' Milt asked cautiously.

'Drunk as a skunk', said Joe.

'Would you like me to come over?'

'No, no. I'll send Lucy home. See you in the morning.'

Hetty was drinking even more defiantly when he returned to the living-room. Ten to one she could scarcely see him by now.

'Now it's Andy', she said to Lucy. 'How's Andrew, Joie?'

'Fine', Joe said. 'I'm gonna run up to see him in the morning.'

'What's the matter? What's wrong?' There was panic in Hetty's voice and she half rose.

'Not a goddam thing. He's got some dope for me on this Senate sub-committee deal.'

Hetty lurched to her feet. 'Now you're not going to mix 'm up in that? You can't be serious.' She was tugging futilely at his sleeve. 'You can't ... can't.'

She turned back to Lucy, her face crumpled, almost hideous, 'He's all I have, Luce. My sweet Andy. He wan'sa be teasher. Simple college teasher. So what? No lions. No tigers. He's not a hunter. But he's such a sweet, tender *giving* boy. He'll be a *good* teasher. *Wonderful* teasher. You think I'm silly, Lucy? I say 'f he wants to be teasher ... lettum! He's such patient boy. Like my poor dear meek father. Joie wants him to come into his business – and *I know why*. Want's 'm to take Carey's place. Can't do it, darling. Can't take one person out 'f your heart, put in a substitute. Carey *wanted* to be in the business. But Carey is *gone*. What do you say, Luce? Don't you think Andy ought to teash if he wants to?'

Lucy said, 'I don't see why not.'

''S bad time to argue, 's not nice of me. I know, 'zif I'm criticising him or his business ... because he's got troubles now. But I'm not. I jus' feel 'f Andy wan's a be teasher, he should. Don' shu think?'

Lucy nodded and patted Hetty's hand. 'I'm sure he will, Het.'

'You know everyone doesn't have to do *exactly* what he says, do they? *Do they?* Why should we all have to do it *his* way? He's so damn persuasive. Oh, Rosie knew what she was doing, didn't she? *Better a nunnery*. At leas' you give your soul to God of your own free will.' She glared at Joe with a fierceness he had never seen before. 'Better a convent. I never understood why Rosie wanted that. But now I do ... That awful house on Elm Street. Oh, clever, clever Rosina. Sister Angelora. Don't they think of the *most* beautiful names?' The fleeting fierceness was gone and Joe was scarcely sure he had seen it.

''Nother thing. When *you* talk of Milton, I'll bet he listens to you, doesn't he? I know Milton. He listens, he hears. With his mind, with his whole being. I jus' bet he does. Well, not when I talk. No ma'am. No one to listen. Not the secret private worrying things I *have* to tell someone.' She glared at Joe. 'Oh sure, I found someone – finally. You di'n't know that, Luce, no ... But I hadda *pay* ... Forty dollars an hour to jus' lie there an' tell this simply wonderful guy, sad little man he was really, anything came into my head. It was such a relief. Terrible, but in funny way, a pleasure. Forty dollars an hour. Worth every penny. An' Joie was glad to pay it, weren't shu, darling? Worth to him not to have to listen.'

'Lookit, Mullaly', Joe broke in. 'You're not yourself. Too much excitement, Si getting sick, we're all shot to hell. How's about wrapping it up?'

'See – see! He won't *listen*. You know how far he'll go. He'll even – he'll even – he'll do *any*thing to shut me up! Oh, not lately, no, no. But he used to.'

'Lookit, Hetty. Will you shut up. Christ, Luce, she said she needed help, she wanted to go to a head shrinker, so okay. I don't believe in all that crap, but if she wanted it, what the hell. Why not? Whatever she wanted.'

'What I want you can't *buy*, Joie. But, I found out some terrifying things from little Dr. Abrams. Terrible things, complicated things. I don't love my husband, Lucy. Not the way I thought I did. He won't let me. Isn't that awful?' Her voice was hollow with pain. 'He doesn't mind. He thinks I'm jus' drunk. Look how he glares at me. Oh, I get so *bored*, Lucy. Bored.' Her voice was hollow. 'The avenging angel. I don't *like* to drink, darling. Ooo, when he gets like this – I don't like him, Lucy. Not one bit.'

Holding a glass of bourbon in one hand, she rose and wove her way past various pieces of furniture to where Joe sat. 'I don't wanna hurt 'm . . . Don't wanna hurt shu, Joie. Specially with all your trouble. But y'know, Luce . . .' Slowly, deliberately, she poured her drink into Joe's lap, listening to the splash against his trousers, while Joe sat and glared at her with something that was almost pity, as if she were out of her mind. Hetty lowered her voice to a whisper, giggled at the sight of what she had done, and pointed to his wet lap. 'You piddled, Joie, oughta be 'shame?' She smiled privately into her empty glass. Then without warning, her face crumpled again, falling into a terrible grimace and folds of flesh. She looked, unexpectedly, a hundred years old.

'Oh, my God, forgive me!' she cried suddenly, and burst into uncontrolled weeping as if her heart would break.

'There, there', Luce said as if to a child. 'Please, Hetty.'

'Oh Lord', Hetty cried. 'What am I going to do? What are we going to do?'

'What you need is a vacation', Luce said. 'Both of you.'

'I have no character. That's my trouble. I hang on for *life*. Life itself. Depend on him. Dear Joie. You know what that makes me? I need him. 'Sn't that ridiculous? We all need him, though, don' we? Isn't that the truth? Milton does, you, Dino, Mammina, everybody. 'S not *all* his fault, then, is it? No ma'am, not by a long shot. But he doesn't need us. Not *me*.'

'Somewhere nice where you can get away and rest and get back on your feet', Lucy said, putting a comforting hand on her shoulder. 'Maybe Palm Springs.'

Hetty put her hands on her face and continued to sob without restraint. Joe stood up and tried to dry his lap, first with a cocktail napkin and then with his handkerchief.

'Oh God', Hetty said, swallowing hard and trying to take control of herself. 'A vacation!' She raised her head. 'He *hates* vacations!' She tried ineffectually to wipe her tears with her knuckles. 'Y'know . . . he doesn't *care*. Not really . . .'

Joe said bitterly, 'Now, Mullaly, you know goddam well who I care plenty about.' He looked at her significantly. 'The people I do give a damn about.'

Hetty exerted great effort to try to keep herself from weeping any more, but without success. Her voice, though full of tears, was harsh, high, surprisingly incisive, an imitation of Joe's. 'Oh, he's so fulluvit. He's fulluvit, Lucy. Big-hearted Ike. You don't know anything about *any*body! You don't know *me*. God knows, not one blessed thing, and God knows you know less about yourself!'

Joe could take no more. 'Come on, Mullaly. You're mean drunk. You're comin' upstairs.'

She tried to push his hand away from her arm. 'No, no *sir*, no, boss. You know, Joie, you mustn't *undercut* me. Just when I'm highest or think I'm getting through, you undercut. It's difficult enough for me to say what I mean, and then when I do, you — Sst. Like that. You know the longes' distance in the world, Lucy? Distance from his bed to mine.' She broke loose from his grasp and, still sobbing, staggered and tried to run towards the diningroom, but he grabbed her and spun her round.

'Cut it now. You've said enough for one night. Christ, what am I supposed to be? A goddam good friend has a heart attack right in my own house, the poor bastid, and now you . . . What the hell you trying to do to me?'

'Let me go', she whispered, and tried in vain to pull away. With his open palm he slapped her one sharp and stunning blow across

L

the cheek. He was surprised himself at how tremendously hard he had hit her. He could hear her gasp, and she slumped unconscious into his arms.

'Help me get her upstairs, Luce.'

After Lucy had gone, Joe sat on the satin spread, mashing an already shredded cigar with his back teeth, watching Hetty's face, drunkenly open-mouthed in sleep, a face not unlike her mother's when the old Bantam hen had been in the agony of her last illness. He sat trying to make head or tail of what had possessed her; in fact, what had happened to them both. He paraded his worries about Hetty on review. The drinking, of course, but not only the drinking. What she said when she got like that, the little flick before she kissed him, the tiny flinch when he touched her. But what was it and when had it happened? Was it Carey's death? God knows she was never right after that. But her drinking had started long before Carey was born, before Joe had met her. Maybe it *was* merely a physical thing inherited from her father. He hoped to God it was, hopeless though that might be. So *he* undercut people, did he? Joe Naples, the guy who built people up beyond what they had ever been . . . What a hell of thing for her to say . . . Lookit the way she lay there sleeping open-mouthed almost as though she had taken ugly pills, though it wasn't easy to uglify such a finely-chiselled, delicate face.

Well, think of something else . . . this goddam Senate investigation . . . Something lousy, but real. He'd better get some sleep. He had to be out of the house by seven at the latest . . .

Twenty-five

JOE, Milt and Rossmore rode a strong tail wind to Boston.
    And who'd have believed that Andy would come to Logan
airport to meet him before nine! Kid must've woke up seven
o'clock, which he did not expect of Andy except maybe if someone
let a nuclear blast go in his ear. And accompanying Andy was Professor Karpeko, a rotund, short, wispy-haired, pink-and smooth-
cheeked man, must've been in his seventies, but preserved in some
kind of juice, gave him lots of bounce. The old professor greeted
him with unexpected warmth, and sitting in the back seat of Andy's
Renault, he kept up a steady chatter all the way back to Cambridge.
Milt sat huddled silent, eyes closed, listening suspiciously. Andy
drove, peeping surreptitiously from the road back to his father and
Professor Karpeko.
    'I surprise you, Mr. Naples, to come out to the airport to greet
you?' The Professor spoke on, breezy as a baby. 'I am a short
sleeper. Six hours, the most. Sometimes four, five. Too much
coffee my wife says. No, Mr. Naples, I never meet you before, is a
pity because I like to meet men of success. You are a man of success.
But that is not why I am here, no. Is also not because of your son.
Very good meticulous student with fine mind, your son – I have
him in my class last year. You know that? Yes . . . What grade
I give you, Naples? Eighty-eight? Is very high grade for me. I am
tough marker. Well, with me I do not go to greet a man at the
airport on the other side of the city early in the morning unless he
is a very old friend or is a question of importance. This is a question
of importance. We are dealing with the heart of good and of evil.'
He paused to emphasize his point with silence, and they drove
through the Summer Street tunnel in the early morning traffic,
hearing only the damp, slapping revolutions of tyres.
    'Good and evil', Karpeko repeated. 'Nothing less, my dear
man. And you know, is not easy for someone like me to decide
which is what. I grew up as a boy in Russia, and my father was a

wealthy man, also by coincidence a builder – he called himself contractor – when I went into the army. I was only sixteen, but I join because we were at war. It was patriotic thing, for God and Tsar. My mother cried when she saw me in uniform and suddenly before I knew what was happening, there was no more war, no Tsar, no army, no officers – officers were being shot by their own men – and people like my father and mother were killed like chickens – by madmen. That was when I looked clearly into the face of evil. Into the eyeball of evil. I do not want to bore you with the story of my life. They wanted my soul. I was invited to be one of them. You know what is the ultimate evil? It is an evil that is unconscious of its own malignancy, blind to its own viciousness. It believes itself good. That is the incurable characteristic. Do I tire you with my sermon, Mr. Naples?'

'Nope.'

'I am glad. Sometimes I put the boys in class to sleep, but not often. I'm prejudiced, you understand – I hate the Bolsheviks. Not the kind of hate that rants and screams, but it's just part of me. Bolshevism is the most corrosive evil in our lifetime, sir. Worse than Hitlerism, because Hitlerism was only a cult, an opportunism, and anyhow it did not survive. But the Bolsheviks not only survive, they prosper and they are most malignant because they think they are noble; but their lies and their treachery, their conspiracy, their cult of brutalism is for them by some upside-down logic for the greater good of mankind. One cannot debate with this kind of evil. One cannot co-exist with it. One can only strangle it where it is found and destroy it wherever one can – if possible without destroying oneself.'

Professor Karpeko spoke almost jauntily, as if he were discussing some obtuse, but intriguing element of international maritime law in a classroom.

'Professor, you just said yourself one hell of a big mouthful. I saw these guys in Italy. They didn't give a damn about anyone. And sneaky! You talk about conspiracy, they got it. They are just going to have it come out their way and they don't give a damn what they do to who. Oh, you and I were made for each other, Professor. We see it the same.'

'Here in Cambridge,' Professor Karpeko said, 'I see this evil corrupt not only boys, but men. Back in the thirties and even in the forties, I watch little cancer cells grow up here and here. We have childish demonstrations on steps of Widener Library, but

behind the demonstrations and silly placards, the real adult conspiracy is at work with roots reaching back to the Kremlin. I fought
them wherever I could because this is no respecter of age. The people
who shot my parents were only boys also.'

Milt's eyes fluttered and he openly stared at the professor.

'This Samuel Poltek your son asks about is a creature I well remember. If I had any idea he is now working for the American
government, I would have done something long ago. He was one
of the deeply malignant ones, that I can promise you. He worked
in a cell with six or seven others right here while he was studying
at law school. Oh, I suspect it even when he was working under
me in the Legal Aid Society. But I can prove it now, even to a
congressional committee.'

Joe Naples looked back at Milt in triumph, 'Okay, Counsellor?'

'And how will you prove it, Professor?' Milt said gently.

It was clear that Milt believed Karpeko was a wackeroo and,
Joe thought reluctantly, the professor probably was exactly that,
and his highly personal feeling about the Bolsheviks might lead
him to extremes created by his own imagination.

'We have here assistant professor at the law school, a man who
was in Poltek's cell – young fellow named Straley – Geoffrey Straley.
He and his wife are good friends of me and my wife. Very talented,
too, don't you think so, Naples?' Andy nodded. 'He teaches constitutional law. You will hear from him the odd way how he comes
to be an expert on constitutional law. He is one of those – how do
you say it – disenchanted? You will talk to him yourself.'

'Good', Joe said.

'For me,' Professor Karpeko continued, 'is still all question of
good and evil. I do not know what you may have done to cause
that the Senate should pry into your affairs. Maybe you have done
some bad things too. But whatever you do, you build houses, you
do not threaten the entire world, that I am sure. If you have acted
here or there against the public interest, let it be brought out in
such a way by men who are interested in America and freedom.
They will bring you to book if that is needed. But the Polteks
must be destroyed. This is how I feel. This is why, when your son
asks me, I am anxious to help.'

'Believe me, Professor', Joe said. 'I didn't do a damn thing.
Nobody has any book they're gonna throw at me.'

'I am glad to hear it', Karpeko said indifferently.

They passed the new Leverett Towers still under construction, crossed Anderson Bridge, went by Eliot House, and headed away from the Charles towards Harvard Square. Boylston Street was alive with boys and girls lugging green bags to classes.

'Ah,' Professor Karpeko said. 'there's a good parking place right in front of the Wursthaus, Naples. Why do we not have a little beer and pretzels? I didn't have breakfast.'

Joe and Milt watched while the round little man put away two huge steinfuls of Heineken's and gobbled half a dozen pretzels, and Andy impatiently sipped a glass of milk. 'You see here is full of students', Karpeko said. 'Teachers all around, but no Bolsheviks this year. We're lucky. No American Bolsheviks. But now Moscow is trying to send us exchange students through the front door. Oooch!' He grimaced and licked the beer suds from his lips. 'Come, gentlemen, we go see Mister Straley and then we are finish, and I go back to work. I have eleven o'clock class.' They drove through the Square and beyond, Joe looking at all the new construction, the foundation for the new medical centre, the Loeb Theatre.

'Jesus', Joe said. 'Old Harvard is bustin' at the seams. What's going on?'

'All the new buildings under this new Programme for Harvard. You made a contribution yourself,' Chuck Rossmore said, 'don't you remember?'

'I did?'

'Fifty thousand', Milt said gloomily. Karpeko's eyes glistened.

'That all?' Joe said. 'God knows you can't do much for fifty whatzis, can you?'

Suddenly he turned on Karpeko. 'Say, Professor, what do you think of my boy wanting to be a professor? You think he'd be any good?'

Karpeko looked surprised. 'You ask *me*? Yes, yes, I think he would be good. He has a keen mind.'

'You like this professor deal your own self? Most of you guys out here are happy? I mean, you really get along here?'

Professor Karpeko suddenly became kittenish and he giggled falsetto. 'Happy? Why not? I *pursue* happiness. Some of us are yes, some no. Same as elsewhere. We have our ulcers, heart conditions, everything like people outside only not quite so bad.'

'I hope you don't mind me asking you, Professor, but how much does a big shot like you make?' He could feel Milt wince behind him.

'Now? I am full professor, eighteen thousand. Is quite adequate.
Also I publish books.'

They had parked in front of an old frame colonial house a block
beyond the glassy Law School dorm.

'I hear you're absolutely top number-one man in the entire
country in international law, is that right?'

'Oh,' Karpeko protested, 'maybe is slight exaggeration. Is
perhaps two or three others.'

'On a lousy eighteen thousand', Joe said. 'No offence, Professor.
It's as tough as workin' for Uncle Sam. Okay, no use standing
around here. If we're going, let's go.'

They stood like a neighbourhood delegation at the front door of
the white house while Professor Karpeko lifted the knocker and
snapped it down twice. A slim, sharp-faced but smiling young
woman answered the door. She wore no make-up, a white shirt and
navy slacks, and cocked her head in frank curiosity. She brought
the glasses perched back on the top of her head down to her eyes
briefly. 'Sacha!' she cried to Karpeko, obviously pleased to see
him. 'Come in, come in. Jeff is just finishing his coffee.' She looked
to the others with the same open curiosity, and Professor Karpeko
introduced them. This was Daphne Straley.

As they walked slowly through the hall towards the kitchen she
said slowly, 'Naples. Joseph Naples. Aren't you the man Sam
Poltek is after?'

'That's me', Joe said. 'Mr. Jason's my attorney, Mr. Rossmore
is my public relations man.'

'That's what I was afraid of', Daphne Straley said softly.

Geoffrey Straley put his coffee down, got up from the kitchen
table and shook hands. Sitting beside him in a high chair was a
two-year-old blonde girl in blue jeans.

'You men go ahead inside,' Daphne said, 'while I put Susan
out in her playpen. Please don't say anything important till I get
back.'

Jeff Straley was a handsome, tall, somewhat lumbering man in
his middle thirties, a contemporary of Poltek's. He sat in the over-
upholstered chair setting his coffee carefully on the table, and the
four-man delegation distributed themselves on the stuffed chairs
and sofa. Joe could remember nothing so goddam solemn since
the night more than twenty-five years ago that the admissions committee from Canoe Hill came to call on him at Elm Street. For a
moment the same shrouded atmosphere hung over the room, but

in a minute or two Daphne was back, and she brought a ray of light in with her. Here was a young broad who was living right and you could feel it just by looking at her. 'Can I get any of you some coffee?' she said.

'Iss no trouble?' Chuck Rossmore hissed, and Daphne shook her head carefully. 'Goot. Thank you.' Daphne pranced out to the kitchen and was back in no time.

'I guess we all know why you're here, Mr. Naples', Jeff Straley said. 'So why don't you just fire away?'

Joe said, 'Yah thanks. I guess my lawyer here has a few questions and Mr. Rossmore may have one or two, and if they forget anything, maybe I'll take a crack at it.'

Milt stiffened and cleared his throat. 'Ah – Mr. Straley, Geoffrey Straley, is it? Ah – you apparently know Sam Poltek pretty well? How well?'

'Oh, I haven't seen Sam in – let's see – perhaps twelve years. Perhaps longer. Sam Poltek and I were close friends at one time. In fact, he was best man at our wedding.'

'I see. And were you friends here at law school?'

'We were in the same class. The first thing about Sam that fascinated me was that he was from the wrong side of the tracks. You know – day student, one of the Boston Latin crowd, poor family, but brilliant as the dickens. I met him at college two years before we came to law school. He hypnotized me. I had just never met anyone like him. We had one common bond, we were both exempted from military service – Four F, he had an ulcer and I had a punctured ear-drum. So even though we travelled in entirely different social circles, I'd rather have spent my time with him than the guys at Porcellian. I was mighty big on the underdog in those days. Sam was sharp and perceptive, had ants in his pants, and was always mad as a wet hen. I'm sure he was deeply discontented. We were still at war then and Russia was our buddy. I don't want to make excuses for him or me, just recalling the atmosphere, you understand. That was early forty-three or four, and I wasn't even mildly surprised when he told me he'd joined the Communist Party.'

'When was that?' Milt was still sceptical.

'Nineteen forty-four. Sometime around December.'

'Did he just *tell* you that or did you see his card?' Rossmore asked, moving forward in his chair.

'Even *I* saw his card', Daphne said. 'He showed it to me before he destroyed it. Sam Poltek was always one for the grand gesture.'

'And he recruited you to do party work?'

'I never thought of it that way', Geoffrey Straley said. 'I was one of those poor rich boys. F.D.R. was my hero. I rebelled against the too-good life, felt guilty about it. In fact, that's when my interest in constitutional law started.'

'How's that?' Milt said.

'Well—' Jeff Straley hesitated and looked at his wife questioningly.

'Jeff, darling,' Daphne said, lighting a cigarette, 'we've been all over it. Go ahead.'

'It was back in the days when the Jenner and the Walter Committees were hauling party members up and asking questions. We had a whole team working on constitutional rights, studying hundreds of cases for constitutionality. Almost every case involved a constitutional question. I must say in all honesty I never had such a good time as I did those days. We were pulling the dragon's tail, and in all due modesty, I was the bright young man of the crowd. By that time, Sam Poltek had quit the party, and as far as I knew had moved out west.'

'Quit the party', Daphne said. 'Oh, yes, he quit the party all right. Tell them how he did that, Jeff. I think that's the key.'

'As a matter of fact, it is,' Jeff said, 'or very frankly I wouldn't be talking to you at all. I guess it was in the early autumn of forty-seven, or maybe late summer. We were having a cook-out at my father's place in Rochester. Daphne and I had just become engaged and I think Sam was a little down in the mouth about that. He had a soft spot for Daph and was rather broken up by our engagement.'

'Well, he never *asked* me', Daphne said tartly.

'I don't know what got into his head – whether he hated himself for being a shrimp or figured that it was simply my Dad's money that had attracted Daph – although she needed no help from my people in that particular – but whatever it was, he was feeling sorry for himself and bitter, and he got pretty tanked up that night.'

Daphne was taking rapid and deep drags on her cigarette, and although her legs were crossed nonchalantly, Joe noticed that she twisted her toes upward in a nervous snap, and remained with her foot tensed, and her eyes steadily on her husband.

'I remember we were watching the steaks sizzle over the charcoal fire and Sam took the card out of his pocket and showed it to me and Daph. "I'm getting rid of this", he said to me and threw it in the fire. "We can't do anything this way," he said, "we're fifty years ahead of our time. But we can pave the way. I'm a better member without it. I can go find my way, however indirectly, to the seat of power, and then I'll be able to do a little useful work. I'll get my licks in for my father and mother and all my relatives and everyone who ever grew up in the Dorchester slums – or any other slums – if it's the last thing I do. So if I seem respectable and talk respectable, and I get to be a public figure, some day, don't think I've betrayed the party, Jeff. Not by a long shot. I don't need party discipline and I know I can do more this way." Not his exact words, I'm sure, but words to that effect.'

'Later he got very drunk and very maudlin,' Daphne added, 'and suggested he and I go off to a hotel and sleep together.'

'Sam disappeared and I never heard of or from him again', Jeff continued. 'If I'd known he was actually working for the government, I think I'd have taken steps to stop him. I just never thought he'd get by a routine FBI security check.'

Professor Karpeko smiled in triumph. Joe felt twenty feet tall and as powerful as a pile driver. He had Polecat's little wagon taken care of.

'Gosh,' Milt said mildly, 'that's tremendously interesting. I just hope it's not too pat.'

'Too pat?' Chuck Rossmore shouted. 'Iss wonderful. People got to understand it, and this they'll understand. If I can, anyone can!'

'And you're willing to testify before a Senate sub-committee?' Andy asked with youthful eagerness.

'I certainly am if I have to', Jeff Straley said. 'The administration here knows all about me. Daph was always miserable about what I was doing, and I broke with the party after I got to know Professor Karpeko here; he opened my eyes to some of what revolution had meant in Russia. Then when the Reds invaded Korea, it was the final push, although mentally I'd quit long before, and when I actually did quit, I had the greatest sense of relief I've ever had. Daph finally made me go to Mr. Pusey with it. There are only two of the original six men in my cell still around. Sam Poltek and I. After Sam and I quit, one was killed in the Korean war, another committed suicide and the other two took off for New York. We simply never heard another word from them again. One was a man named Harry Arons and the other was a chap named Bill Held, who used to be one of Boston's leading patent

attorneys. He was our leader and he had the contacts with outside.'

'Well', Joe said with sudden determination. 'Then you're avail-
able. Thanks for your help.' He got up and the others rose with
him.

'Are you sure I couldn't get any of the rest of you a cup of
coffee?' Daphne said.

'No, thanks', Joe said firmly. 'Look, Milt, maybe you and
Chuck could chew the fat with Professor Karpeko and Mr. Straley
here and get all the details buttoned down. In fact, Milt, maybe
we could retain Mr. Straley here right now. We could use a first-
class constitutional lawyer. How about it, Mr. Straley?'

Jeff seemed taken aback. 'I don't see why not', he said uncertainly.

'I'd like to spend a couple of hours with my son here. I don't
get to see him often enough. See you over at his place around four,
okay, Milt?' And before anyone could do much more than murmur a hasty good-bye, he had grabbed Andy by the arm and they
were out of the door.

'Show me around the joint', Joe said cheerfully. 'I never took
a decent look at this place. You know, I'm planning to build a
college of my own and I might as well see the best.'

They walked around the Yard from Holworthy to Wiggles-
worth – Andy pointing out the buildings – dorms, libraries, classrooms – and describing their purposes. Andy's enthusiasm was
contagious, his pleasure in the place iridescent. It was as if he were
showing off a new home. At University Hall they looked for a
brief instant at the statue of someone who was symbolically John
Harvard and Andy said, 'I can just see you in bronze at Naples U.,
Dad, and underneath they can inscribe the words, "You didn't hear
me so good".' Joe chuckled. Here in the isolation of this university,
criss-crossed by boys and girls going to classes and labs, his difficulties with the United States Senate seemed trivial and unreal.
They walked up into Widener and Andy took his father back into
the endless stacks. 'There's literally miles of books, Dad. Biggest
in the country. It's a collection of the brains of the nation and the
world since the beginning of time.' Here, in places like this, was
the training ground of America's leaders for the next God knows
how many years. To have any part in the training of those brains,
guiding them for the benefit of men, why the building of Naples
University was more than building a hundred cities. Maybe his

not ever getting to Princeton was the best thing that could've happened. It damn well gave him the itch to build Naples U. What the hell, maybe Andy was right. Professor of Government. Why not? Pop, Pop, he thought. Here we are. Take a good look at this kid of mine. You see how we did it, Pop? He's damn well gonna be a professor, and not the kind *you* were talkin' about, but a genuine full-blooded professor at the greatest university in the entire goddam world. For the first time in his life he felt almost as fond of Andy as he had felt of Carey. God, Andy looked like such a kid, so eager, so smooth looking, but, by Christ, as Jock Dennison would say, he'll be a useful citizen.

'Maybe I could meet your girl, Andy', Joe said finally, after they'd had a look through the old houses and Joe had examined the new Quincy House and watched the concrete being poured on Leverett Towers.

'Sure, Dad.' There was a note of surprise in Andy's voice, pleased surprise. 'We'll take her to lunch. She'll be getting back from her phil class about now.' It was beginning to drizzle – typical Cambridge day Andy called it – but they walked over to Radcliffe and met Cynthia Schiller. It was absolutely ridiculous to think that these kids were of an age to be married. Cynthia was not only young, she was tiny. The kid couldn't have been five feet high. There just was nothing to her whatsoever. She had freckles, a little pushed up nose, short, black hair that, if she had been twenty years older, would have been classified as disorderly, but on her it looked great. Her eyes crinkled when she talked, as if damn near everything intrigued her. She said nothing bright or particular, but Joe felt absolutely fascinating in her presence. She was so goddam delighted to meet him and, of course, you didn't need any binoculars to see that she was absolutely nuts about Andy.

They walked back to the Wursthaus for knockwurst, sauerkraut and beer and talked about nothing much until Joe said abruptly, 'Say, Cynthia, what do you think about this teaching business for Andy?'

Cynthia cocked her head. 'Well, Mr. Naples, that's what he wants to do, isn't it? I think it's fine. You know, most of the boys haven't any idea. They don't know what to do, or how to do it. The rich ones, I mean. So they end up in their father's business or practice or whatever and never give it a thought until they're fifty – like my own father.'

'Maybe you got something, Cynthia.'

Andy's whole face lit up. Boy, sometimes he really looked like class. Well, there goes Naples and Son – out of the window. Down the drain. Joe could not deny a sudden chill.

Cynthia had a class then, so Andy and Joe went up to Andy's room at the Law School. Joe took his jacket off, loosened his tie, threw himself on Andy's bed, propping up the pillow, clasped his hands behind his neck and yawned. 'Andy, I must've given you eight million lectures by now. I guess you're goddam tired of listening.'

'Oh, Dad, it's not that bad.' Andy sat down jiggling his foot characteristically. 'Once in a while, you get going about the trials and tribulations of Ninety-eighth Street when you were a boy, but generally —'

Joe laughed. 'Now lookit, kid, this is gonna be no lecture. I want you to hear me good.' He got up, took an Upmann and his lighter out of his pocket, and lay back down again. 'I guess what you'd call this is some kinda bedside confession. Just in case this deal of ours with Poltek doesn't work out a hundred per cent, I don't want you to hear any stuff from someone else or read about your old man in the paper. So here's the poop.' He went through the ritual of biting the cigar and getting it lit. Andy had stopped jiggling his foot and was staring at Joe attentively. He folded his young hands across his stomach and stretched out his feet, sliding down in the chair.

'There's a few things that might sound bad', Joe said. 'There was this guy named Gamboretta – One-eyed Gamboretta. This was God knows how many years ago. He used to know your grandmother in the old country. He was a no-good bastid and one day – well, you know Tony Ferrara —' Joe went along telling the story as he knew it, giving himself none the worst of it, of course, but watching Andy's face carefully. Andy's expression of uncritical interest never changed. Then he told Andy about the time he gave Harold Brice thirty thousand dollars for his campaign. And about Simon Cutler and the ten grand he lent him at Las Vegas. And yes, even about Si and Anna Landos, which was the toughest of all. When he had finished, Joe lay back on the pillow, staring at the ceiling, waiting for Andy to say something, but Andy was silent. To fill the silence Joe said, 'Even your mother don't know a lot of that.'

Andy was silent a while longer. When he spoke, it was slowly, like an elderly professor. 'Dad, I know a little something about

the theory of our system of government. But I also know a few
things about you. Considering your handicaps and your background, you did pretty damn well. In fact, maybe too well. If
you'd been more mediocre, nobody'd have ever bothered you. All
a congressional investigation can really do is focus on symptoms,
try to be the conscience of the country. It's not a bad idea, and
usually I'm for it. But in this case I'd like to help *you*, Pop. I'm
on *your* side. I can take a week or two off and I'd like to be in there
pitching with you.'

Joe chewed on his cigar. Sometimes Andy reminded him of Milt.
Saw both sides of everything. Sometimes three or four sides. Jesus,
when a friend of Joe's was in trouble, Joe Naples saw his side,
absolutely nothing else. All that fair-mindedness was for the birds.
Also it made a guy unfit for genuine thick and thin friendship. How
he'd have loved it if Andy had thrown an arm over his shoulder
and said, 'Pop, I'm going after those no-good bastids with you.'
But, like Andy said, considering the kid's handicaps, his mother,
and the fancy background and all this Veritas he was getting, he
was doing pretty good.

'Okay, kid, you got a deal. You work with Milt and this professor whozis – Straley. In fact, you may learn more constitutional
law this way than going to classes.'

Andy was pleased, and without a word began to pack his shorts
and shirts into a bag and Joe said, 'Here, Andy, pull me up.' His
son gave him a hand and Joe put his tie and coat back on.

'Where's your phone?'

'Right there.'

'What's that guy's name who runs this joint?'

'The Law School?'

'No, no, the whole entire shooting match. Nathan Ducy? Something like Ducy.'

'You mean Pusey?'

'Yah. That's the guy. How do I get hold of him?'

Andy dialled University 8–7600 and handed the phone to his
father. 'Tell her you want to speak to the president's office.'

Joe heard the ring, and a girl's voice answered, 'Harvard.'

'I want to speak to Nathan Pusey', Joe said.

'President's office', a female voice said blandly.

'I want to talk to Nathan Pusey', Joe said. 'This is Joe Naples.'

'Can I help you? The president is on another wire', a new female
voice said, as if to be helpful.

'Lookit,' Joe said, 'I made a pretty good-sized contribution to the place, and I just thought I'd talk it over and see how every little thing is getting along. I got in mind maybe I might give a little more. That's all I had in mind.'

'The name is Naples?'

'Yah.'

A few minutes later it was Mr. Pusey's pleasant voice. 'Good afternoon, Mr. Naples. I'm glad you thought to give me a ring.'

'Well, why not? I'm right here in Cambridge. Say, you busy right at the moment?'

'Why, no, Mr. Naples. I have a free half hour. I'd be delighted to see you.'

'Okay', Joe said. 'I'll be over in five minutes.'

'What are you going to see *him* about, Dad?' Andy's face was screwed up in concern.

'Oh, I just wanna get a line on how you're doing', Joe said as he jabbed his son in the arm.

'Dad, Mr. Pusey doesn't even know I'm alive!'

'Well, Buster, when I get through, he'll know you're alive.'

'You're not planning to do anything wild, Dad, are you?'

'Me? Do I strike you as wild? Lookit, Andy, you don't have to worry about your old man. I've done business with all kinds of people. I ever tell you the time I was down to Washington for a conference with the President?'

'Yes, Dad.'

'Took Carey with me. Yah, I guess you heard that story a coupla times too often.'

Nathan Pusey, the president of Harvard University, smiled amiably. 'Certainly, Mr. Naples. Go ahead and smoke.' Joe looked around the neat, simple, but spacious ground-floor office. Not one bit like his own. Lotta wood and white paint. Covering the centre of the floor was a beat-up Oriental rug without the slightest give, and all the chairs were black wood with those prissy little spokes. In the corner stood a grandfather clock, musta been three, four hundred years old, and on the wall hung only two pictures – five old men sitting together and Benjamin Franklin. Mr. Pusey's desk was a modest table, probably hadn't been changed since the Revolution, all a bit too goddam modest if you asked Joe Naples, but he could be as cool as any college president.

As for Mr. Pusey, although he was exactly Joe's age, he looked almost like a kid, smooth-faced, with a patrician's nose.

'The name is Joe', Joe said. 'I see you're doing a lotta new work here, Mr. Pusey, yessir. I'm interested because I'm planning to build a little college myself. I've been having a look around the place all day. My son goes to the Law School here. Graduated from the college two years ago. Been a lot of progress around here the last couple of years.'

'There's a tremendous amount to be done,' Mr. Pusey said wryly, 'but I'm resigned to the fact there always will be.' It was apparent he was waiting for Joe to state his business.

'We made a little contribution to the fund drive you had going last year', Joe said. 'Fifty thousand. That was last year. I hear you've got about enough to meet your goal.'

Mr. Pusey smiled. 'There's no such thing as *enough*, Mr. Naples, although we're tremendously gratified at our result. I was amazed at the work our alumni did. We raised eighty-six million in three years, including the earned interest. That's a remarkable result in many ways. Other universities have been encouraged to set their sights higher than they would have.'

'Yah', Joe said shortly. 'But never enough, like you say, Nathan.'

Mr. Pusey leaned back in his chair. 'We could use a great deal of unrestricted money. Mr. Bundy for one has a dozen ways of spending it, and usefully. We'd like to expand our freshman seminar programme for one thing. And we want to expand our overseas exchange student programme. We've just begun a programme for exchange students from Africa.' Mr. Pusey spoke with an animation Joe could not understand. Big deal, getting a few black boys in from Africa. These pink-cheeked intellectual guys tickled him.

'Well, I'd like to give a little something more', Joe said. 'Maybe half a million, maybe a million. I just haven't had a chance to make up my mind.'

The university president smiled. 'You can be sure whatever the amount, it will be carefully, and I venture to say wisely, invested.' His smile broke into an easy laugh. 'More carefully, I'm afraid, than the open-handed manner in which you're giving it. I'm sometimes amazed at the impulsive generosity of men like you, sir. Before we actually spend half a million or a million dollars, or even the income on it, heaven knows how many people have had a crack at it.'

'Yah.' Joe laughed too, and blew a smoke ring over the president's head. 'That's the trouble working the way you fellas do –

committees, professors, study groups. Jesus, it's hard to know how you ever get anything done.'

Mr. Pusey said, 'It's slow, but we get quite a lot done.'

'You ask me, it's still bureaucracy', Joe said. 'I don't give a damn if it's the government or a place like this. The goals are fine, but I can't stand it. Too slow. Too many meetings. Too much heavy thinking. But what the hell, I didn't come here to argue. Lookit, Nathan, what's the use kidding around. I'm gonna give you fellows a million bucks.'

'Thank you.'

'And now supposin' I ask you to do a couple of little things for me?'

'Yes?' Mr. Pusey held two fingers at the bridge of his nose and sounded non-committal, almost wary as if this had happened to him a few times before. Joe was on the verge of mentioning Andy, but decided not to do it yet.

'I got a plan', Joe said. 'We wanna build a little college, like I said. Nothing like this place, I realize that. We got around thirty million bucks in our Naples Foundation, and —'

'I'm afraid thirty million dollars, as prodigious a sum as it is, won't take you very far these days', Mr. Pusey said.

'I think we can raise maybe another ten, fifteen million', Joe said. 'The church will probably give us a hand there and you know we don't have to start big. And we have all our land. Lookit *this* place. Started with one guy's library with maybe a hundred books. We can do a hell of a lot better than that, sir. But what we need is advice. Plenty of advice. We gotta get someone to help get our faculty staff set up. Architectural and development advice, administrative help, contacts with the high schools, all that. How to get into the big league. We're going to need advice by the bucketful. That's where you come in.'

'Well, I have rather severe demands on my time,' Mr. Pusey said, 'but we have people here who, I'm sure, would be pleased to help. I'll be glad to have you talk to my assistants, the financial people, the development men, the deans of some of the faculties. But would you be offended if I were to make a suggestion?'

'Shoot.'

'Thirty million is a tidy sum, Mr. Naples, and I certainly don't mean to sound patronizing, but a university is an expensive – uh – hobby. We're spending fifteen million now simply to expand our library facilities. Here – here's a booklet you might like to go

through – it's our annual financial report.' Mr. Pusey reached into
a drawer and produced a crimson-covered booklet. 'What *has*
occurred to me is this: Have you thought of the possibility of
distributing these funds among a number of institutions that are
already functioning? I believe in the long run it would do the most
good and do it most effectively. You could give it to a number of
colleges besides Harvard. Yale, for example, is just starting its
capital fund drive. Dartmouth, Brown, Columbia, Stanford are
all going on extensive fund drives. Then there are research foundations, medical colleges . . .'

Joe was irritated. He hadn't come here for any kind of lecture.
All this guy was trying to do was very simple – deprive him of
immortality. He needed this advice like a second head. He made
an effort to conceal his irritation. 'Sure, sure, I appreciate all that.
We thought of all that. But we decided we wanta build this new
place. If you feel you don't wanta be bothered, why fine.'

'Oh, no', Nathan Pusey said. 'Our people would be delighted to
help.'

Outside Joe saw the drizzling had stopped and the sun was
straining through the clouds.

'My boy Andy's over at the Law School', Joe said. 'Did I
mention that?'

'I believe you did.' Mr. Pusey doodled a moment, then leaned
back.

'He's got a job teaching government here next year', Joe said.

'Oh, I'm pleased to hear it', Mr. Pusey said. 'Now that you
mention it, I do remember meeting him.'

'I've been thinking about that boy', Joe said. 'Andrew. He's
the only son I got. And he'd do a hell of a lot better in *my* business,
am I right?'

'Financially, I have no doubt', Mr. Pusey said pleasantly.

'Well, what kind a future does he have here? Toughest competition in the entire world, and in fifteen, twenty years he might land
a sixteen or eighteen thousand-dollar-a-year job. I mean its absolutely *ridiculous*.'

'If you really believed that, I don't think you'd be here, talking
about the kind of contribution you're talking about. Hundreds of
our men here want to do precisely what they *are* doing,' Mr. Pusey
said, 'and there's no substitute for that. I'd venture to guess that
you're doing what *you* want to do, and that, as much as anything
else, may account for your success, in my view.'

'Yah. Well, sometimes these kids, twenty-one, -two years old don't know what they want. They don't know to come in out of the rain.'

Mr. Pusey smiled. 'I think you underestimate the young men. I'd guess that at twenty-one you knew what you wanted. And see how far you've gone. I sometimes wonder, when I meet a man like you, Mr. Naples, what are the psychological ingredients to his success . . .'

'Hell, that's easy', Joe said laughing. 'I never allowed anything to interfere with my basic sense of insecurity.' He chuckled. 'That's the God's truth, and something I never told anyone outside of you.'

'That may account for more success than we're aware of.' Mr. Pusey laughed.

Joe suddenly took a new tack. 'You got special professorships, special whatzises, chairs?'

'Oh, yes, quite a number.'

'With higher salaries?'

'They vary a bit, but in general we do not have any special chair carrying a stipend higher than other full professorships. One or two get free secretaries, and many of the men earn additional funds by their writing. We expect our faculty to do some creative work.'

'Yah. Tell me, what kinda return you fellows get on your invested capital? I mean on your whatzis, your endowment money?'

'Oh, you'll find all that in the financial report. We average a little better than five per cent these days.'

'Well, this got nothin' to do with what I'm giving you today but I've been thinking maybe of setting up a chair here in honour of my other son Carey. Carey was killed in the Korean war, y'know, and I thought it would be kinda nice.'

'Why, that would be a most generous memorial', Mr. Pusey said.

'Maybe a chair in government', Joe said, and Mr. Pusey looked a little funny. He had skirted as close to what he meant as he dared. With guys like this Nate Pusey, you hadda take it slow and easy.

'I can give you the cheque for a million this afternoon,' Joe said, 'if that's okay. Maybe we oughta have a few pictures taken. Me handin' you the dough. A.P., U.P., all those guys. Would you mind? My public relations man says we could use the publicity for Naples University. Youngest college, oldest college, all that kinda stuff. We could use a little good publicity right now.'

A small cloud passed over Mr. Pusey's face.

'I can have the arrangements made', Mr. Pusey said. 'Perhaps tomorrow we could have a tea at the faculty club, and at that time I can make an announcement about your gift. I'll make some general statement about the importance to Harvard and higher education of gifts like yours. May I have the exact name of the foundation making the grant?'

'Naples Foundation, Naples, New Jersey.' Mr. Pusey wrote it out.

'Oh, yes, Naples. You built that city out there, I understand. What a remarkable achievement.'

'Yah, not bad for a guy who never even finished high school.'

'Will you have your public relations man get in touch with my assistant, Mr. Marlowe?' Mr. Pusey said. 'They can work out the details for the tea.'

'I'll be there', Joe said. 'I'll bring my attorney and my public relations man. I'll have a statement to give 'em myself, okay?'

'I can't tell you how much I've enjoyed meeting you, Mr. Naples', Nathan Pusey was saying.

Twenty-six

A T ten the following Tuesday, after Julius had shaved him and
left, and Joe had made his customary call to the job, telling
Curly to hurry up and get the rest of the window frames to
the site, he received a call from Sam Poltek in Washington. Even
over the wires, he could hear the phony sleaziness in that unctuous
voice. But there was a certain pleasure in hearing the little bastid
oozing self-confidence.

'I thought if it were not inconvenient, p'raps you could come
see us about eleven tomorrow, Mr. Naples. Our investigators just
submitted their preliminary reports, and we thought rather than
go right into a public session, you might want to clear up a few
things for us first.'

'Sure, I'll be there. You want me to bring my lawyer?'

'Oh, I should consider that essential, Mr. Naples.' His voice was
nearly pure oil, the son-of-a-bitch.

'Mr. Poltek. I got a question.'

'Yes?'

'Is this gonna be an executive session of the sub-committee?'
Milt had told him how they do these deals.

'Well, probably Senator Owens will be there and p'raps one or
two other members.'

'Mr. Poltek, I think it would be a good idea if I met you first
without any Senators around, you know what I mean?'

'I don't believe we're going to have time for that, sir.'

'I think you better make time for it, young fellow. Take a little
advice from an old man. This session's for eleven? Suppose me
and my attorney come down and see you in your office first, say
around nine-thirty.' Joe could hear the ominous threat in his own
voice and Sam Poltek could not have missed it.

"Kay, if you wish. See you then. I'm in Room eleven thirteen
in the old Senate Office Building. In the basement.'

The fat was now in the fire.

Joe called Dulian to have the plane ready at seven-thirty, and then he started thinking who he'd better bring along. He didn't know why, exactly, he wanted to be surrounded on this occasion, but he thought he'd better take Milt and Andy, and while he was at it, Chuck Rossmore and Cathy. He put in a call for Jeff Straley and asked him to come to Washington directly from Boston. Jeff was reluctant; he hesitated, but in the end, with almost tired resignation (the die is cast, he must've thought, what the hell) he agreed to join the retinue at the Washington airport. 'We'll take a cab into town together,' Joe said, 'and we'll fill you in on how we're going to do this. I guess you understand the general strategy though. You're no dope.' He was looking forward to Sam Poltek's face when Jeff Straley stepped into that room.

Milt and Andy were going over some of their tactics relating to the statute of limitations and the fifth amendment – studying cases. 'You guys better brief me on what kinda stuff I have to answer and what I don't.' Milt said it was darn short notice, but they'd go over everything they could right after lunch. Better have Rossmore here, too.

Joe called Chuck Rossmore, who was delighted to come. 'That was a hell of a good million-dollar story in the *Times* Sunday, Joe,' the publicity man said with a trace of pride, 'and you looked like a hero galloping on a horse, didn't you? In fact, you looked better than Mr. Pusey.' A million bucks for two columns in the *New York Times*, and now the s.o.b. wanted credit. Joe grunted and asked Rossmore to come over for this afternoon's skull session.

He called Cath in, too, and told her he wanted her to come along. 'Just in case we gotta take notes or dictate some stuff for the papers', Joe said shortly. She nodded and smiled secretly, poor kid.

'You've had calls this morning from representatives of two hospitals and two colleges,' she said, 'including Yale. I suppose the Harvard story encouraged them. That was an awful lot of money to give.'

'Not today, Cath.'

'And there's a Mr. Howard here with his wife waiting to see you. Do you remember you had me call him and ask him to drop in any time? Did you know he was – uh —'

'Oh, that the coloured guy? Send 'em both in, Cath, and ask Milt to join us right away.' A wave of instinctive distaste took possession of him.

Young Malcolm Howard was as black a Negro as there was in

this world. He coulda been from Timbuktu. He was also tall and handsome in a primitive way, wide-nosed and heavy-jawed and he wore a pair of rimless glasses. His wife was light, small, wistful, and nervous as a cat. The guy took Joe's hand and remained standing while Joe sat back. 'Have a seat', he urged, but both visitors murmured and remained on their feet.

'Lookit', Joe said. 'What's the use beatin' around the bush? I got too much respect for you. Lemme come right to the point.' Mr. Howard nodded. 'I don't know whether you can appreciate this, Mr. Howard, Mrs. Howard,' Joe said, leaning back in his chair, 'but before Naples was built, I pictured the whole entire city in my mind. I mean I really *saw* it. The people, the shops schools, churches, everything, and probably it's my own fault. Probably I don't have enough vision, but I just didn't see it with – well, with any coloured families in it. Not a one. You know why I think that was? Because I guess by instinct I just understood no coloured family was gonna be happy here. No one of their own kind, lots of people who'll make trouble for 'em – you know it all as well as I do.'

Mal Howard smiled and his teeth were very white against his black skin. 'Mr. Naples. Let me be equally frank. Just as you saw Naples, I saw something, too, completely, in my mind's eye and it was this: A nice white painted house and a piece of land not too big, but nicely tended and green, for my family – something outside Harlem or Brownsville. That's what I saw. A place of my own where I could water the lawn. Something better for me and my kids and my wife. What I saw doesn't compare with the big vision you saw. It's more modest, it's not much, but I saw it just as you did yours, sharp and clear. When I heard from Mr. Lewin at the lab that he was transferring out to St. Louis and putting his house on the market, I was hearing opportunity strike for the Howard family.'

Mrs. Howard smiled placatingly. 'It's such a convenient and attractive house you built, Mr. Naples. The children love it and it's so easy to take care of.'

'Are you folks out of your heads? You realize what you're doin'?' Joe said. 'You looking for broken windows and burning crosses and insults to your kids and all kinds of trouble for yourself? Can't you picture what's gonna happen? We just don't want things like that in Naples.'

'I thought,' Mr. Howard said, 'that maybe between your idea

of a new model city, which I truly think Naples is, and mine of a new opportunity for myself, the chance to live like a man, we could make a kind of package deal.'

Smart-alecky bastid. Now Joe Naples had Harlem on his back and he wasn't ready for *that* load.

'Mr. Howard. You mind if I talk right out in the open with you?'

'I wish you would.' Mal Howard tensed and blinked, locking his fingers and pulling his palms back.

'Okay. Now this isn't personal, understand, but you're talking to a guy who's got nothing but bad experiences with any whatzis – Negroes. See that?' He showed them the scar on his neck. 'And I've had more labour trouble, more thieving, more lying from coloured guys on my jobs than everyone else put together. Now I'm no dope. I know that don't make every single one of them a liar or a thief, but I just ain't met any I like, that I feel comfortable with or that I'd like to have for a next-door neighbour. It's absolutely *impossible*.'

Mrs. Howard rose. 'I think we should be going, Malcolm. I really do think so.' Her lip trembled.

'Lookit,' Joe said, 'here's Mr. Jason, my lawyer. My God, he's my own brother-in-law. He likes golf as much as I do. But he's Jewish – born Jewish anyhow. Now he don't expect to get into Canoe Hill where I belong. He wouldn't be comfortable there, cause they just don't take any Jews. Now see what I mean? Like this Ralph Bunche business a couple of years ago out at that Forest Hills tennis club. It don't make sense.' Milt had flushed red.

'We're not asking to join a club', Mr. Howard said, holding his wife's elbow. The guy was patient, gotta hand it to him. 'We are asking to buy a decent place to live.'

'Naples is a *club*, don't let anyone kid you about *that*', Joe said. 'We got our own swimming pools, our own club house, our own churches – it's more than a club, it's a hundred per cent world of its own.'

They were backing towards the door. Milt rose and said slowly and kindly, 'Where do you live now, Mr. Howard?'

'A Hundredth Street and Amsterdam Avenue in Manhattan.'

'You like it there?' Milt was looking at Joe.

'Well, it's not bad. We don't have more than one or two muggings a night in the neighbourhood. It isn't that we worry about ourselves, but what bothers us is our boys. We don't look forward to being called by the police one day to come get our son out of the station house or off a slab in the morgue the way the people across the hall did. The boys in our neighbourhood live like animals. Same as we did when we were kids.'

'During World War Two you were in Italy?'

'That's right.'

'See combat?'

'Yes, sir. From Anzio right on up.'

'I hear you won some kind of decoration.'

'Yes, sir. Silver Star.' Same decoration Carey had got.

'And now you're a Ph.D. in chemistry, Mr. Howard?'

Joe realized suddenly what Milt was doing, and he did not like it one bit. This man was the witness and Joe was to be his judge.

'Yes, sir.'

'Must be difficult for you to be a Ph.D. by day and a gutter rat by night', Milt said.

'I'm used to living schizophrenically,' Mr. Howard said, 'but it's harder for Debbie.' He took his wife's elbow. 'She's there in the slums day and night.'

Milt's case rested.

'Mr. Howard!' Joe had risen. The sickness was on him. 'Tell you what. You want that Lewin house? Tell you what I'll do. You're gonna get it!' The little cry that escaped from Mrs. Howard's lips was enough for him, balm.

'Now listen. You're gonna have to trust me. I'm gonna buy that Lewin house my own self and then we'll go to work in the neighbourhood. In a month you can move in. Meanwhile, you tell your attorney to just withdraw your action, hear?'

'Well,' Mr. Howard hesitated, 'I'll have to talk to my attorney.'

'Lookit!' Joe said. 'If I gotta fight the entire NAACP, I'll do it. I know the kinda people get behind these cases. I'm not gonna be forced! But if you want this house, I'm the guy that can get it for you. Now it's clear to me. If this is gonna be a matter of principle, I'm against you. If it's a matter of just people, you and me, I'm for you. You choose it any way you want.'

Mrs. Howard tugged her husband's sleeve. 'May I talk to my husband privately?'

'Sure. Use Mr. Jason's office.' As he showed them to Milt's room, he said lightly, 'Sometimes a guy's gotta rise above his principles. If I can rise above mine, so can you.' And as he stepped out he added, 'Come back to my office when you're ready.'

When Joe got back to his own office, Milt murmured that he
had quite a lot of work to do for tomorrow's meeting with Poltek.
'You seem to have Mr. Howard nicely worked out', he said. 'You
don't need me here.' And Joe detected a note of irritation.

'Fine.'

Ten minutes passed before the Howards returned. Mrs. Howard
was pale, walking separately, not looking at her husband. Mr.
Howard's face was woodenly set, expressionless.

'We think it's very thoughtful of you, Mr. Naples, to want to
do us a kindness, and we thank you, but we've thought it all through.
We can't depend on kindness. We want to buy that house. It's a
right we have. The Lewins are willing to sell it to us. We'll pay
good money for it. Money earned honestly, same as any man's. We
don't want dispensation or patronage. If necessary, we'll wait a
little longer. Sooner or later the courts will act.'

The words were spoken quietly. It was obvious that Mr. Howard
was controlling himself and that what he really wanted to be doing
was to tear the place completely apart.

Joe was on the verge of throwing the bum out, but there was
something about Mrs. Howard, her small tight fists clenched in
fear, not anger, her eyes tear-repelling, that checked Joe's outraged outburst. He looked at the big black young man, who, Ph.D.
and all, was the picture of the untamed. The poor black bastid trying to break the ropes that kept him in the scummy tenement on
Amsterdam Avenue. It was hopeless. Suddenly Joe could smell the
smells, the stifling closeness. He could feel the empty endless black
boredom of Ninety-eighth Street, and in that moment, Mr. Howard
was no longer a black man. Instead of throwing the bum out, Joe
laughed. 'You got inalienable rights, is that what's eatin' you, Mr.
Howard? That's a hot one. I absolutely don't understand that kinda
talk. Lookit, Mr. Howard, I want to tell you something. You're
gonna get this house, you understand? I don't care if you want
it this way or that way. I'm gonna see you get it if it's the last thing
I do, and you'll get it any way you want it. Understood?'

Mr. and Mrs. Howard exchanged surprised glances. 'I *think*
I understand,' Mr. Howard said hesitantly, 'and we are grateful
to you.'

Joe's only impulse was to grab the man's hand and say, 'Christ,
you see! I ain't such a bad guy at that.' He felt like an ageing man
who, having begun to doubt his sexual ability, had just brought wild
pleasure to a girl until then frigid.

Mrs. Howard came to his desk and he stood up. If he could forget the colour, she was a rather attractive woman, with a hell of a figure. 'I cannot tell you how much my husband and I thank you.' She put her hand out and he took it. 'Wait till I tell my boys.' And she slipped her arm through her husband's.

'Only one thing you can do for me', Joe said. 'When you sign your contract for the house, don't noise it around, will you? Gimme a week. Don't record anything. That's all I ask, a week. As long as we're gonna do it, let's do it right. This is damn important and we gotta handle it right. We gotta create the right atmosphere. Give me one week and people around are gonna be as proud as peacocks about the entire deal, instead of sore.'

After they had left, Joe sat staring, first at the portrait of Carey, then at his own hands which he held up before him. He pulled a cigar from the humidor and lit it. At last he said to himself, almost aloud, 'I wish they'd get off my back.' Then he told Cath to ask Milt to return.

'Lookit, Milt, have Larson get up the names of every house-owner within two blocks of the Lewin house. There must be at least sixty-seventy neighbours all around. As soon as we get back from Washington, Hetty and Lucy and you and I will start paying some house calls and do some selling. By the time the Howards move in these people are going to be goddam delighted to have 'em. They'll throw cocktail parties for 'em. Jesus, I really feel like I'll be doin' something useful for a change. And by God,' he mused, purely as an afterthought, 'Chuck Rossmore'll be happy about this, won't he?'

After that there were ten million details to attend to as always. Briefly he looked over the elevation for the Naples University Administration Building again with Dino and admired the new rendering. 'Gorgeous. I'll give it to Chuck tomorrow and he'll make the public announcement Friday.' Dino was delighted.

'We really going ahead then, brother Joe?'

'Yep. We'll have a shovel in the ground in five weeks. Can't sit on thirty million bucks for ever.'

Cathy reported that Simon Cutler was calling from the hospital, and Piggy Banks from Trenton, but Milt advised him, 'Don't talk to these guys.' Which was ridiculous. No need to talk to Piggy, but he hadda talk to Si, the poor bastid was sick as a dog, lying in that lonely hospital room not knowing if he was gonna live or die. He cheered Si up and told him something big was brewing and the whole entire investigation might dry up and blow away tomorrow, if they were lucky, and was there any little thing Si needed, books to read, television, any of that, after all, old Jock Dennison was president of the hospital Board of Trustees, he'd want to be damn sure Si was treated right. And Si was in good hands. He could depend on Jeff Berkman, hell of a fine doctor, Joe had known him thirty years. Si was not to worry about anything. Hear?

There was a call from Hetty. She sounded sober this morning, better than the way he'd seen her the last couple of nights, and at first she was pretty businesslike. She told him that the Wheeler play he'd sunk forty grand in was closing next week, didn't he think that was the smartest thing to do? It was losing money every week and not picking up in spite of the good notices, but the film sale was going through so they'd probably break even. He had to hand it to Hetty. Even the flops she picked broke even. Then a new urgency stirred in her voice.

'Tell me, Joie—' She stopped. She hesitated as she always did when she wanted to say anything gently, and there was something nice that was a new kind of pleading in her voice.

'Yah?'

'Are you in very serious trouble, Joie?'

'Nah!' Joe said. 'Now lookit, I'm going down to Washington tomorrow to tell this jerk where to get off, that's all. And I got this Poltek bird where it hurts the most.'

'Joie, Andy says—'

'Andy! Has that kid been talkin' to you?'

'Darling – he's my *son*.'

'Yah. Well don't worry, for Christ sake.'

'What are you planning to do when you get to Washington with this man Poltek? Whatever it is, Andy's not so sure it will work.'

'Mullaly, you didn't hear me so good. Andy's twenty-three, I'm fifty-two. Okay? I'm still two and a half times as smart.'

Hetty was silent, then in a low voice, 'I'd like to go with you tomorrow, Joie.'

'What for? I'm gonna be busy as hell. We all will.'

'I just want to be there', she said. 'I want to be along, to be part of the family.'

'But this is only a closed session, Mullaly. It'll look ridiculous you goin' in there, in Poltek's office.'

'Then I'll stay in the room just outside', she said. She thought he was going to some kinda hospital instead of a hearing. 'Very near by.' Well, if that's what she wanted. 'And I'll be good. You know what I mean. I'll drink loads of milk shakes and lemonades. I will, Joie, I promise, so you won't have to worry about that.'

'Sure, Mullaly, sure.' Goddam, what do you know, he was touched. 'Okay, okay, okay.'

Of course, it was absolutely nonsensical for Hetty to imply that she was the only one who loved him, as if they all didn't. Andy, Milt, Cath, even Dulian who was flying the plane was the kinda guy who'd lay his life down for Joe, and Chuck Rossmore, the great cynic, Joe suspected, had a sneaking liking for him. Nevertheless, it was something he hadn't expected of Hetty. It was at least ten million years since she said anything like it. In fact, she sounded altogether improved. You wouldn't have thought that for the last six months she was mostly drunk as a skunk. Well, all his trouble was at least good for somebody. Although he would never admit it, Joe had no illusions: he knew he might be getting into waters where indictments lurked, and Hetty, who was no fool, was sure as hell playing the part of Joan of Arc shining up her sword.

There was a call from Martinson at the ball club, which he answered impatiently. That rookie second baseman at Pittsburg, they could get him for ten grand. And they badly needed a second baseman. Joe had seen the boy play early in the year in Philly. He was fast and he could hit. 'How much they paying him?'

'Seventy-four hundred.'

'Good. Make the deal.'

Then there was a short, fat real-estate broker from Atlanta, Georgia, had a site for a new city down there near where the new American Steel Company mill was going up. 'If Levitt can build more than one city, why not you?' the fat man said jovially. He couldn't think about new cities, till he got this bad time behind him.

'Leave all the details, maps, surveys, all that junk. We'll look into it, and thanks a lot for comin' all the way up to see us.'

It went like that all morning. Not a free moment until after lunch, when Joe cut off all calls and closeted himself with Chuck Rossmore, Milt and Andy to go over the ground the sub-committee was likely to cover. Seemed like a waste of time, Joe said, because once Sam Poltek got a load of Jeff Straley, the entire deal was gonna blow right over and you wouldn't be able to find Poltek for ten years. Nevertheless, Milt insisted that they be ready with answers.

To start with, Milt pointed out, if he ever had to testify, Joe was free to plead the Fifth Amendment and refuse to answer questions relating to any matters which might tend to incriminate him. And all things considered, that was the way Milt was leaning. It would discourage the Senators and keep the hearings from becoming a circus. After a while interest would die down. But Joe felt a sharp surge of distaste. Milt, the legal beagle. And suppose he didn't exactly feel like taking the Fifth Amendment?

Well . . . Milt started reluctantly to close in on the problems one by one.

All the stuff on One-eyed Gamboretta, Milt and Andy decided they could ignore. Anything over thirty years old Milt felt could absolutely get thrown out as ancient history. If the question was raised, Joe was to be indignant, get sore as hell and tell them he couldn't remember one goddam thing about it.

The thirty-thousand-dollar contribution he'd made to Harold Brice's campaign back in the forties he might as well admit, although considering that Harold was a fellow Senator the question might never come up. Anyhow, it was one thing the Senators could understand and forgive. It was not illegal, and if the sewage disposal plant for Naples approved by the State Health Commissioner was not up to those ridiculous state specs, it was certainly adequate. No complaints anyhow. The most serious matter was the ten thousand bucks he'd given Simon Cutler in Las Vegas and the deal for him to shack up with Anna Landos. That and the yachting trips and small gifts to the NMIA boys from Trenton – Piggy and the others.

'We only haff to create an image of you,' Rossmore said. 'A public image which can project. You're a generous fellow to a fault. That's our story. You're always doing things for people.'

'Well I am,' Joe said, 'ain't I?' Milt did not look happy. In fact, he appeared worried, almost distressed.

'Yes,' he said, 'I suppose that's the best we can do. Take that house you built for Forney. Oh, we'd better not mention that on account of he's Ev Henderson's nephew and you get all your mortgages from Ev. No, that sounds bad. Well, you put a hell of a lot of time in on the hospital, all the gifts you give your own people at Christmas time, on their birthdays, putting Curly's kid through Penn State. That sort of thing.'

'And how about the cheque he just gave to Harvard?' Rossmore exploded. 'A million bucks.'

'Yes.' Milt still sounded dubious. 'Try to get all that in, but in a kind of offhand way, Joe. You can do that, can't you? Sure you can. And the university here, the Foundation. All that stuff should be helpful.'

'And don't forget, while we're counting virtues, I'm helping a whozis family, Negroes, get a house in Naples. How about that?'

'Are you joking?' Chuck Rossmore said, and his eyes went wide.

'No, sir. What's that guy's name, Milt?'

'Howard.'

'Yah. Malcolm Howard. Big and black as Uncle Tom.'

'We don't have the image here of a man who's corrupting people', Milt said. 'You're no Tony Ferrara. You're just a generous fellow. It can't help but colour their thinking down there.'

'What about the ten G's I loaned Si? You think that might sound a little *too* generous?' Joe laughed.

'You and Si are old friends', Milt said seriously, warming to the subject. 'You've known each other for over thirty years. You've exchanged gifts. He gave you that watch. You've always visited back and forth. You knew him long before he entered the government. He had a sick wife, very sick, who's died since. Awfully nice girl and you were very fond of her.'

'Why I talked Harold Brice into getting Si his first job at NMIA, and the watch the son-of-a-bitch gave me was inscribed, remember that? Something goddam sentimental. He gave it to me at Jock's house. There must've been five witnesses.'

'Do you still have the watch, Dad?' Andy said.

'Sure, somewhere around the house.'

'God,' Milt said, 'try to find it. Do you remember what the inscription said?'

'Nah. We can always put what we want on it.'

'Please', Milt said. 'Try to be serious.'

Round and round they went, talking mostly about the ten thousand and what to say about Anna Landos. They must have talked almost two hours. 'Remember,' Milt warned wearily for the third time, 'they'll have her there testifying, so we'll have to watch our step. Nothing that could conceivably be perjury. You lent him the money and he paid it back all the same evening. You introduced him to Anna. One old friend to another. If that's procurement, I'll eat it. Anna's a big girl.'

'Believe me,' Joe said, 'she doesn't have to tune up *anyone* unless she wants to. Si was a pretty good-lookin' guy those days.'

'And if there's any question as to what would happen if Si hadn't paid the money back,' Milt said, 'you can say it's an iffy question – purely speculative. Don't answer any other way. Fact is he paid you back within four hours.'

'Okay, okay', Joe said impatiently. They went over the ground again and again. It was a little like a rehearsal for a play. Joe learned his lines. The only trouble was he wasn't absolutely sure of the lines of his adversaries.

'Now—' Milt took a deep breath. 'Is there anything else you can think of, anything at all we haven't covered?'

'Nope. Oh, maybe a little petty-larceny stuff.'

By now Milt was somewhat punchy, and his eyes had taken on the opaque glaze of battle fatigue.

'I still say if we want the easiest aftermath – and that's what we have to worry about, Joey, not one of these hoopla hearings – be a good fella and take the Fifth. You want my advice? Now you have it. We have everything to gain and nothing to lose. O.K., you won't be able to stand on your hind legs and roar at the Senators. Better a whimper now than in some little courtroom a year later.'

Joe merely shrugged. You couldn't expect a guy like Milt to change his spots.

'On the other hand,' Milt said, 'the committee could invoke Title Twenty-eight of the Code – a new section – I guess it's section 3486-A, isn't it, Andy? Just passed, at the last session – under which they can give you immunity and make you Tell All under threat of contempt of Congress charges. God forbid. But they'll never do that; too far fetched. I don't think we really have to worry about that.'

Title Twenty-eight, Joe thought. They string you up, they make a Judas of you, they make you cut all your friends of a lifetime into small bloody ribbons, and then they call it Title Twenty-eight, as if it was something respectable.

'Now listen to me', Milt continued. 'You were generous to a fault. Always have been. That's the sum of your story. You like to help people out whether they work for you or the city or the NMIA. It just never seemed wrong to you.'

'Those poor bastids', Joe said. 'How can they live on what the government pays them? It's an outrage, government salaries. I got ball players making three times as much as those poor bastids.'

'That's it, that's it', Milt said. 'You got it.'

'Now you are whistling Dixie', Rossmore said. 'Remember one thing, Joe. You don't win on points. Either you knock them out or they knock you out. Right, counsellor?'

Andy shook his head dolefully. 'Gee, Dad, I'm not so sure. Generosity, yes, but —'

Milt smiled a little under the strain. 'Old John D. Rockefeller used to give dimes to kids.'

'Not to government employees', Andy said gravely.

'Rockefeller didn't *have* any government to worry about those days', Joe said. 'It was a goddam paradise. Nowadays wherever you look, there's the government. Every other guy you meet is workin' for the government.'

'Yes,' Andy said slowly, 'that's exactly it. It makes a difference. The relationship between a citizen and his government today is unique, because when one citizen deals with *all* the citizens, he can't ride high, wide and handsome any more. We have new responsibilities, special and unique. As you say, everyone nowadays deals with the government. Income taxes, social security, old age, the armed forces, radio, television, aeroplane travel. Every business in the country deals with FTC or the Pure Food and Drug people, or NMIA or ICC or SEC. Why in the old days, a scandal like Teapot Dome was big news because it was unique, but nowadays if it's not Goldfine on the hot seat, it's the owner of a TV station, a union big shot, the lipstick makers, airline presidents, house builders, almost anyone. We're in a new era. I'll bet if the Senate and House committees wanted to keep shop open, not a day would pass when they wouldn't uncover one good scandal. It's hard. It requires constant public vigilance.'

''Ey, Andy, whose side you on?' Joe said, laughing.

'I'm on yours, Dad', Andy said in that smooth, quick way. 'But we have to know what's right and what's wrong, don't we, Dad? You want to create a public image. It's got to be a good one. You make yourself sound like a robber baron or a Chinese warlord.'

'Well, what the hell am I? You tell me, I've lost track.'

Milt closed his eyes. 'You're right, Andy, believe thou me. But this is the only image we're going to be able to create of your father. He's not accustomed to big government. He's the tough diamond in the rough – made it all himself, and the hard way. Horatio Alger. Never studied Emily Post, Marquis of Queensbury, or the statutes

M

on various minor matters like those you just mentioned. He ploughed through centre. Bricklayer to master builder. He was building a city, don't you see?'

'*I* see', Rossmore said happily.

'The way you guys talk about me,' Joe said, 'I feel as though I were some kinda inanimate object – and a hell of a big jerk at that. You really want to know what I am? The way I see my own self? I'm a poor slob, and everyone and his uncle takes me coming and going. You ask my own mother. "Pepe's sucha easy mark?" Well, I guess I am an easy mark. Now I don't want you to take this wrong – I swear to Christ I'm not looking for any credit – but look at it. I got my family outa the slums, put my kid brother through architectural school, made a big man outa *him*. Married my kid sister off to *this* guy, helped put *him* through law school' – Milt's eyes clouded and he winced, but Joe ignored him – 'took care of a whole cityful of real washed-up slobs in Italy who couldn't get across the street by themselves. Built *this* town for people who couldn't afford to live anywhere but in a tenement till we came along. Christ, I gave my own blood to Baccio's little kid, I got Anna Landos over here and got her that first job with Trick Potamos, and don't think I ever laid a finger on that kid, cause I didn't; and okay, I loaned a few thousand bucks to Si Cutler, the poor bastid, when his wife was dying. Terrible thing! And this afternoon? I fixed it up so a guy named Howard could move into Naples. A guy as black as the ace of spades, and so's his wife and kids. I oughta have my head examined. Sure everyone says integrate housing, but let someone try it and the walls are down around you like a ton of bricks. So I'm the poor bastid who does it. I'll have every mortgage banker who has paper in Naples on my neck in a week. Oh, very polite, but they'll want to cut my throat. What do I get out of all that? Medals? Hah! Why do I do it? Because I'm some kinda big-hearted hero? Nuts. Lookit, I'm not kidding myself. I don't have the first foggy idea my own self why I do it. I can't help myself. Now all this – this preparation for seeing Poltek tomorrow – well, thank you guys for all the advice. I absolutely think all that'll happen is we'll see Poltek and when he knows we got the goods on him, he'll fall right over on his can and start looking for someone else to pick on. I can be wrong, and if I am, we'll play it by ear, but that's how I see it. So why don't you guys stick close to me and if I got any problems, we'll talk about it right on the spot. Come on, it's time to get home for supper.' He lit a cigar and went to the costumer, got his Eisenhower jacket and put it on.

Milt watched him with alarm. 'We have an awful lot of territory still to go over', he said. 'We've hardly started. I'd like to know more about that trip you made to see the President, all the stuff on housing for Negroes – I'm not even sure I know the full story on that.' But Joe was already waving and out of the door.

Twenty-seven

A MORNING in early November can be as gloomy as an outdoor funeral parlour – and this one was. By seven, everyone showed up at Teterboro – Chuck Rossmore, still sleeping soundly on his feet, Milt, Andy and Hetty, who had come together, and Cathy down from Trenton (she must've got up at five) and, of course, Dulian. But while they unblocked the plane, Dulian kept scowling at the sky as if trying to scare the grey shirt off it. He rammed the earphones over his head and held the receiver to his ear. 'Beechcraft Baker one seven four to tower. What've you got on the weather to Washington? Over.' He listened to the tower's response which the others heard as metallic cacophony.

'Not so hot', Dulian mumbled to Joe.

'Getting better or worse?' Joe said.

'Clearing slowly', he said. 'Can't count on much contact flying on the way down.'

Joe reflected a moment. If he could not get to Washington in time to see Poltek privately, he'd find himself in an executive session. Two hours of delay could be critical. He was counting on knocking Poltek off balance. Once those government boys started taking testimony, that stuff got into the record, even in executive session, the fat was in the fire. That much Milt didn't have to tell him.

'You willing to try it?' Joe said to Dulian.

'Me? Oh, I've flown over four continents. I'll go.' Dulian did not sound exactly happy. Joe reflected it wasn't the same old Dulian. He was too old and wise.

'Lookit', Joe said. 'Why don't the rest of you all do me a favour and drive over to Newark and take a scheduled flight? Eastern has one at ten-thirty. It'll be clearer then. Dulian and I can take the Beech.'

'Not without me you're not going, Joie', Hetty said firmly.

'Ah, Dad, you know Dulian. He's always calamity howling.'

'That's why I continue to be here, able to howl', Dulian said sourly.

Chuck Rossmore, as if by superhuman will, roused himself from his semi-consciousness. 'I get paid very nice fees which does not include any risks to my neck', he said. 'I'm a confirmed coward and I shall be very happy to go to Newark.'

Cathy kept her hands folded in front of her calmly, knowing that they would all do precisely as Joe told them.

Then Milt spoke quietly and Joe could see him sweating. 'I can't think of anything I'd rather do less than fly instrument in a plane without full instrumentation. But, Joe, I can't let you walk into Poltek alone. I just don't trust either you or him. So I tell you what. Let's you and I go with Dulian. The others can join us there at noon. If anything happens, Lucy'll know I got into heaven because I was with you.'

'I don't think it's so funny', Hetty said. 'I'd like to go, too.'

'You didn't hear me so good', Joe said. 'Come on now, like good kids, everyone beat it on over to Newark. I don't dare take any chances with you. As far as I'm concerned, who the hell needs *me*? And Milt, sure, come on along. You're fifty-two. You got nothin' to lose either.' Everyone knew enough not to argue.

It was one of those miserably jumpy flights where their stomachs bounced against the floor like a rubber ball six or eight times a minute, until at last they set down into a pea-soup morning, and although no one said a word, they were happy to touch down on that runway.

Jeff Straley was waiting in Washington for them, and he'd brought his wife Daphne. 'We got a sitter', Daphne said gaily, as if she were going to the April in Paris Ball.

Almost nothing was said in the cab as they headed for the old Senate Office Building, each of the four holding his own thoughts. Even Daphne's bantering stopped as they emerged from National Airport and drove in the fog-grey morning. Traffic was heavy and the cab crawled slowly across the Potomac and into town.

When they saw the familiar Capitol dome, Joe was conscious of the fact that for ten minutes no one had said a word, even his own self. He was beginning to feel sorry for Poltek, who had absolutely no idea what was in store for him. What the hell, Joe thought, it's easy for him, all he's gotta do is lay off me and I'll lay off him. Nobody's trying to destroy him the way the little bastid is doing to me.

Milt paid the driver, inquired of the white-haired man at the information desk, and led the way downstairs. Sam Poltek's office was in the basement, and as they walked through the cheerless halls, Joe had a momentary chill. Hell, sure it would work, it had to work.

The fat girl at the desk wore bifocals. She got up, went inside, and returned briskly. 'Mr. Poltek will be with you in a moment.'

They sat like four mummies looking at their hands, until a buzzer sounded. Miss Bifocals picked up her phone, listened a moment, and said, 'You can go in now, Mr. Naples.'

Joe's stomach tightened as he pushed open the door. Sam Poltek sat like little Napoleon at a desk covered with piles of bulging file folders, arranged not neatly – in fact, in chaos. Six or seven green file cabinets stood ominously behind him, full of derogatory information about God knows who. It was a seedy office, with bare bulbs giving off inadequate light. No wonder all these government people had bad eyes. Uncle Giovanni must be running the place.

'Glad to see you', Sam Poltek said with that sleazy heartiness. He rose and shook hands, clammy hands, too, and sat down again. 'Have a seat.' That stink. They seriously oughta bring Lifebuoy back for this guy.

'I brought my lawyers', Joe said. 'They're right outside there.'

'Oh, by all means, let's have them in here.' Poltek sounded like a cat who was putting on his napkin and getting ready to eat his canary. 'Of course, our place is not so luxuriously appointed. We have no Utrillos on the walls.'

Joe walked back to the door and called to the others, 'Okay, fellas, c'mon in.'

Milt came first and Poltek rose to greet him. Then Poltek saw Jeff and Daphne Straley.

The violent and sudden transformation which Joe had expected in Poltek was confined to a fleeting narrowing of the eyes, the slightest reddening of that sallow face, and then a vague and humourless smile. 'Oh, hello there.' Poltek stood up and put his hand out to Jeff Straley. 'Hiya, fella', as if he were unable to recall his name. He turned to Mrs. Straley, 'Hello, Daph. Glad to see you.'

Milt glanced at Joe.

'You know the Straleys then?' Joe said.

'Oh, yes indeed, Daph and I used to date each other years ago', Sam Poltek said. 'Where're you living now, Daph?'

'In Cambridge. Jeff's teaching constitutional law at Harvard.'

'Oh? I hadn't heard. Sounds like a nice quiet job – nothing like hectic old Washington. We've been making quite a little bit of constitutional law here too – in our own noisy way.' He seemed to be talking to give himself time to think. 'By the way, what are you doing here with this man?' He spat the last two words out as if they were odious.

'Mr. Straley's here as part of my legal team', Joe said quickly.

Sam Poltek sat down again abruptly and his next words were ice water.

'When I have a question to ask you, Mr. Naples, I'll address it to you.' He turned back to Jeff Straley. 'You know, Jeff, we have quite a file on Mr. Naples.' He tapped one of the piles of folders. 'Yes sir, quite a file. Frankly, I'm surprised to see you here in defence of one of the most corrupt men in American business life I've come across, not only on this sub-committee, Jeff, but in all my years at the Justice Department. I have no doubt that when the sub-committee has finished with Mr. Naples, he'll be indicted and tried, and sent to a federal penitentiary.'

'That's quite a mouthful, you arrogant little Communist son-of-a-bitch', Joe said.

Milt closed his eyes and turned away.

Sam Poltek's eyes were now blazing, and he was out of control. 'D'you plan to have me put out of the way like Mr. – uh – what's his name? A' – he looked down at the file in front of him – 'Mr. Gamboretta?'

Milt turned, his eyes pleading with Joe not to respond, then he addressed Poltek. 'Please, Mr. Poltek, couldn't we conduct these proceedings with a little restraint?'

Poltek's voice was high pitched. 'Your man walks in here, counsellor, threatening me, accusing me of Communist affiliations, and you ask *me* for restraint. Well, counsellor, I have seen all kinds of pool, including the dirty, and I know how to handle it.'

Milt was offended. 'Mr. Poltek, I implore you to keep in mind that you are acting as a public servant, and as such —'

'The information I have about *you*, counsellor, is that during the Hendrickson investigation you represented that noble American, Tony Ferrara. And in all the criminal proceedings against him after that, you were constantly at his side. Is that correct?'

'Mr. Poltek, am I under investigation here?' Milt said more quietly. Jeff Straley and Daphne glanced at each other worriedly. Sam Poltek was quick to see the exchange.

'Then in the midst of everything Simon Cutler, one of our key witnesses, and a focal point of corruption, gets what is said to be a heart attack. And what doctor attends him? Why, Mr. Naples's personal physician.

'You know who you're getting into bed with here, Jeff? Here's an attorney who represents one of the greatest, if not the leading criminal in the country, Tony Ferrara. A common gangster. This man Naples, under investigation by the GAPE Committee – well, I simply don't know where to begin. According to our files, he's got away with everything in the book, except murder and we can't be sure of that. According to our files, Ferrara is a silent partner of this man. Is this the team you want to ally yourself with? Will you drag us all down in defence of a character like this? Are these the people who can command one of the greatest minds on constitutional law?'

Milton had turned scarlet. 'This name calling is for children', he said quietly. 'Either you are or are not, have been or have not been a Communist, and Mr. Naples either had or had not trespassed the limits of acceptable business behaviour. The only proper process in our opinion, for any complaint against my client, is the judicial process. Let me state our position as clearly as I can, may I?'

He appeared to have stopped everyone from blowing off any more steam, but they all eyed each other like great circling leopards.

"Kay', Poltek said gruffly. 'State it.'

'We hold this investigation and this sub-committee to be entirely unconstitutional and an abuse of the investigatory powers historically assumed by the Congress and authorized by various acts of the Congress. The frame of reference is too vague. "Good moral character" is too subjective a test for investigation, and the proceeding in our opinion is comparable to a congressional investigation into sex habits or bathroom idiosyncrasies. It invades an area more private than any with which the Congress can be legitimately concerned.'

Poltek said, 'You seriously expect the investigation to stop in its tracks for an argument like that?'

'Every witness – in my opinion, of course – will take this position. They will never answer your questions. Certainly, all your hostile witnesses will not.'

'In my opinion,' Poltek said, slowly taking control of himself, 'if they do that, every one of them will go to the penitentiary for contempt. You remember the ten Hollywood writers who took that position? It's a long gamble, counsellor, and I think you may find many people will prefer to answer a few questions – even unpleasant ones, particularly where no criminal offences are involved.'

'That's the considered attitude of the sub-committee?' Milton said, and Poltek nodded.

Joe had sat quiet during this exchange, which he considered totally inane. Here was this bastid Poltek, not denying he was absolutely a Red, and he was talking as if he were still alive. Sam Poltek must be deaf and pretty dumb at that. Sam Poltek must not have heard too good.

Joe's voice boomed through the room. He had to take over before they began arguing about how many angels could dance on a pinpoint.

'Mr. Poltek. I don't think you understand the position at all. You got everything upside down, which is the way I know you guys operate. We got airtight proof that you *were* a Communist, and maybe still are in your gut, and if that isn't trouble, I don't know what is.' Poltek's face was crimson, but he remained silent, tight-lipped. 'Now listen to me good. All that crap you got in all those files, I don't know what the hell you got in there, and I'd guess damn near all of it is a barrelful of lies, but I got things to do, I got a university to build, I got slums to clear out and new buildings to put up; I'll be goddamned if all that's gonna stop because a little pipsqueak like you, still wet behind the ears, who absolutely don't understand one single thing about what makes this country tick, thinks he's gonna drop me into the sewer. No, sir. You ain't. If you do, you're dead, mister, you're dead in the government and you're dead as a lawyer. And you're too young to die, Mr. Poltek, you're still a kid.' Out of the corner of his eye, Joe saw Jeff Straley looking preoccupied, puzzled, and not happy. He had Poltek on the ropes, but Joe suddenly sensed in Jeff Straley the seeds of disaster, a terrible miscalculation.

Poltek was talking, his face was flushed still, but the words were measured, for he was in retreat. 'It's going to be impossible,' he was saying, 'to avoid questioning you, Mr. Naples. Simply impossible. We've had half a dozen investigators working in the case. We've had people in Jersey, people in California and Las Vegas, people here, people in your office. You can't keep things like this secret. There'd be a tremendous cry of whitewash. No, we'll simply have to ask you questions. No doubt about it. I really think we can ignore some of the stuff in this file that goes back thirty years. It's not terribly relevant in any case. We've been thinking of it merely as atmospheric colour. Well, we can let it go. And I don't think any of the material in our line of questioning actually is going to involve you in any criminal activity, and that's the important phase of these investigations for a witness. Oh, I'd opine you may have a few embarrassing moments, but it's the criminal action which follows these investigations that are so worrisome. Am I right, counsellor?' He addressed Milt, who nodded slowly, in open-eyed amazement. 'I seriously doubt there'd be material of that kind', Poltek said blandly. 'We do have others who were involved in criminal activity, but you aren't among them.'

Milt spoke quickly, in a suppressed voice, trying to be casual. 'May I have a word with my client?'

'Certainly.' Poltek was electric magnanimity, all charged up.

Jeff Straley, Joe and Milt stepped into the hall and started slowly down the corridor, with Daphne trailing. 'He's offering you a deal! Milt whispered excitedly. 'I'd never have believed it, so help me. It worked!'

Joe grinned. 'I know damn well what he offered me. You see, you old sceptical bastid?'

'Joe, I hand it to you', Milt said. 'It's your day. It's all over.' He threw his hands above his head with excitement.

But Joe was now watching Straley closely. Jeff's jaw was working nervously as they walked.

'What's the precise nature of the deal?' Jeff Straley asked.

'He don't bother us, we don't bother him', Joe said slowly and warily.

Jeff Straley squinted. 'I don't know what you have at stake, Mr. Naples. I just don't believe a man like Sam Poltek should have a critical role in the legislative process in this country. Or in the executive branch, either, for that matter.'

'You're a hundred per cent on the right track there, boy', Joe said enthusiastically. 'Bastids like him should be tailors like his old man.'

'But if you're not to bother him, as you say,' Jeff persisted slowly,' 'he remains in a crucial job and distorts an investigation which may have a completely legitimate purpose. He lives to fight another day. I don't see it.'

Joe stopped walking, glared at Straley, caught the tenseness in Daphne's eyes, and then forced a grin. 'Maybe you didn't hear me so good, professor. I retained *you*, sonny. You're my *lawyer*. Your first professional job is to defend me. That's the way I heard it. That's something to do with professional ethics. Once I'm off the hook, *you* want to blow the lid off Sam Poltek, go ahead and blow.'

'But if we give our pledge in my trade, lawyer to lawyer, Mr. Jason and I are bound as attorneys —'

'Mister,' Joe said sharply, 'this man is a Communist. *No*body binds himself to those guys.'

'I'd rather not see him remain on in government', Jeff said, and he wore a long look.

'How come you never did anything about *that* before? You'da saved me lots a trouble, son', Joe said. 'He musta been over in the Justice Department around ninety years.'

'Believe it or not, I never knew about it', Jeff Straley said. 'I thought he'd gone out west. The first I'd heard was when Dr. Karpeko told me.' Jeff Straley peered towards Daphne, who blinked and looked away. 'I'd have to think about it, Mr. Naples', he said slowly.

Joe felt nothing but scorn for this guy, but he tried to look sympathetic. 'Hah! *You* gotta think! I gotta do more than *think*. This boy is on the ropes. He's groggy, ain't he? I'm not so sure I got any great desire to testify about anything whatsoever, at all. What do I want to be on television for? That's not my line. He says "questions that could be embarrassing". What the hell is he *talkin'* about? I got absolutely no interest whatsoever in being even one goddam trifle embarrassed. Right, Milt?'

Milt's face was deeply lined. 'Don't turn him down cold, Joe, whatever you do. Let's play along for time. I can't think this fast – you know me. Why don't I suggest to him that in a routine way he tell the sub-committee he's not ready for us today? That'll give us time. Let's get ourselves a couple of days for reflection. Heck, he can put you off for a few days without anyone on the committee minding one bit. He must have a dozen other witnesses. And believe thou me, secretly I think he'll welcome the suggestion. He's had a nasty surprise today, Joe.'

'Okay,' Joe said, 'sure. We got nothing to lose.' It would give him a chance to talk things over with Tony and with Jock as soon as the old boy got back from Paris.

Milt proved to be right. Poltek jumped at the idea of delay. Sourly he said, 'Can you meet me here next Monday? Ten-thirty?'

'Absolutely', Joe said and, followed by the others, marched out of the office, to step right into Hetty, Andy, Cathy and Rossmore coming down the basement hall searching for Poltek's office. Hetty took Joe's hand and studied his face as though searching for a clue, until Joe laughed and kissed her while Cathy watched woodenly, a thin fixed smile on her face. 'Hearing's postponed', he said. 'Gotta come back Monday morning.'

'What did he have to say, Dad? How did he take it?'

'You don't hear me so good, Andy. Hearing's postponed till Monday. He was knocked bang on his can. Right, Milt?'

'That's not bad, is it, Dad?'

'It ain't bad, Andy', Joe said, winking. 'But it's not perfect either.'

Chuck Rossmore stood with his head bent, and his beady eyes shining. 'Zo. It worked. Anh! Gut.' He raised his head and surveyed the others cheerfully. 'Well, it wass a nice trip. I always luff to get up six o'clock in the morning. I wake up just in time to meet myself falling asleep. Next time I merely kill myself altogether. I must be out of my head. Well, I haff never been to Washington for pleasure. May I invite you all to come to the Washington Monument with me?'

'Chuck,' Joe said, as he walked quickly down the hall, with the others scampering to keep up, 'you are the laziest man God ever made. We got work. Between now and Friday we have to get an announcement out on Naples University. I want it in every Sunday paper and I want coverage in *Time* and *Life* and *Newsweek* and all those kinda magazines. We could even have some guy come down from the *New Yorker* and give me an interview. And that ain't as crazy as it sounds. Don't *you* think I'm a hell of a character to be starting a university? Never even went to college my own self. The *New Yorker* boys oughta like that. *Think* a little bit, man. We're gonna have to move fast. I've got to look like a pure and perfect son-of-a-bitch in shining armour by Monday. Nobody's ever gonna get me mixed up in their mind as if I was some kinda Tony Ferrara type.'

The weather was clearing and by the time they were back out at National Airport, the sun was shining in one of those perfect crisp November days; in an hour, Dulian had them all back at Teterboro in the Beechcraft.

Twenty-eight

ETTY drove Daphne to Easy Street, while Jeff went along with the others back to the office where the lawyers and Andy locked themselves into the law library to continue their research; and to tell the God's honest truth, Joe was goddam glad to get them all out of his hair for a while. How they loved to chew over the same little bit of cud hoping to find some subtle way out or around the problem instead of meeting it on the nose! Just let that little bastid Poltek poke around with him and Joe would need no lawyers whatsoever to advise him exactly what to do.

He leaned back in his chair. This had been a hell of a day so far.

He was glad to be able to spend a few minutes with brother Dino and with Chuck Rossmore getting some of the material ready for Friday's press release. Chuck said he'd have one of his boys do a story, maybe for *Business Week*, on Joe's tremendous and lifetime preoccupation with the state of higher education – featuring his recent contributions to Harvard, Naples University and all that crap.

Chuck reminded him that Father Ritucci had been after him to help with a Parochial Secondary School in Naples – there were five thousand Catholic families in Naples now – and didn't Joe think the Foundation could maybe allocate half a million to old Father Ritucci? By God, he had got his old parish priest from Saint Cecilia's on Ninety-sixth Street transferred out here to Naples (and no easy job talking the bishop into *that*), and it was the least he could do to help the poor bastid out and put that new parochial school across. Tonight would be a good time to tell the priest the news. Joe called the rectory and made the date, and Chuck agreed to have photographers and reporters at St. Theresa's at six-thirty for the entire deal.

Cathy poked her head in while they were talking to hand him a note: Jock Dennison's office had called to confirm their date for tomorrow. Jock would be here at one. Jock wanted to take him to lunch. Joe told Cath to call back and say they'd eat right in the office.

In the early afternoon Joe drove home to talk to Hetty and his sister Lucy while Daphne Straley sat and listened. Joe wanted them to visit the neighbours of the Lewins to prepare them for the Howards, and to get Father Ritucci, the rabbi and the four ministers in on the deal. As he listened to himself talk, he sounded like a member of the NAACP. 'Sure, they got rights. Absolute rights. We're not living in Georgia and we're not living in the nineteenth century. But it's more than rights. These are nice goddam people. He's a research man and she's a trained nurse and they're a hell of a lot nicer than some of the other neighbours – don't say that. But we're either American or we're not. It's time we put up or shut up.'

Hetty squinted and peered up at him. 'You know, Joe, I half think you mean it.'

'Certainly I mean it.' She walked to where he was sitting, put a hand on his cheek, and blinked.

'We'll do it, won't we, Luce?'

'I'd like to help if I may', Daphne said.

Joe never did see his team of attorneys – Milt, the Harvard professor and Andy – that afternoon, and he was just as glad not to. They'd only try to pump him full of more useless instructions if he poked his head in there. No matter what he talked about all day or what the attorneys were hatching up, only one question of substance hung over his head: To take Poltek's offer or not – about as far from a constitutional question as you could get. Joe felt pretty good at judging people, and Poltek was on the run. Should he push the little bastid into a corner and knock him completely out? Tell him testifying at all was one hundred per cent *out*, whatsoever, about *anything*, period? He would not take the stand. Poltek must have nine million other poor bastids lined up all over the country for questioning. Why, the building business alone was absolutely crawling with big and little guys who, to his own knowledge, had made all kinds of crummy deals with all kinds of creepy people in and out of the government. It was in the nature of things. That sub-committee must have files enough to keep it busy until 1975.

No testimony whatever, that was the ticket. No appearance, public or private. But there was just the possibility that Poltek might be right, that it might no longer be within his own control. If so, Poltek's offer was not a bad one at that. Because if Joe turned it down, then the fat would really hit the fire.

Before he made up his mind absolutely, there was one man with some experience in these matters Joe wanted to talk over his problem with. He got into the jeep and started for the Garden State Parkway; he was going to East Orange to see his old friend Tony Ferrara, whom he had not seen face to face for several years, although they talked occasionally on the phone. But you can never really get down to cases except face to face.

Getting into Tony's property was like going through the Maginot line. There were two men in a kind of pillbox at the gate, one of whom telephoned the main house to get the okay to send Joe up; the other got into the car and rode alongside Joe up the quarter-mile long drive.

Tony Ferrara still drank beer at cocktail hour, as well as at all other hours, but now three-quarters of it was gin and the beer was used principally for colouring matter. Tony was seated in one of his new-fangled chairs that look like a big canvas pail, at the far end of his forty-five-foot living-room in his new modern ranch house – the place musta cost him three quarters of a million – and from time to time looked out of his bullet-proof, thermopane glass with which the structure was mostly faced. At the moment Joe arrived, Tony was lifting his gin and beer in a clear Jensen stein and looking at his new little blonde wife who had him on a blitz in a game of gin rummy.

Since Tony had had it in mind to hop into the sack with his new wife right after the card game, he was not exactly delighted to see Joe, but he was not as sour as if it had been anyone else, for Tony had the warmest spot for Joe. 'Knowin' you been my friend for forty years, even makin' me a partner in Naples, makes me feel damn near respectable', he once told Joe, and then added sadly, 'Only I feel a little bad when I realize how easy you made all your dough – *legitimately*, whereas I hadda get into the liquor business, doin' it the hard way. Only remember, Josey boy, you had a big edge on me. You could lay brick. I couldn't do *nothin*'!'

Tony's bodyguard, a slim, middle-aged man with a scar above his lip, served as the butler around the place and he ushered Joe into the living-room. Joe knew him slightly, but not the way he'd known little old George Pedula, who seemed mysteriously to have disappeared a few months ago. Even Tony had no idea where he'd gone.

Tony put down his cards, and looked up with surprise and pleasure. "Ey, Cookie, honey,' he said to his wife, 'I wantcha to meet my oldest extra special friend of mine, Joey Naples.'

'He's the builder one?'

'See?' Tony cried much too enthusiastically. 'You're famous! Where the hell you been, you bastid?'

'How do', blonde Cookie said, completely at home in the house she had moved into less than a week ago. Joe took a good look at her – about five-four, stacked like Marilyn Monroe, equipped with tight skin you wanted to touch all over and which smelled fantastically good, with a generous-featured face including a turned-up nose with wide and quivering nostrils. That skin could drive a man nuts, and in her head was not a thought, but plenty of feeling. She couldn't have been over twenty-five and she was certainly nothing like the first Mrs. Ferrara, Vince's cousin Rosalie Bacciano, may her soul rest in peace.

'I hope you don't mind me coming, Tony, but I got something important I got to talk to you about', Joe said.

'Important to who? You or me?' Tony roared because that was Joe's old line. Then he turned abruptly to the little woman. 'Cookie,' he said, as if he were talking to a favourite lap dog, 'Joey and I need a few minutes to talk things over.'

She put her cards on the table, face down, and smiled sweetly. 'You've got no secrets from me, Sugar.'

Tony's head bobbed like a little boy's. 'You're right, baby, but maybe Joey has.'

'Oh,' she said, 'I guess anything he can tell you he can tell me.'

Tony looked sheepish and turned apologetically to Joe. 'Do you mind, Joey?'

Joe could not believe his senses. He took another look at Tony and was amazed at what he saw now, for the first time. By God, Tony was no longer the conquering hero, but a man atremble. His cheeks were sunken, his eyes glazed. His heart was no longer stout or in the business of command. The realization so appalled Joe that it took a while for it to penetrate. Tony Ferrara, he thought, is an exhausted, beat-up guy. But why? Had it been some kind of erosion he hadn't noticed before, or a sudden blast?

'Hell, I don't care', Joe said magnanimously to Cookie. 'In fact, it's a pleasure to have such a good-looking young broad in the room, I'd rather talk to her than a great big ugly son-of-a-bitch like you any day.'

Tony glowered and Cookie's face remained blank.

At last Tony said slowly, 'Don't worry, Joey. I don't blame you not comin' around these last few years. I'm poison, I know it.'

Joe started to protest, but Tony stopped him.

'Look, Joey, I don't mind, so help me Christ. You're who you are and I'm whom I am; why should you associate with a guy under two indictments who might get shut up any day? I wouldn't do it myself if I could help it.'

'Tony, you old son-of-a-bitch, I feel exactly one hundred per cent the way I always felt—'

'Shu, shu. Well you gotta admit you're takin' to a guy with a hell of a past, right? My future's somethin' else again. Little fuzzy, right?' He laughed as if he had said something hilarious. 'So what I'm wondering,' Tony shouted, 'is what the hell you could possibly want from *me* !'

'Lookit', Joe said, and even as he spoke, he wondered if he should be coming to Tony. 'I got a funny situation with this Senate sub-committee.' He started to tell Tony the Poltek story and when he was half way through, the new Mrs. Ferrara rose quietly and said flatly, 'Could I get you a drink, Mr. Naples?'

'You got some plain table wine?'

'Get him some of that Dago red', Tony said. 'He belongs to that fancy gold club, runs with that Canoe Hill crowd, but he still drinks like a peasant from old Napoli.'

Joe continued. 'My problem, Mr. Antony,' he said, 'is should I make a deal with this commie bastid and testify, or not? Or should I tell him I just don't wanna testify at all? If he won't play my way, or can't, why then I'll blast the son-of-a-bitch out of Washington altogether.'

'What'll he do then?'

'He'll blast me. But I can always prove it's a commie smear. Only I'm just not a hundred per cent sure. Whaddaya say, Tony?'

'You're asking me? What's the Brain say?'

'This is no question for a lawyer', Joe said. 'This is something that's gonna come from the gut.'

'I know. I'm just asking, what does the legal beagle say?'

'Milt thinks I ought to make the deal: Poltek promises not to ask me any questions whatsoever that could interest the Justice Department or the Treasury and I'm supposed to leave him strictly be.'

'That guy Milt,' Tony Ferrara said with a passion that was more exhaustion than anger, 'is fulluvit. So fulluvit! Did you know deep down he *believes* in the *law*? He'll do anything for you if you're a client, but you dast not break the law *after* he's your lawyer. Some of those goddam questions, the easiest way to answer is lie, out and out. What the hell! We useta *kill* guys in the early days. I guess in my life I broke every one of the ten commandments except bowin' down to a graven image, but when it comes to a coupla lies before the Senate Rackets Committee, your friend Milt gets a terrible long look. Damn near starts bawlin', for a while there I think I joined the YMCA, and he says, Tony, all you got to do is keep sayin' I refuse to answer on the grounds of possible self-incrimination. Ain't that a mouthful?'

Cookie was back with a Chianti flask, and Joe thanked her and drank half a tumblerful. 'How can you stand that stuff?' Cookie said admiringly.

'You listen to me, Joe, and watch out for that guy Milt,' Tony said ominously, 'even if he's your brother-in-law.'

'Yah,' Joe said reflectively, 'he sure as hell always hollered like a stuck pig when it came to the smallest shenanigans. Always been like that. I remember back when we were kids, he hollered bloody murder just because I was gonna give Gamboretta a few bucks to lay offa my job.'

'Personally, I love that Milt,' Tony said, 'but I gotta say he's got one hell of a law practice just on me alone. Since I follow his advice and take the Fifth Amendment – Jesus, it was seven years ago – I ain't had a minute's rest.' Tony looked incredibly old and tired. Suddenly for a moment Tony's dull face was animated with the old spark. 'Cookie, honey, do I ever tell you about the time I testify before the Hendrickson Committee on television?'

'No', Cookie said, her eyes shining with approval. 'Tell me.' She musta heard it a million times, but she was kind.

'Well, it was damn near eight years ago', Tony said. 'Right, Joey? Seems like last week.' Joe nodded. He had heard the story a dozen times his own self.

'I was born in 1937', Cookie said. 'I must have been around thirteen at the time. Gosh, if I'd have known I was gonna meet the great Tony Ferrara, I would have come in from my potsy game and watched you on TV.'

'Well, on account of Milt's advice, 'cause I listened to him, I just had to sit there like a horse's ass takin' it from those sancti-monious bastids saying "I'm sorry, Senator, I cannot answer that question 'cause it might tend to incriminate me". And there was one peppery little Senator back there, a funny little guy named Tobey from Vermont or Maine or one of those cold unfriendly states, an' if you ever wanta see a real nut. He kept talkin' about God and the good life. He belonged in some kind of an asylum.

Finally he says to me, "You got any children, Mr Ferrara ?" so I figured I could answer that one. I says, "Yes, sir", and I am very humble to that son-of-a-bitch 'cause after all I am on television, coast to coast, and I don't wanta *look* bad. I gotta think of my public. I don't want people to think I'm arrogant. So then the crazy bastid says, "How do you feel having your children watching this display on television ?" Well, actually Rosalie and I sent both a the kids to Europe a couple of weeks ahead, but I says, very sweet and nice, I says, "Senator, sir, I would give anything in the world not to be here tonight. I'd give a million bucks." And you know that funny little bastid is getting redder and redder because by now he can see I am ribbing him on a national hook-up, coast to coast, and then he practically splits a gut and says, "A life like yours is hardly worth living, is it ?" And I think of all the fine people I know – guys like you, Joey, and Harold Brice and Sam Vogeler on the Jersey Supreme Court and Milt – and all the nice things I'm able to do for my kids, colleges and clothes, and fancy friends, and the great times we had, and even keepin' my old man in booze, and this pipsqueak from New England, without a pot to pee in, talking like that, and I put on a long face and I put my right hand up like in a television courtroom, and I say very slow like, "Senator, crime – does – not – pay", and I got all I can do to keep my thumb away from my nose. The poor bastid almost has apoplexy right in the hearing room, but what can he say ? And the next day, so help me God, he drops dead of a heart attack. Right, Joey ?'

Joe nodded. 'That's what happened.'

'That's rich', Cookie said, and laughed, although it was clear she didn't understand a word of it.

'Coast to coast', Tony roared. 'Kiss my ass, Senator.'

'Why do Senators smile so much ?' Cookie said.

'Well, Senator *Tobey* wasn't smilin' *that* day', Tony said reminiscently. 'He was dyin'.'

'What was so damn wrong with Milt's advice ?' Joe said.

'Why, for Christ's sake, I ain't had a minute's peace from that day to this', Tony said with real passion. 'Seven goddam long years – I been on the run, run, run.' And at last Joe, in his gut, understood Tony's tired face, the terrible tension of hearings, indictments, examinations before trial. Although Tony would be the last to admit it, what had once seemed a kind of joke had stopped being funny a long time ago.

'They must have a million guys workin' in the government,'

Tony said, 'and except for the President and maybe the Secretary of State, they're all working to get Tony Ferrara. They never forgive me for givin' Senator Tobey that apoplexy. But the main thing is if you say you won't answer this or that question because it tends to incriminate you, a million guys down at the Justice Department starts goin' nuts to find the evidence that *will* incriminate you. Those guys never sleep. They work in shifts. Once they get your files, they pass 'em round from one department to the other like dirty pictures – even to the Attorney-General's office here in Jersey. You know I ain't got control of the Attorney-General's office here any more, Joe? This goddam state government of ours is keepin' things outa my hands altogether. Christ, in the early days we kept guys like George Pedula around 'cause we never knew which one of our friends was out to get us. But lemme tell you, Joey, those days were a pleasure compared to these midgets in the Treasury Department and the Justice Department. They fight with paper. It's the worst kind. You don't know when to duck. You don't know where the next shot's comin' from. That old buddy of yours, Milt, the legal beagle, he advised me to pay more than two hundred thousand in back taxes, and I *did* it. You think that did any good? In a pig's ass. It gets worse every day. In fact, it's just no pleasure going to the office any more. There's always at least one subpoena and two investigators waiting for me. I'm up on appeal in two cases right now and I got one indictment against me right here in Jersey on embezzlement. I spend my life in courts and lawyers' offices. It don't hardly seem worth it, I tell ya. No sir, once those guys in Senate get their claws on you, you don't get finished while you're alive. The only time I get any peace is when I'm sleepin'.'

'Poor baby', Cookie said, standing beside her husband and cuddling his head in her long slim hands. 'He does sleep an awful lot.'

'Why not? It's my only pleasure. But don't worry, I ain't licked by a long shot', Tony said. 'Before I go up, I'll drag 'em along for ten more years. That's what Milt's really good for, hah? Honey, get Joey another quart of Dago red, willya?'

When Cookie left, Tony turned confidentially to Joe. 'Luckiest thing I ever did was find her. Ain't she cute? You know me, Joe. I ain't got the strength no more to use my personality. Gimme a girl who's behind in her room rent any time. Well, Cookie not only turns out to be behind, but also she loves me. And she loves sex like it was a new invention. I mean she can *concentrate*. She thinks it's *important*. She enjoys what she's doing.'

The expression on Joe's face must have troubled Tony for he snorted. 'Now you lecherous bastid, you keep your bricklayer hands off her. I'm fifty-three years old and this is mine. I'm not sure it's all worth a hell of a lot without her. So just be nice to her, Joey. It means a hell of a lot to me.'

'You poor bastid', Joe said.

'She's even got me ascared of her', Tony said lightly. Then his face sagged. 'I dunno, maybe I'm grabbin' straws. I just don't know what the hell to do, Joey.' His voice took on an earnestness it had not had before. 'You wanna be a good guy? If anything happens to yours truly, keep an eye on Cookie for me, will ya? She's a good kid, but a goddam infant.'

'What's gonna happen to you, y'old bastid? I thought you were indestructible.'

Tony wiped his face with his open palm. 'Nobody's destroyin' yours truly. But the way I feel, when nobody's dealin' you cards, you might just as well get up from the table. Now don't you say nothin' to Cookie. I don't want her worryin'. She watches me like a hawk as it is. I don't wanna—' He stopped suddenly when he saw Cookie returning with more wine.

Joe was beginning to feel the first quart. 'Thanks, Cookie', he said hazily, but he was thinking he'd make no deal with Poltek. Nosir. He'd never want to end up like his old friend Tony, a hollow man.

He started out to Tony's driveway, waved to the two guards and headed for the rectory of St. Theresa's to leave his cheque with Father Ritucci.

He drove sick at the stomach and depressed by the terrible new knowledge about Tony. His own friend, Tony the Terrible, the stoutest tree in the forest, turned into sawdust by the termites in the United States government. Looked intact, but touch him and he came away in your hands, rotted. Joe shivered.

Twenty-nine

HE looked forward to seeing Jock Dennison more than he cared to admit. Jock's cynical wisdom and superior perception would absolutely expose the ridiculousness of this wild investigation to the numerous sensible men he knew in the U. S. Senate. Jock would put it in perspective for them. Above all, Joe knew Jock would at the very least give him the most affectionate hearing and advice he would ever get from anyone, and *that* he sorely needed.

But when his old friend entered the office somewhat haltingly, Joe's mind did a somersault, and he had to put on a hundred per cent act, grinning like a goddam clown because Jock looked so old and feeble. The poor old bastid was withering up. Even his handshake was a dry rag. All his friends were falling apart.

To reach beyond his own dismay, Joe asked politely about Paris and Jock's old lady; and that seemed to get an unexpected rise out of the old man. 'Remarkable woman', Jock said with enthusiasm. 'Damn near ninety-six and still gadding about! Drinks like a fish. The Ritz bar does something to the old girl, I must say. She claims they're growing old together, she and Paris. She even adores the new small cabs.'

From there Jock moved on to French public affairs. It was the Algerian nonsense that stood between France and salvation. The weirdness of a great nation like France put in jeopardy by a handful of Algerian beasts – Arabs who could neither read nor do long division! De Gaulle stood a giant among pygmies, and if anyone could do the job, he was the one man. Joe nodded, waited for Jock to unwind.

At last the older man paused, walked stiffly to the window, and looked down on the shopping centre. 'What's new here in Naples, my boy?' Jock surely thought of Naples in terms of numbers. House sales, over-age rents in the shopping centre, assessments. Jock had a true IBM mind. Instead, Joe told him about the amenities in the new apartment jobs, about the fantastic equipment in the new hospital wing, about his talk with Nathan Pusey and his decision to break ground for the university. He told him about his plans for a new city of Naples in Pennsylvania, about the ball club and Hetty's new play. He avoided mentioning Mr. Poltek and the Owens sub-committee, trying to decipher Jock's mood, which was if nothing else remote. Yes, preoccupied was what friend Jock was.

'Joe, my boy,' the older man said at last, 'I've been giving some attention to the little fortune I've put together. We may as well face it, my boy, I'm a dying man.' His high and frightened giggle gave Joe the creeps. 'Oh, nothing that has a timetable. But growing older is something a man has to take seriously sooner or later, and I don't like the way my doctor sounds. I've lost forty pounds, Joe. That's not feathers. You have anything to drink in this Philistine office?'

Joe called Cathy and asked her to have lunch brought in. He went to the bar and fixed a Scotch on rocks while Jock hovered behind him and continued to talk.

'I've inherited and accumulated the queerest collection of holdings ever seen. Well, you know what they are – a real estate hodge-podge, enough to drive any executor off his trolley. Office buildings, shopping centres, taxpayers, apartments, even two motels, and to make matters worse, they're spread all over this country, Europe and South America. And to whom would I leave it all? No children, not even a respectable nephew or niece. I've been thinking of all the good I could do right now if it were just plain old-fashioned money. I'd give some of it to Yale, and I hope you won't think I'm being patronizing, Joe, but I'd like to give a good part of it to Naples University. I think it's a fantastic thing you're going to do here. You're being a useful citizen – and I'd like to be part of it, if you don't mind. You've got the guts to dream these things up, and all I want is to go along for the ride. That's not asking too much, is it? Perhaps you could name the library for me or even one of those modern odious lab buildings.'

Joe was touched, his eyes smarting. The nice old bastid.

'But, my boy, in order to do any of that, I simply have to sell everything in sight and quickly. I want to have the fun of giving my money away and see what comes of it. Anything I spend or give away I can enjoy. Whatever I leave I've lost. I estimate I may put together as much as twenty million.'

Joe was about to question the tax wisdom of such a programme, but Cathy came in with lunch and they watched her set the table in silence. With effort she smiled at Jock's withered form and left.

'I know, it means paying three million in capital gains,' Jock said, 'but I don't give a damn about the tax. I want to *see* it. You know what I mean? That's why I'm here, Joe. And the first thing I'd like to sell is my one-third interest in Naples – shopping centre, office building, the apartment houses, the land – everything. I'd like you to buy them.' Joe realized he was staring over his soup at a man who, though speaking casually, was serious and even a bit anxious.

'Name your own price, Joe. Whatever you pay me – less the capital gain – goes to Naples University.' Jock seemed almost short of breath, so eager was he to get to the end of this road.

Joe did not know why, but pity had suddenly left him, and in some way he felt betrayed. Jock's purpose was not clear to him, but his mind filled with faint misgivings.

'Sure, Jock, if that's the way you want it. What the hell, we'll have appraisals made. Yours and mine and we'll take the average. That's probably the best way.'

'I'd just as soon not wait for appraisals, son. I'd like to finish it up in a couple of days.'

'Tell me, Jock, what the hell's the big hurry? You could give your share of Naples to the university in real estate and *they* could sell it and save you the tax. I don't get it.'

'Let's put it this way: I want certainty.'

Now Jock was no senile seventy-four. Shrivelled as he had become, he was as sharp as a cracker.

'Okay, we'll do it *your* way.'

'Thanks.'

'I should be thankin' you on behalf of Naples University.'

Joe poured him a Medoc and took a glass of Chianto himself. They clinked glasses.

'Son-of-a-bitch, you got no idea how glad I am to *see* you', Joe said suddenly. 'You know what I've been through?' And before he knew it, he was pouring out the entire story of the Senate investigation as a child pours out his troubles to his mother. He had just reached his trip to Cambridge when he realized that Jock knew all about it – listening politely, shaking his head in the right places, grimacing and squinting from time to time.

Joe paused. 'What the hell, you know all about it, don't you?'

Jock shrugged. 'Well, you know how word gets around. Paris is only six hours from here.'

'Yah.'

'But I'm fascinated to hear the details. What happened in Cambridge?'

Joe cut it short. There was now something faintly hostile in the way Jock was listening, as if he were doing so against his will.

'Now I gotta make up my mind, Jock. That's where I want your help. Do I testify and trust this bastid Poltek, or do I tell him to take a flying leap at the moon?'

'I should think there are hazards either way', Jock said warily. And Joe realized suddenly and fully, with a deep sinking of disappointment, that Jock was not there to help him.

'You are so damn right, my friend.'

'How can anyone else advise you on a question like that?' Jock said. 'I just don't know what your exposures are.'

'My exposures are the same as anyone's, Jock. Yours, everyone's.'

Jock took his wine glass and drank slowly, looking carefully across at his host. Deliberately he put it down. 'No. I don't think in my case there are any lapses that would engage the interest of the Senate, Joe. No, I'm being quite serious. I have never bribed a federal official, or made alliances with a gangster-run union, or made large political contributions. For over fifty years, I've confined myself to real estate and philanthropy, my boy. I take no special credit because I've never been obliged to engage in such activities, but I take it unkindly you should think that of me.' His voice now had a chill to it.

'Yah. Yah, I guess you're right. Why should you? You were born a millionaire. But how about your old man?'

Jock shrugged. 'My father's been gone for thirty-five years. I don't know what he may or may not have done clawing his way up. But not once during his life was there the slightest cloud on his reputation, not the smallest breath of scandal. And I should hate to think at this late stage – now, when I'm seventy-four, and, well, I won't say feeble – I'd hate to see any mud splattered on the Dennison name.' Jock leaned forward and put his hand over Joe's. For the first time there was an emotional urgency in his voice. 'You wouldn't let that happen to an old friend, would you, Joe?' Jock's voice was almost querulous, childlike.

'What the hell are you *talking* about?' Joe said. Now some irritation had crept into his voice. 'If you didn't have any whatzis – whatever you called 'em – lapses, why worry?'

'You and I are old friends', Jock whispered, and Joe saw fear in those watery eyes for the first time and he thought, this old dying man is worried about his good name, and he hasn't even got a respectable nephew to carry it. The absolutely only one who is left with the damn name is his own self at seventy-four. Oh yah, and his mother at ninety-six. Joe realized he had completely underestimated the magnitude of Jock's interest in his own self.

Jock was smiling – a death's-head smile, Joe thought. 'I know you're under all kinds of tension, my boy. It's to be expected. And I don't mean to sound holier than thou. But listen to me, we've done a lot of things together, you and I. I don't intend to hark back to the beginning, but when you asked me for money, and a million and a quarter was a tidy sum in those days, to help you build your city of Naples, there never was any question about it, was there, my boy?'

'Nope.' The son-of-a-bitch had made only five times his investment, and now he wanted thanks and praise, too. Well he wasn't getting any, not from Naples.

'I've always felt you were more than a son to me. I don't have to tell you. All I ask is that if you *do* decide to testify, couldn't you keep my name out of it? An old name, a spotless, unblemished name, Joe. That's not too much to ask, is it, Joe?'

He made a conscious effort to hide his fury. Jock was some kind of infant pulling his thumb out of his mouth and asking to be taken care of. Joe thought what a jerk I am to expect anything else! The initial shock at the reversal of their roles was wearing off. Okay, then, he had Jock Dennison on his back, too. That was okay with Joe Naples. Fortunately the old man wouldn't weigh a hell of a lot.

Jock spoke quickly, now, almost in relief to have the worst of it behind him, chit-chat, how he expected Yale to use the money he was going to give them – an applied science building and two professorships – one in engineering and one in the theatre. His talk shifted from one subject to another and Joe sat morosely and heard his friend out, trying to act as happy as a clam. The last one in the world now he'd want to know he was troubled was Jock Dennison.

As he was leaving, the old man looked genuinely sad for a fleeting instant before his eyes clouded over again and his slow lids dropped blankly. 'If there's anything I can do to help, please don't hesitate to call on me', he said, and held out his limp hand briefly. Joe was glad to get him to hell out of there.

·   ·   ·   ·   ·

Joe cleared his mind and walked jauntily into Milt's office to tell him he wanted all Jock's interest in Naples transferred to himself immediately – 'before we get into any public hearing. I more or less promised the old bastid he wouldn't be connected with me by the time I have to testify, if I ever have to'. He ignored the puzzled stares of Andy and Jeff Straley.

Milt closed his eyes. He just sat there, eyes closed. At last he mumbled, 'It's impossible. Impossible. Impossible.' He was gibbering. Twenty parcels, Jock would have some hot-shot lawyer, there'd be twenty title searches, no price. Impossible. Appraisals would take a couple of months, minimum. At last he seemed to shake himself and become comprehensible.

'Buddy boy, we have to do first things first. Monday's four days away. You may be on the witness stand a week from now. We have to get on the ball, Joe. You may never be able to make the kind of deal you want with Poltek. If not, you'll testify, and I get the feeling every time we want to go over your testimony, you're not listening. Joe, we have work to do.'

'Okay, okay', Joe said. 'First thing tomorrow. Meanwhile get all that stuff of Jock's over into my name.'

Milt's eyes were closed again. 'We have to get *ready*, Joe. Jeff and Andy and I can't do a single thing without you. Now get a decent night's sleep.' Milt spoke like a nursemaid, his voice shrill. Joe could no longer be trusted to defend himself.

He continued to wail and scold all Thursday afternoon. But to Joe the very idea of defence was poison. All he could think of was Tony, crumpled and crawling. Defence was no posture for Joe Naples.

'Soon as I get a minute, Milt. First thing tomorrow.' Every other job was more important, more immediate, more pressing than trying to recall the things he shouldn't have done in the last thirty years, every one of which he would absolutely do again today. Dimly he foresaw that if he could not win his struggle with Poltek, all these misdeeds Milt was talking about, which were nothing, absolutely nothing in the midst of all the massive working and scheming and struggling he had done to build up Naples, both man and city, would be presented to the country in black headlines out of all sensible context, and God knows what would happen to him after that. There was no way, no defence by which he could ever hope to set the record straight or put it in the right light. Milt oughta know that. Take that business in Las Vegas – one lousy day's work out of maybe a thousand hard working days and nights –

days of persuading Sal Baccio that piecework was the answer for building small houses, of buying the whole goddam timber tract in Heber Springs, Arkansas, from that hillbilly nut billionaire, of setting up the cutting mill in Louisville, of working out the prefab minutiae of the radiant coil heating system. Days of sweat, days of wretched study over microscopic details with Dino, who had struggled over them all with love and intelligence, trying to gain an eighth of an inch in the kitchen wall, squeezing in another six inches of cabinet shelf in the kitchen, or improving the design of the vanitory. I mean, Joe thought, a city does not get built by going out to Las Vegas one day and just putting Si Cutler in your pocket. What the hell is that but simply an annoying detail and one that should've been entirely unnecessary in the first place? But tell that to Sam Poltek or Senator Owens of the Justice Department.

What was the use of stewing stuff like that over in your head or trying to work out excuses with your lawyer? In the end it had to drive you off your wack. No sir. He enjoyed going over the two dormitory buildings with Dino a damn sight more, as modern as Quincy House up at Harvard, each to hold five hundred students, each with its own library and a two-shift dining-room to serve three hundred. He'd call the men's dorm Carey Naples Hall. That would be a hell of a fine monument to Carey.

Gravel Larson had all the bids on the administration building and when they racked up the figures, it looked as if eight hundred and twenty-five thousand would do it all, soup to nuts, including equipment. The dorms would probably run about two and a half million each. The larger of two classroom buildings, including a lecture hall with two hundred seats, and the three-pronged lab, its physics, chemistry and biology-zoology wings jutting out like spider legs, would probably come to around two million.

Before they invested in a stadium, he'd have to travel around and look at some of the other small colleges to see how far they ought to go. Before they could think of a stadium, they needed a gym building, pool, cage, infirmary. It was all on the Foundation report he had ordered to be made three summers ago by that team at Rutgers. Christ, time was running out on him, and there was too damn much to do. He'd put off getting the college started long enough, not doing the one thing he wanted to do, almost afraid of tackling the thing on which his dreams flourished. After all, no one from Father Ritucci to Nathan Pusey quite took him serious, but by God, he was serious. What the hell did he care about putting dough into plays or owning a piece of a ball club, or building another city, or clearing another slum? This was what they'd remember him for. Joe Naples, the kid off Ninety-eighth Street who never got past eleventh grade, Founder of Naples University. Andy was right, he looked forward to that statue of himself in front of the administration building.

Before long now he had to find a college president, and a board of trustees, people he could count on, people who wouldn't fight him at every turn. People who knew the right way to do things, who'd do it the way he wanted when it came to the pinches. But respectable guys. Jesus, all this took time, reflection, thought, calmness, discussions with people like the Harvard and Rutgers boys; but how could he be expected to do anything useful with Milt hounding him every second?

'You'd think just as a matter of self-preservation, Joe, you'd want to do your homework thoroughly. Listen to me, old buddy, you could go to the penitentiary! Have you thought about that? I don't like to cry wolf, but all week you haven't been listening. How do I get *to* you?'

'Okay, okay.'

'When, Joe?'

'Over the week-end. Okay? I'm serious.'

'I hope so. I'll be at your house at ten, with Jeff Straley, and we'll have Andy there, too.'

'Okay.'

Milt was getting to be a real pain in the ass.

He told Larson to let contracts for the administration building and Rossmore to tell the press there'd be a ground-breaking ceremony on December first. That gave the surveyors and engineers three weeks to get ready to dig. Joe felt a wild elation when he gave the instructions, as if by this simple use of words he had liberated himself from the binding restrictions of the workaday world and suddenly grown five full feet.

Nevertheless, when he left the office on Friday, he studied the painting of Carey with special concern. No telling what stuff Poltek had got hold of. But, by God, they were not dragging Carey through the mud, not Poltek, not the entire Senate of the United States. He would call at the vault first thing in the morning and get those letters. Be better to have them handy when they got to Washington, just in case.

.   .   .   .   .

By ten-thirty Saturday morning, the two attorneys and Andy had directed his attention to the case of One-eyed Gamboretta. They were speculating on the evidence Poltek might have unearthed.

'Just remember this is no trial', Milt said grimly. 'Innuendo, suspicion, background colour is all they'll want. Now tell me, when you had this conversation with Tony about getting Gamboretta off your back, was anyone else there?'

'Nope', Joe said. 'Nobody.'

'How about this bodyguard Tony always had? George Pedula, the little guy. Was he around?'

Joe could not recall.

'Where's Pedula now?'

'How the hell do I know? He's gone. Even Tony don't know what happened to him. One day he just didn't show up.'

'How long ago?'

'I dunno. Maybe five, six months ago.'

'Mmmmmm.'

Straley grimaced. 'You think maybe Poltek got to him?'

'It's a possibility we have to reckon with,' Milt said. 'Did you actually say "Get rid of him"?'

Joe blew up. 'Holy Christ, it was thirty years ago! Do you remember exactly one goddam word you said thirty years ago?'

'I – I never—' Milt started to say, then caught himself. 'Let's talk a little about Harold Brice, shall we?'

'Sure', Joe said impatiently. 'I'll talk about anyone.' Milt was trying his patience, and it was a relief to hear the phone ring. Cibulkas came to tell him it was Ev Henderson. Milt was irritated at the interruption, but the hell with *him*.

Ev sounded more remote and cautious than Joe had ever heard him. There was none of that man-to-man squareness in his voice. 'Just wanted to clear this one thing up with you', Ev said. 'Hope you don't mind my calling you at home. It seemed important.'

'What's on your mind, Ev?'

'My nephew tells me you're – ah – well, that one of the engineers over at his place is buying a house in Naples.'

'Yah? So what?'

'You know the fellow I mean, Joe. This man Howard.'

'Yah?'

'Is there anything to it?'

'What about it?' Joe said shortly.

'We're servicing a hundred million in mortgages in your town,

Joe. That's a lot of houses. I think we have a little interest in the matter. Have you given any thought to what this is going to do to property values?'

'Now, Ev,' Joe said slowly, 'what the hell are you *talkin'* about? You think one coloured family is gonna change property value in an entire *city*? There's fourteen thousand homes and two thousand apartments out here. We got ninety *thousand* people. You think four coloured people living in one lousy house —'

'I didn't say anything at all, Joe, not a word. You know it's not one family or four people I'm talking about. It's a hundred families, two or three hundred darky kids in the schools. Can you imagine what that can mean to those folks?'

'Ev, listen.' Joe was as calm as could be with this triple-distilled bastid. 'You mind your bank and I'll mind Naples. Okay? You know goddam well we signed a non-discrimination pledge for NMIA on every mortgage. What d'you expect us to do over here?'

'Sure. I know. Only checking, Joe. Just like to know what's going on. I hear there's a meeting over at one of the neighbours. I think you're going to have trouble.'

'Yah? What neighbour?'

'Fellow named Stringfield at two-o-eight Morning Glory Drive.'

'You kiddin'?'

'I'm not.'

'How'd you hear about it?'

'We have our sources, Joe.' No doubt his fine-feathered nephew, Phil Forney. 'Now look, Joe. I know the score. I know this man Howard is a good man. But I also know he has his case before the Civil Rights Commission, and you're on a spot. They've been damn decent, the Civil Rights people, so far, keeping it out of the press. If you have to let this guy buy a house, okay, you have to. But for God's sake, we don't want a stink. It can't do any of us any good. Let him come in quietly. Not that I think you have much of a chance, at that. But if there is bad publicity, I'm afraid you'll have to look elsewhere for new mortagage money. We can't go to the New York banks with merchandise that's tainted with bad feeling.'

'I see.'

'It's not my doing, Joe. I don't like to talk to you like this.'

'Sure, sure. You're brokenhearted.'

'It's way beyond me, I assure you. I have no personal feeling about Negroes.'

'I got it, Ev. I got the message. Thanks.'

'Any time, Joe.'

'By the way, what time's this guy Stringfield holding this meeting?'

'In about an hour.'

'Thanks, Ev. Maybe I'll go.'

'Why don't you do that? It's worth a try. And you'll get a first-hand feel about how the neighbours are thinking.'

The black-hearted prejudiced no-good bastid.

He'd better get on over to Morning Glory Drive. He knew just how to handle the Stringfields in this world.

In Washington Milt had reserved the presidential suite and six double rooms at the Sheraton Park, and when they arrived and stood in the lobby to register, it looked as if the Naples forces had invaded the Capital – Joe and Hetty, Andy, Dino, Mammina, Milt and Lucy, Chuck Rossmore with a legman named George Bell and a golden-haired stenographer everyone called Puss, Jeff and Daphne Straley, and an agitated Woody Faber, who, facing combat with weak knees, was barely able to remain vertical.

While Milt registered them, Joe took Hetty and Andy to look over the hotel, and from the bar they watched the ice skaters on the new rink. Joe couldn't get far enough away from Milt, who was now as mournful as a funeral.

Chuck followed, like some kind of unnecessary gnat, pleading loudly as he had done all the way down on the train, for Joe to read the press release he had prepared on Poltek. Chuck unlocked his briefcase and passed the two sheets to Joe who took it reluctantly, made a pass at reading it, and shoved it back. 'It's fine, Chuck, fine', he said absently. 'Put it away for God's sake, and watch the skaters.'

There was a young man on the ice who skated backward gracefully, laughing and talking to a pretty girl. 'Jesus, Mullaly', he started to say, then caught himself. The young man reminded him of Carey. Carey had been a hell of a skater. Hetty saw him, too, and turned away quickly.

Mammina and Dino joined them. They had brought Mammina along at Chuck's insistence. ('We don't want anyone to forget your humble beginnings, my boy.') Chuck had even tried to get him to bring Rosina, who was a teaching nun at the Convent of St. Angela, but Jesus, you had to draw the line somewhere in this world.

In the general tension at dinner up in the private dining-room of the gigantic six-room suite, George Bell was making a play for Puss and she cast back happy smiles. Two young people on the loose in a Washington hotel are almost invariably charming and hopeful; they were positively not thinking of Joe Naples, and there was a pang to that – the world had not stopped whirling to await his fate.

When finally all the feverish talk had subsided to a collective whimper, and the rest of the Naples forces had retired to their respective rooms for the night, Andy said a wistful good-night, held Joe's shoulder a moment too long, and left his father slumped glumly in a gold Louis XIV armchair.

Slowly Hetty started to undress. She gave Joe a Seconal, and he was dead asleep three minutes after his head, full of anxiety, had hit the pillow. Hetty, who had taken two Miltowns, sat up in the parlour till three, looking in on him every hour with a satisfaction she scarcely understood. She had not taken a drink since Friday, fortified by her system's new adrenalin. Joie needed caring for, and she was the girl who could damn well do it.

He was aware of her just before he fell off, for a moment only, tremulant and catlike, as though she were afraid he might do something weird, jump out of the window, which was absolutely the last thing *he* had in mind. Then the Seconal put him into a state of unconsciousness.

Suddenly from the depths of a narcotic sleep he was aware of a rattling noise at the end of the long hall. Hetty alongside him was calling, 'Joie, Joie, darling, someone's trying to get in.'

He half sat up, drugged and dull. 'Hmmm? Whozatt?'

'I don't know, darling. Someone's rattling those glass doors in the hall.'

'Well, for God's sake, let 'im in. The son-of-a-bitch, at an hour like this. What time is it anyway?'

'Four-thirty.'

'Jesus.' He dragged himself out of bed, and wearing only pyjama bottoms, stumbled from the bedroom, through the living-room, to the rattling door.

'Who the hell is it?' he called in a muffled growl.

A thin low voice said from the other side of the door, 'It's Harold Brice.'

And, by God, it absolutely was Harold, all six foot six, towering

N

in the doorway. Harold lurched into the parlour and settled raggedly into an armchair.

'It's for Christ sake four-thirty in the morning!' Joe mumbled.

Joe had never seen Harold in such condition. The Senator rose, walked to the wall, and frantically ran his hands over it like a kid looking for a trap door; he lifted down the painting over the fireplace, and in a gesture of vicious triumph, pointed to a tiny microphone hidden in its frame, and grunted. Angrily, he pulled the mike loose from its wiring. 'They think they're playing cops and robbers', he said wryly. 'I suppose we could trace this and find out who these people are, but what good would it do?' Joe was startled. Sure. Poltek would do anything.

'You better have a shot of Scotch, Senator', Joe said. He took the bottle out of Hetty's travelling liquor case, and poured a double into one of the silver shot cups. 'Here, settle down.' Harold drank it without protest.

'I've learned through the committee grapevine that Poltek is trying to tie us together', Harold Brice said.

'Well, what the hell, that's no surprise, is it, Harold? I made a big contribution to your campaign', Joe said. 'Nothin' wrong with that. How'd all the rest of these bastids in the Senate get where they are? And as far as the sewage-disposal plant goes, you and I know it was absolutely a hundred per cent. Those specs were five hundred years behind times. Lookit all the chemicals they invented since those old specs were written. I mean, what the hell have we got to worry about?'

Harold Brice poured himself another Scotch and drank it slowly. 'No. It's that business with Carey.'

Joe felt the blood leave his own face. Involuntarily he turned to the bedroom door and lowered his voice. 'I don't want Carey mixed up in this', he said, and was surprised at his own sudden hoarseness. His throat felt goddam strange.

'It isn't what *you* want,' Harold Brice said angrily, 'or what *I* want. It's what Poltek wants. He's had two men at the Pentagon for three weeks now. They've been all over it with Scotty Manfred. Through the files. He had memoranda of two phone calls I made then – God, it must have been nine years ago. I must've been an idiot. And worse than that, he has a hand-written note I sent Manfred on White House stationery.'

'Jesus, Harold, what the hell did you do a thing like that for?'

'Plain stupidity. I was a neophyte on the White House staff

and I guess we were all pretty cocky. I was so busy I scarcely had a moment to stop and think. You know it's *more* than nine years ago. There were a million things to do. I can simply not recall what I did and did not do.'

'Jesus.' Joe felt hollow in the gut. He wanted to cry. He wanted Harold Brice to go away and not remind him of his own guilt. He was only dimly aware of Harold's ironic smile.

'I don't suppose there's any point in either of us casting the first stone,' the Senator said, 'but isn't it damned amusing in a way. One gives up one's entire private life for public service, I could have made millions at Abbott and Brice, Joe, as many millions as you. But instead I wanted to be the Governor of a great state. Serve all the people, poor guys, rich guys, white, black and brown, not those Madison Avenue freaks. Two tough years in the Far East, two on the White House staff, five in the Senate. It was all satisfying work, and, I like to think, useful work. I enjoy working with ordinary people, Joe, I get a kick out of it. Then one mistake in judgment and everything ends in miscarriage. Washington's a funny place. You never know when you go to sleep at night who's going to be waving your scalp in the morning. Sometimes your closest associates. That's the air we breathe. I won't be able to run for dog catcher when Poltek finishes with me.' He spoke calmly, but with infinite sadness. 'Damned funny when you consider it, don't you think? Here I am chairman of the full committee and there's not a thing I can do about it but wait. And what makes it so utterly ridiculous is that it was nine years ago, wholly irrelevant today. It's damned funny.'

Joe snorted. 'Yah, hysterical. But nothin's gonna touch you, Harold. Here I am trying to do a few useful pieces of work my own self – slum clearance, Naples University, the new hospital wing, alla that, and absolutely the only thing they want to talk about is for God's sake who shot Gamboretta, that was *thirty* years ago, and crap like that. So you explain it to me!'

'Believe me, Joseph, the rest is nothing. They're not interested much in Gamboretta. The big thing is what you and I did for Carey. Can't you see, it reaches right into the White House. They're going to imply you tried to corrupt the *White House*.'

'Yah.' Joe recalled that visit nine years ago to see the President: he saw it in colour, vividly, his only trip to the President's office – in Blair House it was, the White House at the time was under repair. He'd gone down to Lawrenceville to arrange to get Carey

out of school; Carey was just eighteen, and Joe wanted him along.
Let the kid see some high life. The President had been damn nice
about Carey, shook hands, asked the kid a few questions. Then, one
hand on his shiny desk, he had spoken with unusual intensity. 'We
simply have to find a way to get decent housing for our coloured
people, Mr. Naples . . . I've given instructions . . . every assistance
within the limits of the law . . . I personally will thank you for anything you do . . . The country will thank you . . .'

Joe's recollections were interrupted, as he became aware oɪ
Harold Brice's urgent voice. 'So you can see how much like a
quid pro quo it does look – a deal with the Democratic party and
the Administration – oh, how the Republicans will tear into
that.'

Joe was impatient. He didn't want to think about it. Pretty soon
he'd find himself brooding over those letters. He had them with
him – and the citation – letters cold and lifeless and full of mis-
understanding. He had only tried—

'It's all a lotta goddam nonsense. You and I know there's not
one word of truth to the whole entire idea.'

Harold Brice sat silent. At last he said, without inflection or
conviction, 'Oh course. It's absurd. The United States government could never make any such deal. And in the end it didn't.'
The Senator seemed to make an effort to shake himself out of his
mental despair. 'What's more to the point, however, is whether
there's anything to be done.'

Joe took a deep breath. Funny how he'd brought Carey's letters
with him. He wanted to get off the subject, put it away. With a
supreme effort against weariness, Joe tried to sound cheerful. 'Hell,
yes,' he said, 'there's plenty to do. Let me tell you a little about
what I'm doin' about Mr. Poltek, the whiz kid. When I first laid
eyes on him, I thought to myself . . .'

He watched Harold Brice brighten as he talked. Harold took a
Scotch from time to time, and when at last he left, he felt a hell
of a lot better. There was hope. Maybe they could tear Poltek apart
before he pounced on them – pull his fangs. Whatever he said after
that, he'd be biting on his bare gums.

Although Harold was more cheerful, the hidden microphone
and the talk of Carey had left Joe unable to sleep.

Thus it was Milt, by default and almost against his own will,
who began at breakfast to take over active direction of the defence.
Joe was too numbed to make the smallest decision; Hetty even

ordered his food for him. The table for twelve seemed to him this morning to be surrounded by hostile strangers, and he was only dimly aware of Milt's grim chatter. Mammina grumbled, puzzled and distracted by everything she had seen since she arrived in Washington. 'You better itt sometin', she said to Joe. 'Go on, I brekka you neck.' Lucy just peered at her brother and made no effort to hide the anguish she felt for him.

Finally he heard Milt's instructions. 'You'd better get down to see Poltek alone. He can't possibly surrender to a delegation, if there's the slightest chance he might surrender. I'll take Jeff and Andy over to the Justice Department. We'll see if the boys over there have heard anything. You know I'd give anything to know who the number-one dragon is. Have you heard anything from Harold Brice?'

Joe sipped his coffee, looked at Hetty, whose gaze was fixed on her plate of French toast. 'Nah.'

'Don't know if that's good or bad', Milt said glumly.

'What the hell,' Joe said, 'when I finish with Poltek, the whole party will be over. *Finito*.'

Jeff Straley, who had been eating silently, cleared his throat. 'I suppose before we go,' he said, 'I should tell you that Poltek came to see us in our room about one-thirty this morning.'

Joe put his coffee down, took an Uppman from his breast pocket, uncanned it, bit into it and slowly lit the cigar. 'What the hell did *he* want?'

'He implored me, for your sake if not for his, if I had any influence with you, to urge you to accept his offer. He said otherwise his committee had derogatory information about you that could send you to the penitentiary, and although he might not be on hand to use it, his successor would. He also wanted to know what I would do in the event you decided to spill the beans about his past. Would I confirm it. Mostly I think he was appealing to Daph.'

Daphne's eyes were closed in misery.

'What'd you tell him?'

'I reminded him that he and I hadn't been friends for a long time, and at the moment I'm retained by you as counsel.'

'Good. You know where that leaves him.'

'He also wanted to know in the event you were able to work out some kind of accommodation, whether *I* would feel myself obliged to make a statement about him.'

'Yah?'

'I pointed out to him I hadn't made any up to now, but I would expect him to get out of government voluntarily.'

'Perfect', Andy said. 'God, he's a slippery little man, isn't he?'

When breakfast was over, Joe kissed Hetty and Mammina, and on the way to the Senate Office Building in the black chauffeur-driven Cadillac, he dropped Milt, Andy and Jeff at the Justice Department on Twelfth Street and rode in ducal splendour to the Constitution and First Avenue corner of the Senate Office Building. On the way down the cold stairs to the basement, he was conscious of the sound of his own footsteps. He padded through the empty hall to Poltek's office.

Sam Poltek sat like an uneasy fowl behind his littered desk, in his littered office, his eyes feverish and his tell-tale body odour more noticeable than usual. He jumped up when Joe came into his office, his sallow face impassive. Jerking a thumb, he gestured for Joe to sit. For a moment, they eyed each other, fighting cocks across the table.

'Mr. Naples,' Poltek said, leaning back in his armchair, 'I s'pose you've had plenty of time to think everything through. So, p'raps, have I. Are we going to be able to deal with each other?'

Joe blew a smoke ring and tried to settle into one of those awful wooden government chairs. In the end, he had to sit on the edge of it. 'Young fella,' he said slowly, 'I'm nearly fifty-three years old. I don't know a hell of a lot about Washington. Outside the NMIA offices, I'm a babe in the woods. I tell you one thing. I don't like this being under investigation one bit. Not one goddam bit. Oh, at first it was kind of a lark. Not a funny one, but different, you know. I absolutely like to get into all different kinds of things. I always kinda liked testifying before Senate committees before as an expert, but this, you can cut me outa this crap. You want to know what I made up my mind to do? I'm glad to tell you. I don't want to be a witness before this wacked up sub-committee. Not for one second. I don't want to get up there and even give my name, rank and serial number, because once a guy's up there, when he's under attack, you never know. One of these crazy bastid Senators could start askin' stupid questions. You know? You can't guarantee what he might say. Right? And God knows what I might say back. So here's what I suggest. Joe Naples don't testify. And Joe Naples leaves Sam Poltek alone. Period. But if Joe Naples has to testify, you know damn well the absolutely first thing he will testify to. Right? You can be goddamn sure of *that*. He will object to being questioned by a man who once said that he was resigning his membership in the Communist Party in order to do even *better* work for the boys in the Kremlin. You will not only get outa the government, you'll have to clear outa the country. You're in bad shape, son. Is my position clear?'

Poltek was perspiring freely. 'My questions, believe me, Mr. Naples, would be innocuous—'

'No, sir. No sale.'

Sam Poltek rose. 'I suppose you know what you're doing, Naples. You behave as though I were trying to sell you a bill of goods.'

'Maybe you didn't hear me so good. If you got the brains God gave you, you'll do it my way.'

'You're staying at the Sheraton Park?'

'Yop. In the presidential suite.'

'I'll have to think over what you've said. You'll hear from me before the day is out.'

Joe found himself in the hall before he realized it. As he stepped into the dark hall, there was an unexpected and blinding flash full in his face. When Joe's eyes refocused he saw a slender man with a camera running like a goat down the hall, up the stairs, and out into the street.

Thirty

JOE rattled around the six-room presidential suite with Dino and the women, waiting for Milt, Andy and Jeff to return from Justice. Mammina's hovering over him trying to get him to eat something, and Hetty's watching him like a worried swan, not taking her eyes off him, made him jittery.

Lucy and Daphne kept themselves busy in the kitchen supervising the hotel staff preparing lunch.

When he could stand this nonsense no longer, he finally called Chuck Rossmore to come up with his two sidekicks and get his statement on Poltek ready for the papers, because he surely now had the feeling that Poltek had turned him down. He took Chuck, George Bell and Puss, the golden-girl stenographer, into one of the sunrooms, and they sat around on the fussy French furniture trying to pretty up Rossmore's statement on Poltek. Although he had seen it twice, he had never really read it with his mind open, but now he did it.

'I think it's too goddam furious,' he said finally. 'Let's speak more in sorrow. We absolutely gotta be in the right. We're *sorry* this lousy Communist insect worked his way around security right into the Justice Department and then got on this important sub-committee. But it's all part of their technique. We *sympathize* with the Senators who were bamboozled. What these international hoods wanna do is blacken the reputations of any man like Joe Naples who's done a few decent things for the working people. Because there is nothing the Communists want to do more than get ridda the guys who give the people cars, refrigerators, cheap electricity, gas, and decent houses to live in. They hate these guys like poison. Get some stuff like that into it. Make it sound a little more like some kinda statesman talkin'.'

'I like that, Joe.'

For an hour and a half they wrote and rewrote the statement

until Joe was satisfied. Puss was still typing it when Milt, Andy and Jeff returned.

As Milt pulled his coat off in the foyer, Joe thought he had never seen him quite so dejected. Slowly they trailed into the large living-room. They could hear Puss's typewriter going in the sunroom and Chuck's booming voice making corrections.

'Lookit,' Joe said to Hetty hastily, 'why don't you take Mammina and the girls down to Garfinkel's and maybe buy a few good bargains? Dino, look after them. Take the car', Joe said. Dino was happy to go. Hanging around was too gloomy.

'It's serious', Milt said, as soon as the women had left. 'I'm afraid we're number one all right. And, of course, they're out after Si and Harold, too. Nothing like killing birds with stones.'

He settled uneasily into one of the gold chairs, while Andy and Jeff decoated glumly. 'We met a friend of Jeff's over at Justice', Milt said. 'Fred Corrozza. He was quite frank. Poltek's been sending a lot of his material over there, and they're actually preparing a case. In fact, they think they've got a good one. Say, by the way, did you pay Si Cutler's hotel bill in Vegas?'

Joe tried to remember. 'I might've', Joe said. 'When I checked out, I was feeling pretty good – you know, Si winning all that dough and making his connection with Anna. Hell, I musta figured why not make it a clean sweep.'

Milt and Andy exchanged worried glances. 'Well,' Milt said, 'that's one of our worries. They're after us under Title Eighteen, Section 201 of the United States Code, which prohibits giving federal officials anything of value in order merely to influence their decisions. Even to get them to make a good decision. You see? It's a three-year maximum and/or some kind of fine. The Department plans to have a man at our hearings. He's already been assigned.'

'Why, that son-of-a-bitch!' Joe fumed. 'Offering me a deal, and all the time he's nailing me with the Justice Department?'

'I never put much credence in that make-a-deal gambit', Milt said mildly.

'We'll break his goddam back is what', Joe said.

'That I believe you'll do. Yes. I believe you will—'

'Imagine that guy!'

'The only thing is I'd hate to see them attack the tax-free status of the Foundation.'

'How are they gonna do that? The Foundation's absolutely clean, isn't it?'

'We've tried, Joe buddy, we've sure tried, believe thou me. But you never can be sure.'

Milt infuriated him. He could accept almost any development as being reasonably possible. Any question about the Foundation was unthinkable.

'What can they do to the Foundation?' Joe shouted hoarsely, but Milt only shrugged.

'Who knows? They could attack its tax-free status on the grounds that our original deal when we sold the first section to the Foundation was a tax-avoidance subterfuge.'

'Any one tries to get funny with the Foundation better watch himself', Joe said ominously.

'I think you ought to know these things', Milt said.

'Well, I'm not gonna worry. That little Poltek bastid is gonna crumble up like a Uneeda biscuit', Joe said.

'I'd like to think so', Milt said sadly.

At three-thirty, the women returned, and at ten minutes to four, Joe had his jolting answer from Poltek. A stoop-shouldered old man claiming to have a message for Mr. Naples knocked at the glass door.

'Yah? Come in. Yah, I'm Joe Naples.'

'Here you are, sir.'

The old man handed him a blue covered document and shuffled down the hall back towards the lift.

Joseph Naples, Respondent, is summoned to appear as a witness at a public hearing of the Sub-committee on Government Assisted Private Enterprise of the Government Underwriting Committee of the United States Senate. Failure to appear at the time and place indicated may be punishable . . .

It was signed by Senator Owens. Thursday morning at ten a.m. in the United States Senate Hearing Room 12. Joe read the first few lines and handed it to Milt, who looked at it in silent gloom. Andy got up to read it over Milt's shoulder.

'What iss it?' Rossmore shrieked.

'Subpoena', Andy said quietly.

'Well' – Milt's voice was shaken for the first time, more with anger than with worry – 'we have until Thursday morning. By then Sam Poltek has to be destroyed, blow by blow, bit by bit, piece by piece. At least *now* we know what we're doing. The son-of-a-bitch.'

Milt's high pitch was vindictive, warming for the first time to the challenge. He was bitter simply because Joe had not got his own way. Neither of them was accustomed to that, and although Joe had not recovered from the sight of that subpoena, he was somewhat cheered by Milt's new and uncustomary aggressiveness. To Joe's look of surprise, his old friend said, 'Well, I'm fully engaged now, old buddy, *believe thou me*. Don't expect me to be dispassionate and carefully balanced from now on. Washington's a rough place and we're gonna have to play some dirty pool.'

'I'll order some wine', Hetty said.

Joe knew he had stopped dominating events. His wife was tending him as if he were a helpless patient; Milt, Andy, and a total stranger named Jeff Straley were already whispering among themselves about the next steps to be taken. Dimly he was aware that Chuck Rossmore was nodding his approval over the final draft of the release Puss had just finished typing, and he was handing several copies to George Bell. 'Get these to the wire services and all the Washington papers right away. Maybe we can still make the late issues today. If they want to talk to Joe, we'll be here all night.'

But Poltek had beaten them to it. At four-thirty, the phones in the suite started to ring. Two reporters were downstairs to see Mr. Naples. Chuck met them at the door. oozing affability. 'Come in, come in fellowss. Make yourselfss comfortable. Here, Puss, hang these coats up for the boys.'

The two men, one excitable, ugly and stocky, the other a stoop-shouldered pipe smoker, were non-committal. The short one showed Joe and Milt the early-afternoon editions of the *Post*. There was Sam Poltek holding an armful of files. Alongside was a photo of Joe taken that morning hurrying out of the Senate Office Building. A three-column head said, 'SENATE SUB-COMMITTEE COUNSEL RESIGNS'; and the subhead said, 'CHARGES ATTEMPT AT WHITEWASH OF NATION'S LEADING HOME BUILDER'.

The article, under a byline, ran for two columns, an eager reporter's good deed for the day:

Pacing restlessly behind his desk this morning in his basement office in the Senate Office Building, Samuel Poltek, youthful counsel for the Senate Sub-committee on Government Assisted Private Enterprise (GAPE), only recently recruited for his job from the Justice Department, angrily denounced

unnamed senators and 'other persons in high places' for exerting
pressure, both overt and indirect, which he implied threatened to
halt the sub-committee's investigation of Joseph Naples, one of
the nation's leading home builders. Mr. Poltek called it an
attempted whitewash.

Mr. Poltek revealed that he had submitted his resignation as
counsel to the sub-committee in a telephone call to Senator
Richard Owens, this morning. 'Threats have been made,' he
said, 'to smear me personally and rather than embarrass the sub-
committee in an irrelevant and pointless controversy about my
person, which could frustrate the work of the sub-committee, I
have resigned my post on the sub-committee and am turning all
records over to the sub-committee chairman this afternoon with
an urgent request that he appoint new counsel as soon as practic-
able to insure the success of the work of the sub-committee. I felt
that my usefulness as counsel had come to an end when I received
threats from a senator to expose an alleged youthful indiscretion
of mine, when his real purpose is to conceal from public view the
sickening pile of unethical and illegal activities and corruption
which the sub-committee counsel and the staff have uncovered
here.'

Senator Harold Brice is known to have had political support
from Mr. Naples in his successful gubernatorial campaign in New
Jersey's senate seat. Mr. Poltek refused to say if Senator Brice
was one of those who had 'exerted pressure'. When pressed to
reveal the exact nature of the alleged unethical and illegal activities, Mr. Poltek told this reporter, 'the list was too long', but that
everything was 'here in the files'. Senator Owens could not be
reached for comment. His office reported that he was 'not in the
building'.

Mr. Poltek did say as he waved a sheaf of papers at this reporter, 'Our committee's findings are that Mr. Naples has probably engaged in every form of bribery there is, both on a petty
and grand scale; he has resorted to the procurement of a well-
known screen star, female, a national sex symbol, for a government official for immoral purposes. At one time, he even
attempted to corrupt the White House itself in the pursuit of his
personal objectives. This man, who has amassed a huge fortune
with the assistance he received from the United States government through the National Mortgage Insurance Agency, has
given us the Jerry-built city in New Jersey that bears his name.

We have in our files literally thousands of letters of complaint from purchasers of those homes, letters taken from Naples' own files. After using public assistance to make huge profits, this man then contrived a method, the legality of which has already been questioned by some authorities at Internal Revenue, enabling him to keep almost all of these profits under his personal supervision, without paying a cent of taxes, by using the device of a so-called charitable trust in which he is the sole trustee, and with whose funds he has speculated without restraint in Wall Street. Now he is attempting to appear as a public benefactor by distributing this money to private charities, and by building monuments to himself. If ever there was a clear case of private self-aggrandizement and enrichment through the abuse of a government public-assistance programme, then this is such a case, and I might add, far from the only case. The sub-committee and the Senate must examine these programmes and the entrepreneurs who have benefited from them and decide whether the continuation of such programmes under present methods is in the public interest.'

Mr. Poltek refused to say what he meant by his reference to an attempt to 'corrupt the White House', or under which administration the alleged attempt took place.

There was no question in Joe's mind, this guy was a dangerous Red. Lookit the Red phrases and words. Here in one interview Poltek had cast doubt on the Senate, the White House, private builders, the NMIA, and all forms of public assistance. He had made private charity a dirty word and linked it with Wall Street. No question the guy was a craftsman.

Stanley Fullmer's syndicated column, if somewhat obfuscated by the columnist's turgid style, carried the same message as the news story. Joe had become the target of opportunity. Poltek had let loose the termites, to eat sawdust out of every sound institution in the nation.

Milt, of course, could not see it that way at all. Even Andy was sceptical, but Jeff Straley remarked quietly that Sam Poltek was a dedicated man who had managed to do more for his distorted cause by getting his bark in first than he could have by remaining on as counsel for the sub-committee. Now the fat was afire, and before the flames died down, no one could predict who would be seared and who would survive.

Chuck Rossmore uttered a low curse and had Puss give the two reporters copies of the statement they had just prepared.

After a few moments of reading, the stocky man looked up. 'You're charging that Poltek not only was a Communist, but that in effect he still is', he said, wrinkling his forehead in his first show of surprise.

'Yah', Joe said. 'That happens to be my opinion.'

'Just that he's behaving according to a pattern he laid down for himself fifteen years ago when he formally quit the party', Milt said hastily. 'We do not claim that he is at present a member of the party nor that he has been for some years.'

'You better get that straight,' Joe said with a grin, "cause we're dealing with the laws of slander and libel here, and I don't want Mr. Poltek suing me.' The effort of will he needed to produce that grin he could feel in his stomach.

There were other reporters after that, before dinner and after dinner; the phone never stopped ringing; they camped outside the glass doors; Joe must have told the same story twenty times until it became monotonous and he decided they all ought to take in a film. 'Tomorrow and Wednesday, Milt, we'll really do a job. You lawyers can lay down the law for me all day. I got two completely free days.'

Next morning on the floor of the Senate, Harold Brice yielded to his old friend Arthur McLean, the junior Senator and a member of the GAPE sub-committee, for remarks on Poltek's resignation and press conference and Joe's public statement which had appeared on the front pages of the morning papers.

'I want merely to call the attention of the Senate at this time to the principal purpose of the GAPE sub-committee whose authorization and appropriation I supported, and on which I have the privilege of serving. It's altogether proper that we should direct our attention to the question of whether government assistance in various fields is being furnished to persons and firms whose code of conducting their business or their personal lives is or is not beyond reproach. People who depend on assistance from the federal government have to be cleaner, if anything, than those who do not ask for such help. They must be like Caesar's wife. We must by appropriate legislation and by administrative procedures take the necessary action to cut off from government assistance the shysters, the five percenters, the unconscionable profiteers, the men with criminal records, the tinhorns and the chisellers – whether this government assistance is provided by the Small Business Administration, the Department of Agriculture, the National Mortgage Insurance Agency, the Maritime Commission, or whatever.

'At the same time, we would do well to ask ourselves if we want to use this forum to attack without justification the very men who have made substantial contributions to the well-being of the nation, who have, if I may say so without exaggeration, helped make this nation great: The men who have built our homes and ships, and have grown our food. I think of a man like Joseph Naples of New Jersey, who in his lifetime has built or is about to build modern homes and apartments for one-third of a million people, equal to the entire population of the great states of Nevada and Alaska. We have all seen how difficult it is to obtain fine men from private life who are willing to bear the political and personal attacks which are part of serving in government itself. But must the men who are doing a fine job in the private sector of the economy also bear these whips and scorns? Especially when we have reason to believe that these attacks come from a quarter that is, to say the least, surely not motivated by any desire to do this nation any good. I thank the Senator for his courtesy.'

The afternoon papers carried a story, including these senatorial remarks as an afterthought, under the heading: CHAIRMAN SUMMONS SUB-COMMITTEE COUNSEL TO EXECUTIVE SESSION. Joe's prepared statement had surely put the skids on Poltek. At least the country would be rid of that pipsqueak Communist.

These were straws of comfort to which Joe clung, but as Milt said, the remarks were only Harold Brice's way of trying to create a more favourable atmosphere and letting the Naples forces know that in Arthur McLean they had a friend on the GAPE sub-committee to whom they could appeal when the going got rough. Nothing more than that.

Later in the afternoon the sub-committee met in caucus, and reporters outside heard name-calling and shouting as Mr. Poltek apparently took broadside the full wrath of five enraged Senators, who felt they had been betrayed and made fools of. While Poltek did a bit of shouting on his own, it was leaked later, for the most part he played the martyred crusader for truth and justice, and apparently did not flatly deny that he had once held a card in the Communist party. His resignation was accepted, he later told a correspondent for the *St. Louis Post Dispatch* and the man from the *Times*, but not before he had warned the five senators with 'all the seriousness at my command' that ' I would feel it my duty, if the sub-committee cannot come to grips with the material we have assembled on Mr. Naples, Mr. Cutler and Senator Brice, I would feel it my duty to see that the information gets to the public. The public has a right to be informed, but I would be presumptuous in interfering with the investigative process in the United States Senate'. Mr. Poltek closed his interview with the men from the *Post-Dispatch* and the *Times* as soon as they began to ask him probing questions about his own past with the observation, 'That's a matter that can only be categorized as diversionary. What happens to me is not important. Let's not lose our focus. I'm not the one who is under investigation'.

'You will be', the man from the *Post-Dispatch* said acidly.

Joe could scarcely help admiring the weasel. He was ready to flush himself down the nearest drain if it would help eat away at the foundation of American life. Those wacked-up Kamikaze pilots from Japan had nothing on boys like Sam Poltek.

Milt thought it might be a month or more before the sub-committee's new counsel, assuming he were to be appointed at once, could even come to grips with the accumulated evidence. They might just as well go home and let Harold Brice do what in-fighting he could. Andy had to get back to Cambridge anyhow, and so did Jeff. Dino had contracts to let for the administration building. The redevelopment agency chairmen in St. Louis and Philadelphia were becoming restive about delays. Quietly the Naples forces retired from the presidential suite, the issue still much in doubt, and took a full car on the Congressional back to Trenton; by nightfall they were back on Easy Street, getting a big grin from Cibulkas at the front door.

While Andy and Jeff Straley did get back to Cambridge and Dino managed to let the excavating and concrete contracts for the administration building, it was next to impossible for Joe to do anything constructive under this black thunderhead. Two mayors called him to find out what was going on in Washington and what repercussions the hearings would have on their budding and fragile political careers. A scandal-riddled sponsor in a redevelopment project would rub off political poison on everyone. Joe finally gave up talking to all these hyenas. Instead, he visited Si Cutler regularly each morning, spent the afternoons on the apartment job, and in the evenings he and Hetty, who was all sympathetic vibration these days (she never took more than two drinks before dinner), went to a film or got into bed early. It was not a happy time.

When the hearings finally were recalled, in early December, Mammina refused to go back. 'What I'm a gonna do in a Washington? Sitta on my fanny alla day. I waita and I waita and I waita. I no unnerstan' one-a word. Nobody say hello, nobody say notting. I'm justa sitta like-a some kinda statue. I'm-a-*feel* like-a statue. What-a you nidda me for?'

Daphne Straley had no interest in going back either, and Chuck Rossmore dispensed with both his assistants. As for Milt, he was as low in spirit as he ever had been. He did not even bother to respond to Joe's self-cheering comments. Lately his old friend was not even friendly. The Naples forces now were a streamlined, but not happy delegation. The carnival spirit had evaporated.

Thirty-one

THE first person called to testify at the public hearing was to be Anna Landos. The hearing room was brilliant with film klieg lights; photographers were everywhere, but live television had been prohibited.

The new counsel for the sub-committee was a tall, broad, young Californian, with oversized features in a face scarred by several pocks. He had a cheerful leonine face topped with a flowing head of auburn hair, and when he spoke his voice boomed like doomsday. If Sam Poltek had been a weasel, Jonathan Morse was a young and vigorous lion, a Pasadena lawyer who had been Senator Owen's campaign manager and, according to the word, able, tireless, and politically ambitious – which is to say without pity.

Although none of the senators had taken their places at the semi-circular table on the high platform, in the ancient high-ceilinged hearing room, Jonathan Morse sat there shuffling papers in hurried scrutiny. He looked up briefly when Joe came in with Andy, Milt and Jeff Straley, then went back to his papers. Joe was surprised at the size of the crowd. He had testified himself years ago on amendments to the National Housing Acts, but there had never been more than a dozen people in the room. Now they were packed to the window sills. Film cameras were grinding. Two dozen photographers on one side or another flashed away at him as he and Hetty entered the chamber.

They had been sitting almost half an hour when, surrounded by a small knot of photographers, Anna Landos floated in, her hair high in imperial style, brighter red than usual and set off by a white mink stole which fell carelessly from her shoulders. She wore a red wool sheath and matching shoes. Anna smiled to her public, then saw Joe. 'My darling Major!' she called. She shook herself loose from her lawyer, and walked quickly to greet him. 'I'm so sorry, believe me, so sorry, but what can I do? I am a prisoner.'

'Don't use that word.'

Joe tried to smile, but much as he hated giving her the satisfaction, he could feel the cold whiteness in his face. 'Sure, kiddy. You can't help it. You always were a kinda wacky cucaracha.'

'My poor darling', she sighed, touched his arm briefly, smiled, nodded coolly at Hetty and walked to the witness chair, still shaking her head.

Joe saw other faces in the crowd. Many were familiar, sure, Cathy O'Neill's, Curly and Emily di Robert's, Sal Baccio's, a hundred he recognized, but none that he knew. It was the first time the thought occurred to Joe: that although he knew the facts about a hell of a lot of people, he didn't know a one of them. Though years ago he had lain in hotel rooms with Cathy's naked body, he had not the first foggy idea what she liked or wanted. He should have learned more about his own son Andy. Hell, he'd had the chance since the day the kid was born. Milt – Milt seethed under all that calmness, but what was he seething about? Hetty – he oughta know Hetty after thirty years with her, he sure should. But just when he thought he had her pegged, she changed in his face.

What brought them all here? Why weren't they working? Watch 'em feed the monkey in the zoo. Well, he was not gonna be any monkey in any zoo. They would see the same old confident Joe Naples they all depended on.

The five Senators came in, singly, smiling or sombre, shaking hands, waving. The proceedings were neither judicial, nor quite carnival. The skinny guy with the long bald head, cadaverous cheeks, thin lips, was Senator Owens, and the heavy-set, white-haired man was McLean. The other three Senators – Batterson, Gann, and Westlake, were men Joe knew by reputation. At last they were seated, and Anna Landos, her attorney, Lloyd Harris, beside her, was accompanied by the clerk to the witness chair in the well below the high table. Senator Owens pounded the gavel for several minutes.

'Will the photographers please finish taking their pictures and clear this area here. Please clear the area.'

After relative silence was achieved and the flashbulbs subsided, the witness was sworn, her 'I do' rustling with perfumed red. Clearing his throat, the chief counsel began to address his mike.

'We have only a few questions for you, Miss Landos', Jonathan Morse intoned. 'You told us in executive session that you met Joseph Naples in the town of Bellanza. Can you tell us how you came to this country?'

The austere Senators seemed to amuse her. She spoke with animation as if she enjoyed the telling. As she talked, the audience tittered, and she smiled happily, exaggerating the comic aspects of her trip. Even Senator Owens grinned as she described her uniform on the C-47. 'It was so large and baggy that you could not tell if I was a man, woman or child. I could hardly see out of it.'

'And this,' Senator McLean said genially, 'even though it was not strictly speaking legal, and I assume the statute of limitations has run, this was the way Mr. Naples helped to rescue you from the theatre of war and bring you to this country?'

'I would think you would be for ever in his debt', Senator Owens added promptly.

'Oh, I am, Senator. I owe him everything.'

As cameramen continued to swarm like locusts, pleased with her power she cheerfully answered all questions about Las Vegas. Yes, she had become quite friendly with Simon Cutler in Las Vegas. Her infection was significant. Her attorney could see no legitimate interest on the part of the Senate in this matter, but if they were interested, she had nothing to hide. Yes, Mr. Naples had introduced her to Mr. Cutler. No, it was not a blind date. He had merely introduced them after one of her shows. Had Mr. Naples suggested that she 'be accommodating' to Mr. Cutler? Anna Landos's eyes flashed with anger. She could not remember anything like that. Yes, Mr. Naples did say that Mr. Cutler was an old friend. Any friend of Mr. Naples was a friend of Anna Landos. Had he said Mr. Cutler's good will was important to him in his business? She could not really remember. Business was something she did not bother her head about. She was a singer and an actress.

'And a very good one if I may say so', Senator Owens added with gallantry.

In her attention to Mr. Cutler, was she in any way obliging or attempting to please Mr. Naples?

Anna smiled and speaking like a contented cat, said, 'I always please myself. But I think we were all very happy.'

Did she give Mr. Cutler any money from Mr. Naples?

Yes, she recalled dimly. A loan of some kind. In an envelope.

How much?

She did not remember. It was a long time ago and she did not count the money. It was in an envelope. Why did the Senators not ask Mr. Naples or Mr. Cutler? They would probably remember much better. But as she recalled, it was a small sum. Perhaps a few thousand, five or ten. Much less than she made in a week. She did, however, under the prodding of the Committee Counsel recall Si's winning streak and in the end gave a fairly accurate account of the evening. 'Oh, my, yes, my poor Simon was terribly upset when Mr. Naples tried to pull him away from the craps table.' And she described how Si had repaid Joe's loan.

Senator Owens said, 'Thank you. You may step down, Miss Landos.' And the photographers went back into flashing action. 'As a fellow Californian, may I express the appreciation of the sub-committee for your full co-operation.'

'You are very kind, Senator.' Anna Landos smiled the way she had smiled in Las Vegas at Si Cutler. Followed by her attorney, she floated from the chamber, but not before she had thrown a last kiss to Joe. Joe wondered vaguely if she would be back when he testified, to watch his neck wrung like a chicken's.

The second witness was someone Joe had never expected to see again – George Pedula, who testified briefly. He had, he said, for years been the bodyguard and companion of Tony Ferrara, the 'greatest underwoild figure in Joisey'. Over the years George had been at many meetings between Tony and Joe and had driven them about together. 'They was old friends since kids. Mr. Ferrara would do just about anyting for Mr. Naples.'

Could Mr. Pedula recall any specific favour Ferrara had done for Mr. Naples in 1927 in Allenburg?

'Oh, sure. Tony took over the local masons' union in Allenburg and gave it to Mr. Naples.'

How, Senator Batterson asked, does one man give a local union to another?

'Senator, this is back in 1927 and for all I know maybe they're still doing it. They had this man, One-eyed Gamboretta, ran the local union in them days, and I guess he was making troubles for Mr. Naples, because one night I drive Mr. Naples and Mr. Ferrara to this speak —'

'A speak?' young Jonathan Morse asked.

'Yeah, Senator, a speakeasy. I guess maybe that was before your time.' Laughter and the chairman's gavel.

'I am not a Senator', Jonathan Morse said hastily.

'Anyhow, whatever you are, like I say, I sit at the next table and I'm not nosey, but when they get through talkin', Tony says I should send for Hutch. Well, when we send for Hutch, that means

someone's gonna get hit. And three days later One-eyed Gamboretta is hit.'

'Hit? You mean murdered?'

'Well, in those days there was a lot of that, Senator. People
kinda expected it.'

'What ever happened to this man Hutch?'

'Oh, he passed on, Senator, many years ago.'

'Violently?'

'That I don't know. I wasn't there. Usually them guys didn't put
up much of a fight, but *maybe* he was violent.'

'Isn't it dangerous for you to be talking this way, Mr. Pedula?'
Senator Owens asked, almost gently.

'I don't think so. Tony Ferrara is through. He's poison since
Hendrickson. Nobody'll touch him. He got a bad name. Not a bad
guy, either. But that's the way the cookie crumbles.'

George Pedula described in monosyllabic simplicity that meeting
long ago at which Sal Baccio had been named trustee of Allenburg
Mason's Local 812. 'Tony ran the whole show. Yeah, the meetin'.
Nah, he wasn't no mason, but anyone tried askin' questions, he got
his brains beat out and kicked downstairs.'

Simon Cutler's testimony, the chairman announced, was deferred
because of Mr. Cutler's illness, until some date in the future when
the sub-committee's medical consultants were satisfied that he could
testify. The next witness before the sub-committee would be Joseph
Naples, but his testimony was put off one day to give the Senators
an opportunity to vote on the Foreign Aid appropriation.

Joe had been briefed to the ears, and if he followed the advice
of his attorneys, there was now almost nothing he could or would
say. He was to invoke the Fifth Amendment on damn near every
subject. He had listened all week to Jeff Straley and Milt with
miserable submissiveness. Was it, as Milt musta said ten million
times, a matter of survival?

From midnight until four in the morning before he was to testify
Joe paced the parlour of the presidential suite. Twice Hetty called
in to him to come to bed. 'Joie, darling, you really must get some
rest.'

'Okay, okay. Be right in.' Instead, at four o'clock that morning,
he sat down at the fussy Louis XIV writing desk and on Sheraton
Park stationery he began to write longhand, an act that ordinarily
was as impossible for him as advanced calculus. He wrote furiously,
without stopping, until his hand and wrist ached. He wrote until

seven o'clock, took a cold shower, dressed again, and went down to breakfast with Milt, Andy, Jeff and Chuck Rossmore. But he did not mention a word of what he had written. By ten, they were back in the Senate hearing chamber waiting for the proceedings to resume. 'You have your copy of our opening statement?' Milt asked nervously for the millionth time, referring to the carefully drawn statement the lawyers had produced. Joe nodded.

The photographers and the lights no longer bothered Joe. He knew what he had to do now and to hell with it. He found, in fact, that he was anxious to get started.

At last Senator Owens struck the gavel. Joe faced the arc of five Senators above him, and Milt, Jeff Straley, and Andy moved their chairs on either side closer to him and slightly behind. He turned long enough to see Hetty in the front row of spectator seats and winked confidently at her. She smiled back, almost without hope, it seemed to him, but with the kind of expression he hadn't seen on her face in God knows how many years.

Counsel: Will the witness please state his full name?

Naples: You mean the name I was baptized? Giuseppe Angelo Garibaldi Carmine Napoli. Isn't that a duzie of a handle? Right now my name is plain Joseph Naples.

Counsel: And your residence, sir?

Naples: Naples, New Jersey.

Counsel: Mr. Naples, during the last fifteen years how many homes and apartments have you built?

Naples: Oh, I dunno, maybe forty-five thousand.

Counsel: And during this period how much did you or your companies receive in the way of government underwriting – NMIA mortgage insurance or VA guarantees?

Naples: Maybe two hundred million. Maybe more.

Counsel: Now in order for you, as a private entrepreneur, to qualify for this government assistance – and I might say massive assistance it was – did you file anything with any government agency as to your past history – whether you had ever engaged in corrupt practices, whether you had ever been indicted, convicted, imprisoned, or anything like that? Now I'm not implying any of these things, you understand; all I want

	to know is whether the government inquired into anything like that?
Naples:	No, sir.
Counsel:	And to your knowledge did any agency of the Federal Government ever make any independent inquiry of that nature about you?
Naples:	Nope. I'm sure I woulda heard about it.
Chairman:	Do you have a statement you wish to present to the sub-committee at this time?
Naples:	Yes, sir, I do have a statement to make, Senator, but I'd like to make it my own self. I think just putting it in the record takes all the feel out of it.
Senator Owens:	Is it an extensive one?
Naples:	Not very long, no, sir. It might take me a little while to read the thing out loud.

(When Joe took out his hand-written papers Milt jumped out of his seat, put his hand over the mike, tugged at Joe's sleeve, trying to whisper to him, but Joe ignored him and carefully kept the statement beyond his lawyer's reading range.)

Counsel:	Well, perhaps we ought to put it in the record and get on with some of the questions. I know I would like very much to learn a few specific things here and I'm sure the Senators —
Naples:	Mr. Chairman, I'm going to be here probably most of the day, and maybe tomorrow, too, and maybe the next day, if I understand it right. Certainly —
Senator McLean:	Oh there's no great harm in it. Let him read it. But let's get on with it. I for one will not mind if you read your statement, Mr. Naples.
Senator Owens:	Go ahead.

Joe took out the black-rimmed glasses that made him look like some kind of professor, and adjusted them carefully. Frantically Milt handed him his own copy of the freshly typed, carefully prepared disclaimer the three lawyers had composed. Joe took it, impatiently folded it and shoved it into his side pocket. Slowly he held his handwritten statement up, looked through the pages briefly.

'I sure hope I can read my own handwriting. It's awful.' He ignored Milt's hand on his sleeve and all the agitation he sensed behind him, and began to read.

'It's a privilege to have this opportunity to address this sub-committee. I've testified before two Senate sub-committees of Government Underwriting before in connection with housing legislation. My opinion as an expert was asked because the Naples organization has built a lot of housing, maybe more than any other builder in the entire country. But today I understand you're not interested in my opinions as an expert. I gather I'm in the dock this time. Other witnesses have testified publicly or in executive sessions about me, and the question as I understand it is: Am I or is anyone like me fit to receive government assistance, such as that given by NMIA or the Maritime Board or any other government agency? Now my attorney here advises me your entire inquiry in his opinion is absolutely unconstitutional, and for all I know he may be right. I'm not a lawyer. He's advised me not to answer any one of your questions, which he claims have no valid legislative function.' Joe looked up. 'Did I put that all right, Milt? He's nodding yes. Well, that's his legal opinion; he's my chief lawyer and normally I like to take the advice my lawyers give me. But not here or anywhere else am I going to conduct myself like some kind of defendant. I'll answer any question you want to ask. But before that I only want to say this much:

'First, I have a couple of complaints to lodge here as a citizen. The Counsel originally selected by your sub-committee and acting for it was a man who was dedicated to the destruction of our American way of life. He used to be a hard-core Communist and, although he may not be a member of the party right now, he certainly acts like one, and we have a witness here who will tell you that when Sam Poltek resigned from the party, he promised his comrades in the good old cell back in Boston that he would be working for the Cause out here in the legitimate world. Now as a citizen, I protest against any work of our government being put in such hands. And most of all, I object to personally being put on the defensive by such a character. Why, do you know my room at the Sheraton Park was wired? We found a little mike hidden over the fireplace; you would have thought we were in Soviet Russia. I'd like to get all that in the record first.

'I'd also like to say a little something about this sub-committee's work. You men here are doing your jobs. No question about it.

Now, the reason you're here in the first place is not merely because the people elected you to the United States Senate. No, sir. You're here, every last one of you, because you wanted to be. Nobody told you to run for the Senate. You went out and fought for these jobs and it took you all your lives to get them, and now you're here and you're doing your jobs the best you can. I hope nothing is going to stop you. Well, with the greatest respect I'd like you to keep in mind that I have my job to do, too. Nobody told *me* to do it. I thought of it myself and decided I wanted to build houses, the best-designed houses for the lowest price money could buy in this entire country. And after a few years, I wasn't satisfied with building just a few houses. I wanted to build whole cities, full of clean, modern houses with community swimming pools and new schools and churches and hospitals and ball fields and golf courses and tennis courts and a railway station and shopping centres and a little air-port and a fine new university, and once I got *that* idea into my head about the job *I* wanted to do, nothing was gonna stop me, any more than anything is gonna stop you men.

'I have a friend who divides the world as follows: useful citizens and others. I think I've been a useful citizen so far, but it hasn't been easy. No, sir. I remember when I ran a town in military government in Italy and my executive officer was telling me one day he couldn't do this or that because it wasn't authorized by the manual, and I said, "Captain, we're always running high hurdles. You've gotta get over the hurdles somehow."

'Nowadays we've got three ways the people in this world can get what they need. One, we can let the government do the entire job, like Russia does, or two, we can let private industry do the whole job. The first nobody wants. The second won't work in the housing business, any more than it works in lots of other businesses – utilities, farming, radio, shipping, airlines, railways, and whatnot. So, here in this country, we've found this third road, the middle way, and that's the method whereby private industries do the job and the government assists or regulates or co-operates in some way. Naturally that makes things a little complex.

'We have created a funny kinda conflict. You got men like me who want to get the job done. We like profits, sure, that's number one, but we also have a big picture in our minds of what we want to do, and we're not patient men. We want to get the job done. The men in government we have to work with, and this goes for state and city governments, too, they're in no hurry whatsoever. I'm not talkin' about the men on top. I mean the middle crowd – no special vision, just doing their job every day. And they don't want to make mistakes or stick their necks out. Now, I'm not saying they don't do a conscientious job by their lights. They work hard, they work all kinds of hours. But sometimes they hold people like me back. We're in a hurry, but they get so bogged down, they get suspicious about our motives, they can't tell the good guys from the bad guys. What happens? They block the path of progress. And there are hundreds of thousands of these men everywhere.

'Do you know, in New York City right now it takes four or five months to get a set of plans approved? Plans that comply in each and every respect. Well, builders can't wait for such nonsense. So the builder pays off to get action. In New York City, eighty per cent of the men in the building department turned out to be takers. You want plans approved, you want a C.O., you pay, otherwise nothin' happens for months. We don't have time to fight City Hall. And that's not just in New York. You can take my word for it, it's everywhere.

'I was just a kid when my father started taking me down to construction jobs where he used to lay brick. He was an Italian immigrant without too much education, but he was a pretty smart man. One time he said to me, "Pepe, I tell you what makes the wheels go round. Graft." Well, that was a pretty crude way of putting it, and it's not what you'd wanta print in any book for little school kids. But this is the United States Senate and that is the fact of life, and lots of people know it, so someone might as well say it right out loud to you men up here.

'Well, I don't call it graft, but I've come around to believe that pretty near everything we do is worked out on a certain basis. *Gotta* be. That's natural law. Call it Naples' law: You do something for me, I'll do something for you. Even the most absolutely elemental drive in the human animal, sex, say. What are men and women saying to each other? You do something for me and I'll do something for you. Boom. Boom. Pleasure for pleasure. Think about it. In fact, it's truer than the Golden Rule. It's not what *oughta* happen between people, it's what happens. No one knows it better than you gentlemen. You're all politicians. Boss and his workers, man and his wife, Senator and his voters. What is it? The absolutely same whatzis wherever you look. Boom for boom. Naples' law.

'You're the conscience of the country, alla that stuff, but you're never gonna legislate Naples' law out of existence. Not in a million years.

'I can tell you plainly my organization sends out maybe four hundred Christmas presents every year – all the way from a bottle of Scotch to television sets. We send perfume to the girls, transistor radios, gift certificates, all kinds of junk. Costs us maybe ten thousand dollars each Christmas, and we figure it's well worth it.

'Now a lotta these people are working for the government and the government pays 'em, but not enough. I advocate higher salaries for government employees. If you're working for your country, you gotta be living halfway decent. So this is kind of a gesture on our part you might say. I feel sorry for these people, even the girls – they're good. It's a crying shame, and I'm glad to have this opportunity to make a pitch for higher salaries for these people so guys like me won't *have* to send 'em presents at Christmas.

'That's one thing. Then the trouble gets worse with your income-tax set-up. We got an item of deduction called T and E. Travel and Entertainment. So what do we see? Yachts, aeroplanes, gold clubs, credit cards, all the rest. And who's being entertained? Buyers in the big stores, purchasing agents, little guys and big guys at G.E. or A.T.&T. or General Motors. Well, those are all big companies with hundreds a thousands of little stockholders, so entertaining to get people to do something they wouldn't do if they weren't entertained is kinda corruption, too, and graft and all the rest. Every time someone takes a T-and-E deduction, all the taxpayers and all the stockholders are paying for it. What's the difference between entertaining the purchasing agent for General Motors who's buying parts for a tank, and entertaining some colonel in the Corps of Engineers who's buying the entire tank? If T and E is legitimate, then where does legitimacy stop? Maybe you men oughta give that a little more thought. Maybe a little legislation might help right there, I don't know.

'Now let's get down to cases and the NMIA. You give a local office any special or new idea and oh my, everything has to clear through Washington. It's so slow it's painful. It's unnecessary. Now it happens I had a big vision. I wanted to build a whole city. The first brand-new city in America after the war. Well, what do I find? I find a man in Washington whom I'd known for thirty years, an old friend. I helped get his first job in 1935 at the NMIA in Trenton. A man with the best intentions in the world. A man with a big job in Washington, a job where you *need* vision. He

couldn't see building a whole city at once. Well, I don't blame him.
It hadn't been done before. So I tried to make him see that the
government had to gamble a little on this. But he didn't want to
stick his neck out. It was right after the war, it was a time for big
thinking and this friend of mine who was NMIA project director
just wasn't a big man. He asked my advice about some job in Las
Vegas that I had absolutely nothing to do with. I told him Las Vegas
was growing fast. The boys were coming home from service.
They had to have a decent place to live. I told him my advice was
to go ahead in Las Vegas. Take a chance. I explained to him, in my
own case, if I built a city in New Jersey, six thousand houses at one
clip, my costs would then be twenty per cent less than if I went slow.
I could sell houses under eight thousand dollars or rent them for
eighty dollars a month instead of a hundred. I even went to meet
him in Las Vegas and one night I showed him at the craps table how
if you gambled big you could win. If you played safe, you could
only lose. I absolutely persuaded him, and we built the city. And I
turned out to be too conservative. We could have built ten thousand in our first group. The government didn't lose a dime. People
got houses for twenty per cent less. I made money. It was as simple
as that.

'I know you men want to ask me questions and I want to answer
them, but you'll always find the same simple idea, if I maybe did
something you'd take issue with, it was so I could do my job better
and faster. I'm not a reformer, gentlemen. I'm a builder. I tell you
plainly, I've paid inspectors, state officials, all kinds of people,
entertained them, kidded them along, wined 'em and dined 'em,
took 'em on fishing trips, got dates for them. I've done the same
thing with the unions. I did it with small fry and big fry, whoever
had his finger in the dike to block my progress. And I've got absolutely nothing I want to apologize for. I didn't make the system.
You men made it right here in the Congress – the entire idea of
co-operation between private enterprise and government agencies.
It's a good idea and all I do is try to make it work. Anyone who
works with the men in government is bound to run into some little
guys who are scared, or a few who deliberately hold things up
in order to make some builder cough up. And you have to cope
with them somehow. Each time some jerk gets sticky you can't
come running to the international headquarters of a big union or
the state Attorney-General or the Justice Department here, or the
President of the United States. You just won't get anywhere that

way. Half the time law enforcement agencies are in cahoots with these fellas.

'But now you've got this committee. That's good news. I'm glad. It's an opportunity. Here, for the first time, someone can tell the entire story if you let him. I say that's good. But you have to give a man a little help. I'll come back to that later.

'Now I've got one other thing to say. These men with the frightened little minds are usually nice decent people. They stick to their wives, bring up their kids. You couldn't meet a nicer bunch. They're underpaid, they work ridiculously long hours and they get practically no satisfaction out of their jobs. They're the people I run into, and I try to treat them like my own men or my own family. I try to help them out. I try to make life a little better for them. So sometimes the two fit together. The wheels go round. They're happier. Things get done.

'That's the straight story. I'm not gonna try to kid any sub-committee of the United States Senate. This is going on all over, just about everywhere in every business where government and private business work together, although all I know about myself is the housing business. Still, don't we do a great job? We turn out about a million and a half houses a year. My guess is maybe there are a few hundred thousand strictly illegal acts go into those houses every year. This committee is never gonna stop it altogether. Even while I'm sitting here talkin' in the spotlight today with all these cameras on me and a hundred reporters in this room, somewhere around this country *today*, this very hour, dozens of men are paying off or taking public officials to lunch or on boat rides or fixing up their houses or getting them girls or God only knows what. This investigation isn't going to stop it, but it might slow it down and I'm all for that. Any laws you think may help, I'm all for them. I wanna help, that's the kinda guy I happen to be. But if I tell you the entire story, I have to ask you to do one thing for me. You oughta give me immunity from prosecution so I can speak freely without worrying if I'm getting myself into some kinda legal whammy. You got the right to do that under Title Twenty-Eight, Section 3486–A. Otherwise, I stand on my record. I don't think this is a time that calls for modesty. Since 1927 my company's housed three hundred thousand people and nobody we've dealt with, including the people who maybe took those so-called favours, has ever done anything or approved anything that in the end wasn't good for the country. Okay, Mr. Chairman, you want to ask questions, give me just that one little thing and then fire away, as long as we've got the rules of the game set up right.'

All five Senators were in motion. Senator McLean was whispering to Senator Owens, one hand over the mike. Even the hefty counsel kept shaking his head as if to reorganize his mind. But it was only when Joe turned to Milt that he saw total astonishment. Milt's face was white, his hand trembled. 'Mr. Chairman, Mr. Chairman', he was calling, his voice high pitched and quavering.

'Counsellor?'

'May I ask the sub-committee for a brief recess to enable me to consult my client?'

'If the witness so wishes. In any case, the committee will need time to consider the witness's request, and perhaps later to consult with the full committee.'

'Fine', Joe said. 'I don't mind. What's on your mind, Milt?'

Milt rose unsteadily. He was, Joe observed, not only off balance, but angrier than he had ever seen him. Milt, Joe, Andy, Jeff and Chuck Rossmore walked into the corridor and down to the ancient grey-marbled men's room, while Milt sought desperately to control his own trembling. They stood in a little knot beside the urinals.

'Goddam it, Joe . . . what do you think you're doing?'

Joe was easy for the first time since the investigation had started, unworried, and confident. 'I'm doing exactly what you shoulda told me to do in the first place', Joe said. 'Why the hell else do I pay for all this high-priced legal talent?'

Milt's reaction was as violent as he had ever seen. A suppressed, thin-lipped sneer took possession of his face. 'I just can't discuss it', he said at last, with great effort.

'I don't think we ought to get all excited', Jeff Straley said calmly. 'We're not going to have to go back in there to testify for a while. It'll take them two days at least to consult with the full committee.'

'Too late', Milt said, and he seemed almost to be wailing. 'Too late. If they grant him immunity, then he goes in there and spills his guts. We all agreed that if you just refused to answer anything, the chances were ninety-nine out of a hundred you'd be okay. Why get into all this?'

'I'm not gonna refuse to answer questions. What'm I, some kinda criminal? Why should I have to take a chance on going to the pokey for a year or maybe three? You gonna sit in the pokey for me, Milt? I'm takin' *absolutely* no chances. Excuse me. I gotta take a leak.'

'This sets him off as altogether a much better guy', Chuck Rossmore said admiringly. 'Men, I think he's doing just the right thing. I do, Joe. Victim of circumstance. Caught up in a vicious system. I think it's a good jumping-off point.'

'Sure,' Joe said over his shoulder, 'a victim, that's exactly what the hell I am.'

Andy looked first at his father, then at Milt, and dropped his head in confusion.

'I can't discuss it', Milt said, white. 'Let's get back in there.'

The sub-committee filed back from the caucus room within a few minutes, and Senator Owens conferred with his colleagues in last-minute whispers, his hand over the mike, as they settled in. McLean nodded, and the Senators sat back.

'I have to tell the witness that the sub-committee will refer his request to the full committee for action. If there is nothing more the witness or counsel for the witness have for us now, this hearing will stand in recess until ten a.m. Thursday.'

Thirty-two

HAVING taken the step, Joe was impatient. He wanted to get it over with. He did not want to listen to lectures from Milt, Jeff Straley, Andy or even gloating from Chuck Rossmore, who was delighted with what he had done. He wished Chuck would shut up. Chuck's ecstasy was unlimited. The number of columns he would get from the press services, the coverage he would get in the news and picture magazines! 'I bet we get another full page in *Time*. You'll be a hero, Joe. Man on a white horse. Look what you are doing! You are slaying the dragon single-handed. Who is the dragon? Shortsightedness among those bureaucrats, corruption in the unions, petty graft all over the place. You will expose it all. And after showing up a Communist in a sensitive spot in the government! Why, you'll be the greatest guy since Howard Hughes came down here and went up the Hill and knocked off Senator Brewster.' Chuck Rossmore's enthusiasm bored him.

Milt's white anger, however, began to get under his skin – his brother-in-law was unrecognizable. Back at the hotel he was as unpleasant as a man could get, sulking grimly, totally unresponsive. Joe asked him what the hell he was stewing about, but Milt only scowled and shrugged. 'Not a damn thing', he mumbled, and looked significantly at Hetty, who was, however, unresponsive. She mixed drinks and seemed neither to know nor to care about any problem. She simply never left Joe's side.

An hour after they got back to the suite, a call came from Harold Brice. The full committee was meeting in an hour. He had just heard of Joe's position from Senator Owens, and he wondered what Joe intended.

'Why, Harold, I'm surprised you ask me a thing like that. I'm just gonna tell the committee whatever they wanna know. You know me, Harold. I like to be co-operative. Always did.'

'What about Si Cutler?' Harold Brice said, somewhat forlornly.

'What *about* him? *I* don't think Si Cutler did anything so god-dam terrible. It's up to the sub-committee. If they think different or the Attorney-General doesn't like it, well, I'm not gonna tell them *their* business. But personally, I wouldn't worry about it.'

'I see.' Harold's voice took on a flat coldness. 'And the episode involving Carey?'

Joe thought a moment. 'Now, Harold, I don't wanna talk about that. You can keep Carey outa this thing. It's not even relevant. I'm counting on you, Harold.' He could not quite keep the anger out of his voice.

'Joe, be sensible. You know there are two Republicans on the sub-committee who'd like nothing better than to get my scalp.'

'Yah? Well, I thought you boys all belonged to the same club. The way I hear it, it's kinda the most exclusive club in the world.'

'Assume for a moment I can't stop these questions.'

'What the hell do you expect? You want me to perjure myself? You're not suggesting something like that, are you?'

'No.' Harold Brice was quiet now.

'They've got all the goods. That bastid Poltek. You shoulda kept him the hell outa there. All you can do now is get McLean to put his foot down on funny questions.'

'I'll do what I can', Harold Brice said.

The story of Joe's bid for immunity was broadcast by CBS at three o'clock, and before nightfall, there were a dozen calls from Trenton NMIA, from Jock Dennison, from union delegates, from guys on the redevelopment commissions, all pleading one way or another to be kept out of the hearings, some just to safeguard their local reputations, others because they were afraid of criminal legal action or of losing their jobs. Joe explained patiently to each of them that he was only trying to help this wacked-up Senate sub-committee, and he was pretty goddam sure their names would never come up. Si Cutler did not call, probably because he couldn't from the hospital, and Joe was glad of that, because he really did not want to talk to Si and get him all excited, especially considering Si was still goddam sick in a hospital bed. Worrying about this wouldn't do his heart one bit of good.

Phone calls came also from other builders: Ferber in Los Angeles, Morgenfall in Chicago, Korner in Cleveland – all guys he had met at those useless meetings of the American Home Builders Association, and they wanted to know if maybe Joe was out of his head.

'If you spill your guts, Joe, you'll be crucified', Korner said. 'The boys are going to be good and sore.'

'We'll see', Joe said.

Ferber thought Joe might have the right idea. 'Those bastards have held us up for years. Let's clean house, I say.'

Through the phone calls, Milt sat brooding, silent, drinking the Martinis Hetty mixed for him. By seven o'clock, he must've had a dozen or maybe thirteen and, although his eyesight was not too clear, his mind seemed to be focusing brilliantly.

At last Joe hung up on his last call from a thoroughly hysterical Piggy Banks in Trenton, told the hotel operator he wanted no more calls for the night, and turned his attention to Woody Faber, who had sat, separated from the rest, silent and trembling in one of the two small sunrooms, spasmodically looking over ledger books, making notations on a yellow accounting pad, and trying not to listen to the phone calls.

'Woody, you understand what we're doin' now? Anything the committee wants to know, we tell 'em.'

'If that's the way you want it, Joe.' Woody's voice quavered. 'I suppose I ought to expect them to ask me a few – ah – personal questions. You know, about my own record.'

'You got nothing to be ashamed of. You tell 'em you paid your debt to society. You got off the track, you did a little time, okay the slate's clean. Everything you did for *me*, you did because I told you to do it. You ain't been looting the company treasury, Woody, have you, like some of these nuts you read about?' Joe laughed and Woody tried to laugh.

'You know me, Joe. I'd never have the courage.'

'I think you're right about that', Joe said. He left Woody still studying his ledgers in the sunroom and returned to the parlour. 'Now, Milt, what in the hell is eating *you*?'

Milt looked up at him through bloodshot eyes. 'You don't need *me* any more, buddy. Here's old Jeff Straley. Good lawyer. He'll handle the case jus' dandy, b'lieve thou me. You don't need l'il old Milt. *No* sir!' Milt started up from the couch, staggered, almost slipped back, until Joe took his elbow, helped him to his feet.

'Come in here.' He led Milt to the bedroom as the others watched in silence. He closed the door behind them carefully, quietly.

'Lie down, Milt, you'll feel better.'

'Lie down? In the same room as you, ol' buddy? Oh, no, no, no. I'm perf'c'ly okay. I'll jus' *sit* here, if you don' mind.'

'Okay. Now what the hell is *your* problem?'

'Ol' buddy, you're no ol' buddy of mine, not from this day forth, no sir. I don' wanna be self-righteous, b'lieve thou me, I don't. But y'know, I wouldn't trade three of you and two utility outfielders for one Tony Ferrara. Y'know I had no *idea* what Tony was yapping about that day we all landed in ol' Mount Sinai Hospital when we were kids, after Tony took on The Blade. Boy, those were the days! He said you were – what was it? – an untrustworthy bastid, Joe, an', by golly, that's pr'cisely, *gzactly* what you *are*. Oh, I sure can see what he meant, all right, all right. Pusillanimous is the word for Napoli.'

'What the hell are you *talkin'* about? I absolutely don't understand that kinda talk. Everytime I hadda do anything to get the job done, way back in the days when Gamboretta put that first bite on me, *you* were the guy for fightin' it out if it took all summer. Call the cops, sure, call anyone, but never give in. Only there wasn't a goddam soul to tell. Now we got the mighty Senate of the United States waitin' to hear the entire story, beggin' to hear it, and now you say, tell 'em nothin'. I mean, you are *contrary*, Milton.'

Milt lowered his head, studied the floor, and his jaws worked as though he were trying to capture the words. 'It's different', he managed. 'Entirely different.'

'How?' Joe bellowed. 'You were the guy wanted to make Si Cutler the number-one dragon, remember *that*?'

Milt raised his head and stared at Joe for fully sixty seconds. 'I can't discuss it', he said, his voice shaking. 'I can't dis—'

'You kill me', Joe said.

'Joe, buddy – *former* buddy, that is. I admire you. Yes, I do. I admire the bejesus out of you, but I don't admire myself for it worth a damn. So why don't we jus' forget it, and you go on up to the little ol' sub-committee on Thursday an' tell 'em what a hero you are an' how you're gonna clean out corruption. You do that. I never thought you were going to be the knight on the white charger, but by golly you are! Sure, you won't wan' menshun the guy who foun' you the Woodman estate, an' wrote you to hurry back from Italy, ol' buddy, or gave you the notion of goin' in the brick business in the firs' place, 'r the idea for the Foundation to save the tre*men* — dous corporate tax, or who ran the seven million in there up to thirty-one million five hun'red thousan'. Hah?

Nah, what d'you wanna tell 'em all *that*. You might just'z well be the sole, solitary genius on white stallion. I don' *mind* that. I don't *mind* all those years gettin' a living, as long as you felt like doling it out to me. But a bad living at that, was it? No sir, *I* don' mind. My fault much as yours. But Joe, what are you doin' to the *other* guys that helped you? Sure, they're not perfec', but *you're* the one made the goin'. Si Cutler, the poor bastard, Piggy Banks, Sal Baccio, Harold Brice . . . All those fellows *helped* you. Do you know what you are *doin*?'

'Not a damn thing is going to happen to any of 'em', Joe said coldly.

'Oh, sure, sure. Listen, ol' former buddy, get yourself another boy, willya? Be a nice fella, willya? Some other boy with a strong stomach. I'm goin' back to Newark an' defend our old buddy, Tony Ferrara, who was an honest crook. He needs me. He's in trouble.'

Joe felt a wild frustration. It was not animal fear, but it had the same effect. He could scarcely understand what he was doing himself or why. He only knew that whatever was wrong between Milt and himself had to be made right at once. He needed Milt. Everything could be lost if he lost Milt. Words would never do the trick any more. He opened the bedroom door.

"Ey, Woody, c'mere. Bring me my personal chequebook.'

Woody rummaged around and brought the large black book.

'Gimme one a those blank cheques. You gotta pen? What's the date today?'

He wrote furiously. *Pay to the order of Milton Jason. Two hundred fifty thousand dollars and no cents. $250,000.00 Joseph Naples.* The signature scrawl was as illegible as ever.

'Here.' He shoved the cheque at Milt. 'That ain't compensation, that's a straight gift. I don't expect it to make any difference, but you can probably use it. Be my lawyer, don't be my lawyer, suit your own self. I'll pay the gift tax on it, too, goddammit, so it's free and clear. Woody, you make a note a that for next year's return, got it?'

Milt looked at the cheque a long time, trying desperately to think about it. It was equal to all the money Milt had made and spent in the last eight years.

'Okay, Woody, beat it', Joe grunted; and Woody Faber scurried off like a squirrel, back to the sunroom, and returned to pawing his ledger books.

Slowly Milt frowned. Then he closed his eyes, and Joe thought, be a goddam shame to see a man like Milt cry – and for what? A lousy quarter of a million bucks. Milt was entitled to it. Suddenly he felt kind of broken up about it, deeply sentimental. I shoulda thought of it years ago, Joe thought. Milt has been a tower of strength all these years.

Milt shook his head, trying to clear it of the dozen Martinis and the confusion which was about to engulf him.

At last he spoke slowly, and so faintly Joe had trouble hearing him. 'I'm going to keep this, ol' buddy. I look at this li'l piece of paper, an' I think to myself, Lucy an' I can use it. Our girls can use it. Anyway, I've earned it.. Call it anything you want – gift, charity – *I* know I earned it. *You* know it. An' so help me, I've let you do me all the favours I can stand. I 'cept your offer, ol' former buddy. An' thanks for everything. Now go find yourself another boy for *this* case. Jeff Straley'll do jus' fine for you, believe thou me. If I go back to that office from now on, we won't be kiddin' each other.'

Slowly Milt talked on, tears of distress in his eyes. 'Deep down you're a good guy, Joey, I'm convinced of it, but you know what the trouble is? You humiliate me. My entire life is one tremendous humiliation. Oh, not something everyone knew, not out in the open, no, no. Not visible so anyone sees it. Jus' between us. *You* know it, and *I* know it. We're the ones. Like the way you talk to Woody. Hop to it, boy. Beat it, Woody.'

'Why you trying to compare yourself to Woody? My God, you're not on the same planet.'

'Ain' so different, Joey. R'member our very first deal for Dennison, the A & P job? I thought we were partners an' you jus' said, "You're gettin' seventy-five bucks a week!" R'member that time? Humiliation. I knew it. You knew it. 'At's a deep eroder, Joey.

'An' that God-awful, *terrible* house on Elm Street, Lord. Even the day we went to Marge the Barge's. Tellin' me who I could screw an' who I couldn't. I mean that is *humiliation*!'

Joe was speechless. In Milt's present condition it was senseless to talk to him.

'Listen to me, oh Great White Father. You don' unnerstan' me, do you? You don' unnerstan' anyone. You don't hear me so good, do ya? Nah! You spread humiliation like a soothing balm. 'S your speciality. Ask your wife. Oh, sure, you see everyone's needs. Sure, sure, but that's completely altogether different . . .'

'Are you crazy? You don't hear *me* so good, Milt. I understand 'em all! Every goddam one of 'em. That's one thing I do good. Kings and brickies, one and all. If I can't do one other thing, I absolutely know what makes 'em all tick. An' all I try to do is help out.'

'Sure, sure. Okay, Joey. Have it your way.'

'Ah, now Milt. Milton.' His voice pleaded, but his heart hardened and hurt at the same moment. He thought coldly, you do me wrong. My old friend, you do me goddam wrong. I loved you like a brother, I dunno if I ever will again, but that I did. You wanted my sister, okay I got you my sister, even if you were a Jewish boy; hell, my mother woulda thrown you out on your ear. Sure, sure . . . For Christ sake, I supported you through law school, and I'm your biggest client. You *live* offa me. You and your wife and your two daughters *live* offa me. I'm the roots and you're branches up there, alla you guys. You get your water from me and now you're talkin' to me absolutely as if I was from some entirely different universe. Milton, Milton. I'm in trouble. Can't you see I'm in trouble? What in the goddam hell is the *matter* with you? Where is your *loyalty*, brother?

He felt his own eyes smarting, but took care that Milt did not notice. Milt would figure it was phony.

Milt was studying the cheque again, lugubriously. 'Yep, I'm gonna keep it. 'S overdue. 'Cause the way you loved me, Joe, a hell of a lot of cash had to be thrown into the deal. On the other han', let's be fair. Fair's fair. 'S not all your fault. Can't have a padrone without plenty o' peasants, can you? An' tha's us, all right, all right – craven, dependent, miserable *contadini*.

'Well, I sure hope I'll be able to make a living without ol' Joe Naples. What the hell, why not? I'm fifty-two years old. I'm responsible citizen. I prob'ly know my job better 'n any man this country. Expert in NMIA, red'velopment, charitable trusts.' He was whistling in the dark. 'Wouldn't you say I was all that an' more, ol' former buddy?'

'You better be back in the office', Joe said.

'Maybe so. There mus' be more where this came from, eh Joe? What the hell is a quarter of a million bucks to Joe Naples? More dough than Milt Jason could ever hope to keep after taxes, right? Buy and sell, that's you. But not Milt Jason you don't, not this time.'

Milt rose, as if he were in some kinda ridiculous trance. 'See you around, fella. Who knows, maybe I will be back in the office jus' for the hell of it. But regardless, come over and visit your sister and me any ol' time. Luce an' I'll always be at home to you and Hetty. Equal to equal. No one'll ever know what's happen between us. 'Cept you an' me, ol' former buddy. We'll just say you changed counsel. Now *you* try humiliation on for size. And 'bout this investigashun. You haven't got a thing to worry about. You're gonna do great. *Great.*'

He left Joe in the bedroom, said a gentle good-night to Hetty, told Jeff Straley to carry on, and as for himself, he had to get back to New Jersey for a pressing hearing involving Tony Ferrara.

Not until Milt had been gone two full days and the hearings were resumed, did Joe abandon thinking he would show again. It was the damnedest, most mysterious display Joe had encountered in his entire life. Eventually he'd have to get Milt back. Well, sufficient unto the day. He had Lucy going for him, a million attached strings that could never be disentangled. He needed Milt. Milt needed him. Naples' law. He'd have to work something out first chance he got.

Long before Joe was officially notified, Harold Brice called to say the full committee had voted unanimously to recommend to the Senate to grant him the immunity he had requested. 'Now for God's sake,' Harold said, 'be discreet, will you?' The Senate wanted to hear and the country wanted to hear the truth from the horse's mouth.

Thirty-three

So it happened that by the time Joe Naples testified publicly before the GAPE sub-committee, neither he nor the sub-committee had the counsel each had started with; he was testifying
as a friendly witness instead of a hostile one in a fine effort to help
the sub-committee get to the bottom of some practices of corruption and chicanery in the matter of government assistance to
private enterprise, particularly in the housing business.

To the surprise of nobody, Senator Owens reopened the hearings
of his sub-committee with the announcement that because of the
special knowledge and experience of the witness, and the value of
that knowledge to the sub-committee, the full committee had under
Title Twenty-eight of the United States Code granted the witness
immunity from Federal and State prosecution on matters about
which he was to be asked to testify. This action had been taken,
Senator Owens announced, in the public interest.

Joe was relieved that Jeff Straley was emotionally uninvolved in
the hearing. His advice to Joe, largely technical, evidenced little
if any interest in any of the ridiculous ethical or moral problems
which preoccupied Milt, and that was a blessing.

Although Committee Counsel Jonathan Morse treated Joe with
a leonine caution that was not quite acute suspicion, the lines
within the sub-committee were drawn during the first ten minutes
of testimony. It became clear that Senators Owens, McLean and
Batterson, all Democrats, considered Joe Naples a co-operative
witness to be coddled, if not treated with respect; while Orville
Gann and particularly Potter Westlake, both Republicans, addressed
their questions to him like smiling barracudas.

'I am informed, Mr. Naples,' the silver-tongued Senator Westlake began with sonorous affability, 'that in order to obtain National
Mortgage Insurance Agency insurance, sponsors are required to sign
a pledge not to discriminate in the sale or rental of housing on
account of race, creed or colour. This is a solemn pledge made by

builders in order to induce the government to grant its assistance. Can you tell me whether, to your knowledge, this solemn pledge is more honoured in the breach than in the observance, and can you tell me how you yourself have observed it?'

Joe spoke slowly, a performance which took effort, but this first hostile question gave him a sense of unbounded elation. This would set the atmosphere for the hearing.

'Senator, that's a pretty sharp question, I gotta hand it to you. Yes sir, the pledge you are talking about sure is honoured more in the breach. It gets lip service pure and simple. But you can't put the blame on us. We're people like anyone else. There are plenty of ways for the Congress to tie builders to a policy of absolutely one hundred per cent non-discrimination if you want to do it, but you got a lotta southern gentlemen here and every time that old question comes up, you men know the story better than I do. A few Senators from the South just won't have a non-discrimination clause with teeth in it. The people over at NMIA understand that. So do the builders. It's an open secret. So I wouldn't want to make it sound like some kinda moral lapse, as if builders don't observe their solemn pledges and stuff like that, no sir! The trouble is it's all make-believe in the first place.

'Now you ask about me personally. I can tell you recently we had a fine coloured family wanted to move into Naples. One of the finest families you'd ever want to meet, but this is no simple thing. Our mortgagees have threatened to cut off our supply of mortgage funds. We've had all kinds of pressure. Just the same, I and my wife and my sister and a few men in our organization, plus every priest, rabbi and minister in town made it our business to go around house by house like Fuller Brush men telling everyone living within four or five blocks, one by one, what was happening and why, and how important it was and that it was the right thing to do. That's the important thing you have to keep in mind. It's the right thing to do. It took quite a bit of work and thought, and I hadda go to one meeting where I personally guaranteed to make up any loss any of 'em had when they come to resell their houses – that's eighty families I made that deal with. It wasn't easy, no sir, but we did it. That Negro family moved in. There hasn't been one single peep about it in the papers. The neighbours had 'em in to tea. The kids play together an' go to school together. In fact, this is the first public announcement anyone has made about this family, even though their neighbours know all about it.

Its America in action instead of words. I don't want to pat myself on the back, but I say we're proud to be the ones to take the first step.'

Senator Gann peered over his reading glasses at his colleagues, surprise clearly on his features. 'Didn't you tell Mr. Poltek when he came up to Naples that you had no Negro families living in Naples?'

'Did I?' Joe said. 'Well, I might have at that. I never trusted Mr. Poltek. In fact, I'm surprised anyone ever trusted that man.' Let 'em dig that barb out of their hides. 'And if I remember correctly, at the time I talked to Poltek, this family hadn't moved in yet. We were just taking the preliminary steps.'

'You didn't establish your policy of integration because of this investigation, did you Mr. Naples?'

'I didn't do *anything whatsoever* because of this investigation, Senator. The Naples operations, my whole life is an open book. I've got nothing whatsoever to hide.'

Everyone settled back rather comfortably, Joe thought, except the two Republican Senators. From now on Joe had the feeling that they would ask only questions to which they already knew the answers.

The two days of testimony that followed absolutely annoyed the hell outa Joe. It was not the bit on Gamboretta over which they skipped lightly because it was so long ago, but what bothered him most was that he did not like to cause this kind of trouble for his old friends. All he wanted to do was help the sub-committee. He had exactly the information the Senators were looking for; it would absolutely never have been the right thing to hold back. You cannot clean up a mess without a few people getting hurt. Anyhow, it would blow over after a few weeks. If not, well, *Ecco la vita*. All these guys musta known what they were doing when they did it. Men horse around, they gotta pay the consequences.

Nevertheless, he was sore as a boil over the way some of the papers reported his testimony. His description of a few harmless week-end fishing trips at Tom's River when he took Piggy Banks and the boys from Trenton NMIA for bluefish and tuna were made to look like something savage indeed. Did he pay for everything? Well, who else woulda paid? He couldn't seem to get across to these young reporters who were scarcely dry in the diapers how absolutely harmless they'd been. A few guys getting together for a couple of days of fun and fishing. My God, was that *corruption*?

He felt a little insulted, because it made him look like some kinda tightwad. Nevertheless the NMIA Commissioner and the Civil Service Commission promptly announced jointly that a full-scale departmental investigation of the entire Trenton NMIA office was already under way.

Then there was his testimony on Si Cutler. That was difficult. He went to great lengths to mention all the trouble Si was having in those days, trying to get up some sympathy for the poor bastid.

'I mean, this man was under heavy pressure. He had this wife, one of the nicest ladies you'd ever want to meet, and she was suffering from multiple sclerosis, getting a little worse every day. Dying by inches you might say. Terrible thing to live with. Hard to picture it, and more expensive than anything you can think of – hospitals, doctors, special therapy, the entire works. Simon Cutler spent every dime he had on this great woman, but you never heard him complain. Not once. She died, and he was a widower . . . a widower.' He repeated this incantation to pity. 'And all this time he was trying to do an important job for NMIA. You couldn't *help* being sorry for the guy . . . Right now I'm sure the committee knows he's in the hospital with a coronary thrombosis. He's had two attacks, and I don't think this investigation has helped him much. This is a man who is followed by trouble. And he is an old friend; Si and I know each other almost thirty-five years. Why he once gave me this fine watch. Lookit this inscription . . .'' He tried to make as much as possible out of the watch. 'Well, he met me in Las Vegas, I got it right here—' He consulted his book of notes. 'March 18, 1947, according to my records . . .'

'Will you tell the sub-committee exactly what happened out there?' Counsel and the five Senators leaned forward almost imperceptibly.

'Well, when I got out there, who do I find is singing at the Sands Hotel but my old friend Anna Landos . . .'

Yet when the story appeared in the *Washington News*, it completely ignored every point Joe had tried to build up for Si, and blared, 'SENATORS HEAR ABOUT UNIQUE FOUR-HOUR LOAN. BUILDER CHARGES PAYOLA AND GLAMOUR INFLUENCED NMIA.'

The following day the NMIA Commissioner announced that Simon Cutler had been temporarily relieved of his responsibilities, pending the findings of departmental and Civil Service hearings. The Treasury Department said it would investigate whether

federal income taxes had been paid by Mr. Cutler on his gambling
winnings in 1947. Poor old Si was a dead pigeon. Well, Joe would
try to find some spot for old Si when it all blew over. Assuming Si
ever got up outa bed.

On the second day, the Republican Senators made a point of
Joe's relationship with Tony Ferrara to which Joe testified fully.

'But you gentlemen gotta remember Tony and I were friends
since we were ten years old . . .'

'Don't you think, Mr. Naples, that the government has a right
to be concerned when it furnishes two hundred million in mortgage
insurance to an organization one of whose principals is a former
bootlegger, a convicted felon, a manipulator of corrupt union leaders, and according to testimony before the Hendrickson Committee, the leading underworld figure in New Jersey?'

'Not if our own operation is a hundred per cent legitimate, no
sir. Which it was. All we used was his money.'

Senator Gann was all acid. 'How *can* it be legitimate? You
testified about these activities with Mr. Cutler; you've told us about
your control of the unions through Mr. Ferrara, about your influence and Mr. Ferrara's influence with leading figures in the New
Jersey state government. It doesn't sound a hundred per cent
legitimate to me. Or even ten per cent.'

'You're entitled to your opinion on that, Senator.'

'Thanks.' Senator Gann was drier than usual. 'Don't you think
the government has a right to withhold financial help from people
who have put themselves beyond the law? Whose contempt for
law knows almost no limits?'

'I would say it has the right, yes, Senator.'

'I'm glad to hear you say it. Now, when you sell a house to a
family, you do a routine credit check on the buyer, do you not?
You or the bank lending him his mortgage money. If he has a
bad record, if you have reason to believe he's a bad actor, he
doesn't get his home or apartment. Is that correct?'

'More or less, yes, sir', Joe answered.

'Well, don't you think an agency of the government should do
something of the kind with the people it is helping in a material
way? Not just a dollar and cents check, but a character check on
all the principal stockholders in an enterprise – with criminal penalties for withholding the names of particular stockholders or partners or information relating to them? That is what I'm coming
around to thinking.'

'I can't see any harm in that, sir. Probably be a good thing.'

'Were other persons associated with you financially in the building of Naples, sir? Was there anyone besides you and Mr. Ferrara?'

'Yes, sir. There was a third man, but he was completely legitimate. Hundred per cent up-and-up type of gentleman.'

'I wish I felt we could agree on the meaning of that word legitimate, Mr. Naples. Could you tell us the name of this third individual?'

'Mr. Chairman', Jeff Straley interposed. 'It would be an unnecessary embarrassment and hardship for this gentleman, who enjoys the finest of reputations, to be identified in any way with these proceedings. I can tell the sub-committee that the man in question was unaware of the fact that Mr. Ferrara was a partner in the Naples venture because Ferrara's interest was handled entirely by an attorney acting for him. This other gentleman was never actively engaged in the construction of Naples. He was an investor, pure and simple. Unless the committee can indicate some useful purpose in establishing the identity of this individual, I respectfully urge that the matter be passed over.'

The chairman and his colleagues consulted counsel.

'We will not pursue this line at this time', Senator Owens said at last; no doubt Harold Brice had got his hand in for Jock; they had preserved Jock Dennison's good name and his five million buck contribution to Naples University. One thing, Joe thought, you could always say about Joe Naples, once he made a promise, he damn well stuck by it.

On the third day, however, Senator Gann took off after Harold Brice himself. Gently, slowly, like a cobra beginning its lethal winding, he asked how long Joe had known Senator Brice. 'You are a constituent of his, are you not, sir?'

'Not only a constituent, Senator, but a big supporter. I've been supporting Harold Brice since he was Mayor of Allenburg, and that goes back to 1927. We've been close personal friends. I mean we are very close, Senator. About as close as you and Mr. Gillardin or Glen Stewart or any of those other lumber guys out in your own state.'

The answer annoyed Senator Gann, his soft, almost purring voice contrasting to the open and hostile stare.

'I'm sure you're aware, Mr. Naples, that every citizen has a perfect right to consult his Congressman or his Senators, or seek their assistance in any legal business he may have with the federal government. That's part of our job. What we are trying to learn here now is whether the relationship between those in private enterprise who secure government assistance and those in government has resulted in favouritism, special privilege and the like. Our preliminary findings show a surprising number of instances of special privilege for people who customarily deal with various government officers – privileges in areas that have nothing to do with the usual business. We have instances of men who get special income-tax treatment, special treatment of one kind or another over at SEC, and special treatment by the armed forces for their sons. While part of this inquiry is to learn whether some kind of standard should be established for those who receive government assistance, it would also be of interest to learn whether government officers whose agencies are doing business with private citizens should not be stopped from attempting to influence government officers in other federal agencies on behalf of one or another of these private citizens. You understand what I mean? Citizen Y is doing business with Director X at the Maritime Commission. He is having some difficulty at Internal Revenue. Citizen Y asks Director X at the Maritime Commission to intercede, to make a friendly phone call to someone at Internal Revenue. Well, Director X is not Citizen Y's Congressman or Senator. He does not represent him in any way. He certainly has no obligation to make that phone call. The question is, does he even have the right? You see what I'm getting at?'

'I think I do, Senator.'

'In April of 1950, you came to Washington to visit Senator Brice, who at that time was special assistant to the President, is that correct?'

'Yes, sir.'

'Can you tell the sub-committee about that visit?'

'Be glad to, Senator. We were starting our third group of houses in Naples and finishing the shopping centre – we were busier than one-handed jugglers – when I got this call from Harold Brice to come down to Washington to meet the President. Well, frankly, gentlemen, right at that time I needed that like a pair of fish gills. But you don't say no to the President of the United States, so I came on down.'

'Did anyone come with you?'

'Yah. I brought my son Carey. He was at school, at Lawrenceville, and I figured he might come into the business with me in a

few years when he got out of college, and I guess I wanted to show
him how big a man I was, how big our business was, so I brought
him along. I figured he'd get a big bang outa meeting the President.'

'What did the President want?'

'The way Harold Brice explained it to me in his office, the President wanted housing for coloured families. The President thought
if I could make such a big success of Naples, maybe I could find
some way to get coloured housing built in the cities along the eastern
seaboard – from Washington to Newark. That includes Baltimore,
Wilmington, Philadelphia, Newark – where the problems were
the toughest. He thought if I could show the way, other builders
would follow along. It was no easy job, I can tell you that. There
were all kinds of problems, from neighbourhood opposition to
mortgage financing. Nobody wanted this thing. I mean just about
nobody.'

'Did you discuss this matter with the President?'

'That's what I was there for. After Harold and I finished, we
went to see the President and we must've talked maybe an hour.
The President says to me, "Mr. Naples, I've given instructions to
the National Mortgage Insurance Agency and the Housing and
Home Finance Agency to go with you to the limit. Whatever is
permitted by law we will do. If you and the NMIA find you need
new legislation to do the job, let Harold know and we will see what
can be done up on the Hill. Whatever you can do," he says, "the
country will thank you. I will thank you." I don't mind saying I
got a big kick outa that. Me, son of an Italian bricklayer, grew up
in the slums of New York, never even graduated high school, and
here's the President of the entire United States saying I could do
him a favour. I could do the entire country a favour. My son got a
tremendous kick outa that too.'

'Did you build this housing?'

'Well, that's a long story.'

'Did it actually get built?'

'Not by me. No, sir.'

'And did you make any effort to actually build?'

'Sure, we did a fantastic amount of work. We tied up land, about
six different parcels – one in Washington, one in Baltimore, two in
Philadelphia, two in Newark. We decided to build under Section
608, and we had quite a few meetings with the Regional Directors
in Trenton, down in Philadelphia, in Baltimore and here in Wash-

ington. We put three architects and three site planners to work. I guess we must've spent a couple hundred thousand dollars.'

'And were you in touch with Mr. Brice or the President during this period?'

'Well, not the President. But I checked in with Senator Brice now and then to keep him up to date and he kept after me. He was anxious for us to get moving. Finally we submitted our applications to the different NMIA offices, I guess it was around December of 1950.'

'Was this about the time that your son Carey was notified by his draft board of his classification under the Selective Service Act?'

He had always known this was coming, yet Joe felt his throat constrict. He was ready for them. 'Yah. He certainly was.'

'And you were upset about that?'

'You can say that again, Senator. There was a war going on in Korea. Hundreds of boys were getting killed out there every day.'

'Did you ever talk to Mr. Brice about the matter?'

'Yah, I sure did. I talked to anyone who'd listen.'

'At the same time that you were discussing these housing projects for coloured families?'

'It was during the same period.'

'What was the nature of your discussion with Mr. Brice?'

'I just told him I couldn't keep my mind on my work. If my son was gonna be called into active combat, I was just gonna be damn sick about it. In fact, since I was an officer in World War II, I thought I might go back into service my own self.'

'That would have put an end to these proposed projects of yours, is that right?'

'I suppose. I guess we got kind of a one-man outfit. Without me not much happens. I wasn't thinking too clear. I was half outa my mind with worry. I knew this kid. He would do any crazy thing if he ever got to Korea.'

'What was Mr. Brice's reaction?'

'Well, he didn't want anything to interfere with getting that housing built. He said he was close to somebody over at the Pentagon – some General – and he'd see if maybe there wasn't some useful job for Carey right here in this country, once he finished basic training. I thought it might be worth a try. Carey was a bright boy, he could've been useful anywhere.'

'Do you know,' asked Senator Gann, and Joe could see the saliva as the Senator licked his chops, 'do you know if anything of that sort was done?'

'No, sir, not for quite a while. Carey reported out to Dix and then he was sent down to North Carolina for basic training, and nothing happened while he was down there. Meanwhile, I was getting more upset all the time. We were having a lotta difficulties on these coloured housing deals, Neighbourhood associations were giving us a lotta trouble and frankly I couldn't get my mind on the jobs. I had my own worries.'

'You mean your son?'

'Yah. I was actually goin' outa my mind.'

'Was anything ever done by Mr. Brice about your son's army status?'

'Sure. I finally said to him one day, "My God, I've tried everything else, you're working down at the White House, how about you pickin' up a phone?"'

'And he did?'

'I says to him, "Here I am trying to do something for my country, help out in this coloured problem. How about the country doin' something for me?"'

'Mr. Naples, did Mr. Brice, as you have so nicely put it, pick up the phone?'

'Yah, sure. He called this big mucky-muck over at the Pentagon. Manheim or Maxwell or something like that. Some high-ranking civilian.'

'Would it be Mr. Manfred?'

'I wouldn't be surpirsed.'

'And what did Mr. Manfred do?'

'I don't have the foggiest idea, Senator.'

'Isn't it a fact that your son was transferred to the Pentagon as an orderly in Mr. Manfred's office?'

'Yah, that's right.'

'Was this something Mr. Manfred arranged?'

'I just told you, Senator. I don't have the foggiest idea what the General did or didn't arrange.'

'In any case, you felt that the problem of your son had been resolved satisfactorily.'

'Oh, I wouldn't say that, Senator. I spent three years in the army my own self. You never know when some crazy guy'll come along and look at the Pentagon Building and get mad as hell because they're all sitting around, and next day everyone from the third floor up gets shipped to Korea. You know how they'll do that. Nothing is sure in the army. But I felt a lot better.'

'It sounds very much to me, Mr. Naples, as though you were telling the Administration, in effect the Government of the United States, that you would build these apartments, do this job, provided your son were given special and privileged treatment.' Senator Westlake's voice had a cold edge to it.

Joe sat straight up in his seat. 'Senator, you are talkin' about Naples' law.'

'And you were applying this Naples' law of yours to the United States Government? Mr. Naples, do you realize what you are saying?'

Before Joe could reply, Senator Gann entered the fray. 'Didn't it occur to you, Mr. Naples, that at a time when other men's boys were fighting and dying in Korea that your son should not in good conscience be accorded preferential treatment?'

'I was trying to do my job—'

'So were we all!' Senator Gann snapped. 'I was a Representative in the United States Congress, and my son was out there in the front lines of Korea. Nevertheless I did my job.'

'That could be, Senator. But you got no way of measuring these things from person to person. I don't doubt your son means a lot to you, but what I felt for my boy, there just isn't any way whatsoever of describing it. We're a son and a father family. My father and me. Me and my sons. Some people say I spoiled him. I gotta close friend – in fact he's my own brother-in-law – says the way I brought up this boy he hadda turn out bad. I gave him everything. Car, his own speedboat, even found him a girl-friend one time. Nothing was too good for him. You'd think he'd end up some kinda bum. But he was the greatest kid you'd ever want to meet. He worked hard, he played hard, he was the greatest thing in this entire world. Maybe it was unnatural, what I felt, I don't know.'

'I would suggest,' Senator Westlake said dryly, 'that an attempt to use the White House for the purpose you have described is about as undesirable an activity as any I can imagine. I am just wondering if it isn't precisely people like you, Mr. Naples, who think they have a mortgage on the government, whom we ought to consider barring from our public assistance programmes.'

'Now listen, Senator—' Joe's voice was hoarse and shrill. 'I'm not gonna listen to stuff like *that*. There's not a one of you men up there—'

'I would further suggest,' Senator Westlake's voice was now ice, 'that your son, if he was a decent American, would never have lent himself to any such sordid arrangement.' Senator Gann tried to attract Senator Westlake's attention with a motion of his open palm, but the Senator, who was clearly not informed about Carey, continued full tilt. 'I should think if no one else put a stop to all this, the boy himself—'

'Mr. Chairman! Mr. Chairman!' Joe's hoarse, shrill voice was shouting above the sudden babble of voices, with several people attempting to be heard. The Chairman struck his gavel, trying to still the voices.

'The witness is trying to get the attention of the Chair', Senator Owens said to Senator Westlake.

'And I am trying to finish a sentence, Mr. Chairman', Senator Westlake said frigidly.

'Go ahead then, Senator', Owens said.

'I will refrain from any further comment for the moment', Senator Westlake said. 'I think the witness's statements speak for themselves.' Joe was reaching for the letters, scarcely able to see.

'Do you feel, Mr. Naples,' Senator Gann asked blandly, 'that laws which apply to everyone else are somehow not applicable to you?'

'No, sir!' By now Joe was no longer interested and barely able to understand the questions or his answers. 'Mr. Chairman, Senator Westlake has been saying a few things here, I gotta set this record straight. He wants to attack me, okay, I take care of my own self. But he's been trying to say things about my boy, here in public, and the boy's not here to defend himself, so, Mr. Chairman, I'd like to read a few letters here and get this record about my son Carey straightened out!'

'Has the Committee ever seen these letters? Has Counsel examined them?'

The lumbering counsel shook his huge head. 'Are we going to have letters which the sub-committee has never seen introduced here and read into the record?' Senator Gann said, his face flushing. 'I for one do not see it. Nor do I understand the relevance. I am sure Senator Westlake does not intend to impugn the boy's motives.'

'If I have left any derogatory impression,' said Senator Westlake, who by now had been whispered to by Senator Batterson, 'I would like to withdraw any imputations of the kind.'

'Mr. Chairman,' Joe said, his voice now shaking and his mouth tasting like the ashes of an unlit cigar, 'my son has been attacked here publicly. Senator Westlake has made sounds like he was some kinda whining, snivelling kid. This boy is dead, Senator, but these letters here are from him, he's gonna be heard from right here!'

'May I see the letters?' Senator McLean said helpfully and gently leaned forward. An attendant approached the witness, his hand outstretched.

'Senator, I'll be glad to let you see them as soon as I've read 'em. This first—' Joe looked around as three of the Senators started to talk at once, but he did not stop. He heard nothing, understood nothing. 'The first is one he wrote me right after he found out about his transfer to the Pentagon.'

Senator Owens was gavelling again, but Joe never stopped reading. '"Dear Pop", he says. "This place is fabulous. Colonel Furst called me to Division Headquarters this morning, me, a mere recruit, and told me I had special orders to report to the Pentagon next Monday to work in Mr. Manfred's office as an orderly. Sounds like a fantastic break, doesn't it, Pop? Only one thing bothers me. Colonel Furst made a crack I didn't like too much. Actually, he's a terrific guy, Pop, but this kind of made me sore. He said he thought it was nice for me, but personally would not want any son of his to start out with any special treatment in the Army. Pop, do you have any idea what he meant by that?"

'Well, I got in my plane and flew right down to see the kid. I explained to him it was a great break, a guy who works in a General's office is getting a lotta valuable experience, stuff like that, but all he wanted to know was whether we pulled any strings to get him the job. I told him absolutely not. I absolutely lied to him, 'cause I knew what would happen. I thought I had him pretty well convinced, too, till I got this next letter.'

'Mr. Chairman,' Senator Westlake said plaintively now, 'if I have said anything about the witness's son, or implied anything, if I have offended his sensibilities, I wish to apologize, but I do not think this effort by the witness to win sympathy for himself through his son is either useful or relevant, and I don't believe the time of the sub-committee should be consumed—'

Counsel Morse said ponderously, 'I'm inclined to agree with the Senator—'

Joe's voice was nearly a shout. 'Senator, I don't really give a damn what's relevant. My son was killed and he's got no one in this entire world to defend his name. You made some cracks here with Senatorial immunity. He died when he was nineteen years old, he was a kid, and I think as long as the question was raised right here in a Senate sub-committee with all the press services and radio people and film cameras reporting every word, I think that a nineteen-year-old boy has gotta right to be heard, even from the other side of the grave, and I mean to make him heard.'

Joe felt his throat constrict and he tried hard to clear it. Carefully he opened the ageing papers, looked for a moment at Carey's manuscript writing. He focused on the letters to avoid looking elsewhere. Straley had leaned back and turned away.

At last Senator Owens spoke quietly. 'Very well.'

'This is the second letter. "Dear Joe" – sometimes he'd call me Joe. We were closer you might say than the average father and son. "Dear Joe. Everyone here in Washington is fabulous. It's nothing like life in the Army – even the officers are friendly. In fact, I got into Mr. Manfred's office once, and that's like seeing God himself. But I wouldn't want to kid you, Pop. I wouldn't feel right being here by some kind of special arrangement which I'm pretty sure now you arranged. In fact, Pop that's how I got into Mr. Manfred's office – to ask him that very thing, because I had a peculiar feeling about it. Now please don't get sore, Pop. I know your Italian temper. But I've put in for a transfer to paratroops."'

He folded the letter slowly. 'Well, you men can imagine how I felt about *that* deal. And his mother didn't say anything, but I could see how *she* felt.'

Joe folded the letter almost blindly and stuffed it into his side pocket. 'I wanna glassa water', he croaked, and it was brought for him and he drank trying to compose himself. 'Well, back I got in the Beechcraft and flew down here to Washington. I took my boy out to a fancy dinner at the Shoreham and we had a chance to kick things around. I guess I must've done most of the talkin'. I thought I was making good progress, I don't mind telling you. I guess maybe I took unfair advantage of the kid, 'cause we rarely talked serious. We mostly kidded around together. Anyhow, I talked to him like a Dutch uncle. I told him any boy who had parents who were so crazy about him and a big future laid out for him had some kind of obligation to take care of himself and try to stay alive and not go rushing off to join the paratroops. Why, my God, something could happen on a practice jump! I told him someone had to do the job he was doing, so why not him. I practically got on my knees, although I didn't want him to see *that*. He looked at me kinda sympathetic, as if he knew what I was getting at, and I thought I had him sold. I said, "Well, kid, whaddaya say? Is it a deal?" He grinned at me and said, "Pop, this is quite a snow job you're doing. You're a terrific salesman. In fact, you should have been a politician", and stuff like that. But he didn't give me an answer. All he said was, "I heard you, Pop. Gimme a chance to think." But from the way he said it, it sounded like he just wanted time to come around. So I went home pretty relaxed.

'Well, in a couple of days I got this one here.' Joe stopped to clean his glasses. "'Dear Pop. I've been doing heavy thinking, which is quite a job for me, and I've been trying to understand what I feel myself. Why I'm doing what I feel I have to do. I'd like to be honest between us, okay? I've been thinking I was born with a silver spoon in my mouth. When I wanted you, you were always there. I was like a piece of you, but well protected. Sometimes I wonder what I actually am. Am I a yellow guy, a brave guy, a nothing? Am I as good as the next guy? I mean me, myself, not the son of Joe Naples. Lawrenceville, even Princeton won't tell you much – they're all cotton batting. I was beginning to find out about myself during basic training. I started to make it with some of the guys and officers – and on my own. I wanted to get out from under, Pop. I could have gone to O.C.S. But, Pop, you had me moved. I don't think you should have done that. Maybe I'm crazy, but I *want* to get into paratroops and I want to get to Korea. Not to shoot at Koreans, but to see how I'd do. I have to now. I've got to show you but more important, I have to show myself. I'm sorry, Pop. You can't imagine how sorry I am because I wouldn't hurt you for anything in this world, or Mom, but you can't work me like a wind-up gadget that's run on care and maybe even on love. You see, I'm not Milt Jason or Mom or Dino or any of those people. I'm me, Carey Naples, a separate person – not merely an extension of you. It's probably tough for you to believe, Pop, but no one is *really* an extension of you. I feel awful because of you and Mom, and I don't want to be any trouble, but what else can I do? I've already spoken to Mr. Manfred and to Mr. Brice. Some hot shot, your son, calling the White House. I'm being transferred to Fort Bragg next week and will write from there.

Carey

P.S. Please understand that I do not write any of these things in anger, Pop. I don't have any less affection for you, nor ever will as long as I'm still alive.'"

Joe peered at the words he had just read as though he were staring at the evidence of a grotesque crime, unable to take his eyes off the paper, unable to believe what he had read, although it was all indelible, no longer able to see the words through the mist.

'My fault, he says there, gentlemen. My fault, Mr. Chairman. He says it *himself*. My own fault. He's right. I don't believe in any accidents. Maybe this wasn't the only thing that was my fault. I dunno any more, I'm not sure any more. All I was trying to do was to help my own son, you understand? All I'm trying to do now—' Slowly he composed himself. 'Well, there it is in black and white. He had nothing to do with any of it. It was *me*. Trying to run everyone's life he says. He says to me one time, "Pop, you *just can't have your own way.*" That's the first time anyone ever said that to me and got away with it. So he transferred to paratroops. His mother and I, we never had a minute's peace. We never had a minute's sleep. We hardly talked to each other. Whether he was in this country or when he was overseas, I couldn't work. I thought I was goin' crazy. Oh, I went down there to Bragg. I argued with him, I begged the boy, I threatened him and I tried to bribe him. Anything. Well, you could see the kinda kid he was. He had his own ideas. There's no use dragging it out. After a while he wasn't listening. He kidded about it like it was some kinda joke. Here's all the letters, Mr. Chairman. I'd appreciate it if they were entered in the record. There are more letters from Bragg. No use goin' into all that. Then there were two short ones from Korea and then – that's all. Finished. Not another word. Just that telegram. It's all right here. And a long time later this letter came. You mind if I read this into the record, Mr. Chairman?'

The Chairman merely nodded, and Joe read in a monotone, barely audibly.

'"Dear Mr. and Mrs. Naples: It is with the deepest regret I write you concerning the death of your son, Carey, who was killed in action on 4 June 1951 in Korea.

"You have the sincere sympathy of the officers and men of this organization in your bereavement.

"Carey and eight other men, dropped and scattered behind enemy lines, cut off from the body of their main force, were attacked by a superior enemy force. Your son was attacked by an enemy soldier from the brush and was wounded by a pistol shot. Had he withdrawn to safety instead of fighting for the lives of his comrades, he could have saved his own life, but disregarding his own safety, he made a successful attempt to divert the enemy, rising to his feet with complete disregard for his own safety and recklessly exposing himself to concentrated and intense enemy fire. He bayoneted one enemy soldier before he was attacked from behind and mortally wounded, sacrificing himself to enable his companions to scramble to cover and ultimately to rejoin their unit. Though he has passed from us, his memory as a gallant soldier who unhesitatingly disregarded his own safety for the aid and comfort of others will always remain with us. Sincerely yours, Theodore Bramwell, Colonel 12th Airborne Infantry Commanding." They sent us two medals and a fancy citation. Silver Star and the Purple Heart. And they sent us his body. Yah, and we got these dozens of letters from men in his outfit tellin' us what a great guy he was. So he made it. On his own. That's it. That's the kinda man my son was. Let it be in the record.'

He became aware of the clerk who had been standing patiently alongside him, waiting. Joe saw the tremor in his own hand. He must be getting old, he was always havin' the shakes.

Slowly, eyes closed, Joe folded the worn letter he had just read and handed it to the clerk with the others. The hearing room was utterly silent.

Senator Owens sat stiff-faced, his lower jaw working as if he were trying to put it back in joint. At last he leaned forward, conferred first with Senators Gann and Westlake on his right, then with McLean and Batterson on his left. Jonathan Morse left his seat and conferred with the chairman behind hand-covered mikes.

Senator Owens cleared his throat. 'The witness may step down. I don't believe we will have any further questions. The sub-committee will stand in recess until ten a.m. Monday morning.'

Thirty-four

JOE found it difficult simply to get to his feet. The muscles must've atrophied from sitting so goddam long. With tremendous effort he pushed himself erect and looked around uncertainly. Andy put a comforting hand on his father's shoulder, and Joe let it remain there. In a trance he shook hands with Jeff Straley and muttered something about seeing him around. It was difficult to understand it was over. At last he saw Hetty standing beside him smiling the sad kinda smile he had first seen on her at Jock Dennison's thirty-three years ago, as if all you had to do was say boo and she'd be bawling. Alongside her was the little girl Andy was thinking about marrying. Couldn't remember her name.

'Come on, Mullaly,' he said gruffly, 'let's get outa this firetrap.' She took his hand, glanced at Andy, fear in her eyes, and something more – as if they both had to take care of the old man in spite of everything.

'I'm okay, I'm okay. No use standing around here', Joe said. 'Let's get outa here!' As they headed towards the huge doorway, he saw Anna Landos sitting dabbing at her eyes daintily. She looked quickly away when he saw her.

In the aeroplane sitting beside him, Hetty held his cold hand saying nothing until they were circling the airport. 'I'm sure you had to do what you did, Joie. Everything you did. Try to forgive yourself. I do, if you care.'

'*You* know I had to', he said, his voice muffled over the noise of the engines. 'I absolutely had to, every time. I'm glad you realize that, Mullaly.'

'Otherwise,' Hetty said not unkindly, 'who'd help all those poor slobs get in out of the rain?' Hetty was trying only to be nice, to help him. He wished he could bring himself to give a damn.

When they landed at Teterboro, only Cibulkas was at the airport to meet them. They drove in silence to East Street. The phone had been ringing all day, Cibulkas said, but Joe didn't want to talk to anyone. After dinner, Andy and Cynthia had to get back to Cambridge. They kissed Hetty good-bye and Joe went along to see the young people to the car. Cynthia leaned forward impulsively and kissed him. 'Good luck, Mr. Naples.' And she meant it.

Andy said, 'Cynthia and I are getting married in June, Dad.'

'*Well*, what do you know! Congratulations!' He turned and kissed Cynthia formally. 'I think we're getting a good kid, Andy.'

'We talked it all out, Dad, Cyn and I.' Andy was having difficulty saying what he had to say. 'We thought maybe if you wanted to take some time off, take it a little easy for a few months, maybe a whole year, maybe longer, we could take a bigger apartment in Cambridge and you and Mom could live with us for a while. It'll be quiet up there. No one will bother you. You can get some privacy.'

Suddenly Joe began to laugh. 'By God, Andy, I gotta hand it to you. There's plenty of your old man in you. Takin' care of the poor old bastid like that. Kid, you're my boy, but I gotta turn you down.' He shuddered inwardly when he realized how close he had come to wanting to accept. 'As long as I'm breathing in and out, I guess I can manage. But thanks for askin' me. Best thing that happened to me all day.'

'Uncle Milt could take care of things here for a while', Andy said.

'Uncle Milt? Uncle Milt don't know to come in outa the rain.' But he hugged the boy for that. Damn sweet kid. Even had good judgment in girls. Well, if he wanted to be a professor, that was okay. That was his own business. Joe would call Nathan Pusey first thing Monday morning and make a man-to-man proposition: Half a million to Harvard for a chair in government, and a gentlemen's agreement to give the chair to Andy after a few years. Be a hell of a fine surprise for Andy. No one could say he wasn't helping *this* kid out the right way. And if Harvard was too uppity to make the deal, he'd do it with Oberlin or Duke or one of those outfits.

The Sunday papers carried full coverage on the GAPE sub-committee hearings. They ran a picture of Carey, a photo of the painting in Joe's office, but neither he nor Hetty was interested. Then about Sunday noon, Cibulkas rushed into the living-room breathless. 'It's Mrs. Ferrara', he said ominously. 'She wants you to come over right away.'

Joe knew as soon as he heard her voice. 'It's me, Mr. Naples, Cookie Ferrara. Could you come right over? It's awful, awful.

It's Tony. I tried to get Mr. Jason, but he's out. I didn't know who to call. Please.'

'Sure.'

To Hetty he said, 'Something's happened to Tony. I gotta go see if I can do anything.'

Hetty had to come. She was not letting him out of her sight. Okay, why not. Good to have a someone who gave a damn.

To Hetty's query as they drove to East Orange, he said, only, 'I dunno. Sounds like he's sick or something.' He had no idea what to expect when he arrived at Tony's glass house.

Cookie, wildly dishevelled and decosmeticized, looked terrified as she let them in. 'He's in here', she whispered hysterically, and led them into the bedroom. 'I found him in there.' She pointed to a door, and Joe opened a large walk-in closet and there was Tony hanging, like a scarecrow, head down, eyes and mouth open stupidly, dead. Hetty gasped and turned away. Except for her withered mother twenty-five years ago, she had never seen a corpse. Cookie was sobbing softly.

'He wrote this', she said. She picked up a yellow-lined paper that lay on one of the twin beds and handed it to Joe. The note said, 'This is not living. It's not worth it any more, Cookie. Sorry.'

'He was so depressed', Cookie sobbed. 'But I don't see how he was ever able to do it. When he wasn't in court, all he wanted to do was sleep. He was in court all day yesterday and all I did was go out to get a few cold cuts —' Tony stared at them.

'Let's get him down', Joe said and heard his own voice hoarse.

By noon on Monday, at the office, he had received two unpleasant letters from the redevelopment agencies in St. Louis and Philadelphia giving formal notice in almost identical language of cancellation of the Naples contracts because of 'unnecessary and inexcusable delays'.

'These guys must be outa their heads', Joe roared to Cathy. 'After all the work we put in in those towns, helpin' them play politics. What the hell are they thinking?' Cathy merely lowered her head and looked away.

By two o'clock, Milt came in almost as though nothing had ever happened. He had to tell Joe that Piggy Banks had called to say the rumour was that Washington was going to stop processing all Naples NMIA applications. 'Piggy sounded kind of glad', Milt said. Oh, yes, and the Bureau of Internal Revenue had phoned to say they were sending two examiners up on Wednesday for a re-review of all the Naples tax returns, corporate and individual, since 1950, including the Foundation returns. Milt, Joe noticed, tried to speak remotely, like some kind of efficiency machine that didn't give a damn. But deep down he was his old unhappy self. Joe felt kinda sorry for Milt. Milt couldn't change even when he wanted to. 'I'll take them on in the first instance, Joey, if you want me to. I won't bother you unless it gets sticky.'

'Yah. Thanks. I don't wanna see those guys.' Then a flash of anger overtook him. 'I thought those birds were giving me immunity down there. That was my deal.'

Milt blinked and Joe could see his friend was making enormous efforts to appear uninvolved. 'You have immunity from prosecution on all the points you were questioned about. Didn't you notice they asked you nothing about the Foundation or taxes? There's more than one way to skin a cat, Joey. And those boys in Washington are expert cat skinners.'

'Okay. You see the bastids.'

Milt said slowly, 'I can handle the matter, and I'll take care of it if you want. But are you sure you want me to be the one to do it?'

Joe closed his eyes. 'Milt,' he said, 'I'm not sure of anything. Not one single goddam thing. But you do it, will ya?'

'Sure. I'm glad you have that much confidence in me after all. And say, the Attorney-General's office called, too, the state Attorney-General. They'd like to talk with us in Trenton.'

'What the hell for?'

'Well, you testified that there are these pay-offs at every level of government – you know, state, city. That's a lot of territory.'

'So what?'

'Well, you can see that an Attorney-General of New Jersey has no choice. He simply has to find out what you know.'

Joe had no interest in discussing it. 'I gotta go to Tony's funeral this afternoon', he said. 'You coming out with me?'

Milt nodded. 'Nothing could keep me away', he said. 'I admired old Tony.' It was not absolutely the same old Milt and maybe never would be, but he was becoming more like his old self already.

On the drive home from the funeral, Joe felt more tired than he had ever felt in his life. He drove quietly through Naples, past the new apartment job, wondering where he had found the energy to start it. Nothing was fun any more. All he could think of was Tony hanging there. His mind had stopped going. He wanted to get some rest. Cibulkas let him in and he climbed the long stairs to the bedroom where Hetty was getting out of her afternoon bath.

'Joie, darling. Can I have Cibulkas get you some Chianti?'

Joe shook his head. He wanted to pack everything up, get out. 'I'm tired, Mullaly. Just pull down the shades, turn out the lights, close the door, lemme take a nap, willya?' He lay down in the dark on the satin spread without taking his shoes off and she sat on the edge of the bed and untied them for him. She touched his cheek and left quietly, but the gesture meant nothing to him. He lay in the dark, and his future triumphs, like soldiers in a row, passed in formation. By God, he was not gonna be any Tony Ferrara, the termites were not gonna eat his insides out. He pictured the rebuilding of down-town St. Louis and Philadelphia, windowy and bright; the modern university, in brick, glass and stone spread as far as the eye could see; the moment when Andy in cap and gown became the first Carey Naples Professor of Government at Harvard ... Jesus, he'd forgotten to call Pusey, have to do that first thing in the morning ... Now what the hell was he going to tell the Attorney-General in Trenton? And what were those agents from Internal Revenue going to find in his tax returns? The Foundation – He'd have to go to St. Louis and Philadelphia and get reinstated as sponsor, somehow. He could sue the goddam Redevelopment Commissions, hold them up for five years if they weren't co-operative ... They'd damn well know they were in a fight. But, Jesus, he was tired ... he couldn't think of all these things now ... All he wanted to do was sleep.

THE END

JOSEPH VIERTEL

The Last Temptation

Deborah and Victor Marmorek were a happy young couple, people of means, education, and taste. Victor was an engineer and at one time a member of the Davis Cup team for Czechoslovakia. Deborah was the prettiest girl in Vienna, the daughter of an eminent theatrical promoter.

In England, they would probably have continued to live pleasantly. But this was Europe in 1938, where they were ruthlessly stripped of security and pleasure, and flung into a world of crushing degradation and fear. They compromised their souls a thousand times a day, told as many lies – finally to each other – until deceit became a habit, not always noticed, but always present. This was the price of survival.

They fled from Vienna to Prague, then to Rome, and finally to Jerusalem, where they hoped to find peace and recover the decency of their former life.

But years of demoralizing hardship had planted strange forces within them – especially in Victor – and these, combined with events they could not control, brought them to a crisis more horrifying than anything in their past experience.

The Last Temptation is a powerful novel – and a fascinating one. A Literary Guild Selection.

'*No one who reads the book will remain unmoved*' – SUNDAY TIMES

'*. . . excellent can't-put-it-down reading*' – JEWISH CHRONICLE

Obtainable from all good bookshops and libraries.

MARQUIS CHILDS

THE PEACE- -MAKERS

The Peacemakers of this absorbing novel are the representatives of four countries: Great Britain, America, France, and Russia. They have been summoned to Geneva, the traditional meeting-place of peacemakers, where they must urgently resolve a crisis in Tunisia which has brought the world to the brink of war.

Against this background, Marquis Childs, the special political correspondent and commentator, has set his highly topical novel – a story of diplomats, and the women in their lives, faithful and unfaithful, gathered together under a cloud of suspicion and distrust. In this distinguished novel Marquis Childs shows, in masterly fashion, how a desperate crisis can be sparked off, and how diplomacy can resolve – or fail to resolve – the dangers inherent in a society where the balance of power is divided *almost* equally between the two most important countries in the world.

'*Intrigue and excitement behind a foreign ministers' conference in Geneva; written by an expert on international affairs*'
– JOHN O'LONDON'S

'*It is fiction but uncomfortably near to fact*' – THE GUARDIAN

MACDONALD HULL
The Cultured Pearl

In *The Cultured Pearl* Macdonald Hull has again ventured deep behind the bamboo curtain, beyond the gloss of the cosmopolitan pseudo-westernisms of the Tokyo intelligensia to bring into focus the real Japanese culture. This is a penetrating novel of Christopher Mannering's effort to produce in his protégée, Masa Susuki, a gem of the orient, the perfect mixture of Japanese and Western womanhood.

'*A fascinating unusual story of an attempt to bring up a young Japanese girl as the perfect woman . . .*' – BOOKS AND BOOKMEN

Obtainable from all good bookshops and libraries